Zane Grey

THREE COMPLETE WESTERNS

Riders of the Purple Sage

The Last Trail

Yaqui

LP LONGMEADOW PRESS

1996

A Platinum Press Book

This special reprint edition is now republished by:
Longmeadow Press
201 High Ridge Road
Stamford, CT 06904

in association with

Platinum Press Inc.
311 Crossways Park Drive
Woodbury, NY 11797

Published by Longmeadow Press, 201 High Ridge Road, Stamford, CT 06904.
Longmeadow Press and the colophon are trademarks.

Cover design by James C. Romano II

ISBN: 0-681-21682-4

Printed in USA

First Longmeadow Press Edition 1996

0 9 8 7 6 5 4 3 2 1

RIDERS OF THE PURPLE SAGE

CONTENTS

CHAPTER I

A SHARP clip-clop of iron-shod hoofs deadened and died away, and clouds of yellow dust drifted from under the cottonwoods out over the sage.

Jane Withersteen gazed down the wide purple slope with dreamy and troubled eyes. A rider had just left her and it was his message that held her thoughtful and almost sad, awaiting the churchmen who were coming to resent and attack her right to befriend a Gentile.

She wondered if the unrest and strife that had lately come to the little village of Cottonwoods was to involve her. And then she sighed, remembering that her father had founded this remotest border settlement of southern Utah and that he had left it to her. She owned all the ground and many of the cottages. Withersteen House was hers, and the great ranch, with its thousands of cattle, and the swiftest horses of the sage. To her belonged Amber Spring, the water which gave verdure and beauty to the village and made living possible on that wild purple upland waste. She could not escape being involved by whatever befell Cottonwoods.

That year, 1871, had marked a change which had been gradually coming in the lives of the peace-loving Mormons of the border. Glaze—Stone Bridge—Sterling, villages to the north, had risen against the invasion of Gentile settlers and the forays of rustlers. There had been opposition to the one and fighting with the other. And now Cottonwoods had begun to wake and bestir itself and grown hard.

Jane prayed that the tranquillity and sweetness of her life would not be permanently disrupted. She meant to do so much more for her people than she had done. She wanted the sleepy

3

quiet pastoral days to last always. Trouble between the Mormons and the Gentiles of the community would make her unhappy. She was Mormon-born, and she was a friend to poor and unfortunate Gentiles. She wished only to go on doing good and being happy. And she thought of what that great ranch meant to her. She loved it all—the grove of cottonwoods, the old stone house, the amber-tinted water, and the droves of shaggy, dusty horses and mustangs, the sleek, clean-limbed, blooded racers, and the browsing herds of cattle and the lean, sun-browned riders of the sage.

While she waited there she forgot the prospect of untoward change. The bray of a lazy burro broke the afternoon quiet, and it was comfortingly suggestive of the drowsy farmyard, and the open corrals, and the green alfalfa fields. Her clear sight intensified the purple sage-slope as it rolled before her. Low swells of prairie-like ground sloped up to the west. Dark, lonely cedar-trees, few and far between, stood out strikingly, and at long distances ruins of red rocks. Farther on, up the gradual slope, rose a broken wall, a huge monument, looming dark purple and stretching its solitary, mystic way, a wavering line that faded in the north. Here to the westward was the light and color and beauty. Northward the slope descended to a dim line of cañons from which rose an up-flinging of the earth, not mountainous, but a vast heave of purple uplands, with ribbed and fan-shaped walls, castle-crowned cliffs, and gray escarpments. Over it all crept the lengthening, waning afternoon shadows.

The rapid beat of hoofs recalled Jane Withersteen to the question at hand. A group of riders cantered up the lane, dismounted, and threw their bridles. They were seven in number, and Tull, the leader, a tall, dark man, was an elder of Jane's church.

"Did you get my message?" he asked, curtly.

"Yes," replied Jane.

"I sent word I'd give that rider Venters half an hour to come down to the village. He didn't come."

"He knows nothing of it," said Jane. "I didn't tell him. I've been waiting here for you."

"Where is Venters?"

"I left him in the courtyard."

"Here, Jerry," called Tull, turning to his men, "take the gang and fetch Venters out here if you have to rope him."

The dusty-booted and long-spurred riders clanked noisily into the grove of cottonwoods and disappeared in the shade.

"Elder Tull, what do you mean by this?" demanded Jane. "If you must arrest Venters you might have the courtesy to wait till he leaves my home. And if you do arrest him it will be adding insult to injury. It's absurd to accuse Venters of being mixed up in that shooting fray in the village last night. He was with me at the time. Besides, he let me take charge of his guns. You're only using this as a pretext. What do you mean to do to Venters?"

"I'll tell you presently," replied Tull. "But first tell me why you defend this worthless rider?"

"Worthless!" exclaimed Jane, indignantly. "He's nothing of the kind. He was the best rider I ever had. There's not a reason why I shouldn't champion him and every reason why I should. It's no little shame to me, Elder Tull, that through my friendship he has roused the enmity of my people and become an outcast. Besides, I owe him eternal gratitude for saving the life of little Fay."

"I've heard of your love for Fay Larkin and that you intend to adopt her. But—Jane Withersteen, the child is a Gentile!"

"Yes. But, Elder, I don't love the Mormon children any less because I love a Gentile child. I shall adopt Fay if her mother will give her to me."

"I'm not so much against that. You can give the child Mormon teaching," said Tull. "But I'm sick of seeing this fellow Venters hang around you. I'm going to put a stop to it. You've so much love to throw away on these beggars of Gentiles that I've an idea you might love Venters."

Tull spoke with the arrogance of a Mormon whose power could not be brooked and with the passion of a man in whom jealousy had kindled a consuming fire.

"Maybe I do love him," said Jane. She felt both fear and anger stir her heart. "I'd never thought of that. Poor fellow! he certainly needs some one to love him."

"This 'll be a bad day for Venters unless you deny that," returned Tull, grimly.

Tull's men appeared under the cottonwoods and led a young

5

man out into the lane. His ragged clothes were those of an outcast. But he stood tall and straight, his wide shoulders flung back, with the muscles of his bound arms rippling and a blue flame of defiance in the gaze he bent on Tull.

For the first time Jane Withersteen felt Venters's real spirit. She wondered if she would love this splendid youth. Then her emotion cooled to the sobering sense of the issue at stake.

"Venters, will you leave Cottonwoods at once and forever?" asked Tull, tensely.

"Why?" rejoined the rider.

"Because I order it."

Venters laughed in cool disdain.

The red leaped to Tull's dark cheek.

"If you don't go it means your ruin," he said, sharply.

"Ruin!" exclaimed Venters, passionately. "Haven't you already ruined me? What do you call ruin? A year ago I was a rider. I had horses and cattle of my own. I had a good name in Cottonwoods. And now when I come into the village to see this woman you set your men on me. You hound me. You trail me as if I were a rustler. I've no more to lose—except my life."

"Will you leave Utah?"

"Oh! I know," went on Venters, tauntingly, "it galls you, the idea of beautiful Jane Withersteen being friendly to a poor Gentile. You want her all yourself. You're a wiving Mormon. You have use for her—and Withersteen House and Amber Spring and seven thousand head of cattle!"

Tull's hard jaw protruded, and rioting blood corded the veins of his neck.

"Once more. Will you go?"

"No!"

"Then I'll have you whipped within an inch of your life," replied Tull, harshly. "I'll turn you out in the sage. And if you ever come back you'll get worse."

Venters's agitated face grew coldly set and the bronze changed to gray.

Jane impulsively stepped forward. "Oh! Elder Tull!" she cried. "You won't do that!"

Tull lifted a shaking finger toward her.

6

"That 'll do from you. Understand, you'll not be allowed to hold this boy to a friendship that's offensive to your Bishop. Jane Withersteen, your father left you wealth and power. It has turned your head. You haven't yet come to see the place of Mormon women. We've reasoned with you, borne with you. We've patiently waited. We've let you have your fling, which is more than I ever saw granted to a Mormon woman. But you haven't come to your senses. Now, once for all, you can't have any further friendship with Venters. He's going to be whipped, and he's got to leave Utah!"

"Oh! Don't whip him! It would be dastardly!" implored Jane, with slow certainty of her failing courage.

Tull always blunted her spirit, and she grew conscious that she had feigned a boldness which she did not possess. He loomed up now in different guise, not as a jealous suitor, but embodying the mysterious despotism she had known from childhood—the power of her creed.

"Venters, will you take your whipping here or would you rather go out in the sage?" asked Tull. He smiled a flinty smile that was more than inhuman, yet seemed to give out of its dark aloofness a gleam of righteousness.

"I'll take it here—if I must," said Venters. "But by God!—Tull, you'd better kill me outright. That 'll be a dear whipping for you and your praying Mormons. You'll make me another Lassiter!"

The strange glow, the austere light which radiated from Tull's face, might have been a holy joy at the spiritual conception of exalted duty. But there was something more in him, barely hidden, a something personal and sinister, a deep of himself, an engulfing abyss. As his religious mood was fanatical and inexorable, so would his physical hate be merciless.

"Elder, I—I repent my words," Jane faltered. The religion in her, the long habit of obedience, of humility, as well as agony of fear, spoke in her voice. "Spare the boy!" she whispered.

"You can't save him now," replied Tull, stridently.

Her head was bowing to the inevitable. She was grasping the truth, when suddenly there came, in inward constriction, a hardening of gentle forces within her breast. Like a steel bar it was, stiffening all that had been soft and weak in her. She felt a birth

7

in her of something new and unintelligible. Once more her strained gaze sought the sage-slopes. Jane Withersteen loved that wild and purple wilderness. In times of sorrow it had been her strength, in happiness its beauty was her continual delight. In her extremity she found herself murmuring, "Whence cometh my help!" It was a prayer, as if forth from those lonely purple reaches and walls of red and clefts of blue might ride a fearless man, neither creed-bound nor creed-mad, who would hold up a restraining hand in the faces of her ruthless people.

The restless movements of Tull's men suddenly quieted down. Then followed a low whisper, a rustle, a sharp exclamation.

"Look!" said one, pointing to the west.

"A rider!"

Jane Withersteen wheeled and saw a horseman, silhouetted against the western sky, coming riding out of the sage. He had ridden down from the left, in the golden glare of the sun, and had been unobserved till close at hand. An answer to her prayer!

"Do you know him? Does any one know him?" questioned Tull, hurriedly.

His men looked and looked, and one by one shook their heads.

"He's come from far," said one.

"Thet's a fine hoss," said another.

"A strange rider."

"Huh! he wears black leather," added a fourth.

With a wave of his hand, enjoining silence, Tull stepped forward in such a way that he concealed Venters.

The rider reined in his mount, and with a lithe forward-slipping action appeared to reach the ground in one long step. It was a peculiar movement in its quickness and inasmuch that while performing it the rider did not swerve in the slightest from a square front to the group before him.

"Look!" hoarsely whispered one of Tull's companions. "He packs two black-butted guns—low down—they're hard to see—black agin them black chaps."

"A gun-man!" whispered another. "Fellers, careful now about movin' your hands."

The stranger's slow approach might have been a mere leisurely manner of gait or the cramped short steps of a rider unused to

8

walking; yet, as well, it could have been the guarded advance of one who took no chances with men.

"Hello, stranger!" called Tull. No welcome was in this greeting, only a gruff curiosity.

The rider responded with a curt nod. The wide brim of a black sombrero cast a dark shade over his face. For a moment he closely regarded Tull and his comrades, and then, halting in his slow walk, he seemed to relax.

"Evenin', ma'am," he said to Jane, and removed his sombrero with quaint grace.

Jane, greeting him, looked up into a face that she trusted instinctively and which riveted her attention. It had all the characteristics of the range rider's—the leanness, the red burn of the sun, and the set changelessness that came from years of silence and solitude. But it was not these which held her; rather the intensity of his gaze, a strained weariness, a piercing wistfulness of keen, gray sight, as if the man was forever looking for that which he never found. Jane's subtle woman's intuition, even in that brief instant, felt a sadness, a hungering, a secret.

"Jane Withersteen, ma'am?" he inquired.

"Yes," she replied.

"The water here is yours?"

"Yes."

"May I water my horse?"

"Certainly. There's the trough."

"But mebbe if you knew who I was—" He hesitated, with his glance on the listening men. "Mebbe you wouldn't let me water him—though I ain't askin' none for myself."

"Stranger, it doesn't matter who you are. Water your horse. And if you are thirsty and hungry come into my house."

"Thanks, ma'am. I can't accept for myself—but for my tired horse—"

Trampling of hoofs interrupted the rider. More restless movements on the part of Tull's men broke up the little circle, exposing the prisoner Venters.

"Mebbe I've kind of hindered somethin'—for a few moments, perhaps?" inquired the rider.

"Yes," replied Jane Withersteen, with a throb in her voice.

9

She felt the drawing power of his eyes; and then she saw him look at the bound Venters, and at the men who held him, and their leader.

"In this here country all the rustlers an' thieves an' cut-throats an' gun-throwers an' all-round no-good men jest happen to be Gentiles. Ma'am, which of the no-good class does that young feller belong to?"

"He belongs to none of them. He's an honest boy."

"You *know* that, ma'am?"

"Yes—yes."

"Then what has he done to get tied up that way?"

His clear and distinct question, meant for Tull as well as for Jane Withersteen, stilled the restlessness and brought a momentary silence.

"Ask him," replied Jane, her voice rising high.

The rider stepped away from her, moving out with the same slow, measured stride in which he had approached, and the fact that his action placed her wholly to one side, and him no nearer to Tull and his men, had a penetrating significance.

"Young feller, speak up," he said to Venters.

"Here, stranger, this 's none of your mix," began Tull. "Don't try any interference. You've been asked to drink and eat. That's more than you'd have got in any other village of the Utah border. Water your horse and be on your way."

"Easy—easy—I ain't interferin' yet," replied the rider. The tone of his voice had undergone a change. A different man had spoken. Where, in addressing Jane, he had been mild and gentle, now, with his first speech to Tull, he was dry, cool, biting. "I've jest stumbled onto a queer deal. Seven Mormons all packin' guns, an' a Gentile tied with a rope, an' a woman who swears by his honesty! Queer, ain't that?"

"Queer or not, it's none of your business," retorted Tull.

"Where I was raised a woman's word was law. I 'ain't quite outgrowed that yet."

Tull fumed between amaze and anger.

"Meddler, we have a law here something different from woman's whim—Mormon law! . . . Take care you don't transgress it."

"To hell with your Mormon law!"

The deliberate speech marked the rider's further change, this time from kindly interest to an awakening menace. It produced a transformation in Tull and his companions. The leader gasped and staggered backward at a blasphemous affront to an institution he held most sacred. The man Jerry, holding the horses, dropped the bridles and froze in his tracks. Like posts the other men stood, watchful-eyed, arms hanging rigid, all waiting.

"Speak up now, young man. What have you done to be roped that way?"

"It's a damned outrage!" burst out Venters. "I've done no wrong. I've offended this Mormon Elder by being a friend to that woman."

"Ma'am, is it true—what he says?" asked the rider of Jane; but his quiveringly alert eyes never left the little knot of quiet men.

"True? Yes, perfectly true," she answered.

"Well, young man, it seems to me that bein' a friend to such a woman would be what you wouldn't want to help an' couldn't help. . . . What's to be done to you for it?"

"They intend to whip me. You know what that means—in Utah!"

"I reckon," replied the rider, slowly.

With his gray glance cold on the Mormons, with the restive bit-champing of the horses, with Jane failing to repress her mounting agitations, with Venters standing pale and still, the tension of the moment tightened. Tull broke the spell with a laugh, a laugh without mirth, a laugh that was only a sound betraying fear.

"Come on, men!" he called.

Jane Withersteen turned again to the rider.

"Stranger, can you do nothing to save Venters?"

"Ma'am, you ask me to save him—from your own people?"

"Ask you? I beg of you!"

"But you don't dream who you're askin'."

"Oh, sir, I pray you—save him!"

"These are Mormons, an' I . . ."

"At—at any cost—save him. For I—I care for him!"

Tull snarled. "You love-sick fool! Tell your secrets. There'll be a way to teach you what you've never learned. . . . Come men, out of here!"

"Mormon, the young man stays," said the rider.

11

Like a shot his voice halted Tull.

"What!"

"He stays."

"Who'll keep him? He's my prisoner!" cried Tull, hotly.

"Stranger, again I tell you—don't mix here. You've meddled enough. Go your way now or—"

"Listen! . . . He stays."

Absolute certainty, beyond any shadow of doubt, breathed in the rider's low voice.

"Who are you? We are seven here."

The rider dropped his sombrero and made a rapid movement, singular in that it left him somewhat crouched, arms bent and stiff, with the big black gun-sheaths swung round to the fore.

"*Lassiter!*"

It was Venters's wondering, thrilling cry that bridged the fateful connection between the rider's singular position and the dreaded name.

Tull put out a groping hand. The life of his eyes dulled to the gloom with which men of his fear saw the approach of death. But death, while it hovered over him, did not descend, for the rider waited for the twitching fingers, the downward flash of hand that did not come. Tull, gathering himself together, turned to the horses, attended by his pale comrades.

CHAPTER II

VENTERS appeared too deeply moved to speak the gratitude his face expressed. And Jane turned upon the rescuer and gripped his hands. Her smiles and tears seemingly dazed him. Presently, as something like calmness returned, she went to Lassiter's weary horse.

"I will water him myself," she said, and she led the horse to a trough under a huge old cottonwood. With nimble fingers she loosened the bridle and removed the bit. The horse snorted and bent his head. The trough was of solid stone, hollowed out, moss-covered and green and wet and cool, and the clear brown water that fed it spouted and splashed from a wooden pipe.

"He has brought you far to-day?"

"Yes, ma'am, a matter of over sixty miles, mebbe seventy."

"A long ride—a ride that— Ah, he is blind!"

"Yes, ma'am," replied Lassiter.

"What blinded him?"

"Some men once roped an' tied him, an' then held white-iron close to his eyes."

"Oh! Men? You mean devils. . . . Were they your enemies—Mormons?"

"Yes, ma'am."

"To take revenge on a horse! Lassiter, the men of my creed are unnaturally cruel. To my everlasting sorrow I confess it. They have been driven, hated, scourged till their hearts have hardened. But we women hope and pray for the time when our men will soften."

"Beggin' your pardon, ma'am—that time will never come."

"Oh, it will! . . . Lassiter, do you think Mormon women wicked? Has your hand been against them, too?"

"No. I believe Mormon women are the best and noblest, the most long-sufferin', and the blindest, unhappiest women on earth."

"Ah!" She gave him a grave, thoughtful look. "Then you will break bread with me?"

Lassiter had no ready response, and he uneasily shifted his weight from one leg to another, and turned his sombrero round and round in his hands. "Ma'am," he began, presently, "I reckon your kindness of heart makes you overlook things. Perhaps I ain't well known hereabouts, but back up North there's Mormons who'd rest oneasy in their graves at the idea of me sittin' to table with you."

"I dare say. But—will you do it, anyway?" she asked.

"Mebbe you have a brother or relative who might drop in an' be offended, an' I wouldn't want to—"

"I've not a relative in Utah that I know of. There's no one with a right to question my actions." She turned smilingly to Venters. "You will come in, Bern, and Lassiter will come in. We'll eat and be merry while we may."

"I'm only wonderin' if Tull an' his men 'll raise a storm down in the village," said Lassiter, in his last weakening stand.

"Yes, he'll raise the storm—after he has prayed," replied Jane. "Come."

She led the way, with the bridle of Lassiter's horse over her arm. They entered a grove and walked down a wide path shaded by great low-branching cottonwoods. The last rays of the setting sun sent golden bars through the leaves. The grass was deep and rich; welcome contrast to sage-tired eyes. Twittering quail darted across the path, and from a tree-top somewhere a robin sang its evening song, and on the still air floated the freshness and murmur of flowing water.

The home of Jane Withersteen stood in a circle of cottonwoods, and was a flat, long, red-stone structure with a covered court in the center through which flowed a lively stream of amber-colored water. In the massive blocks of stone and heavy timbers and solid doors and shutters showed the hand of a man who had builded against pillage and time; and in the flowers and mosses lining the stone-bedded stream, in the bright colors of rugs and blankets

14

on the court floor, and the cozy corner with hammock and books, and the clean-linened table, showed the grace of a daughter who lived for happiness and the day at hand.

Jane turned Lassiter's horse loose in the thick grass. "You will want him to be near you," she said, "or I'd have him taken to the alfalfa fields." At her call appeared women who began at once to bustle about, hurrying to and fro, setting the table. Then Jane, excusing herself, went within.

She passed through a huge low-ceiled chamber, like the inside of a fort, and into a smaller one where a bright wood-fire blazed in an old open fireplace, and from this into her own room. It had the same comfort as was manifested in the home-like outer court; moreover, it was warm and rich in soft hues.

Seldom did Jane Withersteen enter her room without looking into her mirror. She knew she loved the reflection of that beauty which since early childhood she had never been allowed to forget. Her relatives and friends, and later a horde of Mormon and Gentile suitors, had fanned the flame of natural vanity in her. So that at twenty-eight she scarcely thought at all of her wonderful influence for good in the little community where her father had left her practically its beneficent landlord; but cared most for the dream and the assurance and the allurement of her beauty. This time, however, she gazed into her glass with more than the usual happy motive, without the usual slight conscious smile. For she was thinking of more than the desire to be fair in her own eyes, in those of her friend; she wondered if she were to seem fair in the eyes of this Lassiter, this man whose name had crossed the long, wild brakes of stone and plains of sage, this gentle-voiced, sad-faced man who was a hater and a killer of Mormons. It was not now her usual half-conscious vain obsession that actuated her as she hurriedly changed her riding-dress to one of white, and then looked long at the stately form with its gracious contours, at the fair face with its strong chin and full firm lips, at the dark-blue, proud, and passionate eyes.

"If by some means I can keep him here a few days, a week—he will never kill another Mormon," she mused. "Lassiter! . . . I shudder when I think of that name, of him. But when I look at the man I forget who he is—I almost like him. I remember only that he saved Bern. He has suffered. I wonder what it was—did he love a Mormon woman once? How splendidly he championed us poor misunderstood souls! Somehow he knows—much."

Jane Withersteen joined her guests and bade them to her board. Dismissing her woman, she waited upon them with her own hands. It was a bountiful supper and a strange company. On her right sat the ragged and half-starved Venters; and though blind eyes could have seen what he counted for in the sum of her happiness, yet he looked the gloomy outcast his allegiance had made him, and about him there was the shadow of the ruin presaged by Tull. On her left sat black-leather-garbed Lassiter looking like a man in a dream. Hunger was not with him, nor composure, nor speech, and when he twisted in frequent unquiet movements the heavy guns that he had not removed knocked against the table-legs. If it had been otherwise possible to forget the presence of Lassiter those telling little jars would have rendered it unlikely. And Jane Withersteen talked and smiled and laughed with all the dazzling play of lips and eyes that a beautiful, daring woman could summon to her purpose.

When the meal ended, and the men pushed back their chairs, she leaned closer to Lassiter and looked square into his eyes.

"Why did you come to Cottonwoods?"

Her question seemed to break a spell. The rider arose as if he had just remembered himself and had tarried longer than his wont.

"Ma'am, I have hunted all over the southern Utah and Nevada for—somethin'. An' through your name I learned where to find it —here in Cottonwoods."

"My name! Oh, I remember. You did know my name when you spoke first. Well, tell me where you heard it and from whom?"

"At the little village—Glaze, I think it's called—some fifty miles or more west of here. An' I heard it from a Gentile, a rider who said you'd know where to tell me to find—"

"What?" she demanded, imperiously, as Lassiter broke off.

"Milly Erne's grave," he answered low, and the words came with a wrench.

Venters wheeled in his chair to regard Lassiter in amazement, and Jane slowly raised herself in white, still wonder.

"Milly Erne's grave?" she echoed, in a whisper. "What do you

16

know of Milly Erne, my best-beloved friend—who died in my arms? What were you to her?"

"Did I claim to be anythin'?" he inquired. "I know people—relatives—who have long wanted to know where she's buried. That's all."

"Relatives? She never spoke of relatives, except a brother who was shot in Texas. Lassiter, Milly Erne's grave is in a secret burying-ground on my property."

"Will you take me there? . . . You'll be offendin' Mormons worse than by breakin' bread with me."

"Indeed yes, but I'll do it. Only we must go unseen. To-morrow, perhaps."

"Thank you, Jane Withersteen," replied the rider, and he bowed to her and stepped backward out of the court.

"Will you not stay—sleep under my roof?" she asked.

"No, ma'am, an' thanks again. I never sleep indoors. An' even if I did there's that gatherin' storm in the village below. No, no. I'll go to the sage. I hope you won't suffer none for your kindness to me."

"Lassiter," said Venters, with a half-bitter laugh, "my bed, too, is the sage. Perhaps we may meet out there."

"Mebbe so. But the sage is wide an' I won't be near. Good night."

At Lassiter's low whistle the black horse whinnied, and carefully picked his blind way out of the grove. The rider did not bridle him, but walked beside him, leading him by touch of hand, and together they passed slowly into the shade of the cottonwoods.

"Jane, I must be off soon," said Venters. "Give me my guns. If I'd had my guns—"

"Either my friend or the Elder of my church would be lying dead," she interposed.

"Tull would be—surely."

"Oh, you fierce-blooded, savage youth! Can't I teach you forbearance, mercy? Bern, it's divine to forgive your enemies. 'Let not the sun go down upon thy wrath.' "

"Hush! Talk to me no more of mercy or religion—after to-day. To-day this strange coming of Lassiter left me still a man, and now I'll die a man! . . . Give me my guns."

17

Silently she went into the house, to return with a heavy cartridge-belt and gun-filled sheath and a long rifle; these she handed to him, and as he buckled on the belt she stood before him in silent eloquence.

"Jane," he said, in gentler voice, "don't look so. I'm not going out to murder your churchman. I'll try to avoid him and all his men. But can't you see I've reached the end of my rope? Jane, you're a wonderful woman. Never was there a woman so unselfish and good. Only you're blind in one way. . . . Listen!"

From behind the grove came the clicking sound of horses in a rapid trot.

"Some of your riders," he continued. "It's getting time for the night shift. Let us go out to the bench in the grove and talk there."

It was still daylight in the open, but under the spreading cottonwoods shadows were obscuring the lanes. Venters drew Jane off from one of these into a shrub-lined trail, just wide enough for the two to walk abreast, and in a roundabout way led her far from the house to a knoll on the edge of the grove. Here in a secluded nook was a bench from which, through an opening in the tree-tops, could be seen the sage-slope and the wall of rock and the dim lines of cañons. Jane had not spoken since Venters had shocked her with his first harsh speech; but all the way she had clung to his arm, and now, as he stopped and laid his rifle against the bench, she still clung to him.

"Jane, I'm afraid I must leave you."

"Bern!" she cried.

"Yes, it looks that way. My position is not a happy one—I can't feel right—I've lost all—"

"I'll give you anything you—"

"Listen, please. When I say loss I don't mean what you think. I mean loss of good-will, good name—that which would have enabled me to stand up in this village without bitterness. Well, it's too late. . . . Now, as to the future, I think you'd do best to give me up. Tull is implacable. You ought to see from his intention to-day that— But you can't see. Your blindness—your damned religion! . . . Jane, forgive me—I'm sore within and something rankles. Well, I fear that invisible hand will turn its hidden work to your ruin."

"Invisible hand? Bern!"

"I mean your Bishop." Venters said it deliberately and would not release her as she started back. "He's the law. The edict went forth to ruin me. Well, look at me! It'll now go forth to compel you to the will of the Church."

"You wrong Bishop Dyer. Tull is hard, I know. But then he has been in love with me for years."

"Oh, your faith and your excuses! You can't see what I know—and if you did see it you'd not admit it to save your life. That's the Mormon of you. These elders and bishops will do absolutely any deed to go on building up the power and wealth of their church, their empire. Think of what they've done to the Gentiles here, to me—think of Milly Erne's fate!"

"What do you know of her story?"

"I know enough—all, perhaps, except the name of the Mormon who brought her here. But I must stop this kind of talk."

She pressed his hand in response. He helped her to a seat beside him on the bench. And he respected a silence that he divined was full of woman's deep emotion, beyond his understanding.

It was the moment when the last ruddy rays of the sunset brightened momentarily before yielding to twilight. And for Venters the outlook before him was in some sense similar to a feeling of his future, and with searching eyes he studied the beautiful purple, barren waste of sage. Here was the unknown and the perilous. The whole scene impressed Venters as a wild, austere, and mighty manifestation of nature. And as it somehow reminded him of his prospect in life, so it suddenly resembled the woman near him, only in her there were greater beauty and peril, a mystery more unsolvable, and something nameless that numbed his heart and dimmed his eye.

"Look! A rider!" exclaimed Jane, breaking the silence. "Can that be Lassiter?"

Venters moved his glance once more to the west. A horseman showed dark on the sky-line, then merged into the color of the sage.

"It might be. But I think not—that fellow was coming in. One of your riders, more likely. Yes, I see him clearly now. And there's another."

"I see them, too."

"Jane, your riders seem as many as the bunches of sage. I ran into five yesterday 'way down near the trail to Deception Pass. They were with the white herd."

"You still go to that cañon? Bern, I wish you wouldn't. Oldring and his rustlers live somewhere down there."

"Well, what of that?"

"Tull has already hinted to your frequent trips into Deception Pass."

"I know." Venters uttered a short laugh. "He'll make a rustler of me next. But, Jane, there's no water for fifty miles after I leave here, and the nearest is in the cañon. I must drink and water my horse. There! I see more riders. They are going out."

"The red herd is on the slope, toward the Pass."

Twilight was fast falling. A group of horsemen crossed the dark line of low ground to become more distinct as they climbed the slope. The silence broke to a clear call from an incoming rider, and, almost like the peal of a hunting-horn, floated back the answer. The outgoing riders moved swiftly, came sharply into sight as they topped a ridge to show wild and black above the horizon, and then passed down, dimming into the purple of the sage.

"I hope they don't meet Lassiter," said Jane.

"So do I," replied Venters. "By this time the riders of the night shift know what happened to-day. But Lassiter will likely keep out of their way."

"Bern, who is Lassiter? He's only a name to me—a terrible name."

"Who is he? I don't know, Jane. Nobody I ever met knows him. He talks a little like a Texan, like Milly Erne. Did you note that?"

"Yes. How strange of him to know of her! And she lived here ten years and has been dead two. Bern, what do you know of Lassiter? Tell me what he has done—why you spoke of him to Tull—threatening to become another Lassiter yourself?"

"Jane, I only heard things, rumors, stories, most of which I disbelieved. At Glaze his name was known, but none of the riders or ranchers I knew there ever met him. At Stone Bridge I never heard him mentioned. But at Sterling and villages north of there he was spoken of often. I've never been in a village which he had been known to visit. There were many conflicting stories about him and his doings. Some said he had shot up this and that Mormon village, and others denied it. I'm inclined to believe he has, and you know how Mormons hide the truth. But there was one feature about Lassiter upon which all agree—that he was what riders in this country call a gun-man. He's a man with a marvelous quickness and accuracy in the use of a Colt. And now that I've seen him I know more. Lassiter was born without fear. I watched him with eyes which saw him my friend. I'll never forget the moment I recognized him from what had been told me of his crouch before the draw. It was then I yelled his name. I believe that yell saved Tull's life. At any rate, I know this, between Tull and death then there was not the breadth of the littlest hair. If he or any of his men had moved a finger downward . . ."

Venters left his meaning unspoken, but at the suggestion Jane shuddered.

The pale afterglow in the west darkened with the merging of twilight into night. The sage now spread out black and gloomy. One dim star glimmered in the southwest sky. The sound of trotting horses had ceased, and there was silence broken only by a faint, dry pattering of cottonwood leaves in the soft night wind.

Into this peace and calm suddenly broke the high-keyed yelp of a coyote, and from far off in the darkness came the faint answering note of a trailing mate.

"Hello! the sage-dogs are barking," said Venters.

"I don't like to hear them," replied Jane. "At night, sometimes, when I lie awake, listening to the long mourn or breaking bark or wild howl, I think of you asleep somewhere in the sage, and my heart aches."

"Jane, you couldn't listen to sweeter music, nor could I have a better bed."

"Just think! Men like Lassiter and you have no home, no comfort, no rest, no place to lay your weary heads. Well! . . . Let us be patient. Tull's anger may cool, and time may help us. You might do some service to the village—who can tell? Suppose you discovered the long-unknown hiding-place of Oldring and his band, and told it to my riders? That would disarm Tull's ugly hints and put you in favor. For years my riders have trailed the tracks of stolen cattle. You know as well as I how dearly we've paid for our ranges in this wild country. Oldring drives our cattle down into the network of deceiving cañons, and somewhere far to the north or east he drives them up and out to Utah markets. If you will spend time in Deception Pass try to find the trails."

"Jane, I've thought of that. I'll try."

"I must go now. And it hurts, for now I'll never be sure of seeing you again. But to-morrow, Bern?"

"To-morrow surely. I'll watch for Lassiter and ride in with him."

"Good night."

Then she left him and moved away, a white, gliding shape that soon vanished in the shadows.

Venters waited until the faint slam of a door assured him she had reached the house; and then, taking up his rifle, he noiselessly slipped through the bushes, down the knoll, and on under the dark trees to the edge of the grove. The sky was now turning from gray to blue; stars had begun to lighten the earlier blackness; and from the wide flat sweep before him blew a cool wind, fragrant with the breath of sage. Keeping close to the edge of the cottonwoods, he went swiftly and silently westward. The grove was long, and he had not reached the end when he heard something that brought him to a halt. Low padded thuds told him horses were coming this way. He sank down in the gloom, waiting, listening. Much before he had expected, judging from sound, to his amazement he descried horsemen near at hand. They were riding along the border of the sage, and instantly he knew the hoofs of the horses were muffled. Then the pale star-light afforded him indistinct sight of the riders. But his eyes were keen and used to the dark, and by peering closely he recognized the huge bulk and black-bearded visage of Oldring and the lithe, supple form of the rustler's lieutenant, a masked rider. They passed on; the darkness swallowed them. Then, farther out on the sage, a dark, compact body of horsemen went by, almost without sound, almost like specters, and they, too, melted into the night.

CHAPTER III

NO unusual circumstances was it for Oldring and some of his men to visit Cottonwoods in the broad light of day, but for him to prowl about in the dark with the hoofs of his horses muffled meant that mischief was brewing. Moreover, to Venters the presence of the masked rider with Oldring seemed especially ominous. For about this man there was mystery; he seldom rode through the village, and when he did ride through it was swiftly; riders seldom met by day on the sage; but wherever he rode there always followed deeds as dark and mysterious as the mask he wore. Oldring's band did not confine themselves to the rustling of cattle.

Venters lay low in the shade of the cottonwoods, pondering this chance meeting, and not for many moments did he consider it safe to move on. Then, with sudden impulse, he turned the other way and went back along the grove. When he reached the path leading to Jane's home he decided to go down to the village. So he hurried onward, with quick soft steps. Once beyond the grove he entered the one and only street. It was wide, lined with tall poplars, and under each row of trees, inside the foot-path, were ditches where ran the water from Jane Withersteen's spring.

Between the trees twinkled lights of cottage candles, and far down flared bright windows of the village stores. When Venters got closer to these he saw knots of men standing together in earnest conversation. The usual lounging on the corners and benches and steps was not in evidence. Keeping in the shadow, Venters went closer and closer until he could hear voices. But he could not distinguish what was said. He recognized many Mormons, and looked hard for Tull and his men, but looked in vain.

23

Venters concluded that the rustlers had not passed along the village street. No doubt these earnest men were discussing Lassiter's coming. But Venters felt positive that Tull's intention toward himself that day had not been and would not be revealed. So Venters, seeing there was little for him to learn, began retracing his steps. The church was dark, Bishop Dyer's home next to it was also dark, and likewise Tull's cottage. Upon almost any night at this hour there would be lights here, and Venters marked the unusual omission.

As he was about to pass out of the street to skirt the grove, he once more slunk down at the sound of trotting horses. Presently he descried two mounted men riding toward him. He hugged the shadow of a tree. Again the starlight, brighter now, aided him, and he made out Tull's stalwart figure, and beside him the short, froglike shape of the rider Jerry. They were silent, and they rode on to disappear.

Venters went his way with busy, gloomy mind, revolving events of the day, trying to reckon those brooding in the night. His thoughts overwhelmed him. Up in that dark grove dwelt a woman who had been his friend. And he skulked about her home, gripping a gun stealthily as an Indian, a man without place or people or purpose. Above her hovered the shadow of grim, hidden, secret power. No queen could have given more royally out of a bounteous store than Jane Withersteen gave her people, and likewise to those unfortunates whom her people hated. She asked only the divine right of all women—freedom; to love and to live as her heart willed. And yet prayer and her hope were vain.

"For years I've seen a storm clouding over her and the village of Cottonwoods," muttered Venters, as he strode on. "Soon it 'll burst. I don't like the prospects." That night the villagers whispered in the street—and night-riding rustlers muffled horses— and Tull was at work in secret—and out there in the sage hid a man who meant something terrible—Lassiter!

Venters passed the black cottonwoods, and, entering the sage, climbed the gradual slope. He kept his direction in line with a western star. From time to time he stopped to listen and heard only the usual familiar bark of coyote and sweep of wind and rustle of sage. Presently a low jumble of rocks loomed up darkly somewhat to his right, and, turning that way, he whistled softly.

Out of the rocks glided a dog that leaped and whined about him. He climbed over rough, broken rock, picking his way carefully, and then went down. Here it was darker, and sheltered from the wind. A white object guided him. It was another dog, and this one was asleep, curled up between a saddle and a pack. The animal awoke and thumped his tail in greeting. Venters placed the saddle for a pillow, rolled in his blankets, with his face upward to the stars. The white dog snuggled close to him. The other whined and pattered a few yards to the rise of ground and there crouched on guard. And in that wild covert Venters shut his eyes under the great white stars and intense vaulted blue, bitterly comparing their loneliness to his own, and fell asleep.

When he awoke, day had dawned and all about him was bright steel-gray. The air had a cold tang. Arising, he greeted the fawning dogs and stretched his cramped body, and then, gathering together bunches of dead sage sticks, he lighted a fire. Strips of dried beef held to the blaze for a moment served him and the dogs. He drank from a canteen. There was nothing else in his outfit; he had grown used to a scant fire. Then he sat over the fire, palms outspread, and waited. Waiting had been his chief occupation for months, and he scarcely knew what he waited for, unless it was the passing of the hours. But now he sensed action in the immediate present; the day promised another meeting with Lassiter and Jane, perhaps news of the rustlers; on the morrow he meant to take the trail to Deception Pass.

And while he waited he talked to his dogs. He called them Ring and Whitie; they were sheep-dogs, half collie, half deerhound, superb in build, perfectly trained. It seemed that in his fallen fortunes these dogs understood the nature of their value to him, and governed their affection and faithfulness accordingly. Whitie watched him with somber eyes of love, and Ring, crouched on the little rise of ground above, kept tireless guard. When the sun rose, the white dog took the place of the other, and Ring went to sleep at his master's feet.

By and by Venters rolled up his blankets and tied them and his meager pack together, then climbed out to look for his horse. He saw him, presently, a little way off in the sage, and went to fetch him. In that country, where every rider boasted of a fine mount and was eager for a race, where thoroughbreds dotted the wonderful grazing ranges, Venters rode a horse that was sad proof of his misfortunes.

Then, with his back against a stone, Venters faced the east, and, stick in hand and idle blade, he waited. The glorious sunlight filled the valley with purple fire. Before him, to left, to right, waving, rolling, sinking, rising, like low swells of a purple sea, stretched the sage. Out of the grove of cottonwoods, a green patch on the purple, gleamed the dull red of Jane Withersteen's old stone house. And from there extended the wide green of the village gardens and orchards marked by the graceful poplars; and farther down shone the deep, dark richness of the alfalfa fields. Numberless red and black and white dots speckled the sage, and these were cattle and horses.

So, watching and waiting, Venters let the time wear away. At length he saw a horse rise above a ridge, and he knew it to be Lassiter's black. Climbing to the highest rock, so that he would show against the sky-line, he stood and waved his hat. The almost instant turning of Lassiter's horse attested to the quickness of that rider's eye. Then Venters climbed down, saddled his horse, tied on his pack, and, with a word to his dogs, was about to ride out to meet Lassiter, when he concluded to wait for him there, on higher ground, where the outlook was commanding.

It had been long since Venters had experienced friendly greeting from a man. Lassiter's warmed in him something that had grown cold from neglect. And when he had returned it, with a strong grip of the iron hand that held his, and met the gray eyes, he knew that Lassiter and he were to be friends.

"Venters, let's talk awhile before we go down there," said Lassiter, slipping his bridle. "I ain't in no hurry. Them's sure fine dogs you've got." With a rider's eye he took in the points of Venter's horse, but did not speak his thought. "Well, did anythin' come off after I left you last night?"

Venters told him about the rustlers.

"I was snug hid in the sage," replied Lassiter, "an' didn't see or hear no one. Oldrin's got a high hand here, I reckon. It's no news up in Utah how he holes in cañons an' leaves no track." Lassiter was silent a moment. "Me an' Oldrin' wasn't exactly strangers some years back when he drove cattle into Bostil's Ford, at the head of the Rio Virgin. But he got harassed there an' now he drives some place else."

"Lassiter, you knew him? Tell me, is he Mormon or Gentile?"

"I can't say. I've knowed Mormons who pretended to be Gentiles."

"No Mormon ever pretended that unless he was a rustler," declared Venters.

"Mebbe so."

"It's a hard country for any one, but hardest for Gentiles. Did you ever know or hear of a Gentile prospering in a Mormon community?"

"I never did."

"Well, I want to get out of Utah. I've a mother living in Illinois. I want to go home. It's eight years now."

The older man's sympathy moved Venters to tell his story. He had left Quincy, run off to seek his fortune in the gold fields, had never gotten any farther than Salt Lake City, wandered here and there as helper, teamster, shepherd, and drifted southward over the divide and across the barrens and up the rugged plateau through the passes to the last border settlements. Here he became a rider of the sage, had stock of his own, and for a time prospered, until chance threw him in the employ of Jane Withersteen.

"Lassiter, I needn't tell you the rest."

"Well, it 'd be no news to me. I know Mormons. I've seen their women's strange love an' patience an' sacrifice an' silence an' what I call madness for their idea of God. An' over against that I've seen the tricks of men. They work hand in hand, all together, an' in the dark. No man can hold out against them, unless he takes to packin' guns. For Mormons are slow to kill. That's the only good I ever seen in their religion. Venters, take this from me, these Mormons ain't just right in their minds. Else could a Mormon marry one woman when he already has a wife, an' call it duty?"

"Lassiter, you think as I think," returned Venters.

"How'd it come then that you never throwed a gun on Tull or some of them?" inquired the rider, curiously.

"Jane pleaded with me, begged me to be patient, to overlook. She even took my guns from me. I lost all before I knew it," replied Venters, with the red color in his face. "But, Lassiter, listen.

27

Out of the wreck I saved a Winchester, two Colts, and plenty of shells. I packed these down into Deception Pass. There, almost every day for six months, I have practised with my rifle till the barrel burnt my hands. Practised the draw—the firing of a Colt, hour after hour!"

"Now that's interestin' to me," said Lassiter, with a quick uplift of his head and a concentration of his gray gaze on Venters. "Could you throw a gun before you began that practisin'?"

"Yes. And now . . ." Venters made a lightning-swift movement.

Lassiter smiled, and then his bronzed eyelids narrowed till his eyes seemed mere gray slits. "You'll kill Tull!" He did not question; he affirmed.

"I promised Jane Withersteen I'd try to avoid Tull. I'll keep my word. But sooner or later Tull and I will meet. As I feel now, if he even looks at me I'll draw!"

"I reckon so. There'll be hell down there, presently." He paused a moment and flicked a sage-brush with his quirt. "Venters, seein' as you're considerable worked up, tell me Milly Erne's story."

Venters's agitation stilled to the trace of suppressed eagerness in Lassiter's query.

"Milly Erne's story? Well, Lassiter, I'll tell you what I know. Milly Erne had been in Cottonwoods years when I first arrived there, and most of what I tell you happened before my arrival. I got to know her pretty well. She was a slip of a woman, and crazy on religion. I conceived an idea that I never mentioned—I thought she was at heart more Gentile than Mormon. But she passed as a Mormon, and certainly she had the Mormon woman's locked lips. You know, in every Mormon village there are women who seem mysterious to us, but about Milly there was more than the ordinary mystery. When she came to Cottonwoods she had a beautiful little girl whom she loved passionately. Milly was not known openly in Cottonwoods as a Mormon wife. That she really was a Mormon wife I have no doubt. Perhaps the Mormon's other wife or wives would not acknowledge Milly. Such things happen in these villages. Mormon wives wear yokes, but they get jealous. Well, whatever had brought Milly to this country—love or madness of religion—she repented of it. She gave up teaching the village school. She quit the church. And she began to fight Mormon upbringing for her baby girl. Then the Mormons put on the

28

screws—slowly, as is their way. At last the child disappeared. Lost, was the report. The child was stolen, I know that. So do you. That wrecked Milly Erne. But she lived on in hope. She became a slave. She worked her heart and soul and life out to get back her child. She never heard of it again. Then she sank. . . . I can see her now, a frail thing, so transparent you could almost look through her—white like ashes—and her eyes! . . . Her eyes have always haunted me. She had one real friend—Jane Withersteen. But Jane couldn't mend a broken heart, and Milly died."

For moments Lassiter did not speak, or turn his head.

"The man!" he exclaimed, presently, in husky accents.

"I haven't the slightest idea who the Mormon was," replied Venters; "nor has any Gentile in Cottonwoods."

"Does Jane Withersteen know?"

"Yes. But a red-hot running-iron couldn't burn that name out of her!"

Without further speech Lassiter started off, walking his horse, and Venters followed with his dogs. Half a mile down the slope they entered a luxuriant growth of willows, and soon came into an open space carpeted with grass like deep green velvet. The rushing of water and singing of birds filled their ears. Venters led his comrade to a shady bower and showed him Amber Spring. It was a magnificent outburst of clear, amber water pouring from a dark, stone-lined hole. Lassiter knelt and drank, lingered there to drink again. He made no comment, but Venters did not need words. Next to his horse a rider of the sage loved a spring. And this spring was the most beautiful and remarkable known to the upland riders of southern Utah. It was the spring that made old Withersteen a feudal lord and now enabled his daughter to return the toll which her father had exacted from the toilers of the sage.

The spring gushed forth in a swirling torrent, and leaped down joyously to make its swift way along a willow-skirted channel. Moss and ferns and lilies overhung its green banks. Except for the rough-hewn stones that held and directed the water, this willow thicket and glade had been left as nature had made it.

Below were artificial lakes, three in number, one above the other in banks of raised earth; and round about them rose the lofty green-foliaged shafts of poplar trees. Ducks dotted the glassy surface of the lakes; a blue heron stood motionless on a water-gate; kingfishers darted with shrieking flight along the shady banks; a white hawk sailed above; and from the trees and shrubs came the song of robins and cat-birds. It was all in strange contrast to the endless slopes of lonely sage and the wild rock environs beyond. Venters thought of the woman who loved the birds and the green of the leaves and the murmur of the water.

Next on the slope, just below the third and largest lake, were corrals and a wide stone barn and open sheds and coops and pens. Here were clouds of dust, and cracking sounds of hoofs, and romping colts and heehawing burros. Neighing horses trampled to the corral fences. And from the little windows of the barn projected bobbing heads of bays and blacks and sorrels. When the two men entered the immense barnyard, from all around the din increased. This welcome, however, was not seconded by the several men and boys who vanished on sight.

Venters and Lassiter were turning toward the house when Jane appeared in the lane leading a horse. In riding-skirt and blouse she seemed to have lost some of her statuesque proportions, and looked more like a girl rider than the mistress of Withersteen. She was brightly smiling, and her greeting was warmly cordial.

"Good news," she announced. "I've been to the village. All is quiet. I expected—I don't know what. But there's no excitement. And Tull has ridden out on his way to Glaze."

"Tull gone?" inquired Venters, with surprise. He was wondering what could have taken Tull away. Was it to avoid another meeting with Lassiter that he went? Could it have any connection with the probable nearness of Oldring and his gang?

"Gone, yes, thank goodness," replied Jane. "Now I'll have peace for a while. Lassiter, I want you to see my horses. You are a rider, and you must be a judge of horseflesh. Some of mine have Arabian blood. My father got his best strain in Nevada from Indians who claimed their horses were bred down from the original stock left by the Spaniards."

"Well, ma'am, the one you've been ridin' takes my eye," said Lassiter, as he walked round the racy, clean-limbed, and fine-pointed roan.

"Where are the boys?" she asked, looking about. "Jerd, Paul, where are you? Here, bring out the horses."

The sound of dropping bars inside the barn was the signal for the horses to jerk their heads in the windows, to snort and stamp. Then they came pounding out of the door, a file of thoroughbreds, to plunge about the barnyard, heads and tails up, manes flying. They halted afar off, squared away to look, came slowly forward with whinnies for their mistress, and doubtful snorts for the strangers and their horses.

"Come—come—come," called Jane, holding out her hands. "Why Bells—Wrangle, where are your manners? Come, Black Star—come, Night. Ah, you beauties! My racers of the sage!"

Only two came up to her; those she called Night and Black Star. Venters never looked at them without delight. The first was soft dead black, the other glittering black, and they were perfectly matched in size, both being high and long-bodied, wide through the shoulders, with lithe, powerful legs. That they were a woman's pets showed in the gloss of skin, the fineness of mane. It showed, too, in the light of big eyes and the gentle reach of eagerness.

"I never seen their like," was Lassiter's encomium, "an' in my day I've seen a sight of horses. Now, ma'am, if you was wantin' to make a long an' fast ride across the sage—say to elope—"

Lassiter ended there with dry humor, yet behind that was meaning. Jane blushed and made arch eyes at him.

"Take care, Lassiter, I might think that a proposal," she replied, gaily. "It's dangerous to propose elopement to a Mormon woman. Well, I was expecting you. Now will be a good hour to show you Milly Erne's grave. The day-riders have gone, and the night-riders haven't come in. Bern, what do you make of that? Need I worry? You know I have to be made worry."

"Well, it's not usual for the night shift to ride in so late," replied Venters, slowly, and his glance sought Lassiter's. "Cattle are usually quiet after dark. Still, I've known even a coyote to stampede your white herd."

"I refuse to borrow trouble. Come," said Jane.

They mounted, and, with Jane in the lead, rode down the lane, and, turning off into a cattle trail, proceeded westward. Venters's dogs trotted behind them. On this side of the ranch the outlook was different from that on the other; the immediate foreground was rough and the sage more rugged and less colorful; there were no dark-blue lines of cañons to hold the eye, nor any uprearing rock walls. It was a long roll and slope into gray obscurity. Soon

31

Jane left the trail and rode into the sage, and presently she dismounted and threw her bridle. The men did likewise. Then, on foot, they followed her, coming out at length on the rim of a low escarpment. She passed by several little ridges of earth to halt before a faintly defined mound. It lay in the shade of a sweeping sage-brush close to the edge of the promontory; and a rider could have jumped his horse over it without recognizing a grave.

"Here!"

She looked sad as she spoke, but she offered no explanation for the neglect of an unmarked, uncared-for grave. There was a little bunch of pale, sweet lavender daisies, doubtless planted there by Jane.

"I only come here to remember and to pray," she said. "But I leave no trail!"

A grave in the sage! How lonely this resting-place of Milly Erne! The cottonwoods or the alfalfa fields were not in sight, nor was there any rock or ridge or cedar to lend contrast to the monotony. Gray slopes, tinging the purple, barren and wild, with the wind waving the sage, swept away to the dim horizon.

Lassiter looked at the grave and then out into space. At that moment he seemed a figure of bronze.

Jane touched Venters's arm and led him back to the horses.

"Bern!" cried Jane, when they were out of hearing. "Suppose Lassiter were Milly's husband—the father of that little girl lost so long ago!"

"It might be, Jane. Let us ride on. If he wants to see us again he'll come."

So they mounted and rode out to the cattle trail and began to climb. From the height of the ridge, where they had started down, Venters looked back. He did not see Lassiter, but his glance, drawn irresistibly farther out on the gradual slope, caught sight of a moving cloud of dust.

"Hello, a rider!"

"Yes, I see," said Jane.

"That fellow's riding hard. Jane, there's something wrong."

"Oh yes, there must be. . . . How he rides!"

The horse disappeared in the sage, and then puffs of dust marked his course.

"He's short-cut on us—he's making straight for the corrals."

Venters and Jane galloped their steeds and reined in at the turning of the lane. This lane led down to the right of the grove. Suddenly into its lower entrance flashed a bay horse. Then Venters caught the fast rhythmic beat of pounding hoofs. Soon his keen eye recognized the swing of the rider in his saddle.

"It's Judkins, your Gentile rider!" he cried. "Jane, when Judkins rides like that it means hell!"

CHAPTER IV

DECEPTION PASS

THE rider thundered up and almost threw his foam-flecked horse in the sudden stop. He was a giant form, and with fearless eyes.

"Judkins, you're all bloody!" cried Jane, in affright. "Oh, you've been shot!"

"Nothin' much, Miss Withersteen. I got a nick in the shoulder. I'm some wet an' the hoss's been throwin' lather, so all this ain't blood."

"What's up?" queried Venters, sharply.

"Rustlers sloped off with the red herd."

"Where are my riders?" demanded Jane.

"Miss Withersteen, I was alone all night with the herd. At daylight this mornin' the rustlers rode down. They began to shoot at me on sight. They chased me hard an' far, burnin' powder all the time, but I got away."

"Jud, they meant to kill you," declared Venters.

"Now I wonder," returned Judkins. "They wanted me bad. An' it ain't regular for rustlers to waste time chasin' one rider."

"Thank heaven you got away," said Jane. "But my riders— where are they?"

"I don't know. The night-riders weren't there last night when I rode down, an' this mornin' I met no day-riders."

"Judkins! Bern they've been set upon—killed by Oldring's men!"

"I don't think so," replied Venters, decidedly. "Jane, your riders haven't gone out in the sage."

"Bern, what do you mean?" Jane Withersteen turned deathly pale.

"You remember what I said about the unseen hand?"

34

"Oh! . . . Impossible!"

"I hope so. But I fear—" Venters finished, with a shake of his head.

"Bern, you're bitter; but that's only natural. We'll wait to see what's happened to my riders. Judkins, come to the house with me. Your wound must be attended to."

"Jane, I'll find out where Oldring drives the herd," vowed Venters.

"No, no! Bern, don't risk it now—when the rustlers are in such shooting mood."

"I'm going. Jud, how many cattle in that red herd?"

"Twenty-five hundred head."

"Whew! What on earth can Oldring do with so many cattle? Why, a hundred head is a big steal. I've got to find out."

"Don't go," implored Jane.

"Bern, you want a hoss thet can run. Miss Withersteen, if it's not too bold of me to advise, make him take a fast hoss or don't let him go."

"Yes, yes, Judkins. He must ride a horse that can't be caught. Which one—Black Star—Night?"

"Jane, I won't take either," said Venters, emphatically. "I wouldn't risk losing one of your favorites."

"Wrangle, then?"

"Thet's the hoss," replied Judkins. "Wrangle can outrun Black Star an' Night. You'd never believe it, Miss Withersteen, but I know. Wrangle's the biggest an' fastest hoss on the sage."

"Oh no, Wrangle can't beat Black Star. But, Bern, take Wrangle, if you will go. Ask Jerd for anything you need. Oh, be watchful, careful. . . . God speed you!"

She clasped his hand, turned quickly away, and went down the lane with the rider.

Venters rode to the barn, and, leaping off, shouted for Jerd. The boy came running. Venters sent him for meat, bread, and dried fruits, to be packed in saddlebags. His own horse he turned loose into the nearest corral. Then he went for Wrangle. The giant sorrel had earned his name for a trait the opposite of amiability. He came readily out of the barn, but once in the yard he broke from Venters, and plunged about with ears laid back. Venters had to rope him, and then he kicked down a section of

fence, stood on his hind legs, crashed down and fought the rope.
Jerd returned to lend a hand.

"Wrangle don't git enough work," said Jerd, as the big saddle
went on. "He's unruly when he's corralled, an' wants to run. Wait
till he smells the sage!"

"Jerd, this horse is an iron-jawed devil. I never straddled him
but once. Run? Say, he's swift as wind!"

When Venters's boot touched the stirrup the sorrel bolted,
giving him the rider's flying mount. The swing of this fiery horse
recalled to Venters days that were not really long past, when he
rode into the sage as the leader of Jane Withersteen's riders.
Wrangle pulled hard on a tight rein. He galloped out of the lane,
down the shady border of the grove, and hauled up at the watering-trough, where he pranced and champed his bit. Venters got
off and filled his canteen while the horse drank. The dogs, Ring
and Whitie, came trotting up for their drink. Then Venters re-
mounted and turned Wrangle toward the sage.

A wide, white trail wound away down the slope. One keen,
sweeping glance told Venters that there was neither man nor
horse nor steer within the limit of his vision, unless they were
lying down in the sage. Ring loped in the lead and Whitie loped
in the rear. Wrangle settled gradually into an easy swinging
canter, and Venters's thoughts, now that the rush and flurry of
the start were past, and the long miles stretched before him, reverted to a calm reckoning of late singular coincidences.

There was the night ride of Tull's, which, viewed in the light of
subsequent events, had a look of his covert machinations; Oldring
and his Masked Rider and his rustlers riding muffled horses; the
report that Tull had ridden out that morning with his man Jerry
on the trail to Glaze, the strange disappearance of Jane Withersteen's riders, the unusually determined attempt to kill the one
Gentile still in her employ, an intention frustrated, no doubt, only
by Judkin's magnificent riding of her racer, and lastly the driving
of the red herd. These events, to Venters's color of mind, had a
dark relationship. Remembering Jane's accusation of bitterness,
he tried hard to put aside his rancor in judging Tull. But it was
bitter knowledge that made him see the truth. He had felt the
shadow of an unseen hand; he had watched till he saw its dim
outline, and then he had traced it to a man's hate, to the rivalry

of a Mormon Elder, to the power of a Bishop, to the long, far-reaching arm of a terrible creed. That unseen hand had made its first move against Jane Withersteen. Her riders had been called in, leaving her without help to drive seven thousand head of cattle. But to Venters it seemed extraordinary that the power which had called in these riders had left so many cattle to be driven by rustlers and harried by wolves. For hand in glove with that power was an insatiate greed; they were one and the same.

"What can Oldring do with twenty-five hundred head of cattle?" muttered Venters. "Is he a Mormon? Did he meet Tull last night? It looks like a black plot to me. But Tull and his churchmen wouldn't ruin Jane Withersteen unless the Church was to profit by that ruin. Where does Oldring come in? I'm going to find out about these things."

Wrangle did the twenty-five miles in three hours and walked little of the way. When he had gotten warmed up he had been allowed to choose his own gait. The afternoon had well advanced when Venters struck the trail of the red herd and found where it had grazed the night before. Then Venters rested the horse and used his eyes. Near at hand were a cow and a calf and several yearlings, and farther out in the sage some straggling steers. He caught a glimpse of coyotes skulking near the cattle. The slow, sweeping gaze of the rider failed to find other living things within the field of sight. The sage about him was breast-high to his horse, oversweet with its warm, fragrant breath, gray where it waved to the light, darker where the wind left it still, and beyond the wonderful haze-purple lent by distance. Far across that wide waste began the slow lift of uplands through which Deception Pass cut its tortuous many-cañoned way.

Venters raised the bridle of his horse and followed the broad cattle trail. The crushed sage resembled the path of a monster snake. In a few miles of travel he passed several cows and calves that had escaped the drive. Then he stood on the last high bench of the slope with the floor of the valley beneath. The opening of the cañon showed in a break of the sage, and the cattle trail paralleled it as far as he could see. That trail led to an undiscovered point where Oldring drove cattle into the pass, and many a rider who had followed it had never returned. Venters satisfied himself that the rustlers had not deviated from their usual course, and then he turned at right angles off the cattle trail and made for the head of the pass.

The sun lost its heat and wore down to the western horizon, where it changed from white to gold and rested like a huge ball about to roll on its golden shadows down the slope. Venters watched the lengthening of the rays and bars, and marveled at his own league-long shadow. The sun sank. There was instant shading of brightness about him, and he saw a kind of cold purple bloom creep ahead of him to cross the cañon, to mount the opposite slope and chase and darken and bury the last golden flare of sunlight.

Venters rode into a trail that he always took to get down into the cañon. He dismounted and found no tracks but his own made days previous. Nevertheless he sent the dog Ring ahead and waited. In a little while Ring returned. Whereupon Venters led his horse on to the break in the ground.

The opening into Deception Pass was one of the remarkable natural phenomena in a country remarkable for vast slopes of sage, uplands insulated by gigantic red walls, and deep cañons of mysterious source and outlet. Here the valley floor was level, and here opened a narrow chasm, a ragged vent in yellow walls of stone. The trail down the five hundred feet of sheer depth always tested Venters's nerve. It was bad going for even a burro. But Wrangle, as Venters led him, snorted defiance or disgust rather than fear, and, like a hobbled horse on the jump, lifted his ponderous iron-shod fore hoofs and crashed down over the first rough step. Venters warmed to greater admiration of the sorrel; and, giving him a loose bridle, he stepped down foot by foot. Oftentimes the stones and shale started by Wrangle buried Venters to his knees; again he was hard put to it to dodge a rolling boulder; there were times when he could not see Wrangle for dust, and once he and the horse rode a sliding shelf of yellow, weathered cliff. It was a trail on which there could be no stops, and, therefore, if perilous, it was at least one that did not take long in the descent.

Venters breathed lighter when that was over, and felt a sudden assurance in the success of his enterprise. For at first it had been a reckless determination to achieve something at any cost, and

38

now it resolved itself into an adventure worthy of all his reason and cunning, and keenness of eye and ear.

Piñon pines clustered in little clumps along the level floor of the pass. Twilight had gathered under the walls. Venters rode into the trail and up the cañon. Gradually the trees and caves and objects low down turned black, and this blackness moved up the walls till night enfolded the pass, while day still lingered above. The sky darkened; and stars began to show, at first pale and then bright. Sharp notches of the rim-wall, biting like teeth into the blue, were landmarks by which Venters knew where his camping site lay. He had to feel his way through a thicket of slender oaks to a spring where he watered Wrangle and drank himself. Here he unsaddled and turned Wrangle loose, having no fear that the horse would leave the thick, cool grass adjacent to the spring. Next he satisfied his own hunger, fed Ring and Whitie, and, with them curled beside him, composed himself to await sleep.

There had been a time when night in the high altitude of these Utah uplands had been satisfying to Venters. But that was before the oppression of enemies had made the change in his mind. As a rider guarding the herd he had never thought of the night's wildness and loneliness; as an outcast, now when the full silence set in, and the deep darkness, and trains of radiant stars shone cold and calm, he lay with an ache in his heart. For a year he had lived as a black fox, driven from his kind. He longed for the sound of a voice, the touch of a hand. In the daytime there was riding from place to place, and the gun practice to which something drove him, and other tasks that at least necessitated action; at night, before he won sleep, there was strife in his soul. He yearned to leave the endless sage slopes, the wilderness of cañons; and it was in the lonely night that this yearning grew unbearable. It was then that he reached forth to feel Ring or Whitie, immeasurably grateful for the love and companionship of two dogs.

On this night the same old loneliness beset Venters, the old habit of sad thought and burning unquiet had its way. But from it evolved a conviction that his useless life had undergone a subtle change. He had sensed it first when Wrangle swung him up to the high saddle, he knew it now when he lay in the gateway of Deception Pass. He had no thrill of adventure, rather a gloomy perception of great hazard, perhaps death. He meant to find Oldring's retreat. The rustlers had fast horses, but none that could catch Wrangle. Venters knew no rustler could creep upon him at night when Ring and Whitie guarded his hiding-place. For the rest, he had eyes and ears, and a long rifle and an unerring aim, which he meant to use. Strangely his foreshadowing of change did not hold a thought of the killing of Tull. It related only to what was to happen to him in Deception Pass; and he could no more lift the veil of that mystery than tell where the trails led to in that unexplored cañon. Moreover, he did not care. And at length, tired out by stress of thought, he fell asleep.

When his eyes unclosed, day had come again, and he saw the rim of the opposite wall tipped with the gold of sunrise. A few moments sufficed for the morning's simple camp duties. Near at hand he found Wrangle, and to his surprise the horse came to him. Wrangle was one of the horses that left his viciousness in the home corral. What he wanted was to be free of mules and burros and steers, to roll in dust-patches, and then to run down the wide, open, windy sage-plains, and at night browse and sleep in the cool wet grass of a springhole. Jerd knew the sorrel when he said of him, "Wait till he smells the sage!"

Venters saddled and led him out of the oak thicket, and, leaping astride, rode up the cañon, with Ring and Whitie trotting behind. An old grass-grown trail followed the course of a shallow wash where flowed a thin stream of water. The cañon was a hundred rods wide; its yellow walls were perpendicular; it had abundant sage and a scant growth of oak and piñon. For five miles it held to a comparatively straight bearing, and then began a heightening of rugged walls and a deepening of the floor. Beyond this point of sudden change in the character of the cañon Venters had never explored, and here was the real door to the intricacies of Deception Pass.

He reined Wrangle to a walk, halted now and then to listen, and then proceeded cautiously with shifting and alert gaze. The cañon assumed proportions that dwarfed those of its first ten miles. Venters rode on and on, not losing in the interest of his wide surroundings any of his caution or keen search for tracks or sight of living thing. If there ever had been a trail here, he could not find it. He rode through sage and clumps of piñon trees and grassy plots where long-petaled purple lilies bloomed. He rode through a dark constriction of the pass no wider than the lane in the grove at Cottonwoods. And he came out into a great amphitheater into which jutted huge towering corners of a confluence of intersecting cañons.

Venters sat his horse, and, with a rider's eye, studied this wild cross-cut of huge stone gullies. Then he went on, guided by the course of running water. If it had not been for the main stream of water flowing north he would never have been able to tell which of those many openings was a continuation of the pass. In crossing this amphitheater he went by the mouths of five cañons, fording little streams that flowed into the larger one. Gaining the outlet which he took to be the pass, he rode on again under overhanging walls. One side was dark in shade, the other light in sun. This narrow passageway turned and twisted and opened into a valley that amazed Venters.

Here again was a sweep of purple sage, richer than upon the higher levels. The valley was miles long, several wide, and inclosed by unscalable walls. But it was the background of this valley that so forcibly struck him. Across the sage-flat rose a strange up-flinging of yellow rocks. He could not tell which were close and which were distant. Scrawled mounds of stone, like mountain waves, seemed to roll up to steep bare slopes and towers.

In this plain of sage Venters flushed birds and rabbits, and when he had proceeded about a mile he caught sight of the bobbing white tails of a herd of running antelope. He rode along the edge of the stream which wound toward the western end of the slowly looming mounds of stone. The high slope retreated out of sight behind the nearer projection. To Venters the valley appeared to have been filled in by a mountain of melted stone that had hardened in strange shapes of rounded outline. He followed the stream till he lost it in a deep cut. Therefore Venters quit the dark slit which baffled further search in that direction, and rode out along the curved edge of stone where it met the sage. It was not long before he came to a low place, and here Wrangle readily climbed up.

All about him was ridgy roll of wind-smoothed, rain-washed rock. Not a tuft of grass or a bunch of sage colored the dull rust-yellow. He saw where, to the right, this uneven flow of stone ended in a blunt wall. Leftward, from the hollow that lay at his feet, mounted a gradual slow-swelling slope to a great height topped by leaning, cracked, and ruined crags. Not for some time did he grasp the wonder of that acclivity. It was no less than a mountain-side, glistening in the sun like polished granite, with cedar-trees springing as if by magic out of the denuded surface. Winds had swept it clear of weathered shale, and rains had washed it free of dust. Far up the curved slope its beautiful lines broke to meet the vertical rim-wall, to lose its grace in a different order and color of rock, a stained yellow cliff of cracks and caves and seamed crags. And straight before Venters was a scene less striking but more significant to his keen survey. For beyond a mile of the bare, hummocky rock began the valley of sage, and the mouths of cañons, one of which surely was another gateway into the pass.

He got off his horse, and, giving the bridle to Ring to hold, he commenced a search for the cleft where the stream ran. He was not successful and concluded the water dropped into an underground passage. Then he returned to where he had left Wrangle, and led him down off the stone to the sage. It was a short ride to the opening cañons. There was no reason for a choice of which one to enter. The one he rode into was a clear, sharp shaft in yellow stone a thousand feet deep, with wonderful wind-worn caves low down and high above buttressed and turreted ramparts. Farther on Venters came into a region where deep indentations marked the line of cañon walls. These were huge, cove-like blind pockets extending back to a sharp corner with a dense growth of underbrush and trees.

Venters penetrated into one of these offshoots, and, as he had hoped, he found abundant grass. He had to bend the oak saplings to get his horse through. Deciding to make this a hiding-place if he could find water, he worked back to the limit of the shelving walls. In a little cluster of silver spruces he found a spring. This inclosed nook seemed an ideal place to leave his horse and to camp at night, and from which to make stealthy trips on foot. The thick grass hid his trail; the dense growth of oaks in the opening would serve as a barrier to keep Wrangle in, if, indeed, the luxuriant browse would not suffice for that. So Venters, leaving Whitie with the horse, called Ring to his side, and, rifle in hand, worked his way out to the open. A careful photographing in mind of the formation of the bold outlines of rimrock assured him he would be able to return to his retreat even in the dark.

Bunches of scattered sage covered the center of the cañon, and among these Venters threaded his way with the step of an Indian. At intervals he put his hand on the dog and stopped to listen. There was a drowsy hum of insects, but no other sound disturbed the warm midday stillness. Venters saw ahead a turn, more abrupt than any yet. Warily he rounded this corner, once again to halt bewildered.

The cañon opened fan-shaped into a great oval of green and gray growths. It was the hub of an oblong wheel, and from it, at regular distances, like spokes, ran the outgoing cañons. Here a dull red color predominated over the fading yellow. The corners of wall bluntly rose, scarred and scrawled, to taper into towers and serrated peaks and pinnacled domes.

Venters pushed on more heedfully than ever. Toward the center of this circle the sage-brush grew smaller and farther apart. He was about to sheer off to the right, where thickets and jumbles of fallen rock would afford him cover, when he ran right upon a broad cattle trail. Like a road it was, more than a trail; and the cattle tracks were fresh. What surprised him more, they were wet! He pondered over this feature. It had not rained. The only solution to this puzzle was that the cattle had been driven through water, and water deep enough to wet their legs.

Suddenly Ring growled low. Venters rose cautiously and looked over the sage. A band of straggling horsemen were riding across the oval. He sank down, startled and trembling. "Rustlers!" he muttered. Hurriedly he glanced about for a place to hide. Near at hand there was nothing but sage-brush. He dared not risk crossing the open patches to reach the rocks. Again he peeped over the sage. The rustlers—four—five—seven—eight in all, were approaching, but not directly in line with him. That was relief for a cold deadness which seemed to be creeping inward along his veins. He crouched down with bated breath and held the bristling dog.

He heard the click of iron-shod hoofs on stone, the coarse laughter of men, and then voices gradually dying away. Long moments passed. Then he rose. The rustlers were riding into a cañon. Their horses were tired, and they had several pack animals; evidently they had traveled far. Venters doubted that they were the rustlers who had driven the red herd. Olding's band had split. Venters watched these horsemen disappear under a bold cañon wall.

The rustlers had come from the northwest side of the oval. Venters kept a steady gaze in that direction, hoping, if there were more, to see from what cañon they rode. A quarter of an hour went by. Reward for his vigilance came when he descried three more mounted men, far over to the north. But out of what cañon they had ridden it was too late to tell. He watched the three ride across the oval and round the jutting red corner where the others had gone.

"Up that cañon!" exclaimed Venters. "Oldring's den! I've found it!"

A knotty point for Venters was the fact that the cattle tracks all pointed. The broad trail came from the direction of the cañon into which the rustlers had ridden, and undoubtedly the cattle had been driven out of it across the oval. There were no tracks pointing the other way. It had been in his mind that Oldring had driven the red herd toward the rendezvous, and not from it. Where did that broad trail come down into the pass, and where did it lead? Venters knew he wasted time in pondering the question, but it held a fascination not easily dispelled. For many years Oldring's mysterious entrance and exit to Deception Pass had been all-absorbing topics to sage-riders.

All at once the dog put an end to Venters's pondering. Ring sniffed the air, turned slowly in his tracks with a whine, and then growled. Venters wheeled. Two horsemen were within a hundred yards, coming straight at him. One, lagging behind the other, was Oldring's Masked Rider.

Venters cunningly sank, slowly trying to merge into sage-brush. But, guarded as his action was, the first horse detected it. He stopped short, snorted, and shot up his ears. The rustler bent forward, as if keenly peering ahead. Then, with a swift sweep, he jerked a gun from its sheath and fired.

The bullet zipped through the sage-brush. Flying bits of wood struck Venters, and the hot, stinging pain seemed to lift him in one leap. Like a flash the blue barrel of his rifle gleamed level and he shot once—twice.

The foremost rustler dropped his weapon and toppled from his saddle, to fall with his foot catching in a stirrup. The horse snorted wildly and plunged away, dragging the rustler through the sage.

The Masked Rider huddled over his pommel, slowly swaying to one side, and then, with a faint, strange cry, slipped out of the saddle.

CHAPTER V

VENTERS looked quickly from the fallen rustlers to the cañon where the others had disappeared. He calculated on the time needed for running horses to return to the open, if their riders heard shots. He waited breathlessly. But the estimated time dragged by and no riders appeared. Venters began presently to believe that the rifle reports had not penetrated into the recesses of the cañon, and felt safe for the immediate present.

He hurried to the spot where the first rustler had been dragged by his horse. The man lay in deep grass, dead, jaw fallen, eyes protruding—a sight that sickened Venters. The first man at whom he had ever aimed a weapon he had shot through the heart. With the clammy sweat oozing from every pore Venters dragged the rustler in among some boulders and covered him with slabs of rock. Then he smoothed out the crushed trail in grass and sage. The rustler's horse had stopped a quarter of a mile off and was grazing.

When Venters rapidly strode toward the Masked Rider not even the cold nausea that gripped him could wholly banish curiosity. For he had shot Oldring's infamous lieutenant, whose face had never been seen. Venters experienced a grim pride in the feat. What would Tull say to this achievement of the outcast who rode too often to Deception Pass?

Venters's curious eagerness and expectation had not prepared him for the shock he received when he stood over a slight, dark figure. The rustler wore the black mask that had given him his name, but he had no weapons. Venters glanced at the drooping horse; there were no gun-sheaths on the saddle.

46

"A rustler who didn't pack guns!" muttered Venters. "He wears no belt. He couldn't pack guns in that rig. . . . Strange!"

A low, gasping intake of breath and a sudden twitching of body told Venters the rider still lived.

"He's alive! . . . I've got to stand here and watch him die. And I shot an unarmed man."

Shrinkingly Venters removed the rider's wide sombrero and the black cloth mask. This action disclosed bright chestnut hair, inclined to curl, and a white, youthful face. Along the lower line of cheek and jaw was a clear demarcation, where the brown of tanned skin met the white that had been hidden from the sun.

"Oh, he's only a boy! . . . What! Can he be Oldring's Masked Rider?"

The boy showed signs of returning consciousness. He stirred; his lips moved; a small brown hand clenched in his blouse.

Venters knelt with a gathering horror of his deed. His bullet had entered the rider's right breast, high up to the shoulder. With hands that shook, Venters untied a black scarf and ripped open the blood-wet blouse.

First he saw a gaping hole, dark red against a whiteness of skin, from which welled a slender red stream. Then the graceful, beautiful swell of a woman's breast!

"A woman!" he cried. "A girl! . . . I've killed a girl!"

She suddenly opened eyes that transfixed Venters. They were fathomless blue. Consciousness of death was there, a blended terror and pain, but no consciousness of sight. She did not see Venters. She stared into the unknown.

Then came a spasm of vitality. She writhed in a torture of reviving strength, and in her convulsions she almost tore from Venters's grasp. Slowly she relaxed and sank partly back. The ungloved hand sought the wound, and pressed so hard that her wrist half buried itself in her bosom. Blood trickled between her spread fingers. And she looked at Venters with eyes that saw him.

He cursed himself and the unerring aim of which he had been so proud. He had seen that look in the eyes of a crippled antelope which he was about to finish with his knife. But in her it had infinitely more—a revelation of mortal spirit. The instinctive clinging to life was there, and the divining helplessness and the terrible accusation of the stricken.

"Forgive me! I didn't know!" burst out Venters.

"You shot me—you've killed me!" she whispered, in panting gasps. Upon her lips appeared a fluttering, bloody froth. By that Venters knew the air in her lungs was mixing with blood. "Oh, I knew—it would—come—some day! . . . Oh, the burn! . . . Hold me—I'm sinking—it's all dark. . . . Ah, God! . . . Mercy—"

Her rigidity loosened in one long quiver and she lay back limp, still, white as snow, with closed eyes.

Venters thought then that she died. But the faint pulsation of her breast assured him that life yet lingered. Death seemed only a matter of moments, for the bullet had gone clear through her. Nevertheless, he tore sageleaves from a bush, and, pressing them tightly over her wounds, he bound the black scarf round her shoulder, tying it securely under her arm. Then he closed the blouse, hiding from his sight that blood-stained, accusing breast.

"What—now?" he questioned, with flying mind. "I must get out of here. She's dying—but I can't leave her."

He rapidly surveyed the sage to the north and made out no animate object. Then he picked up the girl's sombrero and the mask. This time the mask gave him as great a shock as when he first removed it from her face. For in the woman he had forgotten the rustler, and this black strip of felt-cloth established the identity of Oldring's Masked Rider. Venters had solved the mystery. He slipped his rifle under her, and, lifting her carefully upon it, he began to retrace his steps. The dog trailed in his shadow. And the horse, that had stood drooping by, followed without a call. Venters chose the deepest tufts of grass and clumps of sage on his return. From time to time he glanced over his shoulder. He did not rest. His concern was to avoid jarring the girl and to hide his trail. Gaining the narrow cañon, he turned and held close to the wall till he reached his hiding-place. When he entered the dense thicket of oaks he was hard put to it to force a way through. But he held his burden almost upright, and by slipping sidewise and bending the saplings he got in. Through sage and grass he hurried to the grove of silver spruces.

He laid the girl down, almost fearing to look at her. Though marble pale and cold, she was living. Venters then appreciated the tax that long carry had been to his strength. He sat down to rest. Whitie sniffed at the pale girl and whined and crept to Venters's feet. Ring lapped the water in the runway of the spring. Presently Venters went out to the opening, caught the horse, and, leading him through the thicket, unsaddled him and tied him with a long halter. Wrangle left his browsing long enough to whinny and toss his head. Venters felt that he could not rest easily till he had secured the other rustler's horse; so, taking his rifle and calling for Ring, he set out. Swiftly yet watchfully he made his way through the cañon to the oval and out to the cattle trail. What few tracks might have betrayed him he obliterated, so only an expert tracker could have trailed him. Then, with many a wary backward glance across the sage, he started to round up the rustler's horse. This was unexpectedly easy. He led the horse to lower ground, out of sight from the opposite side of the oval, along the shadowy western wall, and so on into his cañon and secluded camp.

The girl's eyes were open; a feverish spot burned in her cheeks; she moaned something unintelligible to Venters, but he took the movement of her lips to mean that she wanted water. Lifting her head, he tipped the canteen to her lips. After that she again lapsed into unconsciousness or a weakness which was its counterpart. Venters noted, however, that the burning flush had faded into the former pallor.

The sun set behind the high cañon rim, and a cool shade darkened the walls. Venters fed the dogs and put a halter on the dead rustler's horse. He allowed Wrangle to browse free. This done, he cut spruce boughs and made a lean-to for the girl. Then, gently lifting her upon a blanket, he folded the sides over her. The other blanket he wrapped about his shoulders and found a comfortable seat against a spruce-tree that upheld the little shack. Ring and Whitie lay near at hand, one asleep, the other watchful.

Venters dreaded the night's vigil. At night his mind was active, and this time he had to watch and think and feel beside a dying girl whom he had all but murdered. A thousand excuses he invented for himself, yet not one made any difference in his act or his self-reproach.

It seemed to him that when night fell black he could see her white face so much more plainly.

"She'll go, presently," he said, "and be out of agony—thank God!"

Every little while certainty of her death came to him with a shock; and then he would bend over and lay his ear on her breast. Her heart still beat.

The early night blackness cleared to the cold starlight. The horses were not moving, and no sound disturbed the deathly silence of the cañon.

"I'll bury her here," thought Venters, "and let her grave be as much a mystery as her life was."

For the girl's few words, the look of her eyes, the prayer, had strangely touched Venters.

"She was only a girl," he soliloquized. "What was she to Oldring? Rustlers don't have wives nor sisters nor daughters. She was bad—that's all. But somehow . . . well, she may not have willingly become the companion of rustlers. That prayer of hers to God for mercy! . . . Life is strange and cruel. I wonder if other members of Oldring's gang are women? Likely enough. But what was his game? Oldring's Mask Rider! A name to make villagers hide and lock their doors. A name credited with a dozen murders, a hundred forays, and a thousand stealings of cattle. What part did the girl have in this? It may have served Oldring to create mystery."

Hours passed. The white stars moved across the narrow strip of dark-blue sky above. The silence awoke to the low hum of insects. Venters watched the immovable white face, and as he watched, hour by hour waiting for death, the infamy of her passed from his mind. He thought only of the sadness, the truth of the moment. Whoever she was—whatever she had done—she was young and she was dying.

The after-part of the night wore on interminably. The starlight failed and the gloom blackened to the darkest hour. "She'll die at the gray of dawn," muttered Venters, remembering some old woman's fancy. The blackness paled to gray, and the gray lightened and day peeped over the eastern rim. Venters listened at the breast of the girl. She still lived. Did he only imagine that her heart beat stronger, ever so slightly, but stronger? He pressed his ear closer to her breast. And he rose with his own pulse quickening.

"If she doesn t die soon—she's got a chance—the barest chance —to live," he said.

He wondered if the internal bleeding had ceased. There was no more film of blood upon her lips. But no corpse could have been whiter. Opening her blouse, he untied the scarf, and carefully picked away the sageleaves from the wound in her shoulder. It had closed. Lifting her lightly, he ascertained that the same was true of the hole where the bullet had come out. He reflected on the fact that clean wounds closed quickly in the healing upland air. He recalled instances of riders who had been cut and shot, apparently to fatal issues; yet the blood had clotted, the wounds closed, and they had recovered. He had no way to tell if internal hemorrhage still went on, but he believed that it had stopped. Otherwise she would surely not have lived so long. He marked the entrance of the bullet, and concluded that it had just touched the upper lobe of her lung. Perhaps the wound in the lung had also closed. As he began to wash the blood stains from her breast and carefully rebandage the wound, he was vaguely conscious of a strange, grave happiness in the thought that she might live.

Broad daylight and a hint of sunshine high on the cliff-rim to the west brought him to consideration of what he had better do. And while busy with his few camp tasks he revolved the thing in his mind. It would not be wise for him to remain long in his present hiding-place. And if he intended to follow the cattle trail and try to find the rustlers he had better make a move at once. For he knew that rustlers, being riders, would not make much of a day's or night's absence from camp for one or two of their number; but when the missing ones failed to show up in reasonable time there would be a search. And Venters was afraid of that.

"A good tracker could trail me," he muttered. "And I'd be cornered here. Let's see. Rustlers are a lazy set when they're not on the ride. I'll risk it. Then I'll change my hiding-place."

He carefully cleaned and reloaded his guns. When he rose to go he bent a long glance down upon the unconscious girl. Then, ordering Whitie and Ring to keep guard, he left the camp.

The safest cover lay close under the wall of the cañon, and here through the dense thickets Venters made his slow, listening advance toward the oval. Upon gaining the wide opening he decided to cross it and follow the left wall till he came to the cattle trail.

He scanned the oval as keenly as if hunting for antelope. Then, stooping, he stole from one cover to another, taking advantage of rocks and bunches of sage, until he had reached the thickets under the opposite wall. Once there, he exercised extreme caution in his surveys of the ground ahead, but increased his speed when moving. Dodging from bush to bush, he passed the mouths of two cañons, and in the entrance of a third cañon he crossed a wash of swift, clear water, to come abruptly upon the cattle trail.

It followed the low bank of the wash, and, keeping it in sight, Venters hugged the line of sage and thicket. Like the curves of a serpent the cañon wound for a mile or more and then opened into a valley. Patches of red showed clear against the purple of sage, and farther out on the level dotted strings of red led away to the wall of rock.

"Ha, the red herd!" exclaimed Venters.

Then dots of white and black told him there were cattle of other colors in this inclosed valley. Oldring, the rustler, was also a rancher. Venters's calculating eye took count of stock that out-numbered the red herd.

"What a range!" went on Venters. "Water and grass enough for fifty thousand head, and no riders needed!"

After his first burst of surprise and rapid calculation Venters lost no time there, but slunk again into the sage on his back trail. With the discovery of Oldring's hidden cattle-range had come enlightenment on several problems. Here the rustler kept his stock; here was Jane Withersteen's red herd; here were the few cattle that had disappeared from the Cottonwoods slopes during the last two years. Until Oldring had driven the red herd his thefts of cattle for that time had not been more than enough to supply meat for his men. Of late no drives had been reported from Sterling or the villages north. And Venters knew that the riders had wondered at Oldring's inactivity in that particular field. He and his band had been active enough in their visits to Glaze and Cottonwoods; they always had gold; but of late the amount gambled away and drunk and thrown away in the villages had given rise to much conjecture. Oldring's more frequent visits had resulted in new saloons, and where there had formerly been one raid or shooting fray in the little hamlets there were now many. Perhaps Oldring had another range farther on up the pass, and from there drove the cattle to distant Utah towns where he was little known. But Venters came finally to doubt this. And, from what he had learned in the last few days, a belief began to form in Venters's mind that Oldring's intimidations of the villages and the mystery of the Masked Rider, with his alleged evil deeds, and the fierce resistance offered any trailing riders, and the rustling of cattle—these things were only the craft of the rustler-chief to conceal his real life and purpose and work in Deception Pass.

And like a scouting Indian Venters crawled through the sage of the oval valley, crossed trail after trail on the north side, and at last entered the cañon out of which headed the cattle trail, and into which he had watched the rustlers disappear.

If he had used caution before, now he strained every nerve to force himself to creeping stealth and to sensitiveness of ear. He crawled along so hidden that he could not use his eyes except to aid himself in the toilsome progress through the brakes and ruins of cliff-wall. Yet from time to time, as he rested, he saw the massive red walls growing higher and wilder, more looming and broken. He made note of the fact that he was turning and climbing. The sage and thickets of oak and brakes of alder gave place to piñon pine growing out of rocky soil. Suddenly a low, dull murmur assailed his ears. At first he thought it was thunder, then the slipping of a weathered slope of rock. But it was incessant, and as he progressed it filled out deeper and from a murmur changed into a soft roar.

"Falling water," he said. "There's volume to that. I wonder if it's the stream I lost."

The roar bothered him, for he could hear nothing else. Likewise, however, no rustlers could hear him. Emboldened by this, and sure that nothing but a bird could see him, he arose from his hands and knees to hurry on. An opening in the piñons warned him that he was nearing the height of slope.

He gained it, and dropped low with a burst of astonishment. Before him stretched a short cañon with rounded stone floor bare of grass or sage or tree, and with curved, shelving walls. A broad rippling stream flowed toward him, and at the back of the cañon a waterfall burst from a wide rent in the cliff, and, bounding down in two green steps, spread into a long white sheet.

If Venters had not been indubitably certain that he had entered the right cañon his astonishment would not have been so great. There had been no breaks in the walls, no side cañons entering this one where the rustlers' tracks and the cattle trail had guided him, and, therefore, he could not be wrong. But here the cañon ended, and presumably the trails also.

"That cattle trail headed out of here," Venters kept saying to himself. "It headed out. Now what I want to know is how on earth did cattle ever get in here?"

If he could be sure of anything it was of the careful scrutiny he had given that cattle track, every hoofmark of which headed straight west. He was now looking east at an immense round boxed corner of cañon down which tumbled a thin, white veil of water, scarcely twenty yards wide. Somehow, somewhere, his calculations had gone wrong. For the first time in years he found himself doubting his rider's skill in finding tracks, and his memory of what he had actually seen. In his anxiety to keep under cover he must have lost himself in this offshoot of Deception Pass, and thereby, in some unaccountable manner, missed the cañon with the trails. There was nothing else for him to think. Rustlers could not fly, nor cattle jump down thousand-foot precipices. He was only proving what the sage-riders had long said of this labyrinthine system of deceitful cañons and valleys—trails led down into Deception Pass, but no rider had ever followed them.

On a sudden he heard above the soft roar of the waterfall an unusual sound that he could not define. He dropped flat behind a stone and listened. From the direction he had come swelled something that resembled a strange muffled pounding and splashing and ringing. Despite his nerve the chill sweat began to dampen his forehead. What might not be possible in this stone-walled maze of mystery? The unnatural sound passed beyond him as he lay gripping his rifle and fighting for coolness. Then from the open came the sound, now distinct and different. Venters recognized a hobblebell of a horse, and the cracking of iron on submerged stones, and the hollow splash of hoofs in water.

Relief surged over him. His mind caught again at realities, and curiosity prompted him to peep from behind the rock.

In the middle of the stream waded a long string of packed burros driven by three superbly mounted men. Had Venters met these dark-clothed, dark-visaged, heavily armed men anywhere in Utah, let alone in this robbers' retreat, he would have recognized them as rustlers. The discerning eye of a rider saw the signs of a long, arduous trip. These men were packing in supplies from one of the northern villages. They were tired, and their horses were almost played out, and the burros plodded on, after the manner of their kind when exhausted, faithful and patient, but as if every weary, splashing, slipping step would be their last.

All this Venters noted in one glance. After that he watched with a thrilling eagerness. Straight at the waterfall the rustlers drove the burros, and straight through the middle, where the water spread into a fleecy, thin film like dissolving smoke. Following closely, the rustlers rode into this white mist, showing in bold black relief for an instant, and then they vanished.

Venters drew a full breath that rushed out in brief and sudden utterance.

"Good Heaven! Of all the holes for a rustler! . . . There's a cavern under that waterfall, and a passageway leading out to a cañon beyond. Oldring hides in there. He needs only to guard a trail leading down from the sage-flat above. Little danger of this outlet to the pass being discovered. I stumbled on it by luck, after I had given up. And now I know the truth of what puzzled me most—why that cattle trail was wet!"

He wheeled and ran down the slope, and out to the level of the sage-brush. Returning, he had no time to spare, only now and then, between dashes, a moment when he stopped to cast sharp eyes ahead. The abundant grass left no trace of his trail. Short work he made of the distance to the circle of cañons. He doubted that he would ever see it again; he knew he never wanted to; yet he looked at the red corners and towers with the eyes of a rider picturing landmarks never to be forgotten.

Here he spent a panting moment in a slow-circling gaze of the sage-oval and the gaps between the bluffs. Nothing stirred except the gentle wave of the tips of the brush. Then he pressed on past the mouths of several cañons and over ground new to him, now close under the eastern wall. This latter part proved to be easy traveling, well screened from possible observation from the north and west, and he soon covered it and felt safer in the deepening shade of his own cañon. Then the huge, notched bulge of red rim loomed over him, a mark by which he knew again the deep cove where his camp lay hidden. As he penetrated the thicket, safe again for the present, his thoughts reverted to the girl he had left there. The afternoon had far advanced. How would he find her? He ran into camp, frightening the dogs.

The girl lay with wide-open, dark eyes, and they dilated when he knelt beside her. The flush of fever shone in her cheeks. He lifted her and held water to her dry lips, and felt an inexplicable sense of lightness as he saw her swallow in a slow, choking gulp. Gently he laid her back.

"Who—are—you?" she whispered, haltingly.

"I'm the man who shot you," he replied.

"You'll—not—kill me—now?"

"No, no."

"What—will—you—do—with me?"

"When you get better—strong enough—I'll take you back to the cañon where the rustlers ride through the waterfall."

As with a faint shadow from a flitting wing overhead, the marble whiteness of her face seemed to change.

"Don't—take—me—back—there!"

CHAPTER VI

MEANTIME, at the ranch, when Judkins's news had sent Venters on the trail of the rustlers, Jane Withersteen led the injured man to her house and with skilled fingers dressed the gunshot wound in his arm.

"Judkins, what do you think happened to my riders?"

"I—I'd rather not say," he replied.

"Tell me. Whatever you'll tell me I'll keep to myself. I'm beginning to worry about more than the loss of a herd of cattle. Venters hinted of—but tell me, Judkins."

"Well, Miss Withersteen, I think as Venters thinks—your riders have been called in."

"Judkins! . . . By whom?"

"You know who handles the reins of your Mormon riders."

"Do you dare insinute that my churchmen have ordered in my riders?"

"I ain't insinuatin' nothin', Miss Withersteen," answered Judkins, with spirit. "I know what I'm talking about. I didn't want to tell you."

"Oh, I can't believe that! I'll not believe it! Would Tull leave my herds at the mercy of rustlers and wolves just because—because—? No, no! It's unbelievable."

"Yes, thet particular thing's onheard of around Cottonwoods. But, beggin' pardon, Miss Withersteen, there never was any other rich Mormon woman here on the border, let alone one thet's taken the bit between her teeth."

That was a bold thing for the reserved Judkins to say, but it did not anger her. This rider's crude hint of her spirit gave her a glimpse of what others might think. Humility and obedience had

57

been hers always. But had she taken the bit between her teeth? Still she wavered. And then, with a quick spurt of warm blood along her veins, she thought of Black Star when he got the bit fast between his iron jaws and ran wild in the sage. If she ever started to run! Jane smothered the glow and burn within her, ashamed of a passion for freedom that opposed her duty.

"Judkins, go to the village," she said, "and when you have learned anything definite about my riders please come to me at once."

When he had gone Jane resolutely applied her mind to a number of tasks that of late had been neglected. Her father had trained her in the management of a hundred employees and the working of gardens and fields; and to keep record of the movements of cattle and riders. And beside the many duties she had added to this work was one of extreme delicacy, such as required all her tact and ingenuity. It was an unobtrusive, almost secret aid which she rendered to the Gentile families of the village. Though Jane Withersteen never admitted so to herself, it amounted to no less than a system of charity. But for her invention of numberless kinds of employment, for which there was no actual need, these families of Gentiles, who had failed in a Mormon community, would have starved.

In aiding these poor people Jane thought she deceived her keen churchmen, but it was a kind of deceit for which she did not pray to be forgiven. Equally as difficult was the task of deceiving the Gentiles, for they were as proud as they were poor. It had been a great grief to her to discover how these people hated her people; and it had been a source of great joy that through her they had come to soften in hatred. At any time this work called for a clearness of mind that precluded anxiety and worry; but under the present circumstances it required all her vigor and obstinate tenacity to pin her attention upon her task.

Sunset came, bringing with the end of her labor a patient calmness and power to wait that had not been hers earlier in the day. She expected Judkins, but he did not appear. Her house was always quiet; to-night, however, it seemed unusually so. At supper her women served her with a silent assiduity; it spoke what their sealed lips could not utter—the sympathy of Mormon women. Jerd came to her with the key of the great door of the stone stable, and to make his daily report about the horses. One of his daily duties was to give Black Star and Night and the other racers a ten-mile run. This day it had been omitted, and the boy grew confused in explanations that she had not asked for. She did inquire if he would return on the morrow, and Jerd, in mingled surprise and relief, assured her he would always work for her. Jane missed the rattle and trot, canter and gallop of the incoming riders on the hard trails. Dusk shaded the grove where she walked; the birds ceased singing; the wind sighed through the leaves of the cottonwoods, and the running water murmured down its stone-bedded channel. The glimmering of the first star was like the peace and beauty of the night. Her faith welled up in her heart and said that all would soon be right in her little world. She pictured Venters about his lonely camp-fire sitting between his faithful dogs. She prayed for his safety, for the success of his undertaking.

Early the next morning one of Jane's women brought in word that Judkins wished to speak to her. She hurried out, and in her surprise to see him armed with rifle and revolver, she forgot her intention to inquire about his wound.

"Judkins! Those guns? You never carried guns."

"It's high time, Miss Withersteen," he replied. "Will you come into the grove? It ain't jest exactly safe for me to be seen here."

She walked with him into the shade of the cottonwoods.

"What do you mean?"

"Miss Withersteen, I went to my mother's house last night. While there, some one knocked, an' a man asked for me. I went to the door. He wore a mask. He said I'd better not ride any more for Jane Withersteen. His voice was hoarse an' strange, disguised, I reckon, like his face. He said no more, an' ran off in the dark."

"Did you know who he was?" asked Jane, in a low voice.

"Yes."

Jane did not ask to know; she did not want to know; she feared to know. All her calmness fled at a single thought.

"Thet's why I'm packin' guns," went on Judkins. "For I'll never quit ridin' for you, Miss Withersteen, till you let me go."

"Judkins, do you want to leave me?"

"Do I look thet way? Give me a hoss—a fast hoss, an' send me out on the sage."

"Oh, thank you, Judkins! You're more faithful than my own people. I ought not accept your loyalty—you might suffer more through it. But what in the world can I do? My head whirls. The wrong to Venters—the stolen herd—these masks, threats, this coil in the dark! I can't understand! But I feel something dark and terrible closing in around me."

"Miss Withersteen, it's all simple enough," said Judkins, earnestly. "Now please listen—an' beggin' your pardon—jest turn thet deaf Mormon ear aside, an' let me talk clear an' plain in the other. I went around to the saloons an' the stores an' the loafin' places yesterday. All your riders are in. There's talk of a vigilance band organized to hunt down rustlers. They call themselves 'The Riders.' Thet's the report—thet's the reason given for your riders leavin' you. Strange thet only a few riders of other ranchers joined the band! An' Tull's man, Jerry Card—he's the leader. I seen him an' his hoss. He 'ain't been to Glaze. I'm not easy to fool on the looks of a hoss thet's traveled the sage. Tull an' Jerry didn't ride to Glaze! . . . Well, I met Blake an' Dorn, both good friends of mine, usually, as far as their Mormon lights will let 'em go. But these fellers couldn't fool me, an' they didn't try very hard. I asked them, straight out like a man, why they left you like thet. I didn't forget to mention how you nursed Blake's poor old mother when she was sick, an' how good you was to Dorn's kids. They looked ashamed, Miss Withersteen. An' they jest froze up —thet dark set look thet makes them strange an' different to me. But I could tell the difference between thet first natural twinge of conscience an' the later look of some secret thing. An' the difference I caught was thet they couldn't help themselves. They hadn't no say in the matter. They looked as if their bein' unfaithful to you was bein' faithful to a higher duty. An' there's the secret. Why, it's as plain as—as sight of my gun here."

"Plain! . . . My herds to wander in the sage—to be stolen! Jane Withersteen a poor woman! Her head to be brought low and her spirit broken! . . . Why, Judkins, it's plain enough."

"Miss Withersteen, let me get what boys I can gather, an' hold the white herd. It's on the slope now, not ten miles out—three thousand head, an' all steers. They're wild, an' likely to stampede at the pop of a jack-rabbit's ears. We'll camp right with them, an' try to hold them."

"Judkins, I'll reward you some day for your service, unless all is taken from me. Get the boys and tell Jerd to give you pick of my horses, except Black Star and Night. But—do not shed blood for my cattle nor heedlessly risk your lives."

Jane Withersteen rushed to the silence and seclusion of her room, and there could not longer hold back the bursting of her wrath. She went stone-blind in the fury of a passion that had never before showed its power. Lying upon her bed, sightless, voiceless, she was a writhing, living flame. And she tossed there while her fury burned and burned, and finally burned itself out.

Then, weak and spent, she lay thinking, not of the oppression that would break her, but of this new revelation of self. Until the last few days there had been little in her life to rouse passions. Her forefathers had been Vikings, savage chieftains who bore no cross and brooked no hindrance to their will. Her father had inherited that temper; and at times, like antelope fleeing before fire on the slope, his people fled from his red rages. Jane Withersteen realized that the spirit of wrath and war had lain dormant in her. She shrank from black depths hitherto unsuspected. The one thing in man or woman that she scorned above all scorn, and which she could not forgive, was hate. Hate headed a flaming pathway straight to hell. All in a flash, beyond her control there had been in her a birth of fiery hate. And the man who had dragged her peaceful and loving spirit to this degradation was a minister of God's word, an Elder of her church, the counselor of her beloved Bishop.

The loss of herds and ranges, even of Amber Spring and the Old Stone House, no longer concerned Jane Withersteen; she faced the foremost thought of her life, what she now considered the mightiest problem—the salvation of her soul.

She knelt by her bedside and prayed; she prayed as she had never prayed in all her life—prayed to be forgiven for her sin; to be immune from that dark, hot hate; to love Tull as her minister, though she could not love him as a man; to do her duty by her church and people and those dependent upon her bounty; to hold reverence of God and womanhood inviolate.

When Jane Withersteen rose from that storm of wrath and prayer for help she was serene, calm, sure—a changed woman. She would do her duty as she saw it, live her life as her own truth guided her. She might never be able to marry a man of her choice, but she certainly never would become the wife of Tull. Her churchmen might take her cattle and horses, ranges and fields, her corrals and stables, the house of Withersteen and the water that nourished the village of Cottonwoods; but they could not force her to marry Tull, they could not change her decision or break her spirit. Once resigned to further loss, and sure of herself, Jane Withersteen attained a peace of mind that had not been hers for a year. She forgave Tull, and felt a melancholy regret over what she knew he considered duty, irrespective of his personal feeling for her. First of all, Tull, as he was a man, wanted her for himself; and secondly, he hoped to save her and her riches for his church. She did not believe that Tull had been actuated solely by his minister's zeal to save her soul. She doubted her interpretation of one of his dark sayings—that if she were lost to him she might as well be lost to heaven. Jane Withersteen's common sense took arms against the binding limits of her religion; and she doubted that her Bishop, whom she had been taught had direct communication with God—would damn her soul for refusing to marry a Mormon. As for Tull and his churchmen, when they had harassed her, perhaps made her poor, they would find her unchangeable, and then she would get back most of what she had lost. So she reasoned, true at last to her faith in all men, and in their ultimate goodness.

The clank of iron hoofs upon the stone courtyard drew her hurriedly from her retirement. There, beside his horse, stood Lassiter, his dark apparel and the great black gun-sheaths contrasting singularly with his gentle smile. Jane's active mind took up her interest in him and her half-determined desire to use what charm she had to foil his evident design in visiting Cottonwoods. If she could mitigate his hatred of Mormons, or at least keep him from killing more of them, not only would she be saving her people, but also be leading back this bloodspiller to some semblance of the human.

"Mornin', ma'am," he said, black sombrero in hand.

"Lassiter, I'm not an old woman, or even a madam," she replied, with her bright smile. "If you can't say Miss Withersteen—call me Jane."

"I reckon Jane would be easier. First names are always handy for me."

"Well, use mine, then. Lassiter, I'm glad to see you. I'm in trouble."

Then she told him of Judkins's return, of the driving of the red herd, of Venters's departure on Wrangle, and the calling-in of her riders.

"'Pears to me you're some smilin' an' pretty for a woman with so much trouble," he remarked.

"Lassiter! Are you paying me compliments? But, seriously, I've made up my mind not to be miserable. I've lost much, and I'll lose more. Nevertheless, I won't be sour, and I hope I'll never be unhappy—again."

Lassiter twisted his hat round and round, as was his way, and took his time in replying.

"Women are strange to me. I got to back-trailin' myself from them long ago. But I'd like a game woman. Might I ask, seein' as how you take this trouble, if you're goin' to fight?"

"Fight! How? Even if I would, I haven't a friend except that boy who doesn't dare stay in the village."

"I make bold to say, ma'am—Jane—that there's another, if you want him."

"Lassiter! . . . Thank you. But how can I accept you as a friend? Think! Why, you'd ride down into the village with those terrible guns and kill my enemies—who are also my churchmen."

"I reckon I might be riled up to jest about that," he replied, dryly.

She held out both hands to him.

"Lassiter! I'll accept your friendship—be proud of it—return it —if I may keep you from killing another Mormon."

"I'll tell you one thing," he said, bluntly, as the gray lightning formed in his eyes. "You're too good a woman to be sacrificed as you're goin' to be. . . . No, I reckon you an' me can't be friends on such terms."

In her earnestness she stepped closer to him, repelled yet fascinated by the sudden transition of his moods. That he would fight for her was at once horrible and wonderful.

"You came here to kill a man—the man whom Milly Erne—"

63

"The man who dragged Milly Erne to hell—put it that way!
. . . Jane Withersteen, yes, that's why I came here. I'd tell so
much to no other livin' soul. . . . There 're things such a woman
as you'd never dream of—so don't mention her again. Not till
you tell me the name of the man!"

"Tell you! I? Never!"

"I reckon you will. An' I'll never ask you. I'm a man of strange
beliefs an' ways of thinkin', an' I seem to see into the future an'
feel things hard to explain. The trail I've been followin' for so
many years was twisted an' tangled, but it's straightenin' out now.
An', Jane Withersteen, you crossed it long ago to ease poor Milly's
agony. That, whether you want or not, makes Lassiter your friend.
But you cross it now strangely to mean somethin' to me—God
knows what!—unless by your noble blindness to incite me to
greater hatred of Mormon men."

Jane felt swayed by a strength that far exceeded her own. In
a clash of wills with this man she would go to the wall. If she
were to influence him it must be wholly through womanly allurement. There was that about Lassiter which commanded her respect; she had abhorred his name; face to face with him, she
found she feared only his deeds. His mystic suggestion, his foreshadowing of something that she was to mean to him, pierced
deep into her mind. She believed fate had thrown in her way the
lover or husband of Milly Erne. She believed that through her
an evil man might be reclaimed. His allusion to what he called
her blindness terrified her. Such a mistaken idea of his might un-
leash the bitter, fatal mood she sensed in him. At any cost she
must placate this man; she knew the die was cast, and that if
Lassiter did not soften to a woman's grace and beauty and wiles,
then it would be because she could not make him.

"I reckon you'll hear no more such talk from me," Lassiter went
on, presently. "Now, Miss Jane, I rode in to tell you that your
herd of white steers is down on the slope behind them big ridges.
An' I seen somethin' goin' on that 'd be mighty interestin' to you,
if you could see it. Have you a field-glass?"

"Yes, I have two glasses. I'll get them and ride out with you.
Wait, Lassiter, please," she said, and hurried within. Sending
word to Jerd to saddle Black Star and fetch him to the court, she

then went to her room and changed to the riding-clothes she al
ways donned when going into the sage. In this male attire her
mirror showed her a jaunty, handsome rider. If she expected some
little need of admiration from Lassiter, she had no cause for
disappointment. The gentle smile that she liked, which made of
him another person, slowly overspread his face.

"If I didn't take you for a boy!" he exclaimed. "It's powerful
queer what difference clothes make. Now I've been some scared
of your dignity, like when the other night you was all in white,
but in this rig—"

Black Star came pounding into the court, dragging Jerd half
off his feet, and he whistled at Lassiter's black. But at sight of
Jane all his defiant lines seemed to soften, and with tosses of his
beautiful head he whipped his bridle.

"Down, Black Star, down," said Jane.

He dropped his head, and, slowly lengthening, he bent one
foreleg, then the other, and sank to his knees. Jane slipped her left
foot in the stirrup, swung lightly into the saddle, and Black Star
rose with a ringing stamp. It was not easy for Jane to hold him
to a canter through the grove, and like the wind he broke when
he saw the sage. Jane let him have a couple of miles of free running on the open trail, and then she coaxed him in and waited for
her companion. Lassiter was not long in catching up, and presently they were riding side by side. It reminded her how she used
to ride with Venters. Where was he now? She gazed far down
the slope to the curved purple lines of Deception Pass, and involuntarily shut her eyes with a trembling stir of nameless fear.

"We'll turn off here," Lassiter said, "an' take to the sage a mile
or so. The white herd is behind them big ridges."

"What are you going to show me?" asked Jane. "I'm prepared
—don't be afraid."

He smiled as if he meant that bad news came swiftly enough
without being presaged by speech.

When they reached the lee of a rolling ridge Lassiter dismounted, motioning to her to do likewise. They left the horses
standing, bridles down. Then Lassiter, carrying the field-glasses,
began to lead the way up the slow rise of ground. Upon nearing
the summit he halted her with a gesture.

65

"I reckon we'd see more if we didn't show ourselves against the sky," he said. "I was here less than an hour ago. Then the herd was seven or eight miles south, an' if they 'ain't bolted yet—"

"Lassiter! . . . Bolted?"

"That's what I said. Now let's see."

Jane climbed a few more paces behind him and then peeped over the ridge. Just beyond began a shallow swale that deepened and widened into a valley and then swung to the left. Following the undulating sweep of sage, Jane saw the straggling lines and then the great body of the white herd. She knew enough about steers, even at a distance of four or five miles, to realize that something was in the wind. Bringing her field-glass into use, she moved it slowly from left to right, which action swept the whole herd into range. The stragglers were restless; the more compactly massed steers were browsing. Jane brought the glass back to the big sentinels of the herd, and she saw them trot with quick steps, stop short and toss wide horns, look everywhere, and then trot in another direction.

"Judkins hasn't been able to get his boys together yet," said Jane. "But he'll be there soon. I hope not too late. Lassiter, what's frightening those big leaders?"

"Nothin' jest on the minute," replied Lassiter. "Them steers are quietin' down. They've been scared, but not bad yet. I reckon the whole herd has moved a few miles this way since I was here."

"They didn't browse that distance—not in less than an hour. Cattle aren't sheep."

"No, they jest run it, an' that looks bad."

"Lassiter, what frightened them?" repeated Jane, impatiently.

"Put down your glass. You'll see at first better with a naked eye. Now look along them ridges on the other side of the herd, the ridges where the sun shines bright on the sage. . . . That's right. Now look an' look hard an' wait."

Long-drawn moments of straining sight rewarded Jane with nothing save the low, purple rim of ridge and the shimmering sage.

"It's begun again!" whispered Lassiter, and he gripped her arm. "Watch. . . . There, did you see that?"

"No, no. Tell me what to look for?"

66

"A white flash—a kind of pin-point of quick light—a gleam as from sun shinin' on somethin' white."

Suddenly Jane's concentrated gaze caught a fleeting glint. Quickly she brought her glass to bear on the spot. Again the purple sage, magnified in color and size and wave, for long moments irritated her with its monotony. Then from out of the sage on the ridge flew up a broad, white object, flashed in the sunlight, and vanished. Like magic it was, and bewildered Jane.

"What on earth is that?"

"I reckon there's some one behind that ridge throwin' up a sheet or a white blanket to reflect the sunshine."

"Why?" queried Jane, more bewildered than ever.

"To stampede the herd," replied Lassiter, and his teeth clicked.

"Ah!" She made a fierce, passionate movement, clutched the glass tightly, shook as with the passing of a spasm, and then dropped her head. Presently she raised it to greet Lassiter with something like a smile. "My righteous brethren are at work again," she said, in scorn. She had stifled the leap of her wrath, but for perhaps the first time in her life a bitter derision curled her lips. Lassiter's cool gray eyes seemed to pierce her. "I said I was prepared for anything; but that was hardly true. But why would they—anybody stampede my cattle?"

"That's a Mormon's godly way of bringin' a woman to her knees."

"Lassiter, I'll die before I ever bend my knees. I might be led; I won't be driven. Do you expect the herd to bolt?"

"I don't like the looks of them big steers. But you can never tell. Cattle sometimes stampede as easily as buffalo. Any little flash or move will start them. A rider gettin' down an' walkin' toward them sometimes will make them jump an' fly. Then again nothin' seems to scare them. But I reckon that white flare will do the biz. It's a new one on me, an' I've seen some ridin' an' rustlin'. It jest takes one of them God-fearin' Mormons to think of devilish tricks."

"Lassiter, might not this trick be done by Oldring's men?" asked Jane, ever grasping at straws.

"It might be, but it ain't," replied Lassiter. "Oldring's an honest thief. He don't skulk behind ridges to scatter your cattle to the four winds. He rides down on you, an' if you don't like it you can throw a gun."

Jane bit her tongue to refrain from championing men who at the very moment were proving to her that they were little and mean compared even with rustlers.

"Look! . . . Jane, them leadin' steers have bolted. They're drawin' the stragglers, an' that 'll pull the whole herd."

Jane was not quick enough to catch the details called out by Lassiter, but she saw the line of cattle lengthening. Then, like a stream of white bees pouring from a huge swarm, the steers stretched out from the main body. In a few moments, with astonishing rapidity, the whole herd got into motion. A faint roar of trampling hoofs came to Jane's ears, and gradually swelled; low, rolling clouds of dust began to rise above the sage.

"It's a stampede, an' a hummer," said Lassiter.

"Oh, Lassiter! The herd's running with the valley! It leads into the cañon! There's a straight jump-off!"

"I reckon they'll run into it, too. But that's a good many miles yet. An' Jane, this valley swings round almost north before it goes east. That stampede will pass within a mile of us."

The long, white, bobbing line of steers streaked swiftly through the sage, and a funnel-shaped dust-cloud arose at a low angle. A dull rumbling filled Jane's ears.

"I'm thinkin' of millin' that herd," said Lassiter. His gray glance swept up the slope to the west. "There's some specks an' dust way off toward the village. Mebbe that's Judkins an' his boys. It ain't likely he'll get here in time to help. You'd better hold Black Star here on this high ridge."

He ran to his horse and, throwing off saddle-bags and tightening the cinches, he leaped astride and galloped straight down across the valley.

Jane went for Black Star and, leading him to the summit of the ridge, she mounted and faced the valley with excitement and expectancy. She had heard of milling stampeded cattle, and knew it was a feat accomplished by only the most daring riders.

The white herd was now strung out in a line two miles long. The dull rumble of thousands of hoofs deepened into continuous low thunder, and as the steers swept swiftly closer the thunder became a heavy roll. Lassiter crossed in a few moments the level of the valley to the eastern rise of ground and there waited the coming of the herd. Presently, as the head of the white line reached a point opposite to where Jane stood, Lassiter spurred his black into a run.

Jane saw him take a position on the off side of the leaders of the stampede, and there he rode. It was like a race. They swept on down the valley, and when the end of the white line neared Lassiter's first stand the head had begun to swing round to the west. It swung slowly and stubbornly, yet surely, and gradually assumed a long, beautiful curve of moving white. To Jane's amaze she saw the leaders swinging, turning till they headed back toward her and up the valley. Out to the right of these wild, plunging steers ran Lassiter's black, and Jane's keen eye appreciated the fleet stride and sure-footedness of the blind horse. Then it seemed that the herd moved in a great curve, a huge half-moon, with the points of head and tail almost opposite, and a mile apart. But Lassiter relentlessly crowded the leaders, sheering them to the left, turning them little by little. And the dust-blinded wild followers plunged on madly in the tracks of their leaders. This ever-moving, ever-changing curve of steers rolled toward Jane, and when below her, scarce half a mile, it began to narrow and close into a circle. Lassiter had ridden parallel with her position, turned toward her, then aside, and now he was riding directly away from her, all the time pushing the head of that bobbing line inward.

It was then that Jane, suddenly understanding Lassiter's feat, stared and gasped at the riding of this intrepid man. His horse was fleet and tireless, but blind. He had pushed the leaders around and around till they were about to turn in on the inner side of the end of that line of steers. The leaders were already running in a circle; the end of the herd was still running almost straight. But soon they would be wheeling. Then, when Lassiter had the circle formed, how would he escape? With Jane Withersteen prayer was as ready as praise; and she prayed for this man's safety. A circle of dust began to collect. Dimly, as through a yellow veil, Jane saw Lassiter press the leaders inward to close the gap in the sage. She lost sight of him in the dust; again she thought she saw the black, riderless now, rear and drag himself and fall. Lassiter had been thrown—lost! Then he reappeared running out of the dust into the sage. He had escaped, and she breathed again.

Spellbound, Jane Withersteen watched this stupendous mill-wheel of steers. Here was the milling of the herd. The white running circle closed in upon the open space of sage. And the dust circles closed above into a pall. The ground quaked and the incessant thunder of pounding hoofs rolled on. Jane felt deafened, yet she thrilled to a new sound. As the circle of sage lessened the steers began to bawl, and when it closed entirely there came a great upheaval in the center, and a terrible thumping of heads and clicking of horns. Bawling, climbing, goring, the great mass of steers on the inside wrestled in a crashing din, heaved and groaned under the pressure. Then came a deadlock. The inner strife ceased, and the hideous roar and crash. Movement went on in the outer circle, and that, too, gradually stilled. The white herd had come to a stop, and the pall of yellow dust began to drift away on the wind.

Jane Withersteen waited on the ridge with full and grateful heart. Lassiter appeared, making his weary way toward her through the sage. And up on the slope Judkins rode into sight with his troop of boys. For the present, at least, the white herd would be looked after.

When Lassiter reached her and laid his hand on Black Star's mane, Jane could not find speech.

"Killed—my—hoss," he panted.

"Oh! I'm sorry," cried Jane. "Lassiter! I know you can't replace him, but I'll give you any one of my racers—Bells, or Night, even Black Star."

"I'll take a fast hoss, Jane, but not one of your favorites," he replied. "Only—will you let me have Black Star now an' ride him over there an' head off them fellers who stampeded the herd?"

He pointed to several moving specks of black and puffs of dust in the purple sage.

"I can head them off with this hoss, an' then—"

"Then, Lassiter?"

"They'll never stampede no more cattle."

"Oh! No! No! . . . Lassiter, I won't let you go!"

But a flush of fire flamed in her cheeks, and her trembling hands shook Black Star's bridle, and her eyes fell before Lassiter's.

CHAPTER VII

THE DAUGHTER OF WITHERSTEEN

"LASSITER, will you be my rider?" Jane had asked him.

"I reckon so," he had replied.

Few as the words were, Jane knew how infinitely much they implied. She wanted him to take charge of her cattle and horses and ranges, and save them if that were possible. Yet, though she could not have spoken aloud all she meant, she was perfectly honest with herself. Whatever the price to be paid, she must keep Lassiter close to her; she must shield from him the man who had lured Milly Erne to Cottonwoods. In her fear she so controlled her mind that she did not whisper this Mormon's name to her own soul, she did not even think it. Besides, beyond this thing she regarded as a sacred obligation thrust upon her, was the need of a helper, of a friend, of a champion in this critical time. If she could rule this gun-man, as Venters had called him, if she could even keep him from shedding blood, what strategy to play his name and his presence against the game of oppression her churchmen were waging against her? Never would she forget the effect upon Tull and his men when Venters shouted Lassiter's name. If she could not wholly control Lassiter, then what she could do might put off the fatal day.

One of her safe racers was a dark bay, and she called him Bells because of the way he struck his iron shoes on the stones. When Jerd led out this slender, beautifully built horse Lassiter suddenly became all eyes. A rider's love of a thoroughbred shone in them. Round and round Bells he walked, plainly weakening all the time in his determination not to take one of Jane's favorite racers.

"Lassiter, you're half horse, and Bells sees it already," said Jane,

71

laughing. "Look at his eyes. He likes you. He'll love you, too. How can you resist him? Oh, Lassiter, but Bells can run! It's nip and tuck between him and Wrangle, and only Black Star can beat him. He's too spirited a horse for a woman. Take him. He's yours."

"I jest am weak where a hoss 's concerned," said Lassiter. "I'll take him, an' I'll take your orders, ma'am."

"Well, I'm glad, but never mind the ma'am. Let it still be Jane."

From that hour, it seemed, Lassiter was always in the saddle, riding early and late; and coincident with his part in Jane's affairs the days assumed their old tranquillity. Her intelligence told her this was only the lull before the storm, but her faith would not have it so.

She resumed her visits to the village, and upon one of these she encountered Tull. He greeted her as he had before any trouble came between them, and she, responsive to peace if not quick to forget, met him halfway with manner almost cheerful. He regretted the loss of her cattle; he assured her that the vigilantes which had been organized would soon rout the rustlers; when that had been accomplished her riders would likely return to her.

"You've done a headstrong thing to hire this man Lassiter," Tull went on, severely. "He came to Cottonwoods with evil intent."

"I had to have somebody. And perhaps making him my rider may turn out best in the end for the Mormons of Cottonwoods."

"You mean to stay his hand?"

"I do—if I can."

"A woman like you can do anything with a man. That would be well, and would atone in some measure for the errors you have made."

He bowed and passed on. Jane resumed her walk with conflicting thoughts. She resented Elder Tull's cold, impassive manner that looked down upon her as one who had incurred his just displeasure. Otherwise he would have been the same calm, dark-browed, impenetrable man she had known for ten years. In fact, except when he had revealed his passion in the matter of the seizing of Venters, she had never dreamed he could be other than the grave, reproving preacher. He stood out now a strange, secretive man. She would have thought better of him if he had picked up the threads of their quarrel where they had parted. Was Tull what he appeared to be? The question flung itself involuntarily over Jane Withersteen's inhibitive habit of faith without question. And she refused to answer it. Tull could not fight in the open. Venters had said, Lassiter had said, that her Elder shirked fight and worked in the dark. Just now in this meeting Tull had ignored the fact that he had sued, exhorted, demanded that she marry him. He made no mention of Venters. His manner was that of the minister who had been outraged, but who overlooked the frailties of a woman. Beyond question he seemed unutterably aloof from all knowledge of pressure being brought to bear upon her, absolutely guiltless of any connection with secret power over riders, with night journeys, with rustlers and stampedes of cattle. And that convinced her again of unjust suspicions. But it was convincement through an obstinate faith. She shuddered as she accepted it, and that shudder was the nucleus of a terrible revolt.

Jane turned into one of the wide lanes leading from the main street and entered a huge, shady yard. Here were sweet-smelling clover, alfalfa, flowers, and vegetables, all growing in happy confusion. And like these fresh green things were the dozens of babies, tots, toddlers, noisy urchins, laughing girls, a whole multitude of children of one family. For Collier Brandt, the father of all this numerous progeny, was a Mormon with four wives.

The big house where they lived was old, solid, picturesque, the lower part built of logs, the upper of rough clapboards, with vines growing up the outside stone chimneys. There were many wooden-shuttered windows, and one pretentious window of glass, proudly curtained in white. As this house had four mistresses, it likewise had four separate sections, not one of which communicated with another, and all had to be entered from the outside.

In the shade of a wide, low, vine-roofed porch Jane found Brandt's wives entertaining Bishop Dyer. They were motherly women, of comparatively similar ages, and plain-featured, and just at this moment anything but grave. The Bishop was rather tall, of stout build, with iron-gray hair and beard, and eyes of light blue. They were merry now; but Jane had seen them when they were not, and then she feared him as she had feared her father.

73

The woman flocked around her in welcome.

"Daughter of Withersteen," said the Bishop, gaily, as he took her hand, "you have not been prodigal of your gracious self of late. A Sabbath without you at service! I shall reprove Elder Tull."

"Bishop, the guilt is mine. I'll come to you and confess," Jane replied, lightly; but she felt the undercurrent of her words.

"Mormon love-making!" exclaimed the Bishop, rubbing his hands. "Tull keeps you all to himself."

"No. He is not courting me."

"What? The laggard! If he does not make haste I'll go a-courting myself up to Withersteen House."

There was laughter and further bantering by the Bishop, and then mild talk of village affairs, after which he took his leave, and Jane was left with her friend, Mary Brandt.

"Jane, you're not yourself. Are you sad about the rustling of the cattle? But you have so many, you are so rich."

Then Jane confided in her, telling much, yet holding back her doubts of fear.

"Oh, why don't you marry Tull and be one of us?"

"But, Mary, I don't love Tull," said Jane, stubbornly.

"I don't blame you for that. But, Jane Withersteen, you've got to choose between the love of man and love of God. Often we Mormon women have to do that. It's not easy. The kind of happiness you want I wanted once. I never got it, nor will you, unless you throw away your soul. We've all watched your affair with Venters in fear and trembling. Some dreadful thing will come of it. You don't want him hanged or shot—or treated worse, as that Gentile boy was treated in Glaze for fooling round a Mormon woman. Marry Tull. It's your duty as a Mormon. You'll feel no rapture as his wife—but think of Heaven! Mormon women don't marry for what they expect on earth. Take up the cross, Jane. Remember your father found Amber Spring, built these old houses, brought Mormons here, and fathered them. You are the daughter of Withersteen!"

Jane left Mary Brandt and went to call upon other friends. They received her with the same glad welcome as had Mary, lavished upon her the pent-up affection of Mormon women, and let her go with her ears ringing of Tull, Venters, Lassiter, of duty to God and glory in Heaven.

"Verily," murmured Jane, "I don't know myself when, through all this, I remain unchanged—nay, more fixed of purpose."

She returned to the main street and bent her thoughtful steps toward the center of the village. A string of wagons drawn by oxen was lumbering along. These "sage-freighters," as they were called, hauled grain and flour and merchandise from Sterling; and Jane laughed suddenly in the midst of her humility at the thought that they were her property, as was one of the three stores for which they freighted goods. The water that flowed along the path at her feet, and turned into each cottage-yard to nourish garden and orchard, also was hers, no less her private property because she chose to give it free. Yet in this village of Cottonwoods, which her father had founded and which she maintained, she was not her own mistress; she was not able to abide by her own choice of a husband. She was the daughter of Withersteen. Suppose she proved it, imperiously! But she quelled that proud temptation at its birth.

Nothing could have replaced the affection which the village people had for her; no power could have made her happy as the pleasure her presence gave. As she went on down the street, past the stores with their rude platform entrances, and the saloons, where tired horses stood with bridles dragging, she was again assured of what was the bread and wine of life to her—that she was loved. Dirty boys playing in the ditch, clerks, teamsters, riders, loungers on the corners, ranchers on dusty horses, little girls running errands, and women hurrying to the stores all looked up at her coming with glad eyes.

Jane's various calls and wandering steps at length led her to the Gentile quarter of the village. This was at the extreme southern end, and here some thirty Gentile families lived in huts and shacks and log-cabins and several dilapidated cottages. The fortunes of these inhabitants of Cottonwoods could be read in their abodes. Water they had in abundance, and therefore grass and fruit-trees and patches of alfalfa and vegetable gardens. Some of the men and boys had a few stray cattle, others obtained such intermittent employment as the Mormons reluctantly tendered them. But none of the families was prosperous, many were very poor, and some lived only by Jane Withersteen's beneficence.

As it made Jane happy to go among her own people, so it saddened her to come in contact with these Gentiles. Yet that was not because she was unwelcome; here she was gratefully received by the women, passionately by the children. But poverty and idleness, with their attendant wretchedness and sorrow, always hurt her. That she could alleviate this distress more now than ever before proved the adage that it was an ill wind that blew nobody good. While her Mormon riders were in her employ she had found few Gentiles who would stay with her, and now she was able to find employment for all the men and boys. No little shock was it to have man after man tell her that he dare not accept her kind offer.

"It won't do," said one Carson, an intelligent man who had seen better days. "We've had our warning. Plain and to the point! Now there's Judkins, he packs guns, and he can use them, and so can the daredevil boys he's hired. But they've little responsibility. Can we risk having our homes burned in our absence?"

Jane felt the stretching and chilling of the skin of her face as the blood left it.

"Carson, you and the others rent these houses?" she asked.

"You ought to know, Miss Withersteen. Some of them are yours."

"I know? . . . Carson, I never in my life took a day's labor for rent or a yearling calf or a bunch of grass, let alone gold."

"Bivens, your store-keeper, sees to that."

"Look here, Carson," went on Jane, hurriedly, and now her cheeks were burning. "You and Black and Willet pack your goods and move your families up to my cabins in the grove. They're far more comfortable than these. Then go to work for me. And if aught happens to you there I'll give you money—gold enough to leave Utah!"

The man choked and stammered, and then, as tears welled into his eyes, he found the use of his tongue and cursed. No gentle speech could ever have equaled that curse in eloquent expression of what he felt for Jane Withersteen. How strangely his look and tone reminded her of Lassiter!

"No, it won't do," he said, when he had somewhat recovered himself. "Miss Withersteen, there are things that you don't know, and there's not a soul among us who can tell you."

"I seem to be learning many things, Carson. Well, then, will you let me aid you—say till better times?"

"Yes, I will," he replied, with his face lighting up. "I see what it means to you, and you know what it means to me. Thank you! And if better times ever came I'll be only too happy to work for you."

"Better times will come. I trust God and have faith in man. Good day, Carson."

The lane opened out upon the sage-inclosed alfalfa fields, and the last habitation, at the end of that lane of hovels, was the meanest. Formerly it had been a shed; now it was a home. The broad leaves of a wide-spreading cottonwood sheltered the sunken roof of weathered boards. Like an Indian hut, it had one floor. Round about it were a few scanty rows of vegetables, such as the hand of a weak woman had time and strength to cultivate. This little dwelling-place was just outside the village limits, and the widow who lived there had to carry her water from the nearest irrigation ditch. As Jane Withersteen entered the unfenced yard a child saw her, shrieked with joy, and came tearing toward her with curls flying. This child was a little girl of four called Fay. Her name suited her, for she was an elf, a sprite, a creature so fairy-like and beautiful that she seemed unearthly.

"Muvver sended for oo," cried Fay, as Jane kissed her, "an' oo never tome."

"I didn't know, Fay; but I've come now."

Fay was a child of outdoors, of the garden and ditch and field, and she was dirty and ragged. But rags and dirt did not hide her beauty. The one thin little bedraggled garment she wore half covered her fine, slim body. Red as cherries were her cheeks and lips; her eyes were violet blue, and the crown of her childish loveliness was the curling golden hair. All the children of Cottonwoods were Jane Withersteen's friends; she loved them all. But Fay was dearest to her. Fay had few playmates, for among the Gentile children there were none near her age, and the Mormon children were forbidden to play with her. So she was a shy, wild, lonely child.

"Muvver's sick," said Fay, leading Jane toward the door of the hut.

Jane went in. There was only one room, rather dark and bare, but it was clean and neat. A woman lay upon a bed.

"Mrs. Larkin, how are you?" asked Jane, anxiously.

"I've been pretty bad for a week, but I'm better now."

"You haven't been here all alone—with no one to wait on you?"

"Oh no! My women neighbors are kind. They take turns coming in."

"Did you send for me?"

"Yes, several times."

"But I had no word—no messages ever got to me."

"I sent the boys, and they left word with your women that I was ill and would you please come."

A sudden deadly sickness seized Jane. She fought the weakness, as she fought to be above suspicious thoughts, and it passed, leaving her conscious of her utter impotence. That, too, passed as her spirit rebounded. But she had again caught a glimpse of dark underhand domination, running its secret lines this time into her own household. Like a spider in the blackness of night an unseen hand had begun to run these dark lines, to turn and twist them about her life, to plait and weave a web. Jane Withersteen knew it now, and in the realization further coolness and sureness came to her, and the fighting courage of her ancestors.

"Mrs. Larkin, you're better, and I'm so glad," said Jane. "But may I not do something for you—a turn at nursing, or send you things, or take care of Fay?"

"You're so good. Since my husband's been gone what would have become of Fay and me but for you? It was about Fay that I wanted to speak to you. This time I thought surely I'd die, and I was worried about Fay. Well, I'll be around all right shortly, but my strength's gone and I won't live long. So I may as well speak now. You remember you've been asking me to let you take Fay and bring her up as your daughter?"

"Indeed yes, I remember. I'll be happy to have her. But I hope the day—"

"Never mind that. The day 'll come—sooner or later. I refused your offer, and now I'll tell you why."

"I know why," interposed Jane. "It's because you don't want her brought up as a Mormon."

"No, it wasn't altogether that." Mrs. Larkin raised her thin

78

hand and laid it appealingly on Jane's. "I don't like to tell you. But—it's this: I told all my friends what you wanted. They know you, care for you, and they said for me to trust Fay to you. Women will talk, you know. It got to the ears of Mormons— gossip of your love for Fay and your wanting her. And it came straight back to me, in jealousy, perhaps, that you wouldn't take Fay as much for love of her as because of your religious duty to bring up another girl for some Mormon to marry."

"That's a damnable lie!" cried Jane Withersteen.

"It was what made me hesitate," went on Mrs. Larkin, "but I never believed it at heart. And now I guess I'll let you—"

"Wait! Mrs. Larkin, I may have told little white lies in my life, but never a lie that mattered, that hurt any one. Now believe me. I love little Fay. If I had her near me I'd grow to worship her. When I asked for her I thought only of that love. . . . Let me prove this. You and Fay come to live with me. I've such a big house, and I'm so lonely. I'll help nurse you, take care of you. When you're better you can work for me. I'll keep little Fay and bring her up—without Mormon teaching. When she's grown, if she should want to leave me, I'll send her, and not empty-handed, back to Illinois where you came from. I promise you."

"I knew it was a lie," replied the mother, and she sank back upon her pillow with something of peace in her white, worn face. "Jane Withersteen, may Heaven bless you! I've been deeply grateful to you. But because you're a Mormon I never felt close to you till now. I don't know much about religion as religion, but your God and my God are the same."

CHAPTER VIII

SURPRISE VALLEY

BACK in that strange cañon, which Venters had found indeed a valley of surprises, the wounded girl's whispered appeal, almost a prayer, not to take her back to the rustlers crowned the events of the last few days with a confounding climax. That she should not want to return to them staggered Venters. Presently, as logical thought returned, her appeal confirmed his first impression—that she was more unfortunate than bad—and he experienced a sensation of gladness. If he had known before that Oldring's Masked Rider was a woman his opinion would have been formed and he would have considered her abandoned. But his first knowledge had come when he lifted a white face quivering in a convulsion of agony; he had heard God's name whispered by blood-stained lips; through her solemn and awful eyes he had caught a glimpse of her soul. And just now had come the entreaty to him, "Don't—take—me—back—there!"

Once for all Venters's quick mind formed a permanent conception of this poor girl. He based it, not upon what the chances of life had made her, but upon the revelation of dark eyes that pierced the infinite, upon a few pitiful, halting words that betrayed failure and wrong and misery, yet breathed the truth of a tragic fate rather than a natural leaning to evil.

"What's your name?" he inquired.

"Bess," she answered.

"Bess what?"

"That's enough—just Bess."

The red that deepened in her cheeks was not all the flush of fever. Venters marveled anew, and this time at the tint of shame in her face, at the momentary drooping of long lashes. She might

80

be a rustler's girl, but she was still capable of shame; she might be dying, but she still clung to some little remnant of honor.

"Very well, Bess. It doesn't matter," he said. "But this matters —what shall I do with you?"

"Are—you—a rider?" she whispered.

"Not now. I was once. I drove the Withersteen herds. But I lost my place—lost all I owned—and now I'm—I'm a sort of outcast. My name's Bern Venters."

"You won't—take me—to Cottonwoods—or Glaze? I'd be— hanged."

"No, indeed. But I must do something with you. For it's not safe for me here. I shot that rustler who was with you. Sooner or later he'll be found, and then my tracks. I must find a safer hiding-place where I can't be trailed."

"Leave me—here."

"Alone—to die!"

"Yes."

"I will not." Venters spoke shortly with a kind of ring in his voice.

"What—do you want—to do—with me?" Her whispering grew difficult, so low and faint that Venters had to stoop to hear her.

"Why, let's see," he replied, slowly. "I'd like to take you some place where I could watch by you, nurse you, till you're all right again."

"And—then?"

"Well, it'll be time to think of that when you're cured of your wound. It's a bad one. And—Bess, if you don't want to live—if you don't fight for life—you'll never—"

"Oh! I want—to live! I'm afraid—to die. But I'd rather—die— than go back—to—to—"

"To Oldring?" asked Venters, interrupting her in turn.

Her lips moved in an affirmative.

"I promise not to take you back to him or to Cottonwoods or to Glaze."

The mournful earnestness of her gaze suddenly shone with unutterable gratitude and wonder. And as suddenly Venters found her eyes beautiful as he had never seen or felt beauty. They were as dark blue as the sky at night. Then the flashing changed to a long, thoughtful look, in which there was a wistful, unconscious searching of his face, a look that trembled on the verge of hope and trust.

"I'll try—to live," she said. The broken whisper just reached his ears. "Do what—you want—with me."

"Rest then—don't worry—sleep," he replied.

Abruptly he arose, as if words had been decision for him, and with a sharp command to the dogs he strode from the camp. Venters was conscious of an indefinite conflict of change within him. It seemed to be a vague passing of old moods, a dim coalescing of new forces, a moment of inexplicable transition. He was both cast down and uplifted. He wanted to think and think of the meaning, but he resolutely dispelled emotion. His imperative need at present was to find a safe retreat, and this called for action.

So he set out. It still wanted several hours before dark. This trip he turned to the left and wended his skulking way southward a mile or more to the opening of the valley, where lay the strange scrawled rocks. He did not, however, venture boldly out into the open sage, but clung to the right-hand wall and went along that till its perpendicular line broke into the long incline of bare stone.

Before proceeding farther he halted, studying the strange character of this slope and realizing that a moving black object could be seen far against such background. Before him ascended a gradual swell of smooth stone. It was hard, polished, and full of pockets worn by centuries of eddying rain-water. A hundred yards up began a line of grotesque cedar-trees, and they extended along the slope clear to its most southerly end. Beyond that end Venters wanted to get, and he concluded the cedars, few as they were, would afford some cover.

Therefore he climbed swiftly. The trees were farther up than he had estimated, though he had from long habit made allowance for the deceiving nature of distances in that country. When he gained the cover of cedars he paused to rest and look, and it was then he saw how the trees sprang from holes in the bare rock. Ages of rain had run down the slope, circling, eddying in depressions, wearing deep round holes. There had been dry seasons, accumulations of dust, wind-blown seeds, and cedars rose wonderfully out of solid rock. But these were not beautiful cedars.

They were gnarled, twisted into weird contortions, as if growth were torture, dead at the tops, shrunken, gray, and old. Theirs had been a bitter fight, and Venters felt a strange sympathy for them. This country was hard on trees—and men.

He slipped from cedar to cedar, keeping them between him and the open valley. As he progressed, the belt of trees widened, and he kept to its upper margin. He passed shady pockets half full of water, and, as he marked the location for possible future need, he reflected that there had been no rain since the winter snows. From one of these shady holes a rabbit hopped out and squatted down, laying its ears flat.

Venters wanted fresh meat now more than when he had only himself to think of. But it would not do to fire his rifle there. So he broke off a cedar branch and threw it. He crippled the rabbit, which started to flounder up the slope. Venters did not wish to lose the meat, and he never allowed crippled game to escape, to die lingeringly in some covert. So after a careful glance below, and back toward the cañon, he began to chase the rabbit.

The fact that rabbits generally ran uphill was not new to him. But it presently seemed singular why this rabbit, that might have escaped downward, chose to ascend the slope. Venters knew then that it had a burrow higher up. More than once he jerked over to seize it, only in vain, for the rabbit by renewed effort eluded his grasp. Thus the chase continued on up the bare slope. The farther Venters climbed the more determined he grew to catch his quarry. At last, panting and sweating, he captured the rabbit at the foot of a steeper grade. Laying his rifle on the bulge of rising stone, he killed the animal and slung it from his belt.

Before starting down he waited to catch his breath. He had climbed far up that wonderful smooth slope, and had almost reached the base of yellow cliff that rose skyward, a huge scarred and cracked bulk. It frowned down upon him as if to forbid furthur ascent. Venters bent over for his rifle, and, as he picked it up from where it leaned against the steeper grade, he saw several little nicks cut in the solid stone.

They were only a few inches deep and about a foot apart. Venters began to count them—one—two—three—four—on up to sixteen. That number carried his glance to the top of his first bulging bench of cliff-base. Above, after a more level offset, was still steeper slope, and the line of nicks kept on, to wind round a projecting corner of wall.

A casual glance would have passed by these little dents; if Venters had not known what they signified he would never have bestowed upon them the second glance. But he knew they had been cut there by hand, and, though age-worn, he recognized them as steps cut in the rock by the cliff-dwellers. With a pulse beginning to beat and hammer away his calmness, he eyed that indistinct line of steps, up to where the buttress of wall hid further sight of them. He knew that behind the corner of stone would be a cave or a crack which could never be suspected from below. Chance, that had sported with him of late, now directed him to a probable hiding-place. Again he laid aside his rifle, and, removing boots and belt, he began to walk up the steps. Like a mountain goat, he was agile, sure-footed, and he mounted the first bench without bending to use his hands. The next ascent took grip of fingers as well as toes, but he climbed steadily, swiftly, to reach the projecting corner, and slipped around it. Here he faced a notch in the cliff. At the apex he turned abruptly into a ragged vent that split the ponderous wall clear to the top, showing a narrow streak of blue sky.

At the base this vent was dark, cool, and smelled of dry, musty dust. It zigzagged so that he could not see ahead more than a few yards at a time. He noticed tracks of wildcats and rabbits in the dusty floor. At every turn he expected to come upon a huge cavern full of little square stone houses, each with a small aperture like a staring dark eye. The passage lightened and widened, and opened at the foot of a narrow, steep, ascending chute.

Venters had a moment's notice of the rock, which was of the same smoothness and hardness as the slope below, before his gaze went irresistibly upward to the precipitous walls of this wide ladder of granite. These were ruined walls of yellow sandstone, and so split and splintered, so overhanging with great sections of balancing rim, so impending with tremendous crumbling crags, that Venters caught his breath sharply, and, appalled, he instinctively recoiled as if a step upward might jar the ponderous cliffs from their foundation. Indeed, it seemed that these ruined cliffs were but awaiting a breath of wind to collapse and come tumbling down. Venters hesitated. It would be a foolhardy man who risked his life under the leaning, waiting avalanches of rock in that gigantic split. Yet how many years had they leaned there without falling! At the bottom of the incline was an immense heap of weathered sandstone all crumbling to dust, but there were no huge rocks as large as houses, such as rested so lightly and frightfully above, waiting patiently and inevitably to crash down. Slowly split from the parent rock by the weathering process, and carved and sculptured by ages of wind and rain, they waited their moment. Venters felt how foolish it was for him to fear these broken walls; to fear that, after they had endured for thousands of years, the moment of his passing should be the one for them to slip. Yet he feared it.

"What a place to hide!" muttered Venters. "I'll climb—I'll see where this thing goes. If only I can find water!"

With teeth tight shut he essayed the incline. And as he climbed he bent his eyes downward. This, however, after a little grew impossible; he had to look to obey his eager, curious mind. He raised his glance and saw light between row on row of shafts and pinnacles and crags that stood out from the main wall. Some leaned against the cliff, others against each other; many stood sheer and alone; all were crumbling, cracked, rotten. It was a place of yellow, ragged ruin. The passage narrowed as he went up; it became a slant, hard for him to stick on; it was smooth as marble. Finally he surmounted it, surprised to find the walls still several hundred feet high, and a narrow gorge leading down on the other side. This was a divide between two inclines, about twenty yards wide. At one side stood an enormous rock. Venters gave it a second glance, because it rested on a pedestal. It attracted closer attention. It was like a colossal pear of stone standing on its stem. Around the bottom were thousands of little nicks just distinguishable to the eye. They were marks of stone hatchets. The cliff-dwellers had chipped and chipped away at this boulder till it rested its tremendous bulk upon a mere pin-point of its surface. Venters pondered. Why had the little stone-men hacked away at that big boulder? It bore no semblance to a statue or an idol or a godhead or a sphinx. Instinctively he put his hands on it and pushed; then his shoulder and heaved. The stone seemed to groan, to stir, to grate, and then to move. It tipped a little downward and hung balancing for a long instant, slowly returned, rocked slightly, groaned, and settled back to its former position. Venters divined its significance. It had been meant for defense. The cliff-dwellers, driven by dreaded enemies to this last stand, had cunningly cut the rock until it balanced perfectly, ready to be dislodged by strong hands. Just below it leaned a tottering crag that would have toppled, starting an avalanche on an acclivity where no sliding mass could stop. Crags and pinnacles, splintered cliffs, and leaning shafts and monuments, would have thundered down to block forever the outlet to Deception Pass.

"That was a narrow shave for me," said Venters, soberly. "A balancing rock! The cliff-dwellers never had to roll it. They died, vanished, and here the rock stands, probably little changed. . . . But it might serve another lonely dweller of the cliffs. I'll hide up here somewhere, if I can only find water."

He descended the gorge on the other side. The slope was gradual, the space narrow, the course straight for many rods. A gloom hung between the up-sweeping walls. In a turn the passage narrowed to scarce a dozen feet, and here was darkness of night. But light shone ahead; another abrupt turn brought day again, and then wide open space.

Above Venters loomed a wonderful arch of stone bridging the cañon rims, and through the enormous round portal gleamed and glistened a beautiful valley shining under sunset gold reflected by surrounding cliffs. He gave a start of surprise. The valley was a cove a mile long, half that wide, and its enclosing walls were smooth and stained, and curved inward, forming great caves. He decided that its floor was far higher than the level of Deception Pass and the intersecting cañons. No purple sage colored this valley floor. Instead there were the white of aspens, streaks of branch and slender trunk glistening from the green of leaves, and the darker green of oaks, and through the middle of this forest, from wall to wall, ran a winding line of brilliant green which marked the course of cottonwoods and willows.

"There's water here—and this is the place for me," said Venters. "Only birds can peep over those walls. I've gone Oldring one better."

Venters waited no longer, and turned swiftly to retrace his steps. He named the cañon Surprise Valley and the huge boulder that guarded the outlet Balancing Rock. Going down he did not find himself attended by such fears as had beset him in the climb; still, he was not easy in mind and could not occupy himself with plans of moving the girl and his outfit until he had descended to the notch. There he rested a moment and looked about him. The pass was darkening with the approach of night. At the corner of the wall, where the stone steps turned, he saw a spur of rock that would serve to hold the noose of a lasso. He needed no more aid to scale that place. As he intended to make the move under cover of darkness, he wanted most to be able to tell where to climb up. So, taking several small stones with him, he stepped and slid down to the edge of the slope where he had left his rifle and boots. He placed the stones some yards apart. He left the rabbit lying upon the bench where the steps began. Then he addressed a keen-sighted, remembering gaze to the rim-wall above. It was serrated, and between two spears of rock, directly in line with his position, showed a zigzag crack that at night would let through the gleam of sky. This settled, he put on his belt and boots and prepared to descend. Some consideration was necessary to decide whether or not to leave his rifle there. On the return, carrying the girl and a pack, it would be added encumbrance; and after debating the matter he left the rifle leaning against the bench. As he went straight down the slope he halted every few rods to look up at his mark on the rim. It changed, but he fixed each change in his memory. When he reached the first cedar-tree, he tied his scarf upon a dead branch, and then hurried toward camp, having no more concern about finding his trail upon the return trip.

Darkness soon emboldened and lent him greater speed. It occurred to him, as he glided into the grassy glade near camp and head the whinny of a horse, that he had forgotten Wrangle. The big sorrel could not be gotten into Surprise Valley. He would have to be left here.

Venters determined at once to lead the other horses out through the thicket and turn them loose. The farther they wandered from this cañon the better it would suit him. He easily descried Wrangle through the gloom, but the others were not in sight. Venters whistled low for the dogs, and when they came trotting to him he sent them out to search for the horses, and followed. It soon developed that they were not in the glade nor the thicket.

Venters grew cold and rigid at the thought of rustlers having entered his retreat. But the thought passed, for the demeanor of Ring and Whitie reassured him. The horses had wandered away.

Under the clump of silver spruces a denser mantle of darkness, yet not so thick that Venter's night-practiced eyes could not catch the white oval of a still face. He bent over it with a slight suspension of breath that was both caution lest he frighten her and chill uncertainty of feeling lest he find her dead. But she slept, and he arose to renewed activity.

He packed his saddle-bags. The dogs were hungry, they whined about him and nosed his busy hands; but he took no time to feed them nor to satisfy his own hunger. He slung the saddle-bags over his shoulders and made them secure with his lasso. Then he wrapped the blankets closer about the girl and lifted her in his arms. Wrangle whinnied and thumped the ground as Venters passed him with the dogs. The sorrel knew he was being left behind, and was not sure whether he liked it or not. Venters went on and entered the thicket. Here he had to feel his way in pitch blackness and to wedge his progress between the close saplings. Time meant little to him now that he had started, and he edged along with slow side movement till he got clear of the thicket. Ring and Whitie stood waiting for him. Taking to the open aisles and patches of the sage, he walked guardedly, careful not to stumble or step in dust or strike against spreading sage-branches.

If he were burdened he did not feel it. From time to time, when he passed out of the black lines of shade into the wan starlight, he glanced at the white face of the girl lying in his arms. She had not awakened from her sleep or stupor. He did not rest until he cleared the black gate of the cañon. Then he leaned against a stone breast-high to him and gently released the girl from his hold. His brow and hair and the palms of his hands were wet, and there was a kind of nervous contraction of his muscles. They seemed to ripple and string tense. He had a desire to hurry and no sense of fatigue. A wind blew the scent of sage in his face. The first early blackness of night passed with the brightening of the stars. Somewhere back on his trail a coyote yelped, splitting the dead silence. Venters's faculties seemed singularly acute.

He lifted the girl again and pressed on. The valley afforded

88

better traveling than the cañon. It was lighter, freer of sage, and there were no rocks. Soon, out of the pale gloom shone a still paler thing, and that was the low swell of slope. Venters mounted it, and his dogs walked beside him. Once upon the stone he slowed to snail pace, straining his sight to avoid the pockets and holes. Foot by foot he went up. The weird cedars, like great demons and witches chained to the rock and writhing in silent anguish, loomed up with wide and twisting naked arms. Venters crossed this belt of cedars, skirted the upper border, and recognized the tree he had marked, even before he saw his waving scarf.

Here he knelt and deposited the girl gently, feet first, and slowly laid her out full length. What he feared was to reopen one of her wounds. If he gave her a violent jar, or slipped and fell! But the supreme confidence so strangely felt that night admitted no such blunders.

The slope before him seemed to swell into obscurity, to lose its definite outline in a misty, opaque cloud that shaded into the over-shadowing wall. He scanned the rim where the serrated points speared the sky, and he found the zigzag crack. It was dim, only a shade lighter than the dark ramparts; but he distinguished it, and that served.

Lifting the girl, he stepped upward, closely attending to the nature of the path under his feet. After a few steps he stopped to mark his line with the crack in the rim. The dogs clung closer to him. While chasing the rabbit this slope had appeared interminable to him; now, burdened as he was, he did not think of length or height or toil. He remembered only to avoid a misstep and to keep his direction. He climbed on, with frequent stops to watch the rim, and before he dreamed of gaining the bench he bumped his knees into it, and saw, in the dim gray light, his rifle and the rabbit. He had come straight up without mishap or swerving off his course, and his shut teeth unlocked.

As he laid the girl down in the shallow hollow of the little ridge, with her white face upturned, she opened her eyes. Wide, staring, black, at once like both the night and the stars, they made her face seem still whiter.

"Is—it—you?" she asked, faintly.

"Yes," replied Venters.

"Oh! Where—are we?"

"I'm taking you to a safe place where no one will ever find you. I must climb a little here and call the dogs. Don't be afraid. I'll soon come for you."

She said no more. Her eyes watched him steadily for a moment and then closed. Venters pulled off his boots and then felt for the little steps in the rock. The shade of the cliff above obscured the point he wanted to gain, but he could see dimly a few feet before him. What he had attempted with care he now went at with surpassing lightness. Buoyant, rapid, sure, he attained the corner of wall and slipped around it. Here he could not see a hand before his face, so he groped along, found a little flat space, and there removed the saddle-bags. The lasso he took back with him to the corner and looped the noose over the spur of rock.

"Ring—Whitie—come," he called, softly.

Low whines came up from below.

"Here! Come, Whitie—Ring," he repeated, this time sharply.

Then followed scraping of claws and pattering of feet; and out of the gray gloom below him swiftly climbed the dogs to reach his side and pass beyond.

Venters descended, holding to the lasso. He tested its strength by throwing all his weight upon it. Then he gathered the girl up, and, holding her securely in his left arm, he began to climb, at every few steps jerking his right hand upward along the lasso. It sagged at each forward movement he made, but he balanced himself lightly during the interval when he lacked the support of a taut rope. He climbed as if he had wings, the strength of a giant, and knew not the sense of fear. The sharp corner of cliff seemed to cut out of the darkness. He reached it and the protruding shelf, and then, entering the black shade of the notch, he moved blindly but surely to the place where he had left the saddle-bags. He heard the dogs, though he could not see them. Once more he carefully placed the girl at his feet. Then, on hands and knees, he went over the little flat space, feeling for stones. He removed a number, and, scraping the deep dust into a heap, he unfolded the outer blanket from around the girl and laid her upon this bed. Then he went down the slope again for his boots, rifle, and the rabbit, and, bringing also his lasso with him, he made short work of that trip.

"Are—you—there?" The girl's voice came low from the blackness.

"Yes," he replied, and was conscious that his laboring breast made speech difficult.

"Are we—in a cave?"

"Yes."

"Oh, listen! . . . The waterfall! . . . I hear it! You've brought me back!"

Venters heard a murmuring moan that one moment swelled to a pitch almost softly shrill and the next lulled to a low, almost inaudible sigh.

"That's—wind blowing—in the—cliffs," he panted. "You're far —from Oldring's—cañon."

The effort it cost him to speak made him conscious of extreme lassitude following upon great exertion. It seemed that when he lay down and drew his blanket over him the action was the last before utter prostration. He stretched inert, wet, hot, his body one great strife of throbbing, stinging nerves and bursting veins. And there he lay for a long while before he felt that he had begun to rest.

Rest came to him that night, but no sleep. Sleep he did not want. The hours of strained effort were now as if they had never been, and he wanted to think. Earlier in the day he had dismissed an inexplicable feeling of change; but now, when there was no longer demand on his cunning and strength and he had time to think, he could not catch the illusive thing that had sadly perplexed as well as elevated his spirit.

Above him, through a V-shaped cleft in the dark rim of the cliff, shone the lustrous stars that had been his lonely accusers for a long, long year. To-night they were different. He studied them. Larger, whiter, more radiant they seemed; but that was not the difference he meant. Gradually it came to him that the distinction was not one he saw, but one he felt. In this he divined as much of the baffling change as he thought would be revealed to him then. And as he lay there, with the singing of the cliff-winds in his ears, the white stars above the dark, bold vent, the difference which he felt was that he was no longer alone.

91

CHAPTER IX

SILVER SPRUCE AND ASPENS

THE rest of that night seemed to Venters only a few moments of starlight, a dark overcasting of sky, an hour or so of gray gloom, and then the lighting of dawn.

When he had bestirred himself, feeding the hungry dogs and breaking his long fast, and had repacked his saddle-bags, it was clear daylight, though the sun had not tipped the yellow wall in the east. He concluded to make the climb and descent into Surprise Valley in one trip. To that end he tied his blanket upon Ring and gave Whitie the extra lasso and the rabbit to carry. Then, with the rifle and saddle-bags slung upon his back, he took up the girl. She did not awaken from heavy slumber.

That climb up under the rugged, menacing brows of the broken cliffs, in the face of a grim, leaning boulder that seemed to be weary of its age-long wavering, was a tax on strength and nerve that Venters felt equally with something sweet and strangely exulting in its accomplishment. He did not pause until he gained the narrow divide and there he rested. Balancing Rock loomed huge, cold in the gray light of dawn, a thing without life, yet it spoke silently to Venters: "I am waiting to plunge down, to shatter and crash, roar and boom, to bury your trail, and close forever the outlet to Deception Pass!"

On the descent of the other side Venters had easy going, but was somewhat concerned because Whitie appeared to have succumbed to temptation, and while carrying the rabbit was also chewing on it. And Ring evidently regarded this as an injury to himself, especially as he had carried the heavier load. Presently he snapped at one end of the rabbit and refused to let go. But his action prevented Whitie from further misdoing, and then the two dogs pattered down, carrying the rabbit between them.

Venters turned out of the gorge, and suddenly paused stock-still, astounded at the scene before him. The curve of the great stone bridge had caught the sunrise, and through the magnificent arch burst a glorious stream of gold that shone with a long slant down into the center of Surprise Valley. Only through the arch did any sunlight pass, so that all the rest of the valley lay still asleep, dark green, mysterious, shadowy, merging its level into walls as misty and soft as morning clouds.

Venters then descended, passing through the arch, looking up at its tremendous height and sweep. It spanned the opening to Surprise Valley, stretching in almost perfect curve from rim to rim. Even in his hurry and concern Venters could not but feel its majesty, and the thought came to him that the cliff-dwellers must have regarded it as an object of worship.

Down, down, down Venters strode, more and more feeling the weight of his burden as he descended, and still the valley lay below him. As all other cañons and coves and valleys had deceived him, so had this deep, nestling oval. At length he passed beyond the slope of weathered stone that spread fan-shape from the arch, and encountered a grassy terrace running to the right and about on a level with the tips of the oaks and cottonwoods below. Scattered here and there upon this shelf were clumps of aspens, and he walked through them into a glade that surpassed, in beauty and adaptability for a wild home, any place he had ever seen. Silver spruces bordered the base of a precipitous wall that rose loftily. Caves indented its surface, and there were no detached ledges or weathered sections that might dislodge a stone. The level ground, beyond the spruces, dropped down into a little ravine. This was one dense line of slender aspens from which came the low splashing of water. And the terrace, lying open to the west, afforded unobstructed view of the valley of green tree-tops.

For his camp Venters chose a shady, grassy plot between the silver spruces and the cliff. Here, in the stone wall, had been wonderfully carved by wind or washed by water several deep caves above the level of the terrace. They were clean, dry, roomy.

He cut spruce boughs and made a bed in the largest cave and laid the girl there. The first intimation that he had of her being aroused from sleep or lethargy was a low call for water.

He hurried down into the ravine with his canteen. It was a shallow, grass-green place with aspens growing up everywhere. To his delight he found a tiny brook of swift-running water. Its faint tinge of amber reminded him of the spring at Cottonwoods, and the thought gave him a little shock. The water was so cold it made his fingers tingle as he dipped the canteen. Having returned to the cave, he was glad to see the girl drink thirstily. This time he noted that she could raise her head slightly without his help.

"You were thristy," he said. "It's good water. I've found a fine place. Tell me—how do you feel?"

"There's pain—here," she replied, and moved her hand to her left side.

"Why, that's strange! Your wounds are on your right side. I believe you're hungry. Is the pain a kind of dull ache—a gnawing?"

"It's like—that."

"Then it's hunger." Venters laughed, and suddenly caught himself with a quick breath and felt again the little shock. When had he laughed? "It's hunger," he went on. "I've had that gnaw many a time. I've got it now. But you mustn't eat. You can have all the water you want, but no food just yet."

"Won't I—starve?"

"No, people don't starve easily. I've discovered that. You must lie perfectly still and rest and sleep—for days."

"My hands—are dirty; my face feels—so hot and sticky; my boots hurt." It was her longest speech as yet, and it trailed off in a whisper.

"Well, I'm a fine nurse!"

It annoyed him that he had never thought of these things. But then, awaiting her death and thinking of her comfort were vastly different matters. He unwrapped the blanket which covered her. What a slender girl she was! No wonder he had been able to carry her miles and pack her up that slippery ladder of stone. Her boots were of soft, fine leather, reaching clear to her knees. He recognized the make as one of a bootmaker in Sterling. Her spurs, that he had stupidly neglected to remove, consisted of silver frames and gold chains, and the rowels, large as silver dollars, were fancifully engraved. The boots slipped off rather hard. She wore heavy woollen rider's stockings, half length, and these were pulled up over the ends of her short trousers. Venters took off the stockings to note her little feet were red and swollen. He bathed them. Then he removed his scarf and bathed her face and hands.

"I must see your wounds now," he said, gently.

She made no reply, but watched him steadily as he opened her blouse and untied the bandage. His strong fingers trembled a little as he removed it. If the wounds had reopened! A chill struck him as he saw the angry red bullet-mark, and a tiny stream of blood winding from it down her white breast. Very carefully he lifted her to see that the wound in her back had closed perfectly. Then he washed the blood from her breast, bathed the wound, and left it unbandaged, open to the air.

Her eyes thanked him.

"Listen," he said, earnestly. "I've had some wounds, and I've seen many. I know a little about them. The hole in your back has closed. If you lie still three days the one in your breast will close and you'll be safe. The danger from hemorrhage will be over."

He had spoken with earnest sincerity, almost eagerness.

"Why—do you—want me—to get well?" she asked, wonderingly.

The simple question seemed unanswerable except on grounds of humanity. But the circumstances under which he had shot this strange girl, the shock and realization, the waiting for death, the hope, had resulted in a condition of mind wherein Venters wanted her to live more than he had ever wanted anything. Yet he could not tell why. He believed the killing of the rustler and the subsequent excitement had disturbed him. For how else could he explain the throbbing of his brain, the heat of his blood, the undefined sense of full hours, charged, vibrant with pulsating mystery where once they had dragged in loneliness?

"I shot you," he said, slowly, "and I want you to get well so I shall not have killed a woman. But—for your own sake, too—"

A terrible bitterness darkened her eyes, and her lips quivered.

"Hush," said Venters. "You've talked too much already."

In her unutterable bitterness he saw a darkness of mood that

95

could not have been caused by her present weak and feverish state. She hated the life she had led, that she probably had been compelled to lead. She had suffered some unforgivable wrong at the hands of Oldring. With that conviction Venters felt a flame throughout his body, and it marked the rekindling of fierce anger and ruthlessness. In the past long year he had nursed resentment. He had hated the wilderness—the loneliness of the uplands. He had waited for something to come to pass. It had come. Like an Indian stealing horses he had skulked into the recesses of the cañons. He had found Oldring's retreat; he had killed a rustler; he had shot an unfortunate girl, then had saved her from this unwitting act, and he meant to save her from the consequent wasting of blood, from fever and weakness. Starvation he had to fight for her and for himself. Where he had been sick at the letting of blood, now he remembered it in grim, cold calm. And as he lost that softness of nature, so he lost his fear of men. He would watch for Oldring, biding his time, and he would kill this great black-bearded rustler who had held a girl in bondage, who had used her to his infamous ends.

Venters surmised this much of the change in him—idleness had passed; keen, fierce vigor flooded his mind and body; all that had happened to him at Cottonwoods seemed remote and hard to recall; the difficulties and perils of the present absorbed him, held him in a kind of spell.

First, then, he fitted up the little cave adjoining the girl's room for his own comfort and use. His next work was to build a fireplace of stones and to gather a store of wood. That done, he spilled the contents of his saddle-bags upon the grass and took stock. His outfit consisted of a small-handled axe, a hunting-knife, a large number of cartridges for rifle or revolver, a tin plate, a cup, and a fork and spoon, a quantity of dried beef and dried fruits, and small canvas bags containing tea, sugar, salt, and pepper. For him alone this supply would have been bountiful to begin a sojourn in the wilderness, but he was no longer alone. Starvation in the uplands was not an unheard-of thing; he did not, however, worry at all on that score, and feared only his possible inability to supply the needs of a woman in a weakened and extremely delicate condition.

If there was no game in the valley—a contingency he doubted

—it would not be a great task for him to go by night to Oldring's herd and pack out a calf. The exigency of the moment was to ascertain if there were game in Surprise Valley. Whitie still guarded the dilapidated rabbit, and Ring slept near by under a spruce. Venters called Ring and went to the edge of the terrace, and there halted to survey the valley.

He was prepared to find it larger than his unstudied glances had made it appear; for more than a casual idea of dimensions and a hasty conception of oval shape and singular beauty he had not had time. Again the felicity of the name he had given the valley struck him forcibly. Around the red perpendicular walls, except under the great arc of stone, ran a terrace fringed at the cliff-base by silver spruces; below that first terrace sloped another wider one densely overgrown with aspens, and the center of the valley was a level circle of oaks and alders, with the glittering green line of willows and cottonwood dividing it in half. Venters saw a number and variety of birds flitting among the trees. To his left, facing the stone bridge, an enormous cavern opened in the wall; and low down, just above the tree-tops, he made out a long shelf of cliff-dwellings, with little black, staring windows or doors. Like eyes they were, and seemed to watch him. The few cliff-dwellings he had seen—all ruins—had left him with haunting memory of age and solitude and of something past. He had come, in a way, to be a cliff-dweller himself, and those silent eyes would look down upon him, as if in surprise that after thousands of years a man had invaded the valley. Venters felt sure that he was the only white man who had ever walked under the shadow of the wonderful stone bridge, down into that wonderful valley with its circle of caves and its terraced rings of silver spruce and aspens.

The dog growled below and rushed into the forest. Venters ran down the declivity to enter a zone of light shade streaked with sunshine. The oak-trees were slender, none more than half a foot thick, and they grew close together, intermingling their branches. Ring came running back with a rabbit in his mouth. Venters took the rabbit and, holding the dog near him, stole softly on. There were fluttering of wings among the branches and quick bird-notes, and rustling of dead leaves and rapid patterings. Venters crossed well-worn trails marked with fresh tracks; and when he had stolen on a little farther he saw many birds and running quail, and more rabbits than he could count. He had not penetrated the forest of oaks for a hundred yards, had not approached anywhere near the line of willows and cottonwoods which he knew grew along a stream. But he had seen enough to know that Surprise Valley was the home of many wild creatures.

Venters returned to camp. He skinned the rabbits, and gave the dogs the one they had quarreled over, and the skin of this he dressed and hung up to dry, feeling that he would like to keep it. It was a particularly rich, furry pelt with a beautiful white tail. Venters remembered that but for the bobbing of that white tail catching his eye he would not have espied the rabbit, and he would never have discovered Surprise Valley. Little incidents of chance like this had turned him here and there in Deception Pass; and now they had assumed to him the significance and direction of destiny.

His good fortune in the matter of game at hand brought to his mind the necessity of keeping it in the valley. Therefore he took the axe and cut bundles of aspens and willows, and packed them up under the bridge to the narrow outlet of the gorge. Here he began fashioning a fence, by driving aspens into the ground and lacing them fast with willows. Trip after trip he made down for more building material, and the afternoon had passed when he finished the work to his satisfaction. Wildcats might scale the fence, but no coyote could come in to search for prey, and no rabbits or other small game could escape from the valley.

Upon returning to camp he set about getting his supper at ease, around a fine fire, without hurry or fear of discovery. After hard work that had definite purpose, this freedom and comfort gave him peculiar satisfaction. He caught himself often, as he kept busy round the camp-fire, stopping to glance at the quiet form in the cave, and at the dogs stretched cozily near him, and then out across the beautiful valley. The present was not yet real to him.

While he ate, the sun set beyond a dip in the rim of the curved wall. As the morning sun burst wondrously through a grand arch into this valley, in a golden, slanting shaft, so the evening sun, at the moment of setting, shone through a gap of cliffs, sending down a broad red burst to brighten the oval with a blaze of fire. To Venters both sunrise and sunset were unreal.

A cool wind blew across the oval, waving the tips of oaks, and, while the light lasted, fluttering the aspen leaves into millions of facets of red, and sweeping the graceful spruces. Then with the wind soon came a shade and a darkening, and suddenly the valley was gray. Night came there quickly after the sinking of the sun. Venters went softly to look at the girl. She slept, and her breathing was quiet and slow. He lifted Ring into the cave, with stern whisper for him to stay there on guard. Then he drew the blanket carefully over her and returned to the camp-fire.

Though exceedingly tired, he was yet loath to yield to lassitude, but this night it was not from listening, watchful vigilance; it was from a desire to realize his position. The details of his wild environment seemed the only substance of a strange dream. He saw the darkening rims, the gray oval turning black, the undulating surface of forest, like a rippling lake, and the spear-pointed spruces. He heard the flutter of aspen leaves and the soft, continuous splash of falling water. The melancholy note of a cañon bird broke clear and lonely from the high cliffs. Venters had no name for this night singer, and he had never seen one; but the few notes, always pealing out just at darkness, were as familiar to him as the cañon silence. Then they ceased, and the rustle of leaves and the murmur of water hushed in a growing sound that Venters fancied was not of earth. Neither had he a name for this, only it was inexpressibly wild and sweet. The thought came that it might be a moan of the girl in her last outcry of life, and he felt a tremor shake him. But no! This sound was not human, though it was like despair. He began to doubt his sensitive perceptions, to believe that he half-dreamed what he thought he heard. Then the sound swelled with the strengthening of the breeze, and he realized it was the singing of the wind in the cliffs.

By and by a drowsiness overcame him, and Venters began to nod, half asleep, with his back against a spruce. Rousing himself and calling Whitie, he went to the cave. The girl lay barely visible in the dimness. Ring crouched beside her, and the patting of his tail on the stone assured Venters that the dog was awake and faithful to his duty. Venters sought his own bed of fragrant boughs; and as he lay back, somehow grateful for the comfort and safety, the night seemed to steal away from him and he sank softly into intangible space and rest and slumber.

Venters awakened to the sound of melody that he imagined was only the haunting echo of dream music. He opened his eyes to another surprise of this valley of beautiful surprises. Out of his cave he saw the exquisitely fine foliage of the silver spruces crossing a round space of blue morning sky; and in this lacy leafage fluttered a number of gray birds with black and white stripes and long tails. They were mocking-birds, and they were singing as if they wanted to burst their throats. Venters listened. One long, silver-tipped branch dropped almost to his cave, and upon it, within a few yards of him, sat one of the graceful birds. Venters saw the swelling and quivering of its throat in song. He arose, and when he slid down out of his cave the birds fluttered and flew farther away.

Venters stepped before the opening of the other cave and looked in. The girl was awake, with wide eyes and listening look, and she had a hand on Ring's neck.

"Mocking-birds!" she said.

"Yes," replied Venters, "and I believe they like our company."

"Where are we?"

"Never mind now. After a little I'll tell you."

"The birds woke me. When I heard them—and saw the shiny trees—and the blue sky—and then a blaze of gold dropping down—I wondered—"

She did not complete her fancy, but Venters imagined he understood her meaning. She appeared to be wandering in mind. Venters felt her face and hands and found them burning with fever. He went for water, and was glad to find it almost as cold as if flowing from ice. That water was the only medicine he had, and he put faith in it. She did not want to drink, but he made her swallow, and then he bathed her face and head and cooled her wrists.

The day began with the heightening of the fever. Venters spent the time reducing her temperature, cooling her hot cheeks and temples. He kept close watch over her, and at the least indication of restlessness, that he knew led to tossing and rolling of the body, he held her tightly, so no violent move could reopen her wounds. Hour after hour she babbled and laughed and cried and moaned in delirium; but whatever her secret was she did not reveal it.

Attended by something somber for Venters, the day passed. At night in the cool winds the fever abated and she slept. The second day was a repetition of the first. On the third he seemed to see her wither and waste away before his eyes. That day he scarcely went from her side for a moment, except to run for fresh, cool water; and he did not eat. The fever broke on the fourth day and left her spent and shrunken, a slip of a girl with life only in her eyes. They hung upon Venters with a mute observance, and he found hope in that.

To rekindle the spark that had nearly flickered out, to nourish the little life and vitality that remained in her, was Venters's problem. But he had little resource other than the meat of the rabbits and quail; and from these he made broths and soups as best he could, and fed her with a spoon. It came to him that the human body, like the human soul, was a strange thing and capable of recovering from terrible shocks. For almost immediately she showed faint signs of gathering strength. There was one more waiting day, in which he doubted, and spent long hours by her side as she slept, and watched the gentle swell of her breast rise and fall in breathing, and the wind stir the tangled chestnut curls. On the next day he knew that she would live.

Upon realizing it he abruptly left the cave and sought his accustomed seat against the trunk of a big spruce, where once more he let his glance stray along the sloping terraces. She would live, and the somber gloom lifted out of the valley, and he felt relief that was pain. Then he roused to the call of action, to the many things he needed to do in the way of making camp fixtures and utensils, to the necessity of hunting food, and the desire to explore the valley.

But he decided to wait a few more days before going far from camp, because he fancied that the girl rested easier when she could see him near at hand. And on the first day her languor appeared to leave her in a renewed grip of life. She awoke stronger from each short slumber; she ate greedily, and she moved about in her bed of boughs; and always, it seemed to Venters, her eyes followed him. He knew now that her recovery would be rapid. She talked about the dogs, about the caves, the valley, about how hungry she was, till Venters silenced her, asking her to put off further talk till another time. She obeyed, but she sat up in her bed, and her eyes roved to and fro, and always back to him.

Upon the second morning she sat up when he awakened her, and would not permit him to bathe her face and feed her, which actions she performed for herself. She spoke little, however, and Venters was quick to catch in her the first intimations of thoughtfulness and curiosity and appreciation of her situation. He left camp and took Whitie out to hunt for rabbits. Upon his return he was amazed and somewhat anxiously concerned to see his invalid sitting with her back to a corner of the cave and her bare feet swinging out. Hurriedly he approached, intending to advise her to lie down again, to tell her that perhaps she might overtax her strength. The sun shone upon her, glinting on the little head with its tangle of bright hair and the small, oval face with its pallor, and dark-blue eyes underlined by dark-blue circles. She looked at him and he looked at her. In that exchange of glances he imagined each saw the other in some different guise. It seemed impossible to Venters that this frail girl could be Oldring's Masked Rider. It flashed over him that he had made a mistake which presently she would explain.

"Help me down," she said.

"But—are you well enough?" he protested. "Wait—a little longer."

"I'm weak—dizzy. But I want to get down."

He lifted her—what a light burden now!—and stood her upright beside him, and supported her as she essayed to walk with halting steps. She was like a stripling of a boy; the bright, small head scarcely reached his shoulder. But now, as she clung to his arm, the rider's costume she wore did not contradict, as it had done at first, his feeling of her femininity. She might be the famous Masked Rider of the uplands, she might resemble a boy; but her outline, her little hands and feet, her hair, her big eyes and tremulous lips, and especially a something that Venters felt as a subtle essence rather than what he saw, proclaimed her sex.

She soon tired. He arranged a comfortable seat for her under the spruce that overspread the camp-fire.

"Now tell me—everything," she said.

He recounted all that had happened from the time of his discovery of the rustlers in the cañon up to the present moment.

"You shot me—and now you've saved my life?"

"Yes. After almost killing you I've pulled you through."

"Are you glad?"

"I should say so!"

Her eyes were unusually expressive, and they regarded him steadily; she was unconscious of that mirroring of her emotions, and they shone with gratefulness and interest and wonder and sadness.

"Tell me—about yourself?" she asked.

He made this a briefer story, telling of his coming to Utah, his various occupations till he became a rider, and then how the Mormons had practically driven him out of Cottonwoods, an outcast.

Then, no longer able to withstand his own burning curiosity, he questioned her in turn.

"Are you Oldring's Masked Rider?"

"Yes," she replied, and dropped her eyes.

"I knew it—I recognized your figure—and mask, for I saw you once. Yet I can't believe it! . . . But you never *were* really that rustler, as we riders knew him? A thief—a marauder—a kidnapper of women—a murderer of sleeping riders!"

"No! I never stole—or harmed any one—in all my life. I only rode and rode—"

"But why—why?" he burst out. "Why the name? I understand Oldring made you ride. But the black mask—the mystery—the things laid to your hands—the threats in your infamous name—the night-riding credited to you—the evil deeds deliberately blamed on you and acknowledged by rustlers—even Oldring himself! Why? Tell me why?"

"I never knew that," she answered low. Her drooping head straightened, and the large eyes, larger now and darker, met Venters's with a clear, steadfast gaze in which he read truth. It verified his own conviction.

"Never knew? That's strange! Are you a Mormon?"

"No."

"Is Oldring a Mormon?"

"No."

"Do you—care for him?"

"Yes. I hate his men—his life—sometimes I almost hate him!"

Venters paused in his rapid-fire questioning, as if to brace himself to ask for a truth that would be abhorrent for him to confirm, but which he seemed driven to hear.

"What are—what *were* you to Oldring?"

Like some delicate thing suddenly exposed to blasting heat, the girl wilted; her head dropped, and into her white, wasted cheeks crept the red of shame.

Venters would have given anything to recall that question. It seemed so different—his thought when spoken. Yet her shame established in his mind something akin to the respect he had strangely been hungering to feel for her.

"D—n that question!—forget it!" he cried, in a passion of pain for her and anger at himself. "But once and for all—tell me—I know it, yet I want to hear you say so—you couldn't help yourself?"

"Oh no."

"Well, that makes it all right with me," he went on, honestly. "I—I want you to feel that . . . you see—we've been thrown together—and—and I want to help you—not hurt you. I thought life had been cruel to me, but when I think of yours I feel mean and little for my complaining. Anyway, I was a lonely outcast. And now! . . . I don't see very clearly what it all means. Only we are here—together. We've got to stay here, for long, surely till you are well. But you'll never go back to Oldring. And I'm sure helping you will help me, for I was sick in mind. There's something now for me to do. And if I can win back your strength —then get you away, out of this wild country—help you somehow to a happier life—just think how good that 'll be for me!"

CHAPTER X

LOVE

DURING all these waiting days Venters, with the exception of the afternoon when he had built the gate in the gorge, had scarcely gone out of sight of camp and never out of hearing. His desire to explore Surprise Valley was keen, and on the morning after his long talk with the girl he took his rifle and, calling Ring, made a move to start. The girl lay back in a rude chair of boughs he had put together for her. She had been watching him, and when he picked up the gun and called the dog Venters thought she gave a nervous start.

"I'm only going to look over the valley," he said.

"Will you be gone long?"

"No," he replied, and started off. The incident set him thinking of his former impression that, after her recovery from fever, she did not seem at ease unless he was close at hand. It was fear of being alone, due, he concluded, most likely to her weakened condition. He must not leave her much alone.

As he strode down the sloping terrace, rabbits scampered before him, and the beautiful valley quail, as purple in color as the sage on the uplands, ran fleetly along the ground into the forest. It was pleasant under the trees, in the gold-flecked shade, with the whistle of quail and twittering of birds everywhere. Soon he had passed the limit of his former excursions and entered new territory. Here the woods began to show open glades and brooks running down from the slope, and presently he emerged from shade into the sunshine of a meadow. The shaking of the high grass told him of the running of animals, what species he could not tell, but from Ring's manifest desire to have a chase they were evidently some kind wilder than rabbits. Venters approached the willow and cottonwood belt that he had observed from the height of slope. He penetrated it to find a considerable stream of water and great half-submerged mounds of brush and sticks, and all about him were old and new gnawed circles at the base of the cottonwoods.

"Beaver!" he exclaimed. "By all that's lucky! The meadow's full of beaver! How did they ever get here?"

Beaver had not found a way into the valley by the trail of the cliff-dwellers, of that he was certain; and he began to have more than curiosity as to the outlet or inlet of the stream. When he passed some dead water, which he noted was held by a beaver-dam, there was a current in the stream, and it flowed west. Following its course, he soon entered the oak forest again, and passed through to find himself before massed and jumbled ruins of cliff-wall. There were tangled thickets of wild plum-trees and other thorny growths that made passage extremely laborsome. He found innumerable tracks of wildcats and foxes. Rustlings in the thick undergrowth told him of stealthy movements of these animals. At length his further advance appeared futile, for the reason that the stream disappeared in a split at the base of immense rocks over which he could not climb. To his relief he concluded that though beaver might work their way up the narrow chasm where the water rushed, it would be impossible for men to enter the valley there.

This western curve was the only part of the valley where the walls had been split asunder, and it was a wildly rough and inaccessible corner. Going back a little way, he leaped the stream and headed toward the southern wall. Once out of the oaks he found again the low terrace of aspens, and above that the wide, open terrace fringed by silver spruces. This side of the valley contained the wind or water worn caves. As he pressed on, keeping to the upper terrace, cave after cave opened out of the cliff; now a large one, now a small one. Then yawned, quite suddenly and wonderfully above him, the great cavern of the cliff-dwellers.

It was still a goodly distance, and he tried to imagine, if it appeared so huge from where he stood, what it would be when he got there. He climbed the terrace and then faced a long, gradual ascent of weathered rock and dust, which made climbing too difficult for attention to anything else. At length he entered a zone of shade, and looked up. He stood just within the hollow of a cavern so immense that he had no conception of its real dimensions. The curved roof, stained by ages of leakage, with buff and black and rust-colored streaks, swept up and loomed higher and seemed to soar to the rim of the cliff. Here again was a magnificent arch, such as formed the grand gateway to the valley, only in this instance it formed the dome of a cave instead of the span of a bridge.

Venters passed onward and upward. The stones he dislodged rolled down with strange, hollow crack and roar. He had climbed a hundred rods inward, and yet he had not reached the base of the shelf where the cliff-dwellings rested, a long half-circle of connected stone house, with little dark holes that he had fancied were eyes. At length he gained the base of the shelf, and here found steps cut in the rock. These facilitated climbing, and as he went up he thought how easily this vanished race of men might once have held that stronghold against an army. There was only one possible place to ascend, and this was narrow and steep.

Venters had visited cliff-dwellings before, and they had been in ruins, and of no great character or size but this place was of proportions that stunned him, and it had not been desecrated by the hand of man, nor had it been crumbled by the hand of time. It was a stupendous tomb. It had been a city. It was just as it had been left by its builders. The little houses were there, the smoke-blackened stains of fires, the pieces of pottery scattered about cold hearths, the stone hatchets; and stone pestles and mealing-stones lay beside round holes polished by years of grinding maize—lay there as if they had been carelessly dropped yesterday. But the cliff-dwellers were gone!

Dust! They were dust on the floor or at the foot of the shelf, and their habitations and utensils endured. Venters felt the sublimity of that marvelous vaulted arch, and it seemed to gleam with a glory of something that was gone. How many years had passed since the cliff-dwellers gazed out across the beautiful valley as he was gazing now? How long had it been since women ground grain in those polished holes? What time had rolled by since men of an unknown race lived, loved, fought, and died there? Had an enemy destroyed them? Had disease destroyed them, or only that greatest destroyer—time? Venters saw a long line of blood-red hands painted low down upon the yellow roof of stone. Here was strange portent, if not an answer to his queries. The place oppressed him. It was light, but full of a transparent gloom. It smelled of dust and musty stone, of age and disuse. It was sad. It was solemn. It had the look of a place where silence had become master and was now irrevocable and terrible and could not be broken. Yet, at the moment, from high up in the carved crevices of the arch, floated down the low, strange wail of wind—a knell indeed for all that had gone.

Venters, sighing, gathered up an armful of pottery, such pieces as he thought strong enough and suitable for his own use, and bent his steps toward camp. He mounted the terrace at an opposite point to which he had left. He saw the girl looking in the direction he had gone. His footsteps made no sound in the deep grass, and he approached close without her being aware of his presence. Whitie lay on the ground near where she sat, and he manifested the usual actions of welcome, but the girl did not notice them. She seemed to be oblivious to everything near at hand. She made a pathetic figure drooping there, with her sunny hair contrasting so markedly with her white, wasted cheeks and her hands listlessly clasped and her little bare feet propped in the framework of the rude seat. Venters could have sworn and laughed in one breath at the idea of the connection between this girl and Oldring's Masked Rider. She was the victim of more than accident of fate—a victim to some deep plot the mystery of which burned him. As he stepped forward with a half-formed thought that she was absorbed in watching for his return, she turned her head and saw him. A swift start, a change rather than rush of blood under her white cheeks, a flashing of big eyes that fixed their glance upon him, transformed her face in that single instant of turning; and he knew she had been watching for him, that his return was the one thing in her mind. She did not smile; she did not flush; she did not look glad. All these would have meant little compared to her indefinite expression. Venters grasped the peculiar, vivid, vital something that leaped from her face. It was as if she had been in a dead, hopeless clamp of inaction and feeling, and had been suddenly shot through and through with quivering animation. Almost it was as if she had returned to life.

And Venters thought with lightning swiftness, "I've saved her —I've unlinked her from that old life—she was watching as if

I were all she had left on earth—she belongs to me!" The thought was startlingly new. Like a blow it was in an unprepared moment. The cheery salutation he had ready for her died unborn, and he tumbled the pieces of pottery awkwardly on the grass, while some unfamiliar, deep-seated emotion, mixed with pity and glad assurance of his power to succor her, held him dumb.

"What a load you had!" she said. "Why, they're pots and crocks! Where did you get them?"

Venters laid down his rifle, and, filling one of the pots from his canteen, he placed it on the smoldering campfire.

"Hope it 'll hold water," he said, presently. "Why, there's an enormous cliff-dwelling just across here. I got the pottery there. Don't you think we needed something? That tin cup of mine has served to make tea, broth, soup—everything."

"I noticed we hadn't a great deal to cook in."

She laughed. It was the first time. He liked that laugh, and though he was tempted to look at her, he did not want to show his surprise or his pleasure.

"Will you take me over there, and all around in the valley—pretty soon when I'm well?" she added.

"Indeed I shall. It's a wonderful place. Rabbits so thick you can't step without kicking one out. And quail, beaver, foxes, wildcats. We're in a regular den. But—haven't you ever seen a cliff-dwelling?"

"No. I've heard about them, though. The—the men say the Pass is full of old houses and ruins."

"Why, I should think you'd have run across one in all your riding around," said Venters. He spoke slowly, choosing his words carefully, and he essayed a perfectly casual manner, and pretended to be busy assorting pieces of pottery. She must have no cause again to suffer shame for curiosity of his. Yet never in all his days had he been so eager to hear the details of anyone's life.

"When I rode—I rode like the wind," she replied, "and never had time to stop for anything."

"I remember that day I—I met you in the Pass—how dusty you were, how tired your horse looked. Were you always riding?"

"Oh, no. Sometimes not for months, when I was shut up in the cabin."

Venters tried to subdue a hot tingling.

"You were shut up, then?" he asked, carelessly.

"When Oldring went away on his long trips—he was gone for months sometimes—he shut me up in the cabin."

"What for?"

"Perhaps to keep me from running away. I always threatened that. Mostly, though, because the men got drunk at the villages. But they were always good to me. I wasn't afraid."

"A prisoner! That must have been hard on you?"

"I liked that. As long as I can remember I've been locked up there at times, and those times were the only happy ones I ever had. It's a big cabin, high up on a cliff, and I could look out. Then I had dogs and pets I had tamed, and books. There was a spring inside, and food stored, and the men brought me fresh meat. Once I was there one whole winter."

It now required deliberation on Venters's part to persist in his unconcern and to keep at work. He wanted to look at her, to volley questions at her.

"As long as you can remember—you've lived in Deception Pass?" he went on.

"I've a dim memory of some other place, and women and children; but I can't make anything of it. Sometimes I think till I'm weary."

"Then you can read—you have books?"

"Oh yes, I can read, and write, too, pretty well. Oldring is educated. He taught me, and years ago an old rustler lived with us, and he had been something different once. He was always teaching me."

"So Oldring takes long trips," mused Venters. "Do you know where he goes?"

"No. Every year he drives cattle north of Sterling—then does not return for months. I heard him accused once of living two lives—and he killed the man. That was at Stone Bridge."

Venters dropped his apparent task and looked up with an eagerness he no longer strove to hide.

"Bess," he said, using her name for the first time, "I suspected Oldring was something besides a rustler. Tell me, what's his purpose here in the Pass? I believe much that he has done was to hide his real work here."

"You're right. He's more than a rustler. In fact, as the men say, his rustling cattle is now only a bluff. There's gold in the cañons!"

"Ah!"

"Yes, there's gold, not in great quantities, but gold enough for him and his men. They wash for gold week in and week out. Then they drive a few cattle and go into the villages to drink and shoot and kill—to bluff the riders."

"Drive a few cattle! But, Bess, the Withersteen herd, the red herd—twenty-five hundred head! That's not a few. And I tracked them into a valley near here."

"Oldring never stole the red herd. He made a deal with Mormons. The riders were to be called in, and Oldring was to drive the herd and keep it till a certain time—I won't know when—then drive it back to the range. What his share was I didn't hear."

"Did you hear *why* that deal was made?" queried Venters.

"No. But it was a trick of Mormons. They're full of tricks. I've heard Oldring's men tell about Mormons. Maybe the Withersteen woman wasn't minding her halter! I saw the man who made the deal. He was a little, queer-shaped man, all humped up. He sat his horse well. I heard one of our men say afterward there was no better rider on the sage than this fellow. What was the name? I forget."

"Jerry Card?" suggested Venters.

"That's it. I remember—it's a name easy to remember—and Jerry Card appeared to be on fair terms with Oldring's men."

"I shouldn't wonder," replied Venters, thoughtfully. Verification of his suspicions in regard to Tull's underhand work—for the deal with Oldring made by Jerry Card assuredly had its inception in the Mormon Elder's brain, and had been accomplished through his orders—revived in Venters a memory of hatred that had been smothered by press of other emotions. Only a few days had elapsed since the hour of his encounter with Tull, yet they had been forgotten and now seemed far off, and the interval one that now appeared large and profound with incalculable change in his feelings. Hatred of Tull still existed in his heart; but it had lost its white heat. His affection for Jane Withersteen had not changed in the least; nevertheless, he seemed to view it from another angle and see it as another thing—what, he could not exactly define. The recalling of these two feelings was to Venters like getting glimpses into a self that was gone; and the wonder of them—perhaps the change which was too illusive for him—was the fact that a strange irritation accompanied the memory and a desire to dismiss it from mind. And straightway he did dismiss it, to return to thoughts of his significant present.

"Bess, tell me one more thing," he said. "Haven't you known any women—any young people?"

"Sometimes there were women with the men; but Oldring never let me know them. And all the young people I ever saw in my life was when I rode fast through the villages."

Perhaps that was the most puzzling and thought-provoking thing she had yet said to Venters. He pondered, more curious the more he learned, but he curbed his inquisitive desires, for he saw her shrinking on the verge of that shame, the causing of which had occasioned him such self-reproach. He would ask no more. Still he had to think, and he found it difficult to think clearly. This sad-eyed girl was so utterly different from what it would have been reason to believe such a remarkable life would have made her. On this day he had found her simple and frank, as natural as any girl he had ever known. About her there was something sweet. Her voice was low and well modulated. He could not look into her face, meet her steady, unabashed, yet wistful eyes, and think of her as the woman she had confessed herself. Oldring's Masked Rider sat before him, a girl dressed as a man. She had been made to ride at the head of infamous forays and drives. She had been imprisoned for many months of her life in an obscure cabin. At times the most vicious of men had been her companions; and the vilest of women, if they had not been permitted to approach her, had, at least, cast their shadows over her. But—but in spite of all this—there thundered at Venters some truth that lifted its voice higher than the clamoring facts of dishonor, some truth that was the very life of her beautiful eyes; and it was innocence.

In the days that followed, Venters balanced perpetually in mind this haunting conception of innocence over against the cold and sickening fact of an unintentional yet actual gift. How could it be possible for the two things to be true? He believed the latter to be true, and he would not relinquish his conviction of the former; and these conflicting thoughts augmented the mystery that appeared to be a part of Bess. In those ensuing days, however, it became clear as clearest light that Bess was rapidly regaining strength; that, unless reminded of her long association with Oldring, she seemed to have forgotten it; that, like an Indian who lives solely from moment to moment, she was utterly absorbed in the present.

Day by day Venters watched the white of her face slowly change to brown, and the wasted cheeks fill out by imperceptible degrees. There came a time when he could just trace the line of demarcation between the part of her face once hidden by a mask and that left exposed to wind and sun. When that line disappeared in clear bronze tan it was as if she had been washed clean of the stigma of Oldring's Masked Rider. The suggestion of the mask always made Venters remember; now that it was gone he seldom thought of her past. Occasionally he tried to piece together the several stages of strange experience and to make a whole. He had shot a masked outlaw the very sight of whom had been ill omen to riders; he had carried off a wounded woman whose bloody lips quivered in prayer; he had nursed what seemed a frail, shrunken boy; and now he watched a girl whose face had become strangely sweet, whose dark-blue eyes were ever upon him without boldness, without shyness, but with a steady, grave, and growing light. Many times Venters found the clear gaze embarrassing to him, yet, like wine, it had an exhilarating effect. What did she think when she looked at him so? Almost he believed she had no thought at all. All about her and the present there in Surprise Valley, and the dim yet subtly impending future, fascinated Venters and made him thoughtful as all his lonely vigils in the sage had not.

Chiefly it was the present that he wished to dwell upon; but it was the call of the future which stirred him to action. No idea had he of what that future had in store for Bess and him. He began to think of improving Surprise Valley as a place to live in, for there was no telling how long they would be compelled to stay there. Venters stubbornly resisted the entering into his mind of an insistent thought that, clearly realized, might have made it plain to him that he did not want to leave Surprise Valley at all. But it was imperative that he consider practical matters; and whether or not he was destined to stay long there, he felt the immediate need of a change of diet. It would be necessary for him to go farther afield for a variety of meat, and also that he soon visit Cottonwoods for a supply of food.

It occurred again to Venters that he could go to the cañon where Oldring kept his cattle, and at little risk he could pack out some beef. He wished to do this, however, without letting Bess know of it till after he had made the trip. Presently he hit upon the plan of going while she was asleep.

That very night he stole out of camp, climbed up under the stone bridge, and entered the outlet to the Pass. The gorge was full of luminous gloom. Balancing Rock loomed dark and leaned over the pale descent. Transformed in the shadowy light, it took shape and dimensions of a spectral god waiting—waiting for the moment to hurl himself down upon the tottering walls and close forever the outlet to Deception Pass. At night more than by day Venters felt something fearful and fateful in that rock, and that it had leaned and waited through a thousand years to have somehow to deal with his destiny.

"Old man, if you must roll, wait till I get back to the girl, and then roll!" he said, aloud, as if the stones were indeed a god.

And those spoken words, in their grim note to his ear, as well as contents to his mind, told Venters that he was all but drifting on a current which he had not power nor wish to stem.

Venters exercised his usual care in the matter of hiding tracks from the outlet, yet it took him scarcely an hour to reach Oldring's cattle. Here sight of many calves changed his original intention, and instead of packing out meat he decided to take a calf out alive. He roped one, securely tied its feet, and swung it over his shoulder. Here was an exceedingly heavy burden, but Venters was powerful—he could take up a sack of grain and with ease pitch it over a pack-saddle—and he made long distance without resting. The hardest work came in the climb up to the outlet and on through to the valley. When he had accomplished it, he became fired with another idea that again changed his intention. He would not kill the calf, but keep it alive. He would go back to Oldring's herd and pack out more calves. Thereupon he secured the calf in the best available spot for the moment and turned to make a second trip.

When Venters got back to the valley with another calf, it was close upon daybreak. He crawled into his cave and slept late.

Bess had no inkling that he had been absent from camp nearly all night, and only remarked solicitously that he appeared to be more tired than usual, and more in the need of sleep. In the afternoon Venters built a gate across a small ravine near camp, and here corralled the calves; and he succeeded in completing his task without Bess being any the wiser.

That night he made two more trips to Oldring's range, and again on the following night, and yet another on the next. With eight calves in his corral, he concluded that he had enough; but it dawned upon him then that he did not want to kill one. "I've rustled Oldring's cattle," he said, and laughed. He noted then that all the calves were red. "Red!" he exclaimed. "From the red herd. I've stolen Jane Withersteen's cattle! . . . That's about the strangest thing yet."

One more trip he undertook to Oldring's valley, and this time he roped a yearling steer and killed it and cut out a small quarter of beef. The howling of coyotes told him he need have no apprehension that the work of his knife would be discovered. He packed the beef back to camp and hung it upon a spruce-tree. Then he sought his bed.

On the morrow he was up bright and early, glad that he had a surprise for Bess. He could hardly wait for her to come out. Presently she appeared and walked under the spruce. Then she approached the camp-fire. There was a tinge of healthy red in the bronze of her cheeks, and her slender form had begun to round out in graceful lines.

"Bess, didn't you say you were tired of rabbit?" inquired Venters. "And quail and beaver?"

"Indeed I did."

"What would you like?"

"I'm tired of meat, but if we have to live on it I'd like some beef."

"Well, how does that strike you?" Venters pointed to the quarter hanging from the spruce-tree. "We'll have fresh beef for a few days, then we'll cut the rest into strips and dry it."

"Where did you get that?" asked Bess, slowly.

"I stole that from Oldring."

"You went back to the cañon—you risked—" While she hesitated the tinge of bloom faded out of her cheeks.

"It wasn't any risk, but it was hard work."

"I'm sorry I said I was tired of rabbit. Why! How—When did you get that beef?"

"Last night."

"While I was asleep?"

"Yes."

"I woke last night sometime—but I didn't know."

Her eyes were widening, darkening with thought, and whenever they did so the steady, watchful, seeing gaze gave place to the wistful light. In the former she saw as the primitive woman without thought; in the latter she looked inward, and her gaze was the reflection of a troubled mind. For long Venters had not seen that dark change, that deepening of blue, which he thought was beautiful and sad. But now he wanted to make her think.

"I've done more than pack in that beef," he said. "For five nights I've been working while you slept. I've got eight calves corralled near a ravine. Eight calves, all alive and doing fine!"

"You went five nights!"

All that Venters could make of the dilation of her eyes, her slow pallor, and her exclamation, was fear—fear for herself or for him.

"Yes. I didn't tell you, because I knew you were afraid to be left alone."

"Alone?" She echoed his word, but the meaning of it was nothing to her. She had not even thought of being left alone. It was not, then, fear for herself, but for him. This girl, always slow of speech and action, now seemed almost stupid. She put forth a hand that might have indicated the groping of her mind. Suddenly she stepped swiftly to him, with a look and touch that drove from him any doubt of her quick intelligence or feeling.

"Oldring has men watch the herds—they would kill you. You must never go again!"

When she had spoken, the strength and the blaze of her died, and she swayed toward Venters.

"*Bess, I'll not go again,*" he said, catching her.

She leaned against him, and her body was limp and vibrated to a long, wavering tremble. Her face was upturned to his. Woman's face, woman's eyes, woman's lips—all acutely and blindly and sweetly and terribly truthful in their betrayal! But as her fear was instinctive, so was her clinging to this one and only friend.

Venters gently put her from him and steadied her upon her feet; and all the while his blood raced wild, and a thrilling tingle unsteadied his nerve, and something—that he had seen and felt in her—that he could not understand—seemed very close to him, warm and rich as a fragrant breath, sweet as nothing had ever before been sweet to him.

With all his will Venters strove for calmness and thought and judgment unbiased by pity, and reality unswayed by sentiment. Bess's eyes were still fixed upon him with all her soul bright in that wistful light. Swiftly, resolutely he put out of mind all of her life except what had been spent with him. He scorned himself for the intelligence that made him still doubt. He meant to judge her as she had judged him. He was face to face with the inevitableness of life itself. He saw destiny in the dark, straight path of her wonderful eyes. Here was the simplicity, the sweetness of a girl contending with new and strange and enthralling emotions; here the living truth of innocence; here the blind terror of a woman confronted with the thought of death to her savior and protector. All this Venters saw, but, besides, there was in Bess's eyes a slow-dawning consciousness that seemed about to break out in glorious radiance.

"Bess, are you thinking?" he asked.

"Yes—oh yes!"

"Do you realize we are here alone—man and woman?"

"Yes."

"Have you thought that we may make our way out to civilization, or we may have to stay here—alone—hidden from the world all our lives?"

"I never thought—till now."

"Well, what's your choice—to go—or to stay here—alone with me?"

"Stay!" New-born thought of self, ringing vibrantly in her voice, gave her answer singular power.

Venters trembled, and then swiftly turned his gaze from her face—from her eyes. He knew what she had only half divined—that she loved him.

CHAPTER XI

AT Jane Withersteen's home the promise made to Mrs. Larkin to care for little Fay had begun to be fulfilled. Like a gleam of sunlight through the cottonwoods was the coming of the child to the gloomy house of Withersteen. The big, silent halls echoed with childish laughter. In the shady court, where Jane spent many of the hot July days, Fay's tiny feet pattered over the stone flags and splashed in the amber stream. She prattled incessantly. What difference, Jane thought, a child made in her home! It had never been a real home, she discovered. Even the tidiness and neatness she had so observed, and upon which she had insisted to her women, became, in the light of Fay's smile, habits that now lost their importance. Fay littered the court with Jane's books and papers, and other toys her fancy improvised, and many a strange craft went floating down the little brook.

And it was owing to Fay's presence that Jane Withersteen came to see more of Lassiter. The rider had for the most part kept to the sage. He rode for her, but he did not seek her except on business; and Jane had to acknowledge in pique that her overtures had been made in vain. Fay, however, captured Lassiter the moment he first laid eyes on her.

Jane was present at the meeting, and there was something about it which dimmed her sight and softened her toward this foe of her people. The rider had clanked into the court, a tired yet wary man, always looking for the attack upon him that was inevitable and might come from any quarter; and he had walked right upon little Fay. The child had been beautiful even in her rags and amid the surroundings of the hovel in the sage, but now, in a pretty white dress, with her shining curls brushed and her face clean and rosy, she was lovely. She left her play and looked up at Lassiter.

If there was not an instinct for all three of them in that meeting, an unreasoning tendency toward a closer intimacy, then Jane Withersteen believed she had been subject to a queer fancy. She imagined any child would have feared Lassiter. And Fay Larkin had been a lonely, a solitary elf of the sage, not at all an ordinary child, and exquisitely shy with strangers. She watched Lassiter with great, round, grave eyes, but showed no fear. The rider gave Jane a favorable report of cattle and horses; and as he took the seat to which she invited him, little Fay edged as much as half an inch nearer. Jane replied to his look of inquiry and told Fay's story. The rider's gray, earnest gaze troubled her. Then he turned to Fay and smiled in a way that made Jane doubt her sense of the true relation of things. How could Lassiter smile so at a child when he had made so many children fatherless? But he did smile, and to the gentleness she had seen a few times he added something that was infinitely sad and sweet. Jane's intuition told her that Lassiter had never been a father; but if life ever so blessed him he would be a good one. Fay, also, must have found that smile singularly winning. For she edged closer and closer, and then, by way of feminine capitulation, went to Jane, from whose side she bent a beautiful glance upon the rider.

Lassiter only smiled at her.

Jane watched them, and realized that now was the moment she should seize, if she was ever to win this man from his hatred. But the step was not easy to take. The more she saw of Lassiter the more she respected him, and the greater her respect the harder it became to lend herself to mere coquetry. Yet as she thought of her great motive, of Tull, and of that other whose name she had schooled herself never to think of in connection with Milly Erne's avenger, she suddenly found she had no choice. And her creed gave her boldness far beyond the limit to which vanity would have led her.

"Lassiter, I see so little of you now," she said, and was conscious of heat in her cheeks.

"I've been ridin' hard," he replied.

"But you can't live in the saddle. You come in sometimes. Won't you come here to see me—oftener?"

"Is that an order?"

"Nonsense! I simply ask you to come to see me when you find time."

"Why?"

The query once heard was not so embarrassing to Jane as she might have imagined. Moreover, it established in her mind a fact that there existed actually other than selfish reasons for her wanting to see him. And as she had been bold, so she determined to be both honest and brave.

"I've reasons—only one of which I need mention," she answered. "If it's possible I want to change you toward my people. And on the moment I can conceive of little I wouldn't do to gain that end."

How much better and freer Jane felt after that confession! She meant to show him that there was one Mormon who could play a game or wage a fight in the open.

"I reckon," said Lassiter, and he laughed.

It was the best in her, if the most irritating, that Lassiter always aroused.

"Will you come?" She looked into his eyes, and for the life of her could not quite subdue an imperiousness that rose with her spirit. "I never asked so much of any man—except Bern Venters."

"'Pears to me that you'd run no risk, or Venters, either. But mebbe that doesn't hold good for me."

"You mean it wouldn't be safe for you to be often here? You look for ambush in the cottonwoods?"

"Not that so much."

At this juncture little Fay sidled over to Lassiter.

"Has oo a little dirl?" she inquired.

"No, lassie," replied the rider.

Whatever Fay seemed to be searching for in Lassiter's sun-reddened face and quiet eyes she evidently found. "Oo tan tum to see me," she added, and with that, shyness gave place to friendly curiosity. First his sombrero with its leather band and silver ornaments commanded her attention; next his quirt, and then the clinking, silver spurs. These held her for some time, but presently, true to childish fickleness, she left off playing with them to look for something else. She laughed in glee as she ran her little hands down the slippery, shiny surface of Lassiter's leather chaps. Soon she discovered one of the hanging gun-sheaths, and she dragged it up and began tugging at the huge black handle of the gun. Jane Withersteen repressed an exclamation. What significance there was to her in the little girl's efforts to dislodge that heavy weapon! Jane Withersteen saw Fay's play and her beauty and her love as most powerful allies to her own woman's part in a game that suddenly had acquired a strange zest and a hint of danger. And as for the rider, he appeared to have forgotten Jane in the wonder of this lovely child playing about him. At first he was much the shyer of the two. Gradually her confidence overcame his backwardness, and he had the temerity to stroke her golden curls with a great hand. Fay rewarded his boldness with a smile, and when he had gone to the extreme of closing that great hand over her little brown one, she said, simply, "I like oo!"

Sight of his face then made Jane oblivious for the time to his character as a hater of Mormons. Out of the mother longing that swelled her breast she divined the child hunger in Lassiter.

He returned the next day, and the next; and upon the following he came both at morning and at night. Upon the evening of this fourth day Jane seemed to feel the breaking of a brooding struggle in Lassiter. During all these visits he had scarcely a word to say, though he watched her and played absent-mindedly with Fay. Jane had contented herself with silence. Soon little Fay substituted for the expression of regard, "I like oo," a warmer and more generous one, "I love oo."

Thereafter Lassiter came oftener to see Jane and her little protégée. Daily he grew more gentle and kind, and gradually developed a quaintly merry mood. In the morning he lifted Fay upon his horse and let her ride as he walked beside her to the edge of the sage. In the evening he played with the child at an infinite variety of games she invented, and then, oftener than not, he accepted Jane's invitation to supper. No other visitor came to Withersteen House during those days. So that in spite of watchfulness he never forgot, Lassiter began to show he felt at home there. After the meal they walked into the grove of cottonwoods or up by the lakes, and little Fay held Lassiter's hand as much as she held Jane's. Thus a strange relationship was established, and Jane liked it. At twilight they always returned to the house, where Fay kissed them and went in to her mother. Lassiter and Jane were left alone.

Then, if there were anything that a good woman could do to win a man and still preserve her self-respect, it was something which escaped the natural subtlety of a woman determined to allure. Jane's vanity, that after all was not great, was soon satisfied with Lassiter's silent admiration. And her honest desire to lead him from his dark, blood-stained path would never have blinded her to what she owed herself. But the driving passion of her religion, and its call to save Mormons' lives, one life in particular, bore Jane Withersteen close to an infringement of her womanhood. In the beginning she had reasoned that her appeal to Lassiter must be through the senses. With whatever means she possessed in the way of adornment she enhanced her beauty. And she stooped to artifices that she knew were unworthy of her, but which she deliberately chose to employ. She made of herself a girl in every variable mood wherein a girl might be desirable. In those moods she was not above the methods of an inexperienced though natural flirt. She kept close to him whenever opportunity afforded; and she was forever playfully, yet passionately underneath the surface, fighting him for possession of the great black guns. These he would never yield to her. And so in that manner their hands were often and long in contact. The more of simplicity that she sensed in him the greater the advantage she took.

She had a trick of changing—and it was not altogether voluntary—from this gay, thoughtless, girlish coquettishness to the silence and the brooding, burning mystery of a woman's mood. The strength and passion and fire of her were in her eyes, and she so used them that Lassiter had to see this depth in her, this haunting promise more fitted to her years than to the flaunting guise of a wilful girl.

The July days flew by. Jane reasoned that if it were possible for her to be happy during such a time, then she was happy. Little Fay completely filled a long aching void in her heart. In fettering the hands of this Lassiter she was accomplishing the greatest good of her life, and to do good even in a small way rendered happiness to Jane Withersteen. She had attended the regular Sunday services of her church; otherwise she had not gone to the village for weeks. It was unusual that none of her churchmen or friends had called upon her of late; but it was neglect for which she was glad. Judkins and his boy riders had experienced no difficulty in driving the white herd. So these warm July days were free of worry, and soon Jane hoped she had passed the crisis; and for her to hope was presently to trust, and then to believe. She thought often of Venters, but in a dreamy, abstract way. She spent hours teaching and playing with little Fay. And the activity of her mind centered around Lassiter. The direction she had given her will seemed to blunt any branching off of thought from that straight line. The mood came to obsess her.

In the end, when her awakening came, she learned that she had builded better than she knew. Lassiter, though kinder and gentler than ever, had parted with his quaint humor and his coldness and his tranquillity to become a restless and unhappy man. Whatever the power of his deadly intent toward Mormons, that passion now had a rival, the one equally burning and consuming. Jane Withersteen had one moment of exultation before the dawn of a strange uneasiness. What if she had made of herself a lure, at tremendous cost to him and to her, and all in vain!

That night in the moonlit grove she summoned all her courage and, turning suddenly in the path, she faced Lassiter and leaned close to him, so that she touched him and her eyes looked up to his.

"Lassiter! . . . Will you do anything for me?"

In the moonlight she saw his dark, worn face change, and by that change she seemed to feel him immovable as a wall of stone.

Jane slipped her hands down to the swinging gunsheaths, and when she had locked her fingers around the huge, cold handles of the guns, she trembled as with a chilling ripple over all her body.

"May I take your guns?"

"Why?" he asked, and for the first time to her his voice carried a harsh note. Jane felt his hard, strong hands close round her wrists. It was not wholly with intent that she leaned toward him, for the look of his eyes and the feel of his hands made her weak.

"It's no trifle—no woman's whim—it's deep—as my heart. Let me take them?"

"Why?"

"I want to keep you from killing more men—Mormons. You

must let me save you from more wickedness—more wanton bloodshed—" Then the truth forced itself falteringly from her lips. "You must—let—me—help me to keep my vow to Milly Erne. I swore to her—as she lay dying—that if ever any one came here to avenge her—I swore I would stay his hand. Perhaps I—I alone can save the—the man who—who—Oh, Lassiter! . . . I feel that I can't change you—then soon you'll be out to kill—and you'll kill by instinct—and among the Mormons you kill will be the one—who . . . Lassiter, if you care a little for me—let me—for my sake—let me take your guns!"

As if her hands had been those of a child, he unclasped their clinging grip from the handles of his guns, and, pushing her away, he turned his gray face to her in one look of terrible realization and then strode off into the shadows of the cottonwoods.

When the first shock of her futile appeal to Lassiter had passed, Jane took his cold, silent condemnation and abrupt departure not so much as a refusal to her entreaty as a hurt and stunned bitterness for her attempt at his betrayal. Upon further thought and slow consideration of Lassiter's past actions, she believed he would return and forgive her. The man could not be hard to a woman, and she doubted that he could stay away from her. But at the point where she had hoped to find him vulnerable she now began to fear he was proof against all persuasion. The iron and stone quality that she had early suspected in him had actually cropped out as an impregnable barrier. Nevertheless, if Lassiter remained in Cottonwoods she would never give up her hope and desire to change him. She would change him if she had to sacrifice everything dear to her except hope of heaven. Passionately devoted as she was to her religion, she had yet refused to marry a Mormon. But a situation had developed wherein self paled in the great white light of religious duty of the highest order. That was the leading motive, the divinely spiritual one; but there were other motives, which, like tentacles, aided in drawing her will to the acceptance of a possible abnegation. And through the watches of that sleepless night Jane Withersteen, in fear and sorrow and doubt, came finally to believe that if she must throw herself into Lassiter's arms to make him abide by "Thou shalt not kill!" she would yet do well.

In the morning she expected Lassiter at the usual hour, but she was not able to go at once to the court, so she sent little Fay. Mrs. Larkin was ill and required attention. It appeared that the mother, from the time of her arrival at Withersteen House, had relaxed and was slowly losing her hold on life. Jane had believed that absence of worry and responsibility coupled with good nursing and comfort would mend Mrs. Larkin's broken health. Such, however, was not the case.

When Jane did get out to the court, Fay was there alone, and at the moment embarking on a dubious voyage down the stone-lined amber stream upon a craft of two brooms and a pillow. Fay was as delightfully wet as she could possibly wish to get.

Clatter of hoofs distracted Fay and interrupted the scolding she was gleefully receiving from Jane. The sound was not the light-spirited trot that Bells made when Lassiter rode him into the outer court. This was slower and heavier, and Jane did not recognize in it any of her other horses. The appearance of Bishop Dyer startled Jane. He dismounted with his rapid, jerky motion, flung the bridle, and, as he turned toward the inner court and stalked up on the stone flags, his boots rang. In his authoritative front, and in the red anger unmistakably flaming in his face, he reminded Jane of her father.

"Is that the Larkin pauper?" he asked, bruskly, without any greeting to Jane.

"It's Mrs. Larkin's little girl," replied Jane, slowly.

"I hear you intend to raise the child?"

"Yes."

"Of course you mean to give her Mormon bringing-up?"

"No!"

His questions had been swift. She was amazed at a feeling that some one else was replying for her.

"I've come to say a few things to you." He stopped to measure her with stern, speculative eye.

Jane Withersteen loved this man. From earliest childhood she had been taught to revere and love bishops of her church. And for ten years Bishop Dyer had been the closest friend and counselor of her father, and for the greater part of that period her own friend and Scriptural teacher. Her interpretation of her creed and her religious activity in fidelity to it, her acceptance of mysterious and holy Mormon truths, were all invested in this Bishop. Bishop Dyer as an entity was next to God. He was God's mouthpiece to the little Mormon community at Cottonwoods. God revealed himself in secret to this mortal.

And Jane Withersteen suddenly suffered a paralyzing affront to her consciousness of reverence by some strange, irresistible twist of thought wherein she saw this Bishop as a man. And the train of thought hurdled the rising, crying protests of that other self whose poise she had lost. It was not her Bishop who eyed her in curious measurement. It was a man who tramped into her presence without removing his hat, who had no greeting for her, who had no semblance of courtesy. In looks, as in action, he made her think of a bull stamping cross-grained into a corral. She had heard of Bishop Dyer forgetting the minister in the fury of a common man, and now she was to feel it. The glance by which she measured him in turn momentarily veiled the divine in the ordinary. He looked a rancher; he was booted, spurred, and covered with dust; he carried a gun at his hip, and she remembered that he had been known to use it. But during the long moment while he watched her there was nothing commonplace in the slow-gathering might of his wrath.

"Brother Tull has talked to me," he began. "It was your father's wish that you marry Tull, and my order. You refused him?"

"Yes."

"You would not give up your friendship with that tramp Venters?"

"No."

"But you'll do as I order!" he thundered. "Why, Jane Withersteen, you are in danger of becoming a heretic! You can thank your Gentile friends for that. You face the damning of your soul to perdition."

In the flux and reflux of the whirling torture of Jane's mind, that new, daring spirit of hers vanished in the old habitual order of her life. She was a Mormon, and the Bishop regained ascendance.

"It's well I got you in time, Jane Withersteen. What would your father have said to these goings-on of yours? He would have put you in a stone cage on bread and water. He would have taught you something about Mormonism. Remember, you're a *born*

Mormon. There have been Mormons who turned heretic—damn their souls!—but no born Mormon ever left us yet. Ah, I see your shame. Your faith is not shaken. You are only a wild girl." The Bishop's tone softened. "Well, it's enough that I got to you in time. . . . Now tell me about this Lassiter. I hear strange things."

"What do you wish to know?" queried Jane.

"About this man. You hired him?"

"Yes, he's riding for me. When my riders left me I had to have any one I could get."

"Is it true what I hear—that he's a gun-man, a Mormon-hater, steeped in blood?"

"True—terribly true, I fear."

"But what's he doing here in Cottonwoods? This place isn't notorious enough for such a man. Sterling and the villages north, where there's universal gun-packing and fights every day—where there are more men like him, it seems to me they would attract him most. We're only a wild, lonely border settlement. It's only recently that the rustlers have made killings here. Nor have there been saloons till lately, nor the drifting in of outcasts. Has not this gun-man some special mission here?"

Jane maintained silence.

"Tell me," ordered Bishop Dyer, sharply.

"Yes," she replied.

"Do you know what it is?"

"Yes."

"Tell me that."

"Bishop Dyer, I don't want to tell."

He waved his hand in an imperative gesture of command. The red once more leaped to his face, and in his steel-blue eyes glinted a pin-point of curiosity.

"That first day," whispered Jane, "Lassiter said he came here to find—Milly Erne's grave!"

With downcast eyes Jane watched the swift flow of the amber water. She saw it and tried to think of it, of the stones, of the ferns; but, like her body, her mind was in a leaden vise. Only the Bishop's voice could release her. Seemingly there was silence of longer duration than all her former life.

"For what—else?" When Bishop Dyer's voice did cleave the

silence it was high, curiously shrill, and on the point of breaking. It released Jane's tongue, but she could not lift her eyes.

"To kill the man who persuaded Milly Erne to abandon her home and her husband—and her God!"

With wonderful distinctness Jane Withersteen heard her own clear voice. She heard the water murmur at her feet and flow on to the sea; she heard the rushing of all the waters in the world. They filled her ears with low, unreal murmurings—these sounds that deadened her brain and yet could not break the long and terrible silence. Then, from somewhere—from an immeasurable distance—came a slow, guarded, clinking, clanking step. Into her it shot electrifying life. It released the weight upon her numbed eyelids. Lifting her eyes she saw—ashen, shaken, stricken—not the Bishop but the man! And beyond him, from round the corner came that soft, silvery step. A long black boot with a gleaming spur swept into sight—and then Lassiter! Bishop Dyer did not see, did not hear: he stared at Jane in the throes of sudden revelation.

"Ah, I understand!" he cried, in hoarse accents. "That's why you made love to this Lassiter—to bind his hands!"

It was Jane's gaze riveted upon the rider that made Bishop Dyer turn. Then clear sight failed her. Dizzily, in a blur, she saw the Bishop's hand jerk to his hip. She saw gleam of blue and spout of red. In her ears burst a thundering report. The court floated in darkening circles around her, and she fell into utter blackness.

The darkness lightened, turned to slow-drifting haze, and lifted. Through a thin film of blue smoke she saw the rough-hewn timbers of the court roof. A cool, damp touch moved across her brow. She smelled powder, and it was that which galvanized her suspended thought. She moved, to see that she lay prone upon the stone flags with her head on Lassiter's knee, and he was bathing her brow with water from the stream. The same swift glance, shifting low, brought into range of her sight a smoking gun and splashes of blood.

"Ah-h!" she moaned, and was drifting, sinking again into darkness, when Lassiter's voice arrested her.

"It's all right, Jane. It's all right."

"Did—you—kill—him?" she whispered.

"Who? That fat party who was here? No. I didn't kill him."

"Oh! . . . Lassiter!"

"Say! It was queer for you to faint. I thought you were such a strong woman, not faintish like that. You're all right now—only some pale. I thought you'd never come to. But I'm awkward round women folks. I couldn't think of anythin'."

"Lassiter! . . . the gun there! . . . the blood!"

"So that's troublin' you. I reckon it needn't. You see it was this way. I come round the house an' seen that fat party an' heard him talkin' loud. Then he seen me, an' very impolite goes straight for his gun. He oughtn't have tried to throw a gun on me—whatever his reason was. For that's meetin' me on my own grounds. I've seen runnin' molasses that was quicker 'n him. Now I didn't know who he was, visitor or friend or relation of yours, though I seen he was a Mormon all over, an' I couldn't get serious about shootin'. So I winged him—put a bullet through his arm as he was pullin' at his gun. An' he dropped the gun there, an' a little blood. I told him he'd introduced himself sufficient, an' to please move out of my vicinity. An' he went."

Lassiter spoke with slow, cool, soothing voice, in which there was a hint of levity, and his touch, as he continued to bathe her brow, was gentle and steady. His impassive face, and the kind, gray eyes, further stilled her agitation.

"He drew on you first, and you deliberately shot to cripple him—you wouldn't kill him—you—*Lassiter?*"

"That's about the size of it."

Jane kissed his hand.

All that was calm and cool about Lassiter instantly vanished.

"Don't do that! I won't stand it! An' I don't care a damn who that fat party was."

He helped Jane to her feet and to a chair. Then with the wet scarf he had used to bathe her face he wiped the blood from the stone flags and, picking up the gun, he threw it upon a couch. With that he began to pace the court, and his silver spurs jangled musically, and the great gun-sheaths softly brushed against his leather chaps.

"So—it's true—what I heard him say?" Lassiter asked, presently halting before her. "You made love to me—to bind my hands?"

"Yes," confessed Jane. It took all her woman's courage to meet the gray storm of his glance.

"All these days that you've been so friendly an' like a pardner —all these evenin's that have been so bewilderin' to me—your beauty—an'—an' the way you looked an' came close to me—they were woman's tricks to bind my hands?"

"Yes."

"An' your sweetness that seemed so natural, an' your throwin' little Fay an' me so much together—to make me love the child— all that was for the same reason?"

"Yes."

Lassiter flung his arms—a strange gesture for him.

"Mebbe it wasn't much in your Mormon thinkin', for you to play that game. But to ring the child in—that was hellish!"

Jane's passionate, unheeding zeal began to loom darkly.

"Lassiter, whatever my intention in the beginning, Fay loves you dearly—and I—I've grown to—to like you."

"That's powerful kind of you, now," he said. Sarcasm and scorn made his voice that of a stranger. "An' you sit there an' look me straight in the eyes! You're a wonderful strange woman, Jane Withersteen."

"I'm not ashamed, Lassiter. I told you I'd try to change you."

"Would you mind tellin' me just what you tried?"

"I tried to make you see beauty in me and be softened by it. I wanted you to care for me so that I could influence you. It wasn't easy. At first you were stone-blind. Then I hoped you'd love little Fay, and through that come to feel the horror of making children fatherless."

"Jane Withersteen, either you're a fool or noble beyond my understandin'. Mebbe you're both. I know you're blind. What you meant is one thing—what you *did* was to make me love you."

"Lassiter!"

"I reckon I'm a human bein', though I never loved any one but my sister, Milly Erne. That was long—"

"Oh, are you Milly's brother?"

"Yes, I was, an' I loved her. There never was any one but her in my life till now. Didn't I tell you that long ago I back-trailed myself from women? I was a Texas ranger till—till Milly left home, an' then I became somethin' else—Lassiter! For years I've been a lonely man set on one thing. I came here an' met you. An' now I'm not the man I was. The change was gradual, an' I took no notice of it. I understand now that never-satisfied longin' to see you, listen to you, watch you, feel you near me. It's plain now why you were never out of my thoughts. I've had no thoughts but of you. I've lived an' breathed for you. An' now when I know what it means—what you've done—I'm burnin' up with hell's fire!"

"Oh, Lassiter—no—no—you don't love me that way!" Jane cried.

"If that's what love is, then I do."

"Forgive me! I didn't mean to make you love me like that. Oh, what a tangle of our lives! You—Milly Erne's brother! And I— heedless, mad to melt your heart toward Mormons. Lassiter, I may be wicked but not wicked enough to hate. If I couldn't hate Tull, could I hate you?"

"After all, Jane, mebbe you're only blind—Mormon blind. That only can explain what's close to selfishness—"

"I'm not selfish. I despise the very word. If I were free—"

"But you're not free. Not free of Mormonism. An' in playin' this game with me you've been unfaithful."

"Un-faithful!" faltered Jane.

"Yes, I said unfaithful. You're faithful to your Bishop an' un-faithful to yourself. You're false to your womanhood an' true to your religion. But for a savin' innocence you'd have made your-self low an' vile—betrayin' yourself, betrayin' me—all to bind my hands an' keep me from snuffin' out Mormon life. It's your damned Mormon blindness."

"Is it vile—is it blind—is it only Mormonism to save human life? No, Lassiter, that's God's law, divine, universal for all Christians."

"The blindness I mean is blindness that keeps you from seein' the truth. I've known many good Mormons. But some are blacker than hell. You won't see that even when you know it. Else, why all this blind passion to save the life of that—that. . . ."

Jane shut out the light, and the hands she held over her eyes trembled and quivered against her face.

"Blind—yes, an' let me make it clear an' simple to you," Lassiter went on, his voice losing its tone of anger. "Take, for instance, that idea of yours last night when you wanted my guns. It was good an' beautiful, an' showed your heart—but—why, Jane, it was crazy. Mind I'm assumin' that life to me is as sweet as to any other man. An' to preserve that life is each man's first an' closest thought. Where would any man be on this border without guns? Where, especially, would Lassiter be? Well, I'd be under the sage with thousands of other men now livin' an' sure better men than me. Gun-packin' in the West since the Civil War has growed into a kind of moral law. An' out here on this border it's the difference between a man an' somethin' not a man. Look what your takin' Venters's guns from him all but made him! Why, your churchmen carry guns. Tull has killed a man an' drawed on others. Your Bishop has shot a half dozen men, an' it wasn't through prayers of his that they recovered. An' to-day he'd have shot me if he'd been quick enough on the draw. Could I walk or ride down into Cottonwoods without my guns? This is a wild time, Jane Withersteen, this year of our Lord eighteen seventy-one."

"No time—for a woman!" exclaimed Jane, brokenly. "Oh, Lassiter, I feel helpless—lost—and don't know where to turn. If I *am* blind—then—I need some one—a friend—you, Lassiter—more than ever!"

"Well, I didn't say nothin' about goin' back on you, did I?"

CHAPTER XII

JANE received a letter from Bishop Dyer, not in his own hand-
writing, which stated that the abrupt termination of their interview had left him in some doubt as to her future conduct. A slight
injury had incapacitated him from seeking another meeting at
present, the letter went on to say, and ended with a request
which was virtually a command, that she call upon him at once.

The reading of the letter acquainted Jane Withersteen with
the fact that something within her had all but changed. She
sent no reply to Bishop Dyer nor did she go to see him. On
Sunday she remained absent from the service—for the second
time in years—and though she did not actually suffer there was
a dead-lock of feelings deep within her, and the waiting for a
balance to fall on either side was almost as bad as suffering. She
had a gloomy expectancy of untoward circumstances, and with
it a keen-edged curiosity to watch developments. She had a half-
formed conviction that her future conduct—as related to her
churchmen—was beyond her control and would be governed by
their attitude toward her. Something was changing in her, forming, waiting for decision to make it a real and fixed thing. She
had told Lassiter that she felt helpless and lost in the fateful
tangle of their lives; and now she feared that she was approaching
the same chaotic condition of mind in regard to her religion. It
appalled her to find that she questioned phases of that religion.
Absolute faith had been her serenity. Though leaving her faith
unshaken, her serenity had been disturbed, and now it was
broken by open war between her and her ministers. That something within her—a whisper—which she had tried in vain to hush

had become a ringing voice, and it called to her to wait. She had transgressed no laws of God. Her churchmen, however invested with the power and the glory of a wonderful creed, however they sat in inexorable judgment of her, must now practice toward her the simple, common, Christian virtue they professed to preach, "Do unto others as you would have others do unto you!"

Jane Withersteen, waiting in darkness of mind, remained faithful still. But it was darkness that must soon be pierced by light. If her faith were justified, if her churchmen were trying only to intimidate her, the fact would soon be manifest, as would their failure, and then she would redouble her zeal toward them and toward what had been the best work of her life—work for the welfare and happiness of those among whom she lived, Mormon and Gentile alike. If that secret, intangible power closed its toils round her again, if that great invisible hand moved here and there and everywhere, slowly paralyzing her with its mystery and its inconceivable sway over her affairs, then she would know beyond doubt that it was not chance, nor jealousy, nor intimidation, nor ministerial wrath at her revolt, but a cold and calculating policy thought out long before she was born, a dark, immutable will of whose empire she and all that was hers was but an atom.

Then might come her ruin. Then might come her fall into black storm. Yet she would rise again, and to the light. God would be merciful to a driven woman who had lost her way.

A week passed. Little Fay played and prattled and pulled at Lassiter's big black guns. The rider came to Withersteen House oftener than ever. Jane saw a change in him, though it did not relate to his kindness and gentleness. He was quieter and more thoughtful. While playing with Fay or conversing with Jane he seemed to be possessed of another self that watched with cool, roving eyes, that listened, listened always as if the murmuring amber stream brought messages, and the moving leaves whispered something. Lassiter never rode Bells into the court any more, nor did he come by the lane or the paths. When he appeared it was suddenly and noiselessly out of the dark shadow of the grove.

"I left Bells out in the sage," he said, one day at the end of that week. "I must carry water to him."

134

"Why not let him drink at the trough or here?" asked Jane, quickly.

"I reckon it'll be safer for me to slip through the grove. I've been watched when I rode in from the sage."

"Watched? By whom?"

"By a man who thought he was well hid. But my eyes are pretty sharp. An', Jane," he went on, almost in a whisper, "I reckon it'd be a good idea for us to talk low. You're spied on here by your women."

"Lassiter!" she whispered in turn. "That's hard to believe. My women love me."

"What of that?" he asked. "Of course they love you. But they're Mormon women."

Jane's old, rebellious loyalty clashed with her doubt.

"I won't believe it," she replied, stubbornly.

"Well then, just act natural an' talk natural, an' pretty soon—give them time to hear us—pretend to go over there to the table, an' then quick-like make a move for the door an' open it."

"I will," said Jane, with heightened color. Lassiter was right; he never made mistakes; he would not have told her unless he positively knew. Yet Jane was so tenacious of faith that she had to see with her own eyes, and so constituted that to employ even such small deceit toward her women made her ashamed, and angry for her shame as well as theirs. Then a singular thought confronted her that made her hold up this simple ruse—which hurt her, though it was well justified—against the deceit she had wittingly and eagerly used toward Lassiter. The difference was staggering in its suggestion of that blindness of which he had accused her. Fairness and justice and mercy, that she had imagined were anchor-cables to hold fast her soul to righteousness, had not been hers in the strange, biased duty that had so exalted and confounded her.

Presently Jane began to act her little part, to laugh and play with Fay, to talk of horses and cattle to Lassiter. Then she made deliberate mention of a book in which she kept records of all pertaining to her stock, and she walked slowly toward the table, and when near the door she suddenly whirled and thrust it open. Her sharp action nearly knocked down a woman who had undoubtedly been listening.

"Hester," said Jane, sternly, "you may go home, and you need not come back."

Jane shut the door and returned to Lassiter. Standing unsteadily, she put her hand on his arm. She let him see that doubt had gone, and how this stab of disloyalty pained her.

"Spies! My own women! . . . Oh, miserable!" she cried, with flashing, tearful eyes.

"I hate to tell you," he replied. By that she knew he had long spared her. "It's begun again—that work in the dark."

"Nay, Lassiter—it never stopped!"

So bitter certainty claimed her at last, and trust fled Withersteen House and fled forever. The women who owed much to Jane Withersteen changed not in love for her, nor in devotion to their household work, but they poisoned both by a thousand acts of stealth and cunning and duplicity. Jane broke out once and caught them in strange, stone-faced, unhesitating falsehood. Thereafter she broke out no more. She forgave them because they were driven. Poor, fettered, and sealed Hagars, how she pitied them! What terrible thing bound them and locked their lips, when they showed neither consciousness of guilt toward their benefactress nor distress at the slow wearing apart of long-established and dear ties?

"The blindness again!" cried Jane Withersteen. "In my sisters as in me! . . . O God!"

There came a time when no words passed between Jane and her women. Silently they went about their household duties, and secretly they went about the underhand work to which they had been bidden. The gloom of the house and the gloom of its mistress, which darkened even the bright spirit of little Fay, did not pervade these women. Happiness was not among them, but they were aloof from gloom. They spied and listened; they received and sent secret messengers; and they stole Jane's books and records, and finally the papers that were deeds of her possessions. Through it all they were silent, rapt in a kind of trance. Then one by one, without leave or explanation or farewell, they left Withersteen House, and never returned.

Coincident with this disappearance Jane's gardeners and workers in the alfalfa fields and stable men quit her, not even asking for their wages. Of all her Mormon employees about the great ranch only Jerd remained. He went on with his duty, but talked no more of the change than if it had never occurred.

"Jerd," said Jane, "what stock you can't take care of turn out in the sage. Let your first thought be for Black Star and Night. Keep them in perfect condition. Run them every day and watch them always."

Though Jane Withersteen gave them such liberality, she loved her possessions. She loved the rich, green stretches of alfalfa, and the farms, and the grove, and the old stone house, and the beautiful, ever-faithful amber spring, and every one of a myriad of horses and colts and burros and fowls down to the smallest rabbit that nipped her vegetables; but she loved best her noble Arabian steeds. In common with all riders of the upland sage Jane cherished two material things—the cold, sweet, brown water that made life possible in the wilderness and the horses which were a part of that life. When Lassiter asked her what Lassiter would be without his guns he was assuming that his horse was part of himself. So Jane loved Black Star and Night because it was her nature to love all beautiful creatures—perhaps all living things; and then she loved them because she herself was of the sage and in her had been born and bred the rider's instinct to rely on his four-footed brother. And when Jane gave Jerd the order to keep her favorites trained down to the day it was a half-conscious admission that presaged a time when she would need her fleet horses.

Jane had now, however, no leisure to brood over the coils that were closing round her. Mrs. Larkin grew weaker as the August days began; she required constant care; there was little Fay to look after; and such household work as was imperative. Lassiter put Bells in the stable with the other racers, and directed his efforts to a closer attendance upon Jane. She welcomed the change. He was always at hand to help, and it was her fortune to learn that his boast of being awkward around women had its root in humility and was not true.

His great, brown hands were skilled in a multiplicity of ways which a woman might have envied. He shared Jane's work, and was of especial help to her in nursing Mrs. Larkin. The woman suffered most at night, and this often broke Jane's rest. So it came about that Lassiter would stay by Mrs. Larkin during the day, when she needed care, and Jane would make up the sleep she lost in night-watches. Mrs. Larkin at once took kindly to the gentle Lassiter, and, without ever asking who or what he was, praised him to Jane. "He's a good man and loves children," she said. How sad to hear this truth spoken of a man whom Jane thought lost beyond all redemption! Yet ever and ever Lassiter towered above her, and behind or through his black, sinister figure shone something luminous that strangely affected Jane. Good and evil began to seem incomprehensibly blended in her judgment. It was her belief that evil could not come forth from good; yet here was a murderer who dwarfed in gentleness, patience, and love any man she had ever known.

She had almost lost track of her more outside concerns when early one morning Judkins presented himself before her in the courtyard.

Thin, hard, burnt, bearded, with the dust and sage thick on him, with his leather wrist-bands shining from use, and his boots worn through on the stirrup side, he looked the rider of riders. He wore two guns and carried a Winchester.

Jane greeted him with surprise and warmth, set meat and bread and drink before him; and called Lassiter out to see him. The men exchanged glances, and the meaning of Lassiter's keen inquiry and Judkins's bold reply, both unspoken, was not lost upon Jane.

"Where's your hoss?" asked Lassiter, aloud.

"Left him down the slope," answered Judkins. "I footed it in a ways, an' slept last night in the sage. I went to the place you told me you 'most always slept, but didn't strike you."

"I moved up some, near the spring, an' now I go there nights."

"Judkins—the white herd?" queried Jane, hurriedly.

"Miss Withersteen, I make proud to say I've not lost a steer. Fer a good while after thet stampede Lassiter milled we hed no trouble. Why, even the sage dogs left us. But it's begun agin— thet flashin' of lights over ridge tips, an' queer puffin' of smoke, an' then at night strange whistles an' noises. But the herd's acted magnificent. An' my boys, say, Miss Withersteen, they're only kids, but I ask no better riders. I got the laugh in the village fer takin' them out. They're a wild lot, an' you know boys hev more nerve than grown men, because they don't know what danger is.

I'm not denyin' there's danger. But they glory in it, an' mebbe I like it myself—anyway, we'll stick. We're goin' to drive the herd on the far side of the first break of Deception Pass. There's a great round valley over there, an' no ridges or piles of rocks to aid these stampeders. The rains are due. We'll hev plenty of water fer a while. An' we can hold thet herd from anybody except Oldrin'. I come in fer supplies. I'll pack a couple of burros an' drive out after dark to-night."

"Judkins, take what you want from the store-room. Lassiter will help you. I—I can't thank you enough . . . but—wait."

Jane went to the room that had once been her father's, and from a secret chamber in the thick stone wall she took a bag of gold, and, carrying it back to the court, she gave it to the rider.

"There, Judkins, and understand that I regard it as little for your loyalty. Give what is fair to your boys, and keep the rest. Hide it. Perhaps that would be wisest."

"Oh . . . Miss Withersteen!" ejaculated the rider. "I couldn't earn so much in—in ten years. It's not right—I oughtn't take it."

"Judkins, you know I'm a rich woman. I tell you I've few faithful friends. I've fallen upon evil days. God only knows what will become of me and mine! So take the gold."

She smiled in understanding of his speechless gratitude, and left him with Lassiter. Presently she heard him speaking low at first, then in louder accents emphasized by the thumping of his rifle on the stones. "As infernal a job as even you, Lassiter, ever heerd of."

"Why, son," was Lassiter's reply, "this breakin' of Miss Withersteen may seem bad to you, but it ain't bad—yet. Some of these wall-eyed fellers who look jest as if they was walkin' in the shadow of Christ himself, right down the sunny road, now they can think of things an' do things that are really hell-bent."

Jane covered her ears and ran to her own room, and there like a caged lioness she paced to and fro till the coming of little Fay reversed her dark thoughts.

The following day, a warm and muggy one threatening rain, while Jane was resting in the court, a horseman clattered through the grove and up to the hitching-rack. He leaped off and approached Jane with the manner of a man determined to execute a difficult mission, yet fearful of its reception. In the gaunt, wiry figure and the lean, brown face Jane recognized one of her Mormon riders, Blake. It was he of whom Judkins had long since spoken. Of all the riders ever in her employ Blake owed her the most, and as he stepped before her, removing his hat and making manly efforts to subdue his emotion, he showed that he remembered.

"Miss Withersteen, mother's dead," he said.

"Oh—Blake!" exclaimed Jane, and she could say no more.

"She died free from pain in the end, and she's buried—resting at last, thank God! . . . I've come to ride for you again, if you'll have me. Don't think I mentioned mother to get your sympathy. When she was living and your riders quit, I had to also. I was afraid of what might be done—said to her. . . . Miss Withersteen, we can't talk of—of what's going on now—"

"Blake, do you know?"

"I know a great deal. You understand, my lips are shut. But without explanation or excuse I offer my services. I'm a Mormon —I hope a good one. But—there are some things! . . . It's no use, Miss Withersteen, I can't say any more—what I'd like to. But will you take me back?"

"Blake! . . . You know what it means?"

"I don't care. I'm sick of—of—I'll show you a Mormon who'll be true to you!"

"But, Blake—how terribly you might suffer for that!"

"Maybe. Aren't you suffering now?"

"God knows indeed I am!"

"Miss Withersteen, it's a liberty on my part to speak so, but I know you pretty well—know you'll never give in. I wouldn't if I were you. And I—I must— Something makes me tell you the worst is yet to come. That's all. I absolutely can't say more. Will you take me back—let me ride for you—show everybody what I mean?"

"Blake, it makes me happy to hear you. How my riders hurt me when they quit!" Jane felt the hot tears well to her eyes and splash down upon her hands. "I thought so much of them—tried so hard to be good to them. And not one was true. You've made it easy to forgive. Perhaps many of them really feel as you do, but dare not return to me. Still, Blake, I hesitate to take you back. Yet I want you so much."

"Do it, then. If you're going to make your life a lesson to Mormon women, let me make mine a lesson to the men. Right is right. I believe in you, and here's my life to prove it."

"You hint it may mean your life!" said Jane, breathless and low.

"We won't speak of that. I want to come back. I want to do what every rider aches in his secret heart to do for you. . . . Miss Withersteen, I hoped it'd not be necessary to tell you that my mother on her deathbed told me to have courage. She knew how the thing galled me—she told me to come back. . . . Will you take me?"

"God bless you, Blake! Yes, I'll take you back. And will you —will you accept gold from me?"

"Miss Withersteen!"

"I just gave Judkins a bag of gold. I'll give you one. If you will not take it you must not come back. You might ride for me a few months—weeks—days till the storm breaks. Then you'd have nothing, and be in disgrace with your people. We'll forearm you against poverty, and me against endless regret. I'll give you gold which you can hide—till some future time."

"Well, if it pleases you," replied Blake. "But you know I never thought of pay. Now, Miss Withersteen, one thing more. I want to see this man Lassiter. Is he here?"

"Yes, but, Blake—what— Need you see him? Why?" asked Jane, instantly worried. "I can speak to him—tell him about you."

"That won't do. I want to—I've got to tell him myself. Where is he?"

"Lassiter is with Mrs. Larkin. She is ill. I'll call him," answered Jane, and going to the door she softly called for the rider. A faint, musical jingle preceded his step—then his tall form crossed the threshold.

"Lassiter, here's Blake, an old rider of mine. He has come back to me and he wishes to speak to you."

Blake's brown face turned exceedingly pale.

"Yes, I had to speak to you," he said, swiftly. "My name's Blake. I'm a Mormon and a rider. Lately I quit Miss Withersteen. I've come to beg her to take me back. Now I don't know you, but I know—what you are. So I've this to say to your face. It would never occur to this woman to imagine—let alone suspect

141

me to be a spy. She couldn't think it might just be a low plot to come here and shoot you in the back. Jane Withersteen hasn't that kind of a mind. . . . Well, I've not come for that. I want to help her—to pull a bridle along with Judkins and—and you. The thing is—do you believe me?"

"I reckon I do," replied Lassiter. How this slow, cool speech contrasted with Blake's hot, impulsive words! "You might have saved some of your breath. See here, Blake, cinch this in your mind. Lassiter has met some square Mormons! An' mebbe—"

"Blake," interrupted Jane, nervously anxious to terminate a colloquy that she perceived was an ordeal for him. "Go at once and fetch me a report of my horses."

"Miss Withersteen! . . . You mean the big drove—down in the sage-cleared fields?"

"Of course," replied Jane. "My horses are all there, except the blooded stock I keep here."

"Haven't you heard—then?"

"Heard? No! What's happened to them?"

"They're gone, Miss Withersteen, gone these ten days past. Dorn told me, and I rode down to see for myself."

"Lassiter—did you know?" asked Jane, whirling to him.

"I reckon so. . . . But what was the use to tell you?"

It was Lassiter turning away his face and Blake studying the stone flags at his feet that brought Jane to the understanding of what she betrayed. She strove desperately, but she could not rise immediately from such a blow.

"My horses! My horses! What's become of them?"

"Dorn said the riders report another drive by Oldring. . . . And I trailed the horses miles down the slope toward Deception Pass."

"My red herd's gone! My horses gone! The white herd will go next. I can stand that. But if I lost Black Star and Night, it would be like parting with my own flesh and blood. Lassiter—Blake—am I in danger of losing my racers?"

"A rustler—or—or anybody stealin' hosses of yours would most of all want the blacks," said Lassiter. His evasive reply was affirmative enough. The other rider nodded gloomy acquiescence.

"Oh! Oh!" Jane Withersteen choked, with violent utterance.

"Let me take charge of the blacks?" asked Blake. "One more

rider won't be any great help to Judkins. But I might hold Black Star and Night, if you put such store on their value."

"Value! Blake, I love my racers. Besides, there's another reason why I mustn't lose them. You go to the stables. Go with Jerd every day when he runs the horses, and don't let them out of your sight. If you would please me—win my gratitude, guard my black racers."

When Blake had mounted and ridden out of the court Lassiter regarded Jane with the smile that was becoming rarer as the days sped by.

"'Pears to me, as Blake says, you do put some store on them hosses. Now I ain't gainsayin' that the Arabians are the handsomest hosses I ever seen. But Bells can beat Night, an' run neck an' neck with Black Star."

"Lassiter, don't tease me now. I'm miserable—sick. Bells is fast, but he can't stay with the blacks, and you know it. Only Wrangle can do that."

"I'll bet that big raw-boned brute can more'n show his heels to your black racers. Jane, out there in the sage, on a long chase, Wrangle could kill your favorites."

"No, no," replied Jane, impatiently. "Lassiter, why do you say that so often? I know you've teased me at times, and I believe it's only kindness. You're always trying to keep my mind off worry. But you mean more by this repeated mention of my racers?"

"I reckon so." Lassiter paused, and for the thousandth time in her presence moved his black sombrero round and round, as if counting the silver pieces on the band. "Well, Jane, I've sort of read a little that's passin' in your mind."

"You think I might fly from my home—from Cottonwoods— from the Utah border?"

"I reckon. An' if you ever do an' get away with the blacks I wouldn't like to see Wrangle left here on the sage. Wrangle could catch you. I know Venters had him. But you can never tell. Mebbe he hasn't got him now. . . . Besides—things are happenin', an' somethin' of the same queer nature might have happened to Venters."

"God knows you're right! . . . Poor Bern, how long he's gone! In my trouble I've been forgetting him. But, Lassiter, I've little fear for him. I've heard my riders say he's as keen as a wolf. . . ,

143

As to your reading my thoughts—well, your suggestion makes an actual thought of what was only one of my dreams. I believe I dreamed of flying from this wild borderland, Lassiter. I've strange dreams. I'm not always practical and thinking of my many duties, as you said once. For instance—if I dared—if I dared I'd ask you to saddle the blacks and ride away with me—and hide me."

"Jane!"

The rider's sunburnt face turned white. A few times Jane had seen Lassiter's cool calm broken—when he had met little Fay, when he had learned how and why he had come to love both child and mistress, when he had stood beside Milly Erne's grave. But one and all they could not be considered in the light of his present agitation. Not only did Lassiter turn white—not only did he grow tense, not only did he lose his coolness, but also he suddenly, violently, hungrily took her into his arms and crushed her to his breast.

"Lassiter!" cried Jane, trembling. It was an action for which she took sole blame. Instantly, as if dazed, weakened, he released her. "Forgive me!" went on Jane. "I'm always forgetting your—your feelings. I thought of you as my faithful friend. I'm always making you out more than human . . . only, let me say—I meant that—about riding away. I'm wretched, sick of this—this— Oh, something bitter and black grows on my heart!"

"Jane, the hell—of it," he replied, with deep intake of breath, "is you *can't* ride away. Mebbe realizin' it accounts for my grabbin' you—that way, as much as the crazy boy's rapture your words gave me. I don't understand myself. . . . But the hell of this game is—you *can't* ride away."

"Lassiter! . . . What on earth do you mean? I'm an absolutely free woman."

"You ain't absolutely anythin' of the kind. . . . I reckon I've got to tell you!"

"Tell me all. It's uncertainty that makes me a coward. It's faith and hope—blind love, if you will, that makes me miserable. Every day I awake believing—still believing. The day grows, and with it doubts, fears, and that black bat hate that bites hotter and hotter into my heart. Then comes night—I pray—I pray for all, and for myself—I sleep—and I awake free once more, trustful, faithful, to believe—to hope! Then, O my God! I grow and live a thousand years till night again! . . . But if you want to see me a woman, tell me why I can't ride away—tell me what more I'm to lose—tell me the worst."

"Jane, you're watched. There's no single move of yours, except when you're hid in your house, that ain't seen by sharp eyes. The cottonwood grove's full of creepin', crawlin' men. Like Indians in the grass. When you rode, which wasn't often lately, the sage was full of sneakin' men. At night they crawl under your windows, into the court, an' I reckon into the house. Jane Withersteen, you know, never locked a door! This here grove's a hummin' bee-hive of mysterious happenin's. Jane, it ain't so much that these spies keep out of my way as me keepin' out of theirs. They're goin' to try to kill me. That's plain. But mebbe I'm as hard to shoot in the back as in the face. So far I've seen fit to watch only. This all means, Jane, that you're a marked woman. You can't get away—not now. Mebbe later, when you're broken, you might. But that's sure doubtful. Jane, you're to lose the cattle that's left—your home an' ranch—an' Amber Spring. You can't even hide a sack of gold! For it couldn't be slipped out of the house, day or night, an' hid or buried, let alone be rid off with. You may lose all. I'm tellin' you, Jane, hopin' to prepare you, if the worst does come. I told you once before about that strange power I've got to feel things."

"Lassiter, what can I do?"

"Nothin', I reckon, except know what's comin' an' wait an' be game. If you'd let me make a call on Tull, an' a long-deferred call on—"

"Hush! . . . Hush!" she whispered.

"Well, even that wouldn't help you any in the end."

"What does it mean? Oh, what does it mean? I am my father's daughter—a Mormon, yet I can't see! I've not failed in religion—in duty. For years I've given with a free and full heart. When my father died I was rich. If I'm still rich it's because I couldn't find enough ways to become poor. What am I, what are my possessions to set in motion such intensity of secret oppression?"

"Jane, the mind behind it all is an empire builder."

"But, Lassiter, I would give freely—all I own to avert this—this wretched thing. If I gave—that would leave me with faith still. Surely my—my churchmen think of my soul? If I lose my trust in them—"

"Child, be still!" said Lassiter, with a dark dignity that had in it something of pity. "You are a woman, fine an' big an' strong, an' your heart matches your size. But in mind you're a child. I'll say a little more—then I'm done. I'll never mention this again. Among many thousands of women you're one who has bucked against your churchmen. They tried you out, an' failed of persuasion, an' finally of threats. You meet now the cold steel of a will as far from Christlike as the universe is wide. You're to be broken. Your body's to be held, given to some man, made, if possible, to bring children into the world. But your soul? . . . What do they care for your soul?"

CHAPTER XIII

IN his hidden valley Venters awakened from sleep, and his ears rang with innumerable melodies from full-throated mocking-birds, and his eyes opened wide upon the glorious golden shaft of sunlight shining through the great stone bridge. The circle of cliffs surrounding Surprise Valley lay shrouded in morning mist, a dim blue low down along the terraces, a creamy, moving cloud along the ramparts. The oak forest in the center was a plumed and tufted oval of gold.

He saw Bess under the spruces. Upon her complete recovery of strength she always rose with the dawn. At the moment she was feeding the quail she had tamed. And she had begun to tame the mocking-birds. They fluttered among the branches overhead, and some left off their songs to flit down and shyly hop near the twittering quail. Little gray and white rabbits crouched in the grass, now nibbling, now laying long ears flat and watching the dogs.

Venters's swift glance took in the brightening valley, and Bess and her pets, and Ring and Whitie. It swept over all to return again and rest upon the girl. She had changed. To the dark trousers and blouse she had added moccasins of her own make, but she no longer resembled a boy. No eye could have failed to mark the rounded contours of a woman. The change had been to grace and beauty. A glint of warm gold gleamed from her hair, and a tint of red shone in the clear dark brown of cheeks. The haunting sweetness of her lips and eyes, that earlier had been illusive, a promise, had become a living fact. She fitted harmoniously into that wonderful setting; she was like Surprise Valley—wild and beautiful.

147

Venters leaped out of his cave to begin the day.

He had postponed his journey to Cottonwoods until after the passing of the summer rains. The rains were due soon. But until their arrival and the necessity for his trip to the village he sequestered in a far corner of mind all thought of peril, of his past life, and almost that of the present. It was enough to live. He did not want to know what lay hidden in the dim and distant future. Surprise Valley had enchanted him. In this home of the cliff-dwellers there were peace and quiet and solitude, and another thing, wondrous as the golden morning shaft of sunlight, that he dared not ponder over long enough to understand.

The solitude he had hated when alone he had now come to love. He was assimilating something from this valley of gleams and shadows. From this strange girl he was assimilating more.

The day at hand resembled many days gone before. As Venters had no tools with which to build, or to till the terraces, he remained idle. Beyond the cooking of the simple fare there were no tasks. And as there were no tasks, there was no system. He and Bess began one thing, to leave it; to begin another, to leave that; and then do nothing but lie under the spruces and watch the great cloud-sails majestically move along the ramparts, and dream and dream. The valley was a golden, sunlit world. It was silent. The sighing wind and the twittering quail and the singing birds, even the rare and seldom-occurring hollow crack of a sliding weathered stone, only thickened and deepened that insulated silence.

Venters and Bess had vagrant minds.

"Bess, did I tell you about my horse Wrangle?" inquired Venters.

"A hundred times," she replied.

"Oh, have I? I'd forgotten. I want you to see him. He'll carry us both."

"I'd like to ride him. Can he run?"

"Run? He's a demon. Swiftest horse on the sage! I hope he'll stay in that cañon.

"He'll stay."

They left camp to wander along the terraces, into the aspen ravines, under the gleaming walls. Ring and Whitie wandered in the fore, often turning, often trotting back, open-mouthed and solemn-eyed and happy. Venters lifted his gaze to the grand archway over the entrance to the valley, and Bess lifted hers to follow his, and both were silent. Sometimes the bridge held their attention for a long time. To-day a soaring eagle attracted them.

"How he sails!" exclaimed Bess. "I wonder where his mate is?"

"She's at the nest. It's on the bridge in a crack near the top. I see her often. She's almost white."

They wandered on down the terrace, into the shady, sun-flecked forest. A brown bird fluttered crying from a bush. Bess peeped into the leaves.

"Look! A nest and four little birds. They're not afraid of us. See how they open their mouths. They're hungry."

Rabbits rustled the dead brush and pattered away. The forest was full of a drowsy hum of insects. Little darts of purple, that were running quail, crossed the glades. And a plaintive, sweet peeping came from the coverts. Bess's soft step disturbed a sleeping lizard that scampered away over the leaves. She gave chase and caught it, a slim creature of nameless color but of exquisite beauty.

"Jewel eyes," she said. "It's like a rabbit—afraid. We won't eat you. There—go."

Murmuring water drew their steps down into a shallow shaded ravine where a brown brook brawled softly over mossy stones. Multitudes of strange, gray frogs with white spots and black eyes lined the rocky bank and leaped only at close approach. Then Venters's eye descried a very thin, very long green snake coiled round a sapling. They drew closer and closer till they could have touched it. The snake had no fear and watched them with scintillating eyes.

"It's pretty," said Bess. "How tame! I thought snakes always ran."

"No. Even the rabbits didn't run here till the dogs chased them."

On and on they wandered to the wild jumble of massed and broken fragments of cliff at the west end of the valley. The roar of the disappearing stream dinned in their ears. Into this maze of rocks they threaded a tortuous way, climbing, descending, halting to gather wild plums and great lavender lilies, and going on at the will of fancy. Idle and keen perceptions guided them equally.

"Oh, let us climb there!" cried Bess, pointing upward to a small space of terrace left green and shady between huge abutments of broken cliff. And they climbed to the nook and rested and looked out across the valley to the curling column of blue smoke from their campfire. But the cool shade and the rich grass and the fine view were not what they had climbed for. They could not have told, although whatever had drawn them was well-satisfying. Light, sure-footed as a mountain goat, Bess pattered down at Venters's heels; and they went on, calling the dogs, eyes dreamy and wide, listening to the wind and the bees and the crickets and the birds.

Part of the time Ring and Whitie led the way, then Venters, then Bess; and the direction was not an object. They left the sun-streaked shade of the oaks, brushed the long grass of the meadows, entered the green and fragrant swaying willows, to stop, at length, under the huge old cottonwoods where the beavers were busy.

Here they rested and watched. A dam of brush and logs and mud and stones backed the stream into a little lake. The round, rough beaver houses projected from the water. Like the rabbits, the beavers had become shy. Gradually, however, as Venters and Bess knelt low, holding the dogs, the beavers emerged to swim with logs and gnaw at cottonwoods and pat mud walls with their paddle-like tails, and, glossy and shiny in the sun, to go on with their strange, persistent industry. They were the builders. The lake was a mud-hole, and the immediate environment a scarred and dead region, but it was a wonderful home of wonderful animals.

"Look at that one—he puddles in the mud," said Bess. "And there! See him dive! Hear them gnawing! I'd think they'd break their teeth. How's it they can stay out of the water and under the water?"

And she laughed.

Then Venters and Bess wandered farther, and, perhaps not all unconsciously this time, wended their slow steps to the cave of the cliff-dwellers, where she liked best to go.

The tangled thicket and the long slant of dust and little chips of weathered rock and the steep bench of stone and the worn steps all were arduous work for Bess in the climbing. But she gained the shelf, gasping, hot of cheek, glad of eye, with her hand in Venters's. Here they rested. The beautiful valley glittered below with its millions of wind-turned leaves bright-faced in the sun, and the mighty bridge towered heavenward, crowned with blue sky. Bess, however, never rested for long. Soon she was exploring, and Venters followed; she dragged forth from corners and shelves a multitude of crudely fashioned and painted pieces of pottery, and he carried them. They peeped down into the dark holes of the kivas, and Bess gleefully dropped a stone and waited for the long-coming hollow sound to rise. They peeped into the little globular houses, like mud-wasp nests, and wondered if these had been store-places for grain, or baby cribs, or what; and they crawled into the larger houses and laughed when they bumped their heads on the low roofs, and they dug in the dust of the floors. And they brought from dust and darkness armloads of treasure which they carried to the light. Flints and stones and strange curved sticks and pottery they found; and twisted grass rope that crumbled in their hands, and bits of whitish stone which crushed to powder at a touch and seemed to vanish in the air.

"That white stuff was bone," said Venters, slowly. "Bones of a cliff-dweller."

"No!" exclaimed Bess.

"Here's another piece. Look! . . . Whew! dry, powdery smoke! That's bone."

Then it was that Venters's primitive, childlike mood, like a savage's, seeing, yet unthinking, gave way to the encroachment of civilized thought. The world had not been made for a single day's play or fancy or idle watching. The world was old. Nowhere could be gotten a better idea of its age than in this gigantic silent tomb. The gray ashes in Venters's hand had once been bone of a human being like himself. The pale gloom of the cave had shadowed people long ago. He saw that Bess had received the same shock—could not in moments such as this escape her feeling, living, thinking destiny.

"Bern, people have *lived* here," she said, with wide, thoughtful eyes.

"Yes," he replied.

"How long ago?"

"A thousand years and more."

"What were they?"

"Cliff-dwellers. Men who had enemies and made their homes high out of reach."

"They had to fight?"

"Yes."

"They fought for—what?"

"For life. For their homes, food, children, parents—for their women!"

"Has the world changed any in a thousand years?"

"I don't know—perhaps a little."

"Have men?"

"I hope so—I think so."

"Things crowd into my mind," she went on, and the wistful light in her eyes told Venters the truth of her thoughts. "I've ridden the border of Utah. I've seen people—know how they live— but they must be few of all who are living. I had my books and I studied them. But all that doesn't help me any more. I want to go out into the big world and see it. Yet I want to stay here more. What's to become of us? Are we cliff-dwellers? We're alone here. I'm happy when I don't think. These—these bones that fly into dust—they make me sick and a little afraid. Did the people who lived here once have the same feelings as we have? What was the good of their living at all? They're gone! What's the meaning of it all—of us?"

"Bess, you ask more than I can tell. It's beyond me. Only there was laughter here once—and now there's silence. There was life—and now there's death. Men cut these little steps, made these arrow-heads and mealing-stones, plaited the ropes we found, and left their bones to crumble in our fingers. As far as time is concerned it might all have been yesterday. We're here to-day. Maybe we're higher in the scale of human beings—in intelligence. But who knows? We can't be any higher in the things for which life is lived at all."

"What are they?"

"Why—I suppose relationship, friendship—love."

"Love!"

"Yes. Love of man for woman—love of woman for man. That's the nature, the meaning, the best of life itself."

She said no more. Wistfulness of glance deepened into sadness.

"Come, let us go," said Venters.

Action brightened her. Beside him, holding his hand, she slipped down the shelf, ran down the long, steep slant of sliding stones, out of the cloud of dust, and likewise out of the pale gloom.

"We beat the slide," she cried.

The miniature avalanche cracked and roared, and rattled itself into an inert mass at the base of the incline. Yellow dust like the gloom of the cave, but not so changeless, drifted away on the wind; the roar clapped in echo from the cliff, returned, went back, and came again to die in the hollowness. Down on the sunny terrace there was a different atmosphere. Ring and Whitie leaped around Bess. Once more she was smiling, gay, and thoughtless, with the dream-mood in the shadow of her eyes.

"Bess, I haven't seen that since last summer. Look!" said Venters, pointing to the scalloped edge of rolling purple clouds that peeped over the western wall. "We're in for a storm."

"Oh, I hope not. I'm afraid of storms."

"Are you? Why?"

"Have you ever been down in one of these walled-up pockets in a bad storm?"

"No, now I think of it, I haven't."

"Well, it's terrible. Every summer I get scared to death and hide somewhere in the dark. Storms up on the sage are bad, but nothing to what they are down here in the cañons. And in this little valley—why, echoes can rap back and forth so quick they'll split our ears."

"We're perfectly safe here, Bess."

"I know. But that hasn't anything to do with it. The truth is I'm afraid of lightning and thunder, and thunder-claps hurt my head. If we have a bad storm, will you stay close to me?"

"Yes."

When they got back to camp the afternoon was closing, and it was exceedingly sultry. Not a breath of air stirred the aspen leaves, and when these did not quiver the air was indeed still. The dark-purple clouds moved almost imperceptibly out of the west.

"What have we for supper?" asked Bess.

"Rabbit."

"Bern, can't you think of another new way to cook rabbit?" went on Bess, with earnestness.

"What do you think I am—a magician?" retorted Venters.

"I wouldn't dare tell you. But, Bern, do you want me to turn into a rabbit?"

There was a dark-blue, merry flashing of eyes and a parting of lips; then she laughed. In that moment she was naïve and wholesome.

"Rabbit seems to agree with you," replied Venters. "You are well and strong—and growing very pretty."

Anything in the nature of compliment he had never before said to her, and just now he responded to a sudden curiosity to see its effect. Bess stared as if she had not heard aright, slowly blushed, and completely lost her poise in happy confusion.

"I'd better go right away," he continued, "and fetch supplies from Cottonwoods."

A startlingly swift change in the nature of her agitation made him reproach himself for his abruptness.

"No, no, don't go!" she said. "I didn't mean—that about the rabbit. I—I was only trying to be—funny. Don't leave me all alone!"

"Bess, I must go sometime."

"Wait then. Wait till after the storms."

The purple cloud-bank darkened the lower edge of the setting sun, crept up and up, obscuring its fiery red heart, and finally passed over the last ruddy crescent of its upper rim.

The intense dead silence awakened to a long, low, rumbling roll of thunder.

"Oh!" cried Bess, nervously.

"We've had big black clouds before this without rain," said Venters. "But there's no doubt about that thunder. The storms are coming. I'm glad. Every rider on the sage will hear that thunder with glad ears."

Venters and Bess finished their simple meal and the few tasks around the camp, then faced the open terrace, the valley, and the west, to watch and await the approaching storm.

It required keen vision to see any movement whatever in the purple clouds. By infinitesimal degrees the dark cloud-line merged upward into the golden-red haze of the afterglow of sunset. A shadow lengthened from under the western wall across the valley. As straight and rigid as steel rose the delicate spear-pointed silver spruces; the aspen leaves, by nature pendant and quivering, hung limp and heavy; no slender blade of grass moved. A gentle splashing of water came from the ravine. Then again from out of the west sounded the low, dull, and rumbling roll of thunder.

A wave, a ripple of light, a trembling and turning of the aspen leaves, like the approach of a breeze on the water, crossed the valley from the west; and the lull and the deadly stillness and the sultry air passed away on a cool wind.

The night bird of the cañon, with clear and melancholy notes, announced the twilight. And from all along the cliffs rose the faint murmur and moan and mourn of the wind singing in the caves. The bank of clouds now swept hugely out of the western sky. Its front was purple and black, with gray between, a bulging, mushrooming, vast thing instinct with storm. It had a dark, angry, threatening aspect. As if all the power of the winds were pushing and piling behind, it rolled ponderously across the sky. A red flare burned out instantaneously, flashed from the west to east, and died. Then from the deepest black of the purple cloud burst a boom. It was like the bowling of a huge boulder along the crags and ramparts, and seemed to roll on and fall into the valley to bound and bang and boom from cliff to cliff.

"Oh!" cried Bess, with her hands over her ears. "What did I tell you?"

"Why, Bess, be reasonable!" said Venters.

"I'm a coward."

"Not quite that, I hope. It's strange you're afraid. I love a storm."

"I tell you a storm down in these cañons is an awful thing. I know Oldring hated storms. His men were afraid of them. There was one who went deaf in a bad storm, and never could hear again."

"Maybe I've lots to learn, Bess. I'll lose my guess if this storm isn't bad enough. We're going to have heavy wind first, then lightning and thunder, then the rain. Let's stay out as long as we can."

The tips of the cottonwoods and the oaks waved to the east, and the rings of aspens along the terraces twinkled their myriad of bright faces in fleet and glancing gleam. A low roar rose from the leaves of the forest, and the spruces swished in the rising wind. It came in gusts, with light breezes between. As it increased in strength the lulls shortened in length till there was a strong and steady blow all the time, and violent puffs at intervals, and sudden whirling currents. The clouds spread over the valley, rolling swiftly and low, and twilight faded into a sweeping darkness. Then the singing of the wind in the caves drowned the swift roar of rustling leaves; then the song swelled to a mourning, moaning wail; then with the gathering power of the wind the wail changed to a shriek. Steadily the wind strengthened and constantly the strange sound changed.

The last bit of blue sky yielded to the onsweep of clouds. Like angry surf the pale gleams of gray, amid the purple of that scudding front, swept beyond the eastern rampart of the valley. The purple deepened to black. Broad sheets of lightning flared over the western wall. There were not yet any ropes or zigzag streaks darting down through the gathering darkness. The storm center was still beyond Surprise Valley.

"Listen! . . . Listen!" cried Bess, with her lips close to Venters's ear. "You'll hear Oldring's knell!"

"What's that?"

"Oldring's knell. When the wind blows a gale in the caves it makes what the rustlers call Oldring's knell. They believe it bodes his death. I think he believes so, too. It's not like any sound on earth. . . . It's beginning. Listen!"

The gale swooped down with a hollow unearthly howl. It yelled and pealed and shrilled and shrieked. It was made up of a thousand piercing cries. It was a rising and a moving sound. Beginning at the western break of the valley, it rushed along each gigantic cliff, whistling into the caves and cracks, to mount in power, to bellow a blast through the great stone bridge. Gone, as into an engulfing roar of surging waters, it seemed to shoot back and begin all over again.

It was only wind, thought Venters. Here sped and shrieked the sculptor that carved out the wonderful caves in the cliffs. It was only a gale, but as Venters listened, as his ears became accustomed to the fury and strife, out of it all or through it or above it pealed low and perfectly clear and persistently uniform a strange sound that had no counterpart in all the sounds of the elements. It was not of earth or of life. It was the grief and agony of the gale. A knell of all upon which it blew!

Black night enfolded the valley. Venters could not see his companion, and knew of her presence only through the tightening hold of her hand on his arm. He felt the dogs huddle closer to him. Suddenly the dense, black vault overhead split asunder to a blue-white, dazzling streak of lightning. The whole valley lay vividly clear and luminously bright in his sight. Upreared, vast and magnificent, the stone bridge glimmered like some grand god of storm in the lightning's fire. Then all flashed black again—blacker than pitch—a thick, impenetrable coal-blackness. And there came a ripping, crashing report. Instantly an echo resounded with clapping crash. The initial report was nothing to the echo. It was a terrible, living, reverberating, detonating crash. The wall threw the sound across, and could have made no greater roar if it had slipped in avalanche. From cliff to cliff the echo went in crashing retort and banged in lessening power, and boomed in thinner volume, and clapped weaker and weaker till a final clap could not reach across the waiting cliff.

In the pitchy darkness Venters led Bess, and, groping his way, by feel of hand found the entrance to her cave and lifted her up. On the instant a blinding flash of lightning illumined the cave and all about him. He saw Bess's face white now, with dark, frightened eyes. He saw the dogs leap up, and he followed suit. The golden glare vanished; all was black; then came the splitting crack and the infernal din of echoes.

Bess shrank closer to him and closer, found his hands, and pressed them tightly over her ears, and dropped her face upon his shoulder, and hid her eyes.

Then the storm burst with a succession of ropes and streaks and shafts of lightning, playing continuously, filling the valley with a broken radiance; and the cracking shots followed each other swiftly till the echoes blended in one fearful, deafening crash.

Venters looked out upon the beautiful valley—beautiful now as never before—mystic in its transparent, luminous gloom, weird in the quivering, golden haze of lightning. The dark spruces were tipped with glimmering lights; the aspens bent low in the winds, as waves in a tempest at sea; the forest of oaks tossed wildly and shone with gleams of fire. Across the valley the huge cavern of the cliff-dwellers yawned in the glare, every little black window as clear as at noonday; but the night and the storm added to their tragedy. Flung arching to the black clouds, the great stone bridge seemed to bear the brunt of the storm. It caught the full fury of the rushing wind. It lifted its noble crown to meet the lightnings. Venters thought of the eagles and their lofty nest in a niche under the arch. A driving pall of rain, black as the clouds, came sweeping on to obscure the bridge and the gleaming walls and the shining valley. The lightning played incessantly, streaking down through opaque darkness of rain. The roar of the wind, with its strange knell and the recrashing echoes, mingled with the roar of the flooding rain, and all seemingly were deadened and drowned in a world of sound.

In the dimming pale light Venters looked down upon the girl. She had sunk into his arms, upon his breast, burying her face. She clung to him. He felt the softness of her, and the warmth, and the quick heave of her breast. He saw the dark, slender, graceful outline of her form. A woman lay in his arms! And he held her closer. He who had been alone in the sad, silent watches of the night was not now and never must be again alone. He who had yearned for the touch of a hand felt the long tremble and the heart-beat of a woman. By what strange chance had she come to love him! By what change—by what marvel had she grown into a treasure!

No more did he listen to the rush and roar of the thunder-storm. For with the touch of clinging hands and the throbbing bosom he grew conscious of an inward storm—the tingling of new chords of thought, strange music of unheard, joyous bells, sad dreams dawning to wakeful delight, dissolving doubt, resurging hope, force, fire, and freedom, unutterable sweetness of desire. A storm in his breast—a storm of real love.

CHAPTER XIV

WEST WIND

WHEN the storm abated Venters sought his own cave, and late in the night, as his blood cooled and the stir and throb and thrill subsided, he fell asleep.

With the breaking of dawn his eyes unclosed. The valley lay drenched and bathed, a burnished oval of glittering green. The rain-washed walls glistened in the morning light. Waterfalls of many forms poured over the rims. One, a broad, lacy sheet, thin as smoke, slid over the western notch and struck a ledge in its downward fall, to bound into broader leap, to burst far below into white and gold and rosy mist.

Venters prepared for the day, knowing himself a different man.

"It's a glorious morning," said Bess, in greeting.

"Yes. After the storm the west wind," he replied.

"Last night was I—very much of a baby?" she asked, watching him.

"Pretty much."

"Oh, I couldn't help it!"

"I'm glad you were afraid."

"Why?" she asked, in slow surprise.

"I'll tell you some day," he answered, soberly. Then around the camp-fire and through the morning meal he was silent; afterward he strolled thoughtfully off alone along the terrace. He climbed a great yellow rock raising its crest among the spruces, and there he sat down to face the valley and the west.

"I love her!"

Aloud he spoke—unburdened his heart—confessed his secret. For an instant the golden valley swam before his eyes, and the walls waved, and all about him whirled with tumult within.

"I love her! . . . I understand now."

Reviving memory of Jane Withersteen and thought of the complications of the present amazed him with proof of how far he had drifted from his old life. He discovered that he hated to take up the broken threads, to delve into dark problems and difficulties. In this beautiful valley he had been living a beautiful dream. Tranquillity had come to him, and the joy of solitude, and interest in all the wild creatures and crannies of this incomparable valley—and love. Under the shadow of the great stone bridge God had revealed Himself to Venters.

"The world seems very far away," he muttered, "but it's there—and I'm not yet done with it. Perhaps I never shall be. . . . Only—how glorious it would be to live here always and never think again!"

Whereupon the resurging reality of the present, as if in irony of his wish, steeped him instantly in contending thought. Out of it all he presently evolved these things: he must go to Cottonwoods; he must bring supplies back to Surprise Valley; he must cultivate the soil and raise corn and stock, and, most imperative of all, he must decide the future of the girl who loved him and whom he loved. The first of these things required tremendous effort, the last one, concerning Bess, seemed simply and naturally easy of accomplishment. He would marry her. Suddenly, as from roots of poisonous fire, flamed up the forgotten truth concerning her. It seemed to wither and shrivel up all his joy on its hot, tearing way to his heart. She had been Oldring's Masked Rider. To Venters's question, "What were you to Oldring?" she had answered with scarlet shame and drooping head.

"What do I care who she is or what she was!" he cried, passionately. And he knew it was not his old self speaking. It was this softer, gentler man who had awakened to new thoughts in the quiet valley. Tenderness, masterful in him now, matched the absence of joy and blunted the knife-edge of entering jealousy. Strong and passionate effort of will, surprising to him, held back the poison from piercing his soul.

"Wait! . . . Wait!" he cried, as if calling. His hand pressed his breast, and he might have called to the pang there. "Wait! It's all so strange—so wonderful. Anything can happen. Who am I to judge her? I'll glory in my love for her. But I can't tell it—can't give up to it."

Certainly he could not then decide her future. Marrying her was impossible in Surprise Valley and in any village south of Sterling. Even without the mask she had once worn she would easily have been recognized as Oldring's Rider. No man who had ever seen her would forget her, regardless of his ignorance as to her sex. Then more poignant than all other argument was the fact that he did not want to take her away from Surprise Valley. He resisted all thought of that. He had brought her to the most beautiful and wildest place of the uplands; he had saved her, nursed her back to strength, watched her bloom as one of the valley lilies; he knew her life there to be pure and sweet—she belonged to him, and he loved her. Still these were not all the reasons why he did not want to take her away. Where could they go? He feared the rustlers—he feared the riders—he feared the Mormons. And if he should ever succeed in getting Bess safely away from these immediate perils, he feared the sharp eyes of women and their tongues, the big outside world with its problems of existence. He must wait to decide her future, which, after all, was deciding his own. But between her future and his something hung impending. Like Balancing Rock, which waited darkly over the steep gorge, ready to close forever the outlet to Deception Pass, that nameless thing, as certain yet intangible as fate, must fall and close forever all doubts and fears of the future.

"I've dreamed," muttered Venters, as he rose. "Well, why not? . . . To dream is happiness! But let me just once see this clearly, wholly; then I can go on dreaming till the thing falls. I've got to tell Jane Withersteen. I've dangerous trips to take. I've work here to make comfort for this girl. She's mine. I'll fight to keep her safe from that old life. I've already seen her forget it. I love her. And if a beast ever rises in me I'll burn my hand off before I lay it on her with shameful intent. And, by God! sooner or later I'll kill the man who hid her and kept her in Deception Pass!"

As he spoke the west wind softly blew in his face. It seemed to soothe his passion. That west wind was fresh, cool, fragrant, and it carried a sweet, strange burden of far-off things—tidings of life in other climes, of sunshine asleep on other walls—of other places where reigned peace. It carried, too, sad truth of human hearts and mystery—of promise and hope unquenchable. Surprise Valley was only a little niche in the wide world whence blew that burdened wind. Bess was only one of millions at the mercy of unknown motive in nature and life. Content had come to Venters in the valley; happiness had breathed in the slow, warm air; love as bright as light had hovered over the walls and descended to him; and now on the west wind came a whisper of the eternal triumph of faith over doubt.

"How much better I am for what has come to me!" he exclaimed. "I'll let the future take care of itself. Whatever falls, I'll be ready."

Venters retraced his steps along the terrace back to camp, and found Bess in the old familiar seat, waiting and watching for his return.

"I went off by myself to think a little," he explained.

"You never looked that way before. What—what is it? Won't you tell me?"

"Well, Bess, the fact is I've been dreaming a lot. This valley makes a fellow dream. So I forced myself to think. We can't live this way much longer. Soon I'll simply have to go to Cottonwoods. We need a whole pack train of supplies. I can get—"

"Can you go safely?" she interrupted.

"Why, I'm sure of it. I'll ride through the Pass at night. I haven't any fear that Wrangle isn't where I left him. And once on him—Bess, just wait till you see that horse!"

"Oh, I want to see him—to ride him. But—but, Bern, this is what troubles me," she said. "Will—will you come back?"

"Give me four days. If I'm not back in four days you'll know I'm dead. For that only shall keep me."

"Oh!"

"Bess, I'll come back. There's danger—I wouldn't lie to you—but I can take care of myself."

"Bern, I'm sure—oh, I'm sure of it! All my life I've watched hunted men. I can tell what's in them. And I believe you can ride and shoot and see with any rider of the sage. It's not—not that I—fear."

"Well, what is it, then?"

"Why—why—why should you come back at all?"

"I couldn't leave you here alone."

"You might change your mind when you get to the village—among old friends—"

"I won't change my mind. As for old friends—" He uttered a short, expressive laugh.

"Then—there—there must be a—a woman!" Dark red mantled the clear tan of temple and cheek and neck. Her eyes were eyes of shame, upheld a long moment by intense, straining search for the verification of her fear. Suddenly they drooped, her head fell to her knees, her hands flew to her hot cheeks.

"Bess—look here," said Venters, with a sharpness due to the violence with which he checked his quick, surging emotion.

As if compelled against her will—answering to an irresistible voice—Bess raised her head, looked at him with sad, dark eyes, and tried to whisper with tremulous lips.

"There's no woman," went on Venters, deliberately holding her glance with his. "Nothing on earth, barring the chances of life, can keep me away."

Her face flashed and flushed with the glow of a leaping joy; but like the vanishing of a gleam it disappeared to leave her as he had never beheld her.

"I am nothing—I am lost—I am nameless!"

"Do you *want* me to come back?" he asked, with sudden stern coldness. "Maybe *you* want to go back to Oldring!"

That brought her erect, trembling and ashy pale, with dark, proud eyes and mute lips refuting his insinuation.

"Bess, I beg your pardon. I shouldn't have said that. But you angered me. I intend to work—to make a home for you here—to be a—a brother to you as long as ever you need me. And you must forget what you are—were—I mean, and be happy. When you remember that old life you are bitter, and it hurts me."

"I was happy—I shall be very happy. Oh, you're so good that —that it kills me! If I think, I can't believe it. I grow sick with wondering *why*. I'm only a *let me say it*—only a lost, nameless —girl of the rustlers. *Oldring's Girl*, they called me. That you should save me—be so good and kind—want to make me happy —why, it's beyond belief. No wonder I'm wretched at the thought of your leaving me. But I'll be wretched and bitter no more. I promise you. If only I could repay you even a little—"

"You've repaid me a hundredfold. Will you believe me?"

"Believe you! I couldn't do else."

"Then listen! . . . Saving you, I saved myself. Living here in this valley with you, I've found myself. I've learned to think while I was dreaming. I never troubled myself about God. But God, or some wonderful spirit, has whispered to me here. I absolutely deny the truth of what you say about yourself. I can't explain it. There are things too deep to tell. Whatever the terrible wrongs you've suffered, God holds you blameless. I see that —feel that in you every moment you are near me. I've a mother and a sister 'way back in Illinois. If I could I'd take you to them—to-morrow."

"*If it were true!* Oh, I might—I might lift my head!" she cried.

"Lift it then—you child. For I swear it's true."

She did lift her head with the singular wild grace always a part of her actions, with that old unconscious intimation of innocence which always tortured Venters, but now with something more—a spirit rising from the depths that linked itself to his brave words.

"I've been thinking—too," she cried, with quivering smile and swelling breast. "I've discovered myself—too. I'm young—I'm alive—I'm so full—oh! I'm a woman!"

"Bess, I believe I can claim credit of that last discovery—before you," Venters said, and laughed.

"Oh, there's more—there's something I must tell you."

"Tell it, then."

"When will you go to Cottonwoods?"

"As soon as the storms are past, or the worst of them."

"I'll tell you before you go. I can't now. I don't know how I shall then. But it must be told. I'd never let you leave me without knowing. For in spite of what you say there's a chance you mightn't come back."

Day after day the west wind blew across the valley. Day after day the clouds clustered gray and purple and black. The cliffs sang and the caves rang with Oldring's knell, and the lightning flashed, the thunder rolled, the echoes crashed and crashed, and the rains flooded the valley. Wild flowers sprang up everywhere, swaying with the lengthening grass on the terraces, smiling wanly from shady nooks, peeping wondrously from year-dry crevices of the walls. The valley bloomed into a paradise. Every single moment, from the breaking of the gold bar through the bridge at dawn on to the reddening of rays over the western wall, was one of colorful change. The valley swam in thick, transparent haze, golden at dawn, warm and white at noon, purple in the twilight. At the end of every storm a rainbow curved down into the leaf-bright forest to shine and fade and leave lingeringly some faint essence of its rosy iris in the air.

Venters walked with Bess, once more in a dream, and watched the lights change on the walls, and faced the wind from out of the west.

Always it brought softly to him strange, sweet tidings of far-off things. It blew from a place that was old and whispered of youth. It blew down the grooves of time. It brought a story of the passing hours. It breathed low of fighting men and praying women. It sang clearly the song of love. That ever was the burden of its tidings—youth in the shady woods, waders through the wet meadows, boy and girl at the hedgerow stile, bathers in the booming surf, sweet, idle hours on grassy, windy hills, long strolls down moonlit lanes—everywhere in far-off lands, fingers locked and bursting hearts and longing lips—from all the world tidings of unquenchable love.

Often, in these hours of dreams he watched the girl, and asked himself of what was she dreaming? For the changing light of the valley reflected its gleam and its color and its meaning in the changing light of her eyes. He saw in them infinitely more than he saw in his dreams. He saw thought and soul and nature—strong vision of life. All tidings the west wind blew from distance and age he found deep in those dark-blue depths, and found them mysteries solved. Under their wistful shadow he softened, and in the softening felt himself grow a sadder, a wiser, and a better man.

While the west wind blew its tidings, filling his heart full, teaching him a man's part, the days passed, the purple clouds changed to white, and the storms were over for that summer.

"I must go now," he said.

"When?" she asked.

"At once—to-night."

"I'm glad the time has come. It dragged at me. Go—for you'll come back the sooner."

Late in the afternoon, as the ruddy sun split its last flame in the ragged notch of the western wall, Bess walked with Venters along the eastern terrace, up the long, weathered slope, under the great stone bridge. They entered the narrow gorge to climb around the fence long before built there by Venters. Farther than this she had never been. Twilight had already fallen in the gorge. It brightened to waning shadow in the wider ascent. He showed her Balancing Rock, of which he had often told her, and explained its sinister leaning over the outlet. Shuddering, she looked down the long, pale incline with its closed-in, toppling walls.

"What an awful trail! Did you carry me up here?"

"I did, surely," replied he.

"It frightens me, somehow. Yet I never was afraid of trails. I'd ride anywhere a horse could go, and climb where he couldn't. But there's something fearful here. I feel as—as if the place was watching me."

"Look at this rock. It's balanced here—balanced perfectly. You know I told you the cliff-dwellers cut the rock, and why. But they're gone and the rock waits. Can't you see—feel how it waits here? I moved it once, and I'll never dare again. A strong heave would start it. Then it would fall and bang, and smash that crag, and jar the walls, and close forever the outlet to Deception Pass!"

"Ah! When you come back I'll steal up here and push and push with all my might to roll the rock and close forever the outlet to the Pass!" She said it lightly, but in the undercurrent of her voice was a heavier note, a ring deeper than any ever given mere play of words.

"Bess! . . . You can't dare me! Wait till I come back with supplies—then roll the stone."

"I—was—in—fun." Her voice now throbbed low. "Always you must be free to go when you will. Go now . . . this place presses on me—stifles me."

"I'm going—but you had something to tell me?"

"Yes. . . . Will you—come back?"

"I'll come if I live."

"But—but you mightn't come?"

"That's possible, of course. It'll take a good deal to kill me. A man couldn't have a faster horse or keener dog. And, Bess, I've guns, and I'll use them if I'm pushed. But don't worry."

"I've faith in you. I'll not worry until after four days. Only—because you mightn't come—I *must* tell you—"

She lost her voice. Her pale face, her great, glowing, earnest eyes, seemed to stand alone out of the gloom of the gorge. The dog whined, breaking the silence.

"I *must* tell you—because you mightn't come back," she whispered. "You *must* know what—what I think of your goodness—of you. Always I've been tongue-tied. I seemed not to be grateful. It was deep in my heart. Even now—if I were other than I am —I couldn't tell you. But I'm nothing—only a rustler's girl—nameless—infamous. You've saved me—and I'm—I'm yours to do with as you like. . . . With all my heart and soul—I love you!"

CHAPTER XV

IN the cloudy, threatening, waning summer days shadows lengthened down the sage-slope, and Jane Withersteen likened them to the shadows gathering and closing in around her life.

Mrs. Larkin died, and little Fay was left an orphan with no known relative. Jane's love redoubled. It was the saving brightness of a darkening hour. Fay turned now to Jane in childish worship. And Jane at last found full expression for the mother-longing in her heart. Upon Lassiter, too, Mrs. Larkin's death had some subtle reaction. Before, he had often, without explanation, advised Jane to send Fay back to any Gentile family that would take her in. Passionately and reproachfully and wonderingly Jane had refused even to entertain such an idea. And now Lassiter never advised it again, grew sadder and quieter in his contemplation of the child, and infinitely more gentle and loving. Sometimes Jane had a cold, inexplicable sensation of dread when she saw Lassiter watching Fay. What did the rider see in the future? Why did he, day by day, grow more silent, calmer, cooler, yet sadder in prophetic assurance of something to be?

No doubt, Jane thought, the rider, in his almost superhuman power of foresight, saw behind the horizon the dark, lengthening shadows that were soon to crowd and gloom over him and her and little Fay. Jane Withersteen awaited the long-deferred breaking of the storm with a courage and embittered calm that had come to her in her extremity. Hope had not died. Doubt and fear, subservient to her will, no longer gave her sleepless nights and tortured days. Love remained. All that she had loved she now loved the more. She seemed to feel that she was defiantly flinging the wealth of her love in the face of misfortune and of hate. No day passed but she prayed for all—and most fervently for her enemies. It troubled her that she had lost, or had never gained, the whole control of her mind. In some measure reason and wisdom and decision were locked in a chamber of her brain, awaiting a key. Power to think of some things was taken from her. Meanwhile, abiding a day of judgment, she fought ceaselessly to deny the bitter drops in her cup, to tear back the slow, the intangibly slow growth of a hot, corrosive lichen eating into her heart.

On the morning of August 10th, Jane, while waiting in the court for Lassiter, heard a clear, ringing report of a rifle. It came from the grove, somewhere toward the corrals. Jane glanced out in alarm. The day was dull, windless, soundless. The leaves of the cottonwoods drooped, as if they had foretold the doom of Withersteen House and were now ready to die and drop and decay. Never had Jane seen such shade. She pondered on the meaning of the report. Revolver shots had of late cracked from different parts of the grove—spies taking snap-shots at Lassiter from a cowardly distance! But a rifle report meant more. Riders seldom used rifles. Judkins and Venters were the exceptions she called to mind. Had the men who hounded her hidden in her grove, taken to the rifle to rid her of Lassiter, her last friend? It was probable—it was likely. And she did not share his cool assumption that his death would never come at the hands of a Mormon. Long had she expected it. His constancy to her, his singular reluctance to use the fatal skill for which he was famed—both now plain to all Mormons—laid him open to inevitable assassination. Yet what charm against ambush and aim and enemy he seemed to bear about him! No, Jane reflected, it was not charm; only a wonderful training of eye and ear, and sense of impending peril. Nevertheless that could not forever avail against secret attack.

That moment a rustling of leaves attracted her attention; then the familiar clinking accompaniment of a slow, soft, measured step, and Lassiter walked into the court.

"Jane, there's a fellow out there with a long gun," he said, and, removing his sombrero, showed his head bound in a bloody scarf.

"I heard the shot; I knew it was meant for you. Let me see— you can't be badly injured?"

"I reckon not. But mebbe it wasn't a close call! . . . I'll sit

here in this corner where nobody can see me from the grove."
He untied the scarf and removed it to show a long, bleeding furrow above his left temple.

"It's only a cut," said Jane. "But how it bleeds! Hold your scarf over it just a moment till I come back."

She ran into the house and returned with bandages; and while she bathed and dressed the wound Lassiter talked.

"That fellow had a good chance to get me. But he must have flinched when he pulled the trigger. As I dodged down I saw him run through the trees. He had a rifle. I've been expectin' that kind of gun play. I reckon now I'll have to keep a little closer hid myself. These fellers all seem to get chilly or shaky when they draw a bead on me, but one of them might jest happen to hit me."

"Won't you go away—leave Cottonwoods as I've begged you to—before some one does happen to hit you?" she appealed to him.

"I reckon I'll stay."

"But, oh, Lassiter—your blood will be on my hands!"

"See here, lady, look at your hands now, right now. Aren't they fine, firm, white hands? Aren't they bloody now? Lassiter's blood! That's a queer thing to stain your beautiful hands. But if you could only see deeper you'd find a redder color of blood. Heart color, Jane!"

"Oh! . . . My friend!"

"No, Jane, I'm not one to quit when the game grows hot, no more than you. This game, though, is new to me, an' I don't know the moves yet, else I wouldn't have stepped in front of that bullet."

"Have you no desire to hunt the man who fired at you—to find him—and—and kill him?"

"Well, I reckon I haven't any great hankerin' for that."

"Oh, the wonder of it! . . . I knew—I prayed—I trusted. Lassiter, I almost gave—all myself to soften you to Mormons. Thank God, and thank you, my friend. . . . But, selfish woman that I am, this is no great test. What's the life of one of those sneaking cowards to such a man as you? I think of your great hate toward him who— I think of your life's implacable purpose. Can it be—"

"Wait! . . . Listen!" he whispered. "I hear a hoss."

He rose noiselessly, with his ear to the breeze. Suddenly he pulled his sombrero down over his bandaged head and, swinging his gun-sheaths round in front, he stepped into the alcove.

"It's a hoss—comin' fast," he added.

Jane's listening ear soon caught a faint, rapid, rhythmic beat of hoofs. It came from the sage. It gave her a thrill that she was at a loss to understand. The sound rose stronger, louder. Then came a clear, sharp difference when the horse passed from the sage trail to the hard-packed ground of the grove. It became a ringing run—swift in its bell-like clatterings, yet singular in longer pause than usual between the hoofbeats of a horse.

"It's Wrangle! . . . It's Wrangle!" cried Jane Withersteen. "I'd know him from a million horses!"

Excitement and thrilling expectancy flooded out all Jane Withersteen's calm. A tight band closed round her breast as she saw the giant sorrel flit in reddish-brown flashes across the openings in the green. Then he was pounding down the lane—thundering into the court—crashing his great iron-shod hoofs on the stone flags. Wrangle it was surely, but shaggy and wild-eyed, and sage-streaked, with dust-caked lather staining his flanks. He reared and crashed down and plunged. The rider leaped off, threw the bridle, and held hard on a lasso looped round Wrangle's head and neck. Janet's heart sank as she tried to recognize Venters in the rider. Something familiar struck her in the lofty stature, in the sweep of powerful shoulders. But this bearded, long-haired, unkempt man, who wore ragged clothes patched with pieces of skin, and boots that showed bare legs and feet—this dusty, dark, and wild rider could not possibly be Venters.

"Whoa, Wrangle, old boy! Come down. Easy now. So—so—so. You're home, old boy, and presently you can have a drink of water you'll remember."

In the voice Jane knew the rider to be Venters. He tied Wrangle to the hitching-rack and turned to the court.

"Oh, Bern! . . . You wild man!" she exclaimed.

"Jane—Jane, it's good to see you! Hello, Lassiter! Yes, it's Venters."

Like rough iron his hard hand crushed Jane's. In it she felt the difference she saw in him. Wild, rugged, unshorn—yet how

171

splendid! He had gone away a boy—he had returned a man. He appeared taller, wider of shoulder, deeper-chested, more powerfully built. But was that only her fancy—he had always been a young giant—was the change one of spirit? He might have been absent for years, proven by fire and steel, grown like Lassiter, strong and cool and sure. His eyes—were they keener, more flashing than before?—met hers with clear, frank, warm regard, in which perplexity was not, nor discontent, nor pain.

"Look at me long as you like," he said, with a laugh. "I'm not much to look at. And, Jane, neither you nor Lassiter, can brag. You're paler than I ever saw you. Lassiter, here, he wears a bloody bandage under his hat. That reminds me. Some one took a flying shot at me down in the sage. It made Wrangle run some. . . . Well, perhaps you've more to tell me than I've got to tell you."

Briefly, in few words, Jane outlined the circumstances of her undoing in the weeks of his absence.

Under his beard and bronze she saw his face whiten in terrible wrath.

"Lassiter—what held you back?"

No time in the long period of fiery moments and sudden shocks had Jane Withersteen ever beheld Lassiter as calm and serene and cool as then.

"Jane had gloom enough without my addin' to it by shootin' up the village," he said.

As strange as Lassiter's coolness was Venters's curious, intent scrutiny of them both, and under it Jane felt a flaming tide wave from bosom to temples.

"Well—you're right," he said, with slow pause. "It surprises me a little, that's all."

Jane sensed then a slight alteration in Venters, and what it was, in her own confusion, she could not tell. It had always been her intention to acquaint him with the deceit she had fallen to in her zeal to move Lassiter. She did not mean to spare herself. Yet now, at the moment, before these riders, it was an impossibility to explain.

Venters was speaking somewhat haltingly, without his former frankness. "I found Oldring's hiding-place and your red herd. I learned—I know—I'm sure there was a deal between Tull and

Oldring." He paused and shifted his position and his gaze. He looked as if he wanted to say something that he found beyond him. Sorrow and pity and shame seemed to contend for mastery over him. Then he raised himself and spoke with effort. "Jane, I've cost you too much. You've almost ruined yourself for me. It was wrong, for I'm not worth it. I never deserved such friendship. Well, maybe it's not too late. You must give me up. Mind, I haven't changed. I am just the same as ever. I'll see Tull while I'm here, and tell him to his face."

"Bern, it's too late," said Jane.

"I'll *make* him believe!" cried Venters, violently.

"You ask me to break our friendship?"

"Yes. If you don't, I shall."

"Forever?"

"Forever!"

Jane sighed. Another shadow had lengthened down the sage-slope to cast further darkness upon her. A melancholy sweetness pervaded her resignation. The boy who had left her had returned a man, nobler, stronger, one in whom she divined something unbending as steel. There might come a moment later when she would wonder why she had not fought against his will, but just now she yielded to it. She liked him as well—nay, more, she thought, only her emotions were deadened by the long, menacing wait for the bursting storm.

Once before she had held out her hand to him—when she gave it; now she stretched it tremblingly forth in acceptance of the decree circumstance had laid upon them. Venters bowed over it, kissed it, pressed it hard, and half stifled a sound very like a sob. Certain it was that when he raised his head tears glistened in his eyes.

"Some—women—have a hard lot," he said, huskily. Then he shook his powerful form, and his rags lashed about him. "I'll say a few things to Tull—when I meet him."

"Bern—you'll not draw on Tull? Oh, that must not be! Promise me—"

"I promise you this," he interrupted, in stern passion that thrilled while it terrorized her. "If you say one more word for that plotter I'll kill him as I would a mad coyote!"

Jane clasped her hands. Was this fire-eyed man the one whom

she had once made as wax to her touch? Had Venters become Lassiter and Lassiter Venters?

"I'll—say no more," she faltered.

"Jane, Lassiter once called you blind," said Venters. "It must be true. But I won't upbraid you. Only don't rouse the devil in me by praying for Tull! I'll try to keep cool when I meet him. That's all. Now there's one more thing I want to ask of you— the last. I've found a valley down in the Pass. It's a wonderful place. I intend to stay there. It's so hidden I believe no one can find it. There's good water, and browse, and game. I want to raise corn and stock. I need to take in supplies. Will you give them to me?"

"Assuredly. The more you take the better you'll please me— and perhaps the less my—my enemies will get."

"Venters, I reckon you'll have trouble packin' anythin' away," put in Lassiter.

"I'll go at night."

"Mebbe that wouldn't be best. You'd sure be stopped. You'd better go early in the mornin'—say, just after dawn. That's the safest time to move round here."

"Lassiter, I'll be hard to stop," returned Venters, darkly.

"I reckon so."

"Bern," said Jane, "go first to the riders' quarters and get your- self a complete outfit. You're a—a sight. Then help yourself to whatever else you need—burros, packs, grain, dried fruits, and meat. You must take coffee and sugar and flour—all kinds of supplies. Don't forget corn and seeds. I remember how you used to starve. Please—please take all you can pack away from here. I'll make a bundle for you, which you mustn't open till you're in your valley. How I'd like to see it! To judge by you and Wrangle, how wild it must be!"

Jane walked down into the outer court and approached the sorrel. Upstarting, he laid back his ears and eyed her.

"Wrangle—dear old Wrangle," she said, and put a caressing hand on his matted mane. "Oh, he's wild, but he knows me! Bern, can he run as fast as ever?"

"Run? Jane, he's done sixty miles since last night at dark, and I could make him kill Black Star right now in a ten-mile race."

"He never could," protested Jane. "He couldn't even if he was fresh."

"I reckon mebbe the best hoss 'll prove himself yet," said Lassiter, "an', Jane, if it ever comes to that race I'd like you to be on Wrangle."

"I'd like that, too," rejoined Venters. "But, Jane, maybe Lassiter's hint is extreme. Bad as your prospects are, you'll surely never come to the running point."

"Who knows!" she replied, with mournful smile.

"No, no, Jane, it can't be so bad as all that. Soon as I see Tull there'll be a change in your fortunes. I'll hurry down to the village. . . . Now don't worry."

Jane retired to the seclusion of her room. Lassiter's subtle forecasting of disaster, Venters's forced optimism, neither remained in mind. Material loss weighed nothing in the balance with other losses she was sustaining. She wondered dully at her sitting there, hands folded listlessly, with a kind of numb deadness to the passing of time and the passing of her riches. She thought of Venters's friendship. She had not lost that, but she had lost him. Lassiter's friendship—that was more than love—it would endure, but soon he, too, would be gone. Little Fay slept dreamlessly upon the bed, her golden curls streaming over the pillow. Jane had the child's worship. Would she lose that, too? And if she did, what then would be left? Conscience thundered at her that there was left her religion. Conscience thundered that she should be grateful on her knees for this baptism of fire; that through misfortune, sacrifice, and suffering her soul might be fused pure gold. But the old, spontaneous, rapturous spirit no more exalted her. She wanted to be a woman—not a martyr. Like the saint of old who mortified his flesh, Jane Withersteen had in her the temper for heroic martyrdom, if by sacrificing herself she could save the souls of others. But here the damnable verdict blistered her that the more she sacrificed herself the blacker grew the souls of her churchmen. There was something terribly wrong with her soul, something terribly wrong with her churchmen and her religion. In the whirling gulf of her thought there was yet one shining light to guide her, to sustain her in her hope; and it was that, despite her errors and her frailties and her blindness, she had one absolute and unfaltering hold on ultimate and supreme justice. That was love. "Love your enemies as yourself!" was a divine word, entirely free from any church or creed.

Jane's meditations were disturbed by Lassiter's soft, tinkling step in the court. Always he wore the clinking spurs. Always he was in readiness to ride. She passed out and called him into the huge, dim hall.

"I think you'll be safer here. The court is too open," she said.

"I reckon," replied Lassiter. "An' it's cooler here. The day's sure muggy. Well, I went down to the village with Venters."

"Already! Where is he?" queried Jane, in quick amaze.

"He's at the corrals. Blake's helpin' him get the burros an' packs ready. That Blake is a good fellow."

"Did—did Bern meet Tull?"

"I guess he did," answered Lassiter, and he laughed dryly.

"Tell me! Oh, you exasperate me! You're so cool, so calm! For Heaven's sake, tell me what happened!"

"First time I've been in the village for weeks," went on Lassiter, mildly. "I reckon there 'ain't been more of a show for a long time. Me an' Venters walkin' down the road! It was funny. I ain't sayin' anybody was particular glad to see us. I'm not much thought of hereabouts, an' Venters he sure looks like what you called him, a wild man. Well, there was some runnin' of folks before we got to the stores. Then everybody vamoosed except some surprised rustlers in front of a saloon. Venters went right in the stores an' saloons, an' of course I went along. I don't know which tickled me the most—the actions of many fellers we met, or Venters's nerve. Jane, I was downright glad to be along. You see *that* sort of thing is my element, an' I've been away from it for a spell. But we didn't find Tull in one of them places. Some Gentile feller at last told Venters he'd find Tull in that long buildin' next to Parsons's store. It's a kind of meetin'-room; and sure enough, when we peeped in, it was half full of men.

"Venters yelled: 'Don't anybody pull guns! We ain't come for that!' Then he tramped in, an' I was some put to keep alongside him. There was a hard, scrapin' sound of feet, a loud cry, an' then some whisperin', an' after that stillness you could cut with a knife. Tull was there, an' that fat party who once tried to throw a gun on me, an' other important-lookin' men, an' that little frog-legged feller who was with Tull the day I rode in here. I wish you could have seen their faces, 'specially Tull's an' the fat party's. But there ain't no use of me tryin' to tell you how they looked.

"Well, Venters an' I stood there in the middle of the room, with that batch of men all in front of us, an' not a blamed one of them winked an eyelash or moved a finger. It was natural, of course, for me to notice many of them packed guns. That's a way of mine, first noticin' them things. Venters spoke up, an' his voice sort of chilled an' cut, an' he told Tull he had a few things to say."

Here Lassiter paused while he turned his sombrero round and round, in his familiar habit, and his eyes had the look of a man seeing over again some thrilling spectacle, and under his red bronze there was strange animation.

"Like a shot, then, Venters told Tull that the friendship between you an' him was all over, an' he was leaving your place. He said you'd both of you broken off in the hope of propitiatin' your people, but you hadn't changed your mind otherwise, an' never would.

"Next he spoke up for you. I ain't goin' to tell you what he said. Only—no other woman who ever lived ever had such tribute! You had a champion, Jane, an' never fear that those thick-skulled men don't know you now. It couldn't be otherwise. He spoke the ringin', lightnin' truth. . . . Then he accused Tull of the underhand, miserable robbery of a helpless woman. He told Tull where the red herd was, of a deal made with Oldrin', that Jerry Card had made the deal. I thought Tull was goin' to drop, an' that little frog-legged cuss, he looked some limp an' white. But Venters's voice would have kept anybody's legs from bucklin'. I was stiff myself. He went on an' called Tull—called him every bad name ever known to a rider, an' then some. He cursed Tull. I never hear a man get such a cursin'. He laughed in scorn at the idea of Tull bein' a minister. He said Tull an' a few more dogs of hell builded their empire out of the hearts of such innocent an' God-fearin' women as Jane Withersteen. He called Tull a binder of women, a callous beast who hid behind a mock mantle of righteousness—an' the last an' lowest coward on the face of the earth. To prey on weak women through their religion—that was the last unspeakable crime!

"Then he finished, an' by this time he'd almost lost his voice. But his whisper was enough. 'Tull,' he said, '*she* begged me not to draw on you to-day. *She* would pray for you if you burned her at the stake. . . . But listen! . . . I swear if you and I ever come face to face again, I'll kill you!'

"We backed out of the door then, an' up the road. But nobody follered us."

Jane found herself weeping passionately. She had not been conscious of it till Lassiter ended his story, and she experienced exquisite pain and relief in shedding tears. Long had her eyes been dry, her grief deep; long had her emotions been dumb. Lassiter's story put her on the rack; the appalling nature of Venters's act and speech had no parallel as an outrage; it was worse than bloodshed. Men like Tull had been shot, but had one ever been so terribly denounced in public? Overmounting her horror, an uncontrollable, quivering passion shook her very soul. It was sheer human glory in the deed of a fearless man. It was hot, primitive instinct to live—to fight. It was a kind of mad joy in Venters's chivalry. It was close to the wrath that had first shaken her in the beginning of this war waged upon her.

"Well, well, Jane, don't take it that way," said Lassiter, in evident distress. "I had to tell you. There's some things a feller jest can't keep. It's strange you give up on hearin' that, when all this long time you've been the gamest woman I ever seen. But I don't know women. Mebbe there's reason for you to cry. I know this—nothin' ever rang in my soul an' so filled it as what Venters did. I'd like to have done it, but—I'm only good for throwin' a gun, an' it seems you hate that. . . . Well, I'll be goin' now."

"Where?"

"Venters took Wrangle to the stable. The sorrel's shy a shoe, an' I've got to help hold the big devil an' put on another."

"Tell Bern to come for the pack I want to give him—and—and to say good-by," called Jane, as Lassiter went out.

Jane passed the rest of that day in a vain endeavor to decide what and what not to put in the pack for Venters. This task was the last she would ever perform for him, and the gifts were the last she would ever make him. So she picked and chose and rejected, and chose again, and often paused in sad revery, and began again, till at length she filled the pack.

It was about sunset, and she and Fay had finished supper and were sitting in the court, when Venters's quick steps rang on the stones. She scarcely knew him, for he had changed the tattered garments, and she missed the dark beard and long hair. Still he was not the Venters of old. As he came up the steps she felt herself pointing to the pack, and heard herself speaking words that were meaningless to her. He said good-by; he kissed her, released her, and turned away. His tall figure blurred in her sight, grew dim through dark, streaked vision, and then he vanished.

Twilight fell around Withersteen House, and dusk and night. Little Fay slept; but Jane lay with strained, aching eyes. She heard the wind moaning in the cottonwoods and mice squeaking in the walls. The night was interminably long, yet she prayed to hold back the dawn. What would another day bring forth? The blackness of her room seemed blacker for the sad, entering gray of morning light. She heard the chirp of awakening birds, and fancied she caught a faint clatter of hoofs. Then low, dull, distant, throbbed a heavy gunshot. She had expected it, was waiting for it; nevertheless, an electric shock checked her heart, froze the very living fiber of her bones. That vise-like hold on her faculties apparently did not relax for a long time, and it was a voice under her window that released her.

"Jane! . . . Jane!" softly called Lassiter.

She answered somehow.

"It's all right. Venters got away. I thought mebbe you'd heard that shot, an' I was worried some."

"What was it—who fired?"

"Well—some fool feller tried to stop Venters out there in the sage—an' he only stopped lead! . . . I think it'll be all right. I haven't seen or heard of any other fellers round. Venters 'll go through safe. An', Jane, I've got Bells saddled, an' I'm going to trail Venters. Mind, I won't show myself unless he falls foul of somebody an' needs me. I want to see if this place where he's goin' is safe for him. He says nobody can track him there. I never seen the place yet I couldn't track a man to. Now, Jane, you stay indoors while I'm gone, an' keep close watch on Fay. Will you?"

"Yes! Oh yes!"

"An' another thing, Jane," he continued, then paused for long— "another thing—if you ain't here when I come back—if you're *gone*—don't fear, I'll trail you—I'll find you."

"My dear Lassiter, where could I be gone—as you put it?" asked Jane, in curious surprise.

"I reckon you might be somewhere. Mebbe tied in an old barn —or corralled in some gulch—or chained in a cave! *Milly Erne was*—till she give in! Mebbe that's news to you. . . . Well, if you're gone I'll hunt for you."

"No, Lassiter," she replied, sadly and low. "If I'm gone just forget the unhappy woman whose blinded selfish deceit you repaid with kindness and love."

She heard a deep, muttering curse, under his breath, and then the silvery tinkling of his spurs as he moved away.

Jane entered upon the duties of that day with a settled, gloomy calm. Disaster hung in the dark clouds, in the shade, in the humid west wind. Blake, when he reported, appeared without his usual cheer; and Jerd wore a harassed look of a worn and worried man. And when Judkins put in appearance, riding a lame horse, and dismounted with the cramp of a rider, his dust-covered figure and his darkly grim, almost dazed expression told Jane of dire calamity. She had no need of words.

"Miss Withersteen, I have to report—loss of the—white herd," said Judkins, hoarsely.

"Come, sit down; you look played out," replied Jane, solicitously. She brought him brandy and food, and while he partook of refreshments, of which he appeared badly in need, she asked no questions.

"No one rider—could hev done more—Miss Withersteen," he went on, presently.

"Judkins, don't be distressed. You've done more than any other rider. I've long expected to lose the white herd. It's no surprise. It's in line with other things that are happening. I'm grateful for your service."

"Miss Withersteen, I knew how you'd take it. But if anythin', that makes it harder to tell. You see, a feller wants to do so much fer you, an' I'd got fond of my job. We hed the herd a ways off to the north of the break in the valley. There was a big level an' pools of water an' tip-top browse. But the cattle was in a high nervous condition. Wild—as wild as antelope! You see, they'd been so scared they never slept. I ain't a-goin' to tell you of the many tricks that were pulled off out there in the sage. But there wasn't a day for weeks thet the herd didn't get started to run. We allus managed to ride 'em close an' drive 'em back an' keep 'em bunched. Honest, Miss Withersteen, them steers was *thin*. They was *thin* when water and grass was everywhere. *Thin* at this season—thet 'll tell you how your steers was pestered. Fer instance, one night a strange runnin' streak of fire run right through the herd. That streak was a coyote—*with an oiled an' blazin' tail!* Fer I shot it an' found out. We had hell with the herd that night, an' if the sage an' grass hadn't been wet—we, hosses, steers, an' all would hev burned up. But I said I wasn't goin' to tell you any of the tricks. . . . Strange now, Miss Withersteen, when the stampede did come it was from natural cause—jest a whirlin' devil of dust. You've seen the like often. An' this wasn't no big whirl, fer the dust was mostly settled. It had dried out in a little swale, an' ordinarily no steer would ever hev run fer it. But the herd was nervous an' wild. An' jest as Lassiter said, when that bunch of white steers got to movin' they was as bad as buffalo. I've seen some buffalo stampedes back in Nebraska, an' this bolt of the steers was the same kind.

"I tried to mill the herd jest as Lassiter did. But I wasn't equal to it, Miss Withersteen. I don't believe the rider lives who could hev turned thet herd. We kept along of the herd fer miles, an' more 'n one of my boys tried to get the steers a-millin'. It wasn't no use. We got off level ground, goin' down, an' then the steers ran somethin' fierce. We left the little gullies an' washes level-full of dead steers. Finally I saw the herd was makin' to pass a kind of low pocket between ridges. There was a hog-back—as we used to call 'em—a pile of rocks stickin' up, and I saw the herd was goin' to split round it, or swing out to the left. An' I wanted 'em to go to the right so mebbe we'd be able to drive 'em into the pocket. So, with all my boys except three, I rode hard to turn the herd a little to the right. We couldn't budge 'em. They went on an' split round the rocks, an' the most of 'em was turned sharp to the left by a deep wash we hedn't seen—hed no chance to see.

"The other three boys—Jimmy Vail, Joe Willis, an' thet little Cairns boy—a nervy kid! they, with Cairns leadin', tried to buck thet herd round to the pocket. It was a wild, fool idee. I couldn't do nothin'. The boys got hemmed in between the steers an' the wash—thet they hedn't no chance to see, either. Vail an' Willis was run down right before our eyes. An' Cairns, who rode a fine hoss, he did some ridin' I never seen equaled, an' would hev beat the steers if there'd been any room to run in. I was high up an' could see how the steers kept spillin' by twos an' threes over into the wash. Cairns put his hoss to a place thet was too wide fer any hoss, an' broke his neck an' the hoss's too. We found that out after, an' as fer Vail an' Willis—two thousand steers ran over the poor boys. There wasn't much left to pack home fer buryin! . . . An', Miss Withersteen, thet all happened yesterday, an' I believe, if the white herd didn't run over the wall of the Pass, it's runnin' yet."

On the morning of the second day after Judkins's recital, during which time Jane remained indoors a prey to regret and sorrow for the boy riders, and a new and now strangely insistent fear for her own person, she again heard what she had missed more than she dared honestly confess—the soft, jingling step of Lassiter. Almost overwhelming relief surged through her, a feeling as akin to joy as any she could have been capable of in those gloomy hours of shadow, and one that suddenly stunned her with the significance of what Lassiter had come to mean to her. She had begged him, for his own sake, to leave Cottonwoods. She might yet beg that, if her weakening courage permitted her to dare absolute loneliness and helplessness, but she realized now that if she were left alone her life would become one long, hideous nightmare.

When his soft steps clinked into the hall, in answer to her greeting, and his tall, black-garbed form filled the door, she felt an inexpressible sense of immediate safety. In his presence she lost her fear of the dim passageways of Withersteen House and of every sound. Always it had been that, when he entered the court or the hall, she had experienced a distinctly sickening but gradually lessening shock at sight of the huge black guns swinging at his sides. This time the sickening shock again visited her, it was, however, because a revealing flash of thought told her that it was not alone Lassiter who was thrillingly welcome, but also his fatal weapons. They meant so much. How she had fallen—how broken and spiritless must she be—to have still the same old horror of Lassiter's guns and his name, yet feel somehow a cold, shrinking protection in their law and might and use.

"Did you trail Venters—find his wonderful valley?" she asked, eagerly.

"Yes, an' I reckon it's sure a wonderful place."

"Is he safe there?"

"That's been botherin' me some. I tracked him an' part of the trail was the hardest I ever tackled. Mebbe there's a rustler or somebody in this country who's as good at trackin' as I am. If that's so Venters ain't safe."

"Well—tell me all about Bern and his valley."

To Jane's surprise Lassiter showed disinclination for further talk about his trip. He appeared to be extremely fatigued. Jane reflected that one hundred and twenty miles, with probably a great deal of climbing on foot, all in three days, was enough to tire any rider. Moreover, it presently developed that Lassiter had returned in a mood of singular sadness and preoccupation. She put it down to a moodiness over the loss of her white herd and the now precarious condition of her fortune.

Several days passed, and as nothing happened, Jane's spirits began to brighten. Once in her musings she thought that this tendency of hers to rebound was as sad as it was futile. Meanwhile, she had resumed her walks through the grove with little Fay.

One morning she went as far as the sage. She had not seen the slope since the beginning of the rains, and now it bloomed a rich deep purple. There was a high wind blowing, and the sage tossed and waved and colored beautifully from light to dark. Clouds scudded across the sky and their shadows sailed darkly down the sunny slope.

Upon her return toward the house she went by the lane to the stables, and she had scarcely entered the great open space with its corrals and sheds when she saw Lassiter hurriedly approaching. Fay broke from her and, running to a corral fence, began to pat and pull the long, hanging ears of a drowsy burro.

One look at Lassiter armed her for a blow.

Without a word he led her across the wide yard to the rise of the ground upon which the stable stood.

"Jane—look!" he said, and pointed to the ground.

Jane glanced down, and again, and upon steadier vision made out splotches of blood on the stones, and broad, smooth marks in the dust, leading out toward the sage.

"What made these?" she asked.

"I reckon somebody has dragged dead or wounded men out to where there was hosses in the sage."

"Dead—or—wounded—men!"

"I reckon—Jane, are you strong? Can you bear up?"

His hands were gently holding hers, and his eyes—suddenly she could no longer look into them. "Strong?" she echoed, trembling. "I—I will be."

Up on the stone-flag drive, nicked with the marks made by the iron-shod hoofs of her racers, Lassiter led her, his grasp ever growing firmer.

"Where's Blake—and—and Jerb?" she asked, haltingly.

"I don't know where Jerb is. Bolted, most likely," replied Lassiter, as he took her through the stone door. "But Blake—poor Blake! He's gone forever! . . . Be prepared, Jane."

With a cold prickling of her skin, with a queer thrumming in her ears, with fixed and staring eyes, Jane saw a gun lying at her feet with chamber swung and empty, and discharged shells scattered near.

Outstretched upon the stable floor lay Blake, ghastly white—dead—one hand clutching a gun and the other twisted in his bloody blouse.

"Whoever the thieves were, whether your people or rustlers—Blake killed some of them!" said Lassiter.

"Thieves?" whispered Jane.

"I reckon. Hoss-thieves! . . . Look!" Lassiter waved his hand toward the stalls.

The first stall—Bells's stall—was empty. All the stalls were empty. No racer whinnied and stamped greeting to her. Night was gone! Black Star was gone!

CHAPTER XVI

GOLD

AS Lassiter had reported to Jane, Venters "went through" safely, and after a toilsome journey reached the peaceful shelter of Surprise Valley. When finally he lay wearily down under the silver spruces, resting from the strain of dragging packs and burros up the slope and through the entrance to Surprise Valley, he had leisure to think, and a great deal of the time went in regretting that he had not been frank with his loyal friend, Jane Withersteen.

But, he kept continually recalling, when he had stood once more face to face with her and had been shocked at the change in her and had heard the details of her adversity, he had not had the heart to tell her of the closer interest which had entered his life. He had not lied; yet he had kept silence.

Bess was in transports over the stores of supplies and the outfit he had packed from Cottonwoods. He had certainly brought a hundred times more than he had gone for; enough, surely, for years, perhaps to make permanent home in the valley. He saw no reason why he need ever leave there again.

After a day of rest he recovered his strength and shared Bess's pleasure in rummaging over the endless packs, and began to plan for the future. And in this planning, his trip to Cottonwoods, with its revived hate of Tull and consequent unleashing of fierce passions, soon faded out of mind. By slower degrees his friendship for Jane Withersteen and his contrition drifted from the active preoccupation of his present thought to a place in memory, with more and more infrequent recalls.

And as far as the state of his mind was concerned, upon the second day after his return, the valley, with its golden hues and

185

purple shades, the speaking west wind and the cool, silent night, and Bess's watching eyes with their wonderful light, so wrought upon Venters that he might never have left them at all.

That very afternoon he set to work. Only one thing hindered him upon beginning, though it in no wise checked his delight, and that in the multiplicity of tasks planned to make a paradise out of the valley he could not choose the one with which to begin. He had to grow into the habit of passing from one dreamy pleasure to another, like a bee going from flower to flower in the valley, and he found this wandering habit likely to extend to his labors. Nevertheless, he made a start.

At the outset he discovered Bess to be both a considerable help in some ways and a very great hindrance in others. Her excitement and joy were spurs, inspirations; but she was utterly impracticable in her ideas, and she flitted from one plan to another with bewildering vacillation. Moreover, he fancied that she grew more eager, youthful, and sweet; and he marked that it was far easier to watch her and listen to her than it was to work. Therefore he gave her tasks that necessitated her going often to the cave where he had stored his packs.

Upon the last of these trips, when he was some distance down the terrace and out of sight of camp, he heard a scream, and then the sharp barking of the dogs.

For an instant he straightened up, amazed. Danger for her had been absolutely out of his mind. She had seen a rattlesnake— or a wildcat. Still she would not have been likely to scream at sight of either; and the barking of the dogs was ominous. Dropping his work, he dashed back along the terrace. Upon breaking through a clump of aspens he saw the dark form of a man in the camp. Cold, then hot, Venters burst into frenzied speed to reach his guns. He was cursing himself for a thoughtless fool when the man's tall form became familiar and he recognized Lassiter. Then the reversal of emotions changed his run to a walk; he tried to call out, but his voice refused to carry; when he reached camp there was Lassiter staring at the white-faced girl. By that time Ring and Whitie had recognized him.

"Hello, Venters! I'm makin' you a visit," said Lassiter, slowly. "An' I'm some surprised to see you've a—a young feller for company."

One glance had sufficed for the keen rider to read Bess's real sex, and for once his cool calm had deserted him. He stared till the white of Bess's cheeks flared into crimson. That, if it were needed, was the concluding evidence of her femininity; for it went fittingly with her sun-tinted hair and darkened, dilated eyes, the sweetness of her mouth, and the striking symmetry of her slender shape.

"Heavens! Lassiter!" panted Venters, when he caught his breath. "What relief—it's only you! How—in the name of all— that's wonderful—did you ever get here?"

"I trailed you. We—I wanted to know where you was, if you had a safe place. So I trailed you."

"Trailed me," cried Venters, bluntly.

"I reckon. It was some of a job after I got to them smooth rocks. I was all day trackin' you up to them little cut steps in the rock. The rest was easy."

"Where's your hoss? I hope you hid him."

"I tied him in them queer cedars down on the slope. He can't be seen from the valley."

"That's good. Well, well! I'm completely dumfounded. It was my idea that no man could track me in here."

"I reckon. But if there's a tracker in these uplands as good as me he can find you."

"That's bad. That'll worry me. But, Lassiter, now you're here I'm glad to see you. And—and my companion here is not a young fellow! . . . Bess, this is a friend of mine. He saved my life once."

The embarrassment of the moment did not extend to Lassiter. Almost at once his manner, as he shook hands with Bess, relieved Venters and put the girl at ease. After Venters's words and one quick look at Lassiter, her agitation stilled, and, though she was shy, if she were conscious of anything out of the ordinary in the situation, certainly she did not show it.

"I reckon I'll only stay a little while," Lassiter was saying. "An' if you don't mind troublin', I'm hungry. I fetched some biscuits along, but they're gone. Venters, this place is sure the wonderfullest ever seen. Them cut steps on the slope! That outlet into the gorge! An' it's like climbin' up through hell into heaven to climb through that gorge into this valley! There's a queer-lookin'

187

rock at the top of the passage. I didn't have time to stop. I'm wonderin' how you ever found this place. It's sure interestin'."

During the preparation and eating of dinner Lassiter listened mostly, as was his wont, and occasionally he spoke in his quaint and dry way. Venters noted, however, that the rider showed an increasing interest in Bess. He asked her no questions, and only directed his attention to her while she was occupied and had no opportunity to observe his scrutiny. It seemed to Venters that Lassiter grew more and more absorbed in his study of Bess, and that he lost his coolness in some strange, softening sympathy. Then, quite abruptly, he arose and announced the necessity for his early departure. He said good-by to Bess in a voice gentle and somewhat broken, and turned hurriedly away. Venters accompanied him, and they had traversed the terrace, climbed the weathered slope, and passed under the stone bridge before either spoke again.

Then Lassiter put a great hand on Venters's shoulder and wheeled him to meet a smoldering fire of gray eyes.

"Lassiter, I couldn't tell Jane! I couldn't," burst out Venters, reading his friend's mind. "I tried. But I couldn't. She wouldn't understand, and she has troubles enough. And I love the girl!"

"Venters, I reckon this beats me. I've seen some queer things in my time, too. This girl—who is she?"

"I don't know."

"Don't know! What is she, then?"

"I don't know that, either. Oh, it's the strangest story you ever heard. I must tell you. But you'll never believe."

"Venters, women were always puzzles to me. But for all that, if this girl ain't a child, an' as innocent, I'm no fit person to think of virtue an' goodness in anybody. Are you goin' to be square with her?"

"I am—so help me God!"

"I reckoned so. Mebbe my temper oughtn't led me to make sure. But, man, she's a woman in all but years. She's sweeter 'n the sage."

"Lassiter, I know, I know. And the *hell* of it is that in spite of her innocence and charm she's—she's not what she seems!"

"I wouldn't want to—of course, I couldn't call you a liar, Venters," said the older man.

"What's more, she was Oldring's Masked Rider!"

Venters expected to floor his friend with that statement, but he was not in any way prepared for the shock his words gave. For an instant he was astounded to see Lassiter stunned; then his own passionate eagerness to unbosom himself, to tell the wonderful story, precluded any other thought.

"Son, tell me all about this," presently said Lassiter as he seated himself on a stone and wiped his moist brow.

Thereupon Venters began his narrative at the point where he had shot the rustler and Oldring's Masked Rider, and he rushed through it, telling all, not holding back even Bess's unreserved avowal of her love or his deepest emotions.

"That's the story," he said, concluding. "I love her, though I've never told her. If I did tell her I'd be ready to marry her, and that seems impossible in this country. I'd be afraid to risk taking her anywhere. So I intend to do the best I can for her here."

"The longer I live the stranger life is," mused Lassiter, with downcast eyes. "I'm reminded of somethin' you once said to Jane about hands in her game of life. There's that unseen hand of power, an' Tull's black hand, an' my red one, an' your indifferent one, an' the girl's little brown, helpless one. An', Venters, there's another one that's all-wise an' all-wonderful. *That's* the hand guidin' Jane Withersteen's game of life! . . . Your story's one to daze a far clearer head than mine. I can't offer no advice, even if you asked for it. Mebbe I can help you. Anyway, I'll hold Oldrin' up when he comes to the village, an' find out about this girl. I knew the rustler years ago. He'll remember me."

"Lassiter, if I ever meet Oldring I'll kill him!" cried Venters, with sudden intensity.

"I reckon that 'd be perfectly natural," replied the rider.

"Make him think Bess is dead—as she is to him and that old life."

"Sure, sure, son. Cool down now. If you're goin' to begin pullin' guns on Tull an' Oldin' you want to be cool. I reckon, though, you'd better keep hid here. Well, I must be leavin'."

"One thing, Lassiter. You'll not tell Jane about Bess? Please don't!"

"I reckon not. But I wouldn't be afraid to bet that after she'd got over anger at your secrecy—Venters, she'd be furious once in her life!—she'd think more of you. I don't mind sayin' for myself that I think you're a good deal of a man."

In the further ascent Venters halted several times with the intention of saying good-by, yet he changed his mind and kept on climbing till they reached Balancing Rock. Lassiter examined the huge rock, listened to Venters's idea of its position and suggestion, and curiously placed a strong hand upon it.

"Hold on!" cried Venters. "I heaved at it once and have never gotten over my scare."

"Well, you do seem uncommon nervous," replied Lassiter, much amused. "Now, as for me, why I always had the funniest notion to roll stones! When I was a kid I did it, an' the bigger I got the bigger stones I'd roll. Ain't that funny? Honest—even now I often get off my hoss just to tumble a big stone over a precipice, an' watch it drop, an' listen to it bang an' boom. I've started some slides in my time, an' don't you forget it. I never seen a rock I wanted to roll as bad as this one! Wouldn't there jest be roarin', crashin' hell down that trail?"

"You'd close the outlet forever!" exclaimed Venters. "Well, good-by, Lassiter. Keep my secret and don't forget me. And be mighty careful how you get out of the valley below. The rustlers' cañon isn't more than three miles up the Pass. Now you've tracked me here, I'll never feel safe again."

In his descent to the valley, Venters's emotion, roused to stirring pitch by the recital of his love story, quieted gradually, and in its place came a sober, thoughtful mood. All at once he saw that he was serious, because he would never more regain his sense of security while in the valley. What Lassiter could do another skilful tracker might duplicate. Among the many riders with whom Venters had ridden he recalled no one who could have taken his trail at Cottonwoods and have followed it to the edge of the bare slope in the pass, let alone up that glistening smooth stone. Lassiter, however, was not an ordinary rider. Instead of hunting cattle tracks he had likely spent a goodly portion of his life tracking men. It was not improbable that among Oldring's rustlers there was one who shared Lassiter's gift for trailing. And the more Venters dwelt on this possibility the more perturbed he grew.

Lassiter's visit, moreover, had a disquieting effect upon Bess, and Venters fancied that she entertained the same thought as to future seclusion. The breaking of their solitude, though by a well-meaning friend, had not only dispelled all its dream and much of its charm, but had instilled a canker of fear. Both had seen the footprint in the sand.

Venters did no more work that day. Sunset and twilight gave way to night, and the cañon bird whistled its melancholy notes, and the wind sang softly in the cliffs, and the camp-fire blazed and burned down to red embers. To Venters a subtle difference was apparent in all of these, or else the shadowy change had been in him. He hoped that on the morrow this slight depression would have passed away.

In that measure, however, he was doomed to disappointment. Furthermore, Bess reverted to a wistful sadness that he had not observed in her since her recovery. His attempt to cheer her out of it resulted in dismal failure, and consequently in a darkening of his own mood. Hard work relieved him; still, when the day had passed, his unrest returned. Then he set to deliberate thinking, and there came to him the startling conviction that he must leave Surprise Valley and take Bess with him. As a rider he had taken many chances, and as an adventurer in Deception Pass he had unhesitatingly risked his life; but now he would run no preventable hazard of Bess's safety and happiness, and he was too keen not to see that hazard. It gave him a pang to think of leaving the beautiful valley just when he had the means to establish a permanent and delightful home there. One flashing thought tore in hot temptation through his mind—why not climb up into the gorge, roll Balancing Rock down the trail, and close forever the outlet to Deception Pass? "That was the beast in me—showing his teeth!" muttered Venters, scornfully. "I'll just kill him good and quick! I'll be fair to this girl, if it's the last thing I do on earth!"

Another day went by, in which he worked less and pondered more and all the time covertly watched Bess. Her wistfulness had deepened into downright unhappiness, and that made his task to tell her all the harder. He kept the secret another day, hoping by some chance she might grow less moody, and to his exceeding anxiety she fell into far deeper gloom. Out of his own secret and the torment of it he divined that she, too, had a secret and the keeping of it was torturing her. As yet he had no plan thought out in regard to how or when to leave the valley, but he decided to tell her the necessity of it and to persuade her to go. Furthermore, he hoped his speaking out would induce her to unburden her own mind.

"Bess, what's wrong with you?" he asked.

"Nothing," she answered, with averted face.

Venters took hold of her gently, though masterfully, forced her to meet his eyes.

"You can't look at me and lie," he said. "Now—what's wrong with you? You're keeping something from me. Well, I've got a secret, too, and I intend to tell it presently."

"Oh—I *have* a secret. I was crazy to tell you when you came back. That's why I was so silly about everything. I kept holding my secret back—gloating over it. But when Lassiter came I got an idea—that changed my mind. Then I hated to tell you."

"Are you going to now?"

"Yes—yes. I was coming to it. I tried yesterday, but you were so cold. I was afraid. I couldn't keep it much longer."

"Very well, most mysterious lady, tell your wonderful secret."

"You needn't laugh," she retorted, with a first glimpse of reviving spirit. "I can take the laugh out of you in one second."

"It's a go."

She ran through the spruces to the cave, and returned carrying something which was manifestly heavy. Upon nearer view he saw that whatever she held with such evident importance had been bound up in a black scarf he well remembered. That alone was sufficient to make him tingle with curiosity.

"Have you any idea what I did in your absence?" she asked.

"I imagine you lounged about, waiting and watching for me," he replied, smiling. "I've my share of conceit, you know."

"You're wrong. I worked. Look at my hands." She dropped on her knees close to where he sat, and, carefully depositing the black bundle, she held out her hands. The palms and inside of her fingers were white, puckered, and worn.

"Why, Bess, you've been fooling in the water," he said.

"Fooling? Look here!" With deft fingers she spread open the black scarf, and the bright sun shone upon a dull, glittering heap of gold.

192

"Gold!" he ejaculated.

"Yes, gold! See, pounds of gold! I found it—washed it out of the stream—picked it out grain by grain, nugget by nugget!"

"Gold!" he cried.

"Yes. Now—now laugh at my secret!"

For a long minute Venters gazed. Then he stretched forth a hand to feel if the gold was real.

"*Gold!*" he almost shouted. "Bess, there are hundreds—thousands of dollars' worth here!"

He leaned over to her, and put his hand, strong and clenching now, on hers.

"Is there more where this came from?" he whispered.

"Plenty of it, all the way up the stream to the cliff. You know I've often washed for gold. Then I've heard the men talk. I think there's no great quantity of gold here, but enough for—for a fortune for *you*."

"That—was—your—secret!"

"Yes. I hate gold. For it makes men mad. I've seen them drunk with joy and dance and fling themselves around. I've seen them curse and rave. I've seen them fight like dogs and roll in the dust. I've seen them kill each other for gold."

"Is that why you hated to tell me?"

"Not—not altogether." Bess lowered her head. "It was because I knew you'd never stay here long after you found gold."

"You were afraid I'd leave you?"

"Yes."

"Listen! . . . You great, simple child! Listen . . . You sweet, wonderful, wild, blued-eyed girl! I was tortured by my secret. It was that I knew we—*we* must leave the valley. We can't stay here much longer. I couldn't think how we'd get away—out of the country—or how we'd live, if we ever got out. I'm a beggar. That's why I kept my secret. I'm poor. It takes money to make way beyond Sterling. We couldn't ride horses or burros or walk forever. So while I knew we must go, I was distracted over how to go and what to do. *Now!* We've gold! Once beyond Sterling, we'll be safe from rustlers. We've no others to fear.

"Oh! Listen! Bess!" Venters now heard his voice ringing high and sweet, and he felt Bess's cold hands in his crushing grasp as she leaned toward him pale, breathless. "This is how much I'd leave you! You made me live again! I'll take you away—far away from this wild country. You'll begin a new life. You'll be happy. You shall see cities, ships, people. You shall have anything your heart craves. All the shame and sorrow of your life shall be forgotten—as if they had never been. This is how much I'd leave you here alone—you sad-eyed girl. I love you! Didn't you know it? How could you fail to know it? I love you! I'm free! I'm a man —a man you've made—no more a beggar! . . . Kiss me! This is how much I'd leave you here alone—you beautiful, strange, unhappy girl. But I'll make you happy. What—what do I care for —your past! I love you! I'll take you home to Illinois—to my mother. Then I'll take you to far places. I'll make up all you've lost. Oh, I know you love me—knew it before you told me. And it changed my life. And you'll go with me, not as my companion as you are here, nor my sister, but, Bess, darling! . . . *As my wife!*"

THE plan eventually decided upon by the lovers was for Venters to go to the village, secure a horse and some kind of a disguise for Bess, or at least less striking apparel than her present garb, and to return post-haste to the valley. Meanwhile, she would add to their store of gold. Then they would strike the long and perilous trail to ride out of Utah. In the event of his inability to fetch back a horse for her, they intended to make the giant sorrel carry double. The gold, a little food, saddle blankets, and Venters's guns were to compose the light outfit with which they would make the start.

"I love this beautiful place," said Bess. "It's hard to think of leaving it."

"Hard! Well, I should think so," replied Venters. "Maybe—in years—" But he did not complete in words his thought that might be possible to return after many years of absence and change.

Once again Bess bade Venters farewell under the shadow of Balancing Rock, and this time it was with whispered hope and tenderness and passionate trust. Long after he had left her, all down through the outlet to the Pass, the clinging clasp of her arms, the sweetness of her lips, and the sense of a new and exquisite birth of character in her remained hauntingly and thrillingly in his mind. The girl who had sadly called herself nameless and nothing had been marvelously transformed in the moment of his avowal of love. It was something to think over, something to warm his heart, but for the present it had absolutely to be forgotten so that all his mind could be addressed to the trip so fraught with danger.

He carried only his rifle, revolver, and a small quantity of bread and meat; and thus lightly burdened, he made swift progress down the slope and out into the valley. Darkness was coming on, and he welcomed it. Stars were blinking when he reached his old hiding-place in the split of cañon wall, and by their aid he slipped through the dense thickets to the grassy enclosure. Wrangle stood in the center of it with his head up, and he appeared black and of gigantic proportions in the dim light. Venters whistled softly, began a slow approach, and then called. The horse snorted and, plunging away with dull, heavy sound of hoofs, he disappeared in the gloom. "Wilder than ever!" muttered Venters. He followed the sorrel into the narrowing split between the walls, and presently had to desist because he could not see a foot in advance. As he went back toward the open Wrangle jumped out of an ebony shadow of cliff and like a thunderbolt shot huge and black past him down into the starlit glade. Deciding that all attempts to catch Wrangle at night would be useless, Venters repaired to the shelving rock where he had hidden saddle and blanket, and there went to sleep.

The first peep of day found him stirring, and as soon as it was light enough to distinguish objects, he took his lasso off his saddle and went out to rope the sorrel. He espied Wrangle at the lower end of the cove and approached him in a perfectly natural manner. When he got near enough, Wrangle evidently recognized him, but was too wild to stand. He ran up the glade and on into the narrow lane between the walls. This favored Venters's speedy capture of the horse, so, coiling his noose ready to throw, he hurried on. Wrangle let Venters get to within a hundred feet and then he broke. But as he plunged by, rapidly getting into his stride, Venters made a perfect throw with the rope. He had time to brace himself for the shock; nevertheless, Wrangle threw him and dragged him several yards before halting.

"You wild devil," said Venters, as he slowly pulled Wrangle up. "Don't you know me? Come now—old fellow—so—so—"

Wrangle yielded to the lasso and then to Venters's strong hand. He was as straggly and wild-looking as a horse left to roam free in the sage. He dropped his long ears and stood readily to be saddled and bridled. But he was exceedingly sensitive, and quivered at every touch and sound. Venters led him to the thicket, and, bending the close saplings to let him squeeze through, at length reached the open. Sharp survey in each direction assured him of the usual lonely nature of the cañon; then he was in the saddle, riding south.

Wrangle's long, swinging canter was a wonderful ground-gainer. His stride was almost twice that of an ordinary horse, and his endurance was equally remarkable. Venters pulled him in occasionally, and walked him up the stretches of rising ground and along the soft washes. Wrangle had never yet shown any indication of distress while Venters rode him. Nevertheless, there was now reason to save the horse; therefore Venters did not resort to the hurry that had characterized his former trip. He camped at the last water in the Pass. What distance that was to Cottonwoods he did not know; he calculated, however, that it was in the neighborhood of fifty miles.

Early in the morning he proceeded on his way, and about the middle of the forenoon reached the constricted gap that marked the southerly end of the Pass, and through which led the trail up to the sage-level. He spied out Lassiter's tracks in the dust, but no others, and dismounting, he straightened out Wrangle's bridle and began to lead him up the trail. The short climb, more severe on beast than on man, necessitated a rest on the level above, and during this he scanned the wide purple reaches of slope.

Wrangle whistled his pleasure at the smell of the sage. Remounting, Venters headed up the white trail with the fragrant wind in his face. He had proceeded for perhaps a couple of miles when Wrangle stopped with a suddenness that threw Venters heavily against the pommel.

"What's wrong, old boy?" called Venters, looking down for a loose shoe or a snake or a foot lamed by a picked-up stone. Unrewarded, he raised himself from his scrutiny. Wrangle stood stiff, head high, with his long ears erect. Thus guided, Venters swiftly gazed ahead to make out a dust-clouded, dark group of horsemen riding down the slope. If they had seen him, it apparently made no difference in their speed or direction.

"Wonder who they are!" exclaimed Venters. He was not disposed to run. His cool mood tightened under grip of excitement as he reflected that, whoever the approaching riders were, they could not be friends. He slipped out of the saddle and led Wrangle behind the tallest sage-brush. It might serve to conceal them until the riders were close enough for him to see who they were; after that he would be indifferent to how soon they discovered him.

After looking to his rifle and ascertaining that it was in working order, he watched, and as he watched, slowly the force of a bitter fierceness, long dormant, gathered ready to flame into life. If those riders were not rustlers he had forgotten how rustlers looked and rode. On they came, a small group, so compact and dark that he could not tell their number. How unusual that their horses did not see Wrangle! But such failure, Venters decided, was owing to the speed with which they were traveling. They moved at a swift canter affected more by rustlers than by riders. Venters grew concerned over the possibility that these horsemen would actually ride down on him before he had a chance to tell what to expect. When they were within three hundred yards he deliberately led Wrangle out into the trail.

Then he heard shouts, and the hard scrape of sliding hoofs, and saw horses rear and plunge back with up-flung heads and flying manes. Several little white puffs of smoke appeared sharply against the black background of riders and horses, and shots rang out. Bullets struck far in front of Venters, and whipped up the dust and then hummed low into the sage. The range was great for revolvers, but whether the shots were meant to kill or merely to check advance, they were enough to fire that waiting ferocity in Venters. Slipping his arm through the bridle, so that Wrangle could not get away, Venters lifted his rifle and pulled the trigger twice.

He saw the first horseman lean sideways and fall. He saw another lurch in his saddle and heard a cry of pain. Then Wrangle, plunging in fright, lifted Venters and nearly threw him. He jerked the horse down with a powerful hand and leaped into the saddle. Wrangle plunged again, dragging his bridle, that Venters had not had time to throw in place. Bending over with a swift movement, he secured it and dropped the loop over the pommel. Then, with grinding teeth, he looked to see what the issue would be.

The band had scattered so as not to afford such a broad mark for bullets. The riders faced Venters, some with red-belching guns. He heard a sharper report, and just as Wrangle plunged again he caught the whizz of a leaden missile that would have hit him but for Wrangle's sudden jump. A swift, hot wave, turning cold, passed over Venters. Deliberately he picked out the one rider with a carbine, and killed him. Wrangle snorted shrilly and bolted into the sage. Venters let him run a few rods, then with iron arm checked him.

Five riders, surely rustlers, were left. One leaped out of the saddle to secure his fallen comrade's carbine. A shot from Venters, which missed the man but sent the dust flying over him, made him run back to his horse. Then they separated. The crippled rider went one way; the one frustrated in his attempt to get the carbine rode another; Venters thought he made out a third rider, carrying a strange-appearing bundle and disappearing in the sage. But in the rapidity of action and vision he could not discern what it was. Two riders with three horses swung out to the right. Afraid of the long rifle—a burdensome weapon seldom carried by rustlers or riders—they had been put to rout.

Suddenly Venters discovered that one of the two men last noted was riding Jane Withersteen's horse Bells—the beautiful bay racer she had given to Lassiter. Venters uttered a savage outcry. Then the small, wiry, frog-like shape of the second rider, and the ease and grace of his seat in the saddle—things so strikingly incongruous—grew more and more familiar in Venters's sight.

"*Jerry Card!*" cried Venters.

It was indeed Tull's right-hand man. Such a white hot wrath inflamed Venters that he fought himself to see with clearer gaze.

"It's Jerry Card!" he exclaimed, instantly. "*And he's riding Black Star and leading Night!*"

The long-kindling, stormy fire in Venters's heart burst into flame. He spurred Wrangle, and as the horse lengthened his stride Venters slipped cartridges into the magazine of his rifle till it was once again full. Card and his companion were now half a mile or more in advance, riding easily down the slope. Venters marked the smooth gait, and understood it when Wrangle galloped out of the sage into the broad cattle trail, down which Venters had once tracked Jane Withersteen's red herd. This hardpacked trail, from years of use, was as clean and smooth as a road. Venters saw Jerry Card look back over his shoulder; the other rider did likewise. Then the three racers lengthened their stride to the point where the swinging canter was ready to break into a gallop.

"Wrangle, the race's on," said Venters, grimly. "We'll canter with them and gallop with them and run with them. We'll let them set the pace."

Venters knew he bestrode the strongest, swiftest, most tireless horse ever ridden by any rider across the Utah uplands. Recalling Jane Withersteen's devoted assurance that Night could run neck and neck with Wrangle, and Black Star could show his heels to him, Venters wished that Jane were there to see the race to recover her blacks and in the unqualified superiority of the giant sorrel. Then Venters found himself thankful that she was absent, for he meant that race to end in Jerry Card's death. The first flush, the raging of Venters's wrath, passed, to leave him in sullen, almost cold possession of his will. It was a deadly mood, utterly foreign to his nature, engendered, fostered, and released by the wild passions of wild men in a wild country. The strength in him then—the thing rife in him that was note hate, but something as remorseless—might have been the fiery fruition of a whole lifetime of vengeful quest. Nothing could have stopped him.

Venters thought out the race shrewdly. The rider on Bells would probably drop behind and take to the sage. What he did was of little moment to Venters. To stop Jerry Card, his evil hidden career as well as his present flight, and then to catch the blacks—that was all that concerned Venters. The cattle trail wound for miles and miles down the slope. Venters saw with a rider's keen vision ten, fifteen, twenty miles of clear purple sage. There were no on-coming riders or rustlers to aid Card. His only chance to escape lay in abandoning the stolen horses and creeping away in the sage to hide. In ten miles Wrangle could run Black Star and Night off their feet, and in fifteen he could kill them outright. So Venters held the sorrel in, letting Card make the running. It was a long race that would save the blacks.

In a few miles of that swinging canter Wrangle had crept appreciably closer to the three horses. Jerry Card turned again, and when he saw how the sorrel had gained, he put Black Star to a gallop. Night and Bells, on either side of him, swept into his stride.

Venters loosened the rein on Wrangle and let him break into a gallop. The sorrel saw the horses ahead and wanted to run. But Venters restrained him. And in the gallop he gained more than in the canter. Bells was fast in that gait, but Black Star and Night had been trained to run. Slowly Wrangle closed the gap down to a quarter of a mile, and crept closer and closer.

Jerry Card wheeled once more. Venters distinctly saw the red flash of his red face. This time he looked long. Venters laughed. He knew what passed in Card's mind. The rider was trying to make out what horse it happened to be that thus gained on Jane Withersteen's peerless racers. Wrangle had so long been away from the village that not improbably Jerry had forgotten. Besides, whatever Jerry's qualifications for his fame as the greatest rider of the sage, certain it was that his best point was not far-sightedness. He had not recognized Wrangle. After what must have been a searching gaze he got his comrade to face about. This action gave Venters amusement. It spoke so surely of the fact that neither Card nor the rustler actually knew their danger. Yet if they kept to the trail—and the last thing such men would do would be to leave it—they were both doomed.

This comrade of Card's whirled far around in his saddle, and he even shaded his eyes from the sun. He, too, looked long. Then, all at once, he faced ahead again and, bending lower in the saddle, began to fling his right arm up and down. That flinging Venters knew to be the lashing of Bells. Jerry also became active. And the three racers lengthened out into a run.

"Now, Wrangle!" cried Venters. "Run, you big devil! Run!"

Venters laid the reins on Wrangle's neck and dropped the loop over the pommel. The sorrel needed no guiding on that smooth trail. He was surer-footed in a run than at any other fast gait, and his running gave the impression of something devilish. He might now have been actuated by Venters's spirit; undoubtedly his savage running fitted the mood of his rider. Venters bent forward, swinging with the horse, and gripped his rifle. His eye measured the distance between him and Jerry Card.

In less than two miles of running Bells began to drop behind the blacks, and Wrangle began to overhaul him. Venters anticipated that the rustler would soon take to the sage. Yet he did not. Not improbably he reasoned that the powerful sorrel could more easily overtake Bells in the heavier going outside of the trail.

Soon only a few hundred yards lay between Bells and Wrangle. Turning in his saddle, the rustler began to shoot, and the bullets beat up little whiffs of dust. Venters raised his rifle, ready to take snap shots, and waited for favorable opportunity when Bells was out of line with the forward horses. Venters had it in him to kill these men as if they were skunk-bitten coyotes, but also he had restraint enough to keep from shooting one of Jane's beloved Arabians.

No great distance was covered, however, before Bells swerved to the left, out of line with Black Star and Night. Then Venters, aiming high and waiting for the pause between Wrangle's great strides, began to take snap shots at the rustler. The fleeing rider presented a broad target for a rifle, but he was moving swiftly forward and bobbing up and down. Moreover, shooting from Wrangle's back was shooting from a thunderbolt. And added to that was the danger of a low-placed bullet taking effect on Bells. Yet, despite these considerations, making the shot exceedingly difficult, Venters's confidence, like his implacability, saw a speedy and fatal termination of that rustler's race. On the sixth shot the rustler threw up his arms and took a flying tumble off his horse. He rolled over and over, hunched himself to a half-erect position, fell, and then dragged himself into the sage. As Venters went thundering by he peered keenly into the sage, but caught no sign of the man. Bells ran a few hundred yards, slowed up, and had stopped when Wrangle passed him.

Again Venters began slipping fresh cartridges into the magazine of his rifle, and his hand was so sure and steady that he did not drop a single cartridge. With the eye of a rider and the judgment of a marksman he once more measured the distance between him and Jerry Card. Wrangle had gained, bringing him into rifle range. Venters was hard put to it now not to shoot, but thought it better to withhold his fire. Jerry, who, in anticipation of a running fusillade, had huddled himself into a little twisted ball on Black Star's neck, now surmising that this pursuer would make sure of not wounding one of the blacks, rose to his natural seat in the saddle.

In his mind perhaps, as certainly as in Venters's, this moment was the beginning of the real race.

Venters leaned forward to put his hand on Wrangle's neck;

then backward to put it on his flank. Under the shaggy, dusty hair trembled and vibrated and rippled a wonderful muscular activity. But Wrangle's flesh was still cold. What a cold-blooded brute, thought Venters, and felt in him a love for the horse he had never given to any other. It would not have been humanly possible for any rider, even though clutched by hate or revenge or a passion to save a loved one or fear of his own life, to be astride the sorrel, to swing with his swing, to see his magnificent stride and hear the rapid thunder of his hoofs, to ride him in that race and not glory in the ride.

So, with his passion to kill still keen and unabated, Venters lived out that ride, and drank a rider's sage-sweet cup of wildness to the dregs.

When Wrangle's long mane, lashing in the wind, stung Venters in the cheek, the sting added a beat to his flying pulse. He bent a downward glance to try to see Wrangle's actual stride, and saw only twinkling, darting streaks and the white rush of the trail. He watched the sorrel's savage head, pointed level, his mouth still closed and dry, but his nostrils distended as if he were snorting unseen fire. Wrangle was the horse for a race with death. Upon each side Venters saw the sage merged into a sailing, colorless wall. In front sloped the lay of ground with its purple breadth split by the white trail. The wind, blowing with heavy, steady blast into his face, sickened him with enduring, sweet odor, and filled his ears with a hollow, rushing roar.

Then for the hundredth time he measured the width of space separating him from Jerry Card. Wrangle had ceased to gain. The blacks were proving their fleetness. Venters watched Jerry Card, admiring the little rider's horsemanship. He had the incomparable seat of the upland rider, born in the saddle. It struck Venters that Card had changed his position, or the position of the horses. Presently Venters remembered positively that Jerry had been leading Night on the right-hand side of the trail. The racer was now on the side to the left. No—it was Black Star. But, Venters argued in amaze, Jerry had been mounted on Black Star. Another clearer, keener gaze assured Venters that Black Star was really riderless. Night now carried Jerry Card.

"He's changed from one to the other!" ejaculated Venters, realizing the astounding feat with unstinted admiration. "Changed at full speed! Jerry Card, that's what you've done unless I'm drunk on the smell of sage. But I've got to see the trick before I believe it."

Thenceforth, while Wrangle sped on, Venters glued his eyes to the little rider. Jerry Card rode as only he could ride. Of all the daring horsemen of the uplands, Jerry was the one rider fitted to bring out the greatness of the blacks in that long race. He had them on a dead run, but not yet at the last strained and killing pace. From time to time he glanced backward, as a wise general in retreat calculating his chances and the power and speed of pursuers, and the moment for the last desperate burst. No doubt, Card, with his life at stake, gloried in that race, perhaps more wildly than Venters. For he had been born to the sage and the saddle and the wild. He was more than half horse. Not until the last call—the sudden up-flashing instinct of self-preservation—would he lose his skill and judgment and nerve and the spirit of that race. Venters seemed to read Jerry's mind. That little crime-stained rider was actually thinking of his horses, husbanding their speed, handling them with knowledge of years, glorying in their beautiful, swift, racing stride, and wanting them to win the race when his own life hung suspended in quivering balance. Again Jerry whirled in his saddle and the sun flashed red on his face. Turning, he drew Black Star closer and closer toward Night, till they ran side by side, as one horse. Then Card raised himself in the saddle, slipped out of the stirrups, and, somehow twisting himself, leaped upon Black Star. He did not even lose the swing of the horse. Like a leech he was there in the other saddle, and as the horses separated, his right foot, that had been apparently doubled under him, shot down to catch the stirrup. The grace and dexterity and daring of that rider's act won something more than admiration from Venters.

For the distance of a mile Jerry rode Black Star and then changed back to Night. But all Jerry's skill and the running of the blacks could avail little more against the sorrel.

Venters peered far ahead, studying the lay of the land. Straight-away for five miles the trail stretched, and then it disappeared in hummocky ground. To the right, some few rods, Venters saw a break in the sage, and this was the rim of Deception Pass. Across the dark cleft gleamed the red of the opposite wall. Venters imagined that the trail went down into the Pass somewhere north of those ridges. And he realized that he must and would over·take Jerry Card in this straight course of five miles.

Cruelly he struck his spurs into Wrangle's flanks. A light touch of spur was sufficient to make Wrangle plunge. And now, with a ringing, wild snort, he seemed to double up in muscular convulsions and to shoot forward with an impetus that almost unseated Venters. The sage blurred by, the trail flashed by, and the wind robbed him of breath and hearing. Jerry Card turned once more. And the way he shifted to Black Star showed he had to make his last desperate running. Venters aimed to the side of the trail and sent a bullet puffing the dust beyond Jerry. Venters hoped to frighten the rider and get him to take to the sage. But Jerry returned the shot, and his ball struck dangerously close in the dust at Wrangle's flying feet. Venters held his fire then, while the rider emptied his revolver. For a mile, with Black Star leaving Night behind and doing his utmost, Wrangle did not gain; for another mile he gained little, if at all. In the third he caught up with the now galloping Night and began to gain rapidly on the other black.

Only a hundred yards now stretched between Black Star and Wrangle. The giant sorrel thundered on—and on—and on. In every yard he gained a foot. He was whistling through his nostrils, wringing wet, flying lather, and as hot as fire. Savage as ever, strong as ever, fast as ever, but each tremendous stride jarred Venters out of the saddle! Wrangle's power and spirit and momentum had begun to run him off his legs. Wrangle's great race was nearly won—and run. Venters seemed to see the expanse before him as a vast, sheeted, purple plain sliding under him. Black Star moved in it as a blur. The rider, Jerry Card, appeared a mere dot bobbing dimly. Wrangle thundered on—on—on! Venters felt the increase in quivering, straining shock after every leap. Flecks of foam flew into Venters's eyes, burning him, making him see all the sage as red. But in that red haze he saw, or seemed to see, Black Star suddenly riderless and with broken gait. Wrangle thundered on to change his pace with a violent break. Then Venters pulled him hard. From run to gallop, gallop to canter, canter to trot, trot to walk, and walk to stop, the great sorrel ended his race.

Venters looked back. Black Star stood riderless in the trail. Jerry Card had taken to the sage. Far up the white trail Night came trotting faithfully down. Venters leaped off, still half blind, reeling dizzily. In a moment he had recovered sufficiently to have a care for Wrangle. Rapidly he took off the saddle and bridle. The sorrel was reeking, heaving, whistling, shaking. But he had still the strength to stand, and for him Venters had no fears.

As Venters ran back to Black Star he saw the horse stagger on shaking legs into the sage and go down in a heap. Upon reaching him Venters removed the saddle and bridle. Black Star had been killed on his legs, Venters thought. He had no hope for the stricken horse. Black Star lay flat, covered with bloody froth, mouth wide, tongue hanging, eyes glaring, and all his beautiful body in convulsions.

Unable to stay there to see Jane's favorite racer die, Venters hurried up the trail to meet the other black. On the way he kept a sharp lookout for Jerry Card. Venters imagined the rider would keep well out of range of the rifle, but, as he would be lost on the sage without a horse, not improbably he would linger in the vicinity on the chance of getting back one of the blacks. Night soon came trotting up, hot and wet and run out. Venters led him down near the others, and unsaddling him, let him loose to rest. Night wearily lay down in the dust and rolled, proving himself not yet spent.

Then Venters sat down to rest and think. Whatever the risk, he was compelled to stay where he was, or comparatively near, for the night. The horses must rest and drink. He must find water. He was now seventy miles from Cottonwoods, and, he believed, close to the cañon where the cattle trail must surely turn off and go down into the Pass. After a while he rose to survey the valley.

He was very near to the ragged edge of a deep cañon into which the trail turned. The ground lay in uneven ridges divided by washes, and these sloped into the cañon. Following the cañon line, he saw where its rim was broken by other intersecting cañons, and farther down red walls and yellow cliffs leading toward a deep blue cleft that he made sure was Deception Pass. Walking out a few rods to a promontory, he found where the trail went down. The descent was gradual, along a stone-walled trail, and Venters felt sure that this was the place where Oldring drove cattle into the Pass. There was, however, no indication at all that he ever had driven cattle out at this point. Oldring had many holes to his burrow.

In searching round in the little hollows Venters, much to his relief, found water. He composed himself to rest and eat some bread and meat, while he waited for a sufficient time to elapse so that he could safely give the horses a drink. He judged the hour to be somewhere around noon. Wrangle lay down to rest and Night followed suit. So long as they were down Venters intended to make no move. The longer they rested the better, and the safer it would be to give them water. By and by he forced himself to go over to where Black Star lay, expecting to find him dead. Instead he found the racer partially if not wholly recovered. There was recognition, even fire, in his big black eyes. Venters was overjoyed. He sat by the black for a long time. Black Star presently labored to his feet with a heave and a groan, shook himself, and snorted for water. Venters repaired to the little pool he had found, filled his sombrero, and gave the racer a drink. Black Star gulped it at one draught, as if it were but a drop, and pushed his nose into the hat and snorted for more. Venters now led Night down to drink, and after a further time Black Star also. Then the blacks began to graze.

The sorrel had wandered off down the sage between the trail and the cañon. Once or twice he disappeared in little swales. Finally Venters concluded Wrangle had grazed far enough, and, taking his lasso, he went to fetch him back. In crossing from one ridge to another he saw where the horse had made muddy a pool of water. It occurred to Venters then that Wrangle had drunk his fill, and did not seem the worse for it, and might be anything but easy to catch. And, true enough, he could not come within roping reach of the sorrel. He tried for an hour, and gave up in disgust. Wrangle did not seem so wild as simply perverse. In a quandary Venters returned to the other horses, hoping much, yet doubting more, that when Wrangle had grazed to suit himself he might be caught.

As the afternoon wore away Venters's concern diminished, yet he kept close watch on the blacks and the trail and the sage. There was no telling of what Jerry Card might be capable. Venters sullenly acquiesced to the idea that the rider had been too

207

quick and too shrewd for him. Strangely and doggedly, however, Venters clung to his foreboding of Card's downfall.

The wind died away; the red sun topped the far distant western rise of slope; and the long, creeping purple shadows lengthened. The rims of the cañons gleamed crimson and the deep clefts appeared to belch forth blue smoke. Silence enfolded the scene.

It was broken by a horrid, long-drawn scream of a horse and the thudding of heavy hoofs. Venters sprang erect and wheeled south. Along the cañon rim, near the edge, came Wrangle, once more in thundering flight.

Venters gasped in amazement. Had the wild sorrel gone mad? His head was high and twisted, in a most singular position for a running horse. Suddenly Venters descried a frog-like shape clinging to Wrangle's neck. Jerry Card! Somehow he had straddled Wrangle and now stuck like a huge burr. But it was his strange position and the sorrel's wild scream that shook Venters's nerves. Wrangle was pounding toward the turn where the trail went down. He plunged onward like a blind horse. More than one of his leaps took him to the very edge of the precipice.

Jerry Card was bent forward with his teeth fast in the front of Wrangle's nose! Venters saw it, and there flashed over him a memory of this trick of a few desperate riders. He even thought of one rider who had worn off his teeth in this terrible hold to break or control desperate horses. Wrangle had indeed gone mad. The marvel was what guided him. Was it the half-brute, the more than half-horse instinct of Jerry Card? Whatever the mystery, it was true. And in a few more rods Jerry would have the sorrel turning into the trail leading down into the cañon.

"No—Jerry!" whispered Venters, stepping forward and throwing up the rifle. He tried to catch the little humped, frog-like shape over the sights. It was moving too fast; it was too small. Yet Venters shot once . . . twice . . . the third time . . . four times . . . five! All wasted shots and precious seconds!

With a deep-muttered curse Venters caught Wrangle through the sights and pulled the trigger. Plainly he heard the bullet thud. Wrangle uttered a horrible strangling sound. In swift death action he whirled, and with one last splendid leap he cleared the cañon rim. And he whirled downward with the little frog-like shape clinging to his neck!

There was a pause which seemed never ending, a shock, and an instant's silence.

Then up rolled a heavy crash, a long roar of sliding rocks dying away in distant echo, then silence unbroken.

Wrangle's race was run.

CHAPTER XVIII

SOME forty hours or more later Venters created a commotion **in** Cottonwoods by riding down the main street on Black Star and leading Bells and Night. He had come upon Bells grazing near the body of a dead rustler, the only incident of his quick ride into the village.

Nothing was farther from Venters's mind than bravado. No thought came to him of the defiance and boldness of riding Jane Withersteen's racers straight into the archplotter's stronghold. He wanted men to see the famous Arabians; he wanted men to see them dirty and dusty, bearing all the signs of having been driven to their limit; he wanted men to see and to know that the thieves who had ridden them out into the sage had not ridden them back. Venters had come for that and for more—he wanted to meet Tull face to face; if not Tull, then Dyer; if not Dyer, then anyone in the secret of these master conspirators. Such was Venters's passion. The meeting with the rustlers, the unprovoked attack upon him, the spilling of blood, the recognition of Jerry Card and the horses, the race, and that last plunge of mad Wrangle—all these things, fuel on fuel to the smoldering fire, had kindled and swelled and leaped into living flame. He could have shot Dyer in the midst of his religious services at the altar; he could have killed Tull in front of wives and babes.

He walked the three racers down the broad, green-bordered village road. He heard the murmur of running water from Amber Spring. Bitter waters for Jane Withersteen! Men and women stopped to gaze at him and the horses. All knew him; all knew the blacks and the bay. As well as if it had been spoken, Venters read in the faces of men the intelligence that Jane Withersteen's Arabians had been known to have been stolen. Venters reined in and halted before Dyer's residence. It was a low, long, stone structure resembling Withersteen House. The spacious front yard was green and luxuriant with grass and flowers; gravel walks led to the hugh porch; a well-trimmed hedge of purple sage separated the yard from the church grounds; birds sang in the trees; water flowed musically along the walks; and there were glad, careless shouts of children. For Venters the beauty of this home, and the serenity and its apparent happiness, all turned red and black. For Venters a shade overspread the lawn, the flowers, the old vine-clad stone house. In the music of the singing birds, in the murmur of the running water, he heard an ominous sound. Quiet beauty—sweet music—innocent laughter! By what monstrous abortion of fate did these abide in the shadow of Dyer?

Venters rode on and stopped before Tull's cottage. Women stared at him with white faces and then flew from the porch. Tull himself appeared at the door, bent low, craning his neck. His dark face flashed out of sight; the door banged; a heavy bar dropped with a hollow sound.

Then Venters shook Black Star's bridle, and, sharply trotting, led the other horses to the center of the village. Here at the intersecting streets and in front of the stores he halted once more. The usual lounging atmosphere of that prominenet corner was not now in evidence. Riders and ranchers and villagers broke up what must have been absorbing conversation. There was a rush of many feet, and then the walk was lined with faces.

Venters's glance swept down the line of silent stone-faced men. He recognized many riders and villagers, but none of those he had hoped to meet. There was no expression in the faces turned toward him. All of them knew him, most were inimical, but there were few who were not burning with curiosity and wonder in regard to the return of Jane Withersteen's racers. Yet all were silent. Here were the familiar characteristics—masked feeling—strange secretiveness—expressionless expression of mystery and hidden power.

"Has anybody here seen Jerry Card?" queried Venters, in a loud voice.

In reply there came not a word, not a nod or shake of head,

not so much as dropping eye or twitching lip—nothing but a quiet, stony stare.

"Been under the knife? You've a fine knife-wielder here—one Tull, I believe! . . . Maybe you've all had your tongues cut out?"

This passionate sarcasm of Venters brought no response, and the stony calm was as oil on the fire within him.

"I see some of you pack guns, too!" he added, in biting scorn. In the long, tense pause, strung keenly as a tight wire, he sat motionless on Black Star. "All right," he went on. "Then let some of you take this message to Tull. Tell him I've seen Jerry Card! . . . Tell him Jerry Card *will never return!*"

Thereupon, in the same dead calm, Venters backed Black Star away from the curb, into the street, and out of range. He was ready now to ride up to Withersteen House and turn the racers over to Jane.

"Hello, Venters!" a familiar voice cried, hoarsely, and he saw a man running toward him. It was the rider Judkins who came up and gripped Venters's hand. "Venters, I could hev dropped when I seen them hosses. But thet sight ain't a marker to the looks of you. What's wrong? Hev you gone crazy? You must be crazy to ride in here this way—with them hosses—talkin' thet way about Tull an' Jerry Card."

"Jud, I'm not crazy—only mad clean through," replied Venters.

"Wal, now, Bern, I'm glad to hear some of your old self in your voice. Fer when you come up you looked like the corpse of a dead rider with fire fer eyes. You hed thet crowd too stiff fer throwin' guns. Come, we've got to hev a talk. Let's go up the lane. We ain't much safe here."

Judkins mounted Bells and rode with Venters up to the cottonwood grove. Here they dismounted and went among the trees.

"Let's hear from you first," said Judkins. "You fetched back them hosses. Thet *is* the trick. An', of course, you got Jerry the same as you got Horne."

"Horne!"

"Sure. He was found dead yesterday all chewed by coyotes, an' he'd been shot plumb center."

"Where was he found?"

"At the split down the trail—you know where Oldrin's cattle trail runs off north from the trail to the pass."

212

"That's where I met Jerry and the rustlers. What was Horne doing with them? I thought Horne was an honest cattle-man."

"Lord—Bern, don't ask me thet! I'm all muddled now tryin' to figure things."

Venters told of the fight and the race with Jerry Card and its tragic conclusion.

"I knowed it! I knowed all along that Wrangle was the best hoss!" exclaimed Judkins, with his lean face working and his eyes lighting. "Thet was a race! Lord, I'd like to hev seen Wrangle jump the cliff with Jerry. An' thet was good-by to the grandest hoss an' rider ever on the sage! . . . But, Bern, after you got the hosses why'd you want to bolt right in Tull's face?"

"I want him to know. An' if I can get to him I'll—"

"You can't get near Tull," interrupted Judkins. "Thet vigilante bunch hev taken to bein' bodyguard for Tull an' Dyer, too."

"Hasn't Lassiter made a break yet?" inquired Venters, curiously.

"Naw!" replied Judkins, scornfully. "Jane turned his head. He's mad in love over her—follers her like a dog. He ain't no more Lassiter! He's lost his nerve; he doesn't look like the same feller. It's village talk. Everybody knows it. He hasn't thrown a gun, an' he won't!"

"Jud, I'll bet he does," replied Venters, earnestly. "Remember what I say. This Lassiter is something more than a gun-man. Jud, he's big—he's great! . . . I feel that in him. God help Tull and Dyer when Lassiter does go after them. For horses and riders and stone walls won't save them."

"Wal, hev it your way, Bern. I hope you're right. Nat'rully I've been some sore on Lassiter fer gittin' soft. But I ain't denyin' his nerve, or whatever's great in him thet sort of paralyzes people. No later 'n this mornin' I seen him saunterin' down the lane, quiet an' slow. An' like his guns he comes black—*black*, thet's Lassiter. Wal, the crowd on the corner never batted an eye, an' I'll gamble my hoss thet there wasn't one who hed a heartbeat till Lassiter got by. He went in Snell's saloon, an' as there wasn't no gun play I had to go in, too. An' there, darn my pictures, if Lassiter wasn't standin' to the bar, drinkin' an' talkin' with Oldrin'."

"*Oldring!*" whispered Venters. His voice, as all fire and pulse within him, seemed to freeze.

"Let go my arm!" exclaimed Judkins. "Thet's my bad arm. Sure it was Oldrin'. What the hell's wrong with you, anyway? Venters, I tell you somethin's wrong. You're whiter 'n a sheet. You can't be *scared* of the rustler. I don't believe you've got a scare in you. Wal, now, jest let me talk. You know I like to talk, an' if I'm slow I allus git there sometime. As I said, Lassiter was talkin' chummy with Oldrin'. There wasn't no hard feelin's. An' the gang wasn't payin' no pertic'lar attention. But like a cat watchin' a mouse I hed my eyes on them two fellers. It was strange to me, thet confab. I'm gittin' to think a lot, fer a feller who doesn't know much. There's been some queer deals lately an' this seemed to me the queerest. These men stood to the bar alone, an' so close their big gun-hilts butted together. I seen Oldrin' was some surprised at first, an' Lassiter was cool as ice. They talked, an' presently at somethin' Lassiter said the rustler bawled out a curse, an' then he jest fell up against the bar, an' sagged there. The gang in the saloon looked around an' laughed, an' thet's about all. Finally Oldrin' turned, and it was easy to see somethin' hed shook him. Yes, sir, thet big rustler—you know he's as broad as he is long, an' the powerfulest build of a man—yes, sir, the nerve had been taken out of him. Then, after a little, he began to talk an' said a lot to Lassiter, an' by an' by it didn't take much of an eye to see thet Lassiter was gittin' hit hard. I never seen him anyway but cooler 'n ice—till then. He seemed to be hit harder 'n Oldrin', only he didn't roar out thet way. He jest kind of sunk in, an' looked an' looked, an' he didn't see a livin' soul in thet saloon. Then he sort of come to, an' shakin' hands—mind you, *shakin' hands* with Oldrin'—he went out. I couldn't help thinkin' how easy even a boy could hev dropped the great gun-man then! . . . Wal, the rustler stood at the bar fer a long time, an' he was seein' things far off, too; then he come to an' roared fer whisky, an' gulped a drink thet was big enough to drown me."

"Is Oldring here now?" whispered Venters. He could not speak above a whisper. Judkins's story had been meaningless to him.

"He's at Snell's yet. Bern, I hevn't told you yet thet the rustlers hev been raisin' hell. They shot up Stone Bridge an' Glaze, an' fer three days they've been here drinkin' an' gamblin' an' throwin' of gold. These rustlers hev a pile of gold. If it was gold dust or nugget gold I'd hev reason to think, but it's new coin gold, as if it had jest come from the United States treasury. An' the coin's genuine. Thet's all been proved. The truth is Oldrin's on a rampage. A while back he lost his Masked Rider, an' they say he's wild about thet. I'm wonderin' if Lassiter could hev told the rustler anythin' about thet little masked, hard-ridin' devil. Ride! He was most as good as Jerry Card. An', Bern, I've been wonderin' if you know—"

"Judkins, you're a good fellow," interrupted Venters. "Some day I'll tell you a story. I've no time now. Take the horses to Jane."

Judkins stared, and then, muttering to himself, he mounted Bells, and stared again at Venters, and then, leading the other horses, he rode into the grove and disappeared.

Once, long before, on the night Venters had carried Bess through the cañon and up into Surprise Valley, he had experienced the strangeness of faculties singularly, tinglingly acute. And now the same sensation recurred. But it was different in that he felt cold, frozen, mechanical, incapable of free thought, and all about him seemed unreal, aloof, remote. He hid his rifle in the sage, marking its exact location with extreme care. Then he faced down the lane and strode toward the center of the village. Perceptions flashed upon him, the faint, cold touch of the breeze, a cold, silvery tinkle of flowing water, a cold sun shining out of a cold sky, song of birds and laugh of children, coldly distant. Cold and intangible were all things in earth and heaven. Colder and tighter stretched the skin over his face; colder and harder grew the polished butts of his guns; colder and steadier became his hands as he wiped the clammy sweat from his face or reached low to his gunsheaths. Men meeting him in the walk gave him wide berth. In front of Bevin's store a crowd melted apart for his passage, and their faces and whispers were faces and whispers of a dream. He turned a corner to meet Tull face to face, eye to eye. As once before he had seen this man pale to a ghastly, livid white, so again he saw the change. Tull stopped in his tracks, with right hand raised and shaking. Suddenly it dropped, and he seemed to glide aside, to pass out of Venters's sight. Next he saw many horses with bridles down—all clean-limbed, dark bays or blacks—

rustlers' horses! Loud voices and boisterous laughter, rattle of dice and scrape of chair and clink of gold, burst in mingled din from an open doorway. He stepped inside.

With the sight of smoke-hazed room and drinking, cursing, gambling, dark-visaged men, reality once more dawned upon Venters.

His entrance had been unnoticed, and he bent his gaze upon the drinkers at the bar. Dark-clothed, dark-faced men they all were, burned by the sun, bow-legged as were most riders of the sage, but neither lean nor gaunt. Then Venters's gaze passed to the tables, and swiftly it swept over the hard-featured gamesters, to alight upon the huge, shaggy, black head of the rustler chief.

"*Oldring!*" he cried, and to him his voice seemed to split a bell in his ears.

It stilled the din.

That silence suddenly broke to the scrape and crash of Oldring's chair as he rose; and then, while he passed, a great gloomy figure, again the thronged room stilled in silence yet deeper.

"Oldring, a word with you!" continued Venters.

"Ho! What's this?" boomed Oldring, in frowning scrutiny.

"Come outside, alone. A word for you—*from your Masked Rider!*"

Oldring kicked a chair out of his way and lunged forward with a stamp of heavy boot that jarred the floor. He waved down his muttering, rising men.

Venters backed out of the door and waited, hearing, as no sound had ever before struck into his soul, the rapid, heavy steps of the rustler.

Oldring appeared, and Venters had one glimpse of his great breadth and bulk, his gold-buckled belt with hanging guns, his high-top boots with gold spurs. In that moment Venters had a strange, unintelligible curiosity to see Oldring alive. The rustler's broad brow, his large black eyes, his sweeping beard, as dark as the wing of a raven, his enormous width of shoulder and depth of chest, his whole splendid presence so wonderfully charged with vitality and force and strength, seemed to afford Venters an unutterable fiendish joy because for that magnificent manhood and life he meant cold and sudden death.

"Oldring, Bess is alive! But she's dead to you—dead to the life you made her lead—dead as you will be in one second!"

Swift as lightning Venters's glance dropped from Oldring's rolling eyes to his hands. One of them, the right, swept out, then toward his gun—and Venters shot him through the heart.

Slowly Oldring sank to his knees, and the hand, dragging at the gun, fell away. Venters's strangely acute faculties grasped the meaning of that limp arm, of the swaying hulk, of the gasp and heave, of the quivering beard. But was that awful spirit in the black eyes only one of vitality?

"Man—why—didn't—you—wait? Bess—was—" Oldring's whisper died under his beard, and with a heavy lurch he fell forward.

Bounding swiftly away, Venters fled around the corner, across the street, and, leaping a hedge, he ran through yard, orchard, and garden to the sage. Here, under cover of the tall brush, he turned west and ran on to the place where he had hidden his rifle. Securing that, he again set out into a run, and, circling through the sage, came up behind Jane Withersteen's stable and corrals. With laboring, dripping chest, and pain as of a knife thrust in his side, he stopped to regain his breath, and while resting his eyes roved around in search of a horse. Doors and windows of the stable were open wide and had a deserted look. One dejected, lonely burro stood in the near corral. Strange indeed was the silence brooding over the once happy, noisy home of Jane Withersteen's pets.

He went into the corral, exercising care to leave no tracks, and led the burro to the watering-trough. Venters, though not thirsty, drank till he could drink no more. Then, leading the burro over hard ground, he struck into the sage and down the slope.

He strode swiftly, turning from time to time to scan the slope for riders. His head just topped the level of sage-brush, and the burro could not have been seen at all. Slowly the green of Cottonwoods sank behind the slope, and at last a wavering line of purple sage met the blue of sky.

To avoid being seen, to get away, to hide his trail—these were the sole ideas in his mind as he headed for Deception Pass; and he directed all his acuteness of eye and ear, and the keenness of a rider's judgment for distance and ground, to stern accomplishment of the task. He kept to the sage far to the left of the trail leading into the Pass. He walked ten miles and looked back a thousand times. Always the graceful, purple wave of sage remained wide and lonely, a clear, undotted waste. Coming to a stretch of rocky ground, he took advantage of it to cross the trail and then continued down on the right. At length he persuaded himself that he would be able to see riders mounted on horses before they could see him on the little burro, and he rode bareback.

Hour by hour the tireless burro kept to his faithful, steady trot. The sun sank and the long shadows lengthened down the slope. Moving veils of purple twilight crept out of the hollows and, mustering and forming on the levels, soon merged and shaded into night. Venters guided the burro nearer to the trail, so that he could see its white line from the ridges, and rode on through the hours.

Once down in the Pass without leaving a trail, he would hold himself safe for the time being. When late in the night he reached the break in the sage, he sent the burro down ahead of him, and started an avalanche that all but buried the animal at the bottom of the trail. Bruised and battered as he was, he had a moment's elation, for he had hidden his tracks. Once more he mounted the burro and rode on. The hour was the blackest of the night when he made the thicket which inclosed his old camp. Here he turned the burro loose in the grass near the spring, and then lay down on his old bed of leaves.

He felt only vaguely, as outside things, the ache and burn and throb of the muscles of his body. But a dammed-up torrent of emotion at last burst its bounds, and the hour that saw his release from immediate action was one that confounded him in the reaction of his spirit. He suffered without understanding why. He caught glimpses into himself, into unlit darkness of soul. The fire that had blistered him and the cold which had frozen him now united in one torturing possession of his mind and heart, and like a fiery steed with ice-shod feet, ranged his being, ran rioting through his blood, trampling the resurging good, dragging ever at the evil.

Out of the subsiding chaos came a clear question. What had happened? He had left the valley to go to Cottonwoods. Why?

It seemed that he had gone to kill a man—Oldring! The name riveted his consciousness upon the one man of all men upon earth whom he had wanted to meet. He had met the rustler. Venters recalled the smoky haze of the saloon, the dark-visaged men, the huge Oldring. He saw him step out of the door, a splendid specimen of manhood, a handsome giant with purple-black and sweeping beard. He remembered inquisitive gaze of falcon eyes. He heard himself repeating: *"Oldring, Bess is alive! But she's dead to you,"* and he felt himself jerk, and his ears throbbed to the thunder of a gun, and he saw the giant sink slowly to his knees. Was that only the vitality of him—that awful light in the eyes—only the hard-dying life of a tremendously powerful brute? A broken whisper, strange as death: *"Man—why—didn't—you wait! Bess—was—"* And Oldring plunged face forward, dead.

"I killed him," cried Venters, in remembering shock. "But it wasn't *that*. Ah, the look in his eyes and his whisper!"

Herein lay the secret that had clamored to him through all the tumult and stress of his emotions. What a look in the eyes of a man shot through the heart! It had been neither hate nor ferocity nor fear of men nor fear of death. It had been no passionate, glinting spirit of a fearless foe, willing shot for shot, life for life, but lacking physical power. Distinctly recalled now, never to be forgotten, Venters saw in Oldring's magnificent eyes the rolling of great, glad surprise—softness—love! Then came a shadow and the terrible superhuman striving of his spirit to speak. Oldring, shot through the heart, had fought and forced back death, not for a moment in which to shoot or curse, but to whisper strange words.

What words for a dying man to whisper! Why had not Venters waited? For what? That was no plea for life. It was regret that there was not a moment of life left in which to speak. Bess was— Herein lay renewed torture for Venters. What had Bess been to Oldring? The old question, like a specter, stalked from its grave to haunt him. He had overlooked, he had forgiven, he had loved, and he had forgotten; and now, out of the mystery of a dying man's whisper rose again that perverse, unsatisfied, jealous uncertainty. Bess had loved that splendid, black-crowned giant— by her own confession she had loved him; and in Venters's soul again flamed up the jealous hell. Then into the clamoring hell burst the shot that had killed Oldring, and it rang in a wild, fiendish gladness, a hateful, vengeful joy. That passed to the memory of the love and light in Oldring's eyes and the mystery in his whisper. So the changing, swaying emotions fluctuated in Venters's heart.

This was the climax of his year of suffering and the crucial struggle of his life. And when the gray dawn came he rose, a gloomy, almost heartbroken man, but victor over evil passions. He could not change the past; and, even if he had not loved Bess with all his soul, he had grown into a man who would not change the future he had planned for her. Only, and once for all, he must know the truth, know the worst, stifle all these insistent doubts and subtle hopes and jealous fancies, and kill the past by knowing truly what Bess had been to Oldring. For that matter he knew—he had always known, but he must hear it spoken. Then, when they had safely gotten out of that wild country to take up a new and an absorbing life, she would forget, she would be happy, and through that, in the years to come, he could not but find life worth living.

All day he rode slowly and cautiously up the Pass, taking time to peer around corners, to pick out hard ground and grassy patches, and to make sure there was no one in pursuit. In the night sometime he came to the smooth, scrawled rocks dividing the valley, and here set the burro at liberty. He walked beyond, climbed the slope and the dim, starlit gorge. Then, weary to the point of exhaustion, he crept into a shallow cave and fell asleep.

In the morning, when he descended the trail, he found the sun was pouring a golden stream of light through the arch of the great stone bridge. Surprise Valley, like a valley of dreams, lay mystically soft and beautiful, awakening to the golden flood which was rolling away its slumberous bands of mist, brightening its walled faces.

While yet far off he discerned Bess moving under the silver spruces, and soon the barking of the dogs told him that they had seen him. He heard the mocking-birds singing in the trees, and then the twittering of the quail. Ring and Whitie came bounding toward him, and behind them ran Bess, her hands outstretched.

"Bern! You're back! You're back!" she cried, in joy that rang of her loneliness.

"Yes, I'm back," he said, as she rushed to meet him.

She had reached out for him when suddenly, as she saw him closely, something checked her, and as quickly all her joy fled, and with it her color, leaving her pale and trembling.

"Oh! What's happened?"

"A good deal has happened, Bess. I don't need to tell you what. And I'm played out. Worn out in mind more than body."

"Dear—you look strange to me!" faltered Bess.

"Never mind that. I'm all right. There's nothing for you to be scared about. Things are going to turn out just as we have planned. As soon as I'm rested we'll make a break to get out of the country. Only now, right now, I must know the truth about you."

"Truth about me?" echoed Bess, shrinkingly. She seemed to be casting back into her mind for a forgotten key. Venters himself, as he saw her, received a pang.

"Yes—the truth. Bess, don't misunderstand. I haven't changed that way. I love you still. I'll love you more afterward. Life will be just as sweet—sweeter to us. We'll be—be married as soon as ever we can. We'll be happy—but there's a devil in me. A perverse, jealous devil! Then I've queer fancies. I forgot for a long time. Now all those fiendish little whispers of doubt and faith and fear and hope come torturing me again. I've got to kill them with the truth."

"I'll tell you anything you want to know," she replied, frankly.

"Then, by Heaven! we'll have it over and done with! . . . Bess —did Oldring love you?"

"Certainly he did."

"Did—did you love him?"

"Of course. I told you so."

"How can you tell it so lightly?" cried Venters, passionately. "Haven't you any sense of—of—" He choked back speech. He felt the rush of pain and passion. He seized her in rude, strong hands and drew her close. He looked straight into her dark-blue eyes. They were shadowing with the old wistful light, but they were as clear as the limpid water of the spring. They were earnest, solemn in unutterable love and faith and abnegation. Venters shivered. He knew he was looking into her soul. He knew she could not lie in that moment; but that she might tell the truth, looking at him with those eyes, almost killed his belief in purity.

"What are—what were you to—to Oldring?" he panted, fiercely.

"I am his daughter," she replied, instantly.

Venters slowly let go of her. There was a violent break in the force of his feeling—then creeping blankness.

"What—was it—you said?" he asked, in a kind of dull wonder.

"I am his daughter."

"Oldring's daughter?" queried Venters, with life gathering in his voice.

"Yes."

With a passionately awakening start he grasped her hands and drew her close.

"All the time—you've been Oldring's daughter?"

"Yes, of course all the time—always."

"But Bess, you told me—you let me think—I made out you were—a—so—so ashamed."

"It is my shame," she said, with voice deep and full, and now the scarlet fired her cheek. "I told you—I'm nothing—nameless—just Bess, Oldring's girl!"

"I know—I remember. But I never thought—" he went on, hurriedly, huskily. "That time—when you lay dying—you prayed —you—somehow I got the idea you were bad."

"Bad?" she asked, with a little laugh.

She looked up with a faint smile of bewilderment and the absolute unconsciousness of a child. Venters gasped in the gathering might of the truth. She did not understand his meaning.

"Bess! Bess!" He clasped her in his arms, hiding her eyes against his breast. She must not see his face in that moment. And he held her while he looked out across the valley. In his dim and blinded sight, in the blur of golden light and moving mist, he saw Oldring. She was the rustler's nameless daughter. Oldring had loved her. He had so guarded her, so kept her from women and men and knowledge of life that her mind was as a child's. That was part of the secret—part of the mystery. That was the wonderful truth. Not only was she not bad, but good, pure, innocent above all innocence in the world—the innocence of lonely girlhood.

He saw Oldring's magnificent eyes, inquisitive, searching—

softening. He saw them flare in amaze, in gladness, with love, then suddenly strain in terrible effort of will. He heard Oldring whisper and saw him sway like a log and fall. Then a million bellowing, thundering voices—gunshots of conscience, thunderbolts of remorse—dinned horribly in his ears. He had killed Bess's father. Then a rushing wind filled his ears like a moan of wind in the cliffs, a knell indeed—Oldring's knell.

He dropped to his knees and hid his face against Bess, and grasped her with the hands of a drowning man.

"My God! . . . My God! . . . Oh, Bess! . . . Forgive me! Never mind what I've done—what I've thought. But forgive me. I'll give you my life. I'll live for you. I'll love you. Oh, I do love you as no man ever loved a woman. I want you to know—to remember that I fought a fight for you—however blind I was. I thought—I thought—never mind what I thought—but I loved you—I asked you to marry me. Let that—let me have that to hug to my heart. Oh, Bess, I was driven! And I might have known! I could not rest nor sleep till I had this mystery solved. God! how things work out!"

"Bern, you're weak—trembling—you talk wildly," cried Bess. "You've overdone your strength. There's nothing to forgive. There's no mystery except your love for me. You have come back to me!"

And she clasped his head tenderly in her arms and pressed it closely to her throbbing breast.

CHAPTER XIX

FAY

AT the home of Jane Withersteen Little Fay was climbing Lassiter's knee.

"Does oo love me?" she asked.

Lassiter, who was as serious with Fay as he was gentle and loving, assured her in earnest and elaborate speech that he was her devoted subject. Fay looked thoughtful and appeared to be debating the duplicity of men or searching for a supreme test to prove this cavalier.

"Does oo love my new muvver?" she asked, with bewildering suddenness.

Jane Withersteen laughed, and for the first time in many a day she felt a stir of her pulse and warmth in her cheek.

It was a still drowsy summer of afternoon, and the three were sitting in the shade of the wooded knoll that faced the sage-slope. Little Fay's brief spell of unhappy longing for her mother—the childish, mystic gloom—had passed, and now where Fay was there were prattle and laughter and glee. She had emerged from sorrow to be the incarnation of joy and loveliness. She had grown supernaturally sweet and beautiful. For Jane Withersteen the child was an answer to prayer, a blessing, a possession infinitely more precious than all she had lost. For Lassiter, Jane divined that little Fay had become a religion.

"Does oo love my new muvver?" repeated Fay.

Lassiter's answer to this was a modest and sincere affirmative.

"Why don't oo marry my new muvver an' be my favver?"

Of the thousands of questions put by little Fay to Lassiter that was the first he had been unable to answer.

"Fay—Fay, don't ask questions like that," said Jane.

"Why?"

"Because," replied Jane. And she found it strangely embarrassing to meet the child's gaze. It seemed to her that Fay's violet eyes looked through her with piercing wisdom.

"Oo love him, don't oo?"

"Dear child—run and play," said Jane, "but don't go too far. Don't go from this little hill."

Fay pranced off wildly, joyous over freedom that had not been granted her for weeks.

"Jane, why are children more sincere than grown-up persons?" asked Lassiter.

"Are they?"

"I reckon so. Little Fay there—she sees things as they appear on the face. An Indian does that. So does a dog. An' an Indian an' a dog are most of the time right in what they see. Mebbe a child is always right."

"Well, what does Fay see?" asked Jane.

"I reckon you know. I wonder what goes on in Fay's mind when she sees part of the truth with the wise eyes of a child, an' wantin' to know more, meets with strange falseness from you? Wait! You are false in a way, though you're the best woman I ever knew. What I want to say is this. Fay has taken you're pretendin' to—to care for me for the thing it looks on the face. An' her little formin' mind asks questions. An' the answers she gets are different from the looks of things. So she'll grow up, gradually takin' on that falseness, an' be like the rest of the women, an' men, too. An' the truth of this falseness to life is proved by your appearin' to love me when you don't. Things aren't what they seem."

"Lassiter, you're right. A child should be told the absolute truth. But—is that possible? I haven't been able to do it, and all my life I've loved the truth, and I've prided myself upon being truthful. Maybe that was only egotism. I'm learning much, my friend. Some of those blinding scales have fallen from my eyes. And— and as to caring for you, I think I care a great deal. How much, how little, I couldn't say. My heart is almost broken, Lassiter. So now is not a good time to judge of affection. I can still play and be merry with Fay. I can still dream. But when I attempt serious thought I'm dazed. I don't think. I don't care any more.

I don't pray! . . . Think of that, my friend! But in spite of my numb feeling I believe I'll rise out of all this dark agony a better woman, with greater love of man and God. I'm on the rack now; I'm senseless to all but pain, and growing dead to that. Sooner or later I shall rise out of this stupor. I'm waiting the hour."

"It 'll soon come, Jane," replied Lassiter, soberly. "Then I'm afraid for you. Years are terrible things, an' for years you've been bound. Habit of years is strong as life itself. Somehow, though, I believe as you—that you'll come out of it all a finer woman. I'm waitin', too. An' I'm wonderin'—I reckon, Jane, that marriage between us is out of all human reason?"

"Lassiter! . . . My dear friend! . . . It's impossible for us to marry."

"Why—as Fay says?" inquired Lassiter, with gentle persistence.

"Why! I never thought why. But it's not possible. I am Jane, daughter of Withersteen. My father would rise out of his grave. I'm of Mormon birth. I'm being broken. But I'm still a Mormon woman. And you—you are Lassiter!"

"Mebbe I'm not so much Lassiter as I used to be."

"What was it you said? Habit of years is strong as life itself! You can't change the one habit—the purpose of your life. For you still pack those black guns! You still nurse your passion for blood."

A smile, like a shadow, flickered across his face.

"No."

"Lassiter, I lied to you. But I beg of you—don't you lie to me. I've great respect for you. I believe you're softened toward most, perhaps all, my people except— But when I speak of your purpose, your hate, your guns, I have only him in mind. I don't believe you've changed."

For answer he unbuckled the heavy cartridge-belt, and laid it with the heavy, swing gun-sheaths in her lap.

"Lassiter!" Jane whispered, as she gazed from him to the black, cold guns. Without them he appeared shorn of strength, defenseless, a smaller man. Was she Delilah? Swiftly, conscious of only one motive—refusal to see this man called craven by his enemies—she rose, and with blundering fingers buckled the belt round his waist where it belonged.

"Lassiter, *I* am a coward."

"Come with me out of Utah—where I can put away my guns an' be a man," he said. "I reckon I'll prove it to you then! Come! You've got Black Star back, an' Night an' Bells. Let's take the racers an' little Fay, an' ride out of Utah. The hosses an' the child are all you have left. Come!"

"No, no, Lassiter. I'll never leave Utah. What would I do in the world with my broken fortunes and my broken heart? I'll never leave these purple slopes I love so well."

"I reckon I ought to 've knowed that. Presently you'll be livin' down here in a hovel, an' presently Jane Withersteen will be a memory. I only wanted to have a chance to show you how a man—*any* man—can be better 'n he was. If we left Utah I could prove—I reckon I could prove this thing you call love. It's strange, an' hell an' heaven at once, Jane Withersteen. 'Pears to me that you've thrown away your big heart on love—love of religion an' duty an' churchmen, an' riders an' poor families an' poor children! Yet you can't see what love is—how it changes a person! . . . Listen, an' in tellin' you Milly Erne's story I'll show you how love changed her.

"Milly an' me was children when our family moved from Missouri to Texas, an' we growed up in Texas ways same as if we'd been born there. We had been poor, an' there we prospered. In time the little village where we went became a town, an' strangers an' new families kept movin' in. Milly was the belle them days. I can see her now, a little girl no bigger 'n a bird, an' as pretty. She had the finest eyes, dark blue-black when she was excited, an' beautiful all the time. You remember Milly's eyes! An' she had light-brown hair with streaks of gold, an' a mouth that every feller wanted to kiss.

"An' about the time Milly was the prettiest an' the sweetest, along came a young minister who began to ride some of a race with the other fellers for Milly. An' he won. Milly had always been strong on religion, an' when she met Frank Erne she went in heart an' soul for the salvation of souls. Fact was, Milly, through study of the Bible an' attendin' church an' revivals, went a little out of her head. It didn't worry the old folks none, an' the only worry to me was Milly's everlastin' prayin' an' workin' to save my soul. She never converted me, but we was the best of comrades, an' I reckon no brother an' sister ever loved each other

227

better. Well, Frank Erne an' me hit up a great friendship. He was a strappin' feller, good to look at, an' had the most pleasin' ways. His religion never bothered me, for he could hunt an' fish an' ride an' be a good feller. After buffalo once, he come pretty near to savin' my life. We got to be thick as brothers, an' he was the only man I ever seen who I thought was good enough for Milly. An' the day they were married I got drunk for the only time in my life.

"Soon after that I left home—it seems Milly was the only one who could keep me home—an' I went to the bad, as to prosperin'. I saw some pretty hard life in the Pan Handle, an' then I went North. In them days Kansas an' Nebraska was as bad, come to think of it, as these days right here on the border of Utah. I got to be pretty handy with guns. An' there wasn't many riders as could beat me ridin'. An' I can say all modest-like that I never seen the white man who could track a hoss or a steer or a man with me. Afore I knowed it two years slipped by, an' all at once I got homesick, an' pulled a bridle south.

"Things at home had changed. I never got over that home-comin'. Mother was dead an' in her grave. Father was a silent, broken man, killed already on his feet. Frank Erne was a ghost of his old self, through with workin', through with preachin', almost through with livin', an' Milly was gone! . . . It was a long time before I got the story. Father had no mind left, an' Frank Erne was *afraid* to talk. So I had to pick up what'd happened from different people.

"It 'pears that soon after I left home another preacher come to the little town. An' he an' Frank become rivals. This feller was different from Frank. He preached some other kind of religion, and he was quick an' passionate, where Frank was slow an' mild. He went after people, women specially. In looks he couldn't compare to Frank Erne, but he had power over women. He had a voice, an' he talked an' talked an' preached an' preached. Milly fell under his influence. She became mightily interested in his religion. Frank had patience with her, as was his way, an' let her be as interested as she liked. All religions were devoted to one God, he said, an' it wouldn't hurt Milly none to study a different point of view. So the new preacher often called on Milly, an' sometimes in Frank's absence. Frank was a cattle-man between Sundays.

"Along about this time an incident come off that I couldn't get much light on. A stranger come to town, an' was seen with the preacher. This stranger was a big man with an eye like blue ice, an' a beard of gold. He had money, an' he 'peared a man of mystery, an' the town went to buzzin' when he disappeared about the same time as a young woman known to be mightily interested in the new preacher's religion. Then, presently, along comes a man from somewheres in Illinois, an' he up an' spots this preacher as a famous Mormon proselyter. That ri'led Frank Erne as nothin' ever before, an' from rivals they come to be bitter enemies. An' it ended in Frank goin' to the meetin'-house where Milly was listenin', an' before her an' everybody else he called that preacher —called him, well, almost as hard as Venters called Tull here sometime back. An' Frank followed up that call with a hoss-whippin', an' he drove the proselyter out of town.

"People noticed, so 'twas said, that Milly's sweet disposition changed. Some said it was because she would soon become a mother, an' others said she was pinin' after the new religion. An' there was women who said right out that she was pinin' after the Mormon. Anyway, one mornin' Frank rode in from one of his trips, to find Milly gone. He had no real near neighbors— livin' a little out of town—but those who was nearest said a wagon had gone by in the night, an' they though it stopped at her door. Well, tracks always tell, an' there was the wagon tracks an' hoss tracks an' man tracks. The news spread like wildfire that Milly had run off from her husband. Everybody but Frank believed it an' wasn't slow in tellin' why she run off. Mother had always hated that strange streak of Milly's, takin' up with the new religion as she had, an' she believed Milly ran off with the Mormon. That hastened mother's death, an' she died unforgivin'. Father wasn't the kind to bow down under disgrace or misfortune, but he had surpassin' love for Milly, an' the loss of her broke him.

"From the minute I heard of Milly's disappearance I never believed she went off of her own free will. I knew Milly, an' I knew she *couldn't* have done that. I stayed at home awhile, tryin' to make Frank Erne talk. But if he knowed anythin' then he wouldn't tell it. So I set out to find Milly. An' I tried to get on the trail of that proselyter. I knew if I ever struck a town he'd visited that I'd get a trail. I knew, too, that nothin' short of hell would stop his proselytin'. An' I rode from town to town. I had a blind faith that somethin' was guidin' me. An' as the weeks an' months went by I growed into a strange sort of a man, I guess. Anyway, people were afraid of me. Two yars after that, way over in a corner of Texas, I struck a town where my man had been. He'd jest left. People said he came to that town *without* a woman. I back-trailed my man through Arkansas an' Mississippi, an' the old trail got hot again in Texas. I found the town where he first went after leavin' home. An' here I got track of Milly. I found a cabin where she had given birth to her baby. There was no way to tell whether she'd been kept a prisoner or not. The feller who owned the place was a mean, silent sort of a skunk, an' as I was leavin' I jest took a chance an' left my mark on him. Then I went home again.

"It was to find I hadn't any home, no more. Father had been dead a year. Frank Erne still lived in the house where Milly had left him. I stayed with him awhile, an' I grew old watchin' him. His farm had gone to weed, his cattle had strayed or been rustled, his house weathered till it wouldn't keep out rain nor wind. An' Frank set on the porch and whittled sticks, an' day by day wasted away. There was times when he ranted about like a crazy man, but mostly he was always sittin' an' starin' with eyes that made a man curse. I figured Frank had a secret fear that I needed to know. An' when I told him I'd trailed Milly for near three years an' had got trace of her, an' saw where she'd had her baby, I thought he would drop dead at my feet. An' when he'd come round more natural-like he begged me to *give up* the trail. But he wouldn't explain. So I let him alone, an' watched him day an' night.

"An' I found there was one thing still precious to him, an' it was a little drawer where he kept his papers. This was in the room where he slept. An' it 'peared he seldom slept. But after bein' patient I got the contents of that drawer an' found two letters from Milly. One was a long letter written a few months after her disappearance. She had been bound an' gagged an' dragged away from her home by three men, an' she named them

—Hurd, Metzger, Slack. They was strangers to her. She was taken to the little town where I found trace of her two years after. But she didn't send the letter from that town. There she was penned in. 'Peared that the proselyter, who had, of course, come on the scene, was not runnin' any risks of losin' her. She went on to say that for a time she was out of her head, an' when she got right again all that kept her alive was the baby. It was a beautiful baby, she said, an' all she thought an' dreamed of was somehow to get baby back to its father, an' then she'd thankfully lay down and die. An' the letter ended abrupt, in the middle of a sentence, an' it wasn't signed.

"The second letter was written more than two years after the first. It was from Salt Lake City. It simply said that Milly had heard her brother was on her trail. She asked Frank to tell her brother to give up the search because if he didn't she would suffer in a way too horrible to tell. She didn't beg. She just stated a fact an' made the simple request. An' she ended that letter by sayin' she would soon leave Salt Lake City with the man she had come to love, an' would never be heard of again.

"I recognized Milly's handwritin', an' I recognized her way of puttin' things. But that second letter told me of some great change in her. Ponderin' over it, I felt at last she'd either come to love that feller an' his religion, or some terrible fear made her lie an' say so. I couldn't be sure which. But, of course, I meant to find out. I'll say here, if I'd known Mormons then as I do now I'd left Milly to her fate. For mebbe she was right about what she'd suffer if I kept on her trail. But I was young an' wild them days. First I went to the town where she'd first been taken, an' I went to the place where she'd been kept. I got that skunk who owned the place, an' took him out in the woods, an' made him tell all he knowed. That wasn't much as to length, but it was pure hell's-fire in substance. This time I left him some incapacitated for any more skunk work short of hell. Then I hit the trail for Utah.

"That was fourteen years ago. I saw the incomin' of most of the Mormons. It was a wild country an' a wild time. I rode from town to town, village to village, ranch to ranch, camp to camp. I never stayed long in one place. I never had but one idea. I never rested. Four years went by, an' I knowed every trail in northern Utah. I kept on an' as time went by, an' I'd begun to grow old in my search, I had firmer, blinder faith in whatever was guidin' me. Once I read about a feller who sailed the seven seas an' traveled the world, an' he had a story to tell, an' whenever he seen the man to whom he must tell that story he knowed him on sight. I was like that, only I had a question to ask. An' always I knew the man of whom I must ask. So I never really lost the trail, though for many years it was the dimmest trail ever followed by any man.

"Then come a change in my luck. Along in Central Utah I rounded up Hurd, an' I whispered somethin' in his ear, an' watched his face, an' then throwed a gun against his bowels. An' he died with his teeth so tight shut I couldn't have pried them open with a knife. Slack an' Metzger that same year both heard me whisper the same question, an' neither would they speak a word when they lay dyin'. Long before I'd learned no man of this breed or class—or God knows what—would give up any secrets! I had to see in a man's fear of death the connections with Milly Erne's fate. An' as the years passed at long intervals I would find such a man.

"So as I drifted on the long trail down into southern Utah my name preceded me, an' I had to meet a people prepared for me, an' ready with guns. They made me a gun-man. An' that suited me. In all this time signs of the proselyter an' the giant with the blue-ice eyes an' the gold beard seemed to fade dimmer out of the trail. Only twice in ten years did I find a trace of that mysterious man who had visited the proselyter at my home village. What he had to do with Milly's fate was beyond all hope for me to learn, unless my guidin' spirit led me to him! As for the other man, I knew, as sure as I breathed an' the stars shone an' the wind blew, that I'd meet him some day.

"Eighteen years I've been on the trail. An' it led me to the last lonely villages of the Utah border. Eighteen years! . . . I feel pretty old now. I was only twenty when I hit that trail. Well, as I told you, back here a ways a Gentile said Jane Withersteen could tell me about Milly Erne an' show me her grave!"

The low voice ceased, and Lassiter slowly turned his sombrero round and round, and appeared to be counting the silver ornaments on the band. Jane, leaning toward him, sat as if petrified, listening intently, waiting to hear more. She could have shrieked, but power of tongue and lips were denied her. She saw only this sad, gray, passion-worn man, and she heard only the faint rustling of the leaves.

"Well, I came to Cottonwoods," went on Lassiter, "an' you showed me Milly's grave. An' though your teeth have been shut tighter 'n them of all the dead men lyin' back along that trail, jest the same you told me the secret I've lived these eighteen years to hear! Jane, I said you'd tell me without ever me askin'. I didn't need to ask my question here. The day, you remember, when that fat party throwed a gun on me in your court, an'—"

"Oh! Hush!" whispered Jane, blindly holding up her hands.

"*I seen in your face that Dyer, now a bishop, was the proselyter who ruined Milly Erne!*"

For an instant Jane Withersteen's brain was a whirling chaos, and she recovered to find herself grasping at Lassiter like one drowning. And as if by a lightning stroke she sprang from her dull apathy into exquisite torture.

"*It's a lie!* Lassiter! No, no!" she moaned. "I swear—you're wrong!"

"Stop! You'd perjure yourself! But I'll spare you that. You poor woman! Still blind! Still faithful! . . . Listen. I *know*. Let that settle it. An' I give up my purpose!"

"What is it—you say?"

"I give up my purpose. I've come to see an' feel differently. I can't help poor Milly. An' I've outgrown revenge. I've come to see I can be no judge for men. I can't kill a man jest for hate. Hate ain't the same with me since I loved you and little Fay."

"Lassiter! You mean you won't kill him?" Jane whispered.

"No."

"For my sake?"

"I reckon. I can't understand, but I'll respect your feelin's."

"Because you—oh, because you love me? . . . Eighteen years! You were that terrible Lassiter! And *now*—because you love me?"

"That's it, Jane."

"Oh, you'll make me love you! How can I help but love you? My heart must be stone. But—oh, Lassiter, wait, wait! Give me time. I'm not what I was. Once it was so easy to love. Now it's easy to hate. Wait! My faith in God—*some* God—still lives. By it I see happier times for you, poor passion-swayed wanderer! For me—a miserable, broken woman. I loved your sister Milly. I *will* love you. I can't have fallen so low—I can't be so abandoned by God—that I've no love left to give you. Wait! Let us forget Milly's sad life. Ah, I knew it as no one else on earth! There's one thing I shall tell you—if you are at my death-bed, but I can't speak now."

"I reckon I don't want to hear no more," said Lassiter.

Jane leaned against him; as if some pent-up force had rent its way out, she fell into a paroxysm of weeping. Lassiter held her in silent sympathy. By degrees she regained composure, and she was rising, sensible of being relieved of a weighty burden, when a sudden start on Lassiter's part alarmed her.

"I heard hosses—hosses with muffled hoofs!" he said; and he got up guardedly.

"Where's Fay?" asked Jane, hurriedly glancing round the shady knoll. The bright-haired child, who had appeared to be close all the time, was not in sight.

"Fay!" called Jane.

No answering shout of glee. No patter of flying feet. Jane saw Lassiter stiffen.

"*Fay—oh—Fay!*" Jane almost screamed.

The leaves quivered and rustled; a lonesome cricket chirped in the grass; a bee hummed by. The silence of the waning afternoon breathed hateful portent. It terrified Jane. When had silence been so infernal?

"She's—only—strayed—out—of earshot," faltered Jane, looking at Lassiter.

Pale, rigid as a statue, the rider stood, not in listening, searching posture, but in one of doomed certainty. Suddenly he grasped Jane with an iron hand, and, turning his face from her gaze, he strode with her from the knoll.

"See—Fay played here last—a house of stones an' sticks. . . . An' here's a corral of pebbles with leaves for hosses," said Lassiter, stridently, and pointed to the ground. "Back an' forth she trailed here. . . . See, she's buried somethin'—a dead grasshopper—there's a tombstone . . . here she went, chasin' a lizard—see the tiny streaked trail . . . she pulled bark off this cottonwood . . . look in the dust of the path—the letters you taught her—she's drawn pictures of birds an' hosses an' people. . . . Look, a cross! Oh, Jane, *your* cross!"

Lassiter dragged Jane on, and as if from a book read the meaning of little Fay's trail. All the way down the knoll, through the shrubbery, round and round a cottonwood, Fay's vagrant fancy left records of her sweet musings and innocent play. Long had she lingered round a bird-nest to leave therein the gaudy wing of a butterfly. Long had she played beside the running stream, sending adrift vessels freighted with pebbly cargo. Then she had wandered through the deep grass, her tiny feet scarcely turning a fragile blade, and she had dreamed beside some old faded flowers. Thus her steps led her into the broad lane. The little dimpled imprints of her bare feet showed clean-cut in the dust; they went a little way down the lane; and then, at a point where they stopped, the great tracks of a man led out from the shrubbery and returned.

CHAPTER XX

LASSITER'S WAY

FOOTPRINTS told the story of little Fay's abduction. In anguish Jane Withersteen turned speechlessly to Lassiter, and, confirming her fears, she saw him gray-faced, aged all in a moment, stricken as if by a mortal blow. .

Then all her life seemed to fall about her in wreck and ruin.

"It's all over," she heard her voice whisper. "It's ended. I'm going—I'm going—"

"Where?" demanded Lassiter, suddenly looming darkly over her.

"To—to those cruel men—"

"Speak names!" thundered Lassiter.

"To Bishop Dyer—to Tull," went on Jane, shocked into obedience.

"Well—what for?"

"I want little Fay. I can't live without her. They've stolen her as they stole Milly Erne's child. I must have little Fay. I want only her. I give up. I'll go and tell Bishop Dyer—I'm broken. I'll tell him I'm ready for the yoke—only give me back Fay—and—and I'll marry Tull!"

"*Never!*" hissed Lassiter.

His long arm leaped at her. Almost running, he dragged her under the cottonwoods, across the court, into the huge hall of Withersteen House, and he shut the door with a force that jarred the heavy walls. Black Star and Night and Bells, since their return, had been locked in this hall, and now they stamped on the stone floor.

Lassiter released Jane and like a dizzy man swayed from her with a hoarse cry and leaned shaking against a table where he kept his rider's accoutrements. He began to fumble in his saddle-bags. His action brought a clinking, metallic sound—the rattling of gun-cartridges. His fingers trembled as he slipped cartridges into an extra belt. But as he buckled it over the one he habitually wore his hands became steady. This second belt contained two guns, smaller than the black ones swinging low, and he slipped them round so that his coat hid them. Then he fell to swift action. Jane Withersteen watched him, fascinated but uncomprehending; and she saw him rapidly saddle Black Star and Night. Then he drew her into the light of the huge windows, standing over her, gripping her arm with fingers like cold steel.

"Yes, Jane, it's ended—but you're not goin' to Dyer! . . . *I'm goin' instead!*"

Looking at him—he was so terrible of aspect—she could not comprehend his words. Who was this man with the face gray as death, with eyes that would have made her shriek had she the strength, with the strange, ruthlessly bitter lips? Where was the gentle Lassiter? What was this presence in the hall, about him, about her—this cold, invisible presence?

"Yes, it's ended, Jane," he was saying, so awfully quiet and cool and implacable, "an' I'm goin' to make a little call. I'll lock you in here, an' when I get back have the saddle-bags full of meat an' bread. An' be ready to ride!"

"Lassiter!" cried Jane.

Desperately she tried to meet his gray eyes, in vain; desperately she tried again, fought herself as feeling and thought resurged in torment, and she succeeded; and then she knew.

"No—no—no!" she wailed. "You said you'd foregone your vengeance. You promised not to kill Bishop Dyer."

"If you want to talk to me about him—leave off the Bishop. I don't understand that name, or its use."

"Oh, hadn't you foregone your vengeance on—on Dyer?"

"Yes."

"But—your actions—your words—your guns—your terrible looks! . . . They don't seem foregoing vengeance?"

"Jane, now it's justice."

"You'll—kill him?"

"If God lets me live another hour! If not God—then the devil who drives me!"

"You'll kill him—for yourself—for your vengeful hate?"

"No!"

"For Milly Erne's sake?"

"No."

"For little Fay's?"

"No!"

"Oh—for whose?"

"*For yours!*"

"His blood on my soul!" whispered Jane, and she fell to her knees. This was the long-pending hour of fruition. And the habit of years—the religious passion of her life—leaped from lethargy, and the long months of gradual drifting to doubt were as if they had never been. "If you spill his blood it'll be on my soul—and on my father's. Listen." And she clasped his knees, and clung there as he tried to raise her. "Listen. Am I nothing to you?"

"Woman—don't trifle at words! I love you! An' I'll soon prove it!"

"I'll give myself to you—I'll ride away with you—marry you, if only you'll spare him?"

His answer was a cold, ringing, terrible laugh.

"Lassiter—I'll love you. Spare him!"

"No!"

She sprang up in despairing, breaking spirit, and encircled his neck with her arms, and held him in an embrace that he strove vainly to loosen. "Lassiter, would you kill me? I'm fighting my last fight for the principles of my youth—love of religion, love of father. You don't know—you can't guess the truth, and I can't speak it! I'm losing all. I'm changing. All I've gone through is nothing to this hour. Pity me—help me in my weakness. You're strong again—oh, so cruelly, coldly strong! You're killing me. I see you —feel you as some other Lassiter! My master, be merciful—spare him!"

His answer was a ruthless smile.

She clung the closer to him, and leaned her panting breast on him, and lifted her face to his. "Lassiter, *I do love you!* It's leaped out of my agony. It comes suddenly with a terrible blow of truth. You are a man! I never knew it till now. Some wonderful change came to me when you buckled on these guns and showed that gray, awful face. I loved you then. All my life I've loved, but never as now. No woman can love like a broken woman. If it were not for one thing—just one thing—and yet! I *can't* speak it— I'd glory in your manhood—the lion in you that means to slay for me. Believe me—and spare Dyer. Be merciful—great as it's in you to be great. . . . Oh, listen and believe—I have nothing, but I'm a woman—a beautiful woman, Lassiter—a passionate, loving woman—and I love you! Take me—hide me in some wild place —and love me and mend my broken heart. Spare him and take me away."

She lifted her face closer and closer to his, until their lips nearly touched, and she hung upon his neck, and with strength almost spent pressed and still pressed her palpitating body to his.

"Kiss me!" she whispered, blindly.

"No—not at your price!" he answered. His voice had changed or she had lost clearness of hearing.

"Kiss me! . . . Are you a man? Kiss me and save me!"

"Jane, you never played fair with me. But now you're blisterin' your lips—blackenin' your soul with lies!"

"By the memory of my mother—by my Bible—no! No, I *have* no Bible! But by my hope of heaven I swear I love you!"

Lassiter's gray lips formed soundless words that meant even her love could not avail to bend his will. As if the hold of her arms was that of a child's he loosened it and stepped away.

"Wait! Don't go! Oh, hear a last word! . . . May a more just and merciful God than the God I was taught to worship judge me —forgive me—save me! For I can no longer keep silent! . . . Lassiter, in pleading for Dyer I've been pleading more for my father. My father was a Mormon master, close to the leaders of the church. It was my father who sent Dyer out to proselyte. It was my father who had the blue-ice eye and the beard of gold. It was my father you got trace of in the past years. Truly, Dyer ruined Milly Erne—dragged her from her home—to Utah—to Cottonwoods. *But it was for my father!* If Milly Erne was ever wife of a Mormon that Mormon was my father! I never knew— never will know whether or not she was a wife. Blind I may be, Lassiter—fanatically faithful to a false religion I may have been, but I know justice, and my father is beyond human justice. Surely

239

he is meeting just punishment—somewhere. Always it has appalled me—the thought of your killing Dyer for my father's sins. So I have prayed!"

"Jane, the past is dead. In my love for you I forgot the past. This thing I'm about to do ain't for myself or Milly or Fay. It's not because of anythin' that ever happened in the past, but for what is happenin' right *now. It's for you!* . . . An' listen. Since I was a boy I've never thanked God for anythin'. If there is a God —an' I've come to believe it—I thank Him now for the years that made me Lassiter! . . . I can reach down an' feel these big guns, an' know what I can do with them. An', Jane, only one of the miracles Dyer professes to believe in can save him!"

Again for Jane Withersteen came the spinning of her brain in darkness, and as she whirled in endless chaos she seemed to be falling at the feet of a luminous figure—a man—Lassiter—who had saved her from herself, who could not be changed, who would slay rightfully. Then she slipped into utter blackness.

When she recovered from her faint she became aware that she was lying on a couch near the window in her sitting-room. Her brow felt damp and cold and wet; some one was chafing her hands; she recognized Judkins, and then saw that his lean, hard face wore the hue and look of excessive agitation.

"Judkins!" Her voice broke weakly.

"Aw, Miss Withersteen, you're comin' round fine. Now jest lay still a little. You're all right; everythin's all right."

"Where is—he?"

"Who?"

"Lassiter!"

"You needn't worry none about him."

"Where is he? Tell me—instantly."

"Wal, he's in the other room patchin' up a few triflin' bulletholes."

"Ah! . . . *Bishop Dyer?*"

"When I seen him last—a matter of half an hour ago, he was on his knees. He was some busy, *but* he wasn't prayin'!"

"How strangely you talk! I'll sit up. I'm—well, strong again. Tell me. Dyer on his knees! What was he doing?"

"Wal, beggin' your pardon fer blunt talk, Miss Withersteen, Dyer was on his knees an' *not* prayin'. You remember his big, broad hands? You've seen 'em raised in blessin' over old gray men an' little curly-headed children like—like Fay Larkin! Come to think of thet, I disremember ever hearin' of his liftin' his big hands in blessin' over a *woman*. Wal, when I seen him last—jest a little while ago—he was on his knees, *not* prayin', as I remarked—an' he was pressin' his big hands over some bigger wounds."

"Man, you drive me mad! Did Lassiter kill Dyer?"

"Yes."

"Did he kill Tull?"

"No. Tull's out of the village with most of his riders. He's expected back before evenin'. Lassiter will hev to git away before Tull an' his riders come in. It's sure death fer him here. An' wuss fer you, too, Miss Withersteen. There'll be some of an uprisin' when Tull gits back."

"I shall ride away with Lassiter. Judkins, tell me all you saw—all you know about this killing." She realized, without wonder or amaze, how Judkins's one word, affirming the death of Dyer—that the catastrophe had fallen—had completed the change whereby she had been molded or beaten or broken into another woman. She felt calm, slightly cold, strong as she had not been strong since the first shadow fell upon her.

"I jest saw about all of it, Miss Withersteen, an' I'll be glad to tell you if you'll only hev patience with me," said Judkins, earnestly. "You see, I've been pecooliarly interested, an' nat'rully I'm some excited. An' I talk a lot thet mebbe ain't necessary, but I can't help thet.

"I was at the meetin'-house where Dyer was holdin' court. You know he allus acts as magistrate an' judge when Tull's away. An' the trial was fer tryin' what's left of my boy riders—thet helped me hold your cattle—fer a lot of hatched-up things the boys never did. We're used to thet, an' the boys wouldn't hev minded bein' locked up fer a while, or hevin' to dig ditches, or whatever the judge laid down. You see, I divided the gold you give me among all my boys, an' they all hid it, an' they all feel rich. Howsomever, court was adjourned before the judge passed sentence. Yes, ma'm, court was adjourned some strange an' quick, much as if lightnin' hed struck the meetin'-house.

"I hed trouble attendin' the trial, but I got in. There was a good many people there, all my boys, an' Judge Dyer with his several clerks. Also he hed with him the five riders who've been guardin' him pretty close of late. They was Carter, Wright, Jengessen, an' two new riders from Stone Bridge. I didn't hear their names, but I heard they was handy men with guns an' they looked more like rustlers than riders. Anyway, there they was, the five all in a row.

"Judge Dyer was tellin' Willie Kern, one of my best an' steadiest boys—Dyer was tellin' him how there was a ditch opened near Willie's home lettin' water through his lot, where it hadn't ought to go. An' Willie was tryin' to git a word in to prove he wasn't at home all the day it happened—which was true, as I know—but Willie couldn't git a word in, an' then Judge Dyer went on layin' down the law. An' all to onct he happened to look down the long room. An' if ever any man turned to stone he was thet man.

"Nat'rully I looked back to see what hed acted so powerful strange on the judge. An' there, half-way up the room, in the middle of the wide aisle, stood Lassiter! All white an' black he looked, an' I can't think of anythin' he resembled, onless it's death. Venters made thet same room some still an' chilly when he called Tull; but this was different. I give my word, Miss Withersteen, thet I went cold to my very marrow. I don't know why. But Lassiter had a way about him thet's awful. He spoke a word—a name—I couldn't understand it, though he spoke clear as a bell. I was too excited, mebbe. Judge Dyer must hev understood it, an' a lot more thet was mystery to me, for he pitched forrard out of his chair right onto the platform.

"Then them five riders, Dyer's bodyguards, they jumped up, an' two of them thet I found out afterward were the strangers from Stone Bridge, they piled right out of a winder, so quick you couldn't catch your breath. It was plain they wasn't Mormons.

"Jengessen, Carter, an' Wright eyed Lassiter, for what must hev been a second an' seemed like an hour, an' they went white an' strung. But they didn't weaken nor lose their nerve.

"I hed a good look at Lassiter. He stood sort of stiff, bendin' a little, an' both his arms were crooked, an' his hands looked like a hawk's claws. But there ain't no tellin' how his eyes looked. I know this, though, an' thet is his eyes could read the mind of any man about to throw a gun. An' in watchin' him, of course, I couldn't see the three men go fer their guns. An' though I was lookin' right at Lassiter—lookin' hard—I couldn't see how he

drawed. He was quicker 'n eyesight—thet's all. But I seen the red
spurtin' of his guns, an' heard his shots jest the very littlest instant
before I heard the shots of the riders. An' when I turned, Wright
an' Carter was down, an' Jengessen, who's tough like a steer, was
pullin' the trigger of a wabblin' gun. But it was plain he was shot
through, plumb center. An' sudden he fell with a crash, an' his
gun clattered on the floor.

"Then there was a hell of a silence. Nobody breathed. Sartin
I didn't, anyway. I saw Lassiter slip a smokin' gun back in a belt.
But he hadn't throwed either of the big black guns, an' I thought
thet strange. An' all this was happenin' quick—you can't imagine
how quick.

"There come a scrapin' on the floor an' Dyer got up, his face
like lead. I wanted to watch Lassiter, but Dyer's face, onct I seen
it like thet, glued my eyes. I seen him go fer his gun—why, I could
hev done better, quicker—an' then there was a thunderin' shot
from Lassiter, an' it hit Dyer's right arm, an' his gun went off as
it dropped. He looked at Lassiter like a cornered sage-wolf, an'
sort of howled, an' reached down fer his gun. He'd jest picked
it off the floor an' was raisin' it when another thunderin' shot almost tore thet arm off—so it seemed to me. The gun dropped
again an' he went down on his knees, kind of flounderin' after it.
It was some strange an' terrible to see his awful earnestness. Why
would such a man cling so to life? Anyway, he got the gun with
left hand an' was raisin' it, pullin' trigger in his madness, when
the third thunderin' shot hit his left arm, an' he dropped the gun
again. But thet left arm wasn't useless yet, fer he grabbed up the
gun, an' with a shakin' 'aim thet would hev been pitiful to me—
in any other man—he began to shoot. One wild bullet struck a
man twenty feet from Lassiter. An' it killed thet man, as I seen
afterward. Then come a bunch of thunderin' shots—nine I calki-
lated after, fer they come so quick I couldn't count them—an' I
knew Lassiter hed turned the black guns loose on Dyer.

"I'm tellin' you straight, Miss Withersteen, fer I want you to
know. Afterward you'll git over it. I've seen some soul-rackin'
scenes on this Utah border, but this was the awfulest. I remember
I closed my eyes, an' fer a minute I thought of the strangest
things, out of place there, such as you'd never dream would come
to mind. I saw the sage, an' runnin' hosses—an' thet's the beau·

tifulest sight to me—an' I saw dim things in the dark, an' there was a kind of hummin' in my ears. An' I remember distinctly— fer it was what made all these things whirl out of my mind an' opened my eyes—I remember distinctly it was the smell of gunpowder.

"The court had about adjourned fer thet judge. He was on his knees, an' he wasn't prayin'. He was gaspin' an' tryin' to press his big, floppin', crippled hands over his body. Lassiter had sent all those last thunderin' shots through his body. Thet was Lassiter's way.

"An' Lassiter spoke, an' if I ever forgit his words I'll never forgit the sound of his voice.

" 'Proselyter, I reckon you'd better call quick on thet God who reveals Hisself to you on earth, because He won't be visitin' the place you're goin' to!'

"An' then I seen Dyer look at his big, hangin' hands thet wasn't big enough fer the last work he set them to. An' he looked up at Lassiter. An' then he stared horrible at somethin' thet wasn't Lassiter, nor anyone there, nor the room, nor the branches of purple sage peepin' into the winder. Whatever he seen, it was with the look of a man who *discovers* somethin' too late. Thet's a terrible look! . . . An' with a horrible *understandin'* cry he slid forrard on his face."

Judkins paused in his narrative, breathing heavily while he wiped his perspiring brow.

"Thet's about all," he concluded. "Lassiter left the meetin'-house an' I hurried to catch up with him. He was bleedin' from three gunshots, none of them much to bother him. An' we come right up here. I found you layin' in the hall, an' I hed to work some over you."

Jane Withersteen offered up no prayer for Dyer's soul.

Lassiter's step sounded in the hall—the familiar soft, silver-clinking step—and she heard it with thrilling new emotions in which was a vague joy in her very fear of him. The door opened, and she saw him, the old Lassiter, slow, easy, gentle, cool, yet not exactly the same Lassiter. She rose, and for a moment her eyes blurred and swam in tears.

"Are you—all—all right?" she asked, tremulously.

"I reckon."

244

"Lassiter, I'll ride away with you. Hide me till danger is past—till we are forgotten—then take me where you will. Your people shall be my people, and your God my God!"

He kissed her hand with the quaint grace and courtesy that came to him in rare moments.

"Black Star an' Night are ready," he said, simply.

His quiet mention of the black racers spurred Jane to action. Hurrying to her room, she changed to her rider's suit, packed her jewelry, and the gold that was left, and all the woman's apparel for which there was space in the saddle-bags, and then returned to the hall. Black Star stamped his iron-shod hoofs and tossed his beautiful head, and eyed her with knowing eyes.

"Judkins, I give Bells to you," said Jane. "I hope you will always keep him and be good to him."

Judkins mumbled thanks that he could not speak fluently, and his eyes flashed.

Lassiter strapped Jane's saddle-bags upon Black Star, and led the racers out into the court.

"Judkins, you ride with Jane out into the sage. If you see any riders comin' shout quick twice. An', Jane, *don't look back!* I'll catch up soon. We'll get to the break into the Pass before midnight, an' then wait until mornin' to go down."

Black Star bent his graceful neck and bowed his noble head, and his broad shoulders yielded as he knelt for Jane to mount.

She rode out of the court beside Judkins, through the grove, across the wide lane into the sage, and she realized that she was leaving Withersteen House forever, and she did not look back. A strange, dreamy, calm peace pervaded her soul. Her doom had fallen upon her, but, instead of finding life no longer worth living she found it doubly significant, full of sweetness as the western breeze, beautiful and unknown as the sage-slope stretching its purple sunset shadows before her. She became aware of Judkins's hand touching hers; she heard him speak a husky good-by; then into the place of Bells shot the dead-black, keen, racy nose of Night, and she knew Lassiter rode beside her.

"Don't—look—back!" he said, and his voice, too, was not clear.

Facing straight ahead, seeing only the waving, shadowy sage, Jane held out her gauntleted hand, to feel it enclosed in strong clasp. So she rode on without a backward glance at the beautiful

245

grove of Cottonwoods. She did not seem to think of the past, of what she left forever, but of the color and mystery and wildness of the sage-slope leading down to Deception Pass, and of the future. She watched the shadows lengthen down the slope; she felt the cool west wind sweeping by from the rear; and she wondered at low, yellow clouds sailing swiftly over her and beyond.

"*Don't—look—back!*" said Lassiter.

Thick-driving belts of smoke traveled by on the wind, and with it came a strong, pungent odor of burning wood.

Lassiter had fired Withersteen House! But Jane did not look back.

A misty veil obscured the clear, searching gaze she had kept steadfastly upon the purple slope and the dim lines of cañons. It passed, as passed the rolling clouds of smoke, and she saw the valley deepening into the shades of twilight. Night came on, swift as the fleet racers, and stars peeped out to brighten and grow, and the huge, windy, eastern heave of sage-level paled under a rising moon and turned to silver. Blanched in moonlight, the sage yet seemed to hold its hue of purple and was infinitely more wild and lonely. So the night hours wore on, and Jane Withersteen never once looked back.

CHAPTER XXI

BLACK STAR AND NIGHT

THE time had come for Venters and Bess to leave their retreat. They were at great pains to choose the few things they would be able to carry with them on the journey out of Utah.

"Bern, whatever kind of a pack's this, anyhow?" questioned Bess, rising from her work with reddened face.

Venters, absorbed in his own task, did not look up at all, and in reply said he had brought so much from Cottonwoods that he did not recollect the half of it.

"A woman packed this!" Bess exclaimed.

He scarcely caught her meaning, but the peculiar tone of her voice caused him instantly to rise, and he saw Bess on her knees before an open pack which he recognized as the one given him by Jane.

"By George!" he ejaculated, guiltily, and then at sight of Bess's face he laughed outright.

"A woman packed this," she repeated, fixing woeful, tragic eyes on him.

"Well, is that a crime?"

"There—there *is* a woman, after all!"

"Now Bess—"

"You've lied to me!"

Then and there Venters found it imperative to postpone work for the present. All her life Bess had been isolated, but she had inherited certain elements of the eternal feminine.

"But there *was* a woman and you *did* lie to me," she kept repeating, after he had explained.

"What of that? Bess, I'll get angry at you in a moment. Remember you've been pent up all your life. I venture to say that if

247

you'd been out in the world you'd have had a dozen sweethearts and have told many a lie before this."

"I wouldn't anything of the kind," declared Bess, indignantly.

"Well—perhaps not lie. But you'd have had the sweethearts. You couldn't have helped that—being so pretty."

This remark appeared to be a very clever and fortunate one; and the work of selecting and then of stowing all the packs in the cave went on without further interruption.

Venters closed up the opening of the cave with a thatch of willows and aspens, so that not even a bird or a rat could get in to the sacks of grain. And this work was in order with the precaution habitually observed by him. He might not be able to get out of Utah, and have to return to the valley. But he owed it to Bess to make the attempt, and in case they were compelled to turn back he wanted to find that fine store of food and grain intact. The outfit of implements and utensils he packed away in another cave.

"Bess, we have enough to live here all our lives," he said once, dreamily.

"Shall I go roll Balancing Rock?" she asked, in light speech, but with deep-blue fire in her eyes.

"No—no."

"Ah, you don't forget the gold and the world," she sighed.

"Child, you forget the beautiful dresses and the travel—and everything."

"Oh, I want to go. But I want to stay!"

"I feel the same way."

They let the eight calves out of the corral, and kept only two of the burros Venters had brought from Cottonwoods. These they intended to ride. Bess freed all her pets—the quail and rabbits and foxes.

The last sunset and twilight and night were both the sweetest and saddest they had ever spent in Surprise Valley. Morning brought keen exhilaration and excitement. When Venters had saddled the two burros, strapped on the light packs and the two canteens, the sunlight was dispersing the lazy shadows from the valley. Taking a last look at the caves and the silver spruces, Venters and Bess made a reluctant start, leading the burros. Ring and Whitie looked keen and knowing. Something seemed to drag at Venters's feet and he noticed Bess lagged behind. Never had the climb from terrace to bridge appeared so long.

Not till they reached the opening of the gorge did they stop to rest and take one last look at the valley. The tremendous arch of stone curved clear and sharp in outline against the morning sky. And through it streaked the golden shaft. The valley seemed an enchanted circle of glorious veils of gold and wraiths of white and silver haze and dim, blue, moving shade—beautiful and wild and unreal as a dream.

"We—we can—th—think of it—always—re—remember," sobbed Bess.

"Hush! Don't cry. Our valley has only fitted us for a better life somewhere. Come!"

They entered the gorge and he closed the willow gate. From rosy, golden morning light they passed into cool, dense gloom. The burros pattered up the trail with little hollow-cracking steps. And the gorge widened to narrow outlet and the gloom lightened to gray. At the divide they halted for another rest. Venters's keen, remembering gaze searched Balancing Rock, and the long incline, and the cracked toppling walls, but failed to note the slightest change.

The dogs led the descent; then came Bess leading her burro; then Venters leading his. Bess kept her eyes bent downward. Venters, however, had an irresistible desire to look upward at Balancing Rock. It had always haunted him, and now he wondered if he were really to get through the outlet before the huge stone thundered down. He fancied that would be a miracle. Every few steps he answered to the strange, nervous fear and turned to make sure the rock still stood like a giant statue. And, as he descended, it grew dimmer in his sight. It changed form; it swayed; it nodded darkly; and at last, in his heightened fancy, he saw it heave and roll. As in a dream when he felt himself falling yet knew he would never fall, so he saw this long-standing thunderbolt of the little stone-men plunge down to close forever the outlet to Deception Pass.

And while he was giving way to unaccountable dread imaginations the descent was accomplished without mishap.

"I'm glad that's over," he said, breathing more freely. "I hope

I'm by that hanging rock for good and all. Since almost the moment I first saw it I've had an idea that it was waiting for me. Now, when it does fall, if I'm thousands of miles away, I'll hear it."

With the first glimpses of the smooth slope leading down to the grotesque cedars and out to the Pass, Venters's cool nerve returned. One long survey to the left, then one to the right, satisfied his caution. Leading the burros down to the spur of rock, he halted at the steep incline.

"Bess, here's the bad place, the place I told you about, with the cut steps. You start down, leading your burro. Take your time and hold on to him if you slip. I've got a rope on him and a half-hitch on this point of rock, so I can let him down safely. Coming up here was a killing job. But it'll be easy going down."

Both burros passed down the difficult stairs cut by the cliff-dwellers, and did it without a misstep. After that the descent down the slope and over the mile of scrawled, ripped, and ridged rock required only careful guidance, and Venters got the burros to level ground in a condition that caused him to congratulate himself.

"Oh, if we only had Wrangle!" exclaimed Venters. "But we're lucky. That's the worst of our trail passed. We've only men to fear now. If we get up in the sage we can hide and slip along like coyotes."

They mounted and rode west through the valley and entered the cañon. From time to time Venters walked, leading his burro. When they got by all the cañons and gullies opening into the Pass they went faster and with fewer halts. Venters did not confide in Bess the alarming fact that he had seen horses and smoke less than a mile up one of the intersecting cañons. He did not talk at all. And long after he had passed this cañon and felt secure once more in the certainty that they had been unobserved he never relaxed his watchfulness. But he did not walk any more, and he kept the burros at a steady trot. Night fell before they reached the last water in the Pass and they made camp by starlight. Venters did not want the burros to stray, so he tied them with long halters in the grass near the spring. Bess, tired out and silent, laid her head in a saddle and went to sleep between the two dogs. Venters did not close his eyes. The cañon silence appeared full of the low, continuous hum of insects. He listened until the hum grew into a roar, and then, breaking the spell, once more he heard it low and clear. He watched the stars and the moving shadows, and always his glance returned to the girl's dimly pale face. And he remembered how white and still it had once looked in the starlight. And again stern thought fought his strange fancies. Would all his labor and his love be for naught? Would he lose her, after all? What did the dark shadow around her portend? Did calamity lurk on that long upland trail through the sage? Why should his heart swell and throb with nameless fear? He listened to the silence, and told himself that in the broad light of day he could dispel this leaden-weighted dread.

At the first hint of gray over the eastern rim he awoke Bess, saddled the burros, and began the day's travel. He wanted to get out of the Pass before there was any chance of riders coming down. They gained the break as the first red rays of the rising sun colored the rim.

For once, so eager was he to get up to level ground, he did not send Ring or Whitie in advance. Encouraging Bess to hurry, pulling at his patient, plodding burro, he climbed the soft, steep trail.

Brighter and brighter grew the light. He mounted the last broken edge of rim to have the sun-fired, purple sage-slope burst upon him as a glory. Bess panted up to his side, tugging on the halter of her burro.

"We're up!" he cried, joyously. "There's not a dot on the sage. We're safe. We'll not be seen! Oh, Bess—"

Ring growled and sniffed the keen air and bristled. Venters clutched at his rifle. Whitie sometimes made a mistake, but Ring never. The dull thud of hoofs almost deprived Venters of power to turn and see from where disaster threatened. He felt his eyes dilate as he stared at Lassiter leading Black Star and Night out of the sage, with Jane Withersteen, in rider's costume, close beside them.

For an instant Venters felt himself whirl dizzily in the center of vast circles of sage. He recovered partially, enough to see Lassiter standing with a glad smile and Jane riveted in astonishment.

"Why, Bern!" she exclaimed. "How good it is to see you! We're

riding away, you see. The storm burst—and I'm a ruined woman!
. . . I thought you were alone."

Venters, unable to speak for consternation, and bewildered out
of all sense of what he ought or ought not to do, simply stared at
Jane.

"Son, where are you bound for?" asked Lassiter.

"Not safe—where I was. I'm—we're going out of Utah—back
East," he found tongue to say.

"I reckon this meetin's the luckiest thing that ever happened
to you an' to me—an' to Jane—an' to Bess," said Lassiter, coolly.

"*Bess!*" cried Jane, with a sudden leap of blood to her pale
cheek.

It was entirely beyond Venters to see any luck in that meeting.

Jane Withersteen took one flashing, woman's glance at Bess's
scarlet face, at her slender, shapely form.

"Venters! is this a girl—a woman?" she questioned, in a voice
that stung.

"Yes."

"Did you have her in that wonderful valley?"

"Yes, but Jane—"

"All the time you were gone?"

"Yes, but I couldn't tell—"

"Was it for *her* you asked me to give you supplies? Was it for
her that you wanted to make your valley a paradise?"

"Oh—Jane—"

"Answer me."

"Yes."

"Oh, you liar!" And with these passionate words Jane Withersteen succumbed to fury. For the second time in her life she fell
into the ungovernable rage that had been her father's weakness.
And it was worse than his, for she was a jealous woman—jealous
even of her friends.

As best he could, he bore the brunt of her anger. It was not only
his deceit to her that she visited upon him, but her betrayal by
religion, by life itself.

Her passion, like fire at white heat, consumed itself in little
time. Her physical strength failed, and still her spirit attempted
to go on in magnificent denunciation of those who had wronged
her. Like a tree cut deep into its roots, she began to quiver and

252

shake, and her anger weakened into despair. And her ringing voice sank into a broken, husky whisper. Then, spent and pitiable, upheld by Lassiter's arm, she turned and hid her face in Black Star's mane.

Numb as Venters was when at length Jane Withersteen lifted her head and looked at him, he yet suffered a pang.

"Jane, the girl is innocent!" he cried.

"Can you expect me to believe that?" she asked, with weary, bitter eyes.

"I'm not that kind of a liar. And you know it. If I lied—if I kept silent when honor should have made me speak, it was to spare you. I came to Cottonwoods to tell you. But I couldn't add to your pain. I intended to tell you I had come to love this girl. But, Jane, I hadn't forgotten how good you were to me. I haven't changed at all toward you. I prize your friendship as I always have. But, however it may look to you—don't be unjust. The girl is innocent. Ask Lassiter."

"Jane, she's jest as sweet an' innocent as little Fay," said Lassiter. There was a faint smile upon his face and a beautiful light.

Venters saw, and knew that Lassiter saw, how Jane Withersteen's tortured soul wrestled with hate and threw it—with scorn, doubt, suspicion, and overcame all.

"Bern, if in my misery I accused you unjustly, I crave forgiveness," she said. "I'm not what I once was. Tell me—who is this girl?"

"Jane, she is Oldring's daughter, and his Masked Rider. Lassiter will tell you how I shot her for a rustler, saved her life—all the story. It's a strange story, Jane, as wild as the sage. But it's true—true as her innocence. That you must believe!"

"Oldring's Masked Rider! Oldring's daughter!" exclaimed Jane. "And she's innocent! You ask me to believe much. If this girl is —is what you say, how could she be going away with the man who killed her father?"

"Why did you tell that?" cried Venters, passionately.

Jane's question had roused Bess out of stupefaction. Her eyes suddenly darkened and dilated. She stepped toward Venters and held up both hands as if to ward off a blow.

"Did—did you kill Oldring?"

"I did, Bess, and I hate myself for it. But you know I never dreamed he was your father. I thought he'd wronged you. I killed him when I was madly jealous."

For a moment Bess was shocked into silence.

"But he was my father!" she broke out, at last. "And now I must go back—I can't go with you. It's all over—that beautiful dream. Oh, I *knew* it couldn't come true. You can't take me now."

"If you forgive me, Bess, it'll all come right in the end!" implored Venters.

"It can't be right. I'll go back. After all, I loved him. He was good to me. I can't forget that."

"If you go back to Oldring's men I'll follow you, and then they'll kill me," said Venters, hoarsely.

"Oh no, Bern, you'll not come. Let me go. It's best for you to forget me. I've brought you only pain and dishonor.

She did not weep. But the sweet bloom and life died out of her face. She looked haggard and sad, all at once stunted; and her hands dropped listlessly; and her head drooped in slow, final acceptance of a hopeless fate.

"Jane, look there!" cried Venters, in despairing grief. "Need you have told her? Where was all your kindness of heart? This girl has had a wretched, lonely life. And I'd found a way to make her happy. You've killed it. You've killed something sweet and pure and hopeful, just as sure as you breathe."

"Oh, Bern! It was a slip. I never thought—I never thought!" replied Jane. "How could I tell she didn't know?"

Lassiter suddenly moved forward, and with the beautiful light on his face now strangely luminous, he looked at Jane and Venters and then let his soft, bright gaze rest on Bess.

"Well, I reckon you've all had your say, an' now it's Lassiter's turn. Why, I was jest prayin' for this meetin'. Bess, jest look here."

Gently he touched her arm and turned her to face the others, and then outspread his great hand to disclose a shiny, battered gold locket.

"Open it," he said, with a singularly rich voice.

Bess complied, but listlessly.

"Jane—Venters—come closer," went on Lassiter. "Take a look at the picture. Don't you know the woman?"

Jane, after one glance, drew back.

"Milly Erne!" she cried, wonderingly.

Venters, with tingling pulse, with something growing on him, recognized in the faded miniature portrait the eyes of Milly Erne.

"Yes, that's Milly," said Lassiter, softly. "Bess, did you ever see her face—look hard—with all your heart an' soul?"

"The eyes seem to haunt me," whispered Bess. "Oh, I can't remember—they're eyes of my dreams—but—but—"

Lassiter's strong arm went round her and he bent his head.

"Child, I thought you'd remember her eyes. They're the same beautiful eyes you'd see if you looked in a mirror or a clear spring. They're your mother's eyes. You are Milly Erne's child. Your name is Elizabeth Erne. You're not Oldring's daughter. You're the daughter of Frank Erne, a man once my best friend. Look! Here's his picture beside Milly's. He was handsome, an' as fine an' gallant a Southern gentleman as I ever seen. Frank came of an old family. You come of the best of blood, lass, and blood tells."

Bess slipped through his arm to her knees and hugged the locket to her bosom, and lifted wonderful, yearning eyes.

"It—can't—be—true!"

"Thank God, lass, it *is* true," replied Lassiter. "Jane an' Bern here—they both recognize Milly. They see Milly in you. They're so knocked out they can't tell you, that's all."

"Who are you?" whispered Bess.

"I reckon I'm Milly's brother an' your uncle! . . . Uncle Jim! Ain't that fine?"

"Oh, I can't believe— Don't raise me! Bern, let me kneel. I see truth in your face—in Miss Withersteen's. But let me hear it all— all on my knees. Tell me *how* it's true!"

"Well, Elizabeth, listen," said Lassiter. "Before you was born your father made a mortal enemy of a Mormon named Dyer. They was both ministers an' come to be rivals. Dyer stole your mother away from her home. She gave birth to you in Texas eighteen years ago. Then she was taken to Utah, from place to place, an' finally to the last border settlement—Cottonwoods. You was about three years old when you was taken away from Milly. She never knew what had become of you. But she lived a good while hopin' and prayin' to have you again. Then she gave up an' died. An' I may as well put in here your father died ten years ago. Well, I spent my time tracin' Milly, an' some months back I landed in Cottonwoods. An' jest lately I learned all about you. I had a talk with Oldrin' an' told him you was dead, an' he told me what I had so long been wantin' to know. It was Dyer, of course, who stole you from Milly. Part reason he was sore because Milly refused to give you Mormon teachin', but mostly he still hated Frank Erne so infernally that he made a deal with Oldrin' to take you an' bring you up as an infamous rustler an' rustler's girl. The idea was to break Frank Erne's heart if he ever came to Utah—to show him his daughter with a band of low rustlers. Well—Oldrin' took you, brought you up from childhood, an' then made you his Masked Rider. He made you infamous. He kept that part of the contract, but he learned to love you as a daughter an' never let any but his own men know you was a girl. I heard him say that with my own ears, an' I saw his big eyes grow dim. He told me how he had guarded you always, kept you locked up in his absence, was always at your side or near you on those rides that made you famous on the sage. He said he an' an old rustler whom he trusted had taught you how to read an' write. They selected the books for you. Dyer had wanted you brought up the vilest of the vile! An' Oldrin' brought you up the innocentest of the innocent. He said you didn't know what vileness was. I can hear his big voice tremble now as he said it. He told me how the men—rustlers an' outlaws—who from time to time tried to approach you familiarly—he told me how he shot them dead. I'm tellin' you this 'specially because you've showed such shame—sayin' you was nameless an' all that. Nothin' on earth can be wronger than that idea of yours. An' the truth of it is here. Oldrin' swore to me that if Dyer died, releasin' the contract, he intended to hunt up your father an' give you back to him. It seems Oldrin' wasn't all bad, an' he sure loved you."

Venters leaned forward in passionate remorse.

"Oh, Bess! I know Lassiter speaks the truth. For when I shot Oldring he dropped to his knees and fought with unearthly power to speak. And he said: 'Man—why—didn't—you—wait? Bess was—' Then he fell dead. And I've been haunted by his look and words. Oh, Bess, what a strange, splendid thing for Oldring to do! It all seems impossible. But, dear, you really are not what you thought."

"Elizabeth Erne!" cried Jane Withersteen. "I loved your mother and I see her in you!"

What had been incredible from the lips of men became, in the tone, look, and gesture of a woman, a wonderful truth for Bess. With little tremblings of all her slender body she rocked to and fro on her knees. The yearning wistfulness of her eyes changed to solemn splendor of joy. She believed. She was realizing happiness. And as the process of thought was slow, so were the variations of her expression. Her eyes reflected the transformation of her soul. Dark, brooding, hopeless belief—clouds of gloom— drifted, paled, vanished in glorious light. An exquisite rose flush— a glow—shone from her face as she slowly began to rise from her knees. A spirit uplifted her. All that she had held as base dropped from her.

Venters watched her in joy too deep for words. By it he divined something of what Lassiter's revelation meant to Bess, but he knew he could only faintly understand. That moment when she seemed to be lifted by some spiritual transfiguration was the most beautiful moment of his life. She stood with parted, quivering lips, with hands tightly clasping the locket to her heaving breast. A new conscious pride of worth dignified the old wild, free grace and poise.

"Uncle Jim!" she said, tremulously, with a different smile from any Venters had ever seen on her face.

Lassiter took her into his arms.

"I reckon. It's powerful fine to hear that," replied Lassiter, unsteadily.

Venters, feeling his eyes grow hot and wet, turned away, and found himself looking at Jane Withersteen. He had almost forgotten her presence. Tenderness and sympathy were fast hiding traces of her agitation. Venters read her mind—felt the reaction of her noble heart—saw the joy she was beginning to feel at the happiness of others. And suddenly blinded, choked by his emotions, he turned from her also. He knew what she would do presently; she would make some magnificent amend for her anger; she would give some manifestation of her love; probably all in a moment, as she had loved Milly Erne, so would she love Elizabeth Erne.

"'Pears to me, folks, that we'd better talk a little serious now," remarked Lassiter, at length. "Time flies."

"You're right," replied Venters, instantly. "I'd forgotten time—

place—danger. Lassiter, you're riding away. Jane's leaving Withersteen House?"

"Forever," replied Jane.

"I fired Withersteen House," said Lassiter.

"Dyer?" questioned Venters, sharply.

"I reckon where Dyer's gone there won't be any kidnappin' of girls."

"Ah! I knew it. I told Judkins— And Tull?" went on Venters, passionately.

"Tull wasn't around when I broke loose. By now he's likely on our trail with his riders."

"Lassiter, you're going into the Pass to hide till all this storm blows over?"

"I reckon that's Jane's idea. I'm thinkin' the storm 'll be a powerful long time blowin' over. I was comin' to join you in Surprise Valley. You'll go back now with me?"

"No. I want to take Bess out of Utah. Lassiter, Bess found gold in the valley. We've a saddle-bag full of gold. If we can reach Sterling—"

"Man! how 're you ever goin' to do that? Sterlin' is a hundred miles."

"My plan is to ride on, keeping sharp lookout. Somewhere up the trail we'll take to the sage and go round Cottonwoods and then hit the trail again."

"It's a bad plan. You'll kill the burros in two days."

"Then we'll walk."

"That's more bad an' worse. Better go back down the Pass with me."

"Lassiter, this girl has been hidden all her life in that lonely place," went on Venters. "Oldring's men are hunting me. We'd not be safe there any longer. Even if we would be I'd take this chance to get her out. I want to marry her. She shall have some of the pleasures of life—see cities and people. We've gold—we'll be rich. Why, life opens sweet for both of us. And, by Heaven! I'll get her out or lose my life in the attempt!"

"I reckon if you go on with them burros you'll lose your life all right. Tull will have riders all over this sage. You can't get out on them burros. It's a fool idea. That's not doin' best by the girl. Come with me an' take chances on the rustlers."

Lassiter's cool argument made Venters waver, not in determination to go, but in hope of success.

"Bess, I want you to know. Lassiter says the trip's almost useless now. I'm afraid he's right. We've got about one chance in a hundred to go through. Shall we take it? Shall we go on?"

"We'll go on," replied Bess.

"That settles it, Lassiter."

Lassiter spread wide his hands, as if to signify he could do no more, and his face clouded.

Venters felt a touch on his elbow. Jane stood beside him with a hand on his arm. She was smiling. Something radiated from her, and like an electric current accelerated the motion of his blood.

"Bern, you'd be right to die rather than not take Elizabeth out of Utah—out of this wild country. You must do it. You'll show her the great world, with all its wonders. Think how little she has seen! Think what delight is in store for her! You have gold; you will be free; you will make her happy. What a glorious prospect! I share it with you. I'll think of you—dream of you—pray for you."

"Thank you, Jane," replied Venters, trying to steady his voice. "It does look bright. Oh, if we were only across that wide, open waste of sage!"

"Bern, the trip's as good as made. It'll be safe—easy. It'll be a glorious ride," she said, softly.

Venters stared. Had Jane's troubles made her insane? Lassiter, too, acted queerly, all at once beginning to turn his sombrero round in hands that actually shook.

"You are a rider. She is a rider. This will be the ride of your lives," added Jane, in that same soft undertone, almost as if she were musing to herself.

"Jane!" he cried.

"I give you Black Star and Night!"

"*Black Star and Night!*" he echoed.

"It's done. Lassiter, put our saddle-bags on the burros."

Only when Lassiter moved swiftly to execute her bidding did Venters's clogged brain grasp at literal meanings. He leaped to catch Lassiter's busy hands.

"No, no! What are you doing?" he demanded, in a kind of fury. "I won't take her racers. What do you think I am? It'd be monstrous. Lassiter! stop it, I say! . . . You've got her to save.

You've miles and miles to go. Tull is trailing you. There are rustlers in the Pass. Give me back that saddle-bag!"

"Son—cool down," returned Lassiter, in a voice he might have used to a child. But the grip with which he tore away Venters's grasping hands was that of a giant. "Listen—you fool boy! Jane's sized up the situation. The burros 'll do for us. We'll sneak along an' hide. I'll take your dogs an' your rifle. Why, it's the trick. The blacks are yours, an' sure as I can throw a gun you're goin' to ride safe out of the sage."

"Jane—stop him—please stop him," gasped Venters. "I've lost my strength. I can't do—anything. This is hell for me! Can't you see that? I've ruined you—it was through me you lost all. You've only Black Star and Night left. You love these horses. Oh! I know how you must love them now! And—you're trying to give them to me. To help me out of Utah! To save the girl I love!"

"That will be my glory."

Then in the white, rapt face, in the unfathomable eyes, Venters saw Jane Withersteen in a supreme moment. This moment was one wherein she reached up to the height for which her noble soul had ever yearned. He, after disrupting the calm tenor of her peace, after bringing down on her head the implacable hostility of her churchmen, after teaching her a bitter lesson of life—he was to be her salvation. And he turned away again, this time shaken to the core of his soul. Jane Withersteen was the incarnation of selflessness. He experienced wonder and terror, exquisite pain and rapture. What were all the shocks life had dealt him compared to the thought of such loyal and generous friendship?

And instantly, as if by some divine insight, he knew himself in the remaking—tried, found wanting; but stronger, better, surer —and he wheeled to Jane Withersteen, eager, joyous, passionate, wild, exalted. He bent to her; he left tears and kisses on her hands.

"Jane, I—I can't find words—now," he said. "I'm beyond words. Only—I understand. And I'll take the blacks."

"Don't be losin' no more time," cut in Lassiter. "I ain't certain, but I think I seen a speck up the sage-slope. Mebbe I was mistaken. But, anyway, we must all be movin'. I've shortened the stirrups on Black Star. Put Bess on him."

Jane Withersteen held out her arms.

"Elizabeth Erne!" she cried, and Bess flew to her.

How inconceivably strange and beautiful it was for Venters to see Bess clasped to Jane Withersteen's breast!

Then he leaped astride Night.

"Venters, ride straight on up the slope," Lassiter was saying, "an' if you don't meet any riders keep on till you're a few miles from the village, then cut off in the sage an' go round to the trail. But you'll most likely meet riders with Tull. Jest keep right on till you're jest out of gunshot an' then make your cut-off into the sage. They'll ride after you, but it won't be no use. You can ride, an' Bess can ride. When you're out of reach turn on round to the west, an' hit the trail somewhere. Save the hosses all you can, but don't be afraid. Black Star and Night are good for a hundred miles before sundown, if you have to push them. You can get to Sterlin' by night if you want. But better make it along about to-morrow mornin'. When you get through the notch on the Glaze trail, swing to the right. You'll be able to see both Glaze an' Stone Bridge. Keep away from them villages. You won't run no risk of meetin' any of Oldrin's rustlers from Sterlin' on. You'll find water in them deep hollows north of the Notch. There's an old trail there, not much used, an' it leads to Sterlin'. That's your trail. An' one thing more. If Tull pushes you—or keeps on persistent-like, for a few miles—jest let the blacks out an' lose him an' his riders."

"Lassiter, may we meet again!" said Venters, in a deep voice.

"Son, it ain't likely—it ain't likely. Well, Bess Oldrin'—Masked Rider—Elizabeth Erne—now you climb on Black Star. I've heard you could ride. Well, every rider loves a good horse. An', lass, there never was but one that could beat Black Star."

"Ah, Lassiter, there never was any horse that could beat Black Star," said Jane, with the old pride.

"I often wondered—mebbe Venters rode out that race when he brought back the blacks. Son, was Wrangle the best hoss?"

"No, Lassiter," replied Venters. For this lie he had his reward in Jane's quick smile.

"Well, well, my hoss-sense ain't always right. An' here I'm talkin' a lot, wastin' time. It ain't so easy to find an' lose a pretty niece all in one hour! Elizabeth—good-by!"

"Oh, Uncle Jim! . . . Good-by!"
"Elizabeth Erne, be happy! Good-by," said Jane.
"Good-by—oh—good-by!"
In lithe, supple action Bess swung up to Black Star's saddle.
"Jane Withersteen! . . . Good-by!" called Venters hoarsely.
"Bern—Bess—riders of the purple sage—good-by!"

CHAPTER XXII

BLACK STAR and Night, answering to spur, swept swiftly westward along the white, slow-rising, sage-bordered trail. Venters heard a mournful howl from Ring, but Whitie was silent. The blacks settled into their fleet, long-striding gallop. The wind sweetly fanned Venters's hot face. From the summit of the first low-swelling ridge he looked back. Lassiter waved his hand; Jane waved her scarf. Venters replied by standing in his stirrups and holding high his sombrero. Then the dip of the ridge hid them. From the height of the next he turned once more. Lassiter, Jane, and the burros had disappeared. They had gone down into the Pass. Venters felt a sensation of irreparable loss.

"Bern—look!" called Bess, pointing up the long slope.

A small, dark, moving dot split the line where purple sage met blue sky. That dot was a band of riders.

"Pull the black, Bess."

They slowed from gallop to canter, then to trot. The fresh and eager horses did not like the check.

"Bern, Black Star has great eyesight."

"I wonder if they're Tull's riders. They might be rustlers. But it's all the same to us."

The black dot grew to a dark patch moving under low dust-clouds. It grew all the time, though very slowly. There were long periods when it was in plain sight, and intervals when it dropped behind the sage. The blacks trotted for half an hour, for another half-hour, and still the moving patch appeared to stay on the horizon line. Gradually, however, as time passed, it began to enlarge, to creep down the slope, to encroach upon the intervening distance.

"Bess, what do you make them out?" asked Venters. "I don't think they're rustlers."

"They're sage-riders," replied Bess. "I see a white horse and several grays. Rustlers seldom ride any horses but bays and blacks."

"That white horse is Tull's. Pull the black, Bess. I'll get down and cinch up. We're in for some riding. Are you afraid?"

"Not now," answered the girl, smiling.

"You needn't be. Bess, you don't weigh enough to make Black Star know you're on him. I won't be able to stay with you. You'll leave Tull and his riders as if they were standing still."

"How about you?"

"Never fear. If I can't stay with you I can still laugh at Tull."

"Look, Bern! They've stopped on that ridge. They see us."

"Yes. But we're too far yet for them to make out who we are. They'll recognize the blacks first. We've passed most of the ridges and the thickest sage. Now, when I give the word, let Black Star go and ride!"

Venters calculated that a mile or more still intervened between them and the riders. They were approaching at a swift canter. Soon Venters recognized Tull's white horse, and concluded that the riders had likewise recognized Black Star and Night. But it would be impossible for Tull yet to see that the blacks were not ridden by Lassiter and Jane. Venters noted that Tull and the line of horsemen, perhaps ten or twelve in number, stopped several times and evidently looked hard down the slope. It must have been a puzzling circumstance for Tull. Venters laughed grimly at the thought of what Tull's rage would be when he finally discovered the trick. Venters meant to sheer out into the sage before Tull could possibly be sure who rode the blacks.

The gap closed to a distance to half a mile. Tull halted. His riders came up and formed a dark group around him. Venters thought he saw him wave his arms, and was certain of it when the riders dashed into the sage, to right and left of the trail. Tull had anticipated just the move held in mind by Venters.

"Now Bess!" shouted Venters. "Strike north. Go round those riders and turn west."

Black Star sailed over the low sage, and in a few leaps got into his stride and was running. Venters spurred Night after him. It

264

was hard going in the sage. The horses could run as well there, but keen eyesight and judgment must constantly be used by the riders in choosing ground. And continuous swerving from aisle to aisle between the brush, and leaping little washes and mounds of the pack-rats, and breaking through sage, made rough riding. When Venters had turned into a long aisle he had time to look up at Tull's riders. They were now strung out into an extended line riding northeast. And, as Venters and Bess were holding due north, this meant, if the horses of Tull and his riders had the speed and the staying power, they would head the blacks and turn them back down the slope. Tull's men were not saving their mounts; they were driving them desperately. Venters feared only an accident to Black Star or Night, and skilful riding would mitigate possibility of that. One glance ahead served to show him that Bess could pick a course through the sage as well as he. She looked neither back nor at the running riders, and bent forward over Black Star's neck and studied the ground ahead.

It struck Venters, presently, after he had glanced up from time to time, that Bess was drawing away from him as he had expected. He had, however, only thought of the light weight Black Star was carrying and of his superior speed; he saw now that the black was being ridden as never before, except when Jerry Card lost the race to Wrangle. How easily, gracefully, naturally, Bess sat her saddle! She could ride! Suddenly Venters remembered she had said she could ride. But he had not dreamed she was capable of such superb horsemanship. Then all at once, flashing over him, thrilling him, came the recollection that Bess was Oldring's Masked Rider.

He forgot Tull—the running riders—the race. He let Night have a free rein and felt him lengthen out to suit himself, knowing he would keep to Black Star's course, knowing that he had been chosen by the best rider now on the upland sage. For Jerry Card was dead. And fame had rivaled him with only one rider, and that was the slender girl who now swung so easily with Black Star's stride. Venters had abhorred her notoriety, but now he took passionate pride in her skill, her daring, her power over a horse. And he delved into his memory, recalling famous rides which he had heard related in the villages and round the camp-fires. Oldring's Masked Rider! Many times this strange rider, at once well

265

known and unknown, had escaped pursuers by matchless riding. He had to run the gantlet of vigilantes down the main street of Stone Bridge, leaving dead horses and dead rustlers behind. He had jumped his horse over the Gerber Wash, a deep, wide ravine separating the fields of Glaze from the wild sage. He had been surrounded north of Sterling; and he had broken through the line. How often had been told the story of day stampedes, of night raids, of pursuit, and then how the Masked Rider, swift as the wind, was gone in the sage! A fleet, dark horse—a slender, dark form—a black mask—a driving run down the slope—a dot on the purple sage—a shadowy, muffled steed disappearing in the night!

And this Masked Rider of the uplands had been Elizabeth Erne!

The sweet sage wind rushed in Venters's face and sang a song in his ears. He heard the dull, rapid beat of Night's hoofs; he saw Black Star drawing away, farther and farther. He realized both horses were swinging to the west. Then gunshots in the rear reminded him of Tull. Venters looked back. Far to the side, dropping behind, trooped the riders. They were shooting. Venters saw no puffs or dust, heard no whistling bullets. He was out of range. When he looked back again Tull's riders had given up pursuit. The best they could do, no doubt, had been to get near enough to recognize who really rode the blacks. Venters saw Tull drooping in his saddle.

Then Venters pulled Night out of his running stride. Those few miles had scarcely warmed the black, but Venters wished to save him. Bess turned, and, though she was far away, Venters caught the white glint of her waving hand. He held Night to a trot and rode on, seeing Bess and Black Star, and the sloping upward stretch of sage, and from time to time the receding black riders behind. Soon they disappeared behind a ridge, and he turned no more. They would go back to Lassiter's trail and follow it, and follow in vain. So Venters rode on, with the wind growing sweeter to taste and smell, and the purple sage richer and the sky bluer in his sight; and the song in his ears ringing. By and by Bess halted to wait for him, and he knew she had come to the trail. When he reached her it was to smile at sight of her standing with arms round Black Star's neck.

"Oh, Bern! I love him!" she cried. "He's beautiful; he knows;

266

and how he can run! I've had fast horses. But Black Star! . . . Wrangle never beat him!"

"I'm wondering if I didn't dream that. Bess, the blacks are grand. What it must have cost Jane—ah!—well, when we get out of this wild country with Star and Night, back to my old home in Illinois, we'll buy a beautiful farm with meadows and springs and cool shade. There we'll turn the horses free—free to roam and browse and drink—never to feel a spur again—never to be ridden!"

"I would like that," said Bess.

They rested. Then, mounting, they rode side by side up the white trail. The sun rose higher behind them. Far to the left a low line of green marked the site of Cottonwoods. Venters looked once and looked no more. Bess gazed only straight ahead. They put the blacks to the long, swinging rider's canter, and at times pulled them to a trot, and occasionally to a walk. The hours passed, the miles slipped behind, and the wall of rock loomed in the fore. The Notch opened wide. It was a rugged, stony pass, but with level and open trail, and Venters and Bess ran the blacks through it. An old trail led off to the right, taking the line of the wall, and this Venters knew to be the trail mentioned by Lassiter.

The little hamlet, Glaze, a white and green patch in the vast waste of purple, lay miles down a slope much like the Cottonwoods slope, only this descended to the west. And miles farther west a faint green spot marked the location of Stone Bridge. All the rest of that world was seemingly smooth, undulating sage, with no ragged lines of cañons to accentuate its wildness.

"Bess, we're safe—we're free!" said Venters. "We're alone on the sage. We're half way to Sterling."

"Ah! I wonder how it is with Lassiter and Miss Withersteen."

"Never fear, Bess. He'll outwit Tull. He'll get away and hide her safely. He might climb into Surprise Valley, but I don't think he'll go so far."

"Bern, will we ever find any place like our beautiful valley?"

"No. But, dear, listen. We'll go back some day, after years—ten years. Then we'll be forgotten. And our valley will be just as we left it."

"What if Balancing Rock falls and closes the outlet to the Pass?"

"I've thought of that. I'll pack in ropes and ropes. And if the outlet's closed we'll climb up the cliffs and over them to the valley and go down on rope ladders. It could be done. I know just where to make the climb, and I'll never forget."

"Oh yes, let us go back!"

"It's something sweet to look forward to. Bess, it's like all the future looks to me."

"Call me—Elizabeth," she said, shyly.

"Elizabeth Erne! It's a beautiful name. But I'll never forget Bess. Do you know—have you thought that very soon—by this time to-morrow—you will be Elizabeth Venters?"

So they rode on down the old trail. And the sun sloped to the west, and a golden sheen lay on the sage. The hours sped now; the afternoon waned. Often they rested the horses. The glisten of a pool of water in a hollow caught Venters's eye, and here he unsaddled the blacks and let them roll and drink and browse. When he and Bess rode up out of the hollow the sun was low, a crimson ball, and the valley seemed veiled in purple fire and smoke. It was that short time when the sun appeared to rest before setting, and silence, like a cloak of invisible life, lay heavy on all that shimmering world of sage.

They watched the sun begin to bury its red curve under the dark horizon.

"We'll ride on till late," he said. "Then you can sleep a little, while I watch and graze the horses. And we'll ride into Sterling early to-morrow. We'll be married! . . . We'll be in time to catch the stage. We'll tie Black Star and Night behind—and then—for a country not wild and terrible like this!"

"Oh, Bern! . . . But look! The sun is setting on the sage—the last time for us till we dare come again to the Utah border. Ten years! Oh, Bern, look, so you will never forget!"

Slumbering, fading purple fire burned over the undulating sage ridges. Long streaks and bars and shafts and spears fringed the far western slope. Drifting, golden veils mingled with low, purple shadows. Colors and shades changed in slow, wondrous transformation.

Suddenly Venters was startled by a low, rumbling roar—so low that it was like the roar in a sea-shell.

"Bess, did you hear anything?" he whispered.

"No."

"Listen! . . . Maybe I only imagined— *Ah!*"

Out of the east or north, from remote distance, breathed an infinitely low, continuously long sound—deep, weird, detonating, thundering, deadening—dying.

CHAPTER XXIII

THE FALL OF BALANCING ROCK

THROUGH tear-blurred sight Jane Withersteen watched Venters and Elizabeth Erne and the black racers disappear over the ridge of sage.

"They're gone!" said Lassiter. "An' they're safe now. An' there'll never be a day of their comin' happy lives but what they'll remember Jane Withersteen an'—an' Uncle Jim! . . . I reckon, Jane, we'd better be on our way."

The burros obediently wheeled and started down the break with little, cautious steps, but Lassiter had to leash the whining dogs and lead them. Jane felt herself bound in a feeling that was neither listlessness nor indifference, yet which rendered her incapable of interest. She was still strong in body, but emotionally tired. That hour at the entrance to Deception Pass had been the climax of her suffering—the flood of her wrath—the last of her sacrifice—the supremity of her love—and the attainment of peace. She thought that if she had little Fay she would not ask any more of life.

Like an automaton she followed Lassiter down the steep trail of dust and bits of weathered stone; and when the little slides moved with her or piled around her knees she experienced no alarm. Vague relief came to her in the sense of being enclosed between dark stone walls, deep hidden from the glare of sun, from the glistening sage. Lassiter lengthened the stirrup straps on one of the burros and bade her mount and ride close to him. She was to keep the burro from cracking his little hard hoofs on stones. Then she was riding on between dark, gleaming walls. There were quiet and rest and coolness in this cañon. She noted indifferently that they passed close under shady, bulging shelves of cliff, through patches of grass and sage and thicket and groves of slender trees, and over white, pebbly washes, and around masses of broken rock. The burros trotted tirelessly; the dogs, once more free, pattered tirelessly; and Lassiter led on with never a stop, and at every open place he looked back. The shade under the walls gave place to sunlight. And presently they came to a dense thicket of slender trees, through which they passed to rich, green grass and water. Here Lassiter rested the burros for a little while, but he was restless, uneasy, silent, always listening, peering under the trees. She dully reflected that enemies were behind them—before them; still the thought awakened no dread or concern or interest.

At his bidding she mounted and rode on close to the heels of his burro. The cañon narrowed; the walls lifted their rugged rims higher; and the sun shone down hot from the center of the blue stream of sky above. Lassiter traveled slower, with more exceeding care as to the ground he chose, and he kept speaking low to the dogs. They were now hunting-dogs—keen, alert, suspicious, sniffing the warm breeze. The monotony of the yellow walls broke in change of color and smooth surface, and the rugged outline of rims grew craggy. Splits appeared in deep breaks, and gorges running at right angles, and then the Pass opened wide at a junction of intersecting cañons.

Lassiter dismounted, led his burro, called the dogs close, and proceeded at snail pace through dark masses of rock and dense thickets under the left wall. Long he watched and listened before venturing to cross the mouths of side cañons. At length he halted, tied his burro, lifted a warning hand to Jane, and then slipped away among the boulders, and, followed by the stealthy dogs, disappeared from sight. The time he remained absent was neither short nor long to Jane Withersteen.

When he reached her side again he was pale, and his lips were set in a hard line, and his gray eyes glittered coldly. Bidding her dismount, he led the burros into a covert of stones and cedars, and tied them.

"Jane, I've run into the fellers I've been lookin' for, an' I'm goin' after them," he said.

"Why?" she asked.

"I reckon I won't take time to tell you."

"Couldn't we slip by without being seen?"

"Likely enough. But that ain't my game. An' I'd like to know, in case I don't come back, what you'll do."

"What can I do?"

"I reckon you can go back to Tull. Or stay in the Pass an' be taken off by rustlers. Which 'll you do?"

"I don't know. I can't think very well. But I believe I'd rather be taken off by rustlers."

Lassiter sat down, put his head in his hands, and remained for a few moments in what appeared to be deep and painful thought. When he lifted his face it was haggard, lined, cold as sculptured marble.

"I'll go. I only mentioned that chance of my not comin' back. I'm pretty sure to come."

"Need you risk so much? Must you fight more? Haven't you shed enough blood?"

"I'd like to tell you why I'm goin'," he continued, in coldness he had seldom used to her. She remarked it, but it was the same to her as if he had spoken with his old gentle warmth. "But I reckon I won't. Only, I'll say that mercy an' goodness, such as is in you, though they're the grand things in human nature, can't be lived up to on this Utah border. Life's hell out here. You think— or you used to think—that your religion made this life heaven. Mebbe them scales on your eyes has dropped now. Jane, I wouldn't have you no different, an' that's why I'm going to try to hide you somewhere in this Pass. I'd like to hide many more women, for I've come to see there are more like you among your people. An' I'd like you to see jest how hard an' cruel this border life is. It's bloody. You'd think churches an' churchmen would make it better. They make it worse. You give names to things— bishops, elders, ministers, Mormonism, duty, faith, glory. You dream—or you're driven mad. I'm a man, an' I know. I name fanatics, followers, blind women, oppressors, thieves, ranchers, rustlers, riders. An' we have—what you've lived through these last months. It can't be helped. But it can't last always. An' remember this—some day the border 'll be better, cleaner, for the ways of men like Lassiter!"

She saw him shake his tall form erect, look at her strangely and steadfastly, and then, noiselessly, stealthily slip away amid the rocks and trees. Ring and Whitie, not being bidden to follow, remained with Jane. She felt extreme weariness, yet somehow it did not seem to be of her body. And she sat down in the shade and tried to think. She saw a creeping lizard, cactus flowers, the drooping burros, the resting dogs, an eagle high over a yellow crag. Once the meanest flower, a color, the flight of the bee, or any living thing had given her deepest joy. Lassiter had gone off, yielding to his incurable blood lust, probably to his own death; and she was sorry, but there was no feeling in her sorrow.

Suddenly from the mouth of the cañon just beyond her rang out a clear, sharp report of a rifle. Echoes clapped. Then followed a piercingly high yell of anguish, quickly breaking. Again echoes clapped, in grim imitation. Dull revolver shots—hoarse yells—pound of hoofs—shrill neighs of horses—commingling of echoes—and again silence! Lassiter must be busily engaged, thought Jane, and no chill trembled over her, no blanching tightened her skin. Yes, the border was a bloody place. But life had always been bloody. Men were blood-spillers. Phases of the history of the world flashed through her mind—Greek and Roman wars, dark, mediæval times, the crimes in the name of religion. On sea, on land, everywhere—shooting, stabbing, cursing, clashing, fighting men! Greed, power, oppression, fanaticism, love, hate, revenge, justice, freedom—for these, men killed one another.

She lay there under the cedars, gazing up through the delicate lacelike foliage at the blue sky, and she thought and wondered and did not care.

More rattling shots disturbed the noonday quiet. She heard a sliding of weathered rock, a hoarse shout of warning, a yell of alarm, again the clear, sharp crack of the rifle, and another cry that was a cry of death. Then rifle reports pierced a dull volley of revolver shots. Bullets whizzed over Jane's hiding-place; one struck a stone and whined away in the air. After that, for a time, succeeded desultory shots; and then they ceased under long, thundering fire from heavier guns.

Sooner or later, then, Jane heard the cracking of horses' hoofs on the stones, and the sound came nearer and nearer. Silence intervened until Lassiter's soft, jingling step assured her of his approach. When he appeared he was covered with blood.

"All right, Jane," he said. "I come back. An' don't worry."

With water from a canteen he washed the blood from his face and hands.

"Jane, hurry now. Tear my scarf in two, an' tie up these places. That hole through my hand is some inconvenient, worse 'n this cut over my ear. There—you're doin' fine! Not a bit nervous—no tremblin'. I reckon I ain't done your courage justice. I'm glad you're brave jest now—you'll need to be. Well, I was hid pretty good, enough to keep them from shootin' me deep, but they was slingin' lead close all the time. I used up all the rifle shells, an' then I went after them. Mebbe you heard. It was then I got hit. I had to use up every shell in my own gun, an' they did, too, as I seen. Rustlers an' Mormons, Jane! An' now I'm packin' five bullet holes in my carcass, an' guns without shells. Hurry, now."

He unstrapped the saddle-bags from the burros, slipped the saddles and let them lie, turned the burros loose, and, calling the dogs, led the way through stones and cedars to an open where two horses stood.

"Jane, are you strong?" he asked.

"I think so. I'm not tired," Jane replied.

"I don't mean that way. Can you bear up?"

"I think I can bear anything."

"I reckon you look a little cold an' thick. So I'm preparin' you."

"For what?"

"I didn't tell you why I jest had to go after them fellers. I couldn't tell you. I believe you'd have died. But I can tell you now—if you'll bear up under a shock?"

"Go on, my friend."

"*I've got little Fay!* Alive—bad hurt—but she'll live!"

Jane Withersteen's dead-locked feeling, rent by Lassiter's deep, quivering voice, leaped into an agony of sensitive life.

"Here," he added, and showed her where little Fay lay on the grass.

Unable to speak, unable to stand, Jane dropped on her knees. By that long, beautiful golden hair Jane recognized the beloved Fay. But Fay's loveliness was gone. Her face was drawn and looked old with grief. But she was not dead—her heart beat—and Jane Withersteen gathered strength and lived again.

"You see I jest had to go after Fay," Lassiter was saying, as he knelt to bathe her little pale face. "But I reckon I don't want no more choices like the one I had to make. There was a crippled feller in that bunch, Jane. Mebbe Venters crippled him. Anyway, that's why they were holdin' up here. I seen little Fay first thing, an' was hard put to it to figure out a way to get her. An' I wanted hosses, too. I had to take chances. So I crawled close to their camp. One feller jumped a hoss with little Fay, an' when I shot him, of course she dropped. She's stunned an' bruised—she fell right on her head. Jane, she's comin' to! She ain't bad hurt!"

Fay's long lashes fluttered; her eyes opened. At first they seemed glazed over. They looked dazed by pain. Then they quickened, darkened, to shine with intelligence—bewilderment—memory—and sudden wonderful joy.

"Muvver—Jane!" she whispered.

"Oh, little Fay, little Fay!" cried Jane, lifting, clasping the child to her.

"*Now*, we've got to rustle!" said Lassiter, in grim coolness. "Jane, look down the Pass!"

Across the mounds of rock and sage Jane caught sight of a band of riders filing out of the narrow neck of the Pass; and in the lead was a white horse, which, even at a distance of a mile or more, she knew.

"Tull!" she almost screamed.

"I reckon. But, Jane, we've still got the game in our hands. They're ridin' tired hosses. Venters likely give them a chase. He wouldn't forget that. An' we've fresh hosses."

Hurriedly he strapped on the saddle-bags, gave quick glance to girths and cinches and stirrups, then leaped astride.

"Lift little Fay up," he said.

With shaking arms Jane complied.

"Get back your nerve, woman! This 's life or death now. Mind that. Climb up! Keep your wits. Stick close to me. Watch where your hoss 's goin' an' ride!"

Somehow Jane mounted; somehow found strength to hold the reins, to spur, to cling on, to ride. A horrible quaking, craven fear possessed her soul. Lassiter led the swift flight across the wide space, over washes, through sage, into a narrow cañon where the rapid clatter of hoofs rapped sharply from the walls. The wind roared in her ears; the gleaming cliffs swept by; trail and sage and grass moved under her. Lassiter's bandaged, blood-stained face turned to her; he shouted encouragement; he looked back down the Pass; he spurred his horse. Jane clung on, spurring likewise. And the horses settled from hard, furious gallop into a long-striding, driving run. She had never ridden at anything like that pace; desperately she tried to get the swing of the horse, to be of some help to him in that race, to see the best of the ground and guide him into it. But she failed of everything except to keep her seat in the saddle, and to spur and spur. At times she closed her eyes, unable to bear sight of Fay's golden curls streaming in the wind. She could not pray; she could not rail; she no longer cared for herself. All of life, of good, of use in the world, of hope in heaven centered in Lassiter's ride with little Fay to safety. She would have tried to turn the iron-jawed brute she rode; she would have given herself to that relentless, dark-browed Tull. But she knew Lassiter would turn with her, so she rode on and on.

Whether that run was of moments or hours Jane Withersteen could not tell. Lassiter's horse covered her with froth that blew back in white streams. Both horses ran their limit, were allowed to slow down in time to save them, and went on dripping, heaving, staggering.

"Oh, Lassiter, we must run—we must run!"

He looked back, saying nothing. The bandage had blown from his head, and blood trickled down his face. He was bowing under the strain of injuries, of the ride, of his burden. Yet how cool and gray he looked—how intrepid!

The horses walked, trotted, galloped, ran, to fall again to walk. Hours sped or dragged. Time was an instant—an eternity. Jane Withersteen felt hell pursuing her, and dared not look back for fear she would fall from her horse.

"Oh, Lassiter! Is he coming?"

The grim rider looked over his shoulder, but said no word. Little Fay's golden hair floated on the breeze. The sun shone; the walls gleamed; the sage glistened. And then it seemed the sun vanished, the walls shaded, the sage paled. The horses walked— trotted—galloped—ran—to fall again to walk. Shadows gathered under shelving cliffs. The cañon turned, brightened, opened into long, wide, wall-enclosed valley. Again the sun, lowering in the west, reddened the sage. Far ahead round, scrawled stone appeared to block the Pass.

"Bear up, Jane, bear up!" called Lassiter. "It's our game, if you don't weaken."

"Lassiter! Go on—*alone!* Save little Fay!"

"Only with you!"

"Oh!—I'm a coward—a miserable coward! I can't fight or think or hope or pray! I'm lost! Oh, Lassiter, look back! Is he coming? I'll not—hold out—"

"Keep your breath, woman, an' ride not for yourself or for me, but for Fay!"

A last breaking run across the sage brought Lassiter's horse to a walk.

"He's done," said the rider.

"Oh, no—no!" moaned Jane.

"Look back, Jane, look back. Three—four miles we've come across this valley, an' no Tull yet in sight. Only a few more miles!"

Jane looked back over the long stretch of sage, and found the narrow gap in the wall, out of which came a file of dark horses with a white horse in the lead. Sight of the riders acted upon Jane as a stimulant. The weight of cold, horrible terror lessened. And, gazing forward at the dogs, at Lassiter's limping horse, at the blood on his face, at the rocks growing nearer, last at Fay's golden hair, the ice left her veins, and slowly, strangely, she gained hold of strength that she believed would see her to the safety Lassiter promised. And, as she gazed, Lassiter's horse stumbled and fell.

He swung his leg and slipped from the saddle.

"Jane, take the child," he said, and lifted Fay up. Jane clasped her arms suddenly strong. "They're gainin'," went on Lassiter, as he watched the pursuing riders. "But we'll beat 'em yet."

Turning with Jane's bridle in his hand, he was about to start when he saw the saddle-bag on the fallen horse.

"I've jest about got time," he muttered, and with swift fingers that did not blunder or fumble he loosened the bag and threw it over his shoulder. Then he started to run, leading Jane's horse, and he ran, and trotted, and walked, and ran again. Close ahead now Jane saw a rise of bare rock. Lassiter reached it, searched along the base, and, finding a low place, dragged the weary horse up and over round, smooth stone. Looking backward, Jane saw Tull's white horse not a mile distant, with riders strung out in a long line behind him. Looking forward, she saw more valley to the right, and to the left a towering cliff. Lassiter pulled the horse and kept on.

Little Fay lay in her arms with wide-open eyes—eyes which were still shadowed by pain, but no longer fixed, glazed in terror. The golden curls blew across Jane's lips; the little hands feebly clasped her arm; a ghost of a troubled, trustful smile hovered round the sweet lips. And Jane Withersteen awoke to the spirit of a lioness.

Lassiter was leading the horse up a smooth slope toward cedar-trees of twisted and bleached appearance. Among these he halted.

"Jane, give me the girl an' get down," he said. As if it wrenched him he unbuckled the empty black guns with a strange air of finality. He then received Fay in his arms and stood a moment looking backward. Tull's white horse mounted the ridge of round stone, and several bays or blacks followed. "I wonder what he'll think when he sees them empty guns. Jane, bring your saddle-bag and climb after me."

A glistening, wonderful bare slope, with little holes, swelled up and up to lose itself in a frowning yellow cliff. Jane closely watched her steps and climbed behind Lassiter. He moved slowly. Perhaps he was only husbanding his strength. But she saw drops of blood on the stone, and then she knew. They climbed and climbed without looking back. Her breast labored; she began to feel as if little points of fiery steel were penetrating her side into her lungs. She heard the panting of Lassiter and the quicker panting of the dogs.

"Wait—here," he said.

Before her rose a bulge of stone, nicked with little cut steps, and above that a corner of yellow wall, and overhanging that a vast, ponderous cliff.

The dogs pattered up, disappeared round the corner. Lassiter mounted the steps with Fay, and he swayed like a drunken man, and he too disappeared. But instantly he returned alone, and half ran, half slipped down to her.

Then from below pealed up hoarse shouts of angry men. Tull

and several of his riders had reached the spot where Lassiter had parted with his guns.

"You'll need that breath—mebbe!" said Lassiter, facing downward, with glittering eyes.

"Now, Jane, the last pull," he went on. "Walk up them little steps. I'll follow an' steady you. Don't think. Jest go. Little Fay's above. Her eyes are open. She jest said to me, 'Where's muvver Jane?'"

Without a fear or a tremor or a slip or a touch of Lassiter's hand Jane Withersteen walked up that ladder of cut steps.

He pushed her round the corner of the wall. Fay lay, with wide staring eyes, in the shade of a gloomy wall. The dogs waited. Lassiter picked up the child and turned into a dark cleft. It zigzagged. It widened. It opened. Jane was amazed at a wonderfully smooth and steep incline leading up between ruined, splintered, toppling walls. A red haze from the setting sun filled this passage. Lassiter climbed with slow, measured steps, and blood dripped from him to make splotches on the white stone. Jane tried not to step in his blood, but was compelled, for she found no other footing. The saddle-bag began to drag her down; she gasped for breath; she thought her heart was bursting. Slower, slower yet the rider climbed, whistling as he breathed. The incline widened. Huge pinnacles and monuments of stone stood alone, leaning fearfully. Red sunset haze shone through cracks where the wall had split. Jane did not look high, but she felt the overshadowing of broken rims above. She felt that it was a fearful, menacing place. And she climbed on in heartrending effort. And she fell beside Lassiter and Fay at the top of the incline in a narrow, smooth divide.

He staggered to his feet—staggered to a huge, leaning rock that rested on a small pedestal. He put his hand on it—the hand that had been shot through—and Jane saw blood drip from the ragged hole. Then he fell.

"Jane—I—can't—do—it!" he whispered.

"What?"

"Roll the—stone! . . . All my—life I've loved—to roll stones—an' now I—can't!"

"What of it? You talk strangely. Why roll that stone?"

"I planned to—fetch you here—to roll this stone. See! It'll smash the crags—loosen the walls—close the outlet!"

As Jane Withersteen gazed down that long incline, walled in by crumbling cliffs, awaiting only the slightest jar to make them fall asunder, she saw Tull appear at the bottom and begin to climb. A rider followed him—another—and another.

"See! Tull! The riders!"

"Yes—they'll get us—now."

"Why? Haven't you strength left to roll the stone?"

"Jane—it ain't that—I've lost my nerve!"

"You! . . . Lassiter!"

"I wanted to roll it—meant to—but I—can't. Venters's valley is down behind here. We could—live there. But if I roll the stone— we're shut in for always. I don't dare. I'm thinkin' of you!"

"Lassiter! Roll the stone!" she cried.

He arose, tottering, but with set face, and again he placed the bloody hand on the Balancing Rock. Jane Withersteen gazed from him down the passageway. Tull was climbing. Almost, she thought, she saw his dark, relentless face. Behind him more riders climbed. What did they mean for Fay—for Lassiter—for herself?

"Roll the stone! . . . Lassiter, I love you!"

Under all his deathly pallor, and the blood, and the iron of seared cheek and lined brow, worked a great change. He placed both hands on the rock and then leaned his shoulder there and braced his powerful body.

"Roll the stone!"

It stirred, it groaned, it grated, it moved; and with a slow grinding, as of wrathful relief, began to lean. It had waited ages to fall, and now was slow in starting. Then, as if suddenly instinct with life, it leaped hurtingly down to alight on the steep incline, to bound more swiftly into the air, to gather momentum, to plunge into the lofty leaning crag below. The crag thundered into atoms. A wave of air—a splitting shock! Dust shrouded the sunset red of shaking rims; dust shrouded Tull as he fell on his knees with uplifted arms. Shafts and monuments and sections of wall fell majestically.

From the depths there rose a long-drawn rumbling roar. The outlet to Deception Pass closed forever.

THE LAST TRAIL

CHAPTER I

Twilight of a certain summer day, many years ago, shaded softly down over the wild Ohio valley bringing keen anxiety to a traveler on the lonely river trail. He had expected to reach Fort Henry with his party on this night, thus putting a welcome end to the long, rough, hazardous journey through the wilderness; but the swift, on-coming dusk made it imperative to halt. The narrow, forest-skirted trail, difficult to follow in broad daylight, apparently led into gloomy aisles in the woods. His guide had abandoned him that morning, making excuse that his services were no longer needed; his teamster was new to the frontier, and, altogether, the situation caused him much uneasiness.

"I wouldn't so much mind another night in camp, if the guide had not left us," he said in a low tone to the teamster.

That worthy shook his shaggy head, and growled while he began unhitching the horses.

"Uncle," said a young man, who had clambered out from the wagon, "we must be within a few miles of Fort Henry."

"How d'ye know we're near the fort?" interrupted the teamster, "or safe, either, fer thet matter? I don't know this country."

"The guide assured me we could easily make Fort Henry by sundown."

"Thet guide! I tell ye, Mr. Sheppard——"

"Not so loud. Do not alarm my daughter," cautioned the man who had been called Sheppard.

"Did ye notice anythin' queer about thet guide?" asked the teamster, lowering his voice. "Did ye see how oneasy he was last night? Did it strike ye he left us in a hurry, kind of excited like, in spite of his offhand manner?"

"Yes, he acted odd, or so it seemed to me," replied Sheppard. "How about you, Will?"

"Now that I think of it, I believe he was queer. He behaved like a man who expected somebody, or feared something might happen. I fancied, however, that it was simply the manner of a woodsman."

"Wal, I hev my opinion," said the teamster, in a gruff whisper. "Ye was in a hurry to be a-goin', an' wouldn't take no advice. The fur-trader at Fort Pitt didn't give this guide Jenks no good send off. Said he wasn't well-known round Pitt, 'cept he could handle a knife some."

"What is your opinion?" asked Sheppard, as the teamster paused.

"Wal, the valley below Pitt is full of renegades, outlaws an' hoss-thieves. The redskins ain't so bad as they used to be, but these white fellers are wusser'n ever. This guide Jenks might be in with them, that's all. Mebbe I'm wrong. I hope so. The way he left us looks bad."

"We won't borrow trouble. If we have come all this way without seeing either Indian or outlaw—in fact, without incident—I feel certain we can perform the remainder of the journey in safety." Then Mr. Sheppard raised his voice. "Here, Helen, you lazy girl, come out of that wagon. We want some supper. Will, you gather some firewood, and we'll soon give this gloomy little glen a more cheerful aspect."

As Mr. Sheppard turned toward the canvas-covered wagon a girl leaped lightly down beside him. She was nearly as tall as he.

"Is this Fort Henry?" she asked, cheerily, beginning to dance around him. "Where's the inn? I'm *so* hungry. How glad I am to get out of that wagon! I'd like to run. Isn't this a lonesome, lovely spot?"

A camp-fire soon crackled with hiss and sputter, and fragrant wood-smoke filled the air. Steaming kettle, and savory steaks of venison cheered the hungry travelers, making them forget for the time the desertion of their guide and the fact that they might be lost. The last glow faded entirely out of the western sky. Night enveloped the forest, and the little glade was a bright spot in the gloom.

The flickering light showed Mr. Sheppard to be a well-preserved old man with gray hair and ruddy, kindly face. The nephew had a boyish, frank expression. The girl was a spendid specimen of womanhood. Her large, laughing eyes were as dark as the shadows beneath the trees.

Suddenly a quick start on Helen's part interrupted the merry flow of conversation. She sat bolt upright with half-averted face.

"Cousin, what is the matter?" asked Will, quickly.

Helen remained motionless.

"My dear," said Mr. Sheppard sharply.

"I heard a footstep," she whispered, pointing with trembling finger toward the impenetrable blackness beyond the camp-fire.

All could hear a soft patter on the leaves. Then distinct footfalls broke the silence.

The tired teamster raised his shaggy head and glanced fearfully around the glade. Mr. Sheppard and Will gazed doubtfully toward the foliage; but Helen did not change her position. The travelers appeared stricken by the silence and solitude of the place. The faint hum of insects, and the low moan of the night wind, seemed accentuated by the almost painful stillness.

"A panther, most likely," suggested Sheppard, in a voice which he intended should be reassuring. "I saw one to-day slinking along the trail."

"I'd better get my gun from the wagon," said Will.

"How dark and wild it is here!" exclaimed Helen nervously. "I believe I was frightened. Perhaps I fancied it—there! Again —listen. Ah!"

Two tall figures emerged from the darkness into the circle of light, and with swift, supple steps gained the camp-fire before any of the travelers had time to move. They were Indians, and ˋe brandishing of their tomahawks proclaimed that they were ostile.

"Ugh!" grunted the taller savage, as he looked down upon the defenseless, frightened group.

As the menacing figures stood in the glare of the fire gazing at the party with shifty eyes, they presented a frightful appearance. Fierce lineaments, all the more so because of bars of paint, the hideous, shaven heads adorned with tufts of hair holding a single feather, sinewy, copper-colored limbs suggestive of action and endurance, the general aspect of untamed ferocity, appalled the travelers and chilled their blood.

Grunts and chuckles manifested the satisfaction with which the Indians fell upon the half-finished supper. They caused it to vanish with astonishing celerity, and resembled wolves rather than human beings in their greediness.

Helen looked timidly around as if hoping tc see those who would aid, and the savages regarded her with ill humor. A movement on the part of any member of the group caused muscular hands to steal toward the tomahawks.

Suddenly the larger savage clutched his companion's knee. Then lifting his hatchet, shook it with a significant gesture in

Sheppard's face, at the same time putting a finger on his lips to enjoin silence. Both Indians became statuesque in their immobility. They crouched in an attitude of listening, with heads bent on one side, nostrils dilated, and mouths open.

One, two, three moments passed. The silence of the forest appeared to be unbroken; but ears as keen as those of a deer had detected some sound. The larger savage dropped noiselessly to the ground, where he lay stretched out with his ear to the ground. The other remained immovable; only his beady eyes gave signs of life, and these covered every point.

Finally the big savage rose silently, pointed down the dark trail, and strode out of the circle of light. His companion followed close at his heels. The two disappeared in the black shadows like specters, as silently as they had come.

"Well!" breathed Helen.

"I am immensely relieved!" exclaimed Will.

"What do you make of such strange behavior?" Sheppard asked of the teamster.

"I 'spect they got wind of somebody; most likely thet guide, an 'll be back again. If they ain't, it's because they got switched off by some signs or tokens, skeered, perhaps, by the scent of the wind."

Hardly had he ceased speaking when again the circle of light was invaded by stalking forms.

"I thought so! Here comes the skulkin' varmints," whispered the teamster.

But he was wrong. A deep, calm voice spoke the single word: "Friends."

Two men in the brown garb of woodsmen approached. One approached the travelers; the other remained in the background, leaning upon a long, black rifle.

Thus exposed to the glare of the flames, the foremost woodsman presented a singularly picturesque figure. His costume was
the fringed buckskins of the border. Fully six feet tall, this
lithe-limbed young giant had something of the wild, free grace
of the Indian in his posture.

He surveyed the wondering travelers with dark, grave eyes.

"Did the reddys do any mischief?" he asked.

"No, they didn't harm us," replied Sheppard. "They ate our
supper, and slipped off into the woods without so much as
touching one of us. But, indeed, sir, we are mighty glad to see
you."

Will echoed this sentiment, and Helen's big eyes were fastened
upon the stranger in welcome and wonder.

"We saw your fire blazin' through the twilight, an' came up
just in time to see the Injuns make off."

"Might they not hide in the bushes and shoot us?" asked
Will, who had listened to many a border story at Fort Pitt. "It
seems as if we'd make good targets in this light."

The gravity of the woodsman's face relaxed.

"You will pursue them?" asked Helen.

"They've melted into the night-shadows long ago," he replied. "Who was your guide?"

"I hired him at Fort Pitt. He left us suddenly this morning.
A big man, with black beard and bushy eyebrows. A bit of his
ear had been shot or cut out," Sheppard replied.

"Jenks, one of Bing Legget's border-hawks."

"You have his name right. And who may Bing Legget be?"

"He's an outlaw. Jenks has been tryin' to lead you into a
trap. Likely he expected those Injuns to show up a day or two
ago. Somethin' went wrong with the plan, I reckon. Mebbe he

was waitin' for five Shawnees, an' mebbe he'll never see three of 'em again."

Something suggestive, cold, and grim, in the last words did not escape the listeners.

"How far are we from Fort Henry?" asked Sheppard.

"Eighteen miles as a crow flies; longer by trail."

"Treachery!" exclaimed the old man. "We were no more than that this morning. It is indeed fortunate that you found us. I take it you are from Fort Henry, and will guide us there? I am an old friend of Colonel Zane's. He will appreciate any kindness you may show us. Of course you know him?"

"I am Jonathan Zane."

Sheppard suddenly realized that he was facing the most celebrated scout on the border. In Revolutionary times Zane's fame had extended even to the far Atlantic Colonies.

"And your companion?" asked Sheppard with keen interest. He guessed what might be told. Border lore coupled Jonathan Zane with a strange and terrible character, a border Nemesis, a mysterious, shadowy, elusive man, whom few pioneers ever saw, but of whom all knew.

"Wetzel," answered Zane.

With one accord the travelers gazed curiously at Zane's silent companion. In the dim background of the glow cast by the fire, he stood a gigantic figure, dark, quiet, and yet with something intangible in his shadowy outline.

Suddenly he appeared to merge into the gloom as if he really were a phantom. A warning, "Hist!" came from the bushes.

With one swift kick Zane scattered the camp-fire.

The travelers waited with bated breaths. They could hear nothing save the beating of their own hearts; they could not even see each other.

"Better go to sleep," came in Zane's calm voice. What a relief it was! "We'll keep watch, an' at daybreak guide you to Fort Henry."

CHAPTER II

COLONEL ZANE, a rugged, stalwart pioneer, with a strong, dark face, sat listening to his old friend's dramatic story. At its close a genial smile twinkled in his fine dark eyes.

"Well, well, Sheppard, no doubt it was a thrilling adventure to you," he said. "It might have been a little more interesting, and doubtless would, had I not sent Wetzel and Jonathan to look you up."

"You did? How on earth did you know I was on the border? I counted much on the surprise I should give you."

"My Indian runners leave Fort Pitt ahead of any travelers, and acquaint me with particulars."

"I remembered a fleet-looking Indian who seemed to be asking for information about us, when we arrived at Fort Pitt. I am sorry I did not take the fur-trader's advice in regard to the guide. But I was in such a hurry to come, and didn't feel able to bear the expense of a raft or boat that we might come by river. My nephew brought considerable gold, and I all my earthly possessions."

"All's well that ends well," replied Colonel Zane cheerily. "But we must thank Providence that Wetzel and Jonathan came up in the nick of time."

"Indeed, yes. I'm not likely to forget those fierce savages. How they slipped off into the darkness! I wonder if Wetzel pursued them? He disappeared last night, and we did not see him again. In fact we hardly had a fair look at him. I question if I should recognize him now, unless by his great stature."

"He was ahead of Jonathan on the trail. That is Wetzel's way. In times of danger he is seldom seen, yet is always near. But come, let us go out and look around. I am running up a log cabin which will come in handy for you."

They passed out into the shade of pine and maples. A winding path led down a gentle slope. On the hillside under a spreading tree a throng of bearded pioneers, clad in faded buckskins and wearing white-ringed coonskin caps, were erecting a log cabin.

"Life here on the border is keen, hard, invigorating," said Colonel Zane. "I tell you, George Sheppard, in spite of your gray hair and your pretty daughter, you have come out West because you want to live among men who do things."

"Colonel, I won't gainsay I've still got hot blood," replied Sheppard; "but I came to Fort Henry for land. My old home in Williamsburg has fallen into ruin together with the fortunes of my family. I brought my daughter and my nephew because I wanted them to take root in new soil."

"Well, George, right glad we are to have you. Where are your sons? I remember them, though 'tis sixteen long years since I left old Williamsburg."

"Gone. The Revolution took my sons. Helen is the last of the family."

"Well, well, indeed that's hard. Independence has cost you colonists as big a price as border-freedom has us pioneers. Come, old friend, forget the past. A new life begins for you here, and it will be one which gives you much. See, up goes a cabin; that will soon be your home."

Sheppard's eye marked the sturdy pioneers and a fast diminishing pile of white-oak logs.

"Ho-heave!" cried a brawny foreman.

A dozen stout shoulders sagged beneath a well-trimmed log.

"Ho-heave!" yelled the foreman.

"See, up she goes," cried the colonel, "and to-morrow night she'll shed rain."

They walked down a sandy lane bounded on the right by a wide, green clearing, and on the left by a line of chestnuts and maples, outposts of the thick forests beyond.

"Yours is a fine site for a house," observed Sheppard, taking in the clean-trimmed field that extended up the hillside, a brook that splashed clear and noisy over the stones to tarry in a little grass-bound lake which forced water through half-hollowed logs into a spring house.

"I think so; this is the fourth time I've put up a cabin on this land," replied the colonel.

"How's that?"

"The redskins are keen to burn things."

Sheppard laughed at the pioneer's reply. "It's not difficult, Colonel Zane, to understand why Fort Henry has stood all these years, with you as its leader. Certainly the location for your cabin is the finest in the settlement. What a view!"

High upon a bluff overhanging the majestic, slow-winding Ohio, the colonel's cabin afforded a commanding position from which to view the picturesque valley. Sheppard's eye first caught the outline of the huge, bold, time-blackened fort which frowned protectingly over surrounding log-cabins; then he saw the wide-sweeping river with its verdant islands, golden, sandy bars, and willow-bordered shores, while beyond, rolling pastures of wavy grass merging into green forests that swept upward with slow swell until lost in the dim purple of distant mountains.

"Sixteen years ago I came out of the thicket upon yonder bluff, and saw this valley. I was deeply impressed by its beauty, but more by its wonderful promise."

"Were you alone?"

"I and my dog. There had been a few white men before me on the river; but I was the first to see this glorious valley from the bluff. Now, George, I'll let you have a hundred acres of well-cleared land. The soil is so rich you can raise two crops in one season. With some stock, and a few good hands, you'll soon be a busy man."

"I didn't expect so much land; I can't well afford to pay for it."

"Talk to me of payment when the farm yields an income. Is this young nephew of yours strong and willing?"

"He is, and has gold enough to buy a big farm."

"Let him keep his money, and make a comfortable home for some good lass. We marry our young people early out here. And your daughter, George, is she fitted for this hard border life?"

"Never fear for Helen."

"The brunt of this pioneer work falls on our women. God bless them, how heroic they've been! The life here is rough for a man, let alone a woman. But it is a man's game. We need girls, girls who will bear strong men. Yet I am always saddened when I see one come out on the border."

"I think I knew what I was bringing Helen to, and she didn't flinch," said Sheppard, somewhat surprised at the tone in which the colonel spoke.

"No one knows until he has lived on the border. Well, well,

all this is discouraging to you. Ah! here is Miss Helen with my sister."

The colonel's fine, dark face lost its sternness, and brightened with a smile.

"I hope you rested well after your long ride."

"I am seldom tired, and I have been made most comfortable. I thank you and your sister," replied the girl, giving Colonel Zane her hand, and including both him and his sister in her grateful glance.

The colonel's sister was a slender, handsome young woman, whose dark beauty showed to most effective advantage by the contrast with her companion's fair skin, golden hair, and blue eyes.

Beautiful as was Helen Sheppard, it was her eyes that held Colonel Zane irresistibly. They were unusually large, of a dark purple-blue that changed, shaded, shadowed with her every thought.

"Come, let us walk," Colonel Zane said abruptly, and, with Mr. Sheppard, followed the girls down the path. He escorted them to the fort, showed a long room with little squares cut in the rough-hewn logs, many bullet holes, fire-charred timbers, and dark stains, terribly suggestive of the pain and heroism which the defense of that rude structure had cost.

Under Helen's eager questioning Colonel Zane yielded to his weakness for story-telling, and recited the history of the last siege of Fort Henry; how the renegade Girty swooped down upon the settlement with hundreds of Indians and British soldiers; how for three days of whistling bullets, flaming arrows, screeching demons, fire, smoke, and attack following attack, the brave defenders stood at their posts, there to die before yielding.

"Grand!" breathed Helen, and her eyes glowed. "It was then Betty Zane ran with the powder? Oh! I've heard the story."

"Let my sister tell you of that," said the colonel, smiling.

"You! Was it you?" And Helen's eyes glowed brighter with the light of youth's glory in great deeds.

"My sister has been wedded and widowed since then," said Colonel Zane, reading in Helen's earnest scrutiny of his sister's calm, sad face a wonder if this quiet woman could be the fearless and famed Elizabeth Zane.

Impulsively Helen's hand closed softly over her companion's. Out of the girlish sympathetic action a warm friendship was born.

"I imagine things do happen here," said Mr. Sheppard, hoping to hear more from Colonel Zane.

The colonel smiled grimly.

"Every summer during fifteen years has been a bloody one on the border. The sieges of Fort Henry, and Crawford's defeat, the biggest things we ever knew out here, are matters of history; of course you are familiar with them. But the numberless Indian forays and attacks, the women who have been carried into captivity by renegades, the murdered farmers, in fact, ceaseless war never long directed at any point, but carried on the entire length of the river, are matters known only to the pioneers. Within five miles of Fort Henry I can show you where the laurel bushes grow three feet high over the ashes of two settlements, and many a clearing where some unfortunate pioneer had staked his claim and thrown up a log cabin, only to die fighting for his wife and children. Between here and Fort Pitt there is only one settlement, Yellow Creek, and most of its inhabitants are survivors of abandoned villages farther up the river. Last summer we had the Moravian Massacre, the blackest, most inhuman deed ever committeed. Since then Simon Girty and his bloody redskins have lain low."

"You must always have had a big force," said Sheppard.

"We've managed always to be strong enough, though there never were a large number of men here. During the last siege I had only forty in the fort, counting men, women and boys. But I had pioneers and women who could handle a rifle, and the best bordermen on the frontier."

"Do you make a distinction between pioneers and bordermen?" asked Sheppard.

"Indeed, yes. I am a pioneer; a borderman is an Indian hunter, or scout. For years my cabins housed Andrew Zane, Sam and John McCollock, Bill Metzar, and John and Martin Wetzel, all of whom are dead. Not one saved his scalp. Fort Henry is growing; it has pioneers, rivermen, soldiers, but only two bordermen. Wetzel and Jonathan are the only ones we have left of those great men."

"They must be old," mused Helen, with a dreamy glow still in her eyes.

"Well, Miss Helen, not in years, as you mean. Life here is old in experience; few pioneers, and no bordermen, live to a great age. Wetzel is about forty, and my brother Jonathan still a young man; but both are old in border lore."

Earnestly, as a man who loves his subject, Colonel Zane told his listeners of these two most prominent characters of the border. Sixteen years previously, when but boys in years, they had cast in their lot with his, and journeyed over the Virginian Mountains, Wetzel to devote his life to the vengeful calling he had chosen, and Jonathan to give rein to an adventurous spirit and love of the wilds. By some wonderful chance, by cunning, woodcraft, or daring, both men had lived through the years of border warfare which had brought to a close the careers of all their contemporaries.

For many years Wetzel preferred solitude to companionship; he roamed the wilderness in pursuit of Indians, his life-long foes, and seldom appeared at the settlement except to bring news of an intended raid of the savages. Jonathan also spent much time alone in the woods, or scouting along the river. But of late years a friendship had ripened between the two bordermen. Mutual interest had brought them together on the trail of a noted renegade, and when, after many long days of patient watching and persistent tracking, the outlaw paid an awful penalty for his bloody deeds, these lone and silent men were friends.

Powerful in build, fleet as deer, fearless and tireless, Wetzel's peculiar bloodhound sagacity, ferocity, and implacability, balanced by Jonathan's keen intelligence and judgment caused these bordermen to become the bane of redmen and renegades. Their fame increased with each succeeding summer, until now the people of the settlement looked upon wonderful deeds of strength and of woodcraft as a matter of course, rejoicing in the power and skill with which these men were endowed.

By common consent the pioneers attributed any mysterious deed, from the finding of a fat turkey on a cabin doorstep, to the discovery of a savage scalped and pulled from his ambush near a settler's spring, to Wetzel and Jonathan. All the more did they feel sure of this conclusion because the bordermen never spoke of their deeds. Sometimes a pioneer living on the outskirts of the settlement would be awakened in the morning by a single rifle shot, and on peering out would see a dead Indian lying almost across his doorstep, while beyond, in the dim, gray mist, a tall figure stealing away. Often in the twilight on a summer evening, while fondling his children and enjoying his smoke after a hard day's labor in the fields, this same settler would see the tall, dark figure of Jonathan Zane step noiselessly out of a thicket, and learn that he must take his family and flee at once to the fort for safety. When a settler was murdered, his children carried into captivity by Indians, and the wife given over to the power of some brutal renegade, tragedies wofully frequent on the border, Wetzel and Jonathan took the trail alone. Many a white woman was returned alive and, sometimes, unharmed to her relatives; more than one maiden lived to be captured, rescued, and returned to her lover, while almost numberless were the bones of brutal redmen lying in the deep and gloomy woods, or bleaching on the plains, silent, ghastly reminders of the stern justice meted out by these two heroes.

"Such are my two bordermen, Miss Sheppard. The fort there, and all these cabins, would be only black ashes, save for them, and as for us, our wives and children—God only knows."

"Haven't they wives and children, too?" asked Helen.

"No," answered Colonel Zane, with his genial smile. "Such joys are not for bordermen."

"Why not? Fine men like them deserve happiness," declared Helen.

"It is necessary we have such," said the colonel simply, "and they cannot be bordermen unless free as the air blows. Wetzel and Jonathan have never had sweethearts. I believe Wetzel loved a lass once; but he was an Indian-killer whose hands were red with blood. He silenced his heart, and kept to his chosen, lonely life. Jonathan does not seem to realize that women exist to charm, to please, to be loved and married. Once we twitted him about his brothers doing their duty by the border, whereupon he flashed out: 'My life is the border's: my sweetheart is the North Star!'"

Helen dreamily watched the dancing, dimpling waves that broke on the stones of the river shore. All unconscious of the powerful impression the colonel's recital had made upon her, she was feeling the greatness of the lives of these bordermen, and the glory it would now be for her to share with others the pride in their protection.

"Say, Sheppard, look here," said Colonel Zane, on the return to his cabin, "that girl of yours has a pair of eyes. I can't forget the way they flashed! They'll cause more trouble here among my garrison than would a swarm of redskins."

"No! You don't mean it! Out here in this wilderness?" queried Sheppard doubtfully.

"Well, I do."

"O Lord! What a time I've had with that girl! There was one man especially, back home, who made our lives miserable. He was rich and well born; but Helen would have none of him. He got around me, old fool that I am! Practically stole what was left of my estate, and gambled it away when Helen said she'd die before giving herself to him. It was partly on his account that I brought her away. Then there were a lot of moon-eyed beggars after her all the time, and she's young and full of fire. I hoped I'd marry her to some farmer out here, and end my days in peace."

"Peace? With eyes like those? Never on this green earth," and Colonel Zane laughed as he slapped his friend on the shoulder. "Don't worry, old fellow. You can't help her having those changing dark-blue eyes any more than you can help being proud of them. They have won me, already, susceptible old backwoodsman! I'll help you with this spirited young lady.

I've had experience, Sheppard, and don't you forget it. First, my sister, a Zane all through, which is saying enough. Then as sweet and fiery a little Indian princess as ever stepped in a beaded moccasin, and since, more than one beautiful, impulsive creature. Being in authority, I suppose it's natural that all the work, from keeping the garrison ready against an attack, to straightening out love affairs, should fall upon me. I'll take the care off your shoulders; I'll keep these young dare-devils from killing each other over Miss Helen's favors. I certainly—Hello! There are strangers at the gate. Something's up."

Half a dozen rough-looking men had appeared from round the corner of the cabin, and halted at the gate.

"Bill Elsing, and some of his men from Yellow Creek," said Colonel Zane, as he went toward the group.

"Hullo, Kurnel," was the greeting of the foremost, evidently the leader. "We've lost six head of hosses over our way, an' are out lookin' 'em up."

"The deuce you have! Say, this horse-stealing business is getting interesting. What did you come in for?"

"Wal, we meets Jonathan on the ridge about sunup, an' he sent us back lickety-cut. Said he had two of the hosses corralled, an' mebbe Wetzel could git the others."

"That's strange," replied Colonel Zane thoughtfully.

" 'Pears to me Jack and Wetzel hev some redskins treed, an' didn't want us to spile the fun. Mebbe there wasn't scalps enough to go round. Anyway, we come in, an' we'll hang up here to-day."

"Bill, who's doing this horse-stealing?"

"Damn if I know. It's a mighty pert piece of work. I've a mind it's some slick white fellar, with Injuns backin' him."

Helen noted, when she was once more indoors, that Colonel

Zane's wife appeared worried. Her usual placid expression was gone. She put off the playful overtures of her two bright boys with unusual indifference, and turned to her husband with anxious questioning as to whether the strangers brought news of Indians. Upon being assured that such was not the case, she looked relieved, and explained to Helen that she had seen armed men come so often to consult the colonel regarding dangerous missions and expeditions, that the sight of a stranger caused her unspeakable dread.

"I am accustomed to danger, yet I can never control my fears for my husband and children," said Mrs. Zane. "The older I grow the more of a coward I am. Oh! this border life is sad for women. Only a little while ago my brother Samuel McColloch was shot and scalped right here on the river bank. He was going to the spring for a bucket of water. I lost another brother in almost the same way. Every day during the summer a husband and a father fall victim to some murderous Indian. My husband will go in the same way some day. The border claims them all."

"Bessie, you must not show your fears to our new friend. And, Miss Helen, don't believe she's the coward she would make out," said the colonel's sister smilingly.

"Betty is right, Bess, don't frighten her," said Colonel Zane. "I'm afraid I talked too much to-day. But, Miss Helen, you were so interested, and are such a good listener, that I couldn't refrain. Once for all let me say that you will no doubt see stirring life here; but there is little danger of its affecting you. To be sure I think you'll have troubles; but not with Indians or outlaws."

He winked at his wife and sister. At first Helen did not understand his sally, but then she blushed red all over her fair face.

Some time after that, while unpacking her belongings, she heard the clatter of horses' hoofs on the rocky road, accompanied by loud voices. Running to the window, she saw a group of men at the gate.

"Miss Sheppard, will you come out?" called Colonel Zane's sister from the door. "My brother Jonathan has returned."

Helen joined Betty at the door, and looked over her shoulder.

"Wal, Jack, ye got two on 'em, anyways," drawled a voice which she recognized as that of Elsing's.

A man, lithe and supple, slipped from the back of one of the horses, and, giving the halter to Elsing with a single word, turned and entered the gate. Colonel Zane met him there.

"Well, Jonathan, what's up?"

"There's hell to pay," was the reply, and the speaker's voice rang clear and sharp.

Colonel Zane laid his hand on his brother's shoulder, and thus they stood for a moment, singularly alike, and yet the sturdy pioneer was, somehow, far different from the dark-haired borderman.

"I thought we'd trouble in store from the look on your face," said the colonel calmly. "I hope you haven't very bad news on the first day, for our old friends from Virginia."

"Jonathan," cried Betty when he did not answer the colonel. At her call he half turned, and his dark eyes, steady, strained like those of a watching deer, sought his sister's face.

"Betty, old Jake Lane was murdered by horse thieves yesterday, and Mabel Lane is gone."

"Oh!" gasped Betty; but she said nothing more.

Colonel Zane cursed inaudibly.

"You know, Eb, I tried to keep Lane in the settlement for Mabel's sake. But he wanted to work that farm. I believe horse-

stealing wasn't as much of an object as the girl. Pretty women
are bad for the border, or any other place, I guess. Wetzel has
taken the trail, and I came in because I've serious suspicions—
I'll explain to you alone."

The borderman bowed gravely to Helen, with a natural grace,
and yet a manner that sat awkwardly upon him. The girl,
slightly flushed, and somewhat confused by this meeting with
the man around whom her romantic imagination had already
woven a story, stood in the doorway after giving him a fleeting
glance, the fairest, sweetest picture of girlish beauty ever seen.

The men went into the house; but their voices came distinctly through the door.

"Eb, if Bing Legget or Girty ever see that big-eyed lass, they'll
have her even if Fort Henry has to be burned, an' in case they
do get her, Wetzel an' I'll have taken our last trail."

CHAPTER III

SUPPER over, Colonel Zane led his guests to a side porch, where
they were soon joined by Mrs. Zane and Betty. The host's two
boys, Noah and Sammy, who had preceded them, were now
astride the porch-rail and, to judge by their antics, were riding
wild Indian mustangs.

"It's quite cool," said Colonel Zane; "but I want you to see
the sunset in the valley. A good many of your future neighbors
may come over to-night for a word of welcome. It's the border
custom."

He was about to seat himself by the side of Mr. Sheppard,

on a rustic bench, when a Negro maid appeared in the doorway carrying a smiling, black-eyed baby. Colonel Zane took the child and, holding it aloft, said with fatherly pride:

"This is Rebecca Zane, the first girl baby born to the Zanes, and destined to be the belle of the border."

"May I have her?" asked Helen softly, holding out her arms. She took the child, and placed it upon her knee where its look of solemnity soon changed to one of infantile delight.

"Here come Nell and Jim," said Mrs. Zane, pointing toward the fort.

"Yes, and there comes my brother Silas with his wife, too," added Colonel Zane. "The first couple are James Douns, our young minister, and Nell, his wife. They came out here a year or so ago. James had a brother Joe, the finest young fellow who ever caught the border fever. He was killed by one of the Girtys. His was a wonderful story, and some day you shall hear about the parson and his wife."

"What's the border fever?" asked Mr. Sheppard.

"It's what brought you out here," replied Colonel Zane with a hearty laugh.

Helen gazed with interest at the couple now coming into the yard, and when they gained the porch she saw that the man was big and tall, with a frank, manly bearing, while his wife was a slender little woman with bright, sunny hair, and a sweet, smiling face. They greeted Helen and her father cordially.

Next came Silas Zane, a typical bronzed and bearded pioneer, with his buxom wife. Presently a little group of villagers joined the party. They were rugged men, clad in faded buckskins, and sober-faced women who wore dresses of plain gray linsey. They welcomed the newcomers with simple, homely courtesy. Then six young frontiersmen appeared from around a corner of the cabin, advancing hesitatingly. To Helen they all looked alike, tall, awkward, with brown faces and big hands. When Colonel Zane cheerily cried out to them, they stumbled forward with evident embarrassment, each literally crushing Helen's hand in his horny palm. Afterward they leaned on the rail and stole glances at her.

Soon a large number of villagers were on the porch or in the yard. After paying their respects to Helen and her father they took part in a general conversation. Two or three girls, the latest callers, were surrounded by half a dozen young fellows, and their laughter sounded high above the hum of voices.

Helen gazed upon this company with mingled feelings of relief and pleasure. She had been more concerned regarding the young people with whom her lot might be cast, than the dangers of which others had told. She knew that on the border there was no distinction of rank. Though she came of an old family, and, during her girlhood, had been surrounded by refinement, even luxury, she had accepted cheerfully the reverses of fortune, and was determined to curb the pride which had been hers. It was necessary she should have friends. Warm-hearted, impulsive and loving, she needed to have around her those in whom she could confide. Therefore it was with sincere pleasure she understood how groundless were her fears and knew that if she did not find good, true friends the fault would be her own. She saw at a glance that the colonel's widowed sister was her equal, perhaps her superior, in education and breeding, while Nellie Douns was as well-bred and gracious a little lady as she had ever met. Then, the other girls, too, were charming, with frank wholesomeness and freedom.

Concerning the young men, of whom there were about a dozen, Helen had hardly arrived at a conclusion. She liked the ruggedness, the signs of honest worth which clung to them. Despite her youth, she had been much sought after because of her personal attractions, and had thus added experience to the natural keen intuition all women possess. The glances of several of the men, particularly the bold regard of one Roger Brandt, whom Colonel Zane introduced, she had seen before, and learned to dislike. On the whole, however, she was delighted with the prospect of new friends and future prosperity, and she felt even greater pleasure in the certainty that her father shared her gratification.

Suddenly she became aware that the conversation had ceased. She looked up to see the tall, lithe form of Jonathan Zane as he strode across the porch. She could see that a certain constraint had momentarily fallen upon the company. It was an involuntary acknowledgment of the borderman's presence, of a presence that worked on all alike with a subtle, strong magnetism.

"Ah, Jonathan, come out to see the sunset? It's unusually fine to-night," said Colonel Zane.

With hardly more than a perceptible bow to those present, the borderman took a seat near the rail, and, leaning upon it, directed his gaze westward.

Helen sat so near she could have touched him. She was conscious of the same strange feeling, and impelling sense of power, which had come upon her so strongly at first sight of him. More than that, a lively interest had been aroused in her. This borderman was to her a new and novel character. She was amused at learning that here was a young man absolutely indifferent to the charms of the opposite sex, and although hardly admitting such a thing, she believed it would be possible to win him from his indifference. On raising her eyelids, it was with the unconcern which a woman feigns when suspecting she is being regarded with admiring eyes. But Jonathan Zane might not have known of her presence, for all the attention he paid her. Therefore, having a good opportunity to gaze at this borderman of daring deeds, Helen regarded him closely.

He was clad from head to foot in smooth, soft buckskin which fitted well his powerful frame. Beaded moccasins, leggings bound high above the knees, hunting coat laced and fringed, all had the neat, tidy appearance due to good care. He wore no weapons. His hair fell in a raven mass over his shoulders. His profile was regular, with a long, straight nose, strong chin, and eyes black as night. They were now fixed intently on the valley. The whole face gave an impression of serenity, of calmness.

Helen was wondering if the sad, almost stern, tranquillity of that face ever changed, when the baby cooed and held out its chubby little hands. Jonathan's smile, which came quickly, accompanied by a warm light in the eyes, relieved Helen of an unaccountable repugnance she had begun to feel toward the borderman. That smile, brief as a flash, showed his gentle kindness and told that he was not a creature who had set himself apart from human life and love.

As he took little Rebecca, one of his hands touched Helen's. If he had taken heed of the contact, as any ordinary man might well have, she would, perhaps, have thought nothing about it, but because he did not appear to realize that her hand had been almost inclosed in his, she could not help again feeling his singular personality. She saw that this man had absolutely no thought of her. At the moment this did not awaken resentment, for with all her fire and pride she was not vain; but amusement gave place to a respect which came involuntarily.

Little Rebecca presently manifested the faithlessness peculiar to her sex, and had no sooner been taken upon Jonathan's knee than she cried out to go back to Helen.

"Girls are uncommon coy critters," said he, with a grave smile in his eyes. He handed back the child, and once more was absorbed in the setting sun.

Helen looked down the valley to behold the most beautiful spectacle she had ever seen. Between the hills far to the west, the sky flamed with a red and gold light. The sun was poised above the river, and the shimmering waters merged into a ruddy horizon. Long rays of crimson fire crossed the smooth waters. A few purple clouds above caught the refulgence, until aided by the delicate rose and blue space beyond, they became many hued ships sailing on a rainbow sea. Each second saw a gorgeous transformation. Slowly the sun dipped into the golden flood; one by one the clouds changed from crimson to gold, from gold to rose, and then to gray; slowly all the tints faded until, as the sun slipped out of sight, the brilliance gave way to the soft afterglow of warm lights. These in turn slowly toned down into gray twilight.

Helen retired to her room soon afterward, and, being unusually thoughtful, sat down by the window. She reviewed the events of this first day of her new life on the border. Her impressions had been so many, so varied, that she wanted to distinguish them. First she felt glad, with a sweet, warm thankfulness, that her father seemed so happy, so encouraged by the outlook. Breaking old ties had been, she knew, no child's play for him. She realized also that it had been done solely because there had been nothing left to offer her in the old home, and in a new one were hope and possibilities. Then she was relieved at getting away from the attentions of a man whose persistence had been most annoying to her. From thoughts of her father, and the old life, she came to her new friends of the present. She was so grateful for their kindness. She certainly would do all in her power to win and keep their esteem.

Somewhat of a surprise was it to her, that she reserved for Jonathan Zane the last and most prominent place in her meditations. She suddenly asked herself how she regarded this fighting borderman. She recalled her unbounded enthusiasm for the man as Colonel Zane had told of him; then her first glimpse, and her surprise and admiration at the lithe-limbed young giant; then incredulity, amusement, and respect followed in swift order, after which an unaccountable coldness that was almost resentment. Helen was forced to admit that she did not know how to regard him, but surely he was a man, throughout every inch of his superb frame, and one who took life seriously, with neither thought nor time for the opposite sex. And this last brought a blush to her cheek, for she distinctly remembered she had expected, if not admiration, more than passing notice from this hero of the border.

Presently she took a little mirror from a table near where she sat. Holding it to catch the fast-fading light, she studied her face seriously.

"Helen Sheppard, I think on the occasion of your arrival in a new country a little plain talk will be wholesome. Somehow or other, perhaps because of a crowd of idle men back there in the colonies, possibly from your own misguided fancy, you imagined you were fair to look at. It is well to be undeceived."

Scorn spoke in Helen's voice. She was angry because of having been interested in a man, and allowed that interest to betray her into a girlish expectation that he would treat her as all other men had. The mirror, even in the dim light, spoke more truly than she, for it caught the golden tints of her luxuriant hair, the thousand beautiful shadows in her great, dark eyes, the white glory of a face fair as a star, and the swelling outline of neck and shoulders.

With a sudden fiery impetuosity she flung the glass to the floor, where it was broken into several pieces.

"How foolish of me! What a temper I have!" she exclaimed repentantly. "I'm glad I have another glass. Wouldn't Mr. Jonathan Zane, borderman, Indian fighter, hero of a hundred battles and never a sweetheart, be flattered? No, most decidedly he wouldn't. He never looked at me. I don't think I expected that; I'm sure I didn't want it; but still he might have—Oh! what am I thinking, and he a stranger?"

Before Helen lost herself in slumber on that eventful evening, she vowed to ignore the borderman; assured herself that she did not want to see him again, and, rather inconsistently, that she would cure him of his indifference.

＊　　　＊　　　＊　　　＊　　　＊　　　＊

When Colonel Zane's guests had retired, and the villagers were gone to their homes, he was free to consult with Jonathan.

"Well, Jack," he said, "I'm ready to hear about the horse thieves."

"Wetzel makes it out the man who's runnin' this hoss-stealin' is located right here in Fort Henry," answered the borderman.

The colonel had lived too long on the frontier to show surprise; he hummed a tune while the genial expression faded slowly from his face.

"Last count there were one hundred and ten men at the fort," he replied thoughtfully. "I know over a hundred, and can trust them. There are some new fellows on the boats, and several strangers hanging round Metzar's."

"Pears to Lew an' me that this fellar is a slick customer, an' one who's been here long enough to know our hosses an' where we keep them."

"I see. Like Miller, who fooled us all, even Betty, when he stole our powder and then sold us to Girty," rejoined Colonel Zane grimly.

"Exactly, only this fellar is slicker an' more desperate than Miller."

"Right you are, Jack, for the man who is trusted and betrays us, must be desperate. Does he realize what he'll get if we ever find out, or is he underrating us?"

"He knows all right, an' is matchin' his cunnin' against our'n."

"Tell me what you and Wetzel learned."

The borderman proceeded to relate the events that had occurred during a recent tramp in the forest with Wetzel. While returning from a hunt in a swamp several miles over the ridge, back of Fort Henry, they ran across the trail of three Indians. They followed this until darkness set in, when both laid down to rest and wait for the early dawn, that time most propitious for taking the savage by surprise. On resuming the trail they found that other Indians had joined the party they were tracking. To the bordermen this was significant of some unusual activity directed toward the settlement. Unable to learn anything definite from the moccasin traces, they hurried up on the trail to find that the Indians had halted.

Wetzel and Jonathan saw from their covert that the savages had a woman prisoner. A singular feature about it all was that the Indians remained in the same place all day, did not light a camp-fire, and kept a sharp lookout. The bordermen crept up as close as safe, and remained on watch during the day and night.

Early next morning, when the air was fading from black to

gray, the silence was broken by the snapping of twigs and a tremor of the ground. The bordermen believed another company of Indians was approaching; but they soon saw it was a single white man leading a number of horses. He departed before daybreak. Wetzel and Jonathan could not get a clear view of him owing to the dim light; but they heard his voice, and afterwards found the imprint of his moccasins. They did, however, recognize the six horses as belonging to settlers in Yellow Creek.

While Jonathan and Wetzel were consulting as to what it was best to do, the party of Indians divided, four going directly west, and the others north. Wetzel immediately took the trail of the larger party with the prisoner and four of the horses. Jonathan caught two of the animals which the Indians had turned loose, and tied them in the forest. He then started after the three Indians who had gone northward.

"Well?" Colonel Zane said impatiently, when Jonathan hesitated in his story.

"One got away," he said reluctantly. "I barked him as he was runnin' like a streak through the bushes, an' judged that he was hard hit. I got the hosses, an' turned back on the trail of the white man."

"Where did it end?"

"In that hard-packed path near the blacksmith shop. An' the fellar steps as light as an Injun."

"He's here, then, sure as you're born. We've lost no horses yet, but last week old Sam heard a noise in the barn, and on going there found Betty's mare out of her stall."

"Some one as knows the lay of the land had been after her," suggested Jonathan.

"You can bet on that. We've got to find him before we lose

all the fine horse-flesh we own. Where do these stolen animals go? Indians would steal any kind; but this thief takes only the best."

"I'm to meet Wetzel on the ridge soon, an' then we'll know, for he's goin' to find out where the hosses are taken."

"That'll help some. On the way back you found where the white girl had been taken from. Murdered father, burned cabin, the usual deviltry."

"Exactly."

"Poor Mabel! Do you think this white thief had anything to do with carrying her away?"

"No. Wetzel says that's Bing Legget's work. The Shawnees were members of his gang."

"Well, Jack, what'll I do?"

"Keep quiet an' wait," was the borderman's answer.

Colonel Zane, old pioneer and frontiersman though he was, shuddered as he went to his room. His brother's dark look, and his deadly calmness, were significant.

CHAPTER IV

To THOSE few who saw Jonathan Zane in the village, it seemed as if he was in his usual quiet and dreamy state. The people were accustomed to his silence, and long since learned that what little time he spent in the settlement was not given to sociability. In the morning he sometimes lay with Colonel Zane's dog, Chief, by the side of a spring under an elm tree, and in the afternoon strolled aimlessly along the river bluff, or on the hillside. At night he sat on his brother's porch smoking a long Indian pipe. Since that day, now a week past, when he had returned with the stolen horses, his movements and habits were precisely what would have been expected of an unsuspicious borderman.

In reality, however, Jonathan was not what he seemed. He knew all that was going on in the settlement. Hardly a bird could have entered the clearing unobserved.

At night, after all the villagers were in bed, he stole cautiously about the stockade, silencing with familiar word the bristling watch-hounds, and went from barn to barn, ending his stealthy tramp at the corral where Colonel Zane kept his thoroughbreds.

But all this scouting by night availed nothing. No unusual event occurred, not even the barking of a dog, a suspicious rustling among the thickets, or whistling of a night-hawk had been heard.

Vainly the borderman strained ears to catch some low night-signal given by waiting Indians to the white traitor within the settlement. By day there was even less to attract the sharp-eyed watcher. The clumsy river boats, half raft, half sawn lumber, drifted down the Ohio on their first and last voyage, discharged their cargoes of grain, liquor, or merchandise, and were broken up. Their crews came back on the long overland journey to Fort Pitt, there to man another craft. The garrison at the fort performed their customary duties; the pioneers tilled the fields; the blacksmith scattered sparks, the wheelwright worked industriously at his bench, and the housewives attended to their many cares. No strangers arrived at Fort Henry. The quiet life of the village was uninterrupted.

Near sunset of a long day Jonathan strolled down the sandy, well-trodden path toward Metzar's inn. He did not drink, and consequently seldom visited the rude, dark, ill-smelling bar-room.

When occasion demanded his presence there, he was evidently not welcome. The original owner, a sturdy soldier and pioneer, came to Fort Henry when Colonel Zane founded the settlement, and had been killed during Girty's last attack. His successor, another Metzar, was, according to Jonathan's belief, as bad as the whiskey he dispensed. More than one murder had been committed at the inn; countless fatal knife and tomahawk fights had stained red the hard clay floor; and more than one desperate character had been harbored there. Once Colonel Zane sent Wetzel there to invite a thief and outlaw to quit the settlement, with the not unexpected result that it became necessary the robber be carried out.

Jonathan thought of the bad name the place bore all over the frontier, and wondered if Metzar could tell anything about the horse-thieves. When the borderman bent his tall frame to enter the low-studded door he fancied he saw a dark figure disappear into a room just behind the bar. A roughly-clad, heavily-bearded man turned hastily at the same moment.

"Hullo," he said gruffly.

"H' are you, Metzar. I just dropped in to see if I could make a trade for your sorrel mare," replied Jonathan. Being well aware that the innkeeper would not part with his horse, the borderman had made this announcement as his reason for entering the barroom.

"Nope, I'll allow you can't," replied Metzar.

As he turned to go, Jonathan's eyes roamed around the barroom. Several strangers of shiftless aspect bleared at him.

"They wouldn't steal a pumpkin," muttered Jonathan to himself as he left the inn. Then he added suspiciously, "Metzar was talkin' to some one, an' 'peared uneasy. I never liked Metzar. He'll bear watchin'."

The borderman passed on down the path thinking of what he had heard against Metzar. The colonel had said that the man was prosperous for an innkeeper who took pelts, grain or meat in exchange for rum. The village gossips disliked him because he was unmarried, taciturn, and did not care for their company. Jonathan reflected also on the fact that Indians were frequently coming to the inn, and this made him distrustful of the proprietor. It was true that Colonel Zane had red-skinned visitors, but there was always good reason for their coming. Jonathan had seen, during the Revolution, more than one trusted man proven to be a traitor, and the conviction settled upon him that some quiet scouting would show up the innkeeper as aiding the horse-thieves if not actually in league with them.

"Good evening, Jonathan Zane."

This greeting in a woman's clear voice brought Jonathan out from his reveries. He glanced up to see Helen Sheppard standing in the doorway of her father's cabin.

"Evenin', miss," he said with a bow, and would have passed on.

"Wait." she cried, and stepped out of the door.

He waited by the gate with a manner which showed that such a summons was novel to him.

Helen, piqued at his curt greeting, had asked him to wait without any idea of what she would say. Coming slowly down the path she felt again a subtle awe of this borderman. Regretting her impulsiveness, she lost confidence.

Gaining the gate she looked up intending to speak; but was unable to do so as she saw how cold and grave was his face, and how piercing were his eyes. She flushed slightly, and then, conscious of an embarrassment new and strange to her, blushed rosy red, making, as it seemed to her, a stupid remark about the sunset. When he took her words literally, and said the sunset was fine, she felt guilty of deceitfulness. Whatever Helen's faults, and they were many, she was honest, and because of not having looked at the sunset, but only wanting him to see her as did other men, the innocent ruse suddenly appeared mean and trifling.

Then, with a woman's quick intuition, she understood that coquetries were lost on this borderman, and, with a smile, got the better of her embarrassment and humiliation by telling the truth.

"I wanted to ask a favor of you, and I'm a little afraid."

She spoke with girlish shyness, which increased as he stared at her.

"Why—why do you look at me so?"

"There's a lake over yonder which the Shawnees say is haunted by a woman they killed," he replied quietly. "You'd do for her spirit, so white an' beautiful in the silver moonlight."

"So my white dress makes me look ghostly," she answered lightly, though deeply conscious of surprise and pleasure at such an unexpected reply from him. This borderman might be full of surprises. "Such a time as I had bringing my dresses out here! I don't know when I can wear them. This is the simplest one."

"An' it's mighty new an' bewilderin' for the border," he replied with a smile in his eyes.

"When these are gone I'll get no more except linsey ones," she said brightly, yet her eyes shone with a wistful uncertainty of the future.

"Will you be happy here?"

"I am happy. I have always wanted to be of some use in the world. I assure you, Master Zane, I am not the butterfly I seem. I have worked hard all day, that is, until your sister Betty came over. All the girls have helped me fix up the cabin until it's more comfortable than I ever dreamed one could be on the frontier. Father is well content here, and that makes me happy. I haven't had time for forebodings. The young men of Fort Henry have been—well, attentive; in fact, they've been here all the time."

She laughed a little at this last remark, and looked demurely at him.

"It's a frontier custom," he said.

"Oh, indeed? Do all the young men call often and stay late?"

"They do."

"You didn't," she retorted. "You're the only one who hasn't been to see me."

"I do not wait on the girls," he replied with a grave smile.

"Oh, you don't? Do you expect them to wait on you?" she asked, feeling, now she had made this silent man talk, once more at her ease.

"I am a borderman," replied Jonathan. There was a certain dignity or sadness in his answer which reminded Helen of Colonel Zane's portrayal of a borderman's life. It struck her keenly. Here was this young giant standing erect and handsome before her, as rugged as one of the ash trees of his beloved forest. Who could tell when his strong life might be ended by an Indian's hatchet?

"For you, then, is there no such thing as friendship?" she asked.

"On the border men are serious."

This recalled his sister's conversation regarding the attentions of the young men, that they would follow her, fight for her, and give her absolutely no peace until one of them had carried her to his cabin a bride.

She could not carry on the usual conventional conversation

with this borderman, but remained silent for a time. She realized more keenly than ever before how different he was from other men, and watched closely as he stood gazing out over the river. Perhaps something she had said caused him to think of the many pleasures and joys he missed. But she could not be certain what was in his mind. She was not accustomed to impassive faces and cold eyes with unlit fires in their dark depths. More likely he was thinking of matters nearer to his wild, free life; of his companion Wetzel somewhere out beyond those frowning hills. Then she remembered that the colonel had told her of his brother's love for nature in all its forms; how he watched the shades of evening fall; lost himself in contemplation of the last copper glow flushing the western sky, or became absorbed in the bright stars. Possibly he had forgotten her presence. Darkness was rapidly stealing down upon them. The evening, tranquil and gray, crept over them with all its mystery. He was a part of it. She could not hope to understand him; but saw clearly that his was no common personality. She wanted to speak, to voice a sympathy strong within her; but she did not know what to say to this borderman.

"If what your sister tells me of the border is true, I may soon need a friend," she said, after weighing well her words. She faced him modestly yet bravely, and looked him straight in the eyes. Because he did not reply she spoke again.

"I mean such a friend as you or Wetzel."

"You may count on both," he replied.

"Thank you," she said softly, giving him her hand. "I shall not forget. One more thing. Will you break a borderman's custom, for my sake?"

"How?"

"Come to see me when you are in the settlement?"

Helen said this in a low voice with just a sob in her breath; but she met his gaze fairly. Her big eyes were all aglow, alight with girlish appeal, and yet proud with a woman's honest demand for fair exchange. Promise was there, too, could he but read it, of wonderful possibilities.

"No," he answered gently.

Helen was not prepared for such a rebuff. She was interested in him, and not ashamed to show it. She feared only that he might misunderstand her; but to refuse her proffered friendship, that was indeed unexpected. Rude she thought it was, while from brow to curving throat her fair skin crimsoned. Then her face grew pale as the moonlight. Hard on her resentment had surged the swell of some new emotion strong and sweet. He refused her friendship because he did not dare accept it; because his life was not his own; because he was a borderman.

While they stood thus, Jonathan looking perplexed and troubled, feeling he had hurt her, but knowing not what to say, and Helen with a warm softness in her eyes, the stalwart figure of a man loomed out of the gathering darkness.

"Ah, Miss Helen! Good evening," he said.

"Is it you, Mr. Brandt?" asked Helen. "Of course you know Mr. Zane."

Brandt acknowledged Jonathan's bow with an awkwardness which had certainly been absent in his greeting to Helen. He started slightly when she spoke the borderman's name.

A brief pause ensued.

"Good night," said Jonathan, and left them.

He had noticed Brandt's gesture of surprise, slight though it was, and was thinking about it as he walked away. Brandt may have been astonished at finding a borderman talking to a girl, and certainly, as far as Jonathan was concerned, the incident was without precedent. But, on the other hand, Brandt may have had another reason, and Jonathan tried to study out what it might be.

He gave but little thought to Helen. That she might like him exceedingly well, did not come into his mind. He remembered his sister Betty's gossip regarding Helen and her admirers, and particularly Roger Brandt; but felt no great concern; he had no curiosity to know more of her. He admired Helen because she was beautiful, yet the feeling was much the same he might have experienced for a graceful deer, a full-foliaged tree, or a dark mossy-stoned bend in a murmuring brook. The girl's face and figure, perfect and alluring as they were, had not awakened him from his indifference.

On arriving at his brother's home, he found the colonel and Betty sitting on the porch.

"Eb, who is this Brandt?" he asked.

"Roger Brandt? He's a French-Canadian; came here from Detroit a year ago. Why do you ask?"

"I want to know more about him."

Colonel Zane reflected a moment, first as to this unusual request from Jonathan, and secondly in regard to what little he really did know of Roger Brandt.

"Well, Jack, I can't tell you much; nothing of him before he showed up here. He says he has been a pioneer, hunter, scout, soldier, trader—everything. When he came to the fort we needed men. It was just after Girty's siege, and all the cabins had been burned. Brandt seemed honest, and was a good fellow. Besides, he had gold. He started the river barges, which came from Fort Pitt. He has surely done the settlement good service, and has prospered. I never talked a dozen times to him, and even then, not for long. He appears to like the young people, which is only natural. That's all I know; Betty might tell you more, for he tried to be attentive to her."

"Did he, Betty?" Jonathan asked.

"He followed me until I showed him I didn't care for company," answered Betty.

"What kind of a man is he?"

"Jack, I know nothing against him, although I never fancied him. He's better educated than the majority of frontiersmen; he's good-natured and agreeable, and the people like him."

"Why don't you?"

Betty looked surprised at his blunt question, and then said with a laugh: "I never tried to reason why; but since you have spoken I believe my dislike was instinctive."

After Betty had retired to her room the brothers remained on the porch smoking.

"Betty's pretty keen, Jack. I never knew her to misjudge a man. Why this sudden interest in Roger Brandt?"

The borderman puffed his pipe in silence.

"Say, Jack," Colonel Zane said suddenly, "do you connect Brandt in any way with this horse-stealing?"

"No more than some, an' less than others," replied Jonathan curtly.

Nothing more was said for a time. To the brothers this hour of early dusk brought the same fullness of peace. From gray twilight to gloomy dusk quiet reigned. The insects of night chirped and chorused with low, incessant hum. From out the darkness came the peeping of frogs.

Suddenly the borderman straightened up, and, removing the pipe from his mouth, turned his ear to the faint breeze, while at the same time one hand closed on the colonel's knee with a warning clutch.

Colonel Zane knew what that clutch signified. Some faint noise, too low for ordinary ears, had roused the borderman. The colonel listened, but heard nothing save the familiar evening sounds.

"Jack, what'd you hear?" he whispered.

"Somethin' back of the barn," replied Jonathan, slipping noiselessly off the steps, lying at full length with his ear close to the ground. "Where's the dog?" he asked.

"Chief must have gone with Sam. The old nigger sometimes goes at this hour to see his daughter."

Jonathan lay on the grass several moments; then suddenly he arose much as a bent sapling springs to place.

"I hear footsteps. Get the rifles," he said in a fierce whisper.

"Damn! There is some one in the barn."

"No; they're outside. Hurry, but softly."

Colonel Zane had but just risen to his feet, when Mrs. Zane came to the door and called him by name.

Instantly from somewhere in the darkness overhanging the road, came a low, warning whistle.

"A signal!" exclaimed Colonel Zane.

"Quick, Eb! Look toward Metzar's light. One, two, three, shadows—Injuns!"

"By the Lord Harry! Now they're gone; but I couldn't mistake those round heads and bristling feathers."

"Shawnees!" said the borderman, and his teeth shut hard like steel on flint.

"Jack, they were after the horses, and some one was on the lookout! By God! right under our noses!"

"Hurry," cried Jonathan, pulling his brother off the porch.

Colonel Zane followed the borderman out of the yard, into the road, and across the grassy square.

"We might find the one who gave the signal," said the colonel. "He was near at hand, and couldn't have passed the house."

Colonel Zane was correct, for whoever had whistled would be forced to take one of two ways of escape; either down the straight road ahead, or over the high stockade fence of the fort.

"There he goes," whispered Jonathan.

"Where? I can't see a blamed thing."

"Go across the square, run around the fort, an' head him off on the road. Don't try to stop him for he'll have weapons, just find out who he is."

"I see him now," replied Colonel Zane, as he hurried off into the darkness.

During a few moments Jonathan kept in view the shadow he had seen first come out of the gloom by the stockade, and thence pass swiftly down the road. He followed swiftly, silently. Presently a light beyond threw a glare across the road. He thought he was approaching a yard where there was a fire, and the flames proved to be from pine cones burning in the yard of Helen Sheppard. He remembered then that she was entertaining some of the young people.

The figure he was pursuing did not pass the glare. Jonathan made certain it disappeared before reaching the light, and he knew his eyesight too well not to trust to it absolutely. Advancing nearer the yard, he heard the murmur of voices in gay conversation, and soon saw figures moving about under the trees.

No doubt was in his mind but that the man who gave the signal to warn the Indians, was one of Helen Sheppard's guests.

Jonathan had walked across the street then down the path, before he saw the colonel coming from the opposite direction. Halting under a maple he waited for his brother to approach.

"I didn't meet any one. Did you lose him?" whispered Colonel Zane breathlessly.

"No; he's in there."

"That's Sheppard's place. Do you mean he's hiding there?"

"No!"

Colonel Zane swore, as was his habit when exasperated. Kind and generous man that he was, it went hard with him to believe in the guilt of any of the young men he had trusted. But Jonathan had said there was a traitor among them, and Colonel Zane did not question this assertion. He knew the borderman. During years full of strife, and war, and blood had he lived beside this silent man who said little, but that little was the truth. Therefore Colonel Zane gave way to anger.

"Well, I'm not so damned surprised! What's to be done?"

"Find out what men are there?"

"That's easy. I'll go to see George and soon have the truth."

"Won't do," said the borderman decisively. "Go back to the barn, an' look after the hosses."

When Colonel Zane had obeyed Jonathan dropped to his hands and knees, and swiftly, with the agile movements of an Indian, gained a corner of the Sheppard yard. He crouched in the shade of a big plum tree. Then, at a favorable opportunity, vaulted the fence and disappeared under a clump of lilac bushes.

The evening wore away no more tediously to the borderman, than to those young frontiersmen who were whispering tender or playful words to their partners. Time and patience were the same to Jonathan Zane. He lay hidden under the fragrant lilacs, his eyes, accustomed to the dark from long practice, losing no movement of the guests. Finally it became evident that the party was at an end. One couple took the initiative, and said good night to their hostess.

"Tom Bennet, I hope it's not you," whispered the borderman to himself, as he recognized the young fellow.

A general movement followed, until the merry party were assembled about Helen near the front gate.

"Jim Morrison, I'll bet it's not you," was Jonathan's comment. "That soldier Williams is doubtful; Hart an' Johnson being strangers, are unknown quantities around here, an' then comes Brandt."

All departed except Brandt, who remained talking to Helen in low, earnest tones. Jonathan lay very quietly, trying to decide what should be his next move in the unraveling of the mystery. He paid little attention to the young couple, but could not help overhearing their conversation.

"Indeed, Mr. Brandt, you frontiersmen are not backward," Helen was saying in her clear voice. "I am surprised to learn that you love me upon such short acquaintance, and am sorry, too, for I hardly know whether I even so much as like you."

"I love you. We men of the border do things rapidly," he replied earnestly.

"So it seems," she said with a soft laugh.

"Won't you care for me?" he pleaded.

"Nothing is surer than that I never know what I am going to do," Helen replied lightly.

"All these fellows are in love with you. They can't help it any more than I. You are the most glorious creature. Please give me hope."

"Mr. Brandt, let go my hand. I'm afraid I don't like such impulsive men."

"Please let me hold your hand."

"Certainly not."

"But I will hold it, and if you look at me like that again I'll do more," he said.

"What, bold sir frontiersman?" she returned, lightly still, but in a voice which rang with a deeper note.

"I'll kiss you," he cried desperately.

"You wouldn't dare."

"Wouldn't I though? You don't know us border fellows yet. You come here with your wonderful beauty, and smile at us with that light in your eyes which makes men mad. Oh, you'll pay for it."

The borderman listened to all this love-making half disgusted, until he began to grow interested. Brandt's back was turned to him, and Helen stood so that the light from the pine cones shone on her face. Her eyes were brilliant, otherwise she seemed a woman perfectly self-possessed. Brandt held her hand despite the repeated efforts she made to free it. But she did not struggle violently, or make an outcry.

Suddenly Brandt grasped her other hand, pulling her toward him.

"These other fellows will kiss you, and I'm going to be the first!" he declared passionately.

Helen drew back, now thoroughly alarmed by the man's fierce energy. She had been warned against this very boldness in frontiersmen; but had felt secure in her own pride and dignity. Her blood boiled at the thought that she must exert strength to escape insult. She struggled violently when Brandt bent his head. Almost sick with fear, she had determined to call for help, when a violent wrench almost toppled her over. At the same instant her wrists were freed; she heard a fierce cry, a resounding blow, and then the sodden thud of a heavy body falling. Recovering her balance, she saw a tall figure beside her, and a man in the act of rising from the ground.

"You?" whispered Helen, recognizing the tall figure as Jonathan's.

The borderman did not answer. He stepped forward, slipping his hand inside his hunting frock. Brandt sprang nimbly to his feet, and with a face which, even in the dim light, could be seen distorted with fury, bent forward to look at the stranger. He, too, had his hand within his coat, as if grasping a weapon; but he did not draw it.

"Zane, a lighter blow would have been easier to forget," he cried, his voice clear and cutting. Then he turned to the girl. "Miss Helen, I got what I deserved. I crave your forgiveness, and ask you to understand a man who was once a gentleman. If I am one no longer, the frontier is to blame. I was mad to treat you as I did."

Thus speaking, he bowed low with the grace of a man sometimes used to the society of ladies, and then went out of the gate.

"Where did you come from?" asked Helen, looking up at Jonathan.

He pointed under the lilac bushes.

"Were you there?" she asked wonderingly. "Did you hear all?"

"I couldn't help hearin'."

"It was fortunate for me; but why—why were you there?"

Helen came a step nearer, and regarded him curiously with her great eyes now black with excitement.

The borderman was silent.

Helen's softened mood changed instantly. There was nothing in his cold face which might have betrayed in him a sentiment similar to that of her admirers.

"Did you spy on me?" she asked quickly, after a moment's thought.

"No," replied Jonathan calmly.

Helen gazed in perplexity at this strange man. She did not

know how to explain it; she was irritated, but did her best to conceal it. He had no interest in her, yet had hidden under the lilacs in her yard. She was grateful because he had saved her from annoyance, yet could not fathom his reason for being so near.

"Did you come here to see me?" she asked, forgetting her vexation.

"No."

"What for, then?"

"I reckon I won't say," was the quiet, deliberate refusal.

Helen stamped her foot in exasperation.

"Be careful that I do not put a wrong construction on your strange action," said she coldly. "If you have reasons, you might trust me. If you are only——"

"Sh-s-sh!" he breathed, grasping her wrist, and holding it firmly in his powerful hand. The whole attitude of the man had altered swiftly, subtly. The listlessness was gone. His lithe body became rigid as he leaned forward, his head toward the ground, and turned slightly in a manner that betokened intent listening.

Helen trembled as she felt his powerful frame quiver. Whatever had thus changed him, gave her another glimpse of his complex personality. It seemed to her incredible that with one whispered exclamation this man could change from cold indifference to a fire and force so strong as to dominate her.

Statue-like she remained listening; but hearing no sound, and thrillingly conscious of the hand on her arm.

Far up on the hillside an owl hooted dismally, and an instant later, faint and far away, came an answer so low as to be almost indistinct.

The borderman raised himself erect as he released her.

"It's only an owl," she said in relief.

His eyes gleamed like stars.

"It's Wetzel, an' it means Injuns!"

Then he was gone into the darkness.

CHAPTER V

In the misty morning twilight Colonel Zane, fully armed, paced to and fro before his cabin, on guard. All night he had maintained a watch. He had not considered it necessary to send his family into the fort, to which they had often been compelled to flee. On the previous night Jonathan had come swiftly back to the cabin, and, speaking but two words, seized his weapons and vanished into the black night. The words were "Injuns! Wetzel!" and there were none others with more power to affect hearers on the border. The colonel believed that Wetzel had signaled to Jonathan.

On the west a deep gully with precipitous sides separated the settlement from a high, wooded bluff. Wetzel often returned from his journeying by this difficult route. He had no doubt seen Indian signs, and had communicated the intelligence to Jonathan by their system of night-bird calls. The nearness of the mighty hunter reassured Colonel Zane.

When the colonel returned from his chase of the previous night, he went directly to the stable, there to find that the Indians had made off with a thoroughbred, and Betty's pony. Colonel Zane was furious, not on account of the value of the horses, but because Bess was his favorite bay, and Betty loved nothing more than her pony Madcap. To have such a march stolen on him after he had heard and seen the thieves was indeed hard. High time it was that these horse thieves be run to earth. No Indian had planned these marauding expeditions. An intelligent white man was at the bottom of the thieving, and he should pay for his treachery.

The colonel's temper, however, soon cooled. He realized after thinking over the matter, that he was fortunate it passed off without bloodshed. Very likely the intent had been to get all his horses, perhaps his neighbor's as well, and it had been partly frustrated by Jonathan's keen sagacity. These Shawnees, white leader or not, would never again run such risks.

"It's like a skulking Shawnee," muttered Colonel Zane, "to slip down here under cover of early dusk, when no one but an Indian hunter could detect him. I didn't look for trouble, especially so soon after the lesson we gave Girty and his damned English and redskins. It's lucky Jonathan was here. I'll go back to the old plan of stationing scouts at the outposts until snow flies."

While Colonel Zane talked to himself and paced the path he had selected to patrol, the white mists cleared, and a rosy hue followed the brightening in the east. The birds ceased twittering to break into gay songs, and the cock in the barnyard gave one final clarion-voiced salute to the dawn. The rose in the east deepened into rich red, and then the sun peeped over the eastern hilltops to drench the valley with glad golden light.

A blue smoke curling lazily from the stone chimney of his cabin, showed that Sam had made the kitchen fire, and a little later a rich, savory odor gave pleasing evidence that his wife was cooking breakfast.

"Any sign of Jack?" a voice called from the open door, and Betty appeared.

"Nary sign."

"Of the Indians, then?"

"Well, Betts, they left you a token of their regard," and Colonel Zane smiled as he took a broken halter from the fence.

"Madcap?" cried Betty.

"Yes, they've taken Madcap and Bess."

"Oh, the villains! Poor pony," exclaimed Betty indignantly. "Eb, I'll coax Wetzel to fetch the pony home if he has to kill every Shawnee in the valley."

"Now you're talking, Betts," Colonel Zane replied. "If you could get Lew to do that much, you'd be blessed from one end of the border to the other."

He walked up the road; then back, keeping a sharp lookout on all sides, and bestowing a particularly keen glance at the hillside across the ravine, but could see no sign of the bordermen. As it was now broad daylight he felt convinced that further watch was unnecessary, and went in to breakfast. When he came out again the villagers were astir. The sharp strokes of axes rang out on the clear morning air, and a mellow anvil-clang pealed up from the blacksmith shop. Colonel Zane found his brother Silas and Jim Douns near the gate.

"Morning, boys," he cried cheerily.

"Any glimpse of Jack or Lew?" asked Silas.

"No; but I'm expecting one of 'em any moment."

"How about the Indians?" asked Douns. "Silas roused me out last night; but didn't stay long enough to say more than 'Indians.' "

"I don't know much more than Silas. I saw several of the red devils who stole the horses; but how many, where they've gone, or what we're to expect, I can't say. We've got to wait for Jack or Lew. Silas, keep the garrison in readiness at the fort, and don't allow a man, soldier or farmer, to leave the clearing until further orders. Perhaps there were only three of those Shawnees, and then again the woods might have been full of them. I take it something's amiss, or Jack and Lew would be in by now."

"Here come Sheppard and his girl," said Silas, pointing down the lane. " 'Pears George is some excited."

Colonel Zane had much the same idea as he saw Sheppard and his daughter. The old man appeared in a hurry, which was sufficient reason to believe him anxious or alarmed, and Helen looked pale.

"Ebenezer, what's this I hear about Indians?" Sheppard asked excitedly. "What with Helen's story about the fort being besieged, and this brother of yours routing honest people from their beds, I haven't had a wink of sleep. What's up? Where are the redskins?"

"Now, George, be easy," said Colonel Zane calmly. "And you, Helen, mustn't be frightened. There's no danger. We did have a visit from Indians last night; but they hurt no one, and got only two horses."

"Oh, I'm so relieved that it's not worse," said Helen.

"It's bad enough, Helen," Betty cried, her black eyes flashing, "my pony Madcap is gone."

"Colonel Zane, come here quick!" cried Douns, who stood near the gate.

With one leap Colonel Zane was at the gate, and, following with his eyes the direction indicated by Douns' trembling finger, he saw two tall, brown figures striding down the lane. One carried two rifles, and the other a long bundle wrapped in a blanket.

"It's Jack and Wetzel," whispered Colonel Zane to Jim. "They've got the girl, and by God! from the way that bundle hangs, I think she's dead. Here," he added, speaking loudly, "you women get into the house."

Mrs. Zane, Betty and Helen stared.

"Go into the house!" he cried authoritatively.

Without a protest the three women obeyed.

At that moment Nellie Douns came across the lane; Sam shuffled out from the backyard, and Sheppard arose from his seat on the steps. They joined Colonel Zane, Silas and Jim at the gate.

"I wondered what kept you so late," Colonel Zane said to Jonathan, as he and his companion came up. "You've fetched Mabel, and she's—" The good man could say no more. If he should live an hundred years on the border amid savage murderers, he would still be tender-hearted. Just now he believed the giant borderman by the side of Jonathan held a dead girl, one whom he had danced, when a child, upon his knee.

"Mabel, an' jest alive," replied Jonathan.

"By God! I'm glad!" exclaimed Colonel Zane. "Here, Lew, give her to me."

Wetzel relinquished his burden to the colonel.

"Lew, any bad Indian sign?" asked Colonel Zane as he turned to go into the house.

The borderman shook his head.

"Wait for me," added the colonel.

He carried the girl to that apartment in the cabin which served the purpose of a sitting-room, and laid her on a couch. He gently removed the folds of the blanket, disclosing to view a fragile, white-faced girl.

"Bess, hurry, hurry!" he screamed to his wife, and as she came running in, followed no less hurriedly by Betty, Helen and Nellie, he continued, "Here's Mabel Lane, alive, poor child;

but in sore need of help. First see whether she has any bodily injury. If a bullet must be cut out, or a knife-wound sewed up, it's better she remained unconscious. Betty, run for Bess's instruments, and bring brandy and water. Lively now!" Then he gave vent to an oath and left the room.

Helen, her heart throbbing wildly, went to the side of Mrs. Zane, who was kneeling by the couch. She saw a delicate girl, not over eighteen years old, with a face that would have been beautiful but for the set lips, the closed eyelids, and an expression of intense pain.

"Oh! Oh!" breathed Helen.

"Nell, hand me the scissors," said Mrs. Zane, "and help me take off this dress. Why, it's wet, but, thank goodness! 'tis not with blood. I know that slippery touch too well. There, that's right. Betty, give me a spoonful of brandy. Now heat a blanket, and get one of your linsey gowns for this poor child."

Helen watched Mrs. Zane as if fascinated. The colonel's wife continued to talk while with deft fingers she forced a few drops of brandy between the girl's closed teeth. Then with the adroitness of a skilled surgeon, she made the examination. Helen had heard of this pioneer woman's skill in setting broken bones and treating injuries, and when she looked from the calm face to the steady fingers, she had no doubt as to the truth of what had been told.

"Neither bullet wound, cut, bruise, nor broken bone," said Mrs. Zane. "It's fear, starvation, and the terrible shock."

She rubbed Mabel's hands while gazing at her pale face. Then she forced more brandy between the tightly-closed lips. She was rewarded by ever so faint a color tinging the wan cheeks, to be followed by a fluttering of the eyelids. Then the eyes opened wide. They were large, soft, dark and humid with agony.

Helen could not bear their gaze. She saw the shadow of death, and of worse than death. She looked away, while in her heart rose a storm of passionate fury at the brutes who had made of this tender girl a wreck.

The room was full of women now, sober-faced matrons and grave-eyed girls, yet all wore the same expression, not alone of anger, nor fear, nor pity, but of all combined.

Helen instinctively felt that this was one of the trials of border endurance, and she knew from the sterner faces of the maturer women that such a trial was familiar. Despite all she had been told, the shock and pain were too great, and she went out of the room sobbing.

She almost fell over the broad back of Jonathan Zane who was sitting on the steps. Near him stood Colonel Zane talking with a tall man clad in faded buckskin.

"Lass, you shouldn't have stayed," said Colonel Zane kindly.

"It's—hurt—me—here," said Helen, placing her hand over her heart.

"Yes, I know, I know; of course it has," he replied, taking her hand. "But be brave, Helen, bear up, bear up. Oh! this border is a stern place! Do not think of that poor girl. Come, let me introduce Jonathan's friend, Wetzel!"

Helen looked up and held out her hand. She saw a very tall man with extremely broad shoulders, a mass of raven-black hair, and a white face. He stepped forward, and took her hand in his huge, horny palm, pressing it, he stepped back without speaking. Colonel Zane talked to her in a soothing voice; but she failed to hear what he said. This Wetzel, this Indian-hunter whom she had heard called "Deathwind of the Border," this companion, guide, teacher of Jonathan Zane, this borderman of wonderful deeds, stood before her.

Helen saw a cold face, deathly in its pallor, lighted by eyes sloe-black but like glinting steel. Striking as were these features, they failed to fascinate as did the strange tracings which apparently showed through the white, drawn skin. This first repelled, then drew her with wonderful force. Suffering, of fire, and frost, and iron was written there, and, stronger than all, so potent as to cause fear, could be read the terrible purpose of this man's tragic life.

"You avenged her! Oh! I know you did!" cried Helen, her whole heart leaping with a blaze to her eyes.

She was answered by a smile, but such a smile! Kindly it broke over the stern face, giving a glimpse of a heart still warm beneath that steely cold. Behind it, too, there was something fateful, something deadly.

Helen knew, though the borderman spoke not, that somewhere among the grasses of the broad plains, or on the moss of the wooded hills, lay dead the perpetrators of this outrage, their still faces bearing the ghastly stamp of Deathwind.

CHAPTER VI

Happier days than she had hoped for, dawned upon Helen after the first touch of border sorrow. Mabel Lane did not die. Helen and Betty nursed the stricken girl tenderly, weeping for very joy when signs of improvement appeared. She had remained silent for several days, always with that haunting fear in her eyes, and then gradually came a change. Tender care and nursing had due effect in banishing the dark shadow. One morning after a long sleep she awakened with a bright smile, and from that time her improvement was rapid.

Helen wanted Mabel to live with her. The girl's position was pitiable. Homeless, fatherless, with not a relative on the border, yet so brave, so patient that she aroused all the sympathy in Helen's breast. Village gossip was in substance, that Mabel had given her love to a young frontiersman, by name Alex Bennet, who had an affection for her, so it was said, but as yet had made no choice between her and the other lasses of the settlement. What effect Mabel's terrible experience might have on this lukewarm lover, Helen could not even guess; but she was not hopeful as to the future. Colonel Zane and Betty approved of Helen's plan to persuade Mabel to live with her, and the latter's faint protestations they silenced by claiming she could be of great assistance in the management of the house, therefore it was settled.

Finally the day came when Mabel was ready to go with Helen. Betty had given her a generous supply of clothing, for all her belongings had been destroyed when the cabin was burned. With Helen's strong young arm around her she voiced her gratitude to Betty and Mrs. Zane and started toward the Sheppard home.

From the green square, where the ground was highest, an un-obstructed view could be had of the valley. Mabel gazed down the river to where her home formerly stood. Only a faint, dark spot, like a blur on the green landscape, could be seen. Her soft eyes filled with tears; but she spoke no word.

"She's game and that's why she didn't go under," Colonel Zane said to himself as he mused on the strength and spirit of borderwomen. To their heroism, more than any other thing, he attributed the establishing of homes in this wilderness.

In the days that ensued, as Mabel grew stronger, the girls became very fond of each other. Helen would have been happy at any time with such a sweet companion, but just then, when the poor girl's mind was so sorely disturbed she was doubly glad. For several days, after Mabel was out of danger, Helen's thoughts had dwelt on a subject which caused extreme vexation. She had begun to suspect that she encouraged too many admirers for whom she did not care, and thought too much of a man who did not reciprocate. She was gay and moody in turn. During the moody hours she suspected herself, and in her gay ones, scorned the idea that she might ever care for a man who was indifferent. But that thought once admitted, had a trick of returning at odd moments, clouding her cheerful moods.

One sunshiny morning while the May flowers smiled under the hedge, when dew sparkled on the leaves, and the locust-blossoms shone creamy-white amid the soft green of the trees, the girls set about their much-planned flower gardening. Helen was passionately fond of plants, and had brought a jar of seeds of her favorites all the way from her eastern home.

"We'll plant the morning-glories so they'll run up the porch, and the dahlias in this long row and the nasturtiums in this round bed," Helen said.

"You have some trailing arbutus," added Mabel, "and must have clematis, wild honeysuckle and golden-glow, for they are all sweet flowers."

"This arbutus is so fresh, so dewy, so fragrant," said Helen, bending aside a lilac bush to see the pale, creeping flowers. "I never saw anything so beautiful. I grow more and more in love with my new home and friends. I have such a pretty garden to look into, and I never tire of the view beyond."

Helen gazed with pleasure and pride at the garden with its fresh green and lavender-crested lilacs, at the white-blossomed trees, and the vine-covered log cabins with blue smoke curling from their stone chimneys. Beyond, the great bulk of the fort stood guard above the willow-skirted river, and far away over the winding stream the dark hills, defiant, kept their secrets.

"If it weren't for that threatening fort one could imagine this little hamlet, nestling under the great bluff, as quiet and secure as it is beautiful," said Helen. "But that charred stockade fence with its scarred bastions and these lowering port-holes, always keep me alive to the reality."

"It wasn't very quiet when Girty was here," Mabel replied thoughtfully.

"Were you in the fort then?" asked Helen breathlessly.

"Oh, yes, I cooled the rifles for the men," replied Mabel calmly.

"Tell me all about it."

Helen listened again to a story she had heard many times; but told by new lips it always gained in vivid interest. She never tired of hearing how the notorious renegade, Girty, rode around the fort on his white horse, giving the defenders an hour in which to surrender; she learned again of the attack, when the British soldiers remained silent on an adjoining hillside, while the Indians yelled exultantly and ran about in fiendish glee, when Wetzel began the battle by shooting an Indian chieftain who had ventured within range of his ever fatal rifle. And when it came to the heroic deeds of that memorable siege Helen could not contain her enthusiasm. She shed tears over little Harry Bennet's death at the south bastion where, though riddled with bullets, he stuck to his post until relieved. Clark's race across the roof of the fort to extinguish a burning arrow, she applauded with clapping hands. Her great eyes glowed and burned, but she was silent, when hearing how Wetzel ran alone to a break in the stockade, and there, with an ax, the terrible borderman held at bay the whole infuriated Indian mob until the breach was closed. Lastly Betty Zane's never-to-be-forgotten run with the powder to the relief of the garrison and the saving of the fort was something not to cry over or applaud; but to dream of and to glorify.

"Down that slope from Colonel Zane's cabin is where Betty ran with the powder," said Mabel, pointing.

"Did you see her?" asked Helen.

"Yes, I looked out of a port-hole. The Indians stopped firing at the fort in their eagerness to shoot Betty. Oh, the banging of guns and yelling of savages was one fearful, dreadful roar! Through all that hail of bullets Betty ran swift as the wind."

"I almost wish Girty would come again," said Helen.

"Don't; he might."

"How long has Betty's husband, Mr. Clarke, been dead?" inquired Helen.

"I don't remember exactly. He didn't live long after the siege. Some say he inhaled the flames while fighting fire inside the stockade."

"How sad!"

"Yes, it was. It nearly killed Betty. But we border girls do not give up easily; we must not," replied Mabel, an unquenchable spirit showing through the sadness of her eyes.

Merry voices interrupted them, and they turned to see Betty and Nell entering the gate. With Nell's bright chatter and Betty's wit, the conversation became indeed vivacious, running from gossip to gowns, and then to that old and ever new theme, love. Shortly afterward the colonel entered the gate, with swinging step and genial smile.

"Well, now, if here aren't four handsome lasses," he said with an admiring glance.

"Eb, I believe if you were single any girl might well suspect you of being a flirt," said Betty.

"No girl ever did. I tell you I was a lady-killer in my day," replied Colonel Zane, straightening his fine form. He was indeed handsome, with his stalwart frame, dark, bronzed face and rugged, manly bearing.

"Bess said you were; but that it didn't last long after you saw her," cried Betty, mischief gleaming in her dark eye.

"Well, that's so," replied the colonel, looking a trifle crest-fallen; "but you know every dog has his day." Then advancing to the porch, he looked at Mabel with a more serious gaze as he asked, "How are you to-day?"

"Thank you, Colonel Zane, I am getting quite strong."

"Look up the valley. There's a raft coming down the river," said he softly.

Far up the broad Ohio a square patch showed dark against the green water.

Colonel Zane saw Mabel start, and a dark red flush came over her pale face. For an instant she gazed with an expression of appeal, almost fear. He knew the reason. Alex Bennet was on that raft.

"I came over to ask if I can be of any service?"

"Tell him," she answered simply.

"I say, Betts," Colonel Zane cried, "has Helen's cousin cast any more such sheep eyes at you?"

"Oh, Eb, what nonsense!" exclaimed Betty, blushing furiously.

"Well, if he didn't look sweet at you I'm an old fool."

"You're one anyway, and you're horrid," said Betty, tears of anger glistening in her eyes.

Colonel Zane whistled softly as he walked down the lane. He went into the wheelwright's shop to see about some repairs he was having made on a wagon, and then strolled on down to the river. Two Indians were sitting on the rude log wharf, together with several frontiersmen and rivermen, all waiting for the raft. He conversed with the Indians, who were friendly Chippewas, until the raft was tied up. The first person to leap on shore was a sturdy young fellow with a shock of yellow hair, and a warm, ruddy skin.

"Hello, Alex, did you have a good trip?" asked Colonel Zane of the youth.

"H'are ye, Colonel Zane. Yes, first-rate trip," replied young Bennet. "Say, I've a word for you. Come aside," and drawing Colonel Zane out of earshot of the others, he continued, "I heard this by accident, not that I didn't spy a bit when I got interested, for I did; but the way it came about was all chance. Briefly, there's a man, evidently an Englishman, at Fort Pitt, whom I overheard say he was out on the border after a Sheppard girl. I happened to hear from one of Brandt's men, who rode into Pitt just before we left, that you had new friends here by that name. This fellow was a handsome chap, no common sort, but lordly, dissipated and reckless as the devil. He had a servant traveling with him, a sailor, by his gab, who was about the toughest customer I've met in many a day. He cut a fellow in bad shape at Pitt. These two will be on the next boat, due here in a day or so, according to river and weather conditions, an' I thought, considerin' how unusual the thing was, I'd better tell ye."

"Well, well," said Colonel Zane reflectively. He recalled Sheppard's talk about an Englishman. "Alex, you did well to tell me.

Was the man drunk when he said he came west after a woman?"

"Sure he was," replied Alex. "But not when he spoke the name. Ye see I got suspicious, an' asked about him. It's this way: Jake Wentz, the trader, told me the fellow asked for the Sheppards when he got off the wagon-train. When I first seen him he was drunk, and I heard Jeff Lynn say as how the border was a bad place to come after a woman. That's what made me prick up my ears. Then the Englishman said: 'It is, eh? By God! I'd go to hell after a woman I wanted.' An' Colonel, he looked it, too."

Colonel Zane remained thoughtful while Alex made up a bundle and forced the haft of an ax under the string; but as the young man started away the colonel suddenly remembered his errand down to the wharf.

"Alex, come back here," he said, and wondered if the lad had good stuff in him. The boatman's face was plain, but not evil, and a close scrutiny of it rather prepossessed the colonel.

"Alex, I've some bad news for you," and then bluntly, with his keen gaze fastened on the young man's face, he told of old Lane's murder, of Mabel's abduction, and of her rescue by Wetzel.

Alex began to curse and swear vengeance.

"Stow all that," said the colonel sharply. "Wetzel followed four Indians who had Mabel and some stolen horses. The redskins quarreled over the girl, and two took the horses, leaving Mabel to the others. Wetzel went after these last, tomahawked them, and brought Mabel home. She was in a bad way, but is now getting over the shock."

"Say, what'd we do here without Wetzel?" Alex said huskily,

unmindful of the tears that streamed from his eyes and ran over his brown cheeks. "Poor old Jake! Poor Mabel! Damn me! it's my fault. If I'd 'a done right an' married her as I should, as I wanted to, she wouldn't have had to suffer. But I'll marry her yet, if she'll have me. It was only because I had no farm, no stock, an' only that little cabin as is full now, that I waited."

"Alex, you know me," said Colonel Zane in kindly tones. "Look there, down the clearing half a mile. See that green strip of land along the river, with the big chestnut in the middle and a cabin beyond. There's as fine farming land as can be found on the border, eighty acres, well watered. The day you marry Mabel that farm is yours."

Alex grew red, stammered, and vainly tried to express his gratitude.

"Come along, the sooner you tell Mabel the better," said the colonel with glowing face. He was a good matchmaker. He derived more pleasure from a little charity bestowed upon a deserving person, than from a season's crops.

When they arrived at the Sheppard house the girls were still on the porch. Mabel rose when she saw Alex, standing white and still. He, poor fellow, was embarrassed by the others, who regarded him with steady eyes.

Colonel Zane pushed Alex up on the porch, and said in a low voice: "Mabel, I've just arranged something you're to give Alex. It's a nice little farm, and it'll be a wedding present."

Mabel looked in a bewildered manner from Colonel Zane's happy face to the girls, and then at the red, joyous features of her lover. Only then did she understand, and uttering a strange little cry, put her trembling hands to her bosom as she swayed to and fro.

But she did not fall, for Alex, quick at the last, leaped forward and caught her in his arms.

* * * * * *

That evening Helen denied herself to Mr. Brandt and several other callers. She sat on the porch with her father while he smoked his pipe.

"Where's Will?" she asked.

"Gone after snipe, so he said," replied her father.

"Snipe? How funny! Imagine Will hunting! He's surely catching the wild fever Colonel Zane told us about."

"He surely is."

Then came a time of silence. Mr. Sheppard, accustomed to Helen's gladsome spirit and propensity to gay chatter, noted how quiet she was, and wondered.

"Why are you so still?"

"I'm a little homesick," Helen replied reluctantly.

"No? Well, I declare! This is a glorious country; but not for such as you, dear, who love music and gaiety. I often fear you'll not be happy here, and then I long for the old home, which reminds me of your mother."

"Dearest, forget what I said," cried Helen earnestly. "I'm only a little blue to-day; perhaps not at all homesick."

"Indeed, you always seemed happy."

"Father, I am happy. It's only—only a girl's foolish sentiment."

"I've got something to tell you, Helen, and it has bothered me since Colonel Zane spoke of it to-night. Mordaunt is coming to Fort Henry."

"Mordaunt? Oh, impossible! Who said so? How did you learn?"

"I fear 'tis true, my dear. Colonel Zane told me he had heard of an Englishman at Fort Pitt who asked after us. Moreover,

the fellow answers the description of Mordaunt. I am afraid it
is he, and come after you."

"Suppose he has—who cares? We owe him nothing. He cannot hurt us."

"But, Helen, he's a desperate man. Aren't you afraid of him?"

"Not I," cried Helen, laughing in scorn. "He'd better have a
care. He can't run things with a high hand out here on the
border. I told him I would have none of him, and that ended it."

"I'm much relieved. I didn't want to tell you; but it seemed
necessary. Well, child, good night, I'll go to bed."

Long after Mr. Sheppard had retired Helen sat thinking.
Memories of the past, and of the unwelcome suitor, Mordaunt,
thronged upon her thick and fast. She could see him now with
his pale, handsome face, and distinguished bearing. She had
liked him, as she had other men, until he involved her father,
with himself, in financial ruin, and had made his attention to
her unpleasantly persistent. Then he had followed the fall of
fortune with wild dissipation, and became a gambler and a
drunkard. But he did not desist in his mad wooing. He became
like her shadow, and life grew to be unendurable, until her
father planned to emigrate west, when she hailed the news with
joy. And now Mordaunt had tracked her to her new home.
She was sick with disgust. Then her spirit, always strong, and
now freer for this new, wild life of the frontier, rose within her,
and she dismissed all thoughts of this man and his passion.

The old life was dead and buried. She was going to be happy
here. As for the present, it was enough to think of the little
border village, now her home; of her girl friends; of the quiet
borderman: and, for the moment, that the twilight was somber
and beautiful.

High up on the wooded bluff rising so gloomily over the

village, she saw among the trees something silver-bright. She
watched it rise slowly from behind the trees, now hidden, now
white through rifts in the foliage, until it soared lovely and
grand above the black horizon. The ebony shadows of night
seemed to lift, as might a sable mantle moved by invisible
hands. But dark shadows, safe from the moon-rays, lay under
the trees, and a pale, misty vapor hung below the brow of the
bluff.

Mysterious as had grown the night before darkness yielded
to the moon, this pale, white light flooding the still valley, was
even more soft and strange. To one of Helen's temperament no
thought was needed; to see was enough. Yet her mind was
active. She felt with haunting power the beauty of all before
her; in fancy transporting herself far to those silver-tipped
clouds, and peopling the dells and shady nooks under the hills
with spirits and fairies, maidens and valiant knights. To her
the day was as a far-off dream. The great watch stars grew
wan before the radiant moon; it reigned alone. The immensity
of the world with its glimmering rivers, pensive valleys and
deep, gloomy forests lay revealed under the glory of the clear
light.

Absorbed in this contemplation Helen remained a long time
gazing with dreamy ecstasy at the moonlit valley until a slight
chill disturbed her happy thoughts. She knew she was not alone.
Trembling, she stood up to see, easily recognizable in the moonlight, the tall buckskin-garbed figure of Jonathan Zane.

"Well, sir," she called, sharply, yet with a tremor in her voice.

The borderman came forward and stood in front of her.
Somehow he appeared changed. The long, black rifle, the dull,
glinting weapons made her shudder. Wilder and more untam-
able he looked than ever. The very silence of the forest clung

to him; the fragrance of the grassy plains came faintly from his buckskin garments.

"Evenin', lass," he said in his slow, cool manner.

"How did you get here?" asked Helen presently, because he made no effort to explain his presence at such a late hour.

"I was able to walk."

Helen observed, with a vaulting spirit, one ever ready to rise in arms, that Master Zane was disposed to add humor to his penetrating mysteriousness. She flushed hot and then paled. This borderman certainly possessed the power to vex her, and, reluctantly she admitted, to chill her soul and rouse her fear. She strove to keep back sharp words, because she had learned that this singular individual always gave good reason for his odd actions.

"I think in kindness to me," she said, choosing her words carefully, "you might tell me why you appear so suddenly, as if you had sprung out of the ground."

"Are you alone?"

"Yes. Father is in bed; so is Mabel, and Will has not yet come home. Why?"

"Has no one else been here?"

"Mr. Brandt came, as did some others; but wishing to be alone, I did not see them," replied Helen in perplexity.

"Have you seen Brandt since?"

"Since when?"

"The night I watched by the lilac bush."

"Yes, several times," replied Helen. Something in his tone made her ashamed. "I couldn't very well escape when he called. Are you surprised because after he insulted me I'd see him?"

"Yes."

Helen felt more ashamed.

"You don't love him?" he continued.

Helen was so surprised she could only look into the dark face above her. Then she dropped her gaze, abashed by his searching eyes. But, thinking of his question, she subdued the vague stirrings of pleasure in her breast, and answered coldly:

"No, I do not; but for the service you rendered me I should never have answered such a question."

"I'm glad, an' hope you care as little for the other five men who were here that night."

"I declare, Master Zane, you seem exceedingly interested in the affairs of a young woman whom you won't visit, except as you have come to-night."

He looked at her with his piercing eyes.

"You spied upon my guests," she said, in no wise abashed now that her temper was high. "Did you care so very much?"

"Care?" he asked slowly.

"Yes; you were interested to know how many of my admirers were here, what they did, and what they said. You even hint disparagingly of them."

"True, I wanted to know," he replied; "but I don't hint about any man."

"You are so interested you wouldn't call on me when I invited you," said Helen, with poorly veiled sarcasm. It was this that made her bitter; she could never forget that she had asked this man to come to see her, and he had refused.

"I reckon you've mistook me," he said calmly.

"Why did you come? Why do you shadow my friends? This is twice you have done it. Goodness knows how many times you've been here! Tell me."

The borderman remained silent.

"Answer me," commanded Helen, her eyes blazing. She

actually stamped her foot. "Borderman or not, you have no right to pry into my affairs. If you are a gentleman, tell me why you came here?"

The eyes Jonathan turned on Helen stilled all the angry throbbing of her blood.

"I come here to learn which of your lovers is the dastard who plotted the abduction of Mabel Lane, an' the thief who stole our hosses. When I find the villain I reckon Wetzel an' I'll swing him to some tree."

The borderman's voice rang sharp and cold, and when he ceased speaking she sank back upon the step, shocked, speech-less, to gaze up at him with staring eyes.

"Don't look so, lass; don't be frightened," he said, his voice gentle and kind as it had been hard. He took her hand in his. "You nettled me into replyin'. You have a sharp tongue, lass, and when I spoke I was thinkin' of him. I'm sorry."

"A horse-thief and worse than murderer among my friends!" murmured Helen, shuddering, yet she never thought to doubt his word.

"I followed him here the night of your company."

"Do you know which one?"

"No."

He still held her hand, unconsciously, but Helen knew it well. A sense of his strength came with the warm pressure, and comforted her. She would need that powerful hand, surely, in the evil days which seemed to darken the horizon.

"What shall I do?" she whispered, shuddering again.

"Keep this secret between you an' me."

"How can I? How can I?"

"You must," his voice was deep and low. "If you tell your father, or any one. I might lose the chance to find this man, for,

lass, he's desperate cunnin'. Then he'd go free to rob others an'
mebbe help make off with other poor girls. Lass, keep my secret."

"But he might try to carry me away," said Helen in fearful perplexity.

"Most likely he might," replied the borderman with the smile
that came so rarely.

"Oh! Knowing all this, how can I meet any of these men again?
I'd betray myself."

"No; you've got too much pluck. It so happens you are the one
to help me an' Wetzel rid the border of these hell-bounds, an' you
won't fail. I know a woman when it comes to that."

"I—I help you and Wetzel?"

"Exactly."

"Gracious!" cried Helen, half-laughing, half-crying. "And poor
me with more trouble coming on the next boat."

"Lass, the colonel told me about the Englishman. It'll be bad
for him to annoy you."

Helen thrilled with the depth of meaning in the low voice. Fate
surely was weaving a bond between her and this borderman. She
felt it in his steady, piercing gaze; in her own tingling blood.

Then as her natural courage dispelled with all girlish fears, she
faced him, white, resolute, with a look in her eyes that matched
his own.

"I will do what I can," she said.

CHAPTER VII

WESTWARD from Fort Henry, far above the eddying river, Jonathan Zane slowly climbed a narrow, hazel-bordered, mountain trail. From time to time he stopped in an open patch among the thickets and breathed deep of the fresh, wood-scented air, while his keen gaze swept over the glades near by, along the wooded hillsides, and above at the timber-strewn woodland. This June morning in the wild forest was significant of nature's brightness and joy. Broad-leaved poplars, dense foliaged oaks, and vine-covered maples shaded cool, mossy banks, while between the trees the sunshine streamed in bright spots. It shone silver on the glancing silver-leaf, and gold on the colored leaves of the butternut tree. Dewdrops glistened on the ferns; ripples sparkled in the brooks; spider-webs glowed with wondrous rainbow hues, and the flower of the forest, the sweet, pale-faced daisy, rose above the green like a white star.

Yellow birds flitted among the hazel bushes caroling joyously, and cat-birds sang gaily. Robins called; bluejays screeched in the tall, white oaks; wood-peckers hammered in the dead hard-woods, and crows cawed overhead. Squirrels chattered everywhere. Ruffed grouse rose with great bustle and a whirr, flitting like brown flakes through the leaves. From far above came the shrill cry of a hawk, followed by the wilder scream of an eagle.

Wilderness music such as all this fell harmoniously on the borderman's ear. It betokened the gladsome spirit of his wild friends, happy in the warm sunshine above, or in the cool depths beneath the fluttering leaves, and everywhere in those lonely haunts unalarmed and free.

Familiar to Jonathan, almost as the footpath near his home, was this winding trail. On the height above was a safe rendez-vous, much frequented by him and Wetzel. Every lichen-covered stone, mossy bank, noisy brook and giant oak on the way up this mountain-side, could have told, had they spoken their secrets, stories of the bordermen. The fragile ferns and slender-bladed grasses peeping from the gray and amber mosses, and the flowers that hung from craggy ledges, had wisdom to impart. A borderman lived under the green tree-tops, and, there-fore, all the nodding branches of sassafras and laurel, the grassy slopes and rocky cliffs, the stately ash trees, kingly oaks and dark, mystic pines, together with the creatures that dwelt among them, save his deadly red-skinned foes, he loved. Other affection as close and true as this, he had not known. Hearkening thus with single heart to nature's teachings, he learned her secrets. Certain it was, therefore, that the many hours he passed in the woods apart from savage pursuits, were happy and fruitful.

Slowly he pressed on up the ascent, at length coming into open light upon a small plateau marked by huge, rugged, weather-chipped stones. On the eastern side was a rocky prom-ontory, and close to the edge of this cliff, an hundred feet in sheer descent, rose a gnarled, time and tempest-twisted chest-nut tree. Here the borderman laid down his rifle and knap-sack, and, half-reclining against the tree, settled himself to rest and wait.

This craggy point was the lonely watch-tower of eagles. Here on the highest headland for miles around where the bordermen were wont to meet, the outlook was far-reaching and grand.

Below the gray, splintered cliffs sheered down to meet the

waving tree-tops, and then hill after hill, slope after slope, waved and rolled far, far down to the green river. Open grassy patches, bright little islands in that ocean of dark green, shone on the hillsides. The rounded ridges ran straight, curved, or zigzag, but shaped their graceful lines in the descent to make the valley. Long, purple-hued, shadowy depressions in the wide expanse of foliage marked deep clefts between ridges where dark, cool streams bounded on to meet the river. Lower, where the land was level, in open spaces could be seen a broad trail, yellow in the sunlight, winding along with the curves of the water-course. On a swampy meadow, blue in the distance, a herd of buffalo browsed. Beyond the river, high over the green island, Fort Henry lay peaceful and solitary, the only token of the works of man in all that vast panorama.

Jonathan Zane was as much alone as if one thousand miles, instead of five, intervened between him and the settlement. Loneliness was to him a passion. Other men loved home, the light of woman's eyes, the rattle of dice or the lust of hoarding; but to him this wild, remote promontory, with its limitless view, stretching away to the dim hazy horizon, was more than all the aching joys of civilization.

Hours here, or in the shady valley, recompensed him for the loss of home comforts, the soft touch of woman's hands, the kiss of baby lips, and also for all he suffered in his pitiless pursuits, the hard fare, the steel and blood of a borderman's life.

Soon the sun shone straight overhead, dwarfing the shadow of the chestnut on the rock.

During such a time it was rare that any connected thought came into the borderman's mind. His dark eyes, now strangely luminous, strayed lingeringly over those purple, undulating slopes. This intense watchfulness had no object, neither had his

listening. He watched nothing; he hearkened to the silence. Undoubtedly in this state of rapt absorption his perceptions were
acutely alert; but without thought, as were those of the savage
in the valley below, or the eagle in the sky above.

Yet so perfectly trained were these perceptions that the least
unnatural sound or sight brought him wary and watchful from
his dreamy trance.

The slight snapping of a twig in the thicket caused him to sit
erect, and reach out toward his rifle. His eyes moved among the
dark openings in the thicket. In another moment a tall figure
pressed the bushes apart. Jonathan let fall his rifle, and sank
back against the tree once more. Wetzel stepped over the rocks
toward him.

"Come from Blue Pond?" asked Jonathan as the newcomer
took a seat beside him.

Wetzel nodded as he carefully laid aside his long, black rifle.

"Any Injun sign?" continued Jonathan, pushing toward his
companion the knapsack of eatables he had brought from the
settlement.

"Nary Shawnee track west of this divide," answered Wetzel,
helping himself to bread and cheese.

"Lew, we must go eastward, over Bing Legget's way, to find
the trail of the stolen horses."

"Likely, an' it'll be a long, hard tramp."

"Who's in Legget's gang now beside Old Horse, the Chippewa, an' his Shawnee pard, Wildfire? I don't know Bing; but
I've seen some of his Injuns an' they remember me."

"Never seen Legget but onct," replied Wetzel, "an' that time
I shot half his face off. I've been told by them as have seen him
since, that he's got a nasty scar on his temple an' cheek. He's a
big man an' knows the woods. I don't know who all's in his gang,

nor does anybody. He works in the dark, an' for cunnin' he's got some on Jim Girty, Deerin', an' several more renegades we know of lyin' quiet back here in the woods. We never tackled as bad a gang as his'n; they're all experienced woodsmen, old fighters, an' desperate, outlawed as they be by Injuns an' whites. It wouldn't surprise me to find that it's him an' his gang who are runnin' this hoss-thievin'; but bad or no, we're goin' after 'em."

Jonathan told of his movements since he had last seen his companion.

"An' the lass Helen is goin' to help us," said Wetzel, much interested. "It's a good move. Women are keen. Betty put Miller's schemin' in my eye long 'afore I noticed it. But girls have chances we men'd never get."

"Yes, an' she's like Betts, quicker'n lightnin'. She'll find out this hoss-thief in Fort Henry; but Lew, when we do get him we won't be much better off. Where do them hosses go? Who's disposin' of 'em for this fellar?"

"Where's Brandt from?" asked Wetzel.

"Detroit; he's a French-Canadian."

Wetzel swung sharply around, his eyes glowing like wakening furnaces.

"Bing Legget's a French-Canadian, an' from Detroit. Metzar was once thick with him down Fort Pitt way 'afore he murdered a man an' became an outlaw. We're on the trail, Jack."

"Brandt an' Metzar, with Legget backin' them, an' the horses go overland to Detroit?"

"I calkilate you've hit the mark."

"What'll we do?" asked Jonathan.

"Wait; that's best. We've no call to hurry. We must know the truth before makin' a move, an' as yet we're only suspicious.

This lass'll find out more in a week than we could in a year. But Jack, have a care she don't fall into any snare. Brandt ain't any too honest a lookin' chap, an' them renegades is hell for women. The scars you wear prove that well enough. She's a rare, sweet, bloomin' lass, too. I never seen her equal. I remember how her eyes flashed when she said she knew I'd avenged Mabel. Jack, they're wonderful eyes; an' that girl, however sweet an' good as she must be, is chain-lightnin' wrapped up in a beautiful form. Aren't the boys at the fort runnin' arter her?"

"Like mad; it'd make you laugh to see 'em," replied Jonathan calmly.

"There'll be some fights before she's settled for, an' mebbe arter thet. Have a care for her, Jack, an' see that she don't ketch you."

"No more danger than for you."

"I was ketched onct," replied Wetzel.

Jonathan Zane looked up at his companion. Wetzel's head was bowed; but there was no merriment in the serious face exposed to the borderman's scrutiny.

"Lew, you're jokin'."

"Not me. Some day, when you're ketched good, an' I have to go back to the lonely trail, as I did afore you an' me become friends, mebbe then, when I'm the last borderman, I'll tell you."

"Lew, 'cordin' to the way settlers are comin', in a few more years there won't be any need for a borderman. When the Injuns are all gone where'll be our work?"

" 'Tain't likely either of us'll ever see them times," said Wetzel, "an' I don't want to. Wal, Jack, I'm off now, an' I'll meet you here every other day."

Wetzel shouldered his long rifle, and soon passed out of sight down the mountain-side.

Jonathan arose, shook himself as a big dog might have done, and went down into the valley. Only once did he pause in his descent, and that was when a crackling twig warned him some heavy body was moving near. Silently he sank into the bushes bordering the trail. He listened with his ear close to the ground. Presently he heard a noise as of two hard substances striking together. He resumed his walk, having recognized the grating noise of a deer-hoof striking a rock. Farther down he espied a pair grazing. The buck ran into the thicket; but the doe eyed him curiously.

Less than an hour's rapid walking brought him to the river. Here he plunged into a thicket of willows, and emerged on a sandy strip of shore. He carefully surveyed the river bank, and then pulled a small birch-bark canoe from among the foliage. He launched the frail craft, paddled across the river and beached it under a reedy, over-hanging bank.

The distance from this point in a straight line to his destination was only a mile; but a rocky bluff and a ravine necessitated his making a wide detour. While lightly leaping over a brook his keen eye fell on an imprint in the sandy loam. Instantly he was on his knees. The footprint was small, evidently a woman's, and, what was more unusual, instead of the flat, round moccasin-track, it was pointed, with a sharp, square heel. Such shoes were not worn by border girls. True Betty and Nell had them; but they never went into the woods without moccasins.

Jonathan's experienced eye saw that this imprint was not an hour old. He gazed up at the light. The day was growing short. Already shadows lay in the glens. He would not long have light enough to follow the trail; but he hurried on hoping to find the person who made it before darkness came. He had not traveled many paces before learning that the one who made it was lost.

The uncertainty in those hasty steps was as plain to the borderman's eyes, as if it had been written in words on the sand. The
course led along the brook, avoiding the rough places, and leading into the open glades and glens; but it drew no nearer to the
settlement. A quarter of an hour of rapid trailing enabled Jonathan to discern a dark figure moving among the trees. Abandoning the trail, he cut across a ridge to head off the lost woman.
Stepping out of a sassafras thicket, he came face to face with
Helen Sheppard.

"Oh!" she cried in alarm, and then the expression of terror
gave place to one of extreme relief and gladness. "Oh! Thank
goodness! You've found me. I'm lost!"

"I reckon," answered Jonathan grimly. "The settlement's only
five hundred yards over that hill."

"I was going the wrong way. Oh! suppose you hadn't come!"
exclaimed Helen, sinking on a log and looking up at him with
warm, glad eyes.

"How did you lose your way?" Jonathan asked. He saw
neither the warmth in her eyes nor the gladness.

"I went up the hillside, only a little way, after flowers, keeping
the fort in sight all the time. Then I saw some lovely violets
down a little hill, and thought I might venture. I found such
loads of them I forgot everything else, and I must have walked
on a little way. On turning to go back I couldn't find the little
hill. I have hunted in vain for the clearing. It seems as if I have
been wandering about for hours. I'm so glad you've found me!"

"Weren't you told to stay in the settlement, inside the clearing?" demanded Jonathan.

"Yes," replied Helen, with her head up.

"Why didn't you?"

"Because I didn't choose."

"You ought to have better sense."

"It seems I hadn't," Helen said quietly, but her eyes belied that calm voice.

"You're a headstrong child," Jonathan added curtly.

"Mr. Zane!" cried Helen with pale face.

"I suppose you've always had your own sweet will; but out here on the border you ought to think a little of others, if not of yourself."

Helen maintained a proud silence.

"You might have run right into prowlin' Shawnees."

"That dreadful disaster would not have caused you any sorrow," she flashed out.

"Of course it would. I might have lost my scalp tryin' to get you back home," said Jonathan, beginning to hesitate. Plainly he did not know what to make of this remarkable young woman.

"Such a pity to have lost all your fine hair," she answered with a touch of scorn.

Jonathan flushed, perhaps for the first time in his life. If there was anything he was proud of, it was his long, glossy hair.

"Miss Helen, I'm a poor hand at words," he said, with a pale, grave face. "I was only speakin' for your own good."

"You are exceedingly kind; but need not trouble yourself."

"Say," Jonathan hesitated, looking half-vexed at the lovely, angry face. Then an idea occurred to him. "Well, I won't trouble. Find your way home yourself."

Abruptly he turned and walked slowly away. He had no idea of allowing her to go home alone; but believed it might be well for her to think so. If she did not call him back he would remain near at hand, and when she showed signs of anxiety or fear he could go to her.

Helen determined she would die in the woods, or be captured

by Shawnees, before calling him back. But she watched him. Slowly the tall, strong figure, with its graceful, springy stride, went down the glade. He would be lost to view in a moment, and then she would be alone. How dark it had suddenly become! The gray cloak of twilight was spread over the forest, and in the hollows night already had settled down. A breathless silence pervaded the woods. How lonely! thought Helen, with a shiver. Surely it would be dark before she could find the settlement. What hill hid the settlement from view? She did not know, could not remember which he had pointed out. Suddenly she began to tremble. She had been so frightened before he had found her, and so relieved afterward; and now he was going away.

"Mr. Zane," she cried with a great effort. "Come back."

Jonathan kept slowly on.

"Come back, Jonathan, please."

The borderman retraced his steps.

"Please take me home," she said, lifting a fair face all flushed, tear-stained, and marked with traces of storm. "I was foolish, and silly to come into the woods, and so glad to see you! But you spoke to me—in—in a way no one ever used before. I'm sure I deserved it. Please take me home. Papa will be worried."

Softer eyes and voice than hers never entreated man.

"Come," he said gently, and, taking her by the hand, he led her up the ridge.

Thus they passed through the darkening forest, hand in hand, like a dusky redman and his bride. He helped her over stones and logs, but still held her hand when there was no need of it. She looked up to see him walking, so dark and calm beside her, his eyes ever roving among the trees. Deepest remorse came upon her because of what she had said. There was no sentiment for him in this walk under the dark canopy of the leaves. He realized the responsibility. Any tree might hide a treacherous foe. She would atone for her sarcasm, she promised herself, while walking, ever conscious of her hand in his, her bosom heaving with the sweet, undeniable emotion which came knocking at her heart.

Soon they were out of the thicket, and on the dusty lane. A few moments of rapid walking brought them within sight of the twinkling lights of the village, and a moment later they were at the lane leading to Helen's home. Releasing her hand, she stopped him with a light touch and said:

"Please don't tell papa or Colonel Zane."

"Child, I ought. Some one should make you stay at home."

"I'll stay. Please don't tell. It will worry papa."

Jonathan Zane looked down into her great, dark, wonderful eyes with an unaccountable feeling. He really did not hear what she asked. Something about that upturned face brought to his mind a rare and perfect flower which grew in far-off rocky fastnesses. The feeling he had was intangible, like no more than a breath of fragrant western wind, faint with tidings of some beautiful field.

"Promise me you won't tell."

"Well, lass, have it your own way," replied Jonathan, wonderingly conscious that it was the first pledge ever asked of him by a woman.

"Thank you. Now we have two secrets, haven't we?" she laughed, with eyes like stars.

"Run home now, lass. Be careful hereafter. I do fear for you with such spirit an' temper. I'd rather be scalped by Shawnees than have Bing Legget so much as set eyes on you."

"You would? Why?" Her voice was like low, soft music.

"Why?" he mused. "It'd seem like a buzzard about to light on a doe."

"Good-night," said Helen abruptly, and, wheeling, she hurried down the lane.

CHAPTER VIII

"Jack," said Colonel Zane to his brother next morning, "to-day is Saturday and all the men will be in. There was high jinks over at Metzar's place yesterday, and I'm looking for more to-day. The two fellows Alex Bennet told me about, came on day-before-yesterday's boat. Sure enough, one's a lordly Englishman, and the other, the cussedest-looking little chap I ever saw. They started trouble immediately. The Englishman, his name is Mordaunt, hunted up the Sheppards and as near as I can make out from George's story, Helen spoke her mind very plainly. Mordaunt and Case, that's his servant, the little cuss, got drunk and raised hell down at Metzar's where they're staying. Brandt and Williams are drinking hard, too, which is something unusual for Brandt. They got chummy at once with the Englishman, who seems to have plenty of gold and is fond of gambling. This Mordaunt is a gentleman, or I never saw one. I feel sorry for him. He appears to be a ruined man. If he lasts a week out here I'll be surprised. Case looks ugly, as if he were spoiling to cut somebody. I want you to keep your eye peeled. The day may pass off as many other days of drinking bouts have, without anything serious, and on the other hand there's liable to be trouble."

Jonathan's preparations were characteristic of the borderman. He laid aside his rifle, and, removing his short coat, buckled on a second belt containing a heavier tomahawk and knife than those he had been wearing. Then he put on his hunting frock, or shirt, and wore it loose with the belts underneath, instead of on the outside. Unfastened, the frock was rather full, and gave him the appearance of a man unarmed and careless.

Jonathan Zane was not so reckless as to court danger, nor, like many frontiersmen, fond of fighting for its own sake. Colonel Zane was commandant of the fort, and, in a land where there was no law, tried to maintain a semblance of it. For years he had kept thieves, renegades and outlaws away from his little settlement by dealing out stern justice. His word was law, and his bordermen executed it as such. Therefore Jonathan and Wetzel made it their duty to have a keen eye on all that was happening. They kept the colonel posted, and never interfered in any case without orders.

The morning passed quietly. Jonathan strolled here or loitered there; but saw none of the roisterers. He believed they were sleeping off the effects of their orgy on the previous evening. After dinner he smoked his pipe. Betty and Helen passed, and Helen smiled. It struck him suddenly that she had never looked at him in such a way before. There was meaning in that warm, radiant flash. A little sense of vexation, the source of which he did not understand, stirred in him against this girl; but with it came the realization that her white face and big, dark eyes had risen before him often since the night before. He wished, for the first time, that he could understand women better.

"Everything quiet?" asked Colonel Zane, coming out on the steps.

"All quiet," answered Jonathan.

"They'll open up later, I suspect. I'm going over to Sheppard's for a while, and, later, will drop into Metzar's. I'll make him

haul in a yard or two. I don't like things I hear about his selling
the youngsters rum. I'd like you to be within call."

The borderman strolled down the bluff and along the path
which overhung the river. He disliked Metzar more than his
brother suspected, and with more weighty reason than that of
selling rum to minors. Jonathan threw himself at length on the
ground and mused over the situation.

"We never had any peace in this settlement, an' never will in
our day. Eb is hopeful an' looks at the bright side, always expectin' to-morrow will be different. What have the past sixteen
years been? One long bloody fight, an' the next sixteen won't be
any better. I make out that we'll have a mix-up soon. Metzar an'
Brandt with their allies, whoever they are, will be in it, an' if
Bing Legget's in the gang, we've got, as Wetzel said, a long, hard
trail, which may be our last. More'n that, there'll be trouble about
this chain-lightnin' girl, as Wetzel predicted. Women make trouble anyways; an' when they're winsome an' pretty they cause
more; but if they're beautiful an' fiery, bent on havin' their way,
as this new lass is, all hell couldn't hold a candle to them. We
don't need the Shawnees an' Girtys, an' hoss thieves round this
here settlement to stir up excitin' times, now we've got this dark-
eyed lass. An' yet any fool could see she's sweet, an' good, an'
true as gold."

Toward the middle of the afternoon Jonathan sauntered in
the direction of Metzar's inn. It lay on the front of the bluff,
with its main doors looking into the road. A long, one-story log
structure with two doors, answered as a bar-room. The inn
proper was a building more pretentious, and joined the smaller
one at its western end. Several horses were hitched outside, and
two great oxen yoked to a cumbersome mud-crusted wagon
stood patiently by.

Jonathan bent his tall head as he entered the noisy bar-room. The dingy place reeked with tobacco smoke and the fumes of vile liquor. It was crowded with men. The lawlessness of the time and place was evident. Gaunt, red-faced frontiersmen reeled to and fro across the sawdust floor; hunters and fur-traders, raftsmen and farmers, swelled the motley crowd; young men, honest-faced, but flushed and wild with drink, hung over the bar; a group of sullen-visaged, serpent-eyed Indians held one corner. The black-bearded proprietor dealt out the rum.

From beyond the bar-room, through a door entering upon the back porch, came the rattling of dice. Jonathan crossed the bar-room apparently oblivious to the keen glance Metzar shot at him, and went out upon the porch. This also was crowded, but there was more room because of greater space. At one table sat some pioneers drinking and laughing; at another were three men playing with dice. Colonel Zane, Silas, and Sheppard were among the lookers-on at the game. Jonathan joined them, and gazed at the gamesters.

Brandt he knew well enough; he had seen that set, wolfish expression in the riverman's face before. He observed, however, that the man had flushed cheeks and trembling hands, indications of hard drinking. The player sitting next to Brandt was Williams, one of the garrison, and a good-natured fellow, but garrulous and wickedly disposed when drunk. The remaining player Jonathan at once saw was the Englishman, Mordaunt. He was a handsome man, with fair skin, and long, silken, blond mustache. Heavy lines, and purple shades under his blue eyes, were the unmistakable stamp of dissipation. Reckless, dissolute, bad as he looked, there yet clung something favorable about the man. Perhaps it was his cool, devil-may-care way as he pushed over gold piece after gold piece from the fast diminishing pile before him. His velvet frock and silken doublet had once been elegant; but were now sadly the worse for border roughing.

Behind the Englishman's chair Jonathan saw a short man with a face resembling that of a jackal. The grizzled, stubbly beard, the protruding, vicious mouth, the broad, flat nose, and deep-set, small, glittering eyes made a bad impression on the observer. This man, Jonathan concluded, was the servant, Case, who was so eager with his knife. The borderman made the reflection, that if knife-play was the little man's pastime, he was not likely to go short of sport in that vicinity.

Colonel Zane attracted Jonathan's attention at this moment. The pioneers had vacated the other table, and Silas and Sheppard now sat by it. The colonel wanted his brother to join them.

"Here, Johnny, bring drinks," he said to the serving boy. "Tell Metzar who they're for." Then turning to Sheppard he continued: "He keeps good whiskey; but few of these poor devils ever see it." At the same time Colonel Zane pressed his foot upon that of Jonathan's.

The borderman understood that the signal was intended to call attention to Brandt. The latter had leaned forward, as Jonathan passed by to take a seat with his brother, and said something in a low tone to Mordaunt and Case. Jonathan knew by the way the Englishman and his man quickly glanced up at him, that he had been the subject of the remark.

Suddenly Williams jumped to his feet with an oath.

"I'm cleaned out," he cried.

"Shall we play alone?" asked Brandt of Mordaunt.

"As you like," replied the Englishman, in a tone which showed he cared not a whit whether he played or not.

"I've got work to do. Let's have some more drinks, and play another time," said Brandt.

The liquor was served and drank. Brandt pocketed his pile of Spanish and English gold, and rose to his feet. He was a trifle unsteady; but not drunk.

"Will you gentlemen have a glass with me?" Mordaunt asked of Colonel Zane's party.

"Thank you, some other time, with pleasure. We have our drink now," Colonel Zane said courteously.

Meantime Brandt had been whispering in Case's ear. The little man laughed at something the riverman said. Then he shuffled from behind the table. He was short, his compact build gave promise of unusual strength and agility.

"What are you going to do now?" asked Mordaunt, rising also. He looked hard at Case.

"Shiver my sides, cap'n, if I don't need another drink," replied the sailor.

"You have had enough. Come upstairs with me," said Mordaunt.

"Easy with your hatch, cap'n," grinned Case. "I want to drink with that ther' Injun killer. I've had drinks with buccaneers, and bad men all over the world, and I'm not going to miss this chance."

"Come on; you will get into trouble. You must not annoy these gentlemen," said Mordaunt.

"Trouble is the name of my ship, and she's a trim, fast craft," replied the man.

His loud voice had put an end to the conversation. Men began to crowd in from the bar-room. Metzar himself came to see what had caused the excitement.

The little man threw up his cap, whooped, and addressed himself to Jonathan:

"Injun-killer, bad man of the border, will you drink with a jolly old tar from England?"

Suddenly a silence reigned, like that in the depths of the forest. To those who knew the borderman, and few did not know him, the invitation was nothing less than an insult. But it did not appear to them, as to him, like a pre-arranged plot to provoke a fight.

"Will you drink, redskin-hunter?" bawled the sailor.

"No," said Jonathan in his quiet voice.

"Maybe you mean that against old England?" demanded Case fiercely.

The borderman eyed him steadily, inscrutable as to feeling or intent, and was silent.

"Go out there and I'll see the color of your insides quicker than I'd take a drink," hissed the sailor, with his brick-red face distorted and hideous to look upon. He pointed with a long-bladed knife that no one had seen him draw, to the green sward beyond the porch.

The borderman neither spoke, nor relaxed a muscle.

"Ho! ho! my brave pirate of the plains!" cried Case, and he leered with braggart sneer into the faces of Jonathan and his companions.

It so happened that Sheppard sat nearest to him, and got the full effect of the sailor's hot, rum-soaked breath. He arose with a pale face.

"Colonel, I can't stand this," he said hastily. "Let's get away from that drunken ruffian."

"Who's a drunken ruffian?" yelled Case, more angry than ever. "I'm not drunk; but I'm going to be, and cut some of you white-livered border mates. Here, you old masthead, drink this to my health, damn you!"

The ruffian had seized a tumbler of liquor from the table, and held it toward Sheppard while he brandished his long knife.

White as snow, Sheppard backed against the wall; but did not take the drink.

The sailor had the floor; no one save him spoke a word. The action had been so rapid that there had hardly been time. Colonel Zane and Silas were as quiet and tense as the borderman.

"Drink!" hoarsely cried the sailor, advancing his knife toward Sheppard's body.

When the sharp point all but pressed against the old man, a bright object twinkled through the air. It struck Case's wrist, knocked the knife from his fingers, and, bounding against the wall, fell upon the floor. It was a tomahawk.

The borderman sprang over the table like a huge catamount, and with movement equally quick, knocked Case with a crash against the wall; closed on him before he could move a hand, and flung him like a sack of meal over the bluff.

The tension relieved, some of the crowd laughed, others looked over the embankment to see how Case had fared, and others remarked that for some reason he had gotten off better than they expected.

The borderman remained silent. He leaned against a post, with broad breast gently heaving, but his eyes sparkled as they watched Brandt, Williams, Mordaunt and Metzar. The Englishman alone spoke.

"Handily done," he said, cool and suave. "Sir, yours is an iron hand. I apologize for this unpleasant affair. My man is quarrelsome when under the influence of liquor."

"Metzar, a word with you," cried Colonel Zane curtly.

"Come inside, kunnel," said the innkeeper, plainly ill at ease.

"No; listen here. I'll speak to the point. You've got to stop running this kind of a place. No words, now, you've got to stop. Understand? You know as well as I, perhaps better, the character of your so-called inn. You'll get but one more chance."

"Wal, kunnel, this is a free country," growled Metzar. "I can't help these fellars comin' here lookin' fer blood. I runs an honest place. The men want to drink an' gamble. What's law here? What can you do?"

"You know me, Metzar," Colonel Zane said grimly. "I don't waste words. 'To hell with law!' so you say. I can say that, too. Remember, the next drunken boy I see, or shady deal, or gambling spree, out you go for good."

Metzar lowered his shaggy head and left the porch. Brandt and his friends, with serious faces, withdrew into the bar-room.

The borderman walked around the corner of the inn, and up the lane. The colonel, with Silas and Sheppard, followed in more leisurely fashion. At a shout from some one they turned to see a dusty, bloody figure, with ragged clothes, stagger up from the bluff.

"There's that blamed sailor now," said Sheppard. "He's a tough nut. My! What a knock on the head Jonathan gave him. Strikes me, too, that tomahawk came almost at the right time to save me a whole skin."

"I was furious, but not at all alarmed," rejoined Colonel Zane.

"I wondered what made you so quiet."

"I was waiting. Jonathan never acts until the right moment, and then—well, you saw him. The little villain deserved killing. I could have shot him with pleasure. Do you know, Sheppard, Jonathan's aversion to shedding blood is a singular thing. He'd never kill the worst kind of a white man until driven to it."

"That's commendable. How about Wetzel?"

"Well, Lew is different," replied Colonel Zane with a shudder.

"If I told him to take an ax and clean out Metzar's place—God! what a wreck he'd make of it. Maybe I'll have to tell him, and if I do, you'll see something you can never forget."

CHAPTER IX

ON SUNDAY morning under the bright, warm sun, the little hamlet of Fort Henry lay peacefully quiet, as if no storms had ever rolled and thundered overhead, no roistering ever disturbed its stillness, and no Indian's yell ever horribly broke the quiet.

" 'Tis a fine morning," said Colonel Zane, joining his sister on the porch. "Well, how nice you look! All in white for the first time since—well, you do look charming. You're going to church, of course."

"Yes, I invited Helen and her cousin to go. I've persuaded her to teach my Sunday-school class, and I'll take another of older children," replied Betty.

"That's well. The youngsters don't have much chance to learn out here. But we've made one great stride. A church and a preacher means very much to young people. Next shall come the village school."

"Helen and I might teach our classes an hour or two every afternoon."

"It would be a grand thing if you did! Fancy these tots growing up unable to read or write. I hate to think of it; but the Lord knows I've done my best. I've had my troubles in keeping them alive."

"Helen suggested the day school. She takes the greatest interest in everything and everybody. Her energy is remarkable. She simply must move, must do everything. She overflows with kindness and sympathy. Yesterday she cried with happiness when Mabel told her Alex was eager to be married very soon. I tell you, Eb, Helen is a fine character."

"Yes, good as she is pretty, which is saying some," mused the colonel. "I wonder who'll be the lucky fellow to win her."

"It's hard to say. Not that Englishman, surely. She hates him. Jonathan might. You should see her eyes when he is mentioned."

"Say, Betts, you don't mean it?" eagerly asked her brother.

"Yes, I do," returned Betty, nodding her head positively. "I'm not easily deceived about those things. Helen's completely fascinated with Jack. She might be only a sixteen-year-old girl for the way she betrays herself to me."

"Betty, I have a beautiful plan."

"No doubt; you're full of them."

"We can do it, Betty, we can, you and I," he said, as he squeezed her arm.

"My dear old matchmaking brother," returned Betty, laughing, "it takes two to make a bargain. Jack must be considered."

"Bosh!" exclaimed the colonel, snapping his fingers. "You needn't tell me any young man—any man, could resist that glorious girl."

"Perhaps not; I couldn't if I were a man. But Jack's not like other people. He'd never realize that she cared for him. Besides, he's a borderman."

"I know, and that's the only serious obstacle. But he could scout around the fort, even if he was married. These long, lovely terrible journeys taken by him and Wetzel are mostly unnecessary. A sweet wife could soon make him see that. The border will be civilized in a few years, and because of that he'd better give over hunting for Indians. I'd like to see him married and settle down, like the rest of us, even Isaac. You know Jack's the last of the Zanes, that is, the old Zanes. The difficulty arising from his extreme modesty and bashfulness can easily be overcome."

"How, most wonderful brother?"

"Easy as pie. Tell Jack that Helen is dying of love for him, and tell her that Jack loves—"

"But, dear Eb, that latter part is not true," interposed Betty.

"True, of course it's true, or would be in any man who wasn't as blind as a bat. We'll tell her Jack cares for her; but he is a borderman with stern ideas of duty, and so slow and backward he'd never tell his love even if he had overcome his tricks of ranging. That would settle it with any girl worth her salt, and this one will fetch Jack in ten days, or less."

"Eb, you're a devil," said Betty gaily, and then she added in a more sober vein, "I understand, Eb. Your idea is prompted by love of Jack, and it's all right. I never see him go out of the clearing but I think it may be for the last time, even as on that day so long ago when brother Andrew waved his cap to us, and never came back. Jack is the best man in the world, and I, too, want to see him happy, with a wife, and babies, and a settled occupation in life. I think we might weave a pretty little romance. Shall we try?"

"Try? We'll do it! Now, Betts, you explain it to both. You can do it smoother than I, and telling them is really the finest point of our little plot. I'll help the good work along afterwards. He'll be out presently. Nail him at once."

Jonathan, all unconscious of the deep-laid scheme to make him happy, soon came out on the porch, and stretched his long arms as he breathed freely of the morning air.

"Hello, Jack, where are you bound?" asked Betty, clasping one of his powerful, buckskin-clad knees with her arm.

"I reckon I'll go over to the spring," he replied, patting her dark, glossy head.

"Do you know I want to tell you something, Jack, and it's quite serious," she said, blushing a little at her guilt; but resolute to carry out her part of the plot.

"Well, dear?" he asked as she hesitated.

"Do you like Helen?"

"That is a question," Jonathan replied after a moment.

"Never mind; tell me," she persisted.

He made no answer.

"Well, Jack, she's—she's wildly in love with you."

The borderman stood very still for several moments. Then, with one step he gained the lawn, and turned to confront her.

"What's that you say?"

Betty trembled a little. He spoke so sharply, his eyes were bent on her so keenly, and he looked so strong, so forceful that she was almost afraid. But remembering that she had said only what, to her mind, was absolutely true, she raised her eyes and repeated the words:

"Helen is wildly in love with you."

"Betty, you wouldn't joke about such a thing; you wouldn't lie to me, I know you wouldn't."

"No, Jack dear."

She saw his powerful frame tremble, even as she had seen more than one man tremble, during the siege, under the impact of a bullet.

Without speaking, he walked rapidly down the path toward the spring.

Colonel Zane came out of his hiding-place behind the porch.

and, with a face positively electrifying in its glowing pleasure, beamed upon his sister.

"Gee! Didn't he stalk off like an Indian chief!" he said, chuckling with satisfaction. "By George! Betts, you must have got in a great piece of work. I never in my life saw Jack look like that."

Colonel Zane sat down by Betty's side and laughed softly but heartily.

"We'll fix him all right, the lonely hill-climber! Why, he hasn't a ghost of a chance. Wait until she sees him after hearing your story! I tell you, Betty—why—damme! you're crying!"

He had turned to find her head lowered, while she shaded her face with her hand.

"Now, Betty, just a little innocent deceit like that—what harm?" he said, taking her hand. He was as tender as a woman.

"Oh, Eb, it wasn't that. I didn't mind telling him. Only the flash in his eyes reminded me of—of Alfred."

"Surely it did. Why not? Almost everything brings up a tender memory for some one we've loved and lost. But don't cry, Betty."

She laughed a little, and raised a face with its dark cheeks flushed and tear-stained.

"I'm silly, I suppose; but I can't help it. I cry at least once every day."

"Brace up. Here come Helen and Will. Don't let them see you grieved. My! Helen in pure white, too! This is a conspiracy to ruin the peace of the masculine portion of Fort Henry."

Betty went forward to meet her friends while Colonel Zane continued talking, but now to himself. "What a fatal beauty she has!" His eyes swept over Helen with the pleasure of an artist. The fair richness of her skin, the perfect lips, the wavy, shiny hair, the wondrous dark-blue, changing eyes, the tall figure, slender, but strong and swelling with gracious womanhood, made a picture he delighted in and loved have near him. The girl did not possess for him any of that magnetism, so commonly felt by most of her admirers; but he did feel how subtly full she was of something, which for want of a better term he described in Wetzel's characteristic expression, as "chain-lighting."

. He reflected that as he was so much older, that she, although always winsome and earnest, showed nothing of the tormenting, bewildering coquetry of her nature. Colonel Zane prided himself on his discernment, and he had already observed that Helen had different sides of character for different persons. To Betty, Mabel, Nell, and the children, she was frank, girlish, full of fun and always lovable; to the young men cold; but with a penetrating, mocking promise haunting that coldness, and sometimes sweetly agreeable, often willful, and changeable as April winds. At last the colonel concluded that she needed, as did all other spirited young women, the taming influence of a man whom she loved, a home to care for, and children to soften and temper her spirit.

"Well, young friends, I see you count on keeping the Sabbath," he said cheerily. "For my part, Will, I don't see how Jim Douns can preach this morning, before his laurel blossom and that damask rose."

"How poetical! Which is which?" asked Betty.

"Flatterer!" laughed Helen, shaking her finger.

"And a married man, too!" continued Jerry.

"Well, being married has not affected my poetical sentiment, nor impaired my eyesight."

"But it has seriously inconvenienced your old propensity of making love to the girls. Not that you wouldn't if you dared," replied Betty with mischief in her eye.

"Now, Will, what do you think of that? Isn't it real sisterly regard? Come, we'll go and look at my thoroughbreds," said Colonel Zane.

"Where is Jonathan?" Helen asked presently. "Something happened at Metzar's yesterday. Papa wouldn't tell me, and I want to ask Jonathan."

"Jack is down by the spring. He spends a great deal of his time there. It's shady and cool, and the water babbles over the stones."

"How much alone he is," said Helen.

Betty took her former position on the steps, but did not raise her eyes while she continued speaking. "Yes, he's more alone than ever lately, and quieter, too. He hardly ever speaks now. There must be something on his mind more serious than horse-thieves."

"What?" Helen asked quickly.

"I'd better not tell—you."

A long moment passed before Helen spoke.

"Please tell me!"

"Well, Helen, we think, Eb and I, that Jack is in love for the first time in his life, and with you, you adorable creature. But Jack's a borderman; he is stern in his principles, thinks he is wedded to his border life, and he knows that he has both red and white blood on his hands. He'd die before he'd speak of his love, because he cannot understand that would do any good, even if you loved him, which is, of course, preposterous."

"Loves me!" breathed Helen softly.

She sat down rather beside Betty, and turned her face away. She still held the young woman's hand which she squeezed so tightly as to make its owner wince. Betty stole a look at her, and saw the rich red blood mantling her cheeks, and her full bosom heave.

Helen turned presently, with no trace of emotion except a singular brilliance of the eyes. She was so slow to speak again that Colonel Zane and Will returned from the corral before she found her voice.

"Colonel Zane, please tell me about last night. When papa came home to supper he was pale and very nervous. I knew something had happened. But he would not explain, which made me all the more anxious. Won't you please tell me?"

Colonel Zane glanced again at her, and knew what had happened. Despite her self-possession those tell-tale eyes told her secret. Ever-changing and shadowing with a bounding, rapturous light, they were indeed the windows of her soul. All the emotion of a woman's heart shone there, fear, beauty, wondering appeal, trembling joy, and timid hope.

"Tell you? Indeed I will," replied Colonel Zane, softened and a little remorseful under those wonderful eyes.

No one liked to tell a story better than Colonel Zane. Briefly and graphically he related the circumstances of the affair leading to the attack on Helen's father, and, as the tale progressed, he became quite excited, speaking with animated face and forceful gestures.

"Just as the knife-point touched your father, a swiftly-flying object knocked the weapon to the floor. It was Jonathan's tomahawk. What followed was so sudden I hardly saw it. Like lightning, and flexible as steel, Jonathan jumped over the table, smashed Case against the wall, pulled him up and threw him over the bank. I tell you, Helen, it was a beautiful piece of action; but not, of course, for a woman's eyes. Now that's all. Your father was not even hurt."

"He saved papa's life," murmured Helen, standing like a statue.

She wheeled suddenly with that swift bird-like motion habitual to her, and went quickly down the path leading to the spring.

* * * * * *

Jonathan Zane, solitary dreamer of dreams as he was, had never been in as strange and beautiful a reverie as that which possessed him on this Sabbath morning.

Deep into his heart had sunk Betty's words. The wonder of it, the sweetness, that alone was all he felt. The glory of this girl had begun, days past, to spread its glamour round him. Swept irresistibly away now, he soared aloft in a dream-castle of fancy with its painted windows and golden walls.

For the first time in his life on the border he had entered the little glade and had no eye for the crystal water flowing over the pebbles and mossy stones, or the plot of grassy ground inclosed by tall, dark trees and shaded by a canopy of fresh green and azure blue. Nor did he hear the music of the soft rushing water, the warbling birds, or the gentle sighing breeze moving the leaves.

Gone, vanished, lost to-day was that sweet companionship of nature. That indefinable and unutterable spirit which flowed so peacefully to him from his beloved woods; that something more than merely affecting his senses, which existed for him in the stony cliffs, and breathed with life through the lonely aisles of the forest, had fled before the fateful power of a woman's love and beauty.

A long time that seemed only a moment passed while he leaned against a stone. A light step sounded on the path.

A vision in pure white entered the glade; two little hands pressed his, and two dark-blue eyes of misty beauty shed their light on him.

"Jonathan, I am come to thank you."

Sweet and tremulous, the voice sounded far away.

"Thank me? For what?"

"You saved papa's life. Oh! how can I thank you?"

No voice answered for him.

"I have nothing to give but this."

A flower-like face was held up to him; hands light as thistle-down touched his shoulders; dark-blue eyes glowed upon him with all tenderness.

"May I thank you—so?"

Soft lips met his full and lingeringly.

Then came a rush as of wind, a flash of white, and the patter of flying feet. He was alone in the glade.

CHAPTER X

JUNE passed; July opened with unusually warm weather, and Fort Henry had no visits from Indians or horse-thieves, nor any inconvenience except the hot sun. It was the warmest weather for many years, and seriously dwarfed the settlers' growing corn. Nearly all the springs were dry, and a drouth menaced the farmers.

The weather gave Helen an excuse which she was not slow to adopt. Her pale face and languid air perplexed and worried her father and her friends. She explained to them that the heat affected her disagreeably.

Long days had passed since that Sunday morning when she kissed the borderman. What transports of sweet hope and fear were hers then! How shame had scorched her happiness! Yet

still she gloried in the act. By that kiss had she awakened to a
full consciousness of her love. With insidious stealth and ever-
increasing power this flood had increased to full tide, and, bursting its bonds, surged over her with irresistible strength.

During the first days after the dawning of her passion, she
lived in its sweetness, hearing only melodious sounds chiming
in her soul. The hours following that Sunday were like long
dreams. But as all things reach fruition, so this girlish period
passed, leaving her a thoughtful woman. She began to gather up
the threads of her life where love had broken them, to plan
nobly, and to hope and wait.

Weeks passed, however, and her lover did not come. Betty
told her that Jonathan made flying trips at break of day to hold
council with Colonel Zane; that he and Wetzel were on the
trail of Shawnees with stolen horses, and both bordermen were
in their dark, vengeful, terrible moods. In these later days Helen
passed through many stages of feeling. After the exalting mood
of hot, young love, came reaction. She fell into the depths of
despair. Sorrow paled her face, thinned her cheeks and lent
another shadow, a mournful one, to her great eyes. The constant
repression of emotion, the strain of trying to seem cheerful when
she was miserable, threatened even her magnificent health. She
answered the solicitude of her friends by evasion, and then by
that innocent falsehood in which a sensitive soul hides its secrets.
Shame was only natural, because since the borderman came not,
nor sent her a word, pride whispered that she had wooed him,
forgetting modesty.

Pride, anger, shame, despair, however, finally fled before affection. She loved this wild borderman, and knew he loved her in
return although he might not understand it himself. His simplicity, his lack of experience with women, his hazardous life

and stern duty regarding it, pleaded for him and for her love. For the lack of a little understanding she would never live unhappy and alone while she was loved. Better give a thousand times more than she had sacrificed. He would return to the village some day, when the Indians and the thieves were run down, and would be his own calm, gentle self. Then she would win him, break down his allegiance to this fearful border life, and make him happy in her love.

While Helen was going through one of the fires of life to come out sweeter and purer, if a little pensive and sad, time, which waits not for love, nor life, nor death, was hastening onward, and soon the golden fields of grain were stored. September came with its fruitful promise fulfilled.

Helen entered once more into the quiet, social life of the little settlement, taught her class on Sundays, did all her own work, and even found time to bring a ray of sunshine to more than one sick child's bed. Yet she did not forget her compact with Jonathan, and bent all her intelligence to find some clew that might aid in the capture of the horse-thief. She was still groping in the darkness. She could not, however, banish the belief that the traitor was Brandt. She blamed herself for this, because of having no good reasons for suspicion; but the conviction was there, fixed by intuition. Because a man's eyes were steely gray, sharp like those of a cat's, and capable of the same contraction and enlargement, there was no reason to believe their owner was a criminal. But that, Helen acknowledged with a smile, was the only argument she had. To be sure Brandt had looked capable of anything, the night Jonathan knocked him down; she knew he had incited Case to begin the trouble at Metzar's, and had seemed worried since that time. He had not left the settlement on short journeys, as had been his custom before the affair in the bar-room. And not a horse had disappeared from Fort Henry since that time.

Brandt had not discontinued his attentions to her; if they were less ardent it was because she had given him absolutely to understand that she could be his friend only. And she would not have allowed even so much except for Jonathan's plan. She fancied it was possible to see behind Brandt's courtesy, the real subtle, threatening man. Stripped of his kindliness, an assumed virtue, the iron man stood revealed, cold, calculating, cruel.

Mordaunt she never saw but once and then, shocking and pitiful, he lay dead drunk in the grass by the side of the road, his pale, weary, handsome face exposed to the pitiless rays of the sun. She ran home weeping over this wreck of what had once been so fine a gentleman. Ah! the curse of rum! He had learned his soft speech and courtly bearing in the refinement of a home where a proud mother adored, and gentle sisters loved him. And now, far from the kindred he had disgraced, he lay in the road like a log. How it hurt her! She almost wished she could have loved him, if love might have redeemed. She was more kind to her other admirers, more tolerant of Brandt, and could forgive the Englishman, because the pangs she had suffered through love had softened her spirit.

During this long period the growing friendship of her cousin for Betty had been a source of infinite pleasure to Helen. She hoped and believed a romance would develop between the young widow and Will, and did all in her power, slyly abetted by the matchmaking colonel, to bring the two together.

One afternoon when the sky was clear with that intense blue peculiar to bright days in early autumn, Helen started out toward Betty's, intending to remind that young lady she had promised to hunt for clematis and other fall flowers.

About half-way to Betty's home she met Brandt. He came swinging round a corner with his quick, firm step. She had not seen him for several days, and somehow he seemed different. A brightness, a flash, as of daring expectation, was in his face. The poise, too, of the man had changed.

"Well, I am fortunate. I was just going to your home," he said cheerily. "Won't you come for a walk with me?"

"You may walk with me to Betty's," Helen answered.

"No, not that. Come up the hillside. We'll get some goldenrod. I'd like to have a chat with you. I may go away—I mean I'm thinking of making a short trip," he added hurriedly.

"Please come."

"I promised to go to Betty's."

"You won't come?" His voice trembled with mingled disappointment and resentment.

"No," Helen replied in slight surprise.

"You have gone with the other fellows. Why not with me?" He was white now, and evidently laboring under powerful feelings that must have had their origin in some thought or plan which hinged on the acceptance of his invitation.

"Because I choose not to," Helen replied coldly, meeting his glance fully.

A dark red flush swelled Brandt's face and neck; his gray eyes gleamed balefully with wolfish glare; his teeth were clenched. He breathed hard and trembled with anger. Then, by a powerful effort, he conquered himself; the villainous expression left his face; the storm of rage subsided. Great incentive there must have been for him thus to repress his emotions so quickly. He looked long at her with sinister, intent regard; then, with the laugh of a desperado, a laugh which might have indicated contempt for the failure of his suit, and which was fraught with a world of meaning, of menace, he left her without so much as a salute.

Helen pondered over this sudden change, and felt relieved because she need make no further pretense of friendship. He had shown himself to be what she had instinctively believed. She hurried on toward Betty's, hoping to find Colonel Zane at home, and with Jonathan, for Brandt's hint of leaving Fort Henry, and his evident chagrin at such a slip of speech, had made her suspicious. She was informed by Mrs. Zane that the colonel had gone to a log-raising; Jonathan had not been in for several days, and Betty went away with Will.

"Where did they go?" asked Helen.

"I'm not sure; I think down to the spring."

Helen followed the familiar path through the grove of oaks into the glade. It was quite deserted. Sitting on the stone against which Jonathan had leaned the day she kissed him, she gave way to tender reflection. Suddenly she was disturbed by the sound of rapid footsteps, and looking up, saw the hulking form of Metzar, the innkeeper, coming down the path. He carried a bucket, and meant evidently to get water. Helen did not desire to be seen, and, thinking he would stay only a moment, slipped into a thicket of willows behind the stone. She could see plainly through the foliage. Metzar came into the glade, peered around in the manner of a man expecting to see some one, and then, filling his bucket at the spring, sat down on the stone.

Not a minute elapsed before soft, rapid footsteps sounded in the distance. The bushes parted, disclosing the white, set face and gray eyes of Roger Brandt. With a light spring he cleared the brook and approached Metzar.

Before speaking he glanced around the glade with the fugitive, distrustful glance of a man who suspects even the trees. Then, satisfied by the scrutiny he opened his hunting frock, taking forth a long object which he thrust toward Metzar.

It was an Indian arrow.

Metzar's dull gaze traveled from this to the ominous face of Brandt.

"See there, you! Look at this arrow! Shot by the best Indian on the border into the window of my room. I hadn't been there a minute when it came from the island. God! but it was a great shot!"

"Hell!" gasped Metzar, his dull face quickening with some awful thought.

"I guess it *is* hell," replied Brandt, his face growing whiter and wilder.

"Our game's up?" questioned Metzar with haggard cheek.

"Up? Man! We haven't a day, maybe less, to shake Fort Henry."

"What does it mean?" asked Metzar. He was the calmer of the two.

"It's a signal. The Shawnees, who were in hiding with the horses over by Blueberry swamp, have been flushed by those bordermen. Some of them have escaped; at least one, for no one but Ashbow could shoot that arrow across the river."

"Suppose he hadn't come?" whispered Metzar hoarsely.

Brandt answered him with a dark, shuddering gaze.

A twig snapped in the thicket. Like foxes at the click of a trap, these men whirled with fearsome glances.

"Ugh!" came a low, guttural voice from the bushes, and an Indian of magnificent proportions and somber, swarthy features, entered the glade.

CHAPTER XI

THE savage had just emerged from the river, for his graceful, copper-colored body and scanty clothing were dripping with water. He carried a long bow and a quiver of arrows.

Brandt uttered an exclamation of surprise, and Metzar a curse, as the lithe Indian leaped the brook. He was not young. His swarthy face was lined, seamed, and terrible with a dark impassiveness.

"Paleface-brother-get-arrow," he said in halting English, as his eyes flashed upon Brandt. "Chief-want-make-sure."

The white man leaned forward, grasped the Indian's arm, and addressed him in an Indian language. This questioning was evidently in regard to his signal, the whereabouts of others of the party, and why he took such fearful risks almost in the village. The Indian answered with one English word.

"Deathwind!"

Brandt drew back with drawn, white face, while a whistling breath escaped him.

"I knew it, Metz. Wetzel!" he exclaimed in a husky voice.

The blood slowly receded from Metzar's evil, murky face, leaving it haggard.

"Deathwind-on-Chief's-trail-up-Eagle Rock," continued the Indian. "Deathwind-fooled-not-for-long. Chief-wait-paleface-brothers at Two Islands."

The Indian stepped into the brook, parted the willows, and was gone as he had come, silently.

"We know what to expect," said Brandt in calmer tone as the

daring cast of countenance returned to him. "There's an Indian for you! He got away, doubled like an old fox on his trail, and ran in here to give us a chance at escape. Now you know why Bing Legget can't be caught."

"Let's dig at once," replied Metzar, with no show of returning courage such as characterized his companion.

Brandt walked to and fro with bent brows, like one in deep thought. Suddenly he turned upon Metzar eyes which were brightly hard, and reckless with resolve.

"By Heaven! I'll do it! Listen. Wetzel has gone to the top of Eagle Mountain, where he and Zane have a rendezvous. Even he won't suspect the cunning of this Indian; anyway it'll be after daylight to-morrow before he strikes the trail. I've got twenty-four hours, and more, to get this girl, and I'll do it!"

"Bad move to have weight like her on a march," said Metzar.

"Bah! The thing's easy. As for you, go on, push ahead after we're started. All I ask is that you stay by me until the time to cut loose."

"I ain't agoin' to crawfish now," growled Metzar. "Strikes me, too, I'm losin' more'n you."

"You won't be a loser if you can get back to Detroit with your scalp. I'll pay you in horses and gold. Once we reach Legget's place we're safe."

"What's yer plan about gittin' the gal?" asked Metzar.

Brandt leaned forward and spoke eagerly, but in a low tone.

"Git away on hoss-back?" questioned Metzar, visibly brightening. "Wal, that's some sense. Kin ye trust ther other party?"

"I'm sure I can," rejoined Brandt.

"It'll be a good job, a good job an' all done in daylight, too. Bing Legget couldn't plan better," Metzar said, rubbing his hands.

"We've fooled these Zanes and their fruit-raising farmers for a year, and our time is about up," Brandt muttered. "One more job and we've done. Once with Legget we're safe, and then we'll work slowly back towards Detroit. Let's get out of here now, for some one may come at any moment."

The plotters separated, Brandt going through the grove, and Metzar down the path by which he had come.

* * * * * *

Helen, trembling with horror of what she had heard, raised herself cautiously from the willows where she had lain, and watched the innkeeper's retreating figure. When it had disappeared she gave a little gasp of relief. Free now to run home, there to plan what course must be pursued, she conquered her fear and weakness, and hurried from the glade. Luckily, so far as she was able to tell, no one saw her return. She resolved that she would be cool, deliberate, clever, worthy of the borderman's confidence.

First she tried to determine the purport of this interview between Brandt and Metzar. She recalled to mind all that was said, and supplied what she thought had been suggested. Brandt and Metzar were horse-thieves, aids of Bing Legget. They had repaired to the glade to plan. The Indian had been a surprise. Wetzel had routed the Shawnees, and was now on the trail of this chieftain. The Indian warned them to leave Fort Henry and to meet him at a place called Two Islands. Brandt's plan, presumably somewhat changed by the advent of the red-man, was to steal horses, abduct a girl in broad daylight, and before tomorrow's sunset escape to join the ruffian Legget.

"I am the girl," murmured Helen shudderingly, as she relapsed momentarily into girlish fears. But at once she rose above selfish feelings.

Secondly, while it was easy to determine what the outlaws meant, the wisest course was difficult to conceive. She had promised the borderman to help him, and not speak of anything she learned to any but himself. She could not be true to him if she asked advice. The point was clear; either she must remain in the settlement hoping for Jonathan's return in time to frustrate Brandt's villainous scheme, or find the borderman. Suddenly she remembered Metzar's allusion to a second person whom Brandt felt certain he could trust. This meant another traitor in Fort Henry, another horse-thief, another desperado willing to make off with helpless women.

Helen's spirit rose in arms. She had their secret, and could ruin them. She would find the borderman.

Wetzel was on the trail at Eagle Rock. What for? Trailing an Indian who was then five miles east of that rock? Not Wetzel! He was on that track to meet Jonathan. Otherwise, with the red-skins near the river, he would have been closer to them. He would meet Jonathan there at sunset to-day, Helen decided.

She paced the room, trying to still her throbbing heart and trembling hands.

"I must be calm," she said sternly. "Time is precious. I have not a moment to lose. I will find him. I've watched that mountain many a time, and can find the trail and the rock. I am in more danger here, than out there in the forest. With Wetzel and Jonathan on the mountain side, the Indians have fled it. But what about the savage who warned Brandt? Let me think. Yes, he'll avoid the river; he'll go round south of the settlement, and, therefore, can't see me cross. How fortunate that I have paddled a canoe many times across the river. How glad that I made Colonel Zane describe the course up the mountains!"

Her resolution fixed, Helen changed her skirt for one of buckskin, putting on leggings and moccasins of the same serviceable material. She filled the pockets of a short, rain-proof jacket with biscuits, and, thus equipped, sallied forth with a spirit and exultation she could not subdue. Only one thing she feared, which was that Brandt or Metzar might see her cross the river. She launched her canoe and paddled down stream, under cover of the bluff, to a point opposite the end of the island, then straight across, keeping the island between her and the settlement. Gaining the other shore, Helen pulled the canoe into the willows, and mounted the bank. A thicket of willow and alder made progress up the steep incline difficult, but once out of it she faced a long stretch of grassy meadowland. A mile beyond began the green, billowy rise of that mountain which she intended to climb.

Helen's whole soul was thrown into the adventure. She felt her strong young limbs in accord with her heart.

"Now, Mr. Brandt, horse-thief and girl-snatcher, we'll see," she said with scornful lips. "If I can't beat you now I'm not fit to be Betty Zane's friend; and am unworthy of a borderman's trust."

She traversed the whole length of meadowland close under the shadow of the fringed bank, and gained the forest. Here she hesitated. All was so wild and still. No definite course through the woods seemed to invite, and yet all was open. Trees, trees, dark, immovable trees everywhere. The violent trembling of poplar and aspen leaves, when all others were so calm, struck her strangely, and the fearful stillness awed her. Drawing a deep breath she started forward up the gently rising ground.

As she advanced the open forest became darker, and of wilder aspect. The trees were larger and closer together. Still she made fair progress without deviating from the course she had determined upon. Before her rose a ridge, with a ravine on either side, reaching nearly to the summit of the mountain. Here the underbrush was scanty, the fallen trees had slipped down the side, and the rocks were not so numerous, all of which gave her reason to be proud, so far, of her judgment.

Helen, pressing onward and upward, forgot time and danger, while she reveled in the wonder of the forestland. Birds and squirrels fled before her; whistling and wheezing of alarm, or heavy crashings in the bushes, told of frightened wild beasts. A dull, faint roar, like a distant wind, suggested tumbling waters. A single birch tree, gleaming white among the black trees, enlivened the gloomy forest. Patches of sunlight brightened the shade. Giant ferns, just tinging with autumn colors, waved tips of sculptured perfection. Most wonderful of all were the colored leaves, as they floated downward with a sad, gentle rustle.

Helen was brought to a realization of her hazardous undertaking by a sudden roar of water, and the abrupt termination of the ridge in a deep gorge. Grasping a tree she leaned over to look down. It was fully an hundred feet deep, with impassable walls, green-stained and damp, at the bottom of which a brawling, brown brook rushed on its way. Fully twenty feet wide, it presented an insurmountable barrier to further progress in that direction.

But Helen looked upon it merely as a difficulty to be overcome. She studied the situation, and decided to go to the left because higher ground was to be seen that way. Abandoning the ridge, she pressed on, keeping as close to the gorge as she dared, and came presently to a fallen tree lying across the dark cleft. Without a second's hesitation, for she knew such would be fatal, she stepped upon the tree and started across, looking at nothing but the log under her feet, while she tried to imagine herself walking across the water-gate, at home in Virginia.

She accomplished the venture without a misstep. When safely on the ground once more she felt her knees tremble and a queer, light feeling came into her head. She laughed, however, as she rested a moment. It would take more than a gorge to discourage her, she resolved with set lips, as once again she made her way along the rising ground.

Perilous, if not desperate, work was ahead of her. Broken, rocky ground, matted thicket, and seemingly impenetrable forest, rose darkly in advance. But she was not even tired, and climbed, crawled, twisted and turned on her way upward. She surmounted a rocky ledge, to face a higher ridge covered with splintered, uneven stones, and the fallen trees of many storms. Once she slipped and fell, spraining her wrist. At length this uphill labor began to weary her. To breathe caused a pain in her side and she was compelled to rest.

Already the gray light of coming night shrouded the forest. She was surprised at seeing the trees become indistinct; because the shadows hovered over the thickets, and noted that the dark, dim outline of the ridges was fading into obscurity.

She struggled on up the uneven slope with a tightening at her heart which was not all exhaustion. For the first time she doubted herself, but it was too late. She could not turn back. Suddenly she felt that she was on a smoother, easier course. Not to strike a stone or break a twig seemed unusual. It might be a path worn by deer going to a spring. Then into her troubled mind flashed the joyful thought, she had found a trail.

Soft, wiry grass, springing from a wet soil, rose under her feet. A little rill trickled alongside the trail. Mossy, soft-cushioned stones lay imbedded here and there. Young maples and hickories grew breast-high on either side, and the way wound in and out under the lowering shade of forest monarchs.

Swiftly ascending this path she came at length to a point where it was possible to see some distance ahead. The ascent became hardly noticeable. Then, as she turned a bend of the trail, the light grew brighter and brighter, until presently all was open and clear. An oval space, covered with stones, lay before her. A big, blasted chestnut stood near by. Beyond was the dim, purple haze of distance. Above, the pale, blue sky just faintly rose-tinted by the setting sun. Far to her left the scraggly trees of a low hill were tipped with orange and russet shades. She had reached the summit.

Desolate and lonely was this little plateau. Helen felt immeasurably far away from home. Yet she could see in the blue distance the glancing river, the dark fort, and that cluster of cabins which marked the location of Fort Henry. Sitting upon the roots of the big chestnut tree she gazed around. There were the remains of a small camp-fire. Beyond, a hollow under a shelving rock. A bed of dry leaves lay packed in this shelter. Some one had been here, and she doubted not that it was the borderman.

She was so tired and her wrist pained so severely that she lay back against the tree-trunk, closed her eyes and rested. A weariness, the apathy of utter exhaustion, came over her. She wished the bordermen would hurry and come before she went to sleep.

Drowsily she was sinking into slumber when a long, low rumble aroused her. How dark it had suddenly become! A sheet of pale light flared across the overcast heavens.

"A storm!" exclaimed Helen. "Alone on this mountain-top with a storm coming. Am I frightened? I don't believe it. At least I'm safe from that ruffian Brandt. Oh! if my borderman would only come!"

Helen changed her position from beside the tree, to the hollow under the stone. It was high enough to permit of her sitting upright, and offered a safe retreat from the storm. The bed of leaves was soft and comfortable. She sat there peering out at the darkening heavens.

All beneath her, southward and westward was gray twilight. The settlement faded from sight; the river grew wan and shadowy. The ruddy light in the west was fast succumbing to the rolling clouds. Darker and darker it became, until only one break in the overspreading vapors admitted the last crimson gleam of sunshine over hills and valley, brightening the river until it resembled a stream of fire. Then the light failed, the glow faded. The intense blackness of night prevailed.

Out of the ebon west came presently another flare of light, a quick, spreading flush, like a flicker from a monster candle; it was followed by a long, low, rumbling roll.

Helen felt in those intervals of unutterably vast silence, that she must shriek aloud. The thunder was a friend. She prayed for the storm to break. She had withstood danger and toilsome effort with fortitude; but could not brave this awful, boding, wilderness stillness.

Flashes of lightning now revealed the rolling, pushing, turbulent clouds, and peals of thunder sounded nearer and louder.

A long swelling moan, sad, low, like the uneasy sigh of the sea, breathed far in the west. It was the wind, the ominous warning of the storm. Sheets of light were now mingled with long, straggling ropes of fire, and the rumblings were often broken by louder, quicker detonations.

Then a period, longer than usual, of inky blackness succeeded the sharp flaring of light. A faint breeze ruffled the leaves of the thicket, and fanned Helen's hot cheek. The moan of the wind became more distinct, then louder, and in another instant like the far-off roar of a rushing river. The storm was upon her. Helen shrank closer against the stone, and pulled her jacket tighter around her trembling form.

A sudden, intense, dazzling, blinding, white light enveloped her. The rocky promontory, the weird, giant chestnut tree, the open plateau, and beyond, the stormy heavens, were all luridly clear in the flash of lightning. She fancied it was possible to see a tall, dark figure emerging from the thicket. As the thunderclap rolled and pealed overhead, she strained her eyes into the blackness waiting for the next lightning flash.

It came with brilliant, dazing splendor. The whole plateau and thicket were as light as in the day. Close by the stone where she lay crept the tall, dark figure of an Indian. With starting eyes she saw the fringed clothing, the long, flying hair, and supple body peculiar to the savage. He was creeping upon her.

Helen's blood ran cold; terror held her voiceless. She felt herself sinking slowly down upon the leaves.

CHAPTER XII

THE sun had begun to cast long shadows the afternoon of Helen's hunt for Jonathan, when the borderman, accompanied by Wetzel, led a string of horses along the base of the very mountain she had ascended.

"Last night's job was a good one, I ain't gainsayin'; but the redskin I wanted got away," Wetzel said gloomily.

"He's safe now as a squirrel in a hole. I saw him dartin' among the trees with his white eagle feathers stickin' up like a buck's flag," replied Jonathan. "He can run. If I'd only had my rifle loaded! But I'm not sure he was that arrow-shootin' Shawnee."

"It was him. I saw his bow. We ought'er taken more time an' picked him out," Wetzel replied, shaking his head gravely. "Though mebbe that'd been useless. I think he was hidin'. He's precious shy of his red skin. I've been after him these ten year, an' never ketched him nappin' yet. We'd have done much toward snuffin' out Legget an' his gang if we'd winged the Shawnee."

"He left a plain trail."

"One of his tricks. He's slicker on a trail than any other Injun on the border, unless mebbe it's old Wingenund, the Huron. This Shawnee'd lead us many a mile for nuthin', if we'd stick to his trail. I'm long ago used to him. He's doubled like an old fox, run harder'n a skeered fawn, an', if needs be, he'll lay low as a cunnin' buck. I calkilate once over the mountain, he's made a bee-line east. We'll go on with the hosses, an' then strike across country to find his trail."

"It 'pears to me, Lew, that we've taken a long time in makin' a show against these hoss-thieves," said Jonathan.

"I ain't sayin' much; but I've felt it," replied Wetzel.

"All summer, an' nothin' done. It was more luck than sense that we run into those Injuns with the hosses. We only got three out of four, an' let the best redskin give us the slip. Here fall is nigh on us, with winter comin' soon, an' still we don't know who's the white traitor in the settlement."

"I said it's be a long, an' mebbe, our last trail."

"Why?"

"Because these fellars. red or white, are in with a picked gang of the best woodsmen as ever outlawed the border. We'll get the Fort Henry hoss-thief. I'll back the bright-eyed lass for that."

"I haven't seen her lately, an' allow she'd left me word if she learned anythin'."

"Wal, mebbe it's as well you hain't seen so much of her."

In silence they traveled and, arriving at the edge of the meadow, were about to mount two of the horses, when Wetzel said in a sharp tone:

"Look!"

He pointed to a small, well-defined moccasin track in the black earth on the margin of a rill.

"Lew, it's a woman's, sure's you're born," declared Jonathan.

Wetzel knelt and closely examined the footprint; "Yes, a woman's, an' no Injun."

"What?" Jonathan exclaimed, as he knelt to scrutinize the imprint.

"This ain't half a day old," added Wetzel. "An' not a red-skin's moccasin near. What d'you reckon?"

"A white girl, alone," replied Jonathan as he followed the trail a short distance along the brook. "See, she's makin' up-land. Wetzel, these tracks could hardly be my sister's, an' there's only one other girl on the border whose feet will match 'em! Helen Sheppard has passed here, on her way up the mountain to find you or me."

"I like your reckonin'."

"She's suddenly discovered somethin', Injuns, hoss-thieves, the Fort Henry traitor, or mebbe, an' most likely, some plottin'. Bein' bound to secrecy by me, she's not told my brother. An' it must be call for hurry. She knows we frequent this mountain-top; said Eb told her about the way we get here."

"I'd calkilate about the same."

"What'll you do? Go with me after her?" asked Jonathan. "I'll take the hosses, an' be at the fort inside of an hour. If Helen's gone, I'll tell her father you're close on her trail. Now listen! It'll be dark soon, an' a storm's comin'. Don't waste time on her trail. Hurry up to the rock. She'll be there, if any lass could climb there. If not, come back in the mornin', hunt her trail out, an' find her. I'm thinkin', Jack, we'll find the Shawnee had somethin' to do with this. Whatever happens after I get back to the fort, I'll expect you hard on my trail."

Jonathan bounded across the brook and with an easy lope began the gradual ascent. Soon he came upon a winding path. He ran along this for perhaps a quarter of an hour, until it became too steep for rapid traveling, when he settled down to a rapid walk. The forest was already dark. A slight rustling of the leaves beneath his feet was the only sound, except at long intervals the distant rumbling of thunder.

The mere possibility of Helen's being alone on that mountain seeking him, made Jonathan's heart beat as it never had before. For weeks he had avoided her, almost forgot her. He had conquered the strange, yearning weakness which assailed him after that memorable Sunday, and once more the silent shaded glens, the mystery of the woods, the breath of his wild, free life had claimed him. But now as this evidence of her spirit, her recklessness, was before him, and he remembered Betty's avowal, a pain, which was almost physical, tore at his heart. How terrible it would be if she came to her death through him! He pictured the big, alluring eyes, the perfect lips, the haunting face, cold in death. And he shuddered.

The dim gloom of the woods soon darkened into blackness. The flashes of lightning, momentarily streaking the foliage, or sweeping overhead in pale yellow sheets, aided Jonathan in keeping the trail.

He gained the plateau just as a great flash illumined it, and distinctly saw the dark hollow where he had taken refuge in many a storm, and where he now hoped to find the girl. Picking his way carefully over the sharp, loose stones, he at last put his hand on the huge rock. Another blue-white, dazzling flash enveloped the scene.

Under the rock he saw a dark form huddled, and a face as white as snow, with wide, horrified eyes.

"Lass," he said, when the thunder had rumbled away. He received no answer, and called again. Kneeling, he groped about until touching Helen's dress. He spoke again; but she did not reply.

Jonathan crawled under the ledge beside the quiet figure. He touched her hands; they were very cold. Bending over, he was relieved to hear her heart beating. He called her name, but still she made no reply. Dipping his hand into a little rill that ran beside the stone, he bathed her face. Soon she stirred uneasily, moaned, and suddenly sat up.

" 'Tis Jonathan," he said quickly; "don't be scared."

Another illuminating flare of lightning brightened the plateau.

"Oh! thank Heaven!" cried Helen. "I thought you were an Indian!"

Helen sank trembling against the borderman, who enfolded her in his long arms. Her relief and thankfulness were so great that she could not speak. Her hands clasped and unclasped round his strong fingers. Her tears flowed freely.

The storm broke with terrific fury. A seething torrent of rain and hail came with the rushing wind. Great heaven-broad sheets of lightning played across the black dome overhead. Zigzag ropes, steel-blue in color, shot downward. Crash, and crack, and boom the thunder split and rolled the clouds above. The lightning flashes showed the fall of rain in columns like white waterfalls, borne on the irresistible wind.

The grandeur of the storm awed, and stilled Helen's emotion. She sat there watching the lightning, listening to the peals of thunder, and thrilling with the wonder of the situation.

Gradually the roar abated, the flashes became less frequent, the thunder decreased, as the storm wore out its strength in passing. The wind and rain ceased on the mountain-top almost as quickly as they had begun, and the roar died slowly away in the distance. Far to the eastward flashes of light illumined scowling clouds, and brightened many a dark, wooded hill and valley.

"Lass, how is't I find you here?" asked Jonathan gravely.

With many a pause and broken phrase, Helen told the story of what she had seen and heard at the spring.

"Child, why didn't you go to my brother?" asked Jonathan. "You don't know what you undertook!"

"I thought of everything; but I wanted to find you myself. Besides, I was just as safe alone on this mountain as in the village."

"I don't know but you're right," replied Jonathan thoughtfully. "So Brandt planned to make off with you to-morrow?"

"Yes, and when I heard it I wanted to run away from the village."

"You've done a wondrous clever thing, lass. This Brandt is a bad man, an' hard to match. But if he hasn't shaken Fort Henry by now, his career'll end mighty sudden, an' his bad trails stop short on the hillside among the graves, for Eb will always give outlaws or Injuns decent burial."

"What will the colonel, or anyone, think has become of me?"

"Wetzel knows, lass, for he found your trail below."

"Then he'll tell papa you came after me? Oh! poor papa! I forgot him. Shall we stay here until daylight?"

"We'd gain nothin' by startin' now. The brooks are full, an' in the dark we'd make little distance. You're dry here, an' comfortable. What's more, lass, you're safe."

"I feel perfectly safe, with you," Helen said softly.

"Aren't you tired, lass?"

"Tired? I'm nearly dead. My feet are cut and bruised, my wrist is sprained, and I ache all over. But, Jonathan, I don't care. I am so happy to have my wild venture turn out successfully."

"You can lie here an' sleep while I keep watch."

Jonathan made a move to withdraw his arm, which was still between Helen and the rock but had dropped from her waist.

"I am very comfortable. I'll sit here with you, watching for daybreak. My! how dark it is! I cannot see my hand before my eyes."

Helen settled herself back upon the stone, leaned a very little against his shoulder, and tried to think over her adventure. But her mind refused to entertain any ideas, except those of the present. Mingled with the dreamy lassitude that grew stronger every moment, was a sense of delight in her situation. She was alone on a wild mountain, in the night, with this borderman, the one she loved. By chance and her own foolhardiness this had come about, yet she was fortunate to have it tend to some good beyond her own happiness. All she would suffer from her perilous climb would be aching bones, and, perhaps, a scolding from her father. What she might gain was more than she had dared hope. The breaking up of the horse-thief gang would be a boon to the harassed settlement. How proudly Colonel Zane would smile! Her name would go on that long roll of border honor and heroism. That was not, however, one thousandth part so pleasing, as to be alone with her borderman.

With a sigh of mingled weariness and content, Helen leaned her head on Jonathan's shoulder and fell asleep.

The borderman trembled. The sudden nestling of her head against him, the light caress of her fragrant hair across his cheek, revived a sweet, almost-conquered, almost-forgotten emotion. He felt an inexplicable thrill vibrate through him. No untrodden, ambushed wild, no perilous trail, no dark and bloody encounter had ever made him feel fear as had the kiss of this maiden. He had sternly silenced faint, unfamiliar, yet tender, voices whispering in his heart; and now his rigorous discipline was as if it were not, for at her touch he trembled. Still he did not move away. He knew she had succumbed to weariness, and was fast asleep. He could, gently, without awakening her, have laid her head upon the pillow of leaves; indeed, he thought of doing it, but made no effort. A woman's head softly lying against him was a thing novel, strange, wonderful. For all the power he had then, each tumbling lock of her hair might as well have been a chain linking him fast to the mountain.

With the memory of his former yearning, unsatisfied moods, and the unrest and pain his awakening tenderness had caused him, came a determination to look things fairly in the face, to be just in thought toward this innocent, impulsive girl, and be honest with himself.

Duty commanded that he resist all charm other than that pertaining to his life in the woods. Years ago he had accepted a borderman's destiny, well content to be recompensed by its untamed freedom from restraint; to be always under the trees he loved so well; to lend his cunning and woodcraft in the pioneer's cause; to haunt the savage trails; to live from day to day a menace to the foes of civilization. That was the life he had chosen; it was all he could ever have.

In view of this, justice demanded that he allow no friendship to spring up between himself and this girl. If his sister's belief was really true, if Helen really was interested in him, it must be a romantic infatuation which, not encouraged, would wear itself out. What was he, to win the love of any girl? An unlettered borderman, who knew only the woods, whose life was hard and cruel, whose hands were red with Indian blood, whose vengeance had not spared men even of his own race. He could not believe she really loved him. Wildly impulsive as girls were at times, she had kissed him. She had been grateful, carried away by a generous feeling for him as the protector of her father. When she did not see him for a long time, as he vowed should be the case after he had carried her safely home, she would forget.

Then honesty demanded that he probe his own feelings. Sternly, as if judging a renegade, he searched out in his simple way the truth. This big-eyed lass with her nameless charm would bewitch even a borderman, unless he avoided her. So much he had not admitted until now. Love he had never believed could be possible for him. When she fell asleep her hand had slipped from his arm to his fingers, and now rested there lightly as a leaf. The contact was delight. The gentle night breeze blew a tress of hair across his lips. He trembled. Her rounded shoulder pressed against him until he could feel her slow, deep breathing. He almost held his own breath lest he disturb her rest.

No, he was no longer indifferent. As surely as those pale stars blinked far above, he knew the delight of a woman's presence.

It moved him to study the emotion, as he studied all things, which was the habit of his borderman's life. Did it come from knowledge of her beauty, matchless as that of the mountain-laurel? He recalled the dark glance of her challenging eyes, her tall, supple figure, and the bewildering excitation and magnetism of her presence. Beauty was wonderful, but not everything. Beauty belonged to her, but she would have been irresistible without it. Was it not because she was a woman? That was the secret. She was a woman with all a woman's charm to bewitch, to twine round the strength of men as the ivy encircles the oak; with all a woman's weakness to pity and to guard; with all a woman's wilful burning love, and with all a woman's mystery.

At last so much of life was intelligible to him. The renegade committed his worst crimes because even in his outlawed, homeless state, he could not exist without the companionship, if not the love, of a woman. The pioneer's toil and privation were for a woman, and the joy of loving her and living for her. The Indian brave, when not on the war-path, walked hand in hand with a dusky, soft-eyed maiden, and sang to her of moonlit lakes and western winds. Even the birds and beasts mated. The robins returned to their old nest; the eagles paired once and were constant in life and death. The buck followed the doe through the forest. All nature sang that love made life worth living. Love, then, was everything.

The borderman sat out the long vigil of the night watching the stars, and trying to decide that love was not for him. If Wetzel had locked a secret within his breast, and never in all these years spoke of it to his companion, then surely that companion could as well live without love. Stern, dark, deadly work must stain and blot all tenderness from his life, else it would be unutterably barren. The joy of living, of unharassed freedom he had always known. If a fair face and dark, mournful eyes were to haunt him on every lonely trail, then it were better an Indian should end his existence.

The darkest hour before dawn, as well as the darkest of doubt and longing in Jonathan's life, passed away. A gray gloom obscured the pale, winking stars; the east slowly whitened, then brightened, and at length day broke misty and fresh.

The borderman rose to stretch his cramped limbs. When he turned to the little cavern the girl's eyes were wide open. All the darkness, the shadow, the beauty, and the thought of the past night, lay in their blue depths. He looked away across the valley where the sky was reddening and a pale rim of gold appeared above the hill-tops.

"Well, if I haven't been asleep!" exclaimed Helen, with a low, soft laugh.

"You're rested, I hope," said Jonathan, with averted eyes. He dared not look at her.

"Oh, yes, indeed. I am ready to start at once. How gray, how beautiful the morning is! Shall we be long? I hope papa knows."

In silence the borderman led the way across the rocky plateau, and into the winding, narrow trail. His pale, slightly drawn and stern, face did not invite conversation, therefore Helen followed silently in his footsteps. The way was steep, and at times he was forced to lend her aid. She put her hand in his and jumped lightly as a fawn. Presently a brawling brook, overcrowding its banks, impeded further progress.

"I'll have to carry you across," said Jonathan.

"I'm very heavy," replied Helen, with a smile in her eyes.

She flushed as the borderman put his right arm around her waist. Then a clasp as of steel enclosed her; she felt herself swinging easily into the air, and over the muddy brook.

Farther down the mountain this troublesome brook again crossed the trail, this time much wider and more formidable. Helen looked with some vexation and embarrassment into the borderman's face. It was always the same, stern, almost cold.

"Perhaps I'd better wade," she said hesitatingly.

"Why? The water's deep an' cold. You'd better not get wet."

Helen flushed, but did not answer. With downcast eyes she let herself be carried on his powerful arm.

The wading was difficult this time. The water foamed furiously around his knees. Once he slipped on a stone, and nearly lost his balance. Uttering a little scream Helen grasped at him wildly, and her arm encircled his neck. What was still more trying, when he put her on her feet again, it was found that her hair had become entangled in the porcupine quills on his hunting-coat.

She stood before him while with clumsy fingers he endeavored to untangle the shimmering strands; but in vain. Helen unwound the snarl of wavy hair. Most alluring she was then, with a certain softness on her face, and light and laughter, and something warm in her eyes.

The borderman felt that he breathed a subtle exhilaration which emanated from her glowing, gracious beauty. She radiated with the gladness of life, with an uncontainable sweetness and joy. But, giving no token of his feeling, he turned to march on down through the woods.

From this point the trail broadened, descending at an easier angle. Jonathan's stride lengthened until Helen was forced to walk rapidly, and sometimes run, in order to keep close behind him. A quick journey home was expedient, and in order to accomplish this she would gladly have exerted herself to a greater extent. When they reached the end of the trail where the forest opened clear of brush, finally to merge into the broad, verdant plain, the sun had chased the mist-clouds from the eastern hill-tops, and was gloriously brightening the valley.

With the touch of sentiment natural to her, Helen gazed backward for one more view of the mountain-top. The wall of rugged rock she had so often admired from her window at home, which henceforth would ever hold a tender place of remembrance in her heart, rose out of a gray-blue bank of mist. The long, swelling slope lay clear to the sunshine. With the rays of the sun gleaming and glistening upon the variegated foliage, and upon the shiny rolling haze above, a beautiful picture of autumn splendor was before her. Tall pines, here and there towered high and lonely over the surrounding trees. Their dark, green, graceful heads stood in bold relief above the gold and yellow crests beneath. Maples, tinged from faintest pink to deepest rose, added warm color to the scene, and chestnuts with their brown-white burrs lent fresher beauty to the undulating slope.

The remaining distance to the settlement was short. Jonathan spoke only once to Helen, then questioning her as to where she had left her canoe. They traversed the meadow, found the boat in the thicket of willows, and were soon under the frowning bluff of Fort Henry. Ascending the steep path, they followed the road leading to Colonel Zane's cabin.

A crowd of boys, men and women loitering near the bluff arrested Helen's attention. Struck by this unusual occurrence, she wondered what was the cause of such idleness among the busy pioneer people. They were standing in little groups. Some made vehement gestures, others conversed earnestly, and yet more were silent. On seeing Jonathan, a number shouted and pointed toward the inn. The borderman hurried Helen along the path, giving no heed to the throng.

But Helen had seen the cause of all this excitement. At first glance she thought Metzar's inn had been burned; but a second later it could be seen that the smoke came from a smoldering heap of rubbish in the road. The inn, nevertheless, had been wrecked. Windows stared with that vacantness peculiar to deserted houses. The doors were broken from their hinges. A pile of furniture, rude tables, chairs, beds, and other articles, were heaped beside the smoking rubbish. Scattered around lay barrels and kegs all with gaping sides and broken heads. Liquor had stained the road, where it had been soaked up by the thirsty dust.

Upon a shattered cellar-door lay a figure covered with a piece of rag carpet. When Helen's quick eyes took in this last, she turned away in horror. That motionless form might be Brandt's. Remorse and womanly sympathy surged over her, for bad as the man had shown himself, he had loved her.

She followed the borderman, trying to compose herself. As they neared Colonel Zane's cabin she saw her father, Will, the colonel, Betty, Nell, Mrs. Zane, Silas Zane, and others whom she did not recognize. They were all looking at her. Helen's throat swelled, and her eyes filled when she got near enough to see her father's haggard, eager face. The others were grave. She wondered guiltily if she had done much wrong.

In another moment she was among them. Tears fell as her father extended his trembling hands to clasp her, and as she hid her burning face on his breast, he cried: "My dear, dear child!" Then Betty gave her a great hug, and Nell flew about them like a happy bird. Colonel Zane's face was pale, and wore a clouded, stern expression. She smiled timidly at him through her tears. "Well! well! well!" he mused, while his gaze softened. That was all he said; but he took her hand and held it while he turned to Jonathan.

The borderman leaned on his long rifle, regarding him with expectant eyes.

"Well, Jack, you missed a little scrimmage this morning. Wetzel got in at daybreak. The storm and horses held him up on the other side of the river until daylight. He told me of your suspicions, with the additional news that he'd found a fresh Indian trail on the island just across from the inn. We went down not expecting to find any one awake; but Metzar was hurriedly packing some of his traps. Half a dozen men were there, having probably stayed all night. That little English cuss was one of them, and another, an ugly fellow, a stranger to us, but evidently a woodsman. Things looked bad. Metzar told a decidedly conflicting story. Wetzel and I went outside to talk over the situation, with the result that I ordered him to clean out the place."

Here Colonel Zane paused to indulge in a grim, meaning laugh.

"Well, he cleaned out the place all right. The ugly stranger got rattlesnake-mad, and yanked out a big knife. Sam is hitching up the team now to haul what's left of him up on the hillside. Metzar resisted arrest, and got badly hurt. He's in the guardhouse. Case, who has been drunk for a week, got in Wetzel's way and was kicked into the middle of next week. He's been spitting blood for the last hour, but I guess he's not much hurt. Brandt flew the coop last night. Wetzel found this hid in his room."

Colonel Zane took a long, feathered arrow from where it lay on a bench, and held it out to Jonathan.

"The Shawnee signal! Wetzel had it right," muttered the borderman.

"Exactly. Lew found where the arrow struck in the wall of Brandt's room. It was shot from the island at the exact spot where Lew came to an end of the Indian's trail in the water."

"That Shawnee got away from us."

"So Lew said. Well, he's gone now. So is Brandt. We're well rid of the gang, if only we never hear of them again."

The borderman shook his head. During the colonel's recital his face changed. The dark eyes had become deadly; the square jaw was shut, the lines of the cheek had grown tense, and over his usually expressive countenance had settled a chill, lowering shade.

"Lew thinks Brandt's in with Bing Legget. Well, d—— his black traitor heart! He's a good man for the worst and strongest gang that ever tracked the border."

The borderman was silent; but the furtive, restless shifting of his eyes over the river and island, hill and valley, spoke more plainly than words.

"You're to take his trail at once," added Colonel Zane. "I had Bess put you up some bread, meat and parched corn. No doubt you'll have a long, hard tramp. Good luck."

The borderman went into the cabin, presently emerging with a buckskin knapsack strapped to his shoulder. He set off eastward with a long, swinging stride.

The women had taken Helen within the house where, no doubt, they could discuss with greater freedom the events of the previous day.

"Sheppard," said Colonel Zane, turning with a sparkle in his eyes. "Brandt was after Helen sure as a bad weed grows fast. And certain as death Jonathan and Wetzel will see him cold and quiet back in the woods. That's a border saying, and it means a good deal. I never saw Wetzel so implacable, nor Jonathan so fatally cold but once, and that was when Miller, another traitor, much like Brandt, tried to make away with Betty. It would have chilled your blood to see Wetzel go at that fool this morning. Why did he want to pull a knife on the borderman? It was a sad sight. Well, these things are justifiable. We must protect ourselves, and above all our women. We've had bad men, and a bad man out here is something you cannot yet appreciate, come here and slip into the life of the settlement, because on the border you can never tell what a man is until he proves himself. There have been scores of criminals spread over the frontier, and some better men, like Simon Girty, who were driven to outlaw life. Simon must not be confounded with Jim Girty, absolutely the most fiendish desperado who ever lived. Why, even the Indians feared Jim so much that after his death his skeleton remained unmolested in the glade where he was killed. The place is believed to be haunted now, by all Indians and many white hunters, and I believe the bones stand there yet."

"Stand?" asked Sheppard, deeply interested.

"Yes, it stands where Girty stood and died, upright against a tree, pinned, pinned there by a big knife."

"Heavens, man! Who did it?" Sheppard cried in horror.

Again Colonel Zane's laugh, almost metallic, broke grimly from his lips.

"Who? Why, Wetzel, of course. Lew hunted Jim Girty five long years. When he caught him—God! I'll tell you some other time. Jonathan saw Wetzel handle Jim and his pal, Deering, as if they were mere boys. Well, as I said, the border has had, and still has, its bad men. Simon Girty took McKee and Elliott, the Tories, from Fort Pitt, when he deserted, and ten men besides. They're all, except those who are dead, outlaws of the worst type. The other bad men drifted out here from Lord only knows where. They're scattered all over. Simon Girty, since his crowning black deed, the massacre of the Christian Indians, is in hiding. Bing Legget now has the field. He's a hard nut, a cunning woodsman, and capable leader who surrounds himself with only the most desperate Indians and renegades. Brandt is an agent of Legget's and I'll bet we'll hear from him again."

CHAPTER XIII

JONATHAN traveled toward the east straight as a crow flies. Wetzel's trail as he pursued Brandt had been left designedly plain. Branches of young maples had been broken by the borderman; they were glaring evidences of his passage. On open ground, or through swampy meadows he had contrived to leave other means to facilitate his comrade's progress. Bits of sumach lay strewn along the way, every red, leafy branch a bright marker of the course; crimson maple leaves served their turn, and even long-bladed ferns were scattered at intervals.

Ten miles east of Fort Henry, at a point where two islands lay opposite each other, Wetzel had crossed the Ohio. Jonathan removed his clothing, and tying these, together with his knapsack, to the rifle, held them above the water while he swam the three narrow channels. He took up the trail again, finding here, as he expected, where Brandt had joined the waiting Shawnee chief. The borderman pressed on harder to the eastward.

About the middle of the afternoon signs betokened that Wetzel and his quarry were not far in advance. Fresh imprints in the grass; crushed asters and moss, broken branches with unwithered leaves, and plots of grassy ground where Jonathan saw that the blades of grass were yet springing back to their original position, proved to the borderman's practiced eye that he was close upon Wetzel.

In time he came to a grove of yellow birch trees. The ground was nearly free from brush, beautifully carpeted with flowers and ferns, and, except where bushy windfalls obstructed the way, was singularly open to the gaze for several hundred yards ahead.

Upon entering this wood Wetzel's plain, intentional markings became manifest, then wavered, and finally disappeared. Jonathan pondered a moment. He concluded that the way was so open and clear, with nothing but grass and moss to mark a trail, that Wetzel had simply considered it waste of time for, perhaps, the short length of this grove.

Jonathan knew he was wrong after taking a dozen steps more. Wetzel's trail, known so well to him, as never to be mistaken, sheered abruptly off to the left, and, after a few yards, the distance between the footsteps widened perceptibly. Then came a point where they were so far apart that they could only have been made by long leaps.

On the instant the borderman knew that some unforeseen peril or urgent cause had put Wetzel to flight, and he now bent piercing eyes around the grove. Retracing his steps to where he had found the break in the trail, he followed up Brandt's tracks for several rods. Not one hundred paces beyond where Wetzel had quit the pursuit, were the remains of a camp fire, the embers still smoldering, and moccasin tracks of a small band of

Indians. The trail of Brandt and his Shawnee guide met the others at almost right angles.

The Indian, either by accident or design, had guided Brandt to a band of his fellows, and thus led Wetzel almost into an ambush.

Evidence was not clear, however, that the Indians had discovered the keen tracker who had run almost into their midst.

While studying the forest ahead Jonathan's mind was running over the possibilities. How close was Wetzel? Was he still in flight? Had the savages an inkling of his pursuit? Or was he now working out one of his cunning tricks of woodcraft? The borderman had no other idea than that of following the trail to learn all this. Taking the desperate chances warranted under the circumstances, he walked boldly forward in his comrade's footsteps.

Deep and gloomy was the forest adjoining the birch grove. It was a heavy growth of hardwood trees, interspersed with slender ash and maples, which with their scanty foliage resembled a labyrinth of green and yellow network, like filmy dotted lace, hung on the taller, darker oaks. Jonathan felt safer in this deep wood. He could still see several rods in advance. Following the trail, he was relieved to see that Wetzel's leaps had become shorter and shorter, until they once again were about the length of a long stride. The borderman was, moreover, swinging in a curve to the northeast. This was proof that the borderman had not been pursued, but was making a wide detour to get ahead of the enemy. Five hundred yards farther on the trail turned sharply toward the birch grove in the rear.

The trail was fresh. Wetzel was possibly within signal call; surely within sound of a rifle shot. But even more stirring was the certainty that Brandt and his Indians were inside the circle Wetzel had made.

Once again in sight of the more open woodland, Jonathan crawled on his hands and knees, keeping close to the cluster of ferns, until well within the eastern end of the grove. He lay for some minutes listening. A threatening silence, like the hush before a storm, permeated the wilderness. He peered out from his covert; but, owing to its location in a little hollow, he could not see far. Crawling to the nearest tree he rose to his feet slowly, cautiously.

No unnatural sight or sound arrested his attention. Repeatedly, with the acute, unsatisfied gaze of the borderman who knew that every tree, every patch of ferns, every tangled brush-heap might harbor a foe, he searched the grove with his eyes; but the curly-barked birches, the clumps of colored ferns, the bushy windfalls kept their secrets.

For the borderman, however, the whole aspect of the birch-grove had changed. Over the forest was a deep calm. A gentle, barely perceptible wind sighed among the leaves, like rustling silk. The far-off drowsy drum of a grouse intruded on the vast stillness. The silence of the birds betokened a message. That mysterious breathing, that beautiful life of the woods lay hushed, locked in a waiting, brooding silence. Far away among the somber trees, where the shade deepened into impenetrable gloom, lay a menace, invisible and indefinable.

A wind, a breath, a chill, terribly potent, seemed to pass over the borderman. Long experience had given him intuition of danger.

As he moved slightly, with lynx-eyes fixed on the grove before him, a sharp, clear, perfect bird-note broke the ominous quiet. It was like the melancholy cry of an oriole, short, deep, suggestive of lonely forest dells. By a slight variation in the short call, Jonathan recognized it as a signal from Wetzel. The borderman smiled as he realized that with all his stealth, Wetzel had heard or seen him re-enter the grove. The signal was a warning to stand still or retreat.

Jonathan's gaze narrowed down to the particular point whence had come the signal. Some two hundred yards ahead in this direction were several large trees standing in a group. With one exception, they all had straight trunks. This deviated from the others in that it possessed an irregular, bulging trunk, or else half-shielded the form of Wetzel. So indistinct and immovable was this irregularity, that the watcher could not be certain. Out of line, somewhat, with this tree which he suspected screened his comrade, lay a huge windfall large enough to conceal in ambush a whole band of savages.

Even as he gazed a sheet of flame flashed from this covert. *Crack!*

A loud report followed; then the whistle and zip of a bullet as it whizzed close by his head.

"Shawnee lead!" muttered Jonathan.

Unfortunately the tree he had selected did not hide him sufficiently. His shoulders were so wide that either one or the other was exposed, affording a fine target for a marksman.

A quick glance showed him a change in the knotty tree-trunk; the seeming bulge was now the well-known figure of Wetzel.

Jonathan dodged as some object glanced slantingly before his eyes.

Twang. Whizz. Thud. Three familiar and distinct sounds caused him to press hard against the tree.

A tufted arrow quivered in the bark not a foot from his head.

"Close shave! Damn that arrow-shootin' Shawnee!" muttered Jonathan. "An' he ain't in that windfall either." His eyes searched to the left for the source of this new peril.

Another sheet of flame, another report from the windfall. A bullet sang, close overhead, and, glancing on a branch, went harmlessly into the forest.

"Injuns all around; I guess I'd better be makin' tracks," Jonathan said to himself, peering out to learn if Wetzel was still under cover.

He saw the tall figure straighten up; a long, black rifle rise to a level and become rigid; a red fire belch forth, followed by a puff of white smoke.

Spang!

An Indian's horrible, strangely-breaking death yell rent the silence.

Then a chorus of plaintive howls, followed by angry shouts, rang through the forest. Naked, painted savages darted out of the windfall toward the tree that had sheltered Wetzel.

Quick as thought Jonathan covered the foremost Indian, and with the crack of his rifle saw the redskin drop his gun, stop in his mad run, stagger sideways, and fall. Then the borderman looked to see what had become of his ally. The cracking of the Indian's rifle told him that Wetzel had been seen by his foes.

With almost incredible fleetness a brown figure with long black hair streaming behind, darted in and out among the trees, flashed through the sunlit glade, and vanished in the dark depths of the forest.

Jonathan turned to flee also, when he heard again the twanging of an Indian's bow. A wind smote his cheek, a shock blinded him, an excruciating pain seized upon his breast. A feathered arrow had pinned his shoulder to the tree. He raised his hand to pull it out; but, slippery with blood, it afforded a poor hold for his fingers. Violently exerting himself, with both hands he wrenched away the weapon. The flint-head lacerating his flesh and scraping his shoulder bones caused sharpest agony. The pain gave away to a sudden sense of giddiness; he tried to run; a dark mist veiled his sight; he stumbled and fell. Then he seemed to sink into a great darkness, and knew no more.

When consciousness returned to Jonathan it was night. He lay on his back, and knew because of his cramped limbs that he had been securely bound. He saw the glimmer of a fire, but could not raise his head. A rustling of leaves in the wind told that he was yet in the woods, and the distant rumble of a waterfall sounded familiar. He felt drowsy; his wound smarted slightly, still he did not suffer any pain. Presently he fell asleep.

Broad daylight had come when again he opened his eyes. The blue sky was directly above, and before him he saw a ledge covered with dwarfed pine trees. He turned his head, and saw that he was in a sort of amphitheater of about two acres in extent enclosed by low cliffs. A cleft in the stony wall let out a brawling brook, and served, no doubt, as entrance to the place. Several rude log cabins stood on that side of the enclosure. Jonathan knew he had been brought to Bing Legget's retreat.

Voices attracted his attention, and, turning his head to the other side, he saw a big Indian pacing near him, and beyond, seven savages and three white men reclining in the shade.

The powerful, dark-visaged savage near him he at once recognized as Ashbow, the Shawnee chief, and noted emissary of Bing Legget. Of the other Indians, three were Delawares, and four Shawnees, all veterans, with swarthy, somber faces and glistening heads on which the scalp-locks were trimmed and tufted. Their naked, muscular bodies were painted for the war-path with their strange emblems of death. A trio of white men, nearly as bronzed as their savage comrades, completed the group. One, a desperate-looking outlaw, Jonathan did not know. The blond-bearded giant in the center was Legget. Steel-blue, inhuman eyes, with the expression of a free but hunted animal; a set, mastiff-like jaw, brutal and coarse, individualized him. The last man was the haggard-faced Brandt.

"I tell ye, Brandt, I ain't agoin' against this Injun," Legget was saying positively. "He's the best reddy on the border, an' has saved me scores of times. This fellar Zane belongs to him, an' while I'd much rather see the scout knifed right here an' now, I won't do nothin' to interfere with the Shawnee's plans."

"Why does the redskin want to take him away to his village?" Brandt growled. "All Injun vanity and pride."

"It's Injun ways, an' we can't do nothin' to change 'em."

"But you're boss here. You could make him put this borderman out of the way."

"Wal, I ain't agoin' ter interfere. Anyways, Brandt, the Shawnee'll make short work of the scout when he gits him among the tribe. Injuns is Injuns. It's a great honor fer him to git Zane, an' he wants his own people to figger in the finish. Quite nat'r'l, I reckon."

"I understand all that; but it's not safe for us, and it's courting death for Ashbow. Why don't he keep Zane here until you can spare more than three Indians to go with him? These bordermen can't be stopped. You don't know them, because you're new in this part of the country."

"I've been here as long as you, an' agoin' some, too, I reckon," replied Legget complacently.

"But you've not been hunted until lately by these bordermen, and you've had little opportunity to hear of them except from

Indians. What can you learn from these silent redskins? I tell you, letting this fellow get out of here alive, even for an hour is a fatal mistake. It's two full days' tramp to the Shawnee village. You don't suppose Wetzel will be afraid of four savages? Why, he sneaked right into eight of us, when we were ambushed, waiting for him. He killed one and then was gone like a streak. It was only a piece of pure luck we got Zane."

"I've reason to know this Wetzel, this Deathwind, as the Delawares call him. I never seen him though, an' anyways, I reckon I can handle him if ever I get the chance."

"Man, you're crazy!" cried Brandt. "He'd cut you to pieces before you'd have time to draw. He could give you a tomahawk, then take it away and split your head. I tell you I know! You remember Jake Deering? He came from up your way. Wetzel fought Deering and Jim Girty together, and killed them. You know how he left Girty."

"I'll allow he must be a fighter; but I ain't afraid of him."

"That's not the question. I am talking sense. You've got a chance now to put one of these bordermen out of the way. Do it quick! That's my advice."

Brandt spoke so vehemently that Legget seemed impressed. He stroked his yellow beard, and puffed thoughtfully on his pipe. Presently he addressed the Shawnee chief in the native tongue.

"Will Ashbow take five horses for his prisoner?"

The Indian shook his head.

"How many will he take?"

The chief strode with dignity to and fro before his captive. His dark, impassive face gave no clew to his thoughts; but his lofty bearing, his measured, stately walk were indicative of great pride. Then he spoke in his deep bass:

"The Shawnee knows the woods from the Great Lakes wher the sun sets, to the Blue Hills where it rises. He has met the great paleface hunters. Only for Deathwind will Ashbow trade his captive."

"See? It ain't no use," said Legget, spreading out his hands. "Let him go. He'll outwit the bordermen if any redskin's able to. The sooner he goes the quicker he'll git back, an' we can go to work. You ought'er be satisfied to git the girl——"

"Shut up!" interrupted Brandt sharply.

" 'Pears to me, Brandt, bein' in love hes kinder worked on your nerves. You used to be game. Now you're afeerd of a bound an' tied man who ain't got long to live."

"I fear no man," answered Brandt, scowling darkly. "But I know what you don't seem to have sense enough to see. If this Zane gets away, which is probable, he and Wetzel will clean up your gang."

"Haw! haw! haw!" roared Legget, slapping his knees. "Then you'd hev little chanst of gittin' the lass, eh?"

"All right. I've no more to say," snapped Brandt, rising and turning on his heel. As he passed Jonathan he paused. "Zane, if I could, I'd get even with you for that punch you once gave me. As it is, I'll stop at the Shawnee village on my way west——"

"With the pretty lass," interposed Legget.

"Where I hope to see your scalp drying in the chief's lodge."

The borderman eyed him steadily; but in silence. Words could not so well have conveyed his thought as did the cold glance of dark scorn and merciless meaning.

Brandt shuffled on with a curse. No coward was he. No man ever saw him flinch. But his intelligence was against him as a desperado. While such as these bordermen lived, an outlaw should never sleep, for he was a marked and doomed man. The deadly, cold-pointed flame which scintillated in the prisoner's eyes was only a gleam of what the border felt towards outlaws.

While Jonathan was considering all he had heard, three more Shawnees entered the retreat, and were at once called aside in consultation by Ashbow. At the conclusion of this brief conference the chief advanced to Jonathan, cut the bonds round his feet, and motioned for him to rise. The prisoner complied to find himself weak and sore, but able to walk. He concluded that his wound, while very painful, was not of a serious nature, and that he would be taken at once on the march toward the Shawnee village.

He was correct, for the chief led him, with the three Shawnees following, toward the outlet of the enclosure. Jonathan's sharp eye took in every detail of Legget's rendezvous. In a corral near the entrance, he saw a number of fine horses, and among them his sister's pony. A more inaccessible, natural refuge than Legget's, could hardly have been found in that country. The entrance was a narrow opening in the wall, and could be held by half a dozen against an army of besiegers. It opened, moreover, on the side of a barren hill, from which could be had a good survey of the surrounding forests and plains.

As Jonathan went with his captors down the hill his hopes, which while ever alive, had been flagging, now rose. The long journey to the Shawnee town led through an untracked wilderness. The Delaware villages lay far to the north; the Wyandot to the west. No likelihood was there of falling in with a band of Indians hunting, because this region, stony, barren, and poorly watered, afforded sparse pasture for deer or bison. From the prisoner's point of view this enterprise of Ashbow's was reckless and vainglorious. Cunning as the chief was, he erred in one point, a great warrior's only weakness, love of show, of pride, of his achievement. In Indian nature this desire for fame was as strong as love of life. The brave risked everything to win his eagle feathers, and the matured warrior found death while keeping bright the glory of the plumes he had won.

Wetzel was in the woods, fleet as a deer, fierce and fearless as a lion. Somewhere among those glades he trod, stealthily, with the ears of a doe and eyes of a hawk strained for sound or sight of his comrade's captors. When he found their trail he would stick to it as the wolf to that of a bleeding buck's. The rescue would not be attempted until the right moment, even though that came within rifle-shot of the Shawnee encampment. Wonderful as his other gifts, was the borderman's patience.

CHAPTER XIV

"Good morning, Colonel Zane," said Helen cheerily, coming into the yard where the colonel was at work. "Did Will come over this way?"

"I reckon you'll find him if you find Betty," replied Colonel Zane dryly.

"Come to think of it, that's true," Helen said, laughing. "I've a suspicion Will ran off from me this morning."

"He and Betty have gone nutting."

"I declare it's mean of Will," Helen said petulantly. "I have been wanting to go so much, and both he and Betty promised to take me."

"Say, Helen, let me tell you something," said the colonel, resting on his spade and looking at her quizzically. "I told them we hadn't had enough frost yet to ripen hickory-nuts and chestnuts. But they went anyhow. Will did remember to say if you came along, to tell you he'd bring the colored leaves you wanted."

"How extremely kind of him. I've a mind to follow them."

"Now see here, Helen, it might be a right good idea for you not to," returned the colonel, with a twinkle and a meaning in his eye.

"Oh, I understand. How singularly dull I've been."

"It's this way. We're mighty glad to have a fine young fellow like Will come along and interest Betty. Lord knows we had a time with her after Alfred died. She's just beginning to brighten up now, and, Helen, the point is that young people on the border must get married. No, my dear, you needn't laugh, you'll have to find a husband same as the other girls. It's not here as it was back east, where a lass might have her fling, so to speak, and take her time choosing. An unmarried girl on the border is a positive menace. I saw, not many years ago, two first-rate youngsters, wild with border fire and spirit, fight and kill each other over a lass who wouldn't choose. Like as not, if she had done so, the three would have been good friends, for out here we're like one big family. Remember this, Helen, and as far as Betty and Will are concerned you will be wise to follow our example: Leave them to themselves. Nothing else will so quickly strike fire between a boy and a girl."

"Betty and Will! I'm sure I'd love to see them care for each other." Then with big, bright eyes bent gravely on him she continued, "May I ask, Colonel Zane, who you have picked out for me?"

"There, now you've said it, and that's the problem. I've looked over every marriageable young man in the settlement, except

Jack. Of course you couldn't care for him, a borderman, a fighter and all that; but I can't find a fellow I think quite up to you."

"Colonel Zane, is not a borderman such as Jonathan worthy a woman's regard?" Helen asked a little wistfully.

"Bless your heart, lass, yes!" replied Colonel Zane heartily. "People out here are not as they are back east. An educated man, polished and all that, but incapable of hard labor, or shrinking from dirt and sweat on his hands, or even blood, would not help us in the winning of the West. Plain as Jonathan is, and with his lack of schooling, he is greatly superior to the majority of young men on the frontier. But, unlettered or not, he is as fine a man as ever stepped in moccasins, or any other kind of foot gear."

"Then why did you say—that—what you did?"

"Well, it's this way," replied Colonel Zane, stealing a glance at her pensive, downcast face. "Girls all like to be wooed. Almost every one I ever knew wanted the young man of her choice to outstrip all her other admirers, and then, for a spell, nearly die of love for her, after which she'd give in. Now, Jack, being a borderman, a man with no occupation except scouting, will never look at a girl, let alone make up to her. I imagine, my dear, it'd take some mighty tall courting to fetch home Helen Sheppard a bride. On the other hand, if some pretty and spirited lass, like, say for instance, Helen Sheppard, would come along and just make Jack forget Indians and fighting, she'd get the finest husband in the world. True, he's wild; but only in the woods. A simpler, kinder, cleaner man cannot be found."

"I believe that, Colonel Zane; but where is the girl who would interest him?" Helen asked with spirit. "These bordermen are unapproachable. Imagine a girl interesting that great, cold, stern

Wetzel! All her flatteries, her wiles, the little coquetries that might attract ordinary men, would not be noticed by him, or Jonathan either."

"I grant it'd not be easy, but woman was made to subjugate man, and always, everlastingly, until the end of life here on this beautiful earth, she will do it."

"Do you think Jonathan and Wetzel will catch Brandt?" asked Helen, changing the subject abruptly.

"I'd stake my all that this year's autumn leaves will fall on Brandt's grave."

Colonel Zane's calm, matter-of-fact coldness made Helen shiver.

"Why, the leaves have already begun to fall. Papa told me Brandt had gone to join the most powerful outlaw band on the border. How can these two men, alone, cope with savages, as I've heard they do, and break up such an outlaw band as Legget's?"

"That's a question I've heard Daniel Boone ask about Wetzel, and Boone, though not a borderman in all the name implies, was a great Indian fighter. I've heard old frontiersmen, grown grizzled on the frontier, use the same words. I've been twenty years with that man, yet I can't answer it. Jonathan, of course, is only a shadow of him; Wetzel is the type of these men who have held the frontier for us. He was the first borderman, and no doubt he'll be the last."

"What have Jonathan and Wetzel that other men do not possess?"

"In them is united a marvelously developed woodcraft, with wonderful physical powers. Imagine a man having a sense, almost an animal instinct, for what is going on in the woods. Take for instance the fleetness of foot. That is one of the greatest factors. It is absolutely necessary to run, to get away when to hold ground would be death. Whether at home or in the woods, the bordermen retreat every day. You wouldn't think they practiced anything of the kind, would you? Well, a man can't be great in anything without keeping at it. Jonathan says he exercises to keep his feet light. Wetzel would just as soon run as walk. Think of the magnificent condition of these men. When a dash of speed is called for, when to be fleet of foot is to elude vengeance-seeking Indians, they must travel as swiftly as the deer. The Zanes were all sprinters. I could do something of the kind; Betty was fast on her feet, as that old fort will testify until the logs rot; Isaac was fleet, too, and Jonathan can get over the ground like a scared buck. But, even so, Wetzel can beat him."

"Goodness me, Helen!" exclaimed the colonel's buxom wife, from the window, "don't you ever get tired hearing Eb talk of Wetzel, and Jack, and Indians? Come in with me. I venture to say my gossip will do you more good than his stories."

Therefore Helen went in to chat with Mrs. Zane, for she was always glad to listen to the colonel's wife, who was so bright and pleasant, so helpful and kindly in her womanly way. In the course of their conversation, which drifted from weaving linsey, Mrs. Zane's occupation at the time, to the costly silks and satins of remembered days, and then to matters of more present interest, Helen spoke of Colonel Zane's hint about Will and Betty.

"Isn't Eb a terror? He's the worst matchmatcher you ever saw," declared the colonel's good spouse.

"There's no harm in that."

"No, indeed; it's a good thing, but he makes me laugh, and Betty, he sets her furious."

"The colonel said he had designs on me."

"Of course he has, dear old Eb! How he'd love to see you

happily married. His heart is as big as that mountain yonder. He has given this settlement his whole life."

"I believe you. He has such interest, such zeal for everybody. Only the other day he was speaking to me of Mr. Mordaunt, telling how sorry he was for the Englishman, and how much he'd like to help him. It does seem a pity a man of Mordaunt's blood and attainments should sink to utter worthlessness."

"Yes, 'tis a pity for any man, blood or no, and the world's full of such wrecks. I always liked that man's looks. I never had a word with him, of course; but I've seen him often, and something about him appealed to me. I don't believe it was just his handsome face; still I know women are susceptible that way."

"I, too, liked him once as a friend," said Helen feelingly. "Well, I'm glad he's gone."

"Gone?"

"Yes, he left Fort Henry yesterday. He came to say good-bye to me, and, except for his pale face and trembling hands, was much as he used to be in Virginia. Said he was going home to England, and wanted to tell me he was sorry—for—for all he'd done to make papa and me suffer. Drink had broken him, he said, and surely he looked a broken man. I shook hands with him, and then slipped upstairs and cried."

"Poor fellow!" sighed Mrs. Zane.

"Papa said he left Fort Pitt with one of Metzar's men as a guide."

"Then he didn't take the 'little cuss,' as Eb calls his man Case?"

"No, if I remember rightly papa said Case wouldn't go."

"I wish he had. He's no addition to our village."

Voices outside attracted their attention. Mrs. Zane glanced from the window and said: "There come Betty and Will."

Helen went on the porch to see her cousin and Betty entering the yard, and Colonel Zane once again leaning on his spade.

"Gather any hickory-nuts from birch or any other kind of trees?" asked the colonel grimly.

"No," replied Will cheerily, "the shells haven't opened yet."

"Too bad the frost is so backward," said Colonel Zane with a laugh. "But I can't see that it makes any difference."

"Where are my leaves?" asked Helen, with a smile and a nod to Betty.

"What leaves?" inquired that young woman, plainly mystified.

"Why, the autumn leaves Will promised to gather with me, then changed his mind, and said he'd bring them."

"I forgot," Will replied a little awkwardly.

Colonel Zane coughed, and then, catching Betty's glance, which had begun to flash, he plied his spade vigorously.

Betty's face had colored warmly at her brother's first question; it toned down slightly when she understood that he was not going to tease her as usual, and suddenly, as she looked over his head, it paled white as snow.

"Eb, look down the lane!" she cried.

Two tall men were approaching with labored tread, one half-supporting his companion.

"Wetzel! Jack! and Jack's hurt!" cried Betty.

"My dear, be calm," said Colonel Zane, in that quiet tone he always used during moments of excitement. He turned toward the bordermen, and helped Wetzel lead Jonathan up the walk into the yard.

From Wetzel's clothing water ran, his long hair was disheveled, his aspect frightful. Jonathan's face was white and drawn. His buckskin hunting coat was covered with blood, and the hand which he held tightly against his left breast showed dark red stains.

Helen shuddered. Almost fainting, she leaned against the porch, too horrified to cry out, with contracting heart and a chill stealing through her veins.

"Jack! Jack!" cried Betty, in agonized appeal.

"Betty, it's nothin'," said Wetzel.

"Now, Betts, don't be scared of a little blood," Jonathan said with a faint smile flitting across his haggard face.

"Bring water, shears an' some linsey cloth," added Wetzel, as Mrs. Zane came running out.

"Come inside," cried the colonel's wife, as she disappeared again immediately.

"No," replied the borderman, removing his coat, and, with the assistance of his brother, he unlaced his hunting shirt, pulling it down from a wounded shoulder. A great gory hole gaped just beneath his left collar-bone.

Although stricken with fear, when Helen saw the bronzed, massive shoulder, the long, powerful arm with its cords of muscles playing under the brown skin, she felt a thrill of admiration.

"Just missed the lung," said Mrs. Zane. "Eb, no bullet ever made that hole."

Wetzel washed the bloody wound, and, placing on it a wad of leaves he took from his pocket, bound up the shoulder tightly.

"What made that hole?" asked Colonel Zane.

Wetzel lifted the quiver of arrows Jonathan had laid on the porch, and, selecting one, handed it to the colonel. The flint-head and a portion of the shaft were stained with blood.

"The Shawnee!" exclaimed Colonel Zane. Then he led Wetzel aside, and began conversing in low tones while Jonathan, with Betty holding his arm, ascended the steps and went within the dwelling.

Helen ran home, and, once in her room, gave vent to her emotions. She cried because of fright, nervousness, relief, and joy. Then she bathed her face, tried to rub some color into her pale cheeks, and set about getting dinner as one in a trance. She could not forget that broad shoulder with its frightful wound. What a man Jonathan must be to receive a blow like that and live! Exhausted, almost spent, had been his strength when he reached home, yet how calm and cool he was! What would she not have given for the faint smile that shone in his eyes for Betty?

The afternoon was long for Helen. When at last supper was over she changed her gown, and, asking Will to accompany her, went down the lane toward Colonel Zane's cabin. At this hour the colonel almost invariably could be found sitting on his doorstep puffing a long Indian pipe, and gazing with dreamy eyes over the valley.

"Well, well, how sweet you look!" he said to Helen; then with a wink of his eyelid, "Hello, Willie, you'll find Elizabeth inside with Jack."

"How is he?" asked Helen eagerly, as Will with a laugh and a retort mounted the steps.

"Jack's doing splendidly. He slept all day. I don't think his injury amounts to much, at least not for such as him or Wetzel. It would have finished ordinary men. Bess says if complications don't set in, blood-poison or something to start a fever, he'll be up shortly. Wetzel believes the two of 'em will be on the trail inside of a week."

"Did they find Brandt?" asked Helen in a low voice.

"Yes, they ran him to his hole, and, as might have been expected, it was Bing Legget's camp. The Indians took Jonathan there."

"Then Jack was captured?"

Colonel Zane related the events, as told briefly by Wetzel, that had taken place during the preceding three days.

"The Indian I saw at the spring carried that bow Jonathan brought back. He must have shot the arrow. He was a magnificent savage."

"He was indeed a great, and a bad Indian, one of the craftiest spies who ever stepped in moccasins; but he lies quiet now on the moss and the leaves. Bing Legget will never find another runner like that Shawnee. Let us go indoors."

He led Helen into the large sitting-room where Jonathan lay on a couch, with Betty and Will sitting beside him. The colonel's wife and children, Silas Zane, and several neighbors, were present.

"Here, Jack, is a lady inquiring after your health. Betts, this reminds me of the time Isaac came home wounded, after his escape from the Hurons. Strikes me he and his Indian bride should be about due here on a visit."

Helen forgot every one except the wounded man lying so quiet and pale upon the couch. She looked down upon him with eyes strangely dilated, and darkly bright.

"How are you?" she asked softly.

"I'm all right, thank you, lass," answered Jonathan.

Colonel Zane contrived, with inimitable skill, to get Betty, Will, Silas, Bessie and the others interested in some remarkable news he had just heard, or made up, and this left Jonathan and Helen comparatively alone for the moment.

The wise old colonel thought perhaps this might be the right time. He saw Helen's face as she leaned over Jonathan, and that was enough for him. He would have taxed his ingenuity to the utmost to keep the others away from the young couple.

"I was so frightened," murmured Helen.

"Why?" asked Jonathan.

"Oh! You looked so deathly—the blood, and that awful wound!"

"It's nothin', lass."

Helen smiled down upon him. Whether or no the hurt amounted to anything in the borderman's opinion, she knew from his weakness, and his white, drawn face, that the strain of the march home had been fearful. His dark eyes held now nothing of the coldness and glitter so natural to them. They were weary, almost sad. She did not feel afraid of him now. He lay there so helpless, his long, powerful frame as quiet as a sleeping child's! Hitherto an almost indefinable antagonism in him had made itself felt; now there was only gentleness, as of a man too weary to fight longer. Helen's heart swelled with pity, and tenderness, and love. His weakness affected her as had never his strength. With an involuntary gesture of sympathy she placed her hand softly on his.

Jonathan looked up at her with eyes no longer blind. Pain had softened him. For the moment he felt carried out of himself, as it were, and saw things differently. The melting tenderness of her gaze, the glowing softness of her face, the beauty, bewitched him; and beyond that, a sweet, impelling gladness stirred within him and would not be denied. He thrilled as her fingers lightly, timidly touched his, and opened his broad hand to press hers closely and warmly.

"Lass," he whispered, with a huskiness and unsteadiness unnatural to his deep voice.

Helen bent her head closer to him; she saw his lips tremble, and his nostrils dilate; but an unutterable sadness shaded the brightness in his eyes.

"I love you."

The low whisper reached Helen's ears. She seemed to float dreamily away to some beautiful world, with the music of those words ringing in her ears. She looked at him again. Had she been dreaming? No; his dark eyes met hers with a love that he could no longer deny. An exquisite emotion, keen, strangely sweet and strong, yet terrible with sharp pain, pulsated through her being. The revelation had been too abrupt. It was so wonderfully different from what she had ever dared hope. She lowered her head, trembling.

The next moment she felt Colonel Zane's hand on her chair, and heard him say in a cheery voice:

"Well, well, see here, lass, you mustn't make Jack talk too much. See how white and tired he looks."

CHAPTER XV

IN FORTY-EIGHT hours Jonathan Zane was up and about the cabin as though he had never been wounded; the third day he walked to the spring; in a week he was waiting for Wetzel, ready to go on the trail.

On the eighth day of his enforced idleness, as he sat with Betty and the colonel in the yard, Wetzel appeared on a ridge east of the fort. Soon he rounded the stockade fence, and came straight toward them. To Colonel Zane and Betty, Wetzel's expression was terrible. The stern kindliness, the calm, though cold, gravity of his countenance, as they usually saw it, had disappeared. Yet it showed no trace of his unnatural passion to pursue and slay.

No doubt that terrible instinct, or lust, was at white heat; but it wore a mask of impenetrable stone-gray gloom.

Wetzel spoke briefly. After telling Jonathan to meet him at sunset on the following day at a point five miles up the river, he reported to the colonel that Legget with his band had left their retreat, moving southward, apparently on a marauding expedition. Then he shook hands with Colonel Zane and turned to Betty.

"Good-bye, Betty," he said, in his deep, sonorous voice.

"Good-bye, Lew," answered Betty slowly, as if surprised. "God save you," she added.

He shouldered his rifle, and hurried down the lane, halting before entering the thicket that bounded the clearing, to look back at the settlement. In another moment his dark figure had disappeared among the bushes.

"Betts, I've seen Wetzel go like that hundreds of times, though he never shook hands before; but I feel sort of queer about it now. Wasn't he strange?"

Betty did not answer until Jonathan, who had started to go within, was out of hearing.

"Lew looked and acted the same the morning he struck Miller's trail," Betty replied in a low voice. "I believe, despite his indifference to danger, he realizes that the chances are greatly against him, as they were when he began the trailing of Miller, certain it would lead him into Girty's camp. Then I know Lew has an affection for us, though it is never shown in ordinary ways. I pray he and Jack will come home safe."

"This is a bad trail they're taking up; the worst, perhaps, in border warfare," said Colonel Zane gloomily. "Did you notice how Jack's face darkened when his comrade came? Much of this borderman-life of his is due to Wetzel's influence."

"Eb, I'll tell you one thing," returned Betty, with a flash of her old spirit. "This is Jack's last trail."

"Why do you think so?"

"If he doesn't return he'll be gone the way of all bordermen; but if he comes back once more he'll never get away from Helen."

"Ugh!" exclaimed Zane, venting his pleasure in characteristic Indian way.

"That night after Jack came home wounded," continued Betty, "I saw him, as he lay on the couch, gaze at Helen. Such a look! Eb, she has won."

"I hope so, but I fear, I fear," replied her brother gloomily. "If only he returns, that's the thing! Betts, be sure he sees Helen before he goes away."

"I shall try. Here he comes now," said Betty.

"Hello, Jack!" cried the colonel, as his brother came out in somewhat of a hurry. "What have you got? By George! It's that blamed arrow the Shawnee shot into you. Where are you going with it? What the deuce—Say—Betts, eh?"

Betty had given him a sharp little kick.

The borderman looked embarrassed. He hesitated and flushed. Evidently he would have liked to avoid his brother's question; but the inquiry came direct. Dissimulation with him was impossible.

"Helen wanted this, an' I reckon that's where I'm goin' with it," he said finally, and walked away.

"Eb, you're a stupid!" exclaimed Betty.

"Hang it! Who'd have thought he was going to give her that blamed, bloody arrow?"

*   *   *   *   *   *

As Helen ushered Jonathan, for the first time, into her cosy little sitting-room, her heart began to thump so hard she could hear it.

She had not seen him since the night he whispered the words which gave such happiness. She had stayed at home, thankful beyond expression to learn every day of his rapid improvement, living in the sweetness of her joy, and waiting for him. And now as he had come, so dark, so grave, so unlike a lover to woo, that she felt a chill steal over her.

"I'm so glad you've brought the arrow," she faltered, "for, of course, coming so far means that you're well once more."

"You asked me for it, an' I've fetched it over. To-morrow I'm off on a trail I may never return from," he answered simply, and his voice seemed cold.

An immeasurable distance stretched once more between them. Helen's happiness slowly died.

"I thank you," she said with a voice that was tremulous despite all her efforts.

"It's not much of a keepsake."

"I did not ask for it as a keepsake, but because—because I wanted it. I need nothing tangible to keep alive my memory. A few words whispered to me not many days ago will suffice for remembrance—or—or did I dream them?"

Bitter disappointment almost choked Helen. This was not the gentle, soft-voiced man who had said he loved her. It was the indifferent borderman. Again he was the embodiment of his strange, quiet woods. Once more he seemed the comrade of the cold, inscrutable Wetzel.

"No, lass, I reckon you didn't dream," he replied.

Helen swayed from sick bitterness and a suffocating sense of pain, back to her old, sweet, joyous, tumultuous heart-throbbing.

"Tell me, if I didn't dream," she said softly, her face flashing warm again. She came close to him and looked up with all her heart in her great dark eyes, and love trembling on her red lips.

Calmness deserted the borderman after one glance at her. He paced the floor; twisted and clasped his hands while his eyes gleamed.

"Lass, I'm only human," he cried hoarsely, facing her again.

But only for a moment did he stand before her; but it was long enough for him to see her shrink a little, the gladness in her eyes giving way to uncertainty and a fugitive hope. Suddenly he began to pace the room again, and to talk incoherently. With the flow of words he gradually grew calmer, and, with something of his natural dignity, spoke more rationally.

"I said I loved you, an' it's true, but I didn't mean to speak. I oughtn't have done it. Somethin' made it so easy, so natural like. I'd have died before letting you know, if any idea had come to me of what I was sayin'. I've fought this feelin' for months. I allowed myself to think of you at first, an' there's the wrong. I went on the trail with your big eyes pictured in my mind, an' before I'd dreamed of it you'd crept into my heart. Life has never been the same since—that kiss. Betty said as how you cared for me, an' that made me worse, only I never really believed. To-day I came over here to say good-bye, expectin' to hold myself well in hand; but the first glance of your eyes unmans me. Nothin' can come of it, lass, nothin' but trouble. Even if you cared, an' I don't dare believe you do, nothin' can come of it! I've my own life to live, an' there's no sweetheart in it. Mebbe, as Lew says, there's one in Heaven. Oh! girl, this has been hard on me. I see you always on my lonely tramps; I see your glorious eyes in the sunny fields an' in the woods, at gray twilight, an' when the stars shine brightest. They haunt me. Ah! you're the sweetest lass as ever tormented a man, an' I love you, I love you!"

He turned to the window only to hear a soft, broken cry, and a flurry of skirts. A rush of wind seemed to envelop him. Then two soft, rounded arms encircled his neck, and a golden head lay on his breast.

"My borderman! My hero! My love!"

Jonathan clasped the beautiful, quivering girl to his heart.

"Lass, for God's sake don't say you love me," he implored, thrilling with contact of her warm arms.

"Ah!" she breathed, and raised her head. Her radiant eyes darkly wonderful with unutterable love, burned into his.

He had almost pressed his lips to the sweet red ones so near his, when he drew back with a start, and his frame straightened.

"Am I a man, or only a coward?" he muttered. "Lass, let me think. Don't believe I'm harsh, nor cold, nor nothin' except that I want to do what's right."

He leaned out of the window while Helen stood near him with a hand on his quivering shoulder. When at last he turned, his face was colorless, white as marble, and sad, and set, and stern.

"Lass, it mustn't be; I'll not ruin your life."

"But you will if you give me up."

"No, no, lass."

"I cannot live without you."

"You must. My life is not mine to give."

"But you love me."

"I am a borderman."

"I will not live without you."

"Hush! lass, hush!"

"I love you."

Jonathan breathed hard; once more the tremor, which seemed pitiful in such a strong man, came upon him. His face was gray.

"I love you," she repeated, her rich voice indescribably deep and full. She opened wide her arms and stood before him with heaving bosom, with great eyes dark with woman's sadness, passionate with woman's promise, perfect in her beauty, glorious in her abandonment.

The borderman bowed and bent like a broken reed.

"Listen," she whispered, coming closer to him, "go if you must leave me; but let this be your last trail. Come back to me, Jack, come back to me! You have had enough of this terrible life; you have won a name that will never be forgotten; you have done your duty to the border. The Indians and outlaws will be gone soon. Take the farm your brother wants you to have, and live for me. We will be happy. I shall learn to keep your home. Oh! my dear, I will recompense you for the loss of all this wild hunting and fighting. Let me persuade you, as much for your sake as for mine, for you are my heart, and soul, and life. Go out upon your last trail, Jack, and come back to me."

"An' let Wetzel go always alone?"

"He is different; he lives only for revenge. What are those poor savages to you? You have a better, nobler life opening."

"Lass, I can't give him up."

"You need not; but give up this useless seeking of adventure. That, you know, is half a borderman's life. Give it up, Jack, if not for your own, then for my sake."

"No—no—never—I can't—I won't be a coward! After all these years I won't desert him. No—no——"

"Do not say more," she pleaded, stealing closer to him until she was against his breast. She slipped her arms around his neck. For love and more than life she was fighting now. "Good-bye, my love." She kissed him, a long, lingering pressure of her soft full lips on his. "Dearest, do not shame me further. Dearest Jack, come back to me, for I love you."

She released him, and ran sobbing from the room.

Unsteady as a blind man, he groped for the door, found it, and went out.

CHAPTER XVI

THE longest day in Jonathan Zane's life, the oddest, the most terrible and complex with unintelligible emotions, was that one in which he learned that the wilderness no longer sufficed for him.

He wandered through the forest like a man lost, searching for, he knew not what. Rambling along the shady trails he looked for that contentment which had always been his, but found it not. He plunged into the depths of deep, gloomy ravines; into the fastnesses of heavy-timbered hollows where the trees hid the light of day; he sought the open, grassy hillsides, and roamed far over meadow and plain. Yet something always eluded him. The invisible and beautiful life of all inanimate things sang no more in his heart. The springy moss, the quivering leaf, the tell-tale bark of the trees, the limpid, misty, eddying pools under green banks, the myriads of natural objects from which he had learned so much, and the manifold joyous life around him, no longer spoke with soul-satisfying faithfulness. The environment of his boyish days, of his youth, and manhood, rendered not a sweetness as of old.

His intelligence, sharpened by the pain of new experience, told him he had been vain to imagine that he, because he was a borderman, could escape the universal destiny of human life. Dimly he could feel the broadening, the awakening into a fuller existence, but he did not welcome this new light. He realized that men had always turned, at some time in their lives, to women even as the cypress leans toward the sun. This weakening of the sterner stuff in him; this softening of his heart, and especially the inquietude, and lack of joy and harmony in his old pursuits of the forest trails bewildered him, and troubled him some. Thousands of times his borderman's trail had been crossed, yet never to his sorrow until now when it had been crossed by a woman.

Sick at heart, hurt in his pride, darkly savage, sad, remorseful, and thrilling with awakened passion, all in turn, he roamed the woodland unconsciously visiting the scenes where he had formerly found contentment.

He paused by many a shady glen, and beautiful quiet glade; by gray cliffs and mossy banks, searching with moody eyes for the spirit which evaded him.

Here in the green and golden woods rose before him a rugged, giant rock, moss-stained, and gleaming with trickling water. Tangled ferns dressed in autumn's russet hue lay at the base of the green-gray cliff, and circled a dark, deep pool dotted with yellow leaves. Half-way up, the perpendicular ascent was broken by a protruding ledge upon which waved broad-leaved plants and rusty ferns. Above, the cliff sheered out with many cracks and seams in its weather-beaten front.

The forest grew to the verge of the precipice. A full foliaged oak and a luxuriant maple, the former still fresh with its dark green leaves, the latter making a vivid contrast with its pale yellow, purple-red, and orange hues, leaned far out over the bluff. A mighty chestnut grasped with gnarled roots deep into the broken cliff. Dainty plumes of goldenrod swayed on the brink; red berries, amber moss, and green trailing vines peeped over the edge, and every little niche and cranny sported fragile ferns and pale-faced asters. A second cliff, higher than the first, and more heavily wooded, loomed above, and over it sprayed a transparent film of water, thin as smoke, and iridescent in the sunshine. Far above where the glancing rill caressed the mossy cliff and shone like gleaming gold against the dark branches with their green and red and purple leaves, lay the faint blue of the sky.

Jonathan pulled on down the stream with humbler heart. His favorite waterfall had denied him. The gold that had gleamed there was his sweetheart's hair; the red was of her lips; the dark pool with its lights and shades, its unfathomable mystery, was like her eyes.

He came at length to another scene of milder aspect. An open glade where the dancing, dimpling brook raced under dark hemlocks, and where blood-red sumach leaves, and beech leaves like flashes of sunshine, lay against the green. Under a leaning birch he found a patch of purple asters, and a little apart from them, by a mossy stone, a lonely fringed gentian. Its deep color brought to him the dark blue eyes that haunted him, and once again, like one possessed of an evil spirit, he wandered along the merry water-course.

But finally pain and unrest left him. When he surrendered to his love, peace returned. Though he said in his heart that Helen was not for him, he felt he did not need to torture himself by fighting against resistless power. He could love her without being a coward. He would take up his life where it had been changed, and live it, carrying this bitter-sweet burden always.

Memory, now that he admitted himself conquered, made a toy of him, bringing the sweetness of fragrant hair, and eloquent eyes, and clinging arms, and dewy lips. A thousand-fold harder to fight than pain was the seductive thought that he had but to go back to Helen to feel again the charm of her presence, to see the grace of her person, to hear the music of her voice, to have again her lips on his.

Jonathan knew then that his trial had but begun; that the pain and suffering of a borderman's broken pride and conquered spirit was nothing; that to steel his heart against the joy, the sweetness, the longing of love was everything.

So a tumult raged within his heart. No bitterness, nor wretchedness stabbed him as before, but a passionate yearning, born of memory, and unquenchable as the fires of the sun, burned there.

Helen's reply to his pale excuses, to his duty, to his life, was that she loved him. The wonder of it made him weak. Was not her answer enough? "I love you!" Three words only; but they changed the world. A beautiful girl loved him, she had kissed him, and his life could never again be the same. She had held out her arms to him—and he, cold, churlish, unfeeling brute, had let her shame herself, fighting for her happiness, for the joy that is a woman's divine right. He had been blind; he had not understood the significance of her gracious action; he had never realized until too late, what it must have cost her, what heartburning shame and scorn his refusal brought upon her. If she ever looked tenderly at him again with her great eyes; or leaned toward him with her beautiful arms outstretched, he would fall at her feet and throw his duty to the winds, swearing his love was hers always and his life forever.

So love stormed in the borderman's heart.

Slowly the melancholy Indian-summer day waned as Jonathan

strode out of the woods into a plain beyond, where he was to meet Wetzel at sunset. A smoky haze like a purple cloud lay upon the gently waving grass. He could not see across the stretch of prairie-land, though at this point he knew it was hardly a mile wide. With the trilling of the grasshoppers alone disturbing the serene quiet of this autumn afternoon, all nature seemed in harmony with the declining season. He stood a while, his thoughts becoming the calmer for the silence and loneliness of this breathing meadow.

When the shadows of the trees began to lengthen, and to steal far out over the yellow grass, he knew the time had come, and glided out upon the plain. He crossed it, and sat down upon a huge stone which lay with one shelving end overhanging the river.

Far in the west the gold-red sun, too fiery for his direct gaze, lost the brilliance of its under circle behind the fringe of the wooded hill. Slowly the red ball sank. When the last bright gleam had vanished in the dark horizon Jonathan turned to search wood and plain. Wetzel was to meet him at sunset. Even as his first glance swept around a light step sounded behind him. He did not move, for that step was familiar. In another moment the tall form of Wetzel stood beside him.

"I'm about as much behind as you was ahead of time," said Wetzel. "We'll stay here fer the night, an' be off early in the mornin'."

Under the shelving side of the rock, and in the shade of the thicket, the bordermen built a little fire and roasted strips of deer-meat. Then, puffing at their long pipes they sat for a long time in silence, while twilight let fall a dark, gray cloak over river and plain.

"Legget's move up the river was a blind, as I suspected," said

Wetzel, presently. "He's not far back in the woods from here, an' seems to be waitin' fer somethin' or somebody. Brandt an' seven redskins are with him. We'd hev a good chance at them in the mornin'; now we've got 'em a long ways from their camp, so we'll wait, an' see what deviltry they're up to."

"Mebbe he's waitin' for some Injun band," suggested Jonathan.

"Thar's redskins in the valley an' close to him; but I reckon he's barkin' up another tree."

"Suppose we run into some of these Injuns?"

"We'll hev to take what comes," replied Wetzel, lying down on a bed of leaves.

When darkness enveloped the spot Wetzel lay wrapped in deep slumber, while Jonathan sat against the rock, watching the last flickerings of the camp-fire.

CHAPTER XVII

WILL and Helen hurried back along the river road. Beguiled by the soft beauty of the autumn morning they ventured farther from the fort than ever before, and had been suddenly brought to a realization of the fact by a crackling in the underbrush. Instantly their minds reverted to bears and panthers, such as they had heard invested the thickets round the settlement.

"Oh! Will! I saw a dark form stealing along in the woods from tree to tree!" exclaimed Helen in a startled whisper.

"So did I. It was an Indian, or I never saw one. Walk faster. Once round the bend in the road we'll be within sight of the fort; then we'll run," replied Will. He had turned pale, but maintained his composure.

They increased their speed, and had almost come up to the curve in the road, marked by dense undergrowth on both sides, when the branches in the thicket swayed violently, a sturdy little man armed with a musket appeared from among them.

"Avast! Heave to!" he commanded in a low, fierce voice, leveling his weapon. "One breeze from ye, an' I let sail this broadside."

"What do you want? We have no valuables," said Will, speaking low.

Helen stared at the little man. She was speechless with terror. It flashed into her mind as soon as she recognized the red, evil face of the sailor, that he was the accomplice upon whom Brandt had told Metzar he could rely.

"Shut up! It's not ye I want, nor valuables, but this wench," growled Case. He pushed Will around with the muzzle of the musket, which action caused the young man to turn a sickly white and shrink involuntarily with fear. The hammer of the musket was raised, and might fall at the slightest jar.

"For God's sake! Will, do as he says," cried Helen, who saw murder in Case's eyes. Capture or anything was better than sacrifice of life.

"March!" ordered Case, with the musket against Will's back.

Will hurriedly started forward, jostling Helen, who had preceded him. He was forced to hurry, because every few moments Case pressed the gun to his back or side.

Without another word the sailor marched them swiftly along the road, which now narrowed down to a trail. His intention, no doubt, was to put as much distance between him and the fort as was possible. No more than a mile had been thus traversed when two Indians stepped into view.

"My God! My God!" cried Will as the savages proceeded first to bind Helen's arms behind her, and then his in the same manner. After this the journey was continued in silence, the Indians walking beside the prisoners, and Case in the rear.

Helen was so terrified that for a long time she could not think coherently. It seemed as if she had walked miles, yet did not feel tired. Always in front wound the narrow, leaf-girt trail, and to the left the broad river gleamed at intervals through open spaces in the thickets. Flocks of birds rose in the line of march. They seemed tame, and uttered plaintive notes as if in sympathy.

About noon the trail led to the river bank. One of the savages disappeared in a copse of willows, and presently reappeared carrying a birch-bark canoe. Case ordered Helen and Will into the boat, got in himself, and the savages, taking stations at bow and stern, paddled out into the stream. They shot over under the lee of an island, around a rocky point, and across a strait to another island. Beyond this they gained the Ohio shore, and beached the canoe.

"Ahoy! there, cap'n," cried Case, pushing Helen up the bank before him, and she, gazing upward, was more than amazed to see Mordaunt leaning against a tree.

"Mordaunt, had you anything to do with this?" cried Helen breathlessly.

"I had all to do with it," answered the Englishman.

"What do you mean?"

He did not meet her gaze, nor make reply; but turned to address a few words in a low tone to a white man sitting on a log.

Helen knew she had seen this person before, and doubted not

he was one of Metzar's men. She saw a rude, bark lean-to, the remains of a camp-fire, and a pack tied in blankets. Evidently Mordaunt and his men had tarried here awaiting such developments as had come to pass.

"You white-faced hound!" hissed Will, beside himself with rage when he realized the situation. Bound though he was, he leaped up and tried to get at Mordaunt. Case knocked him on the head with the handle of his knife. Will fell with blood streaming from cut over the temple.

The dastardly act aroused all Helen's fiery courage. She turned to the Englishman with eyes ablaze.

"So you've at last found your level. Border-outlaw! Kill me at once. I'd rather be dead than breathe the same air with such a coward!"

"I swore I'd have you, if not by fair means then by foul," he answered, with dark and haggard face.

"What do you intend to do with me now that I am tied?" she demanded scornfully.

"Keep you a prisoner in the woods till you consent to marry me."

Helen laughed in scorn. Desperate as was the plight, her natural courage had arisen at the cruel blow dealt her cousin, and she faced the Englishman with flashing eyes and undaunted mien. She saw he was again unsteady, and had the cough and catching breath habitual to certain men under the influence of liquor. She turned her attention to Will. He lay as he had fallen, with blood streaming over his pale face and fair hair. While she gazed at him Case whipped out his long knife, and looked up at Mordaunt.

"Cap'n, I'd better loosen a hatch fer him," he said brutally. "He's dead cargo fer us, an' in the way."

He lowered the gleaming point upon Will's chest.

"Oh-h-h!" breathed Helen in horror. She tried to close her eyes but was so fascinated she could not.

"Get up. I'll have no murder," ordered Mordaunt. "Leave him here."

"He's not got a bad cut," said the man sitting on the log. "He'll come to arter a spell, go back to ther fort, an' give an alarm."

"What's that to me?" asked Mordaunt sharply. "We shall be safe. I won't have him with us because some Indian or another will kill him. It's not my purpose to murder any one."

"Ugh!" grunted one of the savages, and pointed eastward with his hand. "Hurry-long-way-go," he said in English. With the Indians in the lead the party turned from the river into the forest.

Helen looked back into the sandy glade and saw Will lying as they had left him, unconscious, with his hands still bound tightly behind him, and blood running over his face. Painful as was the thought of leaving him thus, it afforded her relief. She assured herself he had not been badly hurt, would recover consciousness before long, and, even bound as he was, could make his way back to the settlement.

Her own situation, now that she knew Mordaunt had instigated the abduction, did not seem hopeless. Although dreading Brandt with unspeakable horror, she did not in the least fear the Englishman. He was mad to carry her off like this into the wilderness, but would force her to do nothing. He could not keep her a prisoner long while Jonathan Zane and Wetzel were free to take his trail. What were his intentions? Where was he taking her? Such questions as these, however, troubled Helen more than a little. They brought her thoughts back to the Indians leading the way with lithe and stealthy step. How had

Mordaunt associated himself with these savages? Then, suddenly, it dawned upon her that Brandt also might be in this
scheme to carry her off. She scouted the idea; but it returned.
Perhaps Mordaunt was only a tool; perhaps he himself was being
deceived. Helen turned pale at the very thought. She had never
forgotten the strange, unreadable, yet threatening, expression
which Brandt had worn the day she had refused to walk with
him.

Meanwhile the party made rapid progress through the forest.
Not a word was spoken, nor did any noise of rustling leaves or
crackling twigs follow their footsteps. The savage in the lead
chose the open and less difficult ground; he took advantage of
glades, mossy places, and rocky ridges. This careful choosing was,
evidently, to avoid noise, and make the trail as difficult to follow
as possible. Once he stopped suddenly, and listened.

Helen had a good look at the savage while he was in this position. His lean, athletic figure resembled, in its half-clothed condition, a bronzed statue; his powerful visage was set, changeless
like iron. His dark eyes seemed to take in all points of the forest
before him.

Whatever had caused the halt was an enigma to all save his
red-skinned companion.

The silence of the wood was the silence of the desert. No bird
chirped; no breath of wind sighed in the treetops; even the
aspens remained unagitated. Pale yellow leaves sailed slowly,
reluctantly down from above.

But some faint sound, something unusual had jarred upon the
exquisitely sensitive ears of the leader, for with a meaning shake
of the head to his followers, he resumed the march in a direction
at right angles with the original course.

This caution, and evident distrust of the forest ahead, made

Helen think again of Jonathan and Wetzel. Those great border-men might already be on the trail of her captors. The thought thrilled her. Presently she realized, from another long, silent march through forest thickets, glades, aisles, and groves, over rock-strewn ridges, and down mossy-stoned ravines, that her strength was beginning to fail.

"I can go no further with my arms tied in this way," she declared, stopping suddenly.

"Ugh!" uttered the savage before her, turning sharply. He brandished a tomahawk before her eyes.

Mordaunt hurriedly set free her wrists. His pale face flushed a dark, flaming red when she shrank from his touch as if he were a viper.

After they had traveled what seemed to Helen many miles, the vigilance of the leaders relaxed.

On the banks of the willow-skirted stream the Indian guide halted them, and proceeded on alone to disappear in a green thicket. Presently he reappeared, and motioned for them to come on. He led the way over smooth, sandy paths between clumps of willows, into a heavy growth of alder bushes and prickly thorns, at length to emerge upon a beautiful grassy plot enclosed by green and yellow shrubbery. Above the stream, which cut the edge of the glade, rose a sloping, wooded ridge, with huge rocks projecting here and there out of the brown forest.

Several birch-bark huts could be seen; then two rough bearded men lolling upon the grass, and beyond them a group of painted Indians.

A whoop so shrill, so savage, so exultant, that it seemingly froze her blood, rent the silence. A man, unseen before, came crashing through the willows on the side of the ridge. He leaped the stream with the spring of a wild horse. He was big and broad, with disheveled hair, keen, hard face, and wild, gray eyes.

Helen's sight almost failed her; her head whirled dizzily; it was as if her heart had stopped beating and was become a cold, dead weight. She recognized in this man the one whom she feared most of all—Brandt.

He cast one glance full at her, the same threatening, cool, and evil-meaning look she remembered so well, and then engaged the Indian guide in low conversation.

Helen sank at the foot of a tree, leaning against it. Despite her weariness she had retained some spirit until this direful revelation broke her courage. What worse could have happened? Mordaunt had led her, for some reason that she could not divine, into the clutches of Brandt, into the power of Legget and his outlaws.

But Helen was not one to remain long dispirited or hopeless. As this plot thickened, as every added misfortune weighed upon her, when just ready to give up to despair she remembered the bordermen. Then Colonel Zane's tales of their fearless, implacable pursuit when bent on rescue or revenge, recurred to her, and fortitude returned. While she had life she would hope.

The advent of the party with their prisoner enlivened Legget's gang. A great giant of a man, blond-bearded, and handsome in a wild, rugged, uncouth way, a man Helen instinctively knew to be Legget, slapped Brandt on the shoulder.

"Damme, Roge, if she ain't a regular little daisy! Never seed such a purty lass in my life."

Brandt spoke hurriedly, and Legget laughed.

All this time Case had been sitting on the grass, saying nothing, but with his little eyes watchful. Mordaunt stood near him, his head bowed, his face gloomy.

"Say, cap'n, I don't like this mess," whispered Case to his master. "They ain't no crew fer us. I know men, fer I've sailed the seas, an' you're goin' to get what Metz calls the double-cross."

Mordaunt seemed to arouse from his gloomy reverie. He looked at Brandt and Legget who were now in earnest council. Then his eyes wandered toward Helen. She beckoned him to come to her.

"Why did you bring me here?" she asked.

"Brandt understood my case. He planned this thing, and seemed to be a good friend of mine. He said if I once got you out of the settlement, he would give me protection until I crossed the border into Canada. There we could be married," replied Mordaunt unsteadily.

"Then you meant marriage by me, if I could be made to consent?"

"Of course. I'm not utterly vile," he replied, with face lowered in shame.

"Have you any idea what you've done?"

"Done? I don't understand."

"You have ruined yourself, lost your manhood, become an outlaw, a fugitive, made yourself the worst thing on the border— a girl-thief, and all for nothing."

"No, I have you. You are more to me than all."

"But can't you see? You've brought me out here for Brandt!"

"My God!" exclaimed Mordaunt. He rose slowly to his feet and gazed around like a man suddenly wakened from a dream. "I see it all now! Miserable, drunken wretch that I am!"

Helen saw his face change and lighten as if a cloud of darkness had passed away from it. She understood that love of liquor had made him a party to this plot. Brandt had cunningly worked upon his weakness, proposed a daring scheme; and filled his befogged mind with hopes that, in a moment of clear-sightedness, he would have seen to be vain and impossible. And Helen understood also that the sudden shock of surprise, pain, possible fury, had sobered Mordaunt, probably for the first time in weeks.

The Englishman's face became exceedingly pale. Seating himself on a stone near Case, he bowed his head, remaining silent and motionless.

The conference between Legget and Brandt lasted for some time. When it ended the latter strode toward the motionless figure on the rock.

"Mordaunt, you and Case will do well to follow this Indian at once to the river, where you can strike the Fort Pitt trail," said Brandt.

He spoke arrogantly and authoritatively. His keen, hard face, his steely eyes, bespoke the iron will and purpose of the man.

Mordaunt rose with cold dignity. If he had been a dupe, he was one no longer, as could be plainly read on his calm, pale face. The old listlessness, the unsteadiness had vanished. He wore a manner of extreme quietude; but his eyes were like balls of blazing blue steel.

"Mr. Brandt, I seem to have done you a service, and am no longer required," he said in a courteous tone.

Brandt eyed his man; but judged him wrongly. An English gentleman was new to the border-outlaw.

"I swore the girl should be mine," he hissed.

"Doomed men cannot be choosers!" cried Helen, who had heard him. Her dark eyes burned with scorn and hatred.

All the party heard her passionate outburst. Case arose as if unconcernedly, and stood by the side of his master. Legget and the other two outlaws came up. The Indians turned their swarthy faces.

"Hah! ain't she sassy?" cried Legget.

Brandt looked at Helen, understood the meaning of her words, and laughed. But his face paled, and involuntarily his shifty glance sought the rocks and trees upon the ridge.

"You played me from the first?" asked Mordaunt quietly.

"I did," replied Brandt.

"You meant nothing of your promise to help me across the border?"

"No."

"You intended to let me shift for myself out here in this wilderness?"

"Yes, after this Indian guides you to the river-trail," said Brandt, indicating with his finger the nearest savage.

"I get what you frontier men call 'the double-cross'?"

"That's it," replied Brandt with a hard laugh, in which Legget joined.

A short pause ensued.

"What will you do with the girl?"

"That's my affair."

"Marry her?" Mordaunt's voice was low and quiet.

"No!" cried Brandt. "She flaunted my love in my face, scorned me! She saw that borderman strike me, and by God! I'll get even. I'll keep her here in the woods until I'm tired of her, and when her beauty fades I'll turn her over to Legget."

Scarcely had the words dropped from his vile lips when Mordaunt moved with tigerish agility. He seized a knife from the belt of one of the Indians.

"Die!" he screamed.

Brandt grasped his tomahawk. At the same instant the man who had acted as Mordaunt's guide grasped the Englishman from behind.

Brandt struck ineffectually at the struggling man.

"Fair play!" roared Case, leaping at Mordaunt's second assail-ant. His long knife sheathed its glittering length in the man's breast. Without even a groan he dropped. "Clear the decks!" Case yelled, sweeping round in a circle. All fell back before that whirling knife.

Several of the Indians started as if to raise their rifles; but Legget's stern command caused them to desist.

The Englishman and the outlaw now engaged in a fearful encounter. The practiced, rugged, frontier desperado apparently had found his match in this pale-faced, slender man. His border skill with the hatchet seemed offset by Mordaunt's terrible rage. Brandt whirled and swung the weapon as he leaped around his antagonist. With his left arm the Englishman sought only to protect his head, while with his right he brandished the knife. Whirling here and there they struggled across the cleared space, plunging out of sight among the willows. During a moment there was a sound as of breaking branches; then a dull blow, horrible to hear, followed by a low moan, and then deep silence.

CHAPTER XVIII

A BLACK weight was seemingly lifted from Helen's weary eyelids. The sun shone; the golden forest surrounded her; the brook babbled merrily; but where were the struggling, panting men? She noticed presently, when her vision had grown more clear, that the scene differed entirely from the willow-glade where she had closed her eyes upon the fight. Then came the knowledge that she had fainted, and, during the time of unconsciousness, been moved.

She lay upon a mossy mound a few feet higher than a swiftly running brook. A magnificent chestnut tree spread its leafy branches above her. Directly opposite, about an hundred feet away, loomed a gray, ragged, moss-stained cliff. She noted this particularly because the dense forest encroaching to its very edge excited her admiration. Such wonderful coloring seemed unreal. Dead gold and bright red foliage flamed everywhere.

Two Indians stood near by silent, immovable. No other of Legget's band was visible. Helen watched the red men.

Sinewy, muscular warriors they were, with bodies partially painted, and long, straight hair, black as burnt wood, interwoven with bits of white bone, and plaited around waving eagle plumes. At first glance their dark faces and dark eyes were expressive of craft, cunning, cruelty, courage, all attributes of the savage.

Yet wild as these savages appeared, Helen did not fear them as she did the outlaws. Brandt's eyes, and Legget's, too, when turned on her, emitted a flame that seemed to scorch and shrivel her soul. When the savages met her gaze, which was but seldom, she imagined she saw intelligence, even pity, in their dusky eyes. Certain it was she did not shrink from them as from Brandt.

Suddenly, with a sensation of relief and joy, she remembered Mordaunt's terrible onslaught upon Brandt. Although she could not recollect the termination of that furious struggle, she did recall Brandt's scream of mortal agony, and the death of the other at Case's hands. This meant, whether Brandt was dead or not, that the fighting strength of her captors had been diminished. Surely as the sun had risen that morning, Helen believed Jonathan and Wetzel lurked on the trail of these renegades. She prayed that her courage, hope, strength, might be continued.

"Ugh!" exclaimed one of the savages, pointing across the open space. A slight swaying of the bushes told that some living thing was moving among them, and an instant later the huge frame of the leader came into view. The other outlaw, and Case, followed closely. Farther down the margin of the thicket the Indians appeared; but without the slightest noise or disturbance of the shrubbery.

It required but a glance to show Helen that Case was in high spirits. His repulsive face glowed with satisfaction. He carried a bundle, which Helen saw, with a sickening sense of horror, was made up of Mordaunt's clothing. Brandt had killed the Englishman. Legget also had a package under his arm, which he threw down when he reached the chestnut tree, to draw from his pocket a long, leather belt, such as travelers use for the carrying of valuables. It was evidently heavy, and the musical clink which accompanied his motion proclaimed the contents to be gold.

Brandt appeared next; he was white and held his hand to his breast. There were dark stains on his hunting coat, which he removed to expose a shirt blotched with red.

"You ain't much hurt, I reckon?" inquired Legget solicitously.

"No; but I'm bleeding bad," replied Brandt coolly. He then called an Indian and went among the willows skirting the stream.

"So I'm to be in this border crew?" asked Case, looking up at Legget.

"Sure," replied the big outlaw. "You're a handy fellar, Case, an' after I break you into border ways you will fit in here tip-top. Now you'd better stick by me. When Eb Zane, his brother Jack, an' Wetzel find out this here day's work. hell will be a cool place compared with their whereabouts. You'll be safe with me, an' this is the only place on the border, I reckon, where you can say your life is your own."

"I'm yer mate, cap'n. I've sailed with soldiers, pirates, sailors, an' I guess I can navigate this borderland. Do we mess here? You didn't come far."

"Wal, I ain't pertikuler, but I don't like eatin' with buzzards," said Legget, with a grin. "Thet's why we moved a bit."

"What's buzzards?"

"Ho! ho! Mebbe you'll hev 'em closer'n you'd like, some day, if you'd only know it. Buzzards are fine birds, most particular birds, as won't eat nothin' but flesh, an' white man or Injun is pie fer 'em."

"Cap'n, I've seed birds as wouldn't wait till a man was dead," said Case.

"Haw! haw! you can't come no sailor yarns on this fellar. Wal, now, we've got ther Englishman's gold. One or t'other of us might jest as well hev it all."

"Right yer are, cap'n. Dice, cards, anyways, so long as I knows the game."

"Here, Jenks, hand over yer clickers, an' bring us a flat stone," said Legget, sitting on the moss and emptying the belt in front of him. Case took a small bag from the dark blue jacket that had so lately covered Mordaunt's shoulders, and poured out its bright contents.

"This coat ain't worth keepin'," he said, holding it up. The garment was rent and slashed, and under the left sleeve was a small, blood-stained hole where one of Brandt's blows had fallen. "Hullo, what's this?" muttered the sailor, feeling in the pocket of the jacket. "Blast my timbers, hooray!"

He held up a small, silver-mounted whiskey flask, unscrewed the lid, and lifted the vessel to his mouth.

"I'm kinder thirsty myself," suggested Legget.

"Cap'n, a nip an' no more," Case replied, holding the flask to Legget's lips.

The outlaw called Jenks now returned with a flat stone which he placed between the two men. The Indians gathered around. With greedy eyes they bent their heads over the gamblers, and watched every movement with breathless interest. At each click of the dice, or clink of gold, they uttered deep exclamations.

"Luck's again' ye, cap'n," said Case, skilfully shaking the ivory cubes.

"Hain't I got eyes?" growled the outlaw.

Steadily his pile of gold diminished, and darker grew his face.

"Cap'n, I'm a bad wind to draw," Case rejoined, drinking again from the flask. His naturally red face had become livid, his skin moist, and his eyes wild with excitement.

"Hullo! If them dice wasn't Jenks's, an' I hadn't played afore with him, I'd swear they's loaded."

"You ain't insinuatin' nothin', cap'n?" inquired Case softly, hesitating with the dice in his hands, his evil eyes glinting at Legget.

"No, you're fair enough," growled the leader. "It's my tough luck."

The game progressed with infrequent runs of fortune for the outlaw, and presently every piece of gold lay in a shining heap before the sailor.

"Clean busted!" exclaimed Legget in disgust.

"Can't you find nothin' more?" asked Case.

The outlaw's bold eyes wandered here and there until they rested upon the prisoner.

"I'll play ther lass against yer pile of gold," he growled. "Best two throws out 'en three. See here, she's as much mine as Brandt's."

"Make it half my pile an' I'll go you."

"Nary time. Bet, or give me back what yer win," replied Legget gruffly.

"She's a trim little craft, no mistake," said Case, critically surveying Helen. "All right, cap'n, I've sportin' blood, an' I'll bet. Yer throw first."

Legget won the first cast, and Case the second. With deliberation the outlaw shook the dice in his huge fist, and rattled them out upon the stone. "Hah!" he cried in delight. He had come within one of the highest score possible. Case nonchalantly flipped the little white blocks. The Indians crowded forward, their dusky eyes shining.

Legget swore in a terrible voice which re-echoed from the stony cliff. The sailor was victorious. The outlaw got up, kicked the stone and dice in the brook, and walked away from the group. He strode to and fro under one of the trees. Gruffly he gave an order to the Indians. Several of them began at once to kindle a fire. Presently he called Jenks, who was fishing the dice out of the brook, and began to converse earnestly with him, making fierce gestures and casting lowering glances at the sailor.

Case was too drunk now to see that he had incurred the enmity of the outlaw leader. He drank the last of the rum, and tossed the silver flask to an Indian, who received the present with every show of delight.

Case then with the slow, uncertain movements of a man whose mind is befogged, began to count his gold; but only to gather up a few pieces when they slipped out of his trembling hands to roll on the moss. Laboriously, seriously, he kept at it with the doggedness of a drunken man. Apparently he had forgotten the others. Failing to learn the value of the coins by taking up each in turn, he arranged them in several piles, and began to estimate his wealth in sections.

In the meanwhile Helen, who had not failed to take in the slightest detail of what was going on, saw that a plot was hatching which boded ill to the sailor. Moreover, she heard Legget and Jenks whispering.

"I kin take him from right here 'atwixt his eyes," said Jenks softly, and tapped his rifle significantly.

"Wal, go ahead, only I ruther hev it done quieter," answered Legget. "We're yet a long ways, near thirty miles, from my camp, an' there's no tellin' who's in ther woods. But we've got ter git rid of ther fresh sailor, an' there's no surer way."

Cautiously cocking his rifle, Jenks deliberately raised it to his shoulder. One of the Indian sentinels who stood near at hand, sprang forward and struck up the weapon. He spoke a single word to Legget, pointed to the woods above the cliff, and then resumed his statue-like attitude.

"I told yer, Jenks, that it wouldn't do. The redskin scents somethin' in the woods, an' ther's an Injun I never seed fooled. We mustn't make a noise. Take yer knife an' tomahawk, crawl down below the edge o' the bank an' slip up on him. I'll give half ther gold fer ther job."

Jenks buckled his belt more tightly, gave one threatening glance at the sailor, and slipped over the bank. The bed of the brook lay about six feet below the level of the ground. This afforded an opportunity for the outlaw to get behind Case without being observed. A moment passed. Jenks disappeared round a bend of the stream. Presently his grizzled head appeared above the bank. He was immediately behind the sailor; but still some thirty feet away. This ground must be covered quickly and noiselessly. The outlaw began to crawl. In his right hand he grasped a tomahawk, and between his teeth was a long knife. He looked like a huge, yellow bear.

The savages, with the exception of the sentinel who seemed absorbed in the dense thicket on the cliff, sat with their knees between their hands, watching the impending tragedy.

Nothing but the merest chance, or some extraordinary intervention, could avert Case's doom. He was gloating over his gold. The creeping outlaw made no more noise than a snake. Nearer and nearer he came; his sweaty face shining in the sun; his eyes tigerish; his long body slipping silently over the grass. At length he was within five feet of the sailor. His knotty hands were dug into the sward as he gathered energy for a sudden spring.

At that very moment Case, with his hand on his knife, rose quickly and turned round.

The outlaw, discovered in the act of leaping, had no alternative, and spring he did, like a panther.

The little sailor stepped out of line with remarkable quickness, and as the yellow body whirled past him, his knife flashed blue-bright in the sunshine.

Jenks fell forward, his knife buried in the grass beneath him, and his outstretched hand still holding the tomahawk.

"Tryin' ter double-cross me fer my gold," muttered the sailor, sheathing his weapon. He never looked to see whether or no his blow had been fatal. "These border fellars might think a man as sails the seas can't handle a knife." He calmly began gathering up his gold, evidently indifferent to further attack.

Helen saw Legget raise his own rifle, but only to have it struck aside as had Jenks's. This time the savage whispered earnestly to Legget, who called the other Indians around him.

The sentinel's low throaty tones mingled with the soft babbling of the stream. No sooner had he ceased speaking than the effect of his words showed how serious had been the information, warning or advice. The Indians cast furtive glances toward the woods. Two of them melted like shadows into the red and gold thicket. Another stealthily slipped from tree to tree until he reached the open ground, then dropped into the grass, and was seen no more until his dark body rose under the cliff. He stole along the green-stained wall, climbed a rugged corner, and vanished amid the dense foliage.

Helen felt that she was almost past discernment or thought. The events of the day succeeding one another so swiftly, and fraught with panic, had, despite her hope and fortitude, reduced her to a helpless condition of piteous fear. She understood that the savages scented danger, or had, in their mysterious way, received intelligence such as rendered them wary and watchful.

"Come on, now, an' make no noise," said Legget to Case. "Bring the girl, an' see that she steps light."

"Ay, ay, cap'n," replied the sailor. "Where's Brandt?"

"He'll be comin' soon's his cut stops bleedin'. I reckon he's weak yet."

Case gathered up his goods, and, tucking it under his arm, grasped Helen's arm. She was leaning against the tree, and when he pulled her, she wrenched herself free, rising with difficulty. His disgusting touch and revolting face had revived her sensibilities.

"Yer kin begin duty by carryin' thet," said Case, thrusting the package into Helen's arms. She let it drop without moving a hand.

"I'm runnin' this ship. Yer belong to me," hissed Case, and then he struck her on the head. Helen uttered a low cry of distress, and half staggered against the tree. The sailor picked up the package. This time she took it, trembling with horror.

"Thet's right. Now, give ther cap'n a kiss," he leered, and jostled against her.

Helen pushed him violently. With agonized eyes she appealed to the Indians. They were engaged tying up their packs. Legget looked on with a lazy grin.

"Oh! oh!" breathed Helen as Case seized her again. She tried to scream, but could not make a sound. The evil eyes, the beastly face, transfixed her with terror.

Case struck her twice, then roughly pulled her toward him.

Half-fainting, unable to move, Helen gazed at the heated, bloated face approaching hers.

When his coarse lips were within a few inches of her lips something hot hissed across her brow. Following so closely as to be an accompaniment, rang out with singular clearness the sharp crack of a rifle.

Case's face changed. The hot, surging flush faded; the expression became shaded, dulled into vacant emptiness; his eyes rolled wildly, then remained fixed, with a look of dark surprise. He stood upright an instant, swayed with the regular poise of a falling oak, and then plunged backward to the ground. His face, ghastly and livid, took on the awful calm of death.

A very small hole, reddish-blue round the edges, dotted the center of his temple.

Legget stared aghast at the dead sailor; then he possessed himself of the bag of gold.

"Saved me ther trouble," he muttered, giving Case a kick.

The Indians glanced at the little figure, then out into the flaming thickets. Each savage sprang behind a tree with incredible quickness. Legget saw this, and grasping Helen, he quickly led her within cover of the chestnut.

Brandt appeared with his Indian companion, and both leaped to shelter behind a clump of birches near where Legget stood. Brandt's hawk eyes flashed upon the dead Jenks and Case. Without asking a question he seemed to take in the situation. He stepped over and grasped Helen by the arm.

"Who killed Case?" he asked in a whisper, staring at the little blue hole in the sailor's temple.

No one answered.

The two Indians who had gone into the woods to the right of the stream, now returned. Hardly were they under the trees with their party, when the savage who had gone off alone arose out of the grass in the left of the brook, took it with a flying leap, and darted into their midst. He was the sentinel who had knocked up the weapons, thereby saving Case's life twice. He was lithe and supple, but not young. His grave, shadowy-lined, iron visage showed the traces of time and experience. All gazed at him as at one whose wisdom was greater than theirs.

"Old Horse," said Brandt in English. "Haven't I seen bullet holes like this?"

The Chippewa bent over Case, and then slowly straightened his tall form.

"*Deathwind!*" he replied, answering in the white man's language.

His Indian companions uttered low, plaintive murmurs, not signifying fear so much as respect.

Brandt turned as pale as the clean birch-bark on the tree near him. The gray flare of his eyes gave out a terrible light of certainty and terror.

"Legget, you needn't try to hide your trail," he hissed, and it seemed as if there was a bitter, reckless pleasure in these words. Then the Chippewa glided into the low bushes bordering the creek. Legget followed him, with Brandt leading Helen, and the other Indians brought up the rear, each one sending wild, savage glances into the dark, surrounding forest.

CHAPTER XIX

A DENSE white fog rose from the river, obscuring all objects, when the bordermen rolled out of their snug bed of leaves. The air was cool and bracing, faintly fragrant with dying foliage and the damp, dewy luxuriance of the ripened season. Wetzel pulled from under the protecting ledge a bundle of bark and sticks he had put there to keep dry, and built a fire, while Jonathan fashioned a cup from a green fruit resembling a gourd, filling it at a spring near by.

"Lew, there's a frosty nip in the water this mornin'," said Jonathan.

"I reckon. It's gettin' along into fall now. Any clear, still night'll fetch all the leaves, an' strip the trees bare as burned timber," answered Wetzel, brushing the ashes off the strip of meat he had roasted. "Get a stick, an' help me cook the rest of this chunk of bison. The sun'll be an hour breakin' up thet mist, an' we can't clear out till then. Mebbe we won't have no chance to light another fire soon."

With these bordermen everything pertaining to their lonely lives, from the lighting of a fire to the trailing of a redskin, was singularly serious. No gladsome song ever came from their lips;

there was no jollity around their camp-fire. Hunters had their
moments of rapturous delight; bordermen knew the peace, the
content of the wilderness, but their pursuits racked nerve and
heart. Wetzel had his moments of frenzied joy, but they passed
with the echo of his vengeful yell. Jonathan's happiness, such as
it was, had been to roam the forests. That, before a woman's eyes
had dispelled it, had been enough, and compensated him for
the gloomy, bloody phantoms which haunted him.

The bordermen, having partaken of the frugal breakfast,
stowed in their spacious pockets all the meat that was left, and
were ready for the day's march. They sat silent for a time waiting for the mist to lift. It broke in places, rolled in huge billows,
sailed aloft like great white clouds, and again hung tenaciously
to the river and the plain. Away in the west blue patches of sky
shone through the rifts, and eastward banks of misty vapor
reddened beneath the rising sun. Suddenly from beneath the
silver edge of the rising pall the sun burst gleaming gold, disclosing the winding valley with its steaming river.

"We'll make up stream fer Two Islands, an' cross there if so
be we've reason," Wetzel had said.

Through the dewy dells, avoiding the wet grass and bushes,
along the dark, damp glades with their yellow carpets, under
the thinning arches of the trees, down the gentle slopes of the
ridges, rich with green moss, the bordermen glided like gray
shadows. The forest was yet asleep. A squirrel frisked up an
oak and barked quarrelsomely at these strange, noiseless visitors.
A crow cawed from somewhere overhead. These were the only
sounds disturbing the quiet early hour.

As the bordermen advanced the woods lightened and awoke
to life and joy. Birds sang, trilled, warbled, or whistled their
plaintive songs, peculiar to the dying season, and in harmony

with the glory of the earth. Birds that in earlier seasons would have screeched and fought, now sang and fluttered side by side, in fraternal parade on their slow pilgrimage to the far south.

"Bad time fer us, when the birds are so tame, an' chipper. We can't put faith in them these days," said Wetzel. "Seems like they never was wild. I can tell, 'cept at this season, by the way they whistle an' act in the woods, if there's been any Injuns along the trails."

The greater part of the morning passed thus with the bordermen steadily traversing the forest; here, through a spare and gloomy wood, blasted by fire, worn by age, with many a dethroned monarch of bygone times rotting to punk and duff under the ferns, with many a dark, seamed and ragged king still standing, but gray and bald of head and almost ready to take his place in the forest of the past; there, through a maze of young saplings where each ash, maple, hickory and oak added some new and beautiful hue to the riot of color.

"I just had a glimpse of the lower island, as we passed an opening in the thicket," said Jonathan.

"We ain't far away," replied Wetzel.

The bordermen walked less rapidly in order to proceed with more watchfulness. Every rod or two they stopped to listen.

"You think Legget's across the river?" asked Jonathan.

"He was two days back, an' had his gang with him. He's up to some bad work, but I can't make out what. One thing, I never seen his trail so near Fort Henry."

They emerged at length into a more open forest which skirted the river. At a point still some distance ahead, but plainly in sight, two small islands rose out of the water.

"Hist! What's that?" whispered Wetzel, slipping his hand in Jonathan's arm.

A hundred yards beyond lay a long, dark figure stretched at full length under one of the trees close to the bank.

"Looks like a man," said Jonathan.

"You've hit the mark. Take a good peep roun' now, Jack, fer we're comin' somewhere near the trail we want."

Minutes passed while the patient bordermen searched the forest with their eyes, seeking out every tree within rifle range, or surveyed the level glades, scrutinized the hollows, and bent piercing eyes upon the patches of ferns.

"If there's a redskin around he ain't big enough to hold a gun," said Wetzel, moving forward again, yet still with that same stealthy step and keen caution.

Finally they were gazing down upon the object which had attracted Wetzel's attention.

"Will Sheppard!" cried Jonathan. "Is he dead? What's this mean?"

Wetzel leaned over the prostrate lad, and then quickly turned to his companion.

"Get some water. Take his cap. No, he ain't even hurt bad, unless he's got some wound as don't show."

Jonathan returned with the water, and Wetzel bathed the bloody face. When the gash on Will's forehead was clean, it told the bordermen much.

"Not an hour old, that blow," muttered Wetzel.

"He's comin' to," said Jonathan as Will stirred uneasily and moaned. Presently the lad opened his eyes and sat bolt upright. He looked bewildered for a moment, and felt of his head while gazing vaguely at the bordermen. Suddenly he cried:

"I remember! We were captured, brought here, and I was struck down by that villain Case."

"We? Who was with you?" asked Jonathan slowly.

"Helen. We came after flowers and leaves. While in full sight of the fort I saw an Indian. We hurried back," he cried, and proceeded with broken, panting voice to tell his story.

Jonathan Zane leaped to his feet with face deathly white and eyes blue-black, like burning stars.

"Jack, study the trail while I get the lad acrost the river, an' steered fer home," said Wetzel, and then he asked Will if he could swim.

"Yes; but you will find a canoe there in those willows."

"Come, lad, we've no time to spare," added Wetzel, sliding down the bank and entering the willows. He came out almost immediately with the canoe which he launched.

Will turned that he might make a parting appeal to Jonathan to save Helen; but could not speak. The expression on the borderman's face frightened him.

Motionless and erect Jonathan stood, his arms folded and his white, stern face distorted with the agony of remorse, fear, and anguish, which, even as Will gazed, froze into an awful, deadly look of fateful purpose.

Wetzel pushed the canoe off, and paddled with powerful strokes; he left Will on the opposite bank, and returned as swiftly as he could propel the light craft.

The bordermen met each other's glance, and had little need of words. Wetzel's great shoulders began to sag slightly, and his head lowered as his eyes sought the grass; a dark and gloomy shade overcast his features. Thus he passed from borderman to Deathwind. The sough of the wind overhead among the almost naked branches might well have warned Indians and renegades that Deathwind was on the trail!

"Brandt's had a hand in this, an' the Englishman's a fool!" said Wetzel.

"An hour ahead; can we come up with them before they join Brandt an' Legget?"

"We can try, but like as not we'll fail. Legget's gang is thirteen strong by now. I said it! Somethin' told me—a hard trail, a long trail, an' our last trail."

"It's over thirty miles to Legget's camp. We know the woods, an' every stream, an' every cover," hissed Jonathan Zane.

With no further words Wetzel took the trail on the run, and so plain was it to his keen eyes that he did not relax his steady lope except to stop and listen at regular intervals. Jonathan followed with easy swing. Through forest and meadow, over hill and valley, they ran, fleet and tireless. Once, with unerring instinct, they abruptly left the broad trail and cut far across a wide and rugged ridge to come again upon the tracks of the marching band. Then, in open country they reduced their speed to a walk. Ahead, in a narrow valley, rose a thicket of willows, yellow in the sunlight, and impenetrable to human vision. Like huge snakes the bordermen crept into this copse, over the sand, under the low branches, hard on the trail. Finally, in a light, open space, where the sun shone through a network of yellow branches and foliage, Wetzel's hand was laid upon Jonathan's shoulder.

"Listen! Hear that!" he whispered.

Jonathan heard the flapping of wings, and a low, hissing sound, not unlike that made by a goose.

"Buzzards!" he said, with a dark, grim smile. "Mebbe Brandt has begun our work. Come."

Out into the open they crawled to put to flight a flock of huge black birds with grisly, naked necks, hooked beaks, and long, yellow claws. Upon the green grass lay three half-naked men, ghastly, bloody, in terribly limp and lifeless positions.

"Metzar's man Smith, Jenks, the outlaw, and Mordaunt!"
Jonathan Zane gazed darkly into the steely, sightless eyes of
the traitor. Death's awful calm had set the expression; but the
man's whole life was there, its better part sadly shining forth
among the cruel shadows.

His body was mutilated in a frightful manner. Cuts, stabs,
and slashes told the tale of a long encounter, brought to an end
by one clean stroke.

"Come here, Lew. You've seen men chopped up; but look at
this dead Englishman," called Zane.

Mordaunt lay weltering in a crimson tide. Strangely though,
his face was uninjured. A black bruise showed under his fair
hair. The ghost of a smile seemed to hover around his set lips,
yet almost intangible though it was, it showed that at last he
had died a man. His left shoulder, side and arm showed where
the brunt of Brandt's attack had fallen.

"How'd he ever fight so?" mused Jonathan.

"You never can tell," replied Wetzel. "Mebbe he killed this
other fellar, too; but I reckon not. Come, we must go slow now,
fer Legget is near at hand."

Jonathan brought huge, flat stones from the brook, and laid
them over Mordaunt; then, cautiously he left the glade on Wetzel's trail.

Five hundred yards farther on Wetzel had ceased following
the outlaw's tracks to cross the creek and climb a ridge. He was
beginning his favorite trick of making a wide detour. Jonathan
hurried forward, feeling he was safe from observation. Soon he
distinguished the tall, brown figure of his comrade gliding
ahead from tree to tree, from bush to bush.

"See them maples an' chestnuts down thar," said Wetzel

when Jonathan had come up, pointing through an opening in the foliage. "They've stopped fer some reason."

On through the forest the bordermen glided. They kept near the summit of the ridge, under the best cover they could find, and passed swiftly over this half-circle. When beginning once more to draw toward the open grove in the valley, they saw a long, irregular cliff, densely wooded. They swerved a little, and made for this excellent covert.

They crawled the last hundred yards and never shook a fern, moved a leaf, or broke a twig. Having reached the brink of the low precipice, they saw the grassy meadow below, the straggling trees, the brook, the group of Indians crowding round the white men.

"See that point of rock thar? It's better cover," whispered Wetzel.

Patiently, with no hurry or excitement, they slowly made their difficult way among the rocks and ferns to the vantage point desired. Taking a position like this was one the bordermen strongly favored. They could see everywhere in front, and had the thick woods at their backs.

"What are they up to?" whispered Jonathan, as he and Wetzel lay close together under a mass of grapevine still tenacious of its broad leaves.

"Dicin'," answered Wetzel. "I can see 'em throw; anyways, nothin' but bettin' ever makes redskins act like that."

"Who's playin'? Where's Brandt?"

"I can make out Legget; see his shaggy head. The other must be Case. Brandt ain't in sight. Nursin' a hurt perhaps. Ah! See thar! Over under the big tree as stands dark-like agin the thicket. Thet's an Injun, an' he looks too quiet an' keen to suit me. We'll have a care of him."

"Must be playin' fer Mordaunt's gold."

"Like as not, for where'd them ruffians get any 'cept they stole it."

"Aha! They're gettin' up! See Legget walk away shakin' his big head. He's mad. Mebbe he'll be madder presently," growled Jonathan.

"Case's left alone. He's countin' his winnin's. Jack, look out fer more work took off our hands."

"By gum! See that Injun knock up a leveled rifle."

"I told you, an' thet redskin has his suspicions. He's seen us down along ther ridge. There's Helen, sittin' behind the biggest tree. Thet Injun guard, 'afore he moved, kept us from seein' her."

Jonathan made no answer to this; but his breath literally hissed through his clenched teeth.

"Thar goes the other outlaw," whispered Wetzel, as if his comrade could not see. "It's all up with Case. See the sneak bendin' down the bank. Now, thet's a poor way. It'd better be done from the front, walkin' up natural-like, instead of tryin' to cover thet wide stretch. Case'll see him or hear him sure. Thar, he's up now, an' crawlin'. He's too slow, too slow. Aha! I knew it—Case turns. Look at the outlaw spring! Well, did you see thet little cuss whip his knife? One more less fer us to quiet. Thet makes four, Jack, an' mebbe, soon, it'll be five."

"They're holdin' a council," said Jonathan.

"I see two Injuns sneakin' off into the woods, an' here comes thet guard. He's a keen redskin, Jack, fer we did come light through the brush. Mebbe it'd be well to stop his scoutin'."

"Lew, that villain Case is bullyin' Helen!" cried Jonathan.

"Sh-sh-h," whispered Wetzel.

"See! He's pulled her to her feet. Oh! He struck her! Oh!"

Jonathan leveled his rifle and would have fired, but for the iron grasp on his wrist.

"Hev you lost yer senses? It's full two hundred paces, an' too far fer your piece," said Wetzel in a whisper. "An' it ain't sense to try from here."

"Lend me your gun! Lend me your gun!"

Silently Wetzel handed him the long, black rifle.

Jonathan raised it, but trembled so violently that the barrel wavered like a leaf in the breeze.

"Take it, I can't cover him," groaned Jonathan. "This is new to me. I ain't myself. God! Lew, he struck her again! *Again!* He's tryin' to kiss her! Wetzel, if you're my friend, kill him!"

"Jack, it'd be better to wait, an'——"

"I love her," breathed Jonathan.

The long, black barrel swept up to a level and stopped. White smoke belched from among the green leaves; the report rang throughout the forest.

"Ah! I saw him stop an' pause," hissed Jonathan. "He stands, he sways, he falls! Death for yours, you sailor-beast!"

CHAPTER XX

THE bordermen watched Legget and his band disappear into the thicket adjoining the grove. When the last dark, lithe form glided out of sight among the yellowing copse, Jonathan leaped from the low cliff, and had hardly reached the ground before Wetzel dashed down to the grassy turf.

Again they followed the outlaw's trail, darker-faced, fiercervisaged than ever, with cocked, tightly-gripped rifles thrust well before them, and light feet that scarcely brushed the leaves.

Wetzel halted after a long tramp up and down the ridges, and surveyed with keen intent the lay of the land ahead.

"Sooner or later we'll hear from that redskin as discovered us a ways back," whispered he. "I wish we might get a crack at him afore he hinders us bad. I ain't seen many keener Injuns. It's lucky we fixed ther arrow-shootin' Shawnee. We'd never hev beat thet combination. An' fer all of thet I'm worrin' some about the goin' ahead."

"Ambush?" Jonathan asked.

"Like as not. Legget'll send thet Injun back, an' mebbe more'n him. Jack, see them little footprints? They're Helen's. Look how she's draggin' along. Almost tuckered out. Legget can't travel many more miles to-day. He'll make a stand somewheres, an' lose all his redskins afore he gives up the lass."

"I'll never live through to-night with her in that gang. She'll be saved, or dead, before the stars pale in the light of the moon."

"I reckon we're nigh the end for some of us. It'll be moon-light an hour arter dusk, an' now it's only the middle of the arternoon; we've time enough fer anythin'. Now, Jack, let's not tackle the trail straight. We'll split, an' go round to head 'em off. See thet dead white oak standin' high over thar?"

Jonathan looked out between the spreading branches of a beech, and saw, far over a low meadow, luxuriant with grasses and rushes and bright with sparkling ponds and streams, a dense wood out of which towered a bare, bleached tree-top.

"You slip around along the right side of this meader, an' I'll take the left side. Go slow, an' hev yer eyes open. We'll meet under thet big dead tree. I allow we can see it from anywhere around. We'll leave the trail here, an' take it up farther on.

Legget's goin' straight for his camp; he ain't losin' an inch.
He wants to get in that rocky hole of his'n."

Wetzel stepped off the trail, glided into the woods, and vanished.

Jonathan turned to the right, traversed the summit of the
ridge, softly traveled down its slope, and, after crossing a slow,
eddying, quiet stream, gained the edge of the forest on that
side of the swamp. A fringe of briars and prickly thorns bordered this wood affording an excellent cover. On the right the
land rose rather abruptly. He saw that by walking up a few
paces he could command a view of the entire swamp, as well as
the ridge beyond, which contained Wetzel, and, probably, the
outlaw and his band.

Remembering his comrade's admonition, Jonathan curbed his
unusual impatience and moved slowly. The wind swayed the
tree-tops, and rustled the fallen leaves. Birds sang as if thinking
the warm, soft weather was summer come again. Squirrels
dropped heavy nuts that cracked on the limbs, or fell with a
thud to the ground, and they scampered over the dry earth,
scratching up the leaves as they barked and scolded. Crows
cawed clamorously after a hawk that had darted under the
tree-tops to escape them; deer loped swiftly up the hill, and a
lordly elk rose from a wallow in the grassy swamp, crashing
into the thicket.

When two-thirds around this oval plain, which was a mile
long and perhaps one-fourth as wide, Jonathan ascended the
hill to make a survey. The grass waved bright brown and golden
in the sunshine, swished in the wind, and swept like a choppy
sea to the opposite ridge. The hill was not densely wooded.
In many places the red-brown foliage opened upon irregular
patches, some black, as if having been burned over, others show ·

ing the yellow and purple colors of the low thickets and the gray, barren stones.

Suddenly Jonathan saw something darken one of these sunlit plots. It might have been a deer. He studied the rolling, rounded tree-tops, the narrow strips between the black trunks, and the open places that were clear in the sunshine. He had nearly come to believe he had seen a small animal or bird flit across the white of the sky far in the background, when he distinctly saw dark figures stealing along past a green-gray rock, only to disappear under colored banks of foliage. Presently, lower down, they reappeared and crossed an open patch of yellow fern. Jonathan counted them. Two were rather yellow in color, the hue of buckskin; another, slight of stature as compared with the first, and light gray by contrast. Then six black, slender, gliding forms crossed the space. Jonathan then lost sight of them, and did not get another glimpse. He knew them to be Legget and his band. The slight figure was Helen.

Jonathan broke into a run, completed the circle around the swamp, and slowed into a walk when approaching the big dead tree where he was to wait for Wetzel.

Several rods beyond the lowland he came to a wood of white oaks, all giants rugged and old, with scarcely a sapling intermingled with them. Although he could not see the objective point, he knew from his accurate sense of distance that he was near it. As he entered the wood he swept its whole length and width with his eyes, he darted forward twenty paces to halt suddenly behind a tree. He knew full well that a sharply moving object was more difficult to see in the woods, than one stationary. Again he ran, fleet and light, a few paces ahead to take up a position as before behind a tree. Thus he traversed the forest.

On the other side he found the dead oak of which Wetzel had spoken.

Its trunk was hollow. Jonathan squeezed himself into the blackened space, with his head in a favorable position behind a projecting knot, where he could see what might occur near at hand.

He waited for what seemed to him a long while, during which he neither saw nor heard anything, and then, suddenly, the report of a rifle rang out. A single, piercing scream followed. Hardly had the echo ceased when three hollow reports, distinctly different in tone from the first, could be heard from the same direction. In quick succession short, fierce yells attended rather than succeeded, the reports.

Jonathan stepped out of the hiding-place, cocked his rifle, and fixed a sharp eye on the ridge before him whence those startling cries had come. The first rifle-shot, unlike any other in its short, spiteful, stinging quality, was unmistakably Wetzel's. Zane had heard it, followed many times, as now, by the wild death-cry of a savage. The other reports were of Indian guns, and the yells were the clamoring, exultant cries of Indians in pursuit.

Far down where the open forest met the gloom of the thickets, a brown figure flashed across the yellow ground. Darting among the trees, across the glades, it moved so swiftly that Jonathan knew it was Wetzel. In another instant a chorus of yelps resounded from the foliage, and three savages burst through the thicket almost at right angles with the fleeing borderman, running to intercept him. The borderman did not swerve from his course; but came on straight toward the dead tree, with the wonderful fleetness that so often had served him well.

Even in that moment Jonathan thought of what desperate chances his comrade had taken. The trick was plain. Wetzel had, most likely, shot the dangerous scout, and, taking to his heels, raced past the others, trusting to his speed and their poor marksmanship to escape with a whole skin.

When within a hundred yards of the oak Wetzel's strength apparently gave out. His speed deserted him; he ran awkwardly, and limped. The savages burst out into full cry like a pack of hungry wolves. They had already emptied their rifles at him, and now, supposing one of the shots had taken effect, redoubled their efforts, making the forest ring with their short, savage yells. One gaunt, dark-bodied Indian with a long, powerful, springy stride easily distanced his companions, and, evidently sure of gaining the coveted scalp of the borderman, rapidly closed the gap between them as he swung aloft his tomahawk, yelling the war-cry.

The sight on Jonathan's rifle had several times covered this savage's dark face; but when he was about to press the trigger Wetzel's fleeting form, also in line with the savage, made it extremely hazardous to take a shot.

Jonathan stepped from his place of concealment, and let out a yell that pealed high over the cries of the savages.

Wetzel suddenly dropped flat on the ground.

With a whipping crack of Jonathan's rifle, the big Indian plunged forward on his face.

The other Indians, not fifty yards away, stopped aghast at the fate of their comrade, and were about to seek the shelter of trees when, with his terrible yell, Wetzel sprang up and charged upon them. He had left his rifle where he fell; but his tomahawk glittered as he ran. The lameness had been a trick, for now he covered ground with a swiftness which caused his former progress to seem slow.

The Indians, matured and seasoned warriors though they

were, gave but one glance at this huge, brown figure bearing down upon them like a fiend, and, uttering the Indian name of *Deathwind,* wavered, broke and ran.

One, not so fleet as his companion, Wetzel overtook and cut down with a single stroke. The other gained an hundred-yard start in the slight interval of Wetzel's attack, and, spurred on by a pealing, awful cry in the rear, sped swiftly in and out among the trees until he was lost to view.

Wetzel scalped the two dead savages, and, after returning to regain his rifle, joined Jonathan at the dead oak.

"Jack, you can never tell how things is comin' out. Thet redskin I allowed might worry us a bit, fooled me as slick as you ever saw, an' I hed to shoot him. Knowin' it was a case of runnin', I just cut fer this oak, drew the redskins' fire, an' hed 'em arter me quicker 'n you'd say Jack Robinson. I was hopin' you'd be here; but wasn't sure till I'd seen your rifle. Then I kinder got a kink in my leg jest to coax the brutes on."

"Three more quiet," said Jonathan Zane. "What now?"

"We've headed Legget, an' we'll keep nosin' him off his course. Already he's lookin' fer a safe campin' place for the night."

"There is none in these woods, fer him."

"We didn't plan this gettin' between him an' his camp; but couldn't be better fixed. A mile farther along the ridge, is a campin' place, with a spring in a little dell close under a big stone, an' well wooded. Legget's headin' straight fer it. With a couple of Injuns guardin' thet spot, he'll think he's safe. But I know the place, an' can crawl to thet rock the darkest night thet ever was an' never crack a stick."

*   *   *   *   *   *

In the gray of the deepening twilight Jonathan Zane sat alone. An owl hooted dismally in the dark woods beyond the thicket where the borderman crouched waiting for Wetzel. His listening ear detected a soft, rustling sound like the play of a mole under the leaves. A branch trembled and swung back; a soft footstep followed and Wetzel came into the retreat.

"Well?" asked Jonathan impatiently, as Wetzel deliberately sat down and laid his rifle across his knees.

"Easy, Jack, easy. We've an hour to wait."

"The time I've already waited has been long for me."

"They're thar," said Wetzel grimly.

"How far from here?"

"A half-hour's slow crawl."

"Close by?" hissed Jonathan.

"Too near fer you to get excited."

"Let us go; it's as light now as in the gray of mornin'."

"Mornin' would be best. Injuns get sleepy along towards day. I've ever found thet time the best. But we'll be lucky if we ketch these redskins asleep."

"Lew, I can't wait here all night. I won't leave her longer with that renegade. I've got to free or kill her."

"Most likely it'll be the last," said Wetzel simply.

"Well, so be it then," and the borderman hung his head.

"You needn't worry none, 'bout Helen. I jest had a good look at her, not half an hour back. She's fagged out; but full of spunk yet. I seen thet when Brandt went near her. Legget's got his hands full jest now with the redskins. He's hevin' trouble keepin' them on this slow trail. I ain't sayin' they're skeered; but they're mighty restless."

"Will you take the chance now?"

"I reckon you needn't hev asked thet."

"Tell me the lay of the land."

"Wal, if we get to this rock I spoke 'bout, we'll be right over 'em. It's ten feet high, an' we can jump straight amongst 'em. Most likely two or three'll be guardin' the openin' which is a little ways to the right. Ther's a big tree, the only one, low down by the spring. Helen's under it, half-sittin', half-leanin' against the roots. When I first looked, her hands were free; but I saw Brandt bind her feet. An' he had to get an Injun to help him, fer she kicked like a spirited little filly. There's moss under the tree an' there's where the redskins'll lay down to rest."

"I've got that; now out with your plan."

"Wal, I calkilate it's this. The moon'll be up in about an hour. We'll crawl as we've never crawled afore, because Helen's life depends as much on our not makin' a noise, as it does on fightin' when the time comes. If they hear us afore we're ready to shoot, the lass'll be tomahawked quicker'n lightnin'. If they don't suspicion us, when the right moment comes you shoot Brandt, yell louder'n you ever did afore, leap amongst 'em, an' cut down the first Injun thet's near you on your way to Helen. Swing her over your arm, an' dig into the woods."

"Well?" asked Jonathan when Wetzel finished.

"That's all," the borderman replied grimly.

"An' leave you all alone to fight Legget an' the rest of 'em?"

"I reckon."

"Not to be thought of."

"Ther's no other way."

"There must be! Let me think; I can't, I'm not myself."

"No other way," repeated Wetzel curtly.

Jonathan's broad hand fastened on Wetzel's shoulder and wheeled him around.

"Have I ever left you alone?"

"This's different," and Wetzel turned away again. His voice was cold and hard.

"How is it different? We've had the same thing to do, almost, more than once."

"We've never had as bad a bunch to handle as Legget's. They're lookin' fer us, an' will be hard to beat."

"That's no reason."

"We never had to save a girl one of us loved."

Jonathan was silent.

"I said this'd be my last trail," continued Wetzel. "I felt it, an' I know it'll be yours."

"Why?"

"If you get away with the girl she'll keep you at home, an' it'll be well. If you don't succeed, you'll die tryin', so it's sure your last trail."

Wetzel's deep, cold voice rang with truth.

"Lew, I can't run away an' leave you to fight those devils alone, after all these years we've been together, I can't."

"No other chance to save the lass."

Jonathan quivered with the force of his emotion. His black eyes glittered; his hands grasped at nothing. Once more he was between love and duty. Again he fought over the old battle, but this time it left him weak.

"You love the big-eyed lass, don't you?" asked Wetzel, turning with softened face and voice.

"I have gone mad!" cried Jonathan, tortured by the simple question of his friend. Those big, dear, wonderful eyes he loved so well, looked at him now from the gloom of the thicket. The old, beautiful, soft glow, the tender light, was there, and more, a beseeching prayer to save her.

Jonathan bowed his head, ashamed to let his friend see the tears that dimmed his eyes.

"Jack, we've follered the trail fer years together. Always you've been true an' staunch. This is our last, but whatever bides we'll break up Legget's band to-night, an' the border'll be cleared, mebbe, for always. At least his race is run. Let thet content you. Our time'd have to come, sooner or later, so why not now? I know how it is, that you want to stick by me; but the lass draws you to her. I understand, an' want you to save her. Mebbe you never dreamed it; but I can tell jest how you feel. All the tremblin', an' softness, an' sweetness, an' delight you've got for thet girl, is no mystery to Lew Wetzel."

"You loved a lass?"

Wetzel bowed his head, as perhaps he had never before in all his life.

"Betty—always," he answered softly.

"My sister!" exclaimed Jonathan, and then his hand closed hard on his comrade's, his mind going back to many things, strange in the past, but now explained. Wetzel had revealed his secret.

"An' it's been all my life, since she wasn't higher 'n my knee. There was a time when I might hev been closer to you than I am now. But I was a mad an' bloody Injun hater, so I never let her know till I seen it was too late. Wal, wal, no more of me. I only told it fer you."

Jonathan was silent.

"An' now to come back where we left off," continued Wetzel. "Let's take a more hopeful look at this comin' fight. Sure I said it was my last trail, but mebbe it's not. You can never tell. Feelin' as we do, I imagine they've no odds on us. Never in my life did I say to you, least of all to any one else, what I was goin' to do; but I'll tell it now. If I land uninjured amongst thet bunch, I'll kill them all."

The giant borderman's low voice hissed, and stung. His eyes

glittered with unearthly fire. His face was cold and gray. He spread out his brawny arms and clenched his huge fists, making the muscles of his broad shoulders roll and bulge.

"I hate the thought, Lew, I hate the thought. Ain't there no other way?"

"No other way."

"I'll do it, Lew, because I'd do the same for you; because I have to, because I love her; but God! it hurts."

"Thet's right," answered Wetzel, his deep voice softening until it was singularly low and rich. "I'm glad you've come to it. An' sure it hurts. I want you to feel so at leavin' me to go it alone. If we both get out alive, I'll come many times to see you an' Helen. If you live an' I don't, think of me sometimes, think of the trails we've crossed together. When the fall comes with its soft, cool air, an' smoky mornin's an' starry nights, when the wind's sad among the bare branches, an' the leaves drop down, remember they're fallin' on my grave."

Twilight darkened into gloom; the red tinge in the west changed to opal light; through the trees over a dark ridge a rim of silver glinted and moved.

The moon had risen; the hour was come.

The bordermen tightened their belts, replaced their leggings, tied their hunting coats, loosened their hatchets, looked to the priming of their rifles, and were ready.

Wetzel walked twenty paces and turned. His face was white in the moonlight; his dark eyes softened into a look of love as he gripped his comrade's outstretched hand.

Then he dropped flat on the ground, carefully saw to the position of his rifle, and began to creep. Jonathan kept close at his heels.

Slowly but steadily they crawled, minute after minute. The

hazel-nut bushes above them had not yet shed their leaves; the ground was clean and hard, and the course fatefully perfect for their deadly purpose.

A slight rustling of their buckskin garments sounded like the rustling of leaves in a faint breeze.

The moon came out above the trees and still Wetzel advanced softly, steadily, surely.

The owl, lonely sentinel of that wood, hooted dismally. Even his night eyes, which made the darkness seem clear as day, missed those gliding figures. Even he, sure guardian of the wilderness, failed the savages.

Jonathan felt soft moss beneath him; he was now in the woods under the trees. The thicket had been passed.

Wetzel's moccasin pressed softly against Jonathan's head. The first signal!

Jonathan crawled forward, and slightly raised himself.

He was on a rock. The trees were thick and gloomy. Below, the little hollow was almost in the wan moonbeams. Dark figures lay close together. Two savages paced noiselessly to and fro. A slight form rolled in a blanket lay against a tree.

Jonathan felt his arm gently squeezed.

The second signal!

Slowly he thrust forward his rifle, and raised it in unison with Wetzel's. Slowly he rose to his feet as if the same muscles guided them both.

Over his head a twig snapped. In the darkness he had not seen a low branch.

The Indian guards stopped suddenly, and became motionless as stone.

They had heard; but too late.

With the blended roar of the rifles both dropped, lifeless.

Almost under the spouting flame and white cloud or smoke, Jonathan leaped behind Wetzel, over the bank. His yells were mingled with Wetzel's vengeful cry. Like leaping shadows the bordermen were upon their foes.

An Indian sprang up, raised a weapon, and fell beneath Jonathan's savage blow, to rise no more. Over his prostrate body the borderman bounded. A dark, nimble form darted upon the captive. He swung high a blade that shone like silver in the moonlight. His shrill war-cry of death rang out with Helen's scream of despair. Even as he swung back her head with one hand in her long hair, his arm descended; but it fell upon the borderman's body. Jonathan and the Indian rolled upon the moss. There was a terrific struggle, a whirling blade, a dull blow which silenced the yell, and the borderman rose alone.

He lifted Helen as if she were a child, leaped the brook, and plunged into the thicket.

The noise of the fearful conflict he left behind, swelled high and hideously on the night air. Above the shrill cries of the Indians, and the furious yells of Legget, rose the mad, booming roar of Wetzel. No rifle cracked; but sodden blows, the clash of steel, the threshing of struggling men, told of the dreadful strife.

Jonathan gained the woods, sped through the moonlit glades, and far on under light and shadow.

The shrill cries ceased; only the hoarse yells and the mad roar could be heard. Gradually these also died away, and the forest was still.

CHAPTER XXI

NEXT MORNING, when the mist was breaking and rolling away under the warm rays of the Indian-summer sun, Jonathan Zane beached his canoe on the steep bank before Fort Henry. A pioneer, attracted by the borderman's halloo, ran to the bluff and sounded the alarm with shrill whoops. Among the hurrying, brown-clad figures that answered this summons, was Colonel Zane.

"It's Jack, kurnel, an' he's got her!" cried one.

The doughty colonel gained the bluff to see his brother climbing the bank with a white-faced girl in his arms.

"Well?" he asked, looking darkly at Jonathan. Nothing kindly or genial was visible in his manner now; rather grim and forbidding he seemed, thus showing he had the same blood in his veins as the borderman.

"Lend a hand," said Jonathan. "As far as I know she's not hurt."

They carried Helen toward Colonel Zane's cabin. Many women of the settlement saw them as they passed, and looked gravely at one another, but none spoke. This return of an abducted girl was by no means a strange event.

"Somebody run for Sheppard," ordered Colonel Zane, as they entered his cabin.

Betty, who was in the sitting-room, sprang up and cried: "Oh! Eb! Eb! Don't say she's——"

"No, no, Betts, she's all right. Where's my wife? Ah! Bess, here, get to work."

The colonel left Helen in the tender, skilful hands of his wife and sister, and followed Jonathan into the kitchen.

"I was just ready for breakfast when I heard some one yell," said he. "Come, Jack, eat something."

They ate in silence. From the sitting-room came excited whispers, a joyous cry from Betty, and a faint voice. Then heavy, hurrying footsteps, followed by Sheppard's words of thanksgiving.

"Where's Wetzel?" began Colonel Zane.

The borderman shook his head gloomily.

"Where did you leave him?"

"We jumped Legget's bunch last night, when the moon was about an hour high. I reckon about fifteen miles northeast. I got away with the lass."

"Ah! Left Lew fighting?"

The borderman answered the question with bowed head.

"You got off well. Not a hurt that I can see, and more than lucky to save Helen. Well, Jack, what do you think about Lew?"

"I'm goin' back," replied Jonathan.

"No! no!"

The door opened to admit Mrs. Zane. She looked bright and cheerful. "Hello, Jack; glad you're home. Helen's all right, only faint from hunger and over-exertion. I want something for her to eat—well! you men didn't leave much."

Colonel Zane went into the sitting-room. Sheppard sat beside the couch where Helen lay, white and wan. Betty and Nell were looking on with their hearts in their eyes. Silas Zane was there, and his wife, with several women neighbors.

"Betty, go fetch Jack in here," whispered the colonel in his sister's ear. "Drag him, if you have to," he added fiercely.

The young woman left the room, to reappear directly with her brother. He came in reluctantly.

As the stern-faced borderman crossed the threshold a smile, beautiful to see, dawned in Helen's eyes.

"I'm glad to see you're comin' round," said Jonathan, but he spoke dully as if his mind was on other things.

"She's a little flighty; but a night's sleep will cure that," cried Mrs. Zane from the kitchen.

"What do you think?" interrupted the colonel. "Jack's not satisfied to get back with Helen unharmed, and a whole skin himself; but he's going on the trail again."

"No, Jack, no, no!" cried Betty.

"What's that I hear?" asked Mrs. Zane as she came in. "Jack's going out again? Well, all I want to say is that he's as mad as a March hare."

"Jonathan, look here," said Silas seriously. "Can't you stay home now?"

"Jack, listen," whispered Betty, going close to him. "Not one of us ever expected to see either you or Helen again, and oh! we are so happy. Do not go away again. You are a man; you do not know, you cannot understand all a woman feels. She must sit and wait, and hope, and pray for the safe return of husband or brother or sweetheart. The long days! Oh, the long sleepless nights, with the wail of the wind in the pines, and the rain on the roof! It is maddening. Do not leave us! Do not leave me! Do not leave Helen! Say you will not, Jack."

To these entreaties the borderman remained silent. He stood leaning on his rifle, a tall, dark, strangely sad and stern man.

"Helen, beg him to stay!" implored Betty.

Colonel Zane took Helen's hand, and stroked it. "Yes," he said, "you ask him, lass. I'm sure you can persuade him to stay."

Helen raised her head. "Is Brandt dead?" she whispered faintly.

Still the borderman failed to speak, but his silence was not an affirmative.

"You said you loved me," she cried wildly. "You said you loved me, yet you didn't kill that monster!"

The borderman, moving quickly like a startled Indian, went out of the door.

* * * * * *

Once more Jonathan Zane entered the gloomy, quiet aisles of the forest with his soft, tireless tread hardly stirring the leaves.

It was late in the afternoon when he had long left Two Islands behind, and arrived at the scene of Mordaunt's death. Satisfied with the distance he had traversed, he crawled into a thicket to rest.

Daybreak found him again on the trail. He made a short cut over the ridges and by the time the mist had lifted from the valley he was within stalking distance of the glade. He approached this in the familiar, slow, cautious manner, and halted behind the big rock from which he and Wetzel had leaped. The wood was solemnly quiet. No twittering of birds could be heard. The only sign of life was a gaunt timber-wolf slinking away amid the foliage. Under the big tree the savage who had been killed as he would have murdered Helen, lay a crumpled mass where he had fallen. Two dead Indians were in the center of the glade, and on the other side were three more bloody, lifeless forms. Wetzel was not there, nor Legget, nor Brandt.

"I reckoned so," muttered Jonathan as he studied the scene. The grass had been trampled, the trees barked, the bushes crushed aside.

Jonathan went out of the glade a short distance, and, circling it, began to look for Wetzel's trail. He found it, and near the light footprints of his comrade were the great, broad moccasin tracks of the outlaw. Further searching disclosed the fact that Brandt must have traveled in line with the others.

With the certainty that Wetzel had killed three of the Indians, and, in some wonderful manner characteristic of him, routed the outlaws of whom he was now in pursuit, Jonathan's smoldering emotion burst forth into full flame. Love for his old comrade, deadly hatred of the outlaws, and passionate thirst for their blood, rioted in his heart.

Like a lynx scenting its quarry, the borderman started on the trail, tireless and unswervable. The traces left by the fleeing outlaws and their pursuer were plain to Jonathan. It was not necessary for him to stop. Legget and Brandt, seeking to escape the implacable Nemesis, were traveling with all possible speed, regardless of the broad trail such hurried movements left behind. They knew full well it would be difficult to throw this wolf off the scent; understood that if any attempt was made to ambush the trail, they must cope with woodcraft keener than an Indian's. Flying in desperation, they hoped to reach the rocky retreat, where, like foxes in their burrows, they believed themselves safe.

When the sun sloped low toward the western horizon, lengthening Jonathan's shadow, he slackened pace. He was entering the rocky, rugged country which marked the approach to the distant Alleghenies. From the top of a ridge he took his bearings, deciding that he was within a few miles of Legget's hiding-place.

At the foot of this ridge, where a murmuring brook sped softly over its bed, he halted. Here a number of horses had forded the brook. They were iron-shod, which indicated almost to a certainty, that they were stolen horses, and in the hands of Indians.

Jonathan saw where the trail of the steeds was merged into that of the outlaws. He suspected that the Indians and Legget had held a short council. As he advanced the borderman found only the faintest impression of Wetzel's trail. Legget and Brandt no longer left any token of their course. They were riding the horses.

All the borderman cared to know was if Wetzel still pursued. He passed on swiftly up a hill, through a wood of birches where the trail showed on a line of broken ferns, then out upon a low ridge where patches of grass grew sparsely. Here he saw in this last ground no indication of his comrade's trail; nothing was to be seen save the imprints of the horses' hoofs. Jonathan halted behind the nearest underbrush. This sudden move on the part of Wetzel was token that, suspecting an ambush, he had made a detour somewhere, probably in the grove of birches.

All the while his eyes searched the long, barren reach ahead. No thicket, fallen tree, or splintered rocks, such as Indians utilized for an ambush, could be seen. Indians always sought the densely matted underbrush, a windfall, or rocky retreat and there awaited a pursuer. It was one of the borderman's tricks of woodcraft that he could recognize such places.

Far beyond the sandy ridge Jonathan came to a sloping, wooded hillside, upon which were scattered big rocks, some mossy and lichen-covered, and one, a giant boulder, with a crown of ferns and laurel gracing its flat surface. It was such a place as the savages would select for ambush. He knew, however, that if an Indian had hidden himself there Wetzel would have discovered him. When opposite the rock Jonathan saw a broken fern hanging over the edge. The heavy trail of the horses ran close beside it.

Then with that thoroughness of search which made the

borderman what he was, Jonathan leaped upon the rock. There, lying in the midst of the ferns, lay an Indian with sullen, somber face set in the repose of death. In his side was a small bullet hole.

Jonathan examined the savage's rifle. It had been discharged. The rock, the broken fern, the dead Indian, the discharged rifle, told the story of that woodland tragedy.

Wetzel had discovered the ambush. Leaving the trail, he had tricked the redskin into firing, then getting a glimpse of the Indian's red body through the sights of his fatal weapon, the deed was done.

With greater caution Jonathan advanced once more. Not far beyond the rock he found Wetzel's trail. The afternoon was drawing to a close. He could not travel much farther, yet he kept on, hoping to overtake his comrade before darkness set in. From time to time he whistled; but got no answering signal.

When the tracks of the horses were nearly hidden by the gathering dusk, Jonathan decided to halt for the night. He whistled one more note, louder and clearer, and awaited the result with strained ears. The deep silence of the wilderness prevailed, suddenly to be broken by a faint, far-away, melancholy call of the hermit-thrush. It was the answering signal the borderman had hoped to hear.

Not many moments elapsed before he heard another call, low, and near at hand, to which he replied. The bushes parted noiselessly on his left, and the tall form of Wetzel appeared silently out of the gloom.

The two gripped hands in silence.

"Hev you any meat?" Wetzel asked, and as Jonathan handed him his knapsack, he continued, "I was kinder lookin' fer you. Did you get out all right with the lass?"

"Nary a scratch."

The giant borderman grunted his satisfaction.

"How'd Legget and Brandt get away?" asked Jonathan.

"Cut an' run like scared bucks. Never got a hand on either of 'em."

"How many redskins did they meet back here a spell?"

"They was seven; but now there are only six, an' all snug in Legget's place by this time."

"I reckon we're near his den."

"We're not far off."

Night soon closing down upon the bordermen found them wrapped in slumber, as if no deadly foes were near at hand. The soft night wind sighed dismally among the bare trees. A few bright stars twinkled overhead. In the darkness of the forest the bordermen were at home.

CHAPTER XXII

In Legget's rude log cabin a fire burned low, lightening the forms of the two border outlaws, and showing in the background the dark forms of Indians sitting motionless on the floor. Their dusky eyes emitted a baleful glint, seemingly a reflection of their savage souls caught by the firelight. Legget wore a look of ferocity and sullen fear strangely blended. Brandt's face was hard and haggard, his lips set, his gray eyes smoldering.

"Safe?" he hissed. "Safe you say? You'll see that it's the same now as on the other night, when those border-tigers jumped us and we ran like cowards. I'd have fought it out here, but for you."

"Thet man Wetzel is ravin' mad, I tell you," growled Legget. "I reckon I've stood my ground enough to know I ain't no coward. But this fellar's crazy. He hed the Injuns slashin' each other like a pack of wolves round a buck."

"He's no more mad than you or I," declared Brandt. "I know all about him. His moaning in the woods, and wild yells are only tricks. He knows the Indian nature, and he makes their very superstition and religion aid him in his fighting. I told you what he'd do. Didn't I beg you to kill Zane when we had a chance? Wetzel would never have taken our trail alone. Now they've beat me out of the girl, and as sure as death will round us up here."

"You don't believe they'll rush us here?" asked Legget.

"They're too keen to take foolish chances, but something will be done we don't expect. Zane was a prisoner here; he had a good look at this place, and you can gamble he'll remember."

"Zane must hev gone back to Fort Henry with the girl."

"Mark what I say, he'll come back!"

"Wal, we kin hold this place against all the men Eb Zane may put out."

"He won't send a man," snapped Brandt passionately. "Remember this, Legget, we're not to fight against soldiers, settlers, or hunters; but bordermen—understand—bordermen! Such as have been developed right here on this bloody frontier, and nowhere else on earth. They haven't fear in them. Both are fleet as deer in the woods. They can't be seen or trailed. They can snuff a candle with a rifle ball in the dark. I've seen Zane do it three times at a hundred yards. And Wetzel! He wouldn't waste powder on practicing. They can't be ambushed, or shaken.

off a track; they take the scent like buzzards, and have eyes like eagles."

"We kin slip out of here under cover of night," suggested Legget.

"Well, what then? That's all they want. They'd be on us again by sunset. No! we've got to stand our ground and fight. We'll stay as long as we can; but they'll rout us out somehow, be sure of that. And if one of us pokes his nose out to the daylight, it will be shot off."

"You're sore, an' you've lost your nerve," said Legget harshly. "Sore at me 'cause I got sweet on the girl. Ho! ho!"

Brandt shot a glance at Legget which boded no good. His strong hands clenched in an action betraying the reckless rage in his heart. Then he carefully removed his hunting coat, and examined his wound. He retied the bandage, muttering gloomily, "I'm so weak as to be light-headed. If this cut opens again, it's all day for me."

After that the inmates of the hut were quiet. The huge outlaw bowed his shaggy head for a while, and then threw himself on a pile of hemlock boughs. Brandt was not long in seeking rest. Soon both were fast asleep. Two of the savages passed out with cat-like step, leaving the door open. The fire had burned low, leaving a bed of dead coals. Outside in the dark a waterfall splashed softly.

The darkest hour came, and passed, and paled slowly to gray. Birds began to twitter. Through the door of the cabin the light of day streamed in. The two Indian sentinels were building a fire on the stone hearth. One by one the other savages got up, stretched and yawned, and began the business of the day by cooking their breakfast. It was, apparently, every one for himself.

Legget arose, shook himself like a shaggy dog, and was starting for the door when one of the sentinels stopped him. Brandt, who was now awake, saw the action, and smiled.

In a few moments Indians and outlaws were eating for breakfast roasted strips of venison, with corn meal baked brown, which served as bread. It was a somber, silent group.

Presently the shrill neigh of a horse startled them. Following it, the whip-like crack of a rifle stung and split the morning air. Hard on this came an Indian's long, wailing death-cry.

"Hah!" exclaimed Brandt.

Legget remained immovable. One of the savages peered out through a little port-hole at the rear of the hut. The others continued their meal.

"Whistler'll come in presently to tell us who's doin' thet shootin'," said Legget. "He's a keen Injun."

"He's not very keen now," replied Brandt, with bitter certainty. "He's what the settlers call a good Indian, which is to say, dead!"

Legget scowled at his lieutenant.

"I'll go an' see," he replied and seized his rifle.

He opened the door, when another rifle-shot rang out. A bullet whistled in the air, grazing the outlaw's shoulder, and imbedded itself in the heavy door-frame.

Legget leaped back with a curse.

"Close shave!" said Brandt coolly. "That bullet came, probably, straight down from the top of the cliff. Jack Zane's there. Wetzel is lower down watching the outlet. We're trapped."

"Trapped," shouted Legget with an angry leer. "We kin live here longer'n the bordermen kin. We've meat on hand, an' a good spring in the back of the hut. How'er we trapped?"

"We won't live twenty-four hours," declared Brandt.

"Why?"

"Because we'll be routed out. They'll find some way to do it, and we'll never have another chance to fight in the open, as we had the other night when they came after the girl. From now on there'll be no sleep, no time to eat, the nameless fear of an unseen foe who can't be shaken off, marching by night, hiding and starving by day, until——! I'd rather be back in Fort Henry at Colonel Zane's mercy."

Legget turned a ghastly face toward Brandt. "Look a here. You're takin' a lot of glee in sayin' these things. I believe you've lost your nerve, or the lettin' out of a little blood hes made you wobbly. We've Injuns here, an' ought to be a match fer two men."

Brandt gazed at him with a derisive smile.

"We kin go out an' fight these fellars," continued Legget. "We might try their own game, hidin' an' crawlin' through the woods."

"We two would have to go it alone. If you still had your trusty, trained band of experienced Indians, I'd say that would be just the thing. But Ashbow and the Chippewa are dead; so are the others. This bunch of redskins here may do to steal a few horses; but they don't amount to much against Zane and Wetzel. Besides, they'll cut and run presently, for they're scared and suspicious. Look at the chief; ask him."

The savage Brandt indicated was a big Indian just coming into manhood. His swarthy face still retained some of the frankness and simplicity of youth.

"Chief," said Legget in the Indian tongue. "The great paleface hunter, Deathwind, lies hid in the woods."

"Last night the Shawnee heard the wind of death mourn through the trees," replied the chief gloomily.

"See! What did I say?" cried Brandt. "The superstitious fool! He would begin his death-chant almost without a fight. We can't count on the redskins. What's to be done?"

The outlaw threw himself upon the bed of boughs, and Legget sat down with his rifle across his knees. The Indians maintained the same stoical composure. The moments dragged by into hours.

"Ugh!" suddenly exclaimed the Indian at the end of the hut.

Legget ran to him, and acting upon a motion of the Indian's hand, looked out through the little port-hole.

The sun was high. He saw four of the horses grazing by the brook; then gazed scrutinizingly from the steep waterfall, along the green-stained cliff to the dark narrow cleft in the rocks. Here was the only outlet from the inclosure. He failed to discover anything unusual.

The Indian grunted again, and pointed upward.

"Smoke! There's smoke risin' above the trees," cried Legget. "Brandt, come here. What's thet mean?"

Brandt hurried, looked out. His face paled, his lower jaw protruded, quivered, and then was shut hard. He walked away, put his foot on a bench and began to lace his leggings.

"Wal?" demanded Legget.

"The game's up! Get ready to run and be shot at," cried Brandt with a hiss of passion.

Almost as he spoke the roof of the hut shook under a heavy blow.

"What's thet?" No one replied. Legget glanced from Brandt's cold, determined face to the uneasy savages. They were restless, and handling their weapons. The chief strode across the floor with stealthy steps.

"Thud!"

A repetition of the first blow caused the Indians to jump, and drew a fierce imprecation from their outlaw leader.

Brandt eyed him narrowly. "It's coming to you, Legget. They are shooting arrows of fire into the roof from the cliff. Zane is doin' that. He can make a bow and draw one, too. We're to be burned out. Now, damn you! take your medicine! I wanted you to kill him when you had the chance. If you had done so we'd never have come to this. Burned out, do you get that? Burned out!"

"Fire!" exclaimed Legget. He sat down as if the strength had left his legs.

The Indians circled around the room like caged tigers.

"Ugh!" The chief suddenly reached up and touched the birch-bark roof of the hut.

His action brought the attention of all to a faint crackling of burning wood.

"It's caught all right," cried Brandt in a voice which cut the air like a blow from a knife.

"I'll not be smoked like a ham, fer all these tricky bordermen," roared Legget. Drawing his knife he hacked at the heavy buckskin hinges of the rude door. When it dropped free he measured it against the open space. Sheathing the blade, he grasped his rifle in his right hand and swung the door on his left arm. Heavy though it was he carried it easily. The roughly hewn planks afforded a capital shield for all except the lower portion of his legs and feet. He went out of the hut with the screen of wood between himself and the cliff, calling for the Indians to follow. They gathered behind him, breathing hard, clutching their weapons, and seemingly almost crazed by excitement.

Brandt, with no thought of joining this foolhardy attempt to escape from the inclosure, ran to the little port-hole that he might see the outcome. Legget and his five redskins were running toward the narrow outlet in the gorge. The awkward and futile efforts of the Indians to remain behind the shield were almost pitiful. They crowded each other for favorable positions, but, struggle as they might, one or two were always exposed to the cliff. Suddenly one, pushed to the rear, stopped simultaneously with the crack of a rifle, threw up his arms and fell. Another report, differing from the first, rang out. A savage staggered from behind the speeding group with his hand at his side. Then he dropped into the brook.

Evidently Legget grasped this as a golden opportunity, for he threw aside the heavy shield and sprang forward, closely followed by his red-skinned allies. Immediately they came near the cliff, where the trail ran into the gorge, a violent shaking of the dry ferns overhead made manifest the activity of some heavy body. Next instant a huge yellow figure, not unlike a leaping cata-mount, plunged down with a roar so terrible as to sound in-human. Legget, Indians, and newcomer rolled along the declivity toward the brook in an indistinguishable mass.

Two of the savages shook themselves free, and bounded to their feet nimbly as cats, but Legget and the other redskin became engaged in a terrific combat. It was a wrestling whirl, so fierce and rapid as to render blows ineffectual. The leaves scattered as if in a whirlwind. Legget's fury must have been awful, to judge from his hoarse screams; the Indians' fear mad-dening, as could be told by their shrieks. The two savages ran wildly about the combatants, one trying to level a rifle, the other to get in a blow with a tomahawk. But the movements of the trio, locked in deadly embrace, were too swift.

Above all the noise of the contest rose that strange, thrilling roar.

"Wetzel!" muttered Brandt, with a chill, creeping shudder as he gazed upon the strife with fascinated eyes.

"Bang!" Again from the cliff came that heavy bellow.

The savage with the rifle shrunk back as if stung, and without a cry fell limply in a heap. His companion, uttering a frightened cry, fled from the glen.

The struggle seemed too deadly, too terrible, to last long. The Indian and the outlaw were at a disadvantage. They could not strike freely. The whirling conflict grew more fearful. During one second the huge, brown, bearish figure of Legget appeared on top; then the dark-bodied, half-naked savage, spotted like a hyena, and finally the lithe, powerful, tiger-shape of the borderman.

Finally Legget wrenched himself free at the same instant that the bloody-stained Indian rolled, writhing in convulsions, away from Wetzel. The outlaw dashed with desperate speed up the trail, and disappeared in the gorge. The borderman sped toward the cliff, leaped on a projecting ledge, grasped an overhanging branch, and pulled himself up. He was out of sight almost as quickly as Legget.

"After his rifle," Brandt muttered, and then realized that he had watched the encounter without any idea of aiding his comrade. He consoled himself with the knowledge that such an attempt would have been useless. From the moment the borderman sprang upon Legget, until he scaled the cliff, his movements had been incredibly swift. It would have been hardly possible to cover him with a rifle, and the outlaw grimly understood that he needed to be careful of that charge in his weapon.

"By Heavens, Wetzel's a wonder!" cried Brandt in unwilling admiration. "Now he'll go after Legget and the redskin, while Zane stays here to get me. Well, he'll succeed, most likely, but I'll never quit. What's this?"

He felt something slippery and warm on his hand. It was blood running from the inside of his sleeve. A slight pain made itself felt in his side. Upon examination he found, to his dismay, that his wound had reopened. With a desperate curse he pulled a linsey jacket off a peg, tore it into strips, and bound up the injury as tightly as possible.

Then he grasped his rifle, and watched the cliff and the gorge with flaring eyes. Suddenly he found it difficult to breathe; his throat was parched, his eyes smarted. Then the odor of woodsmoke brought him to a realization that the cabin was burning. It was only now he understood that the room was full of blue clouds. He sank into the corner, a wolf at bay.

Not many moments passed before the outlaw understood that he could not withstand the increasing heat and stifling vapor of the room. Pieces of burning birch dropped from the roof. The crackling above grew into a steady roar.

"I've got to run for it," he gasped. Death awaited him outside the door, but that was more acceptable than death by fire. Yet to face the final moment when he desired with all his soul to live, required almost super-human courage. Sweating, panting, he glared around. "God! Is there no other way?" he cried in agony. At this moment he saw an ax on the floor.

Seizing it he attacked the wall of the cabin. Beyond this partition was a hut which had been used for a stable. Half a dozen strokes of the ax opened a hole large enough for him to pass through. With his rifle, and a piece of venison which hung near, he literally fell through the hole, where he lay choking, almost fainting. After a time he crawled across the floor to a door. Outside was a dense laurel thicket, into which he crawled.

The crackling and roaring of the fire grew louder. He could see the column of yellow and black smoke. Once fairly under way, the flames rapidly consumed the pitch-pine logs. In an hour Legget's cabins were a heap of ashes.

The afternoon waned. Brandt lay watchful, slowly recovering his strength. He felt secure under this cover, and only prayed for night to come. As the shadows began to creep down the sides of the cliffs, he indulged in hope. If he could slip out in the dark he had a good chance to elude the borderman. In the passionate desire to escape, he had forgotten his fatalistic words to Legget. He reasoned that he could not be trailed until daylight; that a long night's march would put him far in the lead, and there was just a possibility of Zane's having gone away with Wetzel.

When darkness had set in he slipped out of the covert and began his journey for life. Within a few yards he reached the brook. He had only to follow its course in order to find the outlet to the glen. Moreover, its rush and gurgle over the stones would drown any slight noise he might make.

Slowly, patiently he crawled, stopping every moment to listen. What a long time he was in coming to the mossy stones over which the brook dashed through the gorge! But he reached them at last. Here if anywhere Zane would wait for him.

With teeth clenched desperately, and an inward tightening of his chest, for at any moment he expected to see the red flame of a rifle, he slipped cautiously over the mossy stones. Finally his hands touched the dewy grass, and a breath of cool wind fanned his hot cheek. He had succeeded in reaching the open. Crawling some rods farther on, he lay still a while and listened. The solemn wilderness calm was unbroken. Rising, he peered about. Behind loomed the black hill with its narrow cleft just discernible. Facing the north star, he went silently out into the darkness.

CHAPTER XXIII

AT DAYLIGHT Jonathan Zane rolled from his snug bed of leaves under the side of a log, and with the flint, steel and punk he always carried, began building a fire. His actions were far from being hurried. They were deliberate, and seemed strange on the part of a man whose stern face suggested some dark business to be done. When his little fire had been made, he warmed some slices of venison which had already been cooked, and thus satisfied his hunger. Carefully extinguishing the fire and looking to the priming of his rifle, he was ready for the trail.

He stood near the edge of the cliff from which he could command a view of the glen. The black, smoldering ruins of the burned cabins defaced a picturesque scene.

"Brandt must have lit out last night, for I could have seen even a rabbit hidin' in that laurel patch. He's gone, an' it's what I wanted," thought the borderman.

He made his way slowly around the edge of the inclosure and clambered down on the splintered cliff at the end of the gorge. A wide, well-trodden trail extended into the forest below. Jonathan gave scarcely a glance to the beaten path before him; but bent keen eyes to the north, and carefully scrutinized the mossy stones along the brook. Upon a little sand bar running out from the bank he found the light imprint of a hand.

"It was a black night. He'd have to travel by the stars, an' north's the only safe direction for him," muttered the borderman.

On the bank above he found oblong indentations in the grass, barely perceptible, but owing to the peculiar position of the blades of grass, easy for him to follow.

"He'd better have learned to walk light as an Injun before he took to outlawin'," said the borderman in disdain. Then he returned to the gorge and entered the inclosure. At the foot of the little rise of ground where Wetzel had leaped upon his quarry, was one of the dead Indians. Another lay partly submerged in the brown water.

Jonathan carried the weapons of the savages to a dry place under a projecting ledge in the cliff. Passing on down the glen, he stopped a moment where the cabins had stood. Not a log remained. The horses, with the exception of two, were tethered in the copse of laurel. He recognized Colonel Zane's thoroughbred, and Betty's pony. He cut them loose, positive they would not stray from the glen, and might easily be secured at another time.

He set out upon the trail of Brandt with a long, swinging stride. To him the outcome of that pursuit was but a question of time. The consciousness of superior endurance, speed, and craft spoke in his every movement. The consciousness of being in right, a factor so powerfully potent for victory, spoke in the intrepid front with which he faced the north.

It was a gloomy November day. Gray, steely clouds drifted overhead. The wind wailed through the bare trees, sending dead leaves scurrying and rustling over the brown earth.

The borderman advanced with a step that covered glade and glen, forest and field, with astonishing swiftness. Long since he had seen that Brandt was holding to the lowland. This did not strike him as singular until for the third time he found the trail lead a short distance up the side of a ridge, then descend, seeking a level. With this discovery came the certainty that Brandt's pace was lessening. He had set out with a hunter's stride, but it had begun to shorten. The outlaw had shirked the hills, and shifted from his northern course. Why? The man was weakening; he could not climb; he was favoring a wound.

What seemed more serious for the outlaw, was the fact that he had left a good trail, and entered the low, wild land north of the Ohio. Even the Indians seldom penetrated this tangled belt of laurel and thorn. Owing to the dry season the swamps were shallow, which was another factor against Brandt. No doubt he had hoped to hide his trail by wading, and here it showed up like the track of a bison.

Jonathan kept steadily on, knowing the farther Brandt penetrated into this wilderness the worse off he would be. The outlaw dared not take to the river until below Fort Henry, which was distant many a weary mile. The trail grew more ragged as the afternoon wore away. When twilight rendered further tracking impossible, the borderman built a fire in a sheltered place, ate his supper, and went to sleep.

In the dim, gray morning light he awoke, fancying he had been startled by a distant rifle shot. He roasted his strips of venison carefully, and ate with a hungry hunter's appreciation, yet sparingly, as befitted a borderman who knew how to keep up his strength upon a long trail.

Hardly had he traveled a mile when Brandt's footprints covered another's. Nothing surprised the borderman; but he had expected this least of all. A hasty examination convinced him that Legget and his Indian ally had fled this way with Wetzel in pursuit.

The morning passed slowly. The borderman kept to the trail like a hound. The afternoon wore on. Over sandy reaches thick with willows, and through long, matted, dried-out cranberry marshes and copses of prickly thorn, the borderman hung to his purpose. His legs seemed never to lose their spring, but his chest began to heave, his head bent, and his face shone with sweat.

At dusk he tired. Crawling into a dry thicket, he ate his scanty meal and fell asleep. When he awoke it was gray daylight. He was wet and chilled. Again he kindled a fire, and sat over it while cooking breakfast.

Suddenly he was brought to his feet by the sound of a rifle shot; then two others followed in rapid succession. Though they were faint, and far away to the west, Jonathan recognized the first, which could have come only from Wetzel's weapon, and he felt reasonably certain of the third, which was Brandt's. There might have been, he reflected grimly, a good reason for Legget's not shooting. However, he knew that Wetzel had rounded up the fugitives, and again he set out.

It was another dismal day, such a one as would be fitting for a dark deed of border justice. A cold, drizzly rain blew from the northwest. Jonathan wrapped a piece of oil-skin around his rifle, breech, and faced the downfall. Soon he was wet to the skin. He kept on, but his free stride had shortened. Even upon his iron muscles this soggy, sticky ground had begun to tell.

The morning passed but the storm did not; the air grew colder and darker. The short afternoon would afford him little time, especially as the rain and running rills of water were obliterating the trail.

In the midst of a dense forest of great cottonwoods and sycamores he came upon a little pond, hidden among the bushes, and shrouded in a windy, wet gloom. Jonathan recognized the place. He had been there in winter hunting bears when all the swampland was locked by ice.

The borderman searched along the banks for a time, then went back to the trail, patiently following it. Around the pond it led to the side of a great, shelving rock. He saw an Indian leaning against this, and was about to throw forward his rifle when the strange, fixed, position of the savage told of the tragedy. A wound extended from his shoulder to his waist. Near by on the ground lay Legget. He, too, was dead. His gigantic frame weltered in blood. His big feet were wide apart; his arms spread, and from the middle of his chest protruded the haft of a knife.

The level space surrounding the bodies showed evidence of a desperate struggle. A bush had been rolled upon and crushed by heavy bodies. On the ground was blood as on the stones and leaves. The blade Legget still clutched was red, and the wrist of the hand which held it showed a dark, discolored band, where it had felt the relentless grasp of Wetzel's steel grip. The dead man's buckskin coat was cut into ribbons. On his broad face a demoniacal expression had set in eternal rigidity; the animal terror of death was frozen in his wide staring eyes. The outlaw chief had died as he had lived, desperately.

Jonathan found Wetzel's trail leading directly toward the river, and soon understood that the borderman was on the track of Brandt. The borderman had surprised the worn, starved, sleepy fugitives in the gray, misty dawn. The Indian, doubtless, was the sentinel, and had fallen asleep at his post never to awaken. Legget and Brandt must have discharged their weapons ineffectually. Zane could not understand why his comrade had missed Brandt at a few rods' distance. Perhaps he had wounded the younger outlaw; but certainly he had escaped while Wetzel had closed in on Legget to meet the hardest battle of his career.

While going over his version of the attack, Jonathan followed Brandt's trail, as had Wetzel, to where it ended in the river. The old borderman had continued on down stream along the sandy shore. The outlaw remained in the water to hide his trail.

At one point Wetzel turned north. This move puzzled Jonathan, as did also the peculiar tracks. It was more perplexing because not far below Zane discovered where the fugitive had left the water to get around a ledge of rock.

The trail was approaching Fort Henry. Jonathan kept on down the river until arriving at the head of the island which lay opposite the settlement. Still no traces of Wetzel! Here Zane lost Brandt's trail completely. He waded the first channel, which was shallow and narrow, and hurried across the island. Walking out upon a sand-bar he signaled with his well-known Indian cry. Almost immediately came an answering shout.

While waiting he glanced at the sand, and there, pointing straight toward the fort, he found Brandt's straggling trail!

CHAPTER XXIV

COLONEL ZANE paced to and fro on the porch. His genial smile had not returned; he was grave and somber. Information had just reached him that Jonathan had hailed from the island, and that one of the settlers had started across the river in a boat.

Betty came out accompanied by Mrs. Zane.

"What's this I hear?" asked Betty, flashing an anxious glance toward the river. "Has Jack really come in?"

"Yes," replied the colonel, pointing to a throng of men on the river bank.

"Now there'll be trouble," said Mrs. Zane nervously. "I wish with all my heart Brandt had not thrown himself, as he called it, on your mercy."

"So do I," declared Colonel Zane.

"What will be done?" she asked. "There! that's Jack! Silas has hold of his arm."

"He's lame. He has been hurt," replied her husband.

A little procession of men and boys followed the borderman from the river, and from the cabins appeared the settlers and their wives. But there was no excitement except among the children. The crowd filed into the colonel's yard behind Jonathan and Silas.

Colonel Zane silently greeted his brother with an iron grip of the hand which was more expressive than words. No unusual sight was it to see the borderman wet, ragged, bloody, worn with long marches, hollow-eyed and gloomy; yet he had never before presented such an appearance at Fort Henry. Betty ran forward, and, though she clasped his arm, shrank back. There was that in the borderman's presence to cause fear.

"Wetzel?" Jonathan cried sharply.

The colonel raised both hands, palms open, and returned his brother's keen glance. Then he spoke. "Lew hasn't come in. He chased Brandt across the river. That's all I know."

"Brandt's here, then?" hissed the borderman.

The colonel nodded gloomily.

"Where?"

"In the long room over the fort. I locked him in there."

"Why did he come here?"

Colonel Zane shrugged his shoulders. "It's beyond me. He said he'd rather place himself in my hands than be run down by Wetzel or you. He didn't crawl; I'll say that for him. He just said, 'I'm your prisoner.' He's in pretty bad shape; barked over the temple, lame in one foot, cut under the arm, starved and worn out."

"Take me to him," said the borderman, and he threw his rifle on a bench.

"Very well. Come along," replied the colonel. He frowned at those following them. "Here, you women, clear out!" But they did not obey him.

It was a sober-faced group that marched in through the big stockade gate, under the huge, bulging front of the fort, and up the rough stairway. Colonel Zane removed a heavy bar from before a door, and thrust it open with his foot. The long guard-room brilliantly lighted by sunshine coming through the portholes, was empty save for a ragged man lying on a bench.

The noise aroused him; he sat up, and then slowly labored to his feet. It was the same flaring, wild-eyed Brandt, only fiercer and more haggard. He wore a bloody bandage round his head. When he saw the borderman he backed, with involuntary, instinctive action, against the wall, yet showed no fear.

In the dark glance Jonathan shot at Brandt shone a pitiless implacability; no scorn, nor hate, nor passion, but something which, had it not been so terrible, might have been justice.

"I think Wetzel was hurt in the fight with Legget," said Jonathan deliberately, "an' ask if you know?"

"I believe he was," replied Brandt readily. "I was asleep when he jumped us, and was awakened by the Indian's yell. Wetzel must have taken a snap shot at me as I was getting up, which accounts, probably, for my being alive. I fell, but did not lose consciousness. I heard Wetzel and Legget fighting, and at last struggled to my feet. Although dizzy and bewildered, I could see to shoot; but missed. For a long time, it seemed to me, I watched that terrible fight, and then ran, finally reaching the river, where I recovered somewhat."

"Did you see Wetzel again?"

"Once, about a quarter of a mile behind me. He was staggering along on my trail."

At this juncture there was a commotion among the settlers crowding behind Colonel Zane and Jonathan, and Helen Sheppard appeared, white, with her big eyes strangely dilated.

"Oh!" she cried breathlessly, clasping both hands around Jonathan's arm. "I'm not too late? You're not going to——"

"Helen, this is no place for you," said Colonel Zane sternly. "This is business for men. You must not interfere."

Helen gazed at him, at Brandt, and then up at the borderman. She did not loose his arm.

"Outside some one told me you intended to shoot him. Is it true?"

Colonel Zane evaded the searching gaze of those strained, brilliant eyes. Nor did he answer.

As Helen stepped slowly back a hush fell upon the crowd. The whispering, the nervous coughing, and shuffling of feet, ceased.

In those around her Helen saw the spirit of the border. Colonel Zane and Silas wore the same look, cold, hard, almost brutal. The women were strangely grave. Nellie Douns' sweet face seemed changed; there was pity, even suffering on it, but no relenting. Even Betty's face, always so warm, piquant, and wholesome, had taken on a shade of doubt, of gloom, of something almost sullen, which blighted its dark beauty. What hurt Helen most cruelly was the borderman's glittering eyes.

She fought against a shuddering weakness which threatened to overcome her.

"Whose prisoner is Brandt?" she asked of Colonel Zane.

"He gave himself up to me, naturally, as I am in authority

here," replied the colonel. "But that signifies little. I can do no less than abide by Jonathan's decree, which, after all, is the decree of the border."

"And that is?"

"Death to outlaws and renegades."

"But cannot you spare him?" implored Helen. "I know he is a bad man; but he might become a better one. It seems like murder to me. To kill him in cold blood, wounded, suffering as he is, when he claimed your mercy. Oh! it is dreadful!"

The usually kind-hearted colonel, soft as wax in the hands of a girl, was now colder and harder than flint.

"It is useless," he replied curtly. "I am sorry for you. We all understand your feelings, that yours are not the principles of the border. If you had lived long here you could appreciate what these outlaws and renegades have done to us. This man is a hardened criminal; he is a thief, a murderer."

"He did not kill Mordaunt," replied Helen quickly. "I saw him draw first and attack Brandt."

"No matter. Come, Helen, cease. No more of this," Colonel Zane cried with impatience.

"But I will not!" exclaimed Helen, with ringing voice and flashing eye. She turned to her girl friends and besought them to intercede for the outlaw. But Nell only looked sorrowfully on, while Betty met her appealing glance with a fire in her eyes that was no dim reflection of her brother's.

"Then I must make my appeal to you," said Helen, facing the borderman. There could be no mistaking how she regarded him. Respect, honor and love breathed from every line of her beautiful face.

"Why do you want him to go free?" demanded Jonathan. "You told me to kill him."

"Oh, I know. But I was not in my right mind. Listen to me, please. He must have been very different once; perhaps had sisters. For their sake give him another chance. I know he has a better nature. I feared him, hated him, scorned him, as if he were a snake, yet he saved me from that monster Legget!"

"For himself!"

"Well, yes, I can't deny that. But he could have ruined me, wrecked me, yet he did not. At least, he meant marriage by me. He said if I would marry him he would flee over the border and be an honest man."

"Have you no other reason?"

"Yes." Helen's bosom swelled and a glory shone in her splendid eyes. "The other reason is, my own happiness!"

Plain to all, if not through her words, from the light in her eyes, that she could not love a man who was a party to what she considered injustice.

The borderman's white face became flaming red.

It was difficult to refuse this glorious girl any sacrifice she demanded for the sake of the love so openly avowed.

Sweetly and pityingly she turned to Brandt: "Will not you help me?"

"Lass, if it were for me you were asking my life I'd swear it yours for always, and I'd be a man," he replied with bitterness; "but not to save my soul would I ask anything of him."

The giant passions, hate and jealousy, flamed in his gray eyes.

"If I persuade them to release you, will you go away, leave this country, and never come back?"

"I'll promise that, lass, and honestly," he replied.

She wheeled toward Jonathan, and now the rosy color chased the pallor from her cheeks.

"Jack, do you remember when we parted at my home; when

you left on this terrible trail, now ended, thank God! Do you remember what an ordeal that was for me? Must I go through it again?"

Bewitchingly sweet she was then, with the girlish charm of coquetry almost lost in the deeper, stranger power of the woman.

The borderman drew his breath sharply; then he wrapped his long arms closely round her. She, understanding that victory was hers, sank weeping upon his breast. For a moment he bowed his face over her, and when he lifted it the dark and terrible gloom had gone.

"Eb, let him go, an' at once," ordered Jonathan. "Give him a rifle, some meat, an' a canoe, for he can't travel, an' turn him loose. Only be quick about it, because if Wetzel comes in, God himself couldn't save the outlaw."

It was an indescribable glance that Brandt cast upon the tearful face of the girl who had saved his life. But without a word he followed Colonel Zane from the room.

The crowd slowly filed down the steps. Betty and Nell lingered behind, their eyes beaming through happy tears. Jonathan, long so cold, showed evidence of becoming as quick and passionate a lover as he had been a borderman. At least, Helen had to release herself from his embrace, and it was a blushing, tear-stained face she turned to her friends.

When they reached the stockade gate Colonel Zane was hurrying toward the river with a bag in one hand, and a rifle and a paddle in the other. Brandt limped along after him, the two disappearing over the river bank.

Betty, Nell, and the lovers went to the edge of the bluff.

They saw Colonel Zane choose a canoe from among a number on the beach. He launched it, deposited the bag in the bottom, handed the rifle and paddle to Brandt, and wheeled about.

The outlaw stepped aboard, and, pushing off slowly, drifted down and out toward mid-stream. When about fifty yards from shore he gave a quick glance around, and ceased paddling. His face gleamed white, and his eyes glinted like bits of steel in the sun.

Suddenly he grasped the rifle, and, leveling it with the swiftness of thought, fired at Jonathan.

The borderman saw the act, even from the beginning, and must have read the outlaw's motive, for as the weapon flashed he dropped flat on the bank. The bullet sang harmlessly over him, imbedding itself in the stockade fence with a distinct thud.

The girls were so numb with horror that they could not even scream.

Colonel Zane swore lustily. "Where's my gun? Get me a gun. Oh! What did I tell you?"

"Look!" cried Jonathan as he rose to his feet.

Upon the sand-bar opposite stood a tall, dark, familiar figure.

"By all that's holy, Wetzel!" exclaimed Colonel Zane.

They saw the giant borderman raise a long, black rifle, which wavered and fell, and rose again. A little puff of white smoke leaped out, accompanied by a clear, stinging report.

Brandt dropped the paddle he had hurriedly begun plying after his traitor's act. His white face was turned toward the shore as it sank forward to rest at last upon the gunwale of the canoe. Then his body slowly settled, as if seeking repose. His hand trailed outside in the water, drooping inert and lifeless. The little craft drifted down stream.

"You see, Helen, it had to be," said Colonel Zane gently. "What a dastard! A long shot, Jack! Fate itself must have glanced down the sights of Wetzel's rifle."

CHAPTER XXV

A YEAR rolled round; once again Indian summer veiled the golden fields and forests in a soft, smoky haze. Once more from the opal-blue sky of autumn nights, shone the great white stars, and nature seemed wrapped in a melancholy hush.

November the third was the anniversary of a memorable event on the frontier—the marriage of the younger borderman.

Colonel Zane gave it the name of "Independence Day," and arranged a holiday, a feast and dance where all the settlement might meet in joyful thankfulness for the first year of freedom on the border.

With the wiping out of Legget's fierce band, the yoke of the renegades and outlaws was thrown off forever. Simon Girty migrated to Canada and lived with a few Indians who remained true to him. His confederates slowly sank into oblivion. The Shawnee tribe sullenly retreated westward, far into the interior of Ohio; the Delawares buried the war hatchet, and smoked the pipe of peace they had ever before refused. For them the dark, mysterious, fatal wind had ceased to moan along the trails, or sigh through tree-tops over lonely Indian camp-fires.

The beautiful Ohio valley had been wrested from the savages and from those parasites who for years had hung around the necks of the red men.

This day was the happiest of Colonel Zane's life. The task he had set himself, and which he had hardly ever hoped to see completed, was ended. The West had been won. What Boone achieved in Kentucky he had accomplished in Ohio and West Virginia.

The feast was spread on the colonel's lawn. Every man, woman and child in the settlement was there. Isaac Zane, with his Indian wife and child, had come from the far-off Huron town. Pioneers from Yellow Creek and eastward to Fort Pitt attended. The spirit of the occasion manifested itself in such joyousness as had never before been experienced in Fort Henry. The great feast was equal to the event. Choice cuts of beef and venison, savory viands, wonderful loaves of bread and great plump pies, sweet cider and old wine, delighted the merry party.

"Friends, neighbors, dear ones," said Colonel Zane, "my heart is almost too full for speech. This occasion, commemorating the day of our freedom on the border, is the beginning of the reward for stern labor, hardship, silenced hearths of long, relentless years. I did not think I'd live to see it. The seed we have sown has taken root; in years to come, perhaps, a great people will grow up on these farms we call our homes. And as we hope those coming afterward will remember us, we should stop a moment to think of the heroes who have gone before. Many there are whose names will never be written on the roll of fame, whose graves will be unmarked in history. But we who worked, fought, bled beside them, who saw them die for those they left behind, will render them all justice, honor and love. To them we give the victory. They were true; then let us, who begin to enjoy the freedom, happiness and prosperity they won with their lives, likewise be true in memory of them, in deed to ourselves, and in grace to God."

By no means the least of the pleasant features of this pleasant day was the fact that three couples blushingly presented themselves before the colonel, and confided to him their sudden conclusions in regard to the felicitousness of the moment. The happy colonel raced around until he discovered Jim Douns, the minister, and there amid the merry throng he gave the brides away, being the first to kiss them.

It was late in the afternoon when the villagers dispersed to their homes and left the colonel to his own circle. With his strong, dark face beaming, he mounted the old porch step.

"Where are my Zane babies?" he asked. "Ah! here you are! Did anybody ever see anything to beat that? Four wonderful babies! Mother, here's your Daniel—if you'd only named him Eb! Silas, come for Silas junior, bad boy that he is. Isaac, take your Indian princess; ah! little Myeerah with the dusky face. Woe be to him who looks into those eyes when you come to age. Jack, here's little Jonathan, the last of the bordermen; he, too, has beautiful eyes, big like his mother's. Ah! well, I don't believe I have left a wish, unless——"

"Unless?" suggested Betty with her sweet smile.

"It might be——" he said and looked at her.

Betty's warm cheek was close to his as she whispered: "Dear Eb!" The rest only the colonel heard.

"Well! By all that's glorious!" he exclaimed, and attempted to seize her; but with burning face Betty fled.

* * * * * *

"Jack, dear, how the leaves are falling!" exclaimed Helen. "See them floating and whirling. It reminds me of the day I lay a prisoner in the forest glade praying, waiting for you."

The borderman was silent.

They passed down the sandy lane under the colored maple trees, to a new cottage on the hillside.

"I am perfectly happy to-day," continued Helen. "Everybody seems to be content, except you. For the first time in weeks I see that shade on your face, that look in your eyes. Jack, you do not regret the new life?"

"My love, no, a thousand times no," he answered, smiling down into her eyes. They were changing, shadowing with thought, bright as in other days, and with an added beauty. The wilful spirit had been softened by love.

"Ah, I know, you miss the old friend."

The yellow thicket on the slope opened to let out a tall, dark man who came down with lithe and springy stride.

"Jack, it's Wetzel!" said Helen softly.

No words were spoken as the comrades gripped hands.

"Let me see the boy?" asked Wetzel, turning to Helen.

Little Jonathan blinked up at the grave borderman with great round eyes, and pulled with friendly, chubby fingers at the fringed buckskin coat.

"When you're a man the forest trails will be corn fields," muttered Wetzel.

The bordermen strolled together up the brown hillside, and wandered along the river bluff. The air was cool; in the west the ruddy light darkened behind bold hills; a blue mist streaming in the valley shaded into gray as twilight fell.

YAQUI

YAQUI

I

SUNSET—it was the hour of Yaqui's watch. Chief of a driven remnant of the once mighty tribe, he trusted no sentinel so well as himself at the end of the day's march. While his braves unpacked the tired horses, and his women prepared the evening meal, and his bronze-skinned children played in the sand, Yaqui watched the bold desert horizon.

Long years of hatred had existed between the Yaquis of upland Sonora and the Mexicans from the east. Like eagles, the Indian tribe had lived for centuries in the mountain fastnesses of the Sierra Madre, free, happy, self-sufficient. But wandering prospectors had found gold in their country and that had been the end of their peace. At first the Yaquis, wanting only the wildness and loneliness of their homes, moved farther and farther back from the ever-encroaching advance of the gold diggers. At last, driven from the mountains into the desert, they realized that gold was the doom of their tribe and they began to fight for their land. Bitter and bloody were the battles; and from father to son this wild, free, proud race bequeathed a terrible hatred.

Yaqui was one of the last great chiefs of his once great tribe. All his life he remembered the words of his father and his grandfather—that the Yaquis must find an unknown and impenetrable hiding place or perish from the earth. When Mexican soldiers at the decree of their government made war upon this tribe, killing those who resisted and making slaves of the captured, Yaqui with his family and followers set out upon a last journey across the Sonoran wilderness. Hateful and fearful of the east, whence this blight of gold diggers and land robbers appeared to come, he had fled toward the setting sun into a waste of desert land unknown to his people—a desert of scorching heat and burning sand and tearing cactus and treacherous lava, where water and wood and grass seemed days apart. Some of the youngest children had died on the way and all except the strong braves were wearing out.

Alone, on a ridge of rising ground, Yaqui faced the back trail and watched with falcon eyes. Miles distant though that horizon was, those desert eyes could have made out horses against the clear sky. He did not gaze steadily, for the Indian method was to flash a look across the spaces, from near to far, and to fix the eye momentarily, to strain the vision and magnify all objects, then to avert the gaze from that direction and presently flash it back again.

Lonely, wild, and grand, the scene seemed one of lifelessness. Only the sun lived, still hot, as it burned red-gold far away on the rugged rim of this desert world. Nothing breathed in that vastness. To Yaqui's ear the silence was music. The red sun slipped down and the desert changed. The golden floor of sand and rock shaded cold to the horizon and above that the sky lost its rose, turning to intense luminous blue. In the far distance the peaks dimmed and vanished in purple. The fire of the western heavens paled and died, and over all the rock-ribbed, sand-encumbered plateau stole a wondrous gray shade. Yaqui watched until that gray changed to black and the horizon line was lost in night. Safe now from pursuers were he and his people until the dawn.

Then, guided by a speck of camp-fire light, he returned to his silent men and moaning women and a scant meal that he divided. Hunger was naught to Yaqui, nor thirst. Four days could he travel the desert without drink, an endurance most of his hardy tribe were trained to. And as for toil, the strength of his giant frame had never reached its limit. But strong chief that he was, when he listened to the moaning women and gazed at the silent, set faces of the children under the starlight he sagged to the sands and, bowing his head, prayed to his gods. He prayed for little—only life, freedom, loneliness, a hidden niche where his people would hear no steps and fear no specters on their trail. Then with unquenchable faith he stretched his great length on the sands; and the night was as a moment.

In the gray of a dawn cold, pure, and silent, with the radiant morning star shining like a silver moon, the long file of Yaquis rode and tramped westward, on down the rugged bare slopes of this unknown desert.

And out of the relentless east, land of enemies, rose the glaring sun. Like magic the frost melted off the rocks and the cool freshness of morning changed to a fiery breath. The sun climbed, and the leagues were as long as the hours. Down into a broad region of lava toiled the fugitives. Travel over the jagged crusts and through the poison-spiked cholla lamed the horses and made walking imperative. Yaqui drove his people before him, and some of the weakest fell by the way.

Out of the hot lava and stinging cactus the Indians toiled and entered a region of bare stone, cut by wind and water into labyrinthine passages where, even if they had left tracks on the hard rocks, few pursuers could have followed them. Yaqui told this to his people, told them he saw sheep on the peaks above and smelled water, and thus urged them on and on league after league toward distant purple heights. Vast and hard as had been the desert behind them, this strange upflung desert before them seemed vaster and grimmer. The trackless way led ever upward by winding passages and gorges—a gloomy and weird region of colored stone. And over all reigned the terrible merciless sun.

Yaqui sacrificed horses to the thirst and hunger of his people and abandoned the horror of toil under the sun to a slower progress by night. Blanched and magnified under the great stars, the iron-bound desert of riven rock, so unreal and weird, brought forth a chant from the lips of Yaqui's women. His braves, stoic like himself, endured and plodded on, lightening burdens of the weaker and eventually carrying the children. That night passed and a day of stupor in the shade of sun-heated rock; another night led the fugitives onward and upward through a maze of shattered cliffs, black and wild. Day dawned once more, showing Yaqui by the pitiless light that only his men could endure much more of this dragging on.

He made camp there and encouraged his people by a faith that had come to him during the night—a whisper from the spirit of his forefathers —to endure, to live, to go to a beautiful end his vision could not see. Then Yaqui stalked alone off into the fastnesses of the rocks and prayed to his

gods for guidance. All about him were silence,
desolation, a gray barren world of rock, a black
barren world of lava. Far as his falcon eye could
see to the north and east and south stretched the
illimitable glaring desert, rough, peaked, spiked,
riven, ghastly with yellow slopes, bleak with its
bare belts, terrible with its fluted and upflung
plateaus, stone faced by endless ramparts and fast
bound to the fading distance. From the west, up
over the dark and forlorn heights, Yaqui heard the
whispers of his dead forefathers.

Another dawn found Yaqui on the great heights
with the sunrise at his back and with another and
more promising world at his feet.

"Land of our forefathers!" he cried out sonor-
ously to his people, gazing mutely down into the
promised land. A vast gray-green valley yawned
at their feet. Leagues of grassy, rock-ribbed, and
tree-dotted slopes led down to a gleaming white
stream, winding like a silver ribbon down the valley, to lose itself far in the lower country, where
the colored desert merged into an immense and
boundless void of hazy blue—the sea.

"Great Water, where the sun sleeps," said
Yaqui with long arm outstretched. "Yaqui's
father's father saw it."

Yaqui carried the boy and led the way down
from the heights. Mountain sheep and wild
horses and deer and quail that had never before

seen man showed no fear of this invasion of their wild home. And Yaqui's people, footsore and starved, gazed round them and, in the seeming safety of this desert-locked valley with its grass and water and wood and abundant game, they took hope again and saw their prayers answered and happiness once more possible. New life flushed their veins. The long slopes, ever greener as they descended, were welcome to aching eyes so tired of the glaring expanses of the desert. For an encampment Yaqui chose the head of the valley. Wide and gently sloping, with a rock-walled spring that was the source of the stream, and large ironwood trees and pines and paloverdes, this lonely hidden spot satisfied the longing in Yaqui's heart. Almost his joy was complete. But never could he feel wholly secure again, even had he wings of an eagle. For Yaqui's keen eyes had seen gold in the sands of the stream; and gold spelled the doom of the Indian. Still Yaqui was grateful and content. Not soon indeed would his people be tracked to this fastness, and perhaps never. He cautioned his braves to save their scant gun ammunition, sending them' out with bows and arrows to kill the tame deer and antelope. The weary squaws no longer chanted the melancholy songs of their woe. The long travel had ended. They unpacked their stores under the wide-spreading pines, made fires to roast the meat that would soon be brought, and attended to the ailments of the few children left to them. Soon the naked little ones, starved and cut and worn as they were, took to the clear cool water like goslings learning to swim.

Yaqui, carrying his rifle, stalked abroad to learn more of this wonderful valley. Stretching at length along the stream, he drank deeply, as an Indian who loved mountain water. The glint of gold in the wet sand did not please him as had the sweetness of the cold water. Grasping up a handful of sand and pebbles, he rubbed and washed it in his palm. Tiny grains of gold and little nuggets of gold! Somewhere up at the head of this valley lay the mother lode from which the gold had washed down.

Yaqui knew that here was treasure for which the white men would spill blood and sell their souls. But to the Indians—the Papagos, the Yumas, the man-eating Seris, and especially to the Yaquis—gold was no more than rock or sand, except that they hated it for the curse of white hunters it lured to the desert. Yaqui had found many a rich vein and ledge and placer of gold. He had hated them, and now more than any other he hated this new discovery. It would be a constant peril to his people. In times of flood this mountain stream would carry grains of gold as far as it flowed down on the desert. Yaqui saw in it a

menace. But there was hope in the fact that many
treasures of the desert heights would never be seen
by white men. His father had told him that. This
gray valley was high, cradled in the rocky uplands, and it might be inaccessible from below.
Yaqui set out to see. His stride was that of the
strongest and tallest of his tribe, and distance
meant little to him. Hunger gnawed at his vitals,
but the long march across the wastes and heights
had not tired him. Yaqui had never known exhaustion. Before the sun stood straight overhead
he had ascertained that this valley of promise was
shut off from the west and that the stream failed
in impassable desert. From north and east he had
traveled, and therefore felt a grim security. But
to the south he turned apprehensive eyes. Long
he tramped and high he climbed, at last to see that
the valley, this land of his forefathers, could be
gained from the south. Range and ridge sloped
gradually to a barren desolate land of sun and
cacti, far as his desert eyes could see. That must
be the land of the Seris, the man-eaters. But it
was a waterless hell in summer. No fear from the
south till the winter rains fell! Yaqui returned to
his camp, reaching there at sunset. There was
joy in the dusky welcoming eyes of his young wife
as she placed fresh meat before him.

"Yaqui's only son will live," she said, and
pointed to the frail boy as he slept. The chief

gazed somberly at the little brown face of his son, the last of his race.

Days passed. With rest and food and water the gloomy spirit of the Yaquis underwent a gradual change. The wild valley was an Indian's happy hunting ground, encompassed by lofty heights known only to sheep and eagles. Like wild animals, all savages, in the peace and loneliness of a secluded region, soon forgot past trials and fears. Still, the chief Yaqui did not forget, but as time passed and nothing disturbed the serenity of this hiding place his vigilance slowly relaxed. The wind and the sun and the solitude and the presence of antelope and wild horses always within sight of camp—these factors of primitive nature had a healing effect upon his sore heart. In the canyons he found graves and bones of his progenitors.

Days passed into weeks. The scarlet blossoms flamed at the long ends of the *ocatilla*; one morning the pale vordes, which had been bare and shiny green, appeared to have burst into full bloom, a yellow flowering that absorbed the sunlight; cacti opened great buds of magenta; from the canyon walls, on inaccessible ledges, hung the exquisite and rare desert flowers, *lluvia d'oro,* shower of gold; and many beautiful flowers lifted their faces out of the tall grasses. This magic of spring did not last long. The flowers faded, died, and blew away on the dry wind; the tall grasses slowly yellowed and bleached. Summer came. The glaring sun blazed over the eastern ramparts, burned white down over the still solemn valley, and sank like a huge ball of fire into the distant hazy sea. With the torrid heat of desert Sonora came a sense of absolute security to the chief Yaqui. His new home was locked in the furnace of the sun-blasted waste land. The clear spring of mountain water sank lower and lower, yet it did not fail. The birds and beasts that visited the valley attested to the nature of the surrounding country. So the time came when Yaqui forgot the strange feeling of distant steps upon his trail.

When autumn came all the valley was dry and gray and withered, except the green line along the stream and the perennial freshness of the cactus plants and the everlasting green of the paloverdes. With the winter season came the rains, and a wave of ever-brightening green flushed the vast valley from its eastern height of slope to the far distant mouth, where it opened into the barren breaks of the desert.

Manifestly the god of the Yaquis had not forgotten them. As the months passed child after child was born to the women of the tribe. Yaqui's dusky-eyed wife bore him a healthy girl baby. As the chief balanced the tiny brown form in his great hand he remembered speech of his own father's: "Son, let the Yaquis go back to the mountains of the setting sun—to a land free from white men and gold and fire water, to the desert valley where deer graze with horses. There let the Yaquis multiply into a great people or perish from the earth."

Yaqui watched his girl baby with a gleam of troubled hope lighting in his face. His father had spoken prophecy. There waved the green grass of the broad valley, dotted with wild horses, antelope, and deer grazing among his stock. Here in his hand lay another child—a woman child—and he had believed his son to be the last of his race. It was not too late. The god of the Indian was good. His branch of the Yaquis would mother and father a great people. But even as he fondled his babe the toe of his moccasin stirred grains of gold in the sand.

Love of life lulled Yaqui back into his dreams. To live, to have his people round him, to see his dusky-eyed wife at her work, to watch the little naked children playing in the grass, to look out over that rolling, endless green valley, so wild, so lonely, so fertile—such a proof of god in the desert —to feel the hot sun and the sweet wind and the cool night, to linger on the heights watching, listening, feeling, to stalk the keen-eyed mountain sheep, to eat fresh meat and drink pure water, to rest through the solemn still noons and sleep away the silent melancholy nights, to enjoy the games of his forefathers—wild games of riding and run-

ning—to steal off alone into the desert and endure
heat, thirst, cold, dust, starvation while he sought
the Indian gods hidden in the rocks, to be free of
the white man whom he recognized as a superior
and a baser being—to live like the eagles—to live
—Yaqui asked no more.

Yaqui laid the baby back in the cradle of its
mother's breast and stalked out as a chief to in-
spire his people.

In that high altitude the morning air was cold,
exhilarating, sweet to breathe and wonderful to
send the blood racing. Some winter mornings
there was just a touch of frost on the leaves. The
sunshine was welcome, the day was short, the night
was long. Yaqui's people reverted to their old
order of happy primitive life before the white man
had come with greed for gold and lust to kill.

The day dawned in which Yaqui took his son out
and put him upon a horse. As horsemen the
Yaquis excelled all other Indian tribes of the
Southwest. Boys were given lessons at an early
age and taught to ride bareback. Thus as youths
they developed exceeding skill and strength.

Some of the braves had rounded up a band of
wild horses and had driven them into a rough
rock-walled triangle, a natural trap, the opening of
which they had closed with a rude fence. On this
morning the Yaquis all assembled to see the wild
horses broken. Yaqui, as an inspiration to his

little son and to the other boys of the tribe, chose the vicious leader of the band as the horse he would first ride and break. High on the rocky wall perched the black-eyed boys, eager and restless, excited and wondering, some of them naked and all of them stretching out tousled black heads with shining ragged hair flying in the wind. The women and girls of the tribe occupied another position along the outcropping of gray wall, their colorful garments lending contrast to the scene.

The inclosure was wide and long, containing both level and uneven ground, some of which was grass and some sand and rock. A few ironwood trees and one huge paloverde, under which Indians were lolling, afforded shade. At the edge of the highest slope began a line of pine trees that reached up to the bare gray heights.

Yaqui had his braves drive the vicious leader of the wild horses out into the open. It was a stallion, of ungainly shape and rusty color, no longer young. With ugly head high, nostrils distended, mouth open and ears up, showing the white of vicious, fiery eyes, it pranced in the middle of the circle drawn by its captors.

Yaqui advanced with his long leather *riata*, and, once clear of the ring of horsemen inclosing the stallion, he waved them back. Then as the wild steed plunged to and fro, seeking for an opening in that circle, Yaqui swung the long noose. He

missed twice. The third cast caught its mark, the
snarling nose of this savage horse. Yaqui hauled
the lasso taut. Then with snort of fright the stallion lunged and reared, pawing the air. Yaqui,
hauling hand over hand, pulled him down and approached him at the same time. Shuddering all
over, breathing with hard snorts, the stallion faced
his captor one moment, as if ready to fight. But
fear predominated. He leaped away. At the end
of that leap, so powerful was the strain on him, he
went down in the sand. Up he sprang, wilder than
ever, and dashed forward, dragging the Indian,
gaining yards of the lasso. But the mounted Yaquis blocked his passage; he had to swerve; and
as he ran desperately in a circle once more the
giant chief hauled hand over hand on the rope.
Suddenly Yaqui bounded in and with a tremendous leap, like the leap of a huge panther, he
gained the back of the stallion and seemed to become fixed there. He dropped the lasso, and with
the first startled jump of the stallion the noose
loosened and slipped off. Except for Yaqui's
great, long brown legs, with their strung bands of
muscle set like steel, the stallion was free.

The stallion bolted for the open. Only the rock
wall checked his headlong flight. Then he
wheeled and ran along the wall, bounding over
rocks and ditches, stretching out until, with magnificent stride, he was running at his topmost

speed. Along one wall and then the other he dashed, round and round and across, until the moment came when panic succeeded to fury, and then his tremendous energies were directed to the displacement of his rider. Wildly he pitched. With head down, legs stiff, feet together, he plunged over the sand, plowing up the dust, and bounding straight up. But he could not unseat his inexorable rider. Yaqui's legs banded his belly and were as steel. Then the stallion, now lashed into white lather of sweat and froth, lunged high to paw the air and scream and plunge down to pitch again. His motions soon lost their energy, though not their fury. Then he reached back with eyes of fire and open mouth to bite. Yaqui's huge fist met him, first on the right, then, as he turned, on the left. Last he plunged to his knees and with rumbling heave of anger he fell on his side, meaning to roll over his rider. But the Yaqui's leg on that side flashed high while his hands twisted hard in the long mane. When the foiled horse rose again Yaqui rose with him, again fixed tight on his back. Another dash and burst of running, wild and blind this time and plainly losing speed, showed the weakening of the stallion. And the time arrived when, spent and beaten, he fell in the sand.

"Let Yaqui's son learn to ride like his father," said the chief to his gleeful, worshiping son.

Then the chief again stalked forth, drawn irresistibly by something in the hour.

"Let Yaqui's son watch and remember to tell his son's son," he said.

He scattered his riders to block the few passages out of the valley and he ordered his son and all the women of the tribe and their children again to climb high on the rocks, there to watch. The Indian gods said this day marked the rejuvenation of their tribe. Let his son, who would be chief some day, and his people, see the great runner of the Yaquis.

Naked except for his moccasins, the giant chief broke into a slow trot that was habitual with him when alone on a trail; and he crossed the stream and the plots of sand, and headed out into the grassy valley where deer grazed with the horses. Yaqui selected the one that appeared largest and strongest of the herd and to it he called in a loud voice, meant as well for the spirit of his forefathers and for his gods, watching and listening from the heights: "Yaqui runs to kill!"

The sleek gray deer left off their grazing and stood at gaze, with long ears erect. Then they bounded off. Yaqui broke from his trot into a long, swinging lope and the length of his stride was such that he seemed to fly over the ground. Up the valley the deer scattered and Yaqui ran in the trail of the one to which he had called. Half a mile off it halted to look back. Then it grazed a little, but soon lifted its head to look again. Yaqui ran on at the same easy, distance-devouring stride. Presently the deer dashed away and kept on until it was a mere speck in Yaqui's eyes. It climbed a deer trail that led over the heights, to be turned back there by one of Yaqui's braves. Then it crossed the wide valley to be turned back by insurmountable cliffs. Yaqui kept it in sight and watched it trot and stop, run and walk and stop again, all the way up the long grassy slope toward the head of the valley.

Here among rocks and trees Yaqui lost sight of his quarry, but he trailed it with scarcely a slackening of his pace. At length, coming out upon a level open bench, he saw the deer he had chosen to run to death. It was looking back.

Down the grassy middle of the vast valley, clear to the mouth where the stream tumbled off into space, across the wide level from slope to slope, back under the beetling heights, Yaqui pursued the doomed deer.

Leagues and leagues of fleet running had availed the deer nothing. It could not shake off the man. More and more the distance between them lessened. Terror now added to the gradual exhaustion of the four-footed creature, designed by Nature to escape its foes. Yaqui, perfect in all the primal attributes of man, was its superior. The race was not to the swift but to the enduring.

Within sight of his people and his little son Yaqui overtook the staggering deer and broke its neck with his naked hands. Then for an instant he stood erect over his fallen quarry, tall gaunt giant, bathed in the weird afterglow of sunset; and he lifted a long arm to the heights, as if calling upon his spirits there to gaze down upon the victory of the red man.

II

IT WAS toward evening of another day, all the hours of which had haunted Yaqui with a nameless oppression. Like a deer that scented a faint strange taint on the pure air Yaqui pointed his sensitive nose toward the east, whence came the soft wind.

Suddenly his strong vision quivered to the movement of distant objects on the southern slope. Halting, he fixed his gaze. Long line of moving dots! Neither deer nor sheep nor antelope traveled in that formation. The objects were men. Yaqui's magnified sight caught the glint of sunset red on shining guns. Mexican soldiers! That nameless haunting fear of the south, long lulled, now had its fulfillment.

Yaqui leaped with gigantic bounds down the slope. Like an antelope he sprang over rocks and dips, and once on the grassy downs he ran the swiftest race of his life. His piercing yells warned his people in time to save them from being surprised by the soldiers. The first shots of combat were fired as he hurdled the several courses of the stream. Yaqui saw the running and crawling forms of men in dusty blue—saw them aim short carbines—saw spurts of flame and puffs of smoke. Yaqui's last few bounds carried him into the stone-walled encampment, and the whistling bullets that missed him told how the line of soldiers were spreading to surround the place. Yaqui flung himself behind the wall and crawled to where his braves knelt with guns and bows ready. Some of them were shooting. The women and children were huddled somewhere out of sight. Steel-jacketed bullets cracked on the rocks and whined away. Yaqui knew how poor was the marksmanship of the Mexicans; nevertheless it seemed to him they were shooting high. The position of the Indians was open to fire from several angles.

During a lull in the firing a hoarse yell pealed out. Yaqui knew Spanish. "Surrender, Yaquis!" was the command. The Yaquis answered by well-aimed bullets that brought sharp cries from the soldiers. Soon the encampment appeared entirely surrounded. Reports came from all sides and bullets whistled high, spatting into the trees. Then occurred another lull in the firing. Again a voice pealed out: "Surrender, Yaquis, save your lives!"

The Indians recognized their doom. Each man had only a few shells for his gun. Many had only bows and arrows. They would be shot like wolves in a trap. But no Yaqui spoke a word.

Nevertheless, when darkness put an end to their shooting there were only a few who had a shell left. The Mexicans grasped the situation and grew bold. They built fires off under the trees. They crept down to the walls and threw stones into the encampment and yelled derisively: "Yaqui dogs!" They kept up a desultory shooting from all sides as if to make known to the Indians that they were surrounded and vigilantly watched.

At dawn the Mexicans began another heavy volleying, firing into the encampment without aim but with deadly intent. Then, yelling their racial hatred of the Yaquis, they charged the camp. It was an unequal battle. Outnumbered and without ammunition the Yaquis fought a desperate but losing fight. One by one they were set upon by several, sometimes by half a dozen, Mexicans and killed or beaten into insensibility.

Yaqui formed the center of several storms of conflict. With clubbed rifle he was like a giant fighting down a horde of little men.

"Kill the big devil!" cried a soldier.

From the thick of that mêlée sounded Spanish curses and maledictions and dull thuds and groans as well. The Yaqui was a match for all that could surround him. A Mexican fired a pistol. Then the officer came running to knock aside the

weapon. He shouted to his men to capture the
Yaqui chief. The Mexicans pressed closer, dodging the sweeping rifle, and one of them plunged
at the heels of the Indian. Another did likewise
and they tripped up the giant, who was then piled
upon by a number of cursing soldiers. Like a mad
bull Yaqui heaved and tossed, but to no avail. He
was overpowered and bound with a lasso, and tied
upright to the paloverde under which he had so
often rested.

His capture ended the battle. And the Mexicans began to run about, searching. Daylight had
come. From under a ledge of rock the Indian
women and children were driven. One lithe,
quick boy eluded the soldiers. He slipped out of
their hands and ran. As he looked back over his
shoulder his dark face shone wildly. It was
Yaqui's son. Like a deer he ran, not heeding the
stern calls to halt. "Shoot!" ordered the officer.
Then the soldiers leveled rifles and began to fire.
Puffs of dust struck up behind, beside and beyond
that flying form. But none hit him. They shot at
him until he appeared to be out of range. And
all eyes watched him flee. Then a last bullet struck
its flying mark. The watchers heard a shrill cry
of agony and saw the lad fall.

All the Indians were tied hand and foot and
herded into a small space and guarded as if they
had been wild cattle.

After several hours of resting and feasting and celebrating what manifestly was regarded as a great victory, the officer ordered the capture of horses and the burning of effects not transportable. Soon the beautiful encampment of the Yaquis was a scene of blackened and smoking ruin. Then, driving the Yaquis in a herd before them, the Mexicans, most of them now mounted on Indian horses, faced the ascent of the slope by which they had entered the valley.

Far down that ragged mountain slope the Mexicans halted at the camp they had left when they made their attack on the Yaquis. Mules and burros, packsaddles and camp duffel occupied a dusty bench upon which there grew a scant vegetation. All round were black slopes of ragged lava and patches of glistening white cholla.

The Yaquis received but little water and food, no blankets to sleep on, no rest from tight bonds, no bandaging of their fly-tormented wounds. But they bore their ills as if they had none.

Yaqui sat with his back to a stone and when unobserved by the guards he would whisper to those of his people nearest him. Impassively but with intent faces they listened. His words had some strange, powerful, sustaining effect. And all the time his inscrutable gaze swept down off the lava heights to the hazy blue gulf of the sea.

Dawn disclosed the fact that two of the Yaquis

were badly wounded and could not be driven to
make a start. Perhaps they meant to force the
death that awaited them farther down the trail;
perhaps they were absorbed in the morbid gloom
of pain and departing strength. At last the officer,
weary of his subordinate's failure to stir these men,
dragged at them himself, kicked and beat them,
cursing the while. "Yaqui dogs! You go to the
henequen fields!"

The older of these wounded Indians, a man of
lofty stature and mien, suddenly arose. Swiftly
his brown arm flashed. He grasped a billet of
wood from a packsaddle and struck the officer
down. The blow lacked force. It was evident
that the Yaqui, for all his magnificent spirit, could
scarcely stand. Excitedly the soldiers yelled, and
some brandished weapons. The officer staggered
to his feet, livid and furious, snarling like a dog,
and ordering his men to hold back, he drew a pistol to kill the Yaqui. The scorn, the contempt, the
serenity of the Indian, instead of rousing his respect, incurred a fury which demanded more than
death.

"You shall walk the cholla torture!" he
shrieked, waving his pistol in the air.

In northwest Mexico, for longer than the oldest
inhabitant could remember, there had been a notorious rumor of the cholla torture that the Yaquis meted out to their Mexican captives. This

cholla torture consisted of ripping the skin off the soles of Mexicans' feet and driving them to walk upon the cactus beds until they died.

The two wounded Indians, with bleeding raw feet, were dragged to the cholla torture. They walked the white, glistening, needle-spiked beds of cholla blind to the cruel jeers and mute wonderment and vile maledictions of their hereditary foes. The giant Yaqui who had struck down the officer stalked unaided across the beds of dry cholla. The cones cracked like live bits of steel. They collected on the Yaqui's feet until he was lifting pads of cactus. He walked erect, with a quivering of all the muscles of his naked bronze body, and his dark face was set in a terrible hardness of scorn for his murderers.

Then when the mass of cactus cones adhering to the Yaqui's feet grew so heavy that he became anchored in his tracks the Mexican officer, with a fury that was not all hate, ordered his soldiers to dispatch these two Indians, who were beyond the reach of a torture hideous and appalling to all Mexicans. Yaqui, the chief, looked on inscrutably, towering above the bowed heads of his women.

This execution sobered the soldiers. Not only extermination did they mean to mete out to the Yaqui, but an extermination of horrible toil, by which the Mexicans were to profit.

Montes, a Brazilian, lolled in the shady spot on
the dock. The hot sun of Yucatan was more than
enough for him. The still air reeked with a hot
pungent odor of henequen. Montes had learned
to hate the smell. He was in Yucatan on a mission
for the Brazilian government and also as an agent
to study the sisal product—an advantageous business for him, to which he had devoted himself with
enthusiasm and energy.

But two unforeseen circumstances had disturbed
him of late and rendered less happy his devotion
to his tasks. His vanity had been piqued, his pride
had been hurt, his heart had been stormed by one of
Mérida's coquettish beauties. And the plight of
the poor Yaqui Indians, slaves in the henequen
fields, had so roused his compassion that he had
neglected his work.

So, as Montes idled there in the shade, with his
legs dangling over the dock, a time came in his reflection when he was confronted with a choice between the longing to go home and a strange desire
to stay. He gazed out into the gulf. The gun-
boat *Esperanza* had come to anchor in the roads
off Progreso. She had a cargo of human freight—
Yaqui Indian prisoners from the wild plateaus of
Northern Sonora—more slaves to be broken in the
terrible henequen fields. At that moment of
Montes's indecision he espied Lieutenant Perez

coming down the dock at the head of a file of
rurales.

Gazing at Perez intently, the Brazilian experienced a slight cold shock of decision. He would
prolong his stay in Yucatan. Strange was the
nameless something that haunted him. Jealous
curiosity, he called it, bitterly. Perez had the
favor of the proud mother of Senorita Dolores
Mendoza, the coquettish beauty who had smiled
upon Montes. She cared no more for Perez than
she cared for him or any of the young bloods of
Merida. But she would marry Perez.

Montes rose and stepped out of the shade. His
commission in Yucatan put him on common
ground with Perez, but he had always felt looked
down upon by this little Yucatecan.

"Buenos dias, senor," replied Perez to his greeting. "More Yaquis."

A barge was made fast to the end of the dock
and the Yaquis driven off and held there in a closely guarded group.

The time came when Perez halted the loading
of henequen long enough to allow the prisoners
to march up the dock between files of *rurales*.
They passed under the shadows of the huge ware-
houses, out into a glaring square where the bare
sand radiated veils of heat.

At an order from Perez, soldiers began separating the Yaqui women and children from the men.

They were formed in two lines. Then Perez went among them, pointing out one, then another.

Montes suddenly grasped the significance of this scene and it had strange effect upon him. Yaqui father and son—husband and wife—mother and child did not yet realize that here they were to be parted—that this separation was forever. Then one young woman, tall, with striking dark face, beautiful with the grace of some wild creature, instinctively divined the truth and she cried out hoarsely. The silence, the stoicism of these Indians seemed broken. This woman had a baby in her arms. Running across the aisle of sand, she faced a huge Yaqui and cried aloud in poignant broken speech. This giant was her husband and the father of that dusky-eyed baby. He spoke, laid a hand on her and stepped out. Perez, who had been at the other end of the aisle, saw the movement and strode toward them.

"Back, Yaqui dogs!" he yelled stridently, and he flashed his bright sword.

With tremendous stride the Yaqui reached Perez and towered over him.

"*Capitan*, let my wife and child go where Yaqui goes," demanded the Indian in deep voice of sonorous dignity. His Spanish was well spoken. His bearing was that of a chief. He asked what seemed his right, even of a ruthless enemy.

But Perez saw nothing but affront to his authority. At his order the *rurales* clubbed Yaqui back into his squad. They would have done the same for the stricken wife, had she not backed away from their threatening advances. She had time for a long agonized look into the terrible face of her husband. Then she was driven away in one squad and he was left in the other.

Montes thought he would forever carry in memory the tragic face of that Yaqui's wife. Indians had hearts and souls the same as white people. It was a ridiculous and extraordinary and base thing to be callous to the truth. Montes had spent not a little time in the pampas among the Gauchos and for that bold race he had admiration and respect. Indeed, coming to think about it, the Gauchos resembled these Yaquis. Montes took the trouble to go among English and American acquaintances he had made in Progreso, and learned more about this oppressed tribe.

The vast plateau of northwestern Mexico, a desert and mountainous region rich in minerals, was the home of the Yaquis. For more than one hundred and sixty years there had been war between the Yaquis and the Mexicans. And recently, following a bloody raid credited to the Yaquis, the government that happened to be in power determined to exterminate them. To that end it was hunting the Indians down, killing those who resisted capture, and sending the rest to the torture of the henequen fields.

But more interesting was the new information that Montes gathered. The Yaquis were an extraordinary, able-bodied, and intelligent people. Most of them spoke Spanish. They had many aboriginal customs and beliefs, but some were Roman Catholics. The braves made better miners and laborers than white men. Moreover, they possessed singular mechanical gifts and quickly learned to operate machines more efficiently than most whites. They possessed wonderful physical development and a marvelous endurance. At sixty years Yaquis had perfectly sound white teeth and hair as black as night. These desert men could travel seventy miles on foot in one day with only a bag of pinole. Water they could do without for days. And it was said that some of the Yaqui runners performed feats of speed, strength, and endurance beyond credence. Montes, remembering the seven-foot stature of that Yaqui chief and the spread of shoulders and the wonder of his spare lithe limbs, thought that he could believe much.

The act of Perez in deliberately parting the chief from his loved ones was cruel and despicable; and it seemed to establish in Montes's mind an excuse for the disgust and hate he had come to feel for the tyrannical little officer. But, being frank with himself, Montes confessed that this act had only fixed a hate he already had acquired.

The Brazilian convinced himself that he had intuitively grasped a portent apparently lost on Perez. One of those silent, intent-faced Yaquis was going to kill this epauleted scion of a rich Yucatecan house. Montes had read it in these faces. He had lived among the blood-spilling Gauchos and he knew the menace of silent fierce savages. And he did not make any bones about the admission to himself that he hoped some Yaqui would kill the peacocked Mexican. Montes had Spanish in him, and something of the raw passion of the Gauchos he admired; and it suited him to absorb this morbid presentiment. The Yaqui chief fascinated him, impelled him. Montes determined to learn where this giant had been sent and to watch him, win his confidence, if such a thing was possible. *Quién sabe?* Montes felt more reasons than one for his desire to get under the skin of this big Yaqui.

III

IN THE interior of Yucatan there were vast barren areas of land fit only for the production of henequen. Nothing but jungle and henequen would grow there. It was a limestone country. The soil could not absorb water. It soaked through. Here and there, miles apart, were *cenotes*, underground caverns full of water, and usually these marked the location of a hacienda of one of the rich planters. The climate was hot, humid, and for any people used to high altitudes it spelled death.

The plantation of Don Sancho Perez, father of the young lieutenant, consisted of fifty thousand acres. It adjoined the hundred-thousand-acre tract of Donna Isabel Mendoza. The old Don was ambitious to merge the plantations into one, so that he could dominate the fiber output of the region. To this end he had long sought to win for his son the hand of Donna Isabel's beautiful daughter.

The big Yaqui Indian who had been wantonly separated from his wife by young Perez was in the squad of prisoners that had been picked out by the young officer to work on his father's plantation.

They were manacled at night and herded like wild beasts into a pen and watched by armed guards. They were routed out at dawn and put to work in the fiber fields. For food they had, each of them, a single lump of coarse soggy bread —one lump once every day. When the weaker among them began to lag, to slow down, to sicken, they were whipped to their tasks.[1]

Yaqui knew that never again would he see his wife and baby—never hear from them—never know what became of them. He was worked like a galley slave, all the harder because of his great strength and endurance. He would be driven until he broke down.

Yaqui's work consisted of cutting henequen fiber leaves. He had a curved machete and he walked down the endless aisles between the lines of great century plants and from each plant he cut the lower circle of leaves. Each plant gave him a heavy load and he carried it to the nearest one of the hand-car tracks that crossed the plantation. The work of other Indians was to push hand cars along these tracks and gather the loads.

It took Yaqui six days to cut along the length

[1] Recently the Mexican government changed its policy toward peon labor in Yucatan, and the Yaquis in Sonora. These Indians are now in the regular Mexican army. [AUTHOR'S NOTE.]

of one aisle. And as far as he could see stretched a vast, hot, green wilderness with its never-ending lines and lanes, its labyrinthine maze of intersecting aisles, its hazy, copper-hued horizons speared and spiked by the great bayonet-like leaves. He had been born and raised on the rugged mountain plateaus far to the north, where the clear, sweet, cold morning air stung and the midday sun was only warm to his back, where there were grass and water and flowers and trees, where the purple canyons yawned and the black peaks searched the sky. Here he was chained in the thick, hot, moist night, where the air was foul, and driven out in the long day under a fiery sun, where the henequen reeked and his breath clogged in his throat and his eyes were burning balls and his bare feet were like rotting hoofs.

The time came when Montes saw that the Yaqui looked no more toward that northland which he would never see again. He dreamed no more hopeless dreams. Somehow he knew when his wife and baby were no more a part of him on the earth. For something within him died and there were strange, silent voices at his elbow. He listened to them. And in the depths of his being there boiled a maelstrom of blood. He worked on and waited.

At night in the close-crowded filthy pen, with the dampness of tropical dews stealing in, and all about him the silent prostrate forms of his stricken people, he lay awake and waited enduringly through the long hours till a fitful sleep came to him. By day in the henequen fields, with the furnace blasts of wind swirling down the aisles, with the moans of his beaten and failing comrades full in his ears, he waited with a Yaqui's patience.

He saw his people beaten and scourged and starved. He saw them sicken and fail—wilt under the hot sun—die in the henequen aisles—and be thrown like dogs into ditches with quicklime. One by one they went and when they were nearly all gone another squad took their places. The Yaqui recognized Indians of other tribes of his race. But they did not know him. He had greatly changed. Only the shell of him was left. And that seemed unbreakable, deathless. He did not tell these newcomers to the fields what torture lay in store for them. He might have been dumb. He only waited, adding day by day, in the horror of the last throes of his old comrades, something more to the hell in his blood. He watched them die and then the beginning of the end for his new comrades. They were doomed. They were to be driven till they dropped. And others would be brought to fill their places, till at last there were no Yaquis left. The sun was setting for his race.

The Yaqui and his fellow toilers had one day of rest—the Sabbath. There was no freedom. And always there were guards and soldiers. Sunday was the day of bull fights in the great corral at the hacienda. And on these occasions Yaqui was given extra work. Montes knew the Indian looked forward to this day. The old Don's son, Lieutenant Perez, would come down from the city to attend the fight. Then surely Yaqui fed his dark soul with more cunning, more patience, more promise.

It was the Yaqui's work to help drag disemboweled and dying horses from the bull ring and to return with sand to cover up the gory spots in the arena. Often Montes saw him look up at the crowded circle of seats and at the box where the gray old Don and his people and friends watched the spectacle. There were handsome women with white lace over their heads and in whose dark and slumberous eyes lurked something that Yaqui knew. It was something that was in the race. Lieutenant Perez was there leaning toward the proud senorita. The Indian watched her with strange intensity. She appeared indifferent to the efforts of the *picadores* and the *banderilleros*, those men in the arena whose duty it was to infuriate the bull for the artist with the sword—the matador. When he appeared the beautiful senorita wakened to interest. But not until there was blood on the bright blade did she show the fire and passion of her nature. It was sight of blood that quickened her. It was death, then, that she wanted to see.

And last the Yaqui let his gaze rivet on the dark, arrogant visage of young Perez. Did not the great chief then become superhuman, or was it only Montes's morbid fancy? When Yaqui turned away, did he not feel a promise of fulfillment in the red haze of the afternoon sun, in the red tinge of the stained sand, in the red and dripping tongue of the tortured bull? Montes knew the Yaqui only needed to live long enough and there would be something. And death seemed aloof from this Indian. The ferocity of the desert was in him and its incalculable force of life. In his eyes had burned a seared memory of the violent thrust with which Perez had driven his wife and baby forever from his sight.

Montes's changed attitude evidently found favor in the proud senorita's eyes. She had but trifled with an earnest and humble suitor; to the advances of a man, bold, ardent, strange, with something unfathomable in his wooing, she was not indifferent. The fact did not cool Montes's passion, but it changed him somehow. The Spanish in him was the part that so ardently loved and hated; his mother had been French, and from her he had inherited qualities that kept him eternally in conflict with his instincts.

Montes had his living quarters in Mérida, where

all the rich henequen planters had town houses. It was not a long horseback ride out to the haciendas of the two families in which Montes had become most interested. His habit of late, after returning from a visit to the henequen fields, had been to choose the early warm hours of the afternoon to call upon Senorita Mendoza. There had been a time when his calls had been formally received by the Donna Isabel, but of late she had persisted in her siesta, leaving Montes to Dolores. Montes had grasped the significance of this—the future of Dolores had been settled and there no longer was risk in leaving her alone. But Montes had developed a theory that the future of any young woman was an uncertainty.

The Mendoza town house stood in the outskirts of fashionable Mérida. The streets were white, the houses were white, the native Mayan women wore white, and always it seemed to Montes as he took the familiar walk that the white sun blazed down on an immaculate city. But there were dark records against the purity of Mérida and the Yaqui slave driving was one of them. The Mendoza mansion had been built with money coming from the henequen fields. It stood high on a knoll, a stately white structure looking down upon a formal garden, where white pillars and statues gleamed among green palms and bowers of red roses. At the entrance, on each side of the wide flagstone walk, stood a huge henequen plant.

On this day the family was in town and Montes expected that the senorita would see him coming. He derived pleasure from the assurance that, compared with Perez, he was someone good to look at. Beside him the officer was a swarthy undersized youth. But Montes failed to see the white figure of the girl and suffered chagrin for his vanity.

The day was warm. As he climbed the high, wide stone steps his brow grew moist and an oppression weighed upon him. Only in the very early morning here in Yucatan did he ever have any energy. The climate was enervating. No wonder it was that servants and people slept away the warmer hours. Crossing the broad stone court and the spacious outside hall, Montes entered the dim, dark, musty parlors and passed through to the patio.

Here all was colorful luxuriance of grass and flower and palm, great still ferns and trailing vines. It was not cool, but shady and moist. Only a soft spray of falling water and a humming of bees disturbed the deep silence. The place seemed drowned in sweet fragrance, rich and subtle, thickening the air so that it was difficult to breathe. In a bower roofed by roses lay Senorita Mendoza, asleep in a hammock.

Softly Montes made his way to her side and

stood looking down at her. As a picture, as something feminine, beautiful and young and soft and fresh and alluring, asleep and therefore sincere, she seemed all that was desirable. Dolores Mendoza was an unusual type for a Yucatecan of Spanish descent. She was blond. Her hair was not golden, yet nearly so; she had a broad, low, beautiful brow, with level eyebrows, and the effect of her closed lids was fascinating with their promise; her nose was small, straight, piquant, with delicate nostrils that showed they could quiver and dilate; her mouth, the best feature of her beauty, was as red as the roses that drooped over her, and its short curved upper lip seemed full, sweet, sensuous. She had the oval face of her class, but fair, not olive-skinned, and her chin, though it did not detract from her charms, was far from being strong. Perhaps her greatest attraction, seen thus in the slumber of abandon, was her slender form, round-limbed and graceful.

Montes gazed at her until he felt a bitterness of revolt against the deceit of Nature. She gladdened all the senses of man. But somehow she seemed false to the effect she created. If he watched her long in this beautiful guise of sleep he would deaden his intelligence. She was not for him. So he pulled a red rose and pushed it against her lips, playfully tapping them until she awoke. Her eyes unclosed. They were a surprise.

They should have been blue, but they were tawny.
Sleepy, dreamy, wonderful cat eyes they were,
clear and soft, windows of the truth of her nature.
Montes suddenly felt safe again, sure of himself.
"Ah, Señor Montes," she said. "You found me
asleep. How long have you been here?"

"A long time, I think," he replied, as he seated
himself on a bench near her hammock. "Watching you asleep, I forgot time. But alas! time flies
—and you awoke."

Dolores laughed. She had perfect white teeth
that looked made to bite and enjoy biting. Her
smile added to her charm.

"Sir, one would think you liked me best asleep."

"I do. You are always beautiful, Dolores. But
when you are asleep you seem sincere. Now you
are—Dolores Mendoza."

"Who is sincere? You are not," she retorted.
"I don't know you any more. You seem to try to
make me dissatisfied with myself."

"So you ought to be."

"Why? Because I cannot run away with you
to Brazil?"

"No. Because you look like an angel but are
not one. Because your beauty, your charm, your
sweetness deceive men. You seem the incarnation
of love and joy."

"Ah!" she cried, stretching out her round arms
and drawing a deep breath that swelled her white

neck. "You are jealous. But I am happy. I
have what I want. I am young and I enjoy. I
love to be admired. I love to be loved. I love
jewels, gowns, all I have, pleasure, excitement,
music, flowers. I love to eat. I love to be idle,
lazy, dreamy. I love to sleep. And you, horrid
man, awake me to make me think."

"That is impossible, Dolores," he replied. "You
cannot think."

"My mind works pretty well. But I'll admit
I'm a little animal—a tawny-eyed cat. So,
Montes, you must stroke me the right way or I will
scratch."

"Well, I'd rather you scratched," said Montes.
"A man likes a woman who loves him tenderly
and passionately one moment and tears his hair
out the next."

"You know, of course, señor," she replied mock-
ingly. "The little Alva girl, for instance. You
admired her. Perhaps she—"

"She is adorable," he returned complacently.
"I go to her for consolation."

Dolores made a sharp passionate gesture, a contrast to her usual languorous movements. Into the
sleepy, tawny eyes shot a dilating fire.

"Have you made love to her?" she demanded.

"Dolores, do you imagine any man could resist
that girl?" he rejoined.

"Have you?" she repeated with heaving breast.

Montes discarded his tantalizing lightness.
"No, Dolores, I have not. I have lived in a torment lately. My love for you seems turning to
hate."

"No!" she cried, extending her hands. She softened. Her lips parted. If there were depths in
her, Montes had sounded them.

"Dolores, tell me the truth," he said, taking her
hands. "You have never been true."

"I am true to my family. They chose Perez for
me to marry—before I ever knew you. It is settled. I shall marry him. But—"

"But! Dolores, you love me?"

She drooped her head. "Yes, señor—lately it
has come to that. Ah! Don't—don't! Montes, I
beg of you! You forget—I'm engaged to Perez."

Montes released her. In her confession and resistance there was proof of his injustice. She was
no nobler than her class. She was a butterfly in
her fancies, a little cat in her greedy joy of physical life. But in her agitation he saw a deeper
spirit.

"Dolores, if I had come first—before Perez—
would you have given yourself to me?" he asked.

"Ah, señor, with all my heart?" she replied softly.

"Dearest—I think I must ask you to forgive me
for—for something I can't confess. And now tell
me—this reception given to-morrow by your

mother—is that to announce your engagement to Perez?"

"Yes and I will be free then till fall—when—when—"

"When you will be married?"

She bowed assent and hesitatingly slid a white hand toward him.

"Fall! It's a long time. Dolores, I must go back to Brazil."

"Ah, señor, that will kill me! Stay!" she entreated.

"But it would be dangerous. Perez dislikes me. I hate him. Something terrible might come of it."

"That is his risk. I have consented to marry him. I will do my duty before and after. But I see no reason why I may not have a little happiness—of my own—until that day comes. Life for me will not contain all I could wish. I told you; now I am happy. But you were included. Señor, if you love me you will remain."

"Dolores, can you think we will not suffer more?" he asked.

"I know we will afterward. But we shall not now."

"Now is perilous to me. To realize you love me! I did not think you capable of it. Listen! something—something might prevent your marriage—or happen afterward. All—all is so uncertain."

"*Quién sabe?*" she whispered; and to the tawny, sleepy languor of her eyes there came a fancy, a dream, a mystic hope.

"Dolores, if Perez were lost to you—one way or another—would you marry me?" he broke out huskily. Not until then had he asked her hand in marriage.

"If such forlorn hope will make you stay—make you happy—yes, Señor Montes," was her answer.

There came a time when Yaqui was needed in the factory where the henequen fiber was extracted from the leaves. He had come to be a valuable machine—an instrument of toil that did not run down or go wrong. One guard said to another: "That big black peon takes a lot of killing!" and then ceased to watch him closely. He might have escaped. He might have crossed the miles and miles of henequen fields to the jungle, and under that dense cover had made his way northward to the coast. Yaqui had many a chance. But he never looked toward the north.

At first they put him to feeding henequen leaves into the maw of a crushing machine. The juicy, sticky, odorous substance of the big twenty-pound leaf was squeezed into a pulp, out of which came the white glistening threads of fiber. These fibers made sisal rope—rope second in quality only to the manila.

By and by he was promoted. They put him in the pressing room to work on the ponderous iron press which was used to make the henequen bales. This machine was a high, strange-looking object, oblong in shape, like a box, opening in the middle from the top down. It had several distinct movements, all operated by levers. Long bundles of henequen were carried in from the racks and laid in the press until it was half full. Then a lever was pulled, the machine closed on the fiber and opened again. This operation was repeated again and again. Then it was necessary for the operator to step from his platform upon the fiber in the machine and stamp it down and jump upon it and press it closely all round. When this had been done the last time the machine seemed wide open and stuffed so full that it would never close. But when the lever was pulled the ponderous steel jaws shut closer and closer and locked. Then the sides fell away, to disclose a great smooth bale of henequen ready for shipment.

The Yaqui learned to operate this press so skillfully that the work was left to him. When his carriers went out to the racks for more fiber he was left alone in the room.

Some strange relation sprang up between Yaqui and his fiber press. For him it never failed to operate. He knew to a strand just how much fiber made a perfect bale. And he became so accurate that his bales were never weighed. They came out glistening, white, perfect to the pound. There was a strange affinity between this massive, steel-jawed engine and something that lived in the Yaqui's heart, implacable and immutable, appalling in its strength to wait, in its power to crush.

IV

'THERE seemed no failing of the endurance of this primitive giant, but his great frame had wasted away until it was a mere hulk. Owing to his value now to the hacienda, Yaqui was given rations in lieu of the ball of soggy bread; they were not, however, what the Indian needed. Montes at last won Yaqui's gratitude.

"Señor, if Yaqui wanted to eat it would be meat he needed," said the chief. Then Montes added meat to the wine, bread, and fruit he secretly brought to the Indian.

When Montes began covert kindnesses to the poor Yaqui slaves the chief showed gratitude and pathos: "Señor Montes is good—but the sun of the Yaquis is setting."

Perez in his triumphant arrogance evidently derived pleasure from being magnanimous to the man he instinctively knew was his rival.

One day at the hacienda when Montes rode up to meet Donna Isabel and Dolores he found them accompanied by Perez and his parents. Almost immediately the young officer suggested gayly:

"Señor, pray carry Dolores off somewhere. My

father has something to plan with Donna Isabel.
It must be a secret from Dolores. Take her a walk
—talk to her, señor—keep her excited—make love
to her!"

"I shall be happy to obey. Will you come,
señorita?" said Montes.

If they expected Dolores to pout, they were mistaken. Her slow, sleepy glance left the face of
her future husband as she turned away silently to
accompany Montes. They walked along the palm-
shaded road, out toward the huge, open, sunny
space that was the henequen domain.

"I hate Perez," she burst out suddenly. "He
meant to taunt you. He thinks I am his slave—a
creature without mind or heart. Señor, make love
to me!"

"You will be his slave—soon," whispered
Montes bitterly.

"Never!" she exclaimed passionately.

They reached the end of the shady road. The
mill was silent. Montes saw the Indian standing
motionless close at hand, in the shade of the henequen racks.

"Dolores, did you mean what you just said?"
asked Montes eagerly.

"That I will never be Perez's slave?"

"No; the other thing you said."

"Yes, I did," she replied. "Make love to me,
señor. It was his wish. I must learn to obey."

With sullen scorn she spoke, not looking at Montes, scarcely realizing the actual purport of her speech. But when Montes took her in his arms she started back with a cry. He held her. And suddenly clasping her tightly he bent his head to kiss the red lips she opened to protest.

"Let me go!" she begged wildly. "Oh—I did not—mean—Montes, not so! Do not make me—"

"Kiss me!" whispered Montes hoarsely, "or I'll never let you go. It was his wish. Come, I dare you—I beg you!"

One wild moment she responded to his kiss, and then she thrust him away.

"Ah, by the saints!" she murmured with hands over her face. "Now I will love you more—my heart will break."

"Dolores, I can't let Perez have you," declared Montes miserably.

"Too late, my dear. I am to be his wife."

"But you love me, Dolores?"

"Alas! too true. I do. Oh, I never knew how well!" she cried.

"Let us run away," he implored eagerly.

Mournfully she shook her head, and looking up suddenly she espied the Yaqui. His great burning cavernous eyes, like black fire, were fixed upon her.

"Oh, that terrible Yaqui," she whispered. "It is he who watches us at the bull fights— Let us go, Montes— Oh, he saw us—he saw me— Come!"

Upon their return to the house the old Don greeted them effusively. He seemed radiant with happiness. He had united two of the first families of Yucatan, which unison would make the greatest henequen plantation. The beautiful señorita had other admirers. But this marriage had unusual advantages. The peculiar location and productiveness of the plantations and the obstacles to greater and quicker output that would be done away with, and the fact that Lieutenant Perez through his military influence could work the fields with peon labor—these facts had carried the balance in favor of the marriage. The old Don manifestly regarded the arrangement as a victory for him which he owed to the henequen, and he had decided to make the wedding day one on which the rich product of the plantation should play a most important part.

"But how to bring in the henequen!" he concluded in perplexity. "I've racked my brain. Son, I leave it to you."

Young Perez magnificently waved the question aside. Possessing himself of his fiancée's reluctant hand, he spoke in a whisper audible to Montes. "We planned the wedding presents. That was the secret. But you shall not see—not know—until we are married!"

Montes dropped his eyes and his brow knit

thoughtfully. Later, as a peon brought his horse, he called Perez aside.

"I've an idea," he said confidentially. "Have Yaqui select the most perfect henequen fiber to make the most beautiful and perfect bale of henequen ever pressed. Have Yaqui place the wedding presents inside the bale before the final pressing. Then send it to Donna Isabel's house after the wedding and open it there."

Young Perez clapped his hands in delight. What a capital plan! He complimented Montes and thanked him and asked him to keep secret the idea. Indeed, the young lieutenant waxed enthusiastic over the plan. It would be unique; it would be fitting to the occasion. Perez would have Yaqui pick over and select from the racks the most perfect fibers, to be laid aside. Perez would go himself to watch Yaqui at his work. He would have Yaqui practice the operation of pressing, so at the momentous hour there could be no hitch. And on the wedding day Perez would carry the presents himself. No hands but his own would be trusted with those jewels, especially the exquisite pearls that were his own particular gift.

At last the day arrived for the wedding. It was to be a holiday. Yaqui alone was not to lie idle. It was to fall to him to press that bale of henequen and to haul it to the bride's home.

But Perez did not receive all his gifts when he

wanted them. Messengers arrived late and some were yet to come. He went to the mill, however, and put Yaqui to work at packing the henequen in the press and building it up. The Indian was bidden to go so far with the bale, leaving a great hole in the middle for the gifts and to have the rest of the fiber all ready to pack and press. Perez would not trust anyone else with his precious secret; he himself would hurry down with the gifts, and secretly, for the manner of presentation was to be a great surprise.

Blue was the sky, white gold the sun, and the breeze waved the palms. But for Montes an invisible shadow hovered over the stately Mendoza mansion where Dolores was to be made a bride. The shadow existed in his mind and took mystic shape—now a vast, copper-hazed, green-spiked plain of henequen, and then the spectral gigantic shape of a toiling man, gaunt, grim, and fire-eyed.

Montes hid his heavy heart behind smiling lips and the speech of a courtier. He steeled himself against a nameless and portending shock, waiting for it even when his mind scorned the delusion.

But the shock did not come at sight of Señorita Dolores, magnificently gowned in white, beautiful, serene, imperious, with her proud, tawny eyes and proud, red lips. Nor when those sleepy strange eyes met his. Nor when the priest ended the ceremony that made her a wife.

He noted when Lieutenant Perez laughingly fought his way out of the crowd and disappeared. Then the unrest of Montes became a haunting suspense.

By and by the guests were directed out to the shaded west terrace, where in the center of the wide stoned space lay a huge white glistening bale of henequen. Beside it stood the giant Yaqui, dark, motionless, aloof. The guests clustered round.

When Montes saw the Yaqui like a statue beside the bale of henequen, he sustained the shock for which he had been waiting. He slipped to the front of the circle of guests.

"Ah!" exclaimed the old Don, eying the bale of henequen with great satisfaction. "This is the surprise our son had in store for us. Here is the jewel case—here are the wedding presents!"

The guests laughed and murmured their compliments.

"Where is Señor Perez?" demanded the Don as he looked round.

"The boy is hiding," replied Donna Isabel. "He wants to watch his bride when she sees the gifts."

"No—he would not be there," declared the old Don in perplexity. Something strange edged into his gladness of the moment. Suddenly he wheeled to the Yaqui. But he never spoke the question on his lips. Slowly he seemed to be blasted by those great black-fired orbs, as piercing as if they had been lightning from hell.

"Hurry, open the bale," cried the bride, her sweet voice trilling above the gay talk.

Yaqui appeared not to hear. Was he looking into the soul of the father of Lieutenant Perez? All about him betrayed almost a superhuman intensity.

"Open the bale," ordered the bride.

Yaqui cut the wire. He did not look at her. The perfectly folded and pressed strands of fiber shook and swelled and moved apart as if in relief. And like a great white jewel case of glistening silken threads the bale of henequen opened.

It commanded a stilling of the gay murmur—a sudden silence that had a subtle effect upon all. The beautiful bride, leaning closer to look, seemed to lose the light of the tawny proud eyes. Her mother froze into a creature of stone. The old Don, in slow strange action, as if his mind had feeble sway over body, bent his gray head away from the gaunt and terrible Yaqui. Something showed blue down under the center strands of the glistening fiber. With a swift flash of his huge black hand, with exceeding violence, Yaqui swept the strands aside. Then from his lips pealed an awful cry. Instead of the jewels, there, crushed and ghastly, lay the bridegroom Perez.